PASS
IN
REVIEW

Sam Moschella

TABLE OF CONTENTS
PASS IN REVIEW

BOOK 1
FROM BOY TO MAN, A CHANGE OF LIFESTYLE

BOOK 2
THE CHANGE FROM BOY TO MAN GOES ON

BOOK 3
WE ARE WITH THE REAL U.S. AIR FORCE

BOOK 4
I WILL FINISH MY HITCH RIGHT HERE

BOOK 5
THE BEST LAID PLANS OF MICE AND MEN

BOOK 7
I JUST BECAME A LIFER

CHAPTER 1

How I Volunteered for the
United States Army

It was an old building, no pillars to give it a regal look, no marble floors to make boots clatter and sandals shoosh, and no air conditioning. It simply had a sign on a stand which read "Chelsea Court". Inside the building's court rooms there were the US flag, and the State flag, but the decor was the same. Old wooden benches for the spectators, tattered tables for the prosecution and the defense and a jury box with chairs just as old as all the other furniture in the room. The court reporter was poised on an elevated platform and on just a slightly higher dais, in a chair that was just about as old as he was, he sat in his not so new robe, THE JUDGE. There was no jury in the box and very few spectators in the audience. Actually there were only seven players in this game: THE JUDGE, the court reporter, the prosecutor, the defense attorney, the bailiff and the two· defendants: Frederico (also known as Fast Freddie) Pacento, and Saverio (also known as The Musher) Muscarello.

After the gavel smacked and the court was called to order, THE JUDGE spoke:

"The last time I saw you two gentlemen before me it was for illegal bookmaking. Fast Freddie interrupts, "Your honor that was a bum rap, we were simply running slips between bookies and the bookies were never pinched!" A smack of the gavel as THE JUDGE continued, "I will not mention some of the other things I read here. The prosecution has presented a most credible case and the defense has not caused me to disbelieve the prosecution. Therefore, it is my verdict that you are both guilty as charged. My sentence is six months confinement at an institution chosen by the Department of Corrections."

Fast Freddie and The Musher never flinched, never even batted an eye. Both knew that someday this day would come.

THE JUDGE then continued," I know it has been tough on you young fellows, what with World War II just ending, all the deserving· veterans returning to their old jobs or looking for a new job, there just has not been many opportunities for you to get a steady, reliable job. Your school records show that your IQ is high, your grades are good and you did some extra-curricula sports. In light of that I am going to give you a choice. I will

3

withhold any finding and seal these records providing that you immediately enlist in the United States Army. What is your choice"?

The Musher, "Judge I will enlist as soon as possible". Fast Freddie, "Judge, I will take the jail". The Musher almost yelled at Fast Freddie, What are you crazy? We never did time, who knows what it is really like. If you listen to the guys on the street, it is Holy Hell". Freddie retorts, "OK smart ass Musher, I will be out in three months, and you will be in for three years. I can stand on my head for three months. Which one of us is the dummy?"

From there, each went on his own way. Each suffering from feelings of a great loss.

CHAPTER 2
I Am Ready to Go to the US Army

It took a couple of days before Musher could go down to the recruiting center to enlist in the Army. Since Musher was only fifteen and a half years old he had to have a birth certificate to make him seventeen. Where Musher lived it was not much of a task to get any paperwork you wanted, of course for a price. Amazing enough, he had graduated high school with very good grades. How did he finish high school so young? He was of Italian ethnicity. The flat had a large kitchen table which was the center of activity. The table top was marble. Musher had five brothers and sisters. Each one did his or her homework on the marble table until it was correct, and then copied it on to paper. There was no such thing as kindergarten, so by the time Musher went to the first· grade at age five, he had already done that work at least three times. The same applied to the second grade and the fourth grade, so Musher went grades 1-3-5 before falling into the normal grade progression.

From the time he was ten he had always had some kind of a job. He never needed to study. When cars were made of metal he wet-sanded cars in a body shop for fifteen cents an hour fifteen hours a week; he worked Saturdays as a delivery boy for a Kosher grocery store doing the things that the Hebrew religion prohibited for its members who were devout to the religion; worked on a bakery truck doing Sunday deliveries; worked as a grocery clerk in an A&P store; was an usher in the local theatre; and worked as a busboy in a restaurant in down town Boston. In the middle of all that he played on his high school championship hockey team.

He had every intention to go to college. By time the first half of his senior year in high school rolled around it was obvious that there was no money for college and he was not going to college. There were no such things as student loans, grants and very few scholarships. He had applied to all the service academies without any success. He hit a low point and just simply quit going to school. Then was when he met Fast Freddie and learned ways to scam money, hustle dog tracks, horse tracks and the local gin mills. It beat the hell out of working and it was good to have money in his pocket.

There wasn't any fanfare as Musher closed the door to the flat. He was dressed in his usual way, with a white T shirt, Levi's, oxblood loafers, white sox and his North Shore Hockey Championship jacket. He had all his

5

worldly possessions in his pockets. A handkerchief, an unopened pack of Lucky Strike cigarettes, two books of matches, eighteen American dollars and fifty-five cents in change. He had the folder full of papers the Army had given him and he was on his way to the train station. United States Army I am ready for you!

CHAPTER 3

The Ride to Basic Training

When Musher walked into the train station it was not very crowded. Hanging above the middle of the station area was a huge banner, 'US ARMY RECRUITS REPORT HERE". Me and four other guys walked over to the banner, a guy in an Army uniform. complete with helmet, billy club, pistol, stripes allover his sleeves and lots of pretty colored ribbons on his chest, nastily said, "Form. a single line. Now"! Unlucky Musher was the first in line. The Monster (as I nicknamed him to myself), took my papers and made markings on them and said, "Step over there and stay there until I tell you otherwise. Do you understand"? Musher's answer: "OK". I thought the Monster was going to burst, his neck got red and his face even redder and he barked, "You will say yes Sergeant, or no Sergeant. Do you understand?" Musher, "Yes Sergeant. Sergeant may I smoke while I am waiting?" Again I thought the Monster would burst. "He spit a deep, loud NO".

For the next four guys he was just about the same. Yelling and chastising as if it were his goal in life to embarrass everyone in front of the world.

After a short time the Monster came to us and said, "Huddle up around me. As friendly as was possible for the Monster, he said, "If you want to smoke go ahead, or as the old Army joke says, smoke if you have too, but if you have two I will have one. In about an hour you will be boarding the train to head for Fort Benning, Georgia. There you will receive your basic training and become soldiers of the US Army. In this folder are your train tickets, your car assignments, your bunk assignments and your meal tickets for eating on the train. I am giving these to Private Muscarello. During the trip Muscarello is in charge. Good luck in your new careers and do not miss boarding the train. Make the US Army proud. ",

My first question to the other four guys: "I have ridden the subway and street cars, have any of you ever ridden a train?" Not a peep from the four of them. Then the usual wise guy speaks up with, "I had a train set, electric, and my Dad and I would pretend we were riding the train". I shoot him a bird. "Since none of us has any real baggage, why don't we go to the gate to wait for the train?" Sitting at the platform, "I figure we should at least know each other's name. I begin, Saverio Muscarello, known on the streets of the North End of Boston as The Musher. You can call me Musher." Next, John

7

Livingston, Lexington, "you can call me John." Next, Jose Rodriguez, known on the streets of Chelsea as The Rod. "You can call me Rod." Next, Anthony Bevilaqua, known on the streets of Revere as Tony Drinkwater. "You can call me Tony Drinkwater."

We hear the All Aboard and go looking for our car. Since there are five of us there is no three two seating arrangement. My other four pair up in two two's. Once again Musher is on his own, but then again there is nothing new about that. As the train rolled South Musher stared out the window in amazement. He had never seen such wide open spaces and so many different animals doing whatever they were doing in those green, green fields. He was equally surprised at the large houses, all looked like they had been painted yesterday. It was a far cry from the look of his home, the third floor walkup with clotheslines hanging from any where they could be tied off. The air in the train was fresh and clean. He wondered what the air would be like outside the train. He just knew it had to be even fresher and cleaner than anything he had ever smelled before.

He had no idea how much time had passed during his daydreaming but he was brought back to earth by a deep voice announcing, "Lunch is now being served in the dining car". His four fellow recruits were staring at him with the "Let's go eat buddy". Musher dug out the lunch meal tickets for that day and waived his group to the dining car. When they reached the dining car again the seating was for four, and the porter in charge waived The Musher to join a family of three. Trying very hard to make his mother proud of him, he sat, properly spread his napkin and announced I am Saverio Muscarello. The father replied promptly, "We are Mister and Missus Bilderbook, and this is our daughter, Emily. We are returning to Georgia from an extended vacation on the continent. Where are you going?" The Musher replied, "I and my four friends as he pointed to their table are United States Army recruits on our way to Fort Benning, Georgia."

The waiter appeared from nowhere and Mr. Bilderbook ordered for his family. Musher gave the waiter the five meal tickets and the waiter handed him a different menu from which to order. The rest of the conversation during the meal was small talk. Musher tried not to stare at Emily but she was somewhere around sixteen and striking. As Mr. Bilderbook was getting up to leave he asked Musher, "Do you play bridge?" Musher thought to himself, If you use fifty- two cards, I can play it! "He spoke, why yes I do." Trying to be modest, he added, "Not as well as Goren or Culbertson, but I do play." "Excellent," said Mr. Bilderbook, "We are in State Room 21C, two cars ahead. The porter will show you. We can spend an excellent afternoon playing bridge."

Musher walked over to his fellow recruits and asked, "Is everything all right? Go back to your seats and behave. I will see you at dinner. I have an engagement for the afternoon to play cards." All four were bursting with questions, "Who are they?" "Did you know them before?" "What kind of cards?" Typical of his upbringing, the caution crept into his head. Are they hustlers? Who cares, the most they could beat me out of is eighteen dollars and fifty cents. Besides it would be worth losing eighteen dollars and fifty cents to just stare at Emily all afternoon.

CHAPTER 4

We Will Be at Fort Benning Today

The afternoon of bridge with the Bilderbook family was fun. They gave me tonic (which I learned I must call soda) and chips. In return I gave them some bridge lessons. As a matter of fact the afternoon went so well that Mr. Bilderbook gave me their home address, telephone number and an open invitation to come visit whenever I could. Needless to say, during the afternoon Emily and I exchanged smiles, winks of encouragement and a message that we would try very hard to see each other again some time. Later I had dinner with the Bilderbook family and we parted from the dining car.

The rest of the night was not quite so good. Somewhere around nine o'clock the porters started converting the Pullman cars to Pullman beds. Each of us had an assigned bed. The porter kept saying if you gentlemen would go to bed now, when you wake up for breakfast, shortly thereafter you will be at Fort Benning. We took the porter's advice and went to bed. Two of my four companions kept moaning that the rolling ride was making them sick and they vomited in their beds. Naturally, the porters cleaned it all and changed bedding. The porter told me that if they were in the lower bunk rather than the higher, they would probably not get sick. Those three of us in the lowers played paper, rock and scissors to see who would give up the lowers. I never really learned that game so I and John from Lexington were the losers. John suddenly decided that he was not going to give up his lower. He changed his mind quickly when I squeezed his balls and slapped his face. The rest of the night was listening to the moaning and trying to sleep.

When the porter came through ringing his loud bell and announcing that breakfast is being served in the dining car, it seemed that no one in a Pullman bed could get out of bed fast enough. In a Pullman car there are very little bathroom facilities. The rush was on. Me, I went to the outside between the cars and smoked a couple of Lucky Strikes. If I could have had a coffee, breakfast would have been complete. By time I finished my smokes the Pullman car was just about empty, the bathroom facility available and I washed and brushed my teeth. Of course brushing my teeth was my index finger and whatever tooth paste extras were lying on the sink top. I strolled to the dining car, had two cups of coffee, two more Lucky Strikes and I was ready for the world.

In less than two hours the porter was coming through the cars announcing, "Fort Benning Station in fifteen minutes."

CHAPTER 5
Maybe Fast Freddie Was Right
Going to Jail

As I stepped off the train it seemed there were at least one thousand of the same Monsters that were at the train station when we first reported in Boston. A thousand of course is an exaggeration, but all I could see was brown uniforms, shiny silver helmets, white belts and billyclubs. Every one of those Monsters was screaming at the top of his lungs, "Fall in on this line, stand at attention." I took a quick glance down the line and there must have been two hundred recruits. One of the monsters started at the end of the line on my left and shouted "Count down! You idiot are number one, say one." To the next person on the right, "You idiot are number two, say two." To the next person on the right, "You idiot are number three, say three." To the next person on the right, "What is your number on the count down?" The quivering recruit said meekly, "Four." The Monster barked, "OK, continue the count down." I could hear the count down getting stronger, five, six, seven and when it got to me I said "Thirty-six." Again, The Monster barked, "Stop the count down. Pick up your bags. Left, Face." Some turned to the left others to the right. Those who turned to the right were berated as if they were dogs who had just shit in the middle of the living room floor. When The Monster got everybody facing the correct way he bellowed, "Take the first step with your left foot, ready, Forward, March; and, he began to count cadence, Left, Right, Left, Right, Left, Right, etc."

It felt like we marched for an hour. I really don't know how long or how far we marched but it seemed that we were doing much better with the Left, Right cadence. As we marched along The Monster, between cadence counts, told us we were now a platoon. He told us that when he wanted us to stop marching he would make sure he had our attention by loudly giving the command Platoon, shortly after which he would say Halt. The command Halt would be given when our right foot was on the ground, after which we would bring down our left foot, stop moving, and bring our right foot up to meet our left. Well the stopping moment came, The Monster did his job but boy was our halt a tangle. The Monster called us names, got us back in our single line, and announced that we were going into The Fun House.

As we got to the top of the stairs entering The Fun House we could clearly see it was nothing more than a barber shop. In this barber shop they gave only one kind of a haircut, cut it down to the scalp. There were no mirrors with which to see what was happening, or what had happened to your hair. Recruits with moustaches or beards were quickly relieved of those facial appendicles.

Following our two minute haircuts we were funneled into another room and told to strip of all clothes leaving any valuables in your clothing. They gave us each a bag in which to place our clothes and marking pens to write our last names on the bag. When one did the clothes packing bit and was naked he was led into what looked like an archway He was told to walk slowly through the archway. At certain points along the archway the delousing began and did not end until just before you stepped out of the archway. From there he stepped into showers which were already running with lukewarm water and soap in the trays. The Monsters kept screaming "Wash it down. No playing with your dick." If The Monsters thought you were in the shower too long, they would order you out. Awaiting your departure from the shower were Monsters handing out towels. "Dry off and step into the next room." It was comical watching the fat boys trying to tuck the towel.

If you have ever seen a military wedding movie where the officers hold their swords up high and crossed and the bride and groom come down the aisle under the swords, that is exactly what the room set up looked like. Only instead of crossed swords held high, there was inoculation stations with white colored uniformed people poised with syringes in their hands. The Monsters barked, "OK, Go down the line." At every step The Musher received an injection in each arm. There were recruits passing out before the first inoculation, part way through the inoculation process and even after receiving all the inoculations.

The Musher thought to himself that it has been a long way since breakfast and nobody seems to care if we eat or not. Cigarettes and coffee are fine for breakfast, but I am hungry. Haven't felt this hungry since I was a little kid and there was not enough food in the house.

Musher's thoughts were interrupted by one of the Monsters herding them into another room. The Monster announced "This is called the Quartermaster. You will be given all the clothes and other necessities that the US Army believes you need. First recruit, step up." The Baby Monsters, the ones without the shiny helmets, billyclubs and white belts, asked your size and gave you full arms worth of clothing ranging from underwear to hat. The Monster barked, "Into the next room and get dressed. Fatigues (which we just learned were work clothes), socks, laced boots, field jacket and hat. I want every button buttoned. Move quickly we have a lot more to do."

Right here The Musher made his first boo-boo, "When do we get to eat, I am starving?"

The Monster's face swelled, his neck looked double in size and bright red, and he screamed, "My name is Master Sergeant Ronald Dupree, I am your Drill Instructor. You may refer to me as Sergeant Dupree or Drill Instructor Dupree. You eat when I say you eat, you sleep when I say you sleep, you shit when I say you shit and if you do anything else it will be because I said to do it! You Smart Ass (looking at Musher), I don't know your name now but very soon I will. For the next thirteen weeks I am your father, mother, brother and sister. I am not your girlfriend so don't try to fuck me. When you write home you can tell them your soul belongs to God, but your ass belongs to me!

The Musher thought, MAYBE FAST FREDDIE WAS RIGHT?

CHAPTER 6
The First Day Goes On

When The Monster said "Fall Out" (I don't care what he says we may refer to him as, unless I am forced to orally refer to him, he will always be in my head as The Monster) we all hustled out of the Fun House and stood in our line. The Monster instructed "Left Face, if you are taller than the man in front of you step in line in front of him." It took a while but eventually we had the tallest in the front of the line and the shortest at the end of the line. The Monster, "I told you that you that you are a platoon. We will now divide the platoon into four squads. You four tallest men form a line in front of me. You next four tallest men fall in behind these four, your tallest man on the left facing me. You next four tallest men fall in behind these eight, your tallest man on the left facing me." The Monster repeated those instructions until we had four columns of nine recruits each, with each column ranging in height from the tallest at the head of the column and the shortest as the last man in the column.

Again, The Monster, "The squads are numbered one through four. The squad on my left is First Squad, next is Second Squad and you figure out which is the third and fourth squad. If you have any trouble (looking at The Musher) Smart Ass will be glad to help you. For now, the tallest man in each squad will be known as the Squad Leader. If I give the commands, Platoon, Column Left, that means that the next time the squads leaders right foot hits the ground, each squad leader will pivot his right foot ninety degrees, bring his left foot forward and continue marching along. When the second row of the squads reaches the spot where the squad leaders did their pivot, the second row will do the same. That execution will continue until each row of the squads has executed the move and the platoon is moving straight ahead."

The Monster, "Remember the commands, Platoon, Halt. When you hear Halt, the next time your left foot hits the ground stop moving and bring your right foot up next to your left foot. Now, let's try marching to the Mess Hall for something to eat. Step off on your left foot. Platoon, Forward March." and The Monster counted cadence, Left, Right, Left, Right and so on. Fortunately on the way to the Mess Hall we only needed to make one Column Left. It was sloppy and brought forth lots of screams from The Monster but at the Mess Hall we did a fairly descent Halt. The Monster," Fall out and into the chow line by squads, no talking while in the chow line and remember you can take all you want, but you must eat all you take. You will see instructions on what to do with your tray and utensils when you finish eating."

CHAPTER 7
The First Day Goes On and Goes On

The chow was not at all bad, but those metal trays. They had indentures in the tray which were designed to keep the foods from running together. I had meat loaf and gravy, mashed potatoes, cream kernel corn, two bread rolls and ice cream for dessert. By the time I could get a glass of milk, coffee was not permitted to recruits, the gravy was in the ice cream and the corn was in the mashed potatoes. The knife, fork and spoon were cheap metal and big enough for the Jolly Green Giant. Still it was food and I was hungry. I had had worse meals in my young life. Surely as The Monster had said there were signs on where to put your tray and utensils. Since everyone had to eat whatever they took there was no swill barrel for the pigs.

As we exited the Mess Hall, standing there facing our platoon was the joy of the day, The Monster. When our full platoon was in place, The Monster commanded Forward March. Since none of us knew where we were going we blindly tried to march to his cadence and make columns left or right as he directed. He had not instructed how to make a column right as he had for a column left and we certainly made a mess of the first two or three column right commands. At the end of our march we were at a building marked Quartermaster II. The Monster had taken us the very long way to get next to The Fun House. The Monster, "You will fall out by squads. Inside they will issue you a laundry bag, a mattress, a mattress cover (better known in the Army as a Fart Sack), a pillow, two pillow cases, two sheets and two blankets. When you get yours, get out of the building and fall in right here. If you choose to put your items on the Georgia Red Clay that is up to you. Remember, only the sheets will be exchanged on laundry day. Laundry exchange day is by the way seven days from tomorrow. First squad lead the way, second, third and fourth squads follow at a reasonable distance. No talking while in the line." Being that I was third in the first squad I followed my squad leader. The people inside were some more Baby Monsters, you know the ones without the shiny helmet, white web belt and billystick; however, they had the same nasty dispositions as the real grownup Monsters.

I got my gear and went outside to the fall in area. The gear was bulky and hard to hold. I did not want to lay my gear in the Georgia Red Clay so I asked for help from another member of my squad, the Chelsea guy, The Rod. We opened up one sheet and were able to put in all but the mattress

17

and tie off the sheet. Then we did the same for The Rod's gear. It was not a perfect solution, but I could hold all my gear and keep it off the ground. At that moment The Monster came and stood in front of me. The Monster, "Not bad thinking. What is your name soldier?" I rousted my most deep street voice and said, "Saverio Muscarello." He gave me his most vicious look and said, "It makes no difference what your name is, for as long as you are with me you will answer to the name SmartAss. Is that clear?"

CHAPTER 8

The First Day Finally Ends

When all members of the platoon were present The Monster marched us off in a new direction. Soon we came into an area of two story buildings called barracks. The Monster halted the platoon in front of one of the barracks and said, "This will be your home for the next thirteen weeks. That is it will be your home unless you are kicked out of the Army before then, or for some other reason the Army discharges you and sends you back home to your mama. This platoon will reside on the first floor. There are two rows, each with nine double deck bunks. There are no bunk assignments. Each recruit will take a bunk and until I make some different bunk assignments, it will be his bunk for the entire period of basic training. Is that clear? Are there any questions? OK, when I say fall out go get a bunk." Because The Rod from Chelsea and I were in the same squad we decided to take an upper and lower so that we could watch each others back. We chose one in the middle of the row so that in most events we would neither be first, nor would we be last. How do we decide who gets the lower? We don't have a coin to toss so we compromised. I take the lower and if in a day or so The Rod is not comfortable in the upper we would talk about it again.

Just about the time when all the bunk choices had been made, in strode The Monster and six more Monsters. The Monster spoke," My six friends are here to teach you the correct way to make your bed. You will give them your closest attention or I shall make you rue the day you were born. Gentlemen you may proceed with the instruction." Guys like me had never made a bed in our lives. The Monsters showed how to use the Fart Sack, put on the lower sheet making sure it had "hospital corners." They showed how to put on the upper sheet, and then put on one blanket with "hospital corners". Where to place your covered pillow, and then what I thought was the most difficult part, using the second blanket to make a pillow cover. I must admit, my bunk looked very, very good; and ever so inviting. The six Monsters had done their job and left the barracks.

Again The Monster, "There is a community latrine (bathroom to us civilians) on each floor. You may only use the one on this floor, the first floor. All lights except for a small light in the latrine will be turned off at 2200 hours (10 P.M to us civilians). The time is now 2115 hours (9:15 P.M. to us civilians). Your personal belongings are in the room across from the

latrine. You may get them and use the time until 2200 hours as you choose."
With that The Monster left the barracks.

The scramble to get our personal belongings would have equaled the great California Gold Rush. Me personally, I just wanted my Lucky Strike cigarettes. There were No Smoking signs posted in the barracks so I went outside on the steps and smoked three cigarettes in succession. Not a bad way to end the day.

The Musher thought, MAYBE FAST FREDDIE WAS NOT RIGHT? Just about then The Monster reappeared in the barracks yelling, "Three minutes to lights out." True to his words he snapped off all the lights and in parting said, "Goodnight Ladies, sleep tight."

CHAPTER 9

Day Two of Basic Training

Like so many of the members of his platoon The Musher had trouble falling asleep. The groaning, the farting and in some cases the crying was not what kept him awake. What kept him awake was the question, "Will everyday be like today?" As for the noises, when eight people lived in a cold water three room flat you learn to ignore any noises and anything else when it is time to sleep. At some point he went off to slumberland It seemed only seconds later all the barracks lights went on, The Monster was banging his billyclub on the lid of a garbage can, and yelling in his loudest voice, "Drop your cocks, grab your socks and get out of your bunk." At that point Musher noticed that there was another Monster with The Monster. The Monster proclaimed, "This is Corporal Ramos Texico, he is your Assistant Drill Instructor. Any orders coming from him are the same as if they came from me." In his head Musher immediately named Texico, "The Junior Monster, and from hereinafter referred to as TJM"

The platoon was scrambling to get into uniform. When it looked like the platoon was fully clothed The Monster spoke again, "Put on your field jacket and fall in outside by squad. Come on, move it." After I put on my field jacket I grabbed my money, cigarettes and matches and stufffed them into the jacket. Maybe all Monsters, Junior Monsters and Baby Monsters were not totally honest.

As I went through the barrack door there stood The Monster. Everyone else was formed by squad. The Monster barked, "Smart Ass, do you think you have special permission to do as you please just because you are so smart? As of right now you are on latrine duty until I tell you otherwise. Get your ass in the ranks." With that pearl, The Monster marched us off to the mess hall for breakfast. Like everything else with The Monster he took us via the longest route and drilling us all the way. At the Mess Hall he gave his little speech. "It is now 0600 hours (6 A.M.) and the next time you will see food will be at the noon meal. I suggest that those of you who have lived on cigarettes and coffee for breakfast reconsider the cigarettes and coffee and eat a normal American breakfast. Fall out by squads into the line, second squad first, third squad next and by now you should have figured out which squad goes last. When you finish eating fall in at this location. No talking in line. Go!"

Breakfast was all right. I had scrambled eggs, meat they said was pork sausage, fried potatoes, buttered toast and cold milk. Musher had never had that kind of breakfast. Yea, many times around one or two o'clock in the morning after a hard nights fucking around, he had had that kind of a meal and coffee; but, never, never for breakfast. Eventually the full platoon was in place. Once more The Monster marched us, obviously the long way around, to a place we already knew, Quartermaster II. The Monster spoke, "Inside they will issue you physical training shorts and shirt, two pair of athletic socks, a jockstrap, a foot locker, a pair of sneakers, a pad lock with two keys, another towel, and another laundry bag. You are to fit it all in your foot locker, put one key in the locker, pad lock your foot locker and put the other key in your pocket. Third squad will go first, and if you have not figured out the rotation by now you are a bigger bunch of stupid assholes than I first thought. Remember no talking in the line. Third squad, Go."

"Time to go" barked The Monster as the platoon had formed some semblance of four squads. It was comical to see the platoon. Some guys dropped their locker, others were trying to balance them on their head as they had seen Asians and Africans do in the movies. The rest of us tried anything just to make it to wherever The Monster was taking us. The Monster must have been in a good mood because we could tell it was the shortest distance to our barracks and he was not doing a lot of cadence counting. "Fall out, you have a ten minute latrine break and then stand by your bunk."

The Musher didn't care about a latrine break. What he cared about in the latrine was a chance to have a couple of Lucky Strike cigarettes. Just about the time the match would touch the cigarette The Musher heard a voice, "I don't reckon you supposed to smoke in here. You will get us all in trouble again." The Musher ignored him and took a deep drag from his Lucky Strike and slowly exhaled the nerve settling good tasting smoke. The voice said, "Iffin you don't put out that cigarette, I am going to stomp your ass." Mr. Cool, The Musher replies, "Tell you what hillbilly, take five minutes to go get a flashlight and a lunch, I'll smoke some cigarettes and when you get back, I will not only stomp your ass, but I will make sure the shit comes out your dick. Is that a deal or not?" Poor hillbilly, ready to fight, he took a boxer's stance, slight crouch, one fist held at eleven o'clock position and the other at the two o'clock position, elbows in and chin down. At that moment, The Musher kicked him in the balls, threw a punch to his adam's apple and dragged him by the hair and put his face in a commode, which he then flushed. The Musher moved away by three commodes (you have to understand the latrine was a row of twelve commodes on one side and a

22

twenty foot piss trough on the other), he lit another cigarette and waited for hillbilly to rejoin the world.

Just as Musher finished his cigarette came the order, "Stand By Your Bunk". The Musher strolled out of the latrine wondering, but not caring, if hillbilly would drown.

Through the barracks door came the Monster, TJM, and five more Monsters. The Monster announced, you all will be divided into six teams each with its own instructor and you will make your bunk and remake your bunk until you make your bunk in such a way as to please the United States Army; then you are going to learn how to properly mount and tie your laundry bag on the aisle bar of your bunk; then you are going to learn how to properly display the items which will be in your foot locker; then you will learn how the United States Army insists you hang clothes on the rack behind your bunk; then you will learn how to place your shoes under your bunk; and lastly, you will learn from me that your foot locker is never to be left unlocked when you are not there. I repeat your foot locker is never to be left unlocked when you are not there. Instructors take over."

Midway in the barracks a Monster Instructor called for The Monster. "Sergeant it seems this group is one soldier short." The Monster looked at the group, "What is his name and where is he?" One member of the group said "Brad Randolph", another member, "The last thing he said was that he was going to the latrine." To the Monster Instructor, "carry on with this group". With that The Monster headed for the latrine. As he entered the latrine he saw a soldier sitting on the floor, resting against a commode and wet down his chest. "I take it you are Randolph. You look like you have been dumped in a commode." With that Randolph's eyes started to tear and he began sobbing. "Who did this to you?" No answer. "I would guess the smart ass Muscarello except he is only half your size." Randolph's tearing, sobbing and crying became louder and stronger. "Was it Muscarello?" Randolph nodded his head up and down. "OK, pull yourself together and join your group." Amazingly enough all those things that The Monster said they would learn in the barracks, they did learn. They were not perfect in their execution but it was obvious they would be.

The platoon wrapped up in barracks training just in time to fall in for lunch. The Monster avoided looking at the Musher and did not speak directly to him. The march to chow (he adopted the Army slang for a meal) was uneventful. Marching maneuvers, cadence counting and The Monster's speech at the Mess Hall. When the platoon got back to its barracks The Monster gave instructions." Fall out, get into your athletic clothes, square away your area and be back here in ten minutes. Do not be late".

I knew I wasn't going to be late to fall in. I wasn't going to be the first, but I was not going to be the last. By now the story had spread among the platoon how Musher beat Randolph's ass, stuck him in a commode and left him to drown. If the platoon knew it, then certainly The Monster knew it. He had not said a word or even looked directly at Musher.

For the next two hours we did PT (Physical Training). Jumping jacks, knee bends, squats, push ups, sit ups and a few others. The Monster and TJM drifted between the ranks chastising and yelling for more effort. Musher was not the least bit concerned. He could feel the sweat running and he was still breathing normally. He thought to himself, keep it up guys you are making me feel better by the minute.

When the platoon got back to the barracks The Monster gave his instructions: "You have thirty minutes to shower, change into fatigues, square away your area and standby to fall in. If you must smoke, smoke in the latrine. Make sure you flush the butts down a commode but don't worry about any ashes or mess you leave. Smart Ass is the latrine orderly and he will take care of the cleaning. Now Smart Ass needs a helper, who among you wants to volunteer to be his helper?" A voice boomed out, "I do!" It was The Rod. The Monster looked shocked, "Why in the hell would you want to do that?" The Rod boomed out equally loud, "Because I've got his back!"

Musher and Rod headed into the shower and as Musher lit up Rod just sat and watched the other members of the platoon. The showers were on the same motif as the commodes, fourteen shower heads in a line with only a small space between them. When Musher finished his cigarette and he and Rod went into the shower room all the positions were in use. Musher exclaimed, "Which two of you are finished?" Suddenly four positions emptied and Musher and Rod simply took their choice, back to back.

Following an hour and one half of Close Order Drill, sharpening the platoon's marching skills, The Monster halted the drill. He spoke, "You are looking better but you are a far cry from representing the Fort Benning Drill Team. Today we will march to the Headquarters complex for a retreat ceremony. A retreat ceremony is the proper lowering of the flag of the United States and indicates the closure of another day on the post. During the lowering the bugler will play retreat and the ceremony will conclude with the firing of a blank round cannon. I want you to present yourselves as soldiers of the United States Army and do us all proud."

Retreat was breathtaking. All the shining helmets, the immaculately dressed honor guards, the bayonets glistening in the evening sun, the slow tempo with which the flag was lowered, the Bugler blowing soft sounds and

24

finally the roar of the cannon. The sensation reminded him of his first kiss. It sent tingles up and down his spine.

In an almost whispered tone The Monster said, "Forward March". All the way to the Mess Hall The Monster counted soft cadence and when we arrived there he simply said, "OK you know the rotation, no talking in line and form here when you're finished. Remember you can take all you want but you must eat all you take. Go." Away went the fourth squad. When it came my turn on the actual chow line, I had some mashed potatoes and the next item was meat in gravy. I asked the mess server what it was and he said, "steak". May I have two pieces and he graciously put on the second piece. With the way those trays ran your food together I simply got some corn, a roll and a glass of milk. I sat at the table, cut off a piece of steak, put it in my mouth, took one chew and gagged. From the other end of the table came a loud laugh, it was one of the southern boys in the platoon. "Smart Ass Boy, that is liver. Here in the south they call it nigger steak." The commotion caused two Mess Sergeants to be standing over me pointing to the, "Take all you want, but you must eat all you take". The Rod offered to help me eat all I had taken but the two Mess Sergeants were adamant about the fact that help was not part of the rule. The next fifteen minutes were undoubtedly the worst fifteen minutes I had ever had. I got it all into my stomach, and I was determined I would not give them the satisfaction of being sick. That determination only lasted long enough for me to get out of the Mess Hall, off the asphalt assembly area and onto the grass where I upchucked and upchucked until I thought I would drop. I managed to fall in and march back to the barracks. All I could think of was let me lie down and with any luck die.

In front of our barracks, The Monster: "You recruits have worked so hard today that as a reward we are going to have a G.I. (Government Issue) Party. So if you will fall out and stand by your bunks, I shall be right in with the refreshments. Remember, stand by your bunks, do not sit on them, do not lie down on them, just stand." With Rod's help I made it up the barrack steps and fortunately there was a pillar next to my bunk. Rod propped me there as I awaited the worse.

CHAPTER 10
There Is Nothing Like a Party
To End Day Two of Basic Training

In a few minutes the doorway was filled by The Monster and TJM. In their hands they carried mop buckets, mops, scrub brushes, rags and G.I. lye soap. The Monster had an ear to ear smile as he proclaimed, "Recruits, a G.I. Party is designed to make clean and sanitary the quarters in which the recruits are billeted. I and Sergeant Texico will be close by and when you believe this barracks is ready for inspection you just tell us and we shall inspect. The entire latrine is the responsibility of Smart Ass and his helper. OK Smartass, you and your helper get your gear and head for the latrine. The rest of you decide how you are going to get this barracks clean and sanitary. Remember, the sooner this barracks passes inspection, the sooner this day ends. With that The Monster and TJM left the barracks.

Musher's vomiting and dry heaves had completely drawn him down. The Rod practically carried Musher into the latrine, shutting all doors behind him. He took Musher into the shower area, put two of the clothing benches together, stripped his fatigues to make a pillow for Musher and spoke gently,"Buddy, lay here until you feel better. Rod has done enough shit work in his life to make this a walk in the park. Remember, I've got your back." With that Rod began the scrubbing process. Musher had no notion of how much time had passed since Rod lay him down but he was waking up and now believed he would live. He got up went to Rod gave him a big hug and said, "Let me in the game. You are working too hard."

When they thought the latrine was as clean and sanitary as they could make it they sought out The Monster. The Monster walked into the shower area, unscrewed one of the shower heads and pointed, "Look at the buildup minerals clogging this shower head. You need to clear them all." He turned on his heel, "call me when you are ready for inspection" and he left the latrine. It dawned on Musher and Rod that no matter how hard they worked The Monster could always find a way to not pass their inspection. Still there is the problem, how to clear mineral deposits from fourteen shower heads. They decided Rod should go into the barracks bay, see what he could see that might do the trick for these holes and just simply appropriate it for their use. They knew that if Musher went out there it would lead to a brawl and Musher was not ready for that yet.

Rod returned shortly showing three ball point pens. "Don't know who donated them but they were just lying there calling me." Rod had lots of experience with items "falling off a truck". So they unscrewed all the shower heads, sat on the clothing benches and leisurely dug out the mineral buildup. After all, they knew The Monster would find something else they needed to do.

The Musher asked Rod, "Before we seek out The Monster, how is the rest of the platoon doing in the barracks?" Rod, "They look like they are working hard but don't seem to be organized." They called for The Monster to inspect.

The first thing The Monster checked was the shower heads, all fourteen of them. He went on, "You two are resourceful and tough. You both will probably make good infantrymen. You SmartAss if you could keep your mouth shut and temper in control you would make it. Helper, you have what it takes to be an infantry killer. I pass your inspection. The rest of your platoon is struggling to get it right. You two have two choices, you can go and assist the rest of the platoon or you can go sit on the barracks steps and relax. Which is it?" Before Musher could speak Rod did. "Fuck em and feed 'em frijoles. You didn't see any of those pussies stepping up to help us!" The Monster left, Musher said to Rod, "That prick is driving the wedge deeper between me and you and the rest of the platoon." Rod repeated, "Fuck em and feed 'em frijoles." With that they went to sit on the barracks steps.

About and hour and half later the rest of the platoon passed inspection and The Monster left the area. Musher didn't wait for lights out he crawled into his bed and was out like a light in a matter of seconds.

CHAPTER 11
Day Three of Basic Training

The platoon was getting smarter. When The Monster and TJM came in at five o'clock in the morning turning on all the lights and banging the garbage can lids, most of the platoon was already awake. Musher was on his feet, had made his bunk (US Army compliant) and was busily getting dressed. Naturally in a group of thirty-six guys there are those who just cannot move with the rest of the unit. The Monster was on their case trying to hustle them along without causing them to fail. The march to breakfast and breakfast itself went without a hitch. After breakfast we began a routine that would last for three weeks.

- Make sure the barracks was in inspection order.
- Two hours of close order drill and its attendant military commands.
- Back to the barracks, change into physical training gear.
- Two hours of physical training.
- Back to the barracks, change into fatigues. Lunch
- Two hours of close order drill and its attendant military commands.
- Back to the barracks, change into physical training gear.
- Two hours of physical training.
- Back to the barracks, change into fatigues. Dinner

After dinner a class was held in the barracks on such subjects as General Orders and the Articles of War. You must recall that in those years there was no such thing as the Uniform Code of Military Justice (UCMJ). Before the UCMJ commanders at different echelons in the pecking order could, on simply their own word, either promote enlisted men to whatever grade they chose if such grade existed in their echelon table of organization, or reduce (Army calls it bust) any enlisted man to any enlisted rank they chose.

When class ended, we were given one hour of free time to write letters (something the Army encouraged) or just generally relax. Smoking was restricted to the latrine or outside the barracks

During those three weeks we lost five members of our platoon. Either they could not handle the daily schedule or were released by the Army for some other reason. The platoon was reinforced by six soldiers who had been part way through basic training but did not complete the training. For example, there are a number of cases where the soldier was injured and had to leave his platoon. Maybe there was a situation at his home which without him his family could not stay together as a family; and when he got his problem solved he returned to basic training. The question which hung is if we lost five from our platoon, why did we gain six? Why??

CHAPTER 12
Day Four of Basic Training

Getting up to the tune of The Monster's garbage can lids has become even easier. The platoon hustles through the bed making, teeth brushing, squaring away the area and falling out. The six new replacements for the platoon were standing in front of the formation. The Monster eyeballed the platoon and inserted five of the replacements into various squad positions. The sixth replacement stood alone in front of The Monster. The Monster spoke,"This is Private Antonio Bartolucci. He has had many more weeks of basic training than you all have. Just as the other five replacements will, Bartoluccci will complete his basic training with this platoon. Because his training is beyond yours, not to mention his height, he will be the Guidon Bearer for this platoon. His marching position will be one normal step in front of the fourth squad leader. The TJM came from the barracks carrying a pole with a flag on it. TJM gave it to The Monster who told us this is a Guidon. The flag is your flag. It has inscribed on the flag your platoon name, 656th Infantry Training Platoon. What is the purpose of the guidon? The guidon bearer keeps the cadence of the march; and, whenever the platoon is given a prepatory order the flag goes high in the air. The flag is brought down when the execution order is given. For those of you who feel it might be easy to be the guidon bearer just remember he carries it between his thumb and first three fingers. When the platoon forms the guidon bearer will position himself in front of the first squad and on my first preparatory marching command, the guidon bearer will post to his position in front of the fourth squad. It is nice to have your own flag but remember every time the platoon screws up everyone will know it was the 656th. With that The Monster barked "Forward" (the guidon bearer posted to his position and raised the flag high into the air,) "March". Down came the flag and as the platoon stepped off it was almost as if you could feel a new pride in the platoon.

The march to the mess hall was invigorating. The chow was good and everyone seemed eager to get back into formation. During the march to the barracks The Monster taught us our first ditty. The Monster began, "I don't know but I've been told", the platoon chimed in, "Eskimo pussy is mighty cold", The Monster, "left –o right -o left".

At the barracks we got ready for our daily routine:
- Make sure the barracks was in inspection order.

- Two hours of close order drill and its attendant military commands.
- Back to the barracks, change into physical training gear.
- Two hours of physical training.
- Back to the barracks, change into fatigues.
- Lunch
- Two hours of close order drill and its attendant military commands.
- Back to the barracks, change into physical training gear.
- Two hours of physical training.
- Back to the barracks, change into fatigues
- Dinner

When we got back to the barracks after evening chow, The Monster announced, "There will be no evening class training tonight. You are free to do as you please until lights out at 2200 hours (10 P.M. to you civilians). I shall be back for the bed check." With that he left the area.

The Musher could not wait to sit with Rod on the barrack steps and smoke his Lucky Strikes. In a couple of minutes they were joined by the guidon bearer Antonio Bartolucci. They welcomed him to sit, offered him a cigarette and struck the match for him. The Musher made the introductions, "I am called Musher and this is my goombah, The Rod." Bartolucci said, "I have already heard about you two. Musher you kicked the shit out of guy twice your size and almost drowned him in a commode. Rod you faced down Master Sergeant Dupree by telling him you had Musher's back. I want us to be a trio. I come from Steubenville, Ohio. I am short but a decent dirty fighter. I am loyal to my friends and will walk through fire with them if that is what they need. I know a little more about basic training than you two do and I can be some help." Then it is settled said Musher and Rod together, "Among ourselves we shall be The Monster Eaters." Bart did not understand the significance of the brand until Musher explained just who the monsters were.

The Musher thought to himself, **MAYBE FREDDIE WAS NOT RIGHT. THESE TWO GUYS SEEM LIKE OUR KIND OF STREET PEOPLE!**

CHAPTER 13

Days Five and Six of Basic Training

The morning awakenings, the march to and from the mess hall, the breakfast and return to the barracks area were wholly unremarkable. Only today, the daily routine changed and no one knew for how long. The new routine:
- Make sure the barracks was in inspection order.
- Three hours of classroom training on various subjects such as sex hygiene, army command units, basic arithmetic and what to expect as a soldier when you leave the fort.
- Back to the barracks, change into physical training gear.
- One hour of physical training.
- Back to the barracks, change into fatigues.
- Chow (notice how Army I am becoming)
- Two hours of close order drill and its attendant military commands.
- Back to the barracks, change into physical training gear.
- Two hours of physical training.
- Back to the barracks, change into fatigues
- Chow

The after dinner schedule was also different. We were given homework which was to be completed and brought back to class the next day. We were allowed two hours to do the home work. When you finished whether it was in two hours or less, the remaining time to lights out was at our disposal. The homework was so simple it took Musher fifteen minutes to do it and his two members of The Monster Eaters ten minutes to copy it. Our after chow nights were pleasant.

I did notice I was getting tired and bored with the simple routines.

CHAPTER 14

Day Seven of Basic Training

It was just before 0500 hours and Musher lay in his sack (another Army term he picked up from The Monster instead of bunk) waiting for The Monster and his gang to come through the barracks door in their usually quiet manner. At least fifteen minutes went by before someone in the barracks said "It is 0530, do you think they all died?" A quick response from somewhere, "No such luck!" Guys were getting up, going to the latrine and crawling back in the sack. Nobody in the platoon was getting up and starting any routine.

Sometime later The Monster and TJM appeared in the barracks. The Monster began, "In case you did not know it today is Sunday. I know I forgot to tell you this but on Sunday training eases off, we have a late breakfast and everybody, I repeat everybody goes to church. The Army likes it soldiers to go to church. Now, square away your area, dress in your best fatigues and please fall in as quickly as possible. The guidon will remain in the barracks." The shock in the platoon was very noticeable. No one was talking. They were moving through their tasks like robots.

The march to the mess hall was quiet, soft cadence, no singing and marching commands were almost a whisper. At the mess hall The Monster spoke," Today is very different, it is now 0730 hours, you will be allowed forty-five minutes to have your breakfast. There is also another exception, recruits may have coffee. There will be no talking in line but you may talk at your breakfast table. Remember, take all you want but you must eat all you take. Assemble here after breakfast. First squad, go."

Coming off the serving line The Monster Eaters sat together drinking coffee and not caring how much they ate. They took very little food so that they would have more time to drink coffee. Bart spoke in low tones, "Listen guys when we leave the mess hall The Monster and TJM will be asking what is your religion of choice. As of this moment you are Methodists. If you say Catholics to The Monster or TJM then you go to a Catholic mass which is a lot of kneeling, standing and sitting. If you say Methodist then you go to the Protestant service which is all sitting. This is my first but not last contribution to The Monster Eaters." The three of them drank coffee and chewed on toast until they were sure they needed to leave or be late for formation. Just as surely as Brad had warned them they were asked their choice of religion; and just as surely they answered Methodist. The

33

formation had been divided into Catholics and all others. There were a good number of Catholics. The all others ranged from Protestants to Muslims to Hebrews.

The Monster took the Catholics and marched off, TJM took the All Others and they too marched off. Church was quiet, peaceful and very different from any Catholic mass Musher remembered. He thought to himself, wouldn't my mother be proud to know I went to church. I don't know how she would react to the fact that it was a Protestant church. After church TJM marched the All Others back to the barracks. Again, the march to the barracks was quiet, soft cadence, no singing and marching commands were almost a whisper.

We had no sooner got up the barracks steps than The Monster bellowed, "Fall in, and bring the guidon." As the platoon was forming The Monster continued, "I told you on Sunday that the training eases off; however, I never said it stops. Platoon, Forward, March". For the next two and one half hours the platoon executed close order drill and learned new close order drill maneuvers. Enroute to the barracks The Monster taught us another ditty. The Monster (making sure his first word came when our left foot was on the way to the ground), "Jody was there when you left, Jody was there on the phone, Jody is gone from your home, and Jody ain't moving alone. Count cadence count." As the left foot of the platoon came down the platoon musically did the cadence count; one, two, three four, one, two, three, four. The Monster again, "Break it down." Again when the left foot of the platoon came down the platoon musically did the cadence count breakdown; one, two, hesitation as the left foot touched for the second time and then as the right foot was about to hit, in rapid succession, three, four.

At the barracks TJM gave the order to fall-out, change to fatigues and standby to fall in. Musher changed quickly and went into the latrine to have a smoke. Lo and behold who was there but Brad Randolph, The Defender of Clean Air. Musher took a Lucky Strike, inhaled deeply and exhaled the smoke right at Brad Randolph. "Hillbilly you got a problem? For you hillbilly, last time was only a preview of what happens to little guys who fuck with me. Take your choice, make a move or get the fuck out of this latrine!" With that Randolph turned on his heels and walked out. As Musher glanced at Randolph, Randolph passed the other two members of The Monster Eaters who were in rumble ready stance. Came the command to fall-in.

TJM herded the platoon to chow and back again to the barracks. Waiting on the barracks steps was The Monster. He spoke with a jovial tone, "Today has been a fun Sunday. I can think of no better way to end the day than with a bone tickling G.I. party. I have a couple of assignment changes. Effective immediately Private Randolph you are the new keeper of the latrine. Private Randolph needs a helper, is there a volunteer?" To no one's surprise there was not a sound from the platoon. The Monster injected, "In the absence of such camaderie I appoint Private Benjamin Jackson. Private Jackson your appointment is effective now." Private Benjamin Jackson, Stoney as he was known in the platoon, was one of three black soldiers in the platoon. It seems the President of the United States, Harry Truman, was doing token integration in preparation for full removal of segregation in the armed forces. Stoney wasn't exactly a tall guy but when naked you could see the ripples of muscle and the solidity of his body. At this moment the way he leered at The Monster Musher thought that with further investigation Stoney could be a candidate for membership in the exclusive club, The Monster Eaters. The Monster did not even give Stoney a second look as he turned to leave the barracks with a loud message, "Call me when you are ready for inspection."

As people were getting buckets, brushes, etc., most of the platoon was standing around looking like they had their thumb up their ass. The Musher got on his foot locker and called for quiet. His call was echoed by The Rod and Tony B. When the platoon silenced Musher went on. "My intelligence, The Rod here, said you guys took so long to pass inspection not because you were not working hard, but because you were not working smart. I have a few suggestions. We divide this barracks into four parts. Part 1, the support pillars and cross beams. Part 2, the windows and the ledges. Part 3, one half of the floor from the entryway to the middle. Part 4, the remaining portion of the floor. Squad leaders will be in charge of their part and control their squads. Does anyone object to this plan? We will assign the parts in accordance to squad number. Believe me guys, there will be a lot more of these G.I. parties and in our normal squad rotation we will all get a chance to do each part. As for me, Rod and Bart we shall be a floaters. Wherever we see lagging we shall jump in and give that squad a boost. If there are no questions let's get at it."

The squads grabbed their equipment, went to their area and worked at breakneck speed. By and large the squad leaders were controlling their work effort. There was for sure two things happened at that G.I. party, The Musher became the unquestioned recruit platoon leader; and, his two associates, Rod and Bart, were there to support his decisions via of whatever means necessary.

When Musher thought the barrack was inspection ready he sent the first squad leader to get The Monster. Typical of the G.I. party The Monster pointed out some deficiencies in the cleaning then left. Musher pacified the platoon by telling them that this is the norm for G.I. parties. The platoon pitched in to clear the deficiencies and Musher sent the second squad leader to get The Monster. After his inspection The Monster said they passed and they were free until lights out. The two guys doing the latrine had not finished so the latrine was off limits until they passed inspection.

CHAPTER 15

The Second Week of Basic Training

The morning awakenings, the march to the mess hall and the breakfast went rather smoothly. The Monster did his share of ass chewing (another Army term for being rebuked and chastised) and made his usual speech at the mess hall. When the platoon was formed after breakfast we did not return to the barracks. Instead The Monster marched us to a building brightly marked as "The Armory".

The Monster spoke." Inside this building you will be issued your dog tags (Army slang for identification tags), a black marking pen, a second pair of fatigues, a third pair of sox, a helmet, a helmet liner, a web belt, a canteen with eating utensils, a bayonet with scabbard, and a US Army M1A1 caliber .30 rifle. When you sign for these items you must be sure the serial number of your rifle is the same as the serial number for which you sign. As always my same rules apply. No talking in the line. Second squad, Go."

When Musher left the Armory he actually started to feel as if he were in the United States Army.

The march to the barracks was not very smooth what with everyone loaded with gear that was difficult to manage. Fortunately before we left the armory area The Monster taught us how to shoulder sling a rifle. At the barracks he ordered us in to store our gear, lay our rifle on the sack and fall-in.

Today, the daily routine changed again. The new routine:
- Make sure the barracks was in inspection order.
- Three hours of field training with our rifle. Training on the Infantry Manual of Arms. Training to name every part of the rifle's composition, and to explain the function of that part. Training so that blindfolded we could disassemble the rifle and reassemble the rifle in less than one minute. Training called "dry fire" where one is taught to sight the rifle on the target and squeeze the trigger, not pull the trigger.
- Back to the barracks to stow rifles and gear.
- Chow
- Two hours of close order drill bearing our rifles.
- Back to the barracks, change into physical training gear.
- Two hours of physical training.
- Back to the barracks to stow rifles and gear.

- Chow

The post–chow training class was the explanation of dog tags and the fact that you must wear them at all times. The Monster stressed the reasons why the two dog tags were on separate chains, why they were oval shaped and why each had small notches grooved into the dog tags. In a softer voice he continued, when a soldier is killed the short chain tag is taken from his body to return to graves registration to verify his death. The long chain tag is used when the soldier's mouth can be propped open and placed between his teeth. The notches serve to allow placing the tag between the upper and lower teeth and shutting the mouth with the tag showing. Rigor mortis keeps the tag in place.

"Today you were given a black marking pen. You will mark all your clothing with the last four digits of your serial number. In case you cannot remember your serial number it is on your dog tags. You will place the marking so that it may not be seen when you are wearing your clothing. This Friday is laundry day. Any clothes you send to the laundry which are not marked will not be returned to you. Begin by marking your laundry bag. That marking may be visible when the bag is not mounted on your bed.

That's it for tonight. Lights out in two hours." With that The Monster left the barracks.

CHAPTER 16

The Second Week of Basic Training

Tuesday and Wednesday daytime activities were clones of the Monday activities, rifle training and physical training. The post dinner chow meetings were quite different. Each member of the platoon spent the next three hours disassembling, cleaning and reassembling his rifle. During all that effort TJM walked within the platoon, checking the assembly work, asking questions about the rifle components and their functions. The manner in which TJM conversed, screaming and berating gave solid evidence that he would one day be a full grown monster.

After breakfast on Thursday morning as usual we returned to the barracks. There The Monster instructed we make sure the barracks was in inspection order, put on our helmet liners instead of hats, bring our rifles and fall-in, because today the platoon would go to the rifle range. In addition, the platoon would actually fire live rounds at a stationary target. "Platoon, Prepare to sling rifles, Left shoulder, Sling." (some confusion but generally not bad). It is only a short three mile march to the range so lets get started, For…ward, March."

At the rifle range The Monster turned the platoon over to a Range Safety Non-Commissioned Officer (NCO). He was a master sergeant who never gave his name and spoke clearly but softly. The range safety rules were thoroughly explained. When he finished his explanations four additional range safety NCO's joined the group. Each NCO took a section to the firing line. On the line the platoon was familiarized with the targets, were shown the proper standing, kneeling and prone shooting positions and how to use the rifle sling to aid steadiness. The platoon was ordered to the prone shooting position. The platoon had had so much "dry fire" training that when the section NCO handed each one a live caliber thirty round and instructed "Lock and Load" , you could hear rifle bolts open and slam shut. The next loud notice came from the section NCO's at either end of the firing line, "Ready on the Left, Ready on the Right." The senior Range Safety NCO gave the command, "Fire". The noise from thirty-seven rifles reverberated inside the helmet liners. The target results were displayed. Some had completely missed the target and no one had scored a bullseye. The shooting exercise was repeated three times from each shooting position. The scoring improved but the platoon did not have a Buffalo Bill. "Clear rifles", commanded the senior Range Safety NCO. Each platoon member backed up one step from the firing line. The senior Range Safety NCO again, "Inspection Arms". Each platoon member brought his rifle to port arms (a diagonal angle across the chest) locked the bolt open, and waited for the inspector. The section NCOs went from soldier to soldier ensuring there were no rounds in the chamber. One by one the section NCOs bellowed, "Clear". Once more the senior Range Safety Officer, "Close bolts, fall-out and police the brass." Police the brass meant pickup all the empty shell casings and place them in the proper receptacles.

The Monster awaited the platoon in the staging area "You did quite well for a bunch of first time firing dumb-ass recruits. You didn't kill or wound anybody. Take heart, you will improve. Today we will have chow in a field kitchen. A field kitchen is a bunch of tents where cooks do the best they can with portable gas stoves. Eating at a field kitchen is a little more relaxed than the mess hall. You can talk in line; however, you can take all you want but you must eat all you take. After eating you will take your trays and utensils to the G.I. cans (regular garbage cans but like everything else Government Issue) and follow the instructions. There are no tents, tables or chairs for anyone except the soldiers permanently assigned to the firing range. You will put your ass down wherever you can. Of course, you can always stand if you do not want to dirty your pretty fatigues. By the way, you can smoke here in the great outdoors. Third squad. Go."

The Monster Eaters recounted the firing line experience. Each could not believe he fired so poorly. They swore an oath to improve. Chow was not bad, Musher was not sure what it exactly was but it did not gag him so it definitely was not liver. There was an additional advantage to eating lightly. It gave him more time to enjoy his Lucky Strikes. He noted they were almost all gone and he must find a way to get more.

Fall-in! The Musher was putting out his cigarette when The Monster appeared before him. He took the cigarette from Musher and said, "Didn't you hear me call fall-in?" Before Musher could answer The Monster kicked him in the ass and said, "Move it!" Musher turned and charged at The Monster. Just as quickly The Monster rotated, grabbed Musher's arm and threw him at the formation. He stood there and watched as Musher got to his feet and made another charge. As Musher approached The Monster he rolled onto the ground towards The Monster hoping to sweep him off his feet. The Monster again was too quick. He made a vertical leap and as Musher rolled by stepped towards Musher and kicked him in the ass again. The Monster spoke contempetioushly, "SmartAss you ain't fucking with one of these kids or one of the tough guys in your neighborhood, you are fucking with a United States Army combat soldier who has killed men with rifle, bayonet,

40

knife and bare hands. If you are so stupid as to try me again come on. I can do this all day. Now get off your ass and fall-in."

Musher was thumped and he made his way into the formation.

Despite The Monster's actions with Musher, he opened his left hand and there was the remnant of Musher's cigarette. "The Army like its properties clean. The Army hates to see cigarette butts on its grounds. When you smoke and want to put out your cigarette you must "field strip" the butt. To field strip the butt you tear open the butt, spread the remaining tobacco into the air, roll the remaining cigarette paper into a ball and you may either eat the paper ball or stash it on your person until you can dispose of it in a trash receptacle. Is there a question on how to dispose of a cigarette butt using the field strip method? Hearing none let us begin our short walk to the barracks. For...ward, March." The Musher was sore from his encounter with The Monster but he knew, he knew he would make it back under his own steam. He thought, some day Monster, some day.

"It's 1600 hours. Fall-out, shower, shave and get into clean fatigues. Load all your laundry into your laundry bag for drop off tomorrow. You are allowed two hundred pieces per month. Don't send so much that you have nothing left for the next seven days. Remember anything that does not have the last four digits of your serial number marked on the item, the item will not be returned. Mount your second laundry bag in the same place and in the same manner from which you took your first laundry bag. Stand by to fall out. We are going to retreat."

The shower, two Lucky Strikes and clean clothes brought Musher back to life. Rod sounded patronizing with, "he caught you off guard, etc." Bart consoled, "We'll get him for this." The barracks undertone was all about how The Monster had kicked Musher's ass three times. Musher decided to attack. Standing on his foot locker he announced, "When you saw me get my ass kicked today it was by a better, more skilled fighter. None of you are in that class! If any of you believe you are then tell me and we shall dance the tune. You may never hear the music again. I am not as forgiving as the Senior Drill Instructor. I shall rip your heart out and feed it to the rats living below this barracks. Those of you who want to dance, the line forms right here." No one moved in the direction of The Musher.

Retreat was as wonderful as the first time. The platoon marched away with its head higher, its steps more crisp and the stride of winners. Chow went without incident The return to the barracks was just as charged with enthusiasm as when the platoon left the Retreat Ceremony.

The Monster spoke, "Tonight we will work on our rifles. Disassemble, clean, assemble and then do it again. Each man will successfully do the exercise twenty-five times. Those of you who finish the exercise quicker than the others will help those who are having difficulty. That is not a request, it is an order. You march like a team, you do physical training like a team, but you are not a team. Each of you watches out for himself. In combat if you are not a team you have no one to rely on, and no one relies on you. Very soon everyone is dead. Figure out why this platoon is not a team, and solve the problem. Lord knows I have tried and cannot."

At each stage of the exercise either The Monster or TJM would inspect that stage and if satisfactory give permission to go on to the next phase of the exercise. Musher and Rod were good at this exercise but no matter how fast they worked because of the waiting for the inspection they were averaging five and one half minutes per successful exercise. One did not need to be a rocket scientist and multiply five and one half times twenty five. One hundred thirty seven and one half minutes, or otherwise stated two and one quarter hours. Probably two of the most qualified recruits to undertake this exercise cannot finish this exercise before lights out.

Right here Musher made another serious boo-boo. He approached The Monster and asked, "Permission to speak to the Senior Drill Instructor?" "Speak SmartAss." Musher expounded, "My bunkmate and I are probably the two most qualified recruits to do your exercise. Despite the fact that no matter how quickly and how well we do a phase we must wait for inspection to proceed to the next phase. Individually one complete rotation of the system takes us five and one half minutes. Twenty-five such rotations will take two and one quarter hours for both him and me. There is no way we can complete the exercise before lights out, not to mention how many in the platoon will not complete even half the exercise." The Monster, "Listen to me Smartass. Don't you think that with as many recruits as we have run through this training that we don't know that no recruit, no matter how good or how bad he may be at this exercise, can ever complete the exercise before lights out. I heard about your organization of the G.I. party and your foot locker speech after I kicked your ass three times. You heard me say tonight that this platoon is not a team. You heard me lie when I said I did not know why. The reason is simple: There is no common belief. Their frustrations and anger are pointed in every direction and they change daily. I am sure you noticed how they behave when we march away from retreat. Their backs are straight, their arm swings are correct, they stay in step and react to commands like old soldiers. Have you figured out why? I will tell you why. When they leave the retreat they have a common belief, God and Country. At that moment they would do anything to preserve that belief. It's a belief that makes heroes and medal winners. Recruit Platoon 656 needs a common belief. I think you are the man to give it to them. I know how you feel about me and as a Drill Instructor there is at least one in every new bunch of recruits that has that hate. You can channel their hate towards me and salt it to keep it strong. When it is strong enough each one will do anything for someone in the platoon just to keep me from getting a small victory. As they grow accustomed to helping each other it will become a habit and the individualism will be gone. Are you willing to test your leadership ability or not?" The Musher shook his head up and down. The Monster continued, "Don't you expect any special treatment from me. You will catch your share of hell but somewhere along the line you will be pleasantly surprised. Now get your ass back to your exercise."

The Musher sat down next to Rod and began the exercise. Rod was bursting to know what happened. The Musher was silent thinking how am I going to get Rod and Bart involved without them knowing what The Monster had said. He guessed he could count on them being loyal followers without asking too many questions. His thoughts were interrupted by TJM's announcement. "Complete the rotation you are doing then stand by your bunk with your rifle."

The Monster: "I am not pleased with the results of this exercise. We will do it again very soon. For tonight you may have free time until lights out. Tonight you will take your rifle to bed with you." He turned and on the way to leave the barracks he could be heard to say, "See you at bed check".

Musher could not wait for a cigarette. He was lighting up as he passed through the latrine doors. After the third cigarette he came back to the platoon bay, stripped, grabbed his rifle and crawled into the sack. This has been a hell of a day.

CHAPTER 17

Friday, the Second Week of Basic Training

Sleeping with a rifle is not easy, but it is better than not sleeping at all. When The Monster and company began their garbage lid orchestral symphony The Monster bellowed, "Come on, out of those sacks. Leave your rifle in the sack to be warm and comfy." With that The Monster and his cohorts left the barracks. As Musher was getting dressed he decided this might be a good time to begin his "the 656th hates The Monster" campaign. In tones loud enough to be heard by the platoon Musher whined, "Will that prick ever stop acting as if he was God. Lord knows the son of a bitch doesn't have to try to make us all feel like shit every time he opens his mouth." The undertones assured Musher that there were already some recruits in his new campaign.

The march to and from chow and the chow itself was standard. The normal ass chewing and bitching about the way the platoon looked when marching. Outside the barracks The Monster announced, "Get inside, square away your area, then fall out with rifle, helmet with helmet liner and web belt with scabbard bayonet attached. Move it. Go."

The platoon marched along a dirt road until they were deep in the middle of the Georgia woods. A space of about two hundred feet by two hundred feet had been cleared and was covered with pine mulch. The Monster began, "Fall-out and make a circle. Sit and listen. This is where you will learn the use of the bayonet." Talking (instructing) through each move The Monster demonstrated the crouch position, both the left and right parry positions, the rifle butt head smash position and the death issuing bayonet thrust. He repeated his instruction and demonstration two more times. When he finished his second demonstration he ordered the platoon to fall in the center of the pine mulched area. He gave the command, "Open Ranks, Hut." Some of the platoon members lost their footing and The Monster barked, "The slippery surface provided by the mulch is why we train in this area. Combat does not always come on smooth surfaces." For the next forty-five minutes The Monster put the platoon through bayonet drill. Each of the five bayonet moves was repeated, repeated and repeated.

The Monster, "Fall-in". The platoon assembled at its original point and he commanded, "Left shoulder Arms, Forward, March." About a half mile away the platoon halted, was given at ease and told to look down range. Among the trees there were heavily packed straw bodies at various intervals and positions. "You are about to use all the training you have received today. Some of those dummies require a head smash, some a parry and other a death thrust. We will run the exercise by squad and as each squad member finishes he will return to this fall-in area. Platoon, Attention! Prepare to Fix Bayonets (with that command each member withdraws his bayonet from its scabbard), then comes the execution command, Fix Bayonets." That was sight to see, some platoon members dropped their bayonets and others did not have a clue how to attach the bayonet to the rifle. The real sight though was the fact that those members of the platoon who knew what to do and how to do it were actually helping those members who were having difficulty. Both Musher and The Monster smiled inside. Fourth squad, Attack!" As each squad went through the exercise they were surprised to find that also in among the trees were Monsters. The Monsters criticized techniques and forcefulness, sometimes stopping a platoon member to demonstrate the proper way to use the bayonet. When all four squads had finished the exercise once The Monster announced we would break for chow. He reminded us that we knew the rules for a field kitchen and that anyone who broke those rules would be treated harshly. Within fifteen minutes we were standing in the chow line. The food conglomeration was known as Sheppard's Pie. It was a mixture of hamburger meat, mashed potatoes and covered with cheese. That and a couple of slices of bread and a glass of milk are enough for any man. The Monster Eaters found a patch of ground and they were joined by the two black men Stoney Jackson and his buddy Tinman Woods. They were welcomed. The conversation centered on what assholes all the monsters were and The Monster was the biggest of them all. Musher was down to his last two Lucky Strikes. Nobody else in the group smokes so Musher thought he best smoke one and save the other. Their gathering was broken by, "656th, mount up and fall-in".

The platoon marched back to the mulch area. There was a weapons carrier, a pickup truck that has been strenghtend to carry troops, ammunition, etc., parked on the edge of the mulch area. "Third squad, empty the equipment from that weapons carrier and put it along the edge of the mulch area." The equipment was football type helmets with full face mask, a chest protector like a baseball catcher's protector, heavy shin pads, heavy gloves and a barbell shaped pole with large nerf balls on either end of the pole.

The Monster, "It is important that you learn to use the bayonet positions against a live enemy. Unfortunately we don't have any live enemies with which to practice and the US Army would take a very dim view if I allowed one or more of you to be killed during training. This is our substitute. We dress you out in the equipment you have been staring at, I select two opponents and they contest the battle of the bayonets. The contest is over when one is on the ground and cannot get up, in the rare case when one of the participants cries Uncle or I stop the contest. Are there any questions? Privates Washington and Dunn you will dress the combatants. Do I have two volunteers for the first contest? Hearing none, Privates Brent and Conseco. Get outfitted."

Neither of these two privates was a very big guy. In all the protective gear they looked like the dog trainers you would see in the movies. The Monster called them to the center of the area. He gave the French command," En Garde." The contestants assumed the parry position and tried circling each other. Brent tried a death thrust, Washington parried and gave Brent a rifle butt head smash. Brent dropped to the ground like a tree struck by lightning. He did not move. The Monster was quickly at his side taking off the helmet and pouring water on his face. Brent came around and The Monster walked him to the edge of the area and propped him against a tree.

"In real combat Brent would be dead. The next pair, Taylor and Bartolucci." Taylor was a least six inches taller then Bart. At the En Garde command Bart faked a thrust to Taylor and when Taylor tried to parry to counter, Bart kicked him square in the balls. As Taylor doubled up Bart moved in and gave him two quick rifle butt head smashes. The Monster yelled, "Contest over." Two of the platoon helped Taylor to sit under the tree beside Brent.

The exercise went on for almost two more hours. Neither Musher nor Rod was called to participate. The Monster brought the platoon back to the bayonet range. He pointed out, "Remember, some of those dummies require a head smash, some a parry and others a death thrust. We will run the exercise by squad and as each squad member finishes he will return to this fall-in area. Platoon, Attention! Prepare to Fix Bayonets, Fix Bayonets." This time it was different, nobody dropped a bayonet and nobody was having difficulty. affixing the bayonet on the rifle. "First squad...Attack!" Two or three more times through the bayonet course and the platoon headed for home

The march to the barracks was a drag. Just about everybody was beat from a very hard day. At the barracks The Monster proclaimed, "Your laundry should be in the general room. Place you rifle in the rifle rack, dirty clothes in the laundry bag, shower, get into some clean clothes and standby to fall-out." Musher decided he better smoke his last Lucky Strike now. He needed it and he may not get a chance later.

After the shower, that heavy helmet and helmet liner off his head, the web belt and bayonet hung behind his bunk, clean clothes and a smoke Musher felt like he was in the world again. He was still troubled by how he would get some cigarettes. Rod leaned over to him, "Why do you think we were not called in the bayonet combat exercise?" The Musher looked at him and said, "He probably knows we are the two meanest sons-of-bitches in the valley and he does not need any more incidents like Brent."

Fall-In. Off to chow and back again to the barracks. "Today was a hard day on your rifle. You will disassemble your rifle, clean it, reassemble it and when you think it is ready for inspection either I or Sergeant Texico will do the honors. When your rifle passes inspection you will be free to square away your area, put all your clothes where they belong and you might even consider writing a letter to your family or friends. The Army likes you to write letters. The folks back home want to know how well you are doing."

In less than ten minutes Musher and Rod had done the deed with the rifles and the rifles passed inspection. There were still some platoon members who were having a hard time with their rifle. The Musher and Rod went throughout the platoon helping those who needed help and in less than an hour every rifle in the platoon passed inspection

The platoon was in a jovial mood. They were not huddled in small groups but instead were sharing jokes and stories. Brad Randolph sidled up next to Musher," I hear you are out of smokes. Would you care to step outside with me and have a smoke?" Musher was not exactly sure what was happening but inside he knew he could handle this hillbilly anytime he wanted to. On the barracks step Randolph pulled from his pocket what he called "the makings". The makings were cigarette papers and a small pouch of Bull Durham tobacco. Randolph deftly placed the cigarette paper between his index finger and the middle finger of his left hand. From the Bull Durham pouch he spread tobacco on about three quarters of the length of the cigarette paper. With those two fingers and his thumb he rolled the paper into a cylinder. He brought the cylinder to his mouth and wet the closing edge of the cylinder with his tongue; then twisted one end of the cylinder closed. In almost the same movement he put the open end of the cylinder in his mouth, lit a match to the cigarette and took a deep drag. Musher stared at him in amazement. Musher used almost all the cigarette papers before he made one cigarette that he could light and actually get three drags before it fell apart.

Randolph slipped away only to return very quickly with a new package of cigarette papers and a pouch of Bull Durham. He handed them to Musher. "No need to thank me, where I come from very few people can afford to smoke what we call tailor mades. Where I live the makings cost five cents each. Keep trying you will get it. Why, I didn't learn to roll my own cigarettes until I was almost seven years old. Good night Musher."

The Musher sat outside trying to roll cigarettes. He managed to get a drag here, two drags there and once almost four drags. In any case it was strong tobacco and it tasted good. Besides, it was time to turn in. In bed he could hear his Uncle Fanucci, the Mafia bookie, "you only gain strength when you make peace with your enemies."

CHAPTER 18

Saturday, the Second Week
of Basic Training

When the morning serenade began and the platoon was on its feet, The Monster gave his instructions. "Get in to your PT (physical training) gear, square away your area and fall-out. The march to the mess hall was standard, the chow was standard and the reformation of the platoon was standard. Without any other words The Monster ordered, "Platoon, Atten-Hut...Forward, March." We must have gone at least three miles before we came onto an immense sports complex. Tennis courts, basketball courts, softball diamonds, a track meet setup and even weight lifting equipment.

"Today is a PT sports day. The Army does not care in which sports you participate but everyone in the platoon must participate in at least one sport. You are expected to play your chosen sport or sports for the next three and one half hours. Anyone noticed not participating with a degree of sincerity will lose his privilege to go to the Post Exchange (PX) store later today. If the platoon gives the impression it is not sincerely playing sports the entire platoon will lose its PX privilege. You can play any game you know or you can make up new games. The goal is three and one half hours of sincere sports participation. You are your own referees and umpires. You are the rule makers for the sport. I and Sergeant Texico will roam the area to measure the sincerity of play. Fall-out and get at it."

Musher concluded, I am no good at basketball, I don't like track, I cannot play tennis, I have never been a weight lifter, I guess the decision has been made for me. As the old Italians would say, Softball it is. Wanting that PX privilege where he could get cigarettes, tooth paste, a tooth brush, a razor and some Bull Durham, he yelled loudly, "Softball players to the diamonds." Musher had played enough stick ball on the streets of Boston and had many times sneaked in to see the Red Sox at Fenway Park. He quickly organized his eighteen players. You eight take off your tops and you are the Skins. You eight get over there and you are the Shirts. You two, Randolph you are the balls and strikes umpire and you Collingsworth are the middle infield umpire. Does anyone have any catching experience. Some hands went up on both sides. He selected one from each side and told them they would change positions with the other catchers after three innings. Does anyone have any pitching experience. This time at least five hands went up on one side, and none on the other. He pointed to the five hands, you and you come over to the Shirts. You and you go over to the Skins. We will change pitchers every three innings. Everyone will get a chance to play. That also includes you Randolph and you Collingsworth. I need three infielders and three outfielders. Just about all hands went up. He pointed to each team alternately, you left field, you center field and you right field. For the Shirts I will play shortstop, pointing to Jackson, you will play first base and then pointing to Tinman, you will play second base. You three remaining infielder Skins, decide among yourselves who will play what position. Remember everyone will play and we will change positions every three innings. The sports complex lockers were filled with high quality equipment. Musher thought, "Wouldn't Freddie like just one hour here? I wonder how he's doing?" The two pitchers flipped a coin to see who would bat first. At that point Randolph bellowed, "Play ball!".

The players were not bad at all. There were a lot of errors made and a lot of base hits because of the minimum field coverage It took almost two hours to play three complete innings. At the end of the three innings the score was Skins 21, Shirts 18. A real pitcher's duel. The day was hot and the guys were doing a lot of running. Musher called for a ten minute water break while the players switched positions. The Monster came by and said, "They look sincere but they don't look like ball players." Without thinking Musher said, "The fucking rules didn't say that had to be good ball players." Before anyone could imagine The Monster slapped Musher in the face. "Smartass aren't you ever going to learn? Get back out there and play ball or whatever it is you are doing." With that The Monster turned and walked away. You could smell and taste the hate from the teams to the Senior Drill Instructor.

Musher spoke to the teams, "Look guys, he is only trying to provoke us into losing our PX privilege. Let's not let him. As my friend Rod would say, "Fuck him and feed him frijoles. Let's get back out there and put on a good show." They never finished another three innings. The game was called when the loudspeaker bellowed, "Store all equipment and return to the staging area."

The march to the barracks was solemn. Everyone in the platoon knew about the slapping incident. The Monster, "Take a shower, clean fatigues and standby to fall in." When Musher opened his foot locker to get a towel there on the top shelf were three packs of Lucky Strikes, six books of matches, a toothbrush and a tube of tooth paste. Since Musher did not believe in fairies, he concluded that The Monster was somehow trying to say, "You did well Smartass."

After chow the platoon went back to the barracks in anticipation of going to the PX. The Monster, "Make sure your area is squared away, and that you have American money to buy anything at the PX. You will have one hour in the PX. Everyone will be allowed to go to the PX except Smartass. He has volunteered to bleach and scrub the front and back steps to the barracks." The Rod broke in, "Sergeant I don't have any money. I will stay here and help Private Muscarello." Other voices chimed in with the same sentiment as Rod's. The Monster: "When you fall-out those of you who wish to go to the PX have five minutes to come out and fall-in. Fall-out." Six minutes passed and not one soldier had come out of the 656th Barracks. The Monster went into the barracks and said, "It would be a shame to waste a Saturday afternoon. What say soldiers, let's have a G.I. Party." The platoon had a G.I. Party that lasted all the way until it was time to go to chow. That night after chow the platoon had rifle exercises until just before lights out.

CHAPTER 19

Our First Kitchen Police (KP)
of Basic Training

Saturday had been a physically and mentally rough day. With the strenuous morning at the sports complex, the afternoon G.I. Party and the after chow rifle exercises, the entire platoon just dragged itself to bed. It seemed to Musher as if he had just closed his eyes when The Monster and TJM were flashing lights off and on and extra loudly beating the garbage can lids. "Come on girls, out of those sacks. It is already 0200 hours (2 A.M.) and we do not want to be late for our three o'clock duty in the mess hall. Sorry I forgot to tell you that the 656th has Kitchen Police (KP) duty today."

As we marched to the mess hall it was as if more than half the platoon was sleep walking. The Monster brought us into the general dining hall and turned us over to the mess sergeants. The Monster told the mess sergeants, I will come by for them about 1900 hours (7 P.M.).

As the mess sergeants approached it was the same two who had stood over Musher in the liver incident. He hoped they would not remember him. That hope was short lived. These two did not look like mess sergeants. They were tall and lean and looked like the type who would run a field kitchen without any bullshit from anyone. The taller of the two said, "I remember you. You're the one the DI calls Smartass. I have just the job for you." The other mess sergeant was handing out assignments. "You eight are in the dining room. Make sure there are salt, pepper and napkins on the table. You six are on the toast makers. Keep loading the bread onto and off the toast maker and the bread wrapping paper policed up. You fourteen will fly the China Clipper. When the dirty trays and utensils are placed in the disposal area you will get them, stack them in the wooden carriers and put them in line to go through the super hot steam sanitizing cleaner. You eight will do pots and pans. You will scrub them clean and rinse them in scalding hot water before placing them in the clean pots and pans racks. You Smartass will clean grease traps. You know what a grease trap is? They are those places along the drainage lines where all the grease and slime accumulate. There are sixty-four such grease traps in this dining hall. You will clean them all. If you don't finish today I am sure your DI will let us have you again tomorrow. Now this dining hall opens for troops at 0500 hours. If you want breakfast get it now. There will be no time to eat later."

52

The only people Musher saw all day were these two sergeants called "KP Pushers". They roamed the dining hall making sure every KP'er was doing his job. They had a particular interest in Musher. The only tools for emptying the grease traps were some pieces of board and your hands. When the KP Pusher told him to break for lunch, no matter how much he scrubbed he did not feel clean and could not get rid of the grease trap smell. Lunch for him was on the back steps of the mess hall with his buddies, Lucky Strikes. Again, after who knows how many more grease traps, around 1630 hours the KP Pusher told him to break for chow. No matter how he scrubbed he could not face eating food with his hands. To the mess hall back steps and chow with his buddies Lucky Strikes. It was 1800 hours when Musher told the KP Pusher that all sixty-four grease traps had been cleaned. The KP Pusher brought the mess sergeant who said," I'm sorry, it was not sixty-four it is sixty-six. You still have the two out on the back steps of the dining hall." Musher lost it, he grabbed the mess sergeant and yelled, "Is this a game to you? I am not a pig and you will not treat me this way!" The KP Pusher put a half-nelson on Musher and held him that way until the military police arrived.

The Monster showed up at the guardhouse (you and me know it as jail). He visited Musher. "I have signed for your release in my custody. I don't know where we will go from here but for now let's get you out of here, a shower, some clean clothes, some food and a few Lucky Strikes." The Monster drove Musher to the barracks in his personal car. As he let Musher out he said, "I will have some sandwiches and coffee sent here from the mess hall and you try to take it easy until morning."

Musher entered the barracks and the entire platoon went silent. He stripped his clothes, grabbed a towel and headed for the shower. The warm water felt good to his body. There was a knock at the shower entrance and there stood David Storm. He held one of those fancy shaving kits that Musher had seen in the expensive stores in Boston. Storm almost whispered, "In this case are some excellent shampoos, soaps and colognes. Please feel free to use whatever you want and as much as you want." With that he turned and left the shower. Musher opened the case and got a whiff of a very masculine content. He used the shampoo liberally, scrubbed with the soap and repeated the process. Just about the time he was ready to leave the shower Rod showed up with clean clothes. While he dressed Musher smoked another Lucky Strike. When they went into the platoon area the platoon was chanting Musher, Musher. On Musher's foot locker sat two sandwiches and two cups of coffee. The Musher was choked. He walked to David Storm to hand him his shaving kit. "I thank you Storm, I have never used anything as fancy as that. I thank all the rest of you for your support. If you will forgive me I am so hungry I could eat the South end out of a North bound skunk."

CHAPTER 20
Basic Training Discipline— Do I Deserve a Break?

The mood in the platoon was somber from the time they got out of the sack until the platoon came back from chow.

As usual The Monster gave his morning guidance. "I know this will make you sad but I will not be with you today. Your day will be guided by Sergeant Texico. You will spend your morning at the firing range. The afternoon will be devoted to bayonet training. By now you know what gear you need for that training. Smartass will not be with you this morning. He and I have an appointment with the Fort Benning Adjutant General regarding the incident at the mess hall. There will be lawyers there. Let's hope for a favorable decision. Sergeant Texico they are all yours and may God help you."

TJM certainly trying to impress the The Monster barked, "You heard the man. Fall out and get to it. Be back in formation in fifteen minutes."

When the platoon obeyed TJM Musher realized he was standing alone with The Monster. The Monster and Musher got into The Monster's car. Command headquarters was well over to the other side of the fort. As they drove by command headquarters The Monster made no effort to stop. "We are very early, about an hour and a half early. Let's stop at the small PX Coffee Shop and have a cup and a cigarette." Inside and settled The Monster said,"Muscarello (the first time he had called Musher anything but Smartass) I am not sure what is going to happen. Last night I talked with the mess sergeant and convinced him to be with us this morning to tell how he had intentionally exerted pressure on you. He will admit he went too far and will say he is partially at fault. I also wrote a brief memorandum to the Adjutant General regarding you, your abilities and your youth. I wanted you to know this so that when we appear before the Adjutant General you will be on your best behavior and above all no smart ass remarks. You are facing charges which could get you a General Court Martial, a Dishonorable Discharge and at a minimum three years of hard labor in the US Army prison at Fort Leavenworth, Kansas. Am I clear? Do you have any questions? OK then, drink your coffee and enjoy your Luckies."

On the way to Command Headquarters The Monster told him to remember his General Orders, "I shall salute all officers and colors not cased." As they walked up the entryway to Command Headquarters Musher tried hard to stride as The Monster did. When The Monster saluted, Musher saluted. He lost count how many times he saluted. Inside the building The Monster went to the Reception Desk. In low tones he spoke, "Master Sergeant Dupree and detail to report to the Adjutant General." The reception sergeant told him 3rd floor, pointed to a bank of elevators and told him to go right up. As they stepped off the elevator the entryway was marble and dark wood. There were at least a dozen heavy chairs lining the wall. The Monster pointed to one and whispered to Musher,"Sit." The Monster went to the reception desk and repeated, "Master Sergeant Dupree and detail to report to the Adjutant General. (AG)" The desk sergeant spoke in a low tone, "Take a seat. He will call you when he is ready."

About that time Master Sergeant Willy Williams, the mess sergeant, came off the elevator. The Monster waived him to sit beside Musher. Master Sergeant Williams nodded to The Monster and took the seat next to me. With a half smile he leaned towards me and said, "Kid I am going to try to help you. I know I was extra rough on you." There the three of them sat in silence like when the nuns were watching you in church. Musher didn't know how long they sat but he was dying for a smoke and his nerves seemed to be coming unglued. Finally the desk sergeant announced "You may go in now." As they stood up The Monster whispered, "Hang in there kid."

The Monster led them in and the three of them formed a line in front of the Adjutant General's desk. Musher could feel that this room was much larger than the waiting room. The officer behind the desk, Brigadier General Quincy Nichols, US Military Academy, Class of 1941, stared at The Monster. The Monster raised one hand in salute and reported, "Master Sergeant Dupree and detail reports as instructed." The AG pointed to a chair across the way in which sat another officer with and eagle on his shoulder. The AG continued, "This is Colonel Salvatore Mucci, the chief law officer for this command. I have read the military police reports of the incident and on the surface it looks like this private, without provocation, attacked a senior non-commissioned officer. Colonel Mucci agrees that a General Court Martial would only take one day, and this private would get a DD (Dishonorable Discharge) and serve a healthy sentence at Fort Leavenworth. Sergeant Dupree I granted this interview because MSgt Williams says he was partially to blame for the incident; and, your memorandum expounded the youth, background and leadership potential of this private. Do either of you two sergeants have anything to add? You private would you like to speak in your own defense?" Musher could barely get the words out of his mouth, "No Sir." You are excused, "Wait outside."

The wait seemed interminable. Despite the air conditioning Musher's fatigues were sweat soaked. He thought about going to an Army prison for three or more years and it scared him to death. The reception desk buzzer rang, "The AG will see you now." The Monster led them in and the three of them reformed a line in front of the AG's desk. "Here is my decision: Private Muscarello will return to his platoon subject to the following conditions, (1) If the private gets into trouble again and comes before me he will most certainly be court-martialed, get a DD and go to Army prison; (2) For the remainder of his basic training, whenever his platoon is excused from duty the private will perform an additional two hours duty on that day. Private Muscarello do you have anything to say?" Once more Musher could barely get the words out of his mouth, "No Sir."

The AG concluded, "Private Muscarello you owe this break to Master Sergeant Dupree. When I was a Second Lieutenant fresh out of the Academy I was thrown into combat. Sergeant Dupree was the platoon sergeant. He kept me from making mistakes and actually covered up the ones I made. This is a repayment to him, not you! Dismissed!" The Monster saluted and they left the room. They couldn't get on the elevator quick enough, out of the building quick enough and to the The Monster's car quick enough. As MSgt Williams headed for his car The Monster said, "Thanks Willy, I owe you a big one." In the car with the air conditioning running Musher asked for permission to smoke. The Monster drew Lucky Strikes from his pocket, gave one to Musher and lit them both from his Zippo (the gasoline burning cigarette lighter which is the standard for military personnel). They cracked the windows and just sat there and smoked without talking at all. After a couple of cigarettes The Monster suggested lunch where they had had coffee. During the ride to the PX, during his lunch of a cheeseburger, fries and a coco cola, (a real treat for a recruit) and during the ride back to the barracks area, Musher unsuccessfully tried to find the words to thank The Monster. At the barracks The Monster told him, "Change into other fatigues, get your rifle, helmet, helmet liner and bayonet gear and fall out." From there the two of them marched to the bayonet area where The Monster assumed command. The rest of the day was bayonet drills. At one point he gave them a twenty minute water and smoke break. The Musher could not wait to hear how it went on the rifle range. The platoon could not wait to hear how things went with the AG.

After chow and the return to the barracks The Monster excused the platoon from any further duty that day. When the platoon went into the barracks Musher picked up a bucket, a mop and soap and headed for the latrine. The platoon looked at him and Rod spoke, "Let me help." Musher got on his foot locker and said, "One of the conditions for me to avoid court martial, a dishonorable discharge and not less than three years in the US Army prison at Fort Leavenworth, is that whenever the platoon is excused from duty I will do an additional two hours detail duty on that day. Unless one or more of you want me to serve that sentence you must be tolerant of my punishment." He never mentioned what the mess sergeant had done and why the AG had let him off so lightly

CHAPTER 21

Weeks Three, Four, Five and Six
of Basic Training

The platoon was in a definite routine. When The Monster and TJM came in at five o'clock in the morning turning on all the lights and banging the garbage can lids, most of the platoon was already awake. Musher was on his feet, had made his bunk and was already dressed. The daily formations and the chow visits to the mess hall were also routine. That doesn't mean The Monster had stopped chewing ass and embarrassing recruits. Musher was still doing his daily two hour extra duty every day and it seemed nobody in the platoon even noticed it anymore. What the platoon did notice was that Musher was behaving like a model recruit soldier.

There were benefits to the routine schedule. The days were spent attending classroom instruction on various subjects, being on the rifle range improving their shooting skills, doing close order drill until the platoon marched as one, playing games at physical training and best of all, there was very little duty after the evening meal. Saturdays were scheduled for a morning G.I. Party, chow and permission to roam Fort Benning until 1600 hours. The permission allowed them to visit the PX. Sundays were as was the first Sunday, late breakfast, church and chow. These Sundays had one exception from the first Sunday, after chow, no duty for the rest of the day. The Musher still did his extra duty of two hours every day.

The Monster Eaters sat on the barracks steps and agreed that something is not right. This is too easy.

The next morning after the platoon had returned from chow The Monster told them to fall-out, square away your area and stand by your bunk. Moments later The Monster and TJM entered the barracks. The Monster was carrying a clipboard. "You have successfully finished Phase I of your basic training. You are qualified in all the skills of an infantryman. Some of you are exceptionally qualified. Today you will enter into Phase II. Some of you will finish Phase II as part of the curriculum at an Army technical training school. If I call your name you will pack all your gear. Later today there will be platoon orderly clerks here with your orders. Trucks will transport you to either the bus station or the train depot. The orderly clerks will board you in accordance with your orders. He started reading the list. Of the thirty-seven recruits in the platoon, only thirteen had been chosen to go to a technical school. The rest of you men are the salt of the United States Army. You will finish Phase II in the program known as "Advanced Infantry." You will be dispersed among various platoons in your new companies. You must pack and be ready to go at 1100 hours. The clerks will be here with your orders and the trucks to transport you. I have one last thing to do. He took another clipboard from TJM. Many of you qualified on the rifle range as either Marksman or Sharpshooter. Looking at your first day at the range and anyone would seriously doubt if you should even be given a rifle. For your shooting skill you are awarded the shooting badge. Look at Sergeant Texico see how he wears the badge. When I call your name Sergeant Texico will give you the appropriate badge. He began, Marksmen, David Storm and called another name until he called nineteen names and had exhausted the marksman list. Sharpshooters, Brad Randolph, Jose Rodriguez and Saverio Muscarello. Sharpshooters, Marksmen, I am proud of you."

Of the twenty-two recruits awarded a shooting badge only one of the thirteen going to a technical school had even qualified as a marksman. The twenty-four recruits going to Advanced Infantry looked at the tech school choices with the look that says, "Yes Pussy, you are going to school because you cannot cut it here with the real soldiers."

The Monster made his last comments before leaving, "To say I and Sergeant Texico have enjoyed your company would be a lie. We have not. We must give credit where credit is due. You are a team. You have overcome virtually every obstacle we have thrown at you and you have put up with the abuse. We congratulate you on successfully completing Phase I. We wish you the best of luck and maybe some day we will serve together. Take care and keep your head down." A turn from the platoon and they went out the barracks door.

When they were gone Musher headed straight for the latrine and his Lucky Strikes. Shortly he was joined by the other two members of The Monster Eaters. They thought, "Calling ourselves Monster Eaters, boy was that name a misnomer!" Bartolucci apologized for being selected for technical training. Rod assured him, "You are just too smart for us street guys." Musher consoled himself with you know you are as smart as any of those pussies. He felt like The Monster fucked him but down deep he knew that The Monster was probably his best friend in this fort.

As Musher was packing his gear he came upon an envelope. Inside the note said "I have told your new platoon sergeant that you have finished Phase I of your basic training and therefore you have finished your daily extra duty. He and I were at Bastogne together. He is hard but fair. Keep your head down and make me proud."

FREDDIE, MAYBE YOU WERE RIGHT, BUT MAYBE YOU WERE WRONG.

CHAPTER 22
Phase II of Basic Training:
A New Beginning

The truck carrying the Phase II trainees stopped in front of what looked like a fancy tent. Musher would later learn that this type "building" was called "a hooch". It was built with an elevated wooden floor, wooden half walls, heavy plastic upper walls and a wood roof. In the hot season the heavy plastic upper walls were swapped for screening. The sign in front of the company headquarters read "C" Company, 112th Infantry, Reinforced. Commanding Officer (CO) Captain Ned Bailey, Company Sergeant Major (CSM) Master Sergeant Luther Wallace.

The six Phase II Trainees unloaded and formed a line in front of the company headquarters. The CSM came out of the company hooch and the trainees came to attention. The CSM spoke, "Count Off". The CSM made assignments. Number one to Platoon "A", numbers two and three to Platoon "B", four and five to Platoon "C" and the last man to Platoon "D"." At ease. Standby here and someone from your platoon will come and give you a hand getting to your new quarters. You will not meet the CO today. Your platoon sergeant will decide what you will do for the rest of the day. You may smoke while you wait."

The Rod and The Musher were ecstatic about the fact that they would be in the same platoon. Platoon Sergeants came and went until only Musher and Rod were left standing in front of the company headquarters. From some distance down the company street a voice barked, "Trainees, A_Ten Hut!" Strutting, not marching and not walking, towards them was a huge black man. He was accompanied by two other soldiers. His fatigues were so perfect you could dice an apple with the creases. His boots were so shined that you could use them as a mirror. His sleeves bore the stripes of a Master Sergeant. In his deepest voice he told them, "I am Master Sergeant Willard Nelson. I am your platoon sergeant. These two gentlemen are Corporal (Cpl) Walters, the first squad leader and Private First Class (PFC) Devine, assistant first squad leader. These two gentlemen will assist you getting to your quarters where you will unpack and square away your area. You have no duty until we form for chow. Any questions? Good. Squad leader take charge of the detail." He did an about face and went into the company headquarters.

In the platoon hooch there were two empty bunks. An upper and a lower. Rod looked at Musher and said, "Hell I am accustomed to the upper. You take the lower," Another deference to the man who had been the untitled recruit leader of the 656th.

They had plenty of time for SSS (shit, shower and shave in the Army vernacular). Musher even had time for a Lucky. He noticed that throughout the platoon bay there were red cans mounted on various posts and stenciled in bold white letters the word BUTTS. Each can had a small amount of water in it and a whole lot of cigarette butts. He presumed smoking in the barracks was allowed. He sat on his foot locker and enjoyed his Lucky Strikes. He disposed of the butts in one of the red cans.

Later as the rest of the platoon came in each one came to Musher and Rod to introduce himself. It was all a matter of nicknames and Musher knew he would never remember them all. Each offered any assistance he could give to make the transition to an advanced infantry unit easier. There was a ring of sincerity in their offers. The call for fall-in to chow formation came from Platoon Leader (PL) Master Sergeant Nelson. The squad leaders adjusted their squads so that Musher and Rod were in the right position for their height. As they marched away the cadence was solid and most of the ditties Musher did not know. At the mess hall, a different one from the one Musher was accustomed to using the PL did not make any speech. He simply gave the fall-out command. The squads filed into the line in order and they chatted and chatted until they got to the actual chow serving line. There were still signs every where "Take all that you want but you must eat all that you take."

It was a good meal, scrambled eggs, fried ham steak, fried potatoes, toast and ice cream for dessert. The seating was by squad and the squad leader made sure that Musher and Rod were separated by three positions. When the squad leader saw Musher with milk he asked if Musher did not drink coffee. With a bobbing head Musher nodded yes. The squad leader told him to go get some. There is no recruit restriction here.

When the platoon got back to the barracks, without any speech the PL dismissed the platoon. Inside the barracks Musher's squad leader, Cpl Walters, spoke to him and Rod. "With the exception of night maneuvers or operations, we are pretty much left alone after chow, Saturday afternoons and Sundays. That does not relieve you of your responsibility to maintain personal hygiene, your area and above all the cleanliness and condition of your rifle. If you play by those rules life in "C" Company can be very pleasant. You can smoke in the barracks any time you are not on duty in the barracks. Sergeant Miller, the Assistant Platoon Leader (APL) will talk to you about your other duties in and out of the barracks. Any questions? No, enjoy your free time."

Truthfully Musher did not know what to do with his free time. He didn't write letters or read books. Instead he spent his free time smoking, taking care of his rifle, his gear and taking long, hot showers.

CHAPTER 23
Life at Advanced Infantry Training

Reveille was at 0630 hours. The squad leaders made sure their squad members were ready. There was no command to fall-out. The platoon knew when to drift out of the hooch and form for reveille. When the PL came the formation went to attention. The squad leaders reported, "All present or accounted for." The platoon went and returned from chow without incident. Musher was still in awe of the relaxed attitude in the platoon. The PL, "You two, Rodriguez and Muscarello, report to the CSM."

At the company orderly room the other four recruits were already there and seated. The CSM directed them to chairs. "Today you will meet the CO. This is the only time you will meet the CO unless you are here for discipline that I cannot handle. In all my time in the Army I have not encountered a discipline case which I could not and did not handle. You will only speak to a Commissioned Officer in response to a question he may ask you. For any answer the first word out of your mouth will be Sir, and the last word out of your mouth will be Sir. Do you understand?" He did not wait for an answer. "Your PL and I will control your lives. You will not get a pass from this fort unless your PL recommends it and I approve it. Now we are going in to meet the CO. You will stand at attention and say, Sir, Private, speak your last name, reports as ordered."

The CO's office was certainly nowhere near the luxurious office of the AG. The CO spoke, "I am always glad to see new recruits in the company. If you were not already capable infantrymen you would not be sent to us. We will make you better. We will make you leaner and meaner. If there are not any questions the CSM will get you moving in the company. Dismissed." The recruits marched out in single file and the CSM saluted the CO. He closed the CO's door behind them. "You did well in there. You kept your mouths shut and you looked pretty good considering what the Army has to work with. Return to your platoon. There will be someone there to give you instructions."

Musher and Rod did not stride to the hooch but neither did they march. They moved briskly with a whispered cadence. Inside the hooch they found Sergeant Miller, the Assistant Platoon Leader. The APL jumped directly into the subject at hand. There is a bulletin board at the entry to the hooch and another one in front of the orderly room Those boards will list extra duty detail assignments for a two week period. It is your responsibility to check those boards and tell your squad leader when you will be at an assigned detail. You are expected to pull KP. All soldiers below the rank of Corporal pull KP. You are expected to pull guard duty. You are expected to pull hooch fire watch. You are expected to pull latrine duty. You are expected to clean the hooch butt cans. You are expected to vigorously participate in G.I. parties. You will be briefed on how to do these assignments before being placed on an assigned duty. You most probably will not be detailed for more than two in a two week period; however, those who need additional training will certainly receive it. For any questions look to your squad leader. The chain of command is simple, there's you, then your squad leader, then me, then the PL, then the CSM and at the very top, the CO. No one has ever needed to see the CO on a discipline matter. Relax until your squad leader gets here and he will take over. Good Luck and welcome to the 112th."

For the next two weeks Musher was a model soldier. After that the downhill slide began. Hard liquor was not allowed in the hooch but there was always some there. Musher began drinking with some of the older guys. He began playing poker with them. He refused to deal because he did not want to be accused of cheating, but he rubbed their noses in their losses. He kept winning and he kept insulting the players. He taunted them by saying that when he was in the fifth grade the kids in school were better poker players. Animosity was built between Musher and a large segment of the platoon. Musher was barely passing the academic subjects, he was just about always the last soldier to fall in to any formation and one Sunday when the platoon was on a Fort Benning roaming pass he missed the evening chow formation.

The PL invoked platoon discipline. When the rest of the platoon went to evening chow he kept Musher. He had Musher double-timing (twice the speed of regular marching) on the company street with full field pack and his nine pound Garand rifle at high port. He did this four nights in row making sure that Musher was not excused until the mess hall had finished serving chow. On the fourth night Musher went to the PX Cafeteria to get some food. Sitting by himself at a corner table his eyes traveled throughout the PX. There on the wall was a large poster of a soldier with a leather helmet on, a leather jacket, sun glasses and white scarf. The poster proclaimed, "Do you have a high school diploma? Transfer to the new United States Air Force and win your wings as an aerial gunner. See your platoon leader for eligibility and submission of transfer papers."

The next day Musher went through the chain of command, squad leader and APL. He told them the matter was personal until he was in the presence

66

of the PL. He told the PL of his poster sighting and how he thought he would better serve the country as an aerial gunner. The PL was happy to hear that Musher wanted out of the Army and into the new Unites States Air Force. In essence Musher wanted to go and the United States Army would be glad to see him go. The PL excused him from formation and marched him to the company orderly room. As Musher waited outside the PL went in and spoke to the CSM. Musher was brought into the orderly room where a stack of papers were completed and signed. When the package was completed Musher was sent back to the hooch to wait for the PL. The CSM placed the package in the hands of a runner to take to Command Personnel. Later that day Musher was discharged from the Army for the convenience of the government; and sworn in again as an airman in the new United States Air Force. He signed all the papers without reading them, went to the hooch and packed all the gear that he would take on departure from Fort Benning,. He was given a folder full of papers to present to the USAF upon arrival, bus tickets and cash travel allowance, taken to the bus station and was on his way within twelve hours of his request. *He never said goodbye to anyone. Surely Company "C" and the US Army would greatly miss him.*

STRIPES ON A JACKASS WON'T MAKE A ZEBRA

THE CHANGE FROM BOY TO MAN GOES ON

BOOK 2

CHAPTER 24
So You Want To Be a Fly Boy

The ride from Fort Benning to Big Springs, Texas had taken around twelve hours. Musher ate a little bit, smoked a little bit and slept a little bit. All in all the ride wasn't that bad. When he stepped off the bus in Big Springs at 0800 hours in that US Army winter uniform the sweat began running over him like a waterfall. The temperature must be at least one hundred. He saw a bus that said Piute Air Force Base. He grabbed his gear and ran into the air conditioned bus. He tried to give his papers to the driver but the driver just told him to hold them. The signs in the bus said smoking was allowed. Musher sat back, lit a Lucky and waited for the bus to go. The ride to Piute AFB (called Piute by everybody) took almost an hour and must have been at least forty miles from Big Springs. When the bus pulled up in front of this huge building marked Processing Center, the driver told them to get their gear, go on inside and find a seat. When the room filled there must have been at least one hundred fifty soldiers and sailors. There were no marines in the group.

The room was called to attention as a Brigadier General stepped onto the platform. He began, "Seats gentlemen please. I welcome you to the 3910th Aerial Gunners Flying Training Group. My name is Bill Martin. You are the first of what we hope will be many transferees to become aerial gunners. This is not a basic training facility. Each of you has had either basic or boot training and is accustomed to the way of the military. As for regulations and discipline we have ours just as the other services have theirs. Play by the rules and all will go well. When I am finished your flight instructors will form you into as many flights of seventy-eight personnel as possible. From this moment on you will be referred to as airmen. When the flights are formed you will be taken to what is in the US Air Force called Base Supply. There you will discard your present uniforms and be issued flying suits as your daily wear. In addition you will receive new boots, new undergarments, socks, towels, sun glasses, a baseball cap, air force blue naturally, and what ever other items the US Air Force believes you need. Again, welcome to the 3910th Aerial Gunners Flying Training Group." As he turned to leave the platform, a commanding voice barked, Ten-Hut.

When the flight instructors were satisfied that they had done as good as job as possible, they marched the airmen to Base Supply. The flight instructor spoke, "Leave your gear out here, go inside and form a single line." Not one single person was less than soaking wet inside their uniform. When the flight instructor came in he said, "Listen up. There are small waterproof bags at the beginning of the line. Take one and put your valuables in it. We know how hot you are so we want you to shed your clothes and take a cool shower. Be especially sure to drink lots of the cool shower water, run lots of cool water on the top of your head and on the back of your neck. We do not want you to dehydrate and pass out on us your first day." Musher thought is it possible somebody cares about us grunts (the infantry name for the cannon fodder privates). Dressed in a clean flying suit with sunglasses and a baseball cap Musher felt like a new person. When the flight came out of Base Supply parked there were a number of what is called a Six-By. A large covered truck which can seat and carry twenty-four persons. The flight instructor, "Grab your gear and get aboard. Too hot to march to the barracks."

"This barracks has two floors, thirty eight bunks on each floor. There are no assigned bunks. Pick one, store your gear on it and fall out here as quickly as possible. We do not want to miss lunch."

The Musher headed upstairs and as far back in the bay as he could get. He stored his gear on a lower bunk and made his way back out to the formation. The trucks were gone. The flight instructor, "You gentlemen did not expect taxi service. After all, we are in the military." The march to the dining hall (the USAF does not have mess halls) was short but very hot. Musher's first look at the dining hall astounded him. The hall was filled with tables for four. Each table had a table cloth, condiments, napkins and utensils laid out at each seating position. Also on the table were a large pitcher of ice water and a large pitcher of iced tea. Indented metal trays were not used in the serving line. There were trays upon which you could place your dishes, glasses and cups to take them to your table. Like a cafeteria once you off loaded your tray onto the table a silently moving person picked up your tray. The food was basically the same quality as it had been in the Army, and it was generally good, but there were no signs saying, "Take all you want but you must eat all you take." Musher sat with three other guys from the flight. The get to know each other would come later. When you finished eating another one of those silently moving persons would pick up the dirty dishes and you were free to leave the dining hall. The formation outside the dining hall was loose until all the flight had finished. If you were among the early finishers you could have a smoke while waiting.

The flight did a fall-out into the barracks. The Musher went upstairs to his bunk and found his gear had been moved to the top bunk. Patiently he waited for the culprit to make his way to the bunk. He was a big guy, at least two inches taller and twenty-five pounds heavier than Musher. "Did you not see my gear on the lower bunk?" "Yeah I saw it but I want the lower bunk." Without hesitating Musher kicked him the in the balls, kicked him twice in the face and dragged him to the top of the stairs by the neck of his flying suit. At the top of the stairs the Musher told him, "Who gives a fuck what you want", pushed him down the flight of stairs and returned to put his gear on the lower bunk. The other guy's gear he threw out the fire escape door at the back of the bay. The rest of the flight stared at him in disbelief. Musher continued his attack "Is there anyone else who wants my bunk or is not happy with the way I solve problems? This is your time to step up or shut up." Not a murmur in the bay.

Moments later the flight instructor was in the bay demanding, "What went on here?" No one spoke. Musher stepped forward and said, "These floors must be slippery, he fell down the stairs." No one corrected him and Musher knew his place was established in the flight, at least with those in the upper bay.

That afternoon our senior flight instructor announced, "My name is Staff Sergeant Buddy Hamrick. I am a Louisiana Cagean and have only been in the new USAF for four months. I was a Drill Instructor at Fort Benning but I am working to put those habits behind me. Occasionally I will erupt so you must overlook that just as I will try to overlook your little misgivings. I need four squad leaders. The four of you who transferred in here as PFC's and became Airman Third Class overnight will be the squad leaders. You Airmen Second Class Waterford, formerly Corporal Waterford, will be the barracks chief. You and the squad leaders won't get any extra pay or privileges. Let's take the rest of the afternoon to square away our area, make up your bunks and feel free to use the showers to cool off. I will see you for evening dining formation. We fall-in at 1700 hours. There will be no one to hold your hand so make sure you are conscious of the time." As he turned to leave he said, "Airman Muscarello please come out to the back steps with me."

As Musher closed the door behind him, Hamrick asked, "Is it true you and Airman Delgado had words about your bunk selection?"

"Yes it is true, we had a few words."

"Is it true that you pushed him down the stairs?"

"Sergeant ask anyone in the flight if that is true. The floor in the bay is very slippery."

"Is it true that you threw his gear out this door onto the barracks area?"

"That is true. I figured if he decided not to come upstairs again it would be easier for him down on the ground."

"You need to know that Airman Delgado is in the Base Hospital in serious condition."

"I am sorry to hear that, I hope he recovers well."

"OK Muscarello, I don't believe a word of your bullshit but no one in the flight will confirm the stories."

"Let's put it this way Sergeant Hamrick, this is probably one of my little misgivings which you will forgive." The dinner formation went smoothly. The march to the dining hall was hot but considerably cooler than it was at noon. Again Musher was amazed at the dining hall and its service. Upon return to the barracks Sergeant Hamrick dismissed the flight and told them they were on their own until 0600 hours reveille.

The Musher thought, MAYBE FAST FREDDIE WAS NOT RIGHT?

CHAPTER 25

How Long Can the Good Life Last?

The next three weeks morning classes were on learning the nomenclature, the disassembly, assembly and care and cleaning of the Caliber 30 Machine gun, the 50 Caliber Machine Gun and the 20 Millimeter Cannon. The classes included the ammunition for those guns, machine gun belt loading and the various ammunition cans for various combat aircraft. The flight was given practical tests for the practical tasks and written tests for absorbed knowledge. Not having made less than perfect scores on both the practical and knowledge test Musher was number one in the flight

The flight had been issued new PT gear. The afternoons were devoted to physical training. The USAF did not spend much time worrying about close order drill or the marching manual. On occasion the flight was given homework for the following day's classes. With the exception of the regular weekly G.I. Party scheduled for after dinner on Thursday the flight had free time each night. Every Saturday the Group conducted a Group parade. All the flights dressed in their new air force khaki uniforms passed in review for Brigadier Martin and his guests. It was a proud time for the group and the new airmen.

Any of the airmen who were not scheduled for any duty between noon Saturday and 2000 hours Sunday could apply for a pass to leave the air base. The First Sergeant of each squadron decided who could go and who could not. There were scheduled busses which left the air base for Big Springs at 1300 and 1500 hours Saturday; and, the last bus left Big Springs for the air base at 1700 hours Sunday. Musher calculated a least two plus hours round trip on the bus and he was underage to drink. Staying here on the air base had many advantages: There were no inspections; He did not need to make his bunk unless he wanted to. There was no lights out curfew. He could shower as often as he wanted to and stay in the shower as long as he wanted to. The base movies were first run and the ticket, popcorn and a cold drink only cost thirty-five cents. There were no dining formations he could just walk in the dining hall during service hours. There was no mandatory church attendance on Sunday and, he could afford to smoke all the Lucky Strikes he wanted to.

When Musher went into the barracks he was surprised at the number of airmen who elected not to try for a pass. He was standing by his bunk when an airman came up to him and said, "My name is Juan Garcia, my friends call me Mex. I would like you to call me Mex. Some of us were getting ready to walk to the dining hall. Would you care to join us?" Musher thought why not? The five of them headed to the dining hall. Inside the dining hall the tables were set for four. Musher anticipated that this would be like in the dining car on the train. The other four would sit together and he would be eating alone. Immediately Mex grabbed another chair and utensils and made it a table for five. No one in the dining room cared. In the serving line the lead serving attendant told them that today's meal would be C Rations (The C stood for Combat, it was what was issued to troops in the field) The meal was two small hamburger patties covered in a thick gravy. Two Hard Tack biscuits (Hard Tack because they were as hard as a rock) and a chocolate bar. There is only black coffee and water to drink today. We have plenty so don't be bashful about coming back for seconds." The meal wasn't that bad. The conversation was light and as the airmen were leaving the dining hall each was handed a three pack of Lucky Strikes cigarettes. The three packs were boldly marked "Free to our combat soldiers". As it was, none of his dining partners smoked and each handed his three pack to Musher.

Mex spoke, "The base bus stop is right here. We could jump on and be at the movie in time for the 1830 showing. Are we game?" When the bus came they all jumped on. The movie was OK but the popcorn and soda (notice Musher did not say tonic) were great. After the movie the group went next door to the PX cafeteria and had a three two beer (otherwise known as Oklahoma beer because it was so weak you would drown drinking it before you could ever get drunk).

It was 2130 when the group got back to the barracks. He had time for a cool shower before calling it a day.

CHAPTER 26
We Are Becoming Gunners

Today we would start firing real machine guns at stationary targets. When we arrived at the shooting range each of us was issued and signed for a leather helmet and goggles. The helmet was equipped with an internal headset. We were told that the helmet and goggles is to an airman what a rifle is to an infantryman. Musher thought he would have no trouble double timing with his helmet and goggles because he remembered what it had been like to double time with the nine pound M1A1 Garand rifle.

Each shooting position had concrete side walls which were at least eight feet high. Each shooting position had its own shooting instructor. On the concrete floor of the shooting position were painted colored squares, yellow if you were the shooter and red if you were the shooting instructor. Various ammunition cans were placed along the interior walls.

The shooting instructor began, "My name is Staff Sergeant Michaels. I was a B-17 waist gunner during World War II. You have been shown the movies on how we dressed for combat flights, shown that there were no windows in the waist positions and how we aimed and fired by instinct. My personal formal training to be an aerial gunner lasted three days. Uncle Sam wanted the B-17 in England so we trained as a crew while flying across the Atlantic Ocean. I tell you this so you don't think I am one of those jokers from a headquarters who has never had the shit scared out of him in combat. Did I ever shoot down a German aircraft, I kind of doubt it but there was one mission where I swore I shot down two. Unfortunately nobody confirmed the kills. Let's get started."

Sergeant Michaels questioned Musher about the machine gun itself, its caliber, the type ammunition to load and the mechanics of loading the ammunition. Satisfied that this airman had done his home work Sgt Michaels took him to the gun to load the ammo. Looking out of the front of the shooting position they could see stationary targets some three hundred yards away. "This gun is a fixed mount. The lateral movement is limited to ten degrees from either side of stationary. Upon my command you will fire as directed to either the left, right or center target. A full lateral movement either left or right will take you completely off target. You will fire only one short burst for each command. A short burst will expend three to five rounds. Given that firing discipline how many short bursts can be expected from each can of ammunition?"

Musher hesitated and then spoke, "If all the bursts were three we could expect three hundred nine bursts. If all the bursts were five we could expect just about one hundred eighty five bursts. If the average burst was four, we could expect two hundred thirty-one plus bursts."

"Very well done airman, let's get back to the shooting."

"Lock and load. Safeties Off." Musher reached for the bolt charger as he had done so many times before during training. The bolt came back smoothly and as it slid forward it took the first round into the chamber. He released the safety. "Ready to fire, on my command, fire left, fire." The gun bucked in Musher's hands, links flew up and bounced off the wall and the noise was deafening. Thank God for the helmet and goggles. He had completely missed the target.

Sergeant Michaels told Musher to clear his weapon. Musher opened the belt feeder and removed the linked rounds on the gunbelt. Then he jacked the bolt to kick out the one round in the chamber. Without being told Musher picked up the links and the brass putting them in their respective recovery containers,

"That's all right airman. You just did not coordinate your thumbs on the spade grip triggers". Musher remembered from class, a spade grip is like taking the two inserts from rolls of toilet paper and joining them together with a piece of iron so that you have a funning looking rectangle. To that conglomeration attach two unsynchronized triggers. When it is attached to a machine gun the toilet paper inserts are used to elevate and azimuth the gun, and the gun fires when either one of the triggers is squeezed. Independent squeeze on either one of the triggers will pull the gun azimuth in the direction of the trigger squeezed. Musher looked at Sergeant Michaels with the eyes of a puppy who had just shit on the living room floor.

"Let's do it again airman. Lock and load. Safeties Off." Once again Musher reached for the bolt charger. The bolt came back smoothly and as it slid forward it took the first round into the chamber. He released the safety.

"Ready to fire, on my command, fire center, fire." Musher concentrated on coordinating his thumb squeeze on the triggers. Once again he had completely missed the target. Without being told Musher picked up the links and the brass putting them in their respective recovery containers,

"This time you made the other most common mistake. You did not have a firm enough clasp on the spade grip. The gun muzzle slipped upward and you fired completely over the target.

"Let's do it again airman. Lock and load. Safeties Off. Ready to fire, on my command, fire left, fire." Musher concentrated and all three rounds tore through the left hand target.

"Let's see if that was just a lucky accident. Lock and load. Safeties Off. Ready to fire, on my command, fire left and right, fire." Musher concentrated and each round tore through the left hand and right hand targets. The shooting continued and the targets were changed again and again.

"Very good airman. You have passed my tests. Police the area and return to your flight."

After lunch in the field kitchen, the rest of the afternoon was devoted to the caliber 30 Machine Gun. Thanks to his morning training from Sergeant Michaels Musher walked through the exercises.

When the flight formed for dinner there were seventeen less members in the flight. Sergeant Hamrick explained that they had failed the exercises at the machine gun range. Those seventeen had been relocated to different living quarters. They were living in a place called The Casual Barracks. There they would await assignments to a different air base in a different US Air Force specialty. They were still obligated to finish their USAF enlistment and could not return to the service from which they transferred.

That evening in the barracks all discussion centered around the lost seventeen. When the conversation got around to being required to complete their USAF enlistment, one member said," Hardly seems fair that we were required to enlist in the Air Force for three years and they only got to stay here for almost a month." The Musher's ears perked up. "Say that again, you know the part about the enlistment."

"When you left Benning didn't you sign a stack of papers you didn't read? Didn't they tell you that you had been Honorably Discharged from the United States Army and you were now sworn in as a member of the United States Air Force? I am sure they did. None of us closely read the papers we signed. You look at your copies and you will find your USAF enlistment is for three years from the date the Army discharged you."

Musher went to his footlocker, dug out the papers and sure enough he had a three year enlistment in the USAF. There was some consolation, his time in the military would only be extended by a little more than three months. He would be discharged on July 3, 1950. He didn't sleep too well that night.

CHAPTER 27

How High Is Up?

The next entire morning was spent doing Physical Training. There was a short period of controlled calisthenics followed by the branch off for games. The flight was down to sixty men. The flight was divided into two parts, and then divided into two parts again. Sergeant Hamrick had two basketballs. He said to two of the fifteen man groups, off with your tops you are the skins. You other two groups are the shirts. He tossed one basketball to each of the skin groups. Here are the rules, there are no rules. There are no referees and no fouls. Each game will be for one hundred points. The match will be won by the group which wins five games. One point will be scored each time you can get the ball through your opponents net. There are no times out. With this whistle I will stop play for a water break when I think it necessary. Break off and be ready for the tip off. The groups went onto two courts where the skins stared at the shirts and the shirts stared at the skins.

Sergeant Hamrick came to one of the courts and tossed the ball for a tip off. There were so many bodies after the ball Sergeant Hamrick barely escaped with his life. At the other court he experienced the same near doom.

As the games progressed the tactics became rougher. A knee to the back, a slap at the head, a chop to the ribs and just about anything else you could think of. Sergeant Hamrick could hear the score being called out and then argued by the other team. By the time each team was in the fifty points neighborhood there was blood flowing and eyes blackened. Sergeant Hamrick blew his whistle loudly.

"Take fifteen for water and rest."

When the water had cooled their heads and most of the bleeding had stopped the flight had figured out what Sergeant Hamrick had done. He was measuring who was aggressive, who was timid and who just generally played like it was for a trophy or something. Musher had stayed on the perimeter of the game, avoiding the big clashes and out of the sight of Sergeant Hamrick.

Sergeant Hamrick put them back out to play. Only this time he rotated the teams. The skins that played the shirts in the first session would play the other shirts group in the second session. Similarly the other skins and shirts would rotate. He let them go at it for another forty-five minutes then blew his whistle. "Water break, clean up and fall-in". Without further comment he marched them back to the barracks. "When you fall out take a shower, clean flying suits and bring your helmet and goggles. You have thirty minutes."

Musher couldn't wait to get to his Lucky Strikes.

In thirty minutes the flight formation was complete and they marched off to lunch.

Having enjoyed another meal Sergeant Hamrick marched them away and within less than two miles they were halted in front of a building bearing the sign "High Altitude Tolerance Testing and Decompression Chamber." The flight filed in quietly and took seats in a small auditorium. Shortly after they were seated a tall, immaculately dressed Captain came to the microphone. "My name is Doctor Hammersmith and I am the Officer in Charge of this facility. You aerial gunner trainees are here this afternoon for two reasons, one to test your oxygen high altitude tolerance and two, to see how you would handle an emergency decompression in a pressurized aircraft cabin. You will be shown three short films. The first film is about your oxygen mask and its use with your helmet. The second film is how the human body reacts when it is deprived of oxygen. The third film is a visualization of a rapid decompression and what sequential actions the personnel in the compartment should take. Total time for all three films is less than one hour. Our chamber can only service twenty-five persons at one time. When I leave members of my staff will divide your flight for your first ride in a Barometric Pressure Chamber." As he turned to leave a voice boomed, "Ten Hut"

The chamber instructors divided the flight. Each instructor took his group and insured that they knew how an oxygen mask attached to a flight helmet. Enroute to the chamber as each flight member passed a work station each flight member was issued an oxygen mask. "You will sign for this mask and it will be your property as long as you are at this school."

The entry way to the chamber looked like a hatch that you would see in a submarine movie. When the last student and the chamber instructors had entered one of the chamber instructors closed the heavy metal door and spun a wheel to make the enclosure air tight. Along each side of the chamber were small desks and chairs.

From a low platform at the front of the chamber the Senior Chamber Instructor spoke. "Welcome to my castle. I am Master Sergeant Jean Vieux. Please take your helmet intercom cord and connect it in the port marked Intercom. Can everyone hear me in their helmet? Good. Now take your oxygen mask hose and connect it in the port circled in green. The oxygen is flowing. Bring your mask to your face and take a few breaths. Is there anyone who did not feel the sensation of fresh air entering their body? Good.

Let's begin the exercise. Because we are at sea level the chamber is not pressurized. The chamber will pressurize as we ascend. At the ten thousand foot level we shall put on our oxygen masks. The basic rule is O_2 (the symbol for oxygen) Over Ten. We shall continue to ascend and be pressurized to thirty thousand feet. During the ascent I want you to take the chalk on your desk and write your first and last name. At fifteen thousand feet you will take off your mask but continue to write your first and last name. Is that clear? Good. Write your name on the desktop. We are at fifteen thousand feet. Release one side of your mask and let it hang from your helmet.

The flight complied and in a very few moments the writing was what was best described as "discombobbled". The chamber instructors were constantly monitoring the flight. Those members who seemed more strongly affected than others had their oxygen masks rejoined and they started back to normal. In a couple of instances flight members fought the chamber instructors who were trying to rejoin the masks. The flight members actions bordered on panic.

Sergeant Vieux began again. "The chamber pressure has been reduced to ten thousand feet. You may release one side of your mask. During our descent to sea level while the chamber is still pressurized a diaphragm will burst just as if one of the doors had blown off an aircraft or gunner's bubble had burst while the aircraft was pressurized. There will be a very loud noise and you will feel pressure in your ears. The chamber will fill with mist." At that precise moment there was a loud bang and the chamber filled with mist. The flight immediately secured the mask and breathed oxygen. "You were given this demonstration so that you know what a rapid decompression looks and feels like. When we are back on the ground Doctor Hammersmith will give each of you a quick ear and nose examination. We are now at sea level, unlock the hatch and when you file out form a line in the room on your right. Thank you for flying on Hammersmith's Airline."

The examination was quick and Doctor Hammersmith made some notes in his log.

Since Musher had been in the first group he would have a considerable wait for the rest of the flight. Sergeant Hamrick told them that if they wished to smoke they must go outside. They must be sure to field strip cigarette butts and if necessary eat the remaining paper.

An hour and a half later the flight was marching to the barracks. At dismissal Sergeant Hamrick said, "Cool off, clean up and I will see you at evening dining formation."

At evening formation there were seven less left in the flight. Sergeant Hamrick flippantly said, "They are living at The Casual Barracks Hotel."

CHAPTER 28
The Targets Are Moving

We were at a different machine gun range. Parked along side the small administrative building were a series of weapons carriers. On the bed of each was mounted a caliber 30 machine gun turret. The senior Range Officer, Master Sergeant William Tell (so help me that was his real name) gave the range briefing. "Today you will be shooting from a moving vehicle at a moving target. Per usual you will listen closely to the Range Safety NCO who will be with you at the shooting position and you will follow his orders without question. Each of you will have four tries and each try will be scored. Your cumulative score will decide what the training group does with you. The road is not smooth and your targets will vary speeds. If you apply what you have leaned in the classroom and your training shooting at stationary targets, I know each of you will do well. You first twelve stand by the weapons carriers numbered one through twelve. First twelve fall-out."

Musher's luck was holding out. He was number five of the first twelve. A tall black man approached him and Musher snapped to attention. The big man spoke, "At ease airman, I am Airman First Class Ritter (an A1C who in the Army would be a buck sergeant). I am your Range Safety NCO. Let me familiarize you with this shooting vehicle. The speed of this vehicle during the run will vary from ten miles an hour to forty miles an hour. It is important that before the run begins you are securely harnessed in the turret You will get your orders from me through the headset in your helmet. The turret is manually controlled by the gunner for lateral and azimuth movement. Lateral movement is limited to thirty degrees in either direction. The azimuth limitation is ten degrees. The machine gun is a standard caliber 30 M1A1. The ammunition is belt fed from a mounted ammunition can. The target may be a truck, a train or a building. You will fire in short bursts and if you do not and you expend all your ammo before the run is completed, your score for the remaining targets will be zero. Each target will only be counted to the point where you ran out of ammo. Do you have any questions?" Musher knew better than to ask any questions.

"All right then climb aboard." Under A1C Ritter's supervision Musher mounted an ammunition can to the machine gun. He harnessed himself in the turret. He put on his helmet and goggles. "Can you hear me airman. From this point on I talk, you listen and you carry out instructions. Any questions? Are you ready to roll?" Musher nodded his head yes. The driver stepped into the vehicle and Weapons Carrier 5 went to the starting line. The starter's flag dropped and WC5 moved onto the unpaved road. About a half mile down the road WC5 pulled into a revetment. AIC Ritter instructed, "Aim at the dirt wall, charge your gun and fire a short burst." Musher complied. "It looks like we are ready to roll. Remember the targets will be on our right side and may appear at any time. When you sight a target fire at will. Good luck airman."

There were no words that Musher could use to explain the experience. WC5 bumped up and down, targets appeared from nowhere and Musher tried to get two bursts off at each target. He did not know if he hit any targets. Suddenly A1C Ritter called, "Cease fire". WC5 was now on a paved road, had made a one hundred eighty degree turn and was headed for the staging area. Enroute to the staging area WC5 pulled into a revetment where Musher cleared the gun and ejected the chambered round. At the staging area A1C Ritter thanked the driver. He had Musher remove his helmet, goggles and unharness himself. When Musher stepped down from the turret to the WC5 bed he was totally soaked and a little unsteady on his feet. A1C Ritter handed a canteen full of cold water. Musher really wanted a cigarette.

A1C Ritter had Musher unload the ammo can and count the number of rounds left in the can. The original count, unbeknown to Musher was two hundred fifty. Musher had finished the run with seventy rounds left in the can. A1C Ritter smiled and said, "I don't have the vaguest idea how many hits you had or if you had any hits at all. I liked the way you stood in the turret and concentrated on your shooting the moving target. Let's police up WC5 and take it to the wash rack."

At the wash rack A1C Ritter said, "Before we do anything else why don't we have a smoke?" Musher's Luckies were so wet they crumbled as he tried to get one out the pack. A1C Ritter offered him a Camel. Musher thought thank you it is no time for me to be choosy. In Boston they would have said he was smoking "SE's", somebody else's. Together they washed down WC5 and took it back to the staging area.

After lunch A1C Ritter and Musher made three more runs. Each run became easier and Musher finished with less ammo in the can. After all the flight finished their rounds, the WC's were policed, cleaned and neat. The flight was formed and told to be at ease while awaiting the shooting results.

When Master Sergeant Tell appeared with a clipboard in hand the flight came to attention. Sergeant Tell spoke, "It was possible to score one thousand points, Four runs at two hundred fifty probable points per run. The top shooter, Airman Muscarello scored seven hundred eight. The passing grade was a score of five hundred fifty. Unfortunately twenty-one of you failed to achieve that score. I will give the list to Sergeant Hamrick and he will post it in your barracks. Congratulations Airman Muscarello."

Sergeant Hamrick, "Right face, For...ward March. At the barracks fall-out, take a shower, get in clean clothes and I will see you at the dinner formation." He strode into the barracks and posted the list on the bulletin board. When the flight formed for dinner there were twenty-one less members in the flight. No explanation was necessary. What had been a flight of seventy-eight was now a flight of thirty-nine.

CHAPTER 29
Our First Day to Fly

In the parachute shop we watched the riggers (the guys who fill the packs to make the parachutes work) diligently packing chutes. We were issued a parachute and shown the log book for when it was last packed and how to identify the packer. In the center of the shop was a huge sign, "If it doesn't work bring it back and we will give you another."

As the flight marched to the training area Musher felt like he had made it. As if he were looking in a mirror he could see himself in his helmet, goggles, sunglasses, white scarf and a freshly pressed flying suit. If they could only see him in the bucket now. The bucket was the local pool hall in Boston where Musher had spent so much of his time.

The senior instructor announced, "Today you will not be shooting. Instead you will take a number of short flights to test your physical stability. Your pilot will put the aircraft through a series of vigorous maneuvers. Each flight will only be about fifteen minutes. Familiarize yourself with shooting position. During all flights all cockpits will be open." This time he was not so lucky. He was in the third group. Those members who would be required to wait their turn were marched to a covered staging area where they were allowed to smoke and drink cool water. The wait was not very long until it became Musher's time to fly.

The aircraft was called a T-6 Flight Trainer. It had been used to train pilots during World War II. The ground crew assisted Musher into the firing position and made sure he was well harnessed and buckled in. They plugged in his helmet headset, made sure his oxygen mask hose was securely connected to the oxygen port and then cleared the aircraft. The engine roared and the pilot said on the intercom, "Unless you have a reason we should not go, let us be gone. There is no control stick in your position. In real combat aircraft there would be one." The aircraft taxied towards the runway and as the aircraft turned on the runway apron Musher heard, "Tower (Flight Control Tower) this is Flight Trainer One Two Eight ready for take off." Control Tower responds, "You are cleared for takeoff, have a smooth flight." Musher listened to his pilot, "Flaps twenty-five, engine to one hundred ten percent, brakes released." The aircraft lurched forward. The pilot guided the aircraft onto the runway and was rolling for takeoff. As the aircraft broke ground he heard his pilot again, "Gear up and checked, Flaps up." They climbed to seven thousand feet when Musher heard his pilot again. "There is no requirement for an oxygen mask at this level; however, for training purposes secure your mask Airman my job is to make you as uncomfortable as possible. I will take this aircraft through a series of violent maneuvers for just that purpose. If you get sick try not to throw up in your mask. I can see you in my rear view mirror. Are you ready or do you want to return to base?" Musher nodded his head and gave a thumbs up sign. "At any time during this flight you want to return to base wave your arms frantically."

With that the maneuvers began. Aircraft barrel rolls, tight turns, steep dives, loops, stalls and recoveries. All packed into less than ten minutes. Sometimes Musher's eyes felt like they were in the back of his head and his stomach was in his mouth. There was no comparing this ride to any roller coaster ride on Revere Beach or any other beach. The aircraft leveled at five thousand feet and pilot asked, "Are you all right?" Musher nodded yes and the pilot turned towards the base. The landing was smooth and Musher had not gotten sick. On the ramp the ground crew released his harness, unbuckled him, made the equipment disconnections and helped him step out of the cockpit onto the wing. His legs felt like jelly but he had not gotten sick. When he was back in the staging area drinking cool water it dawned on him that he did not want a cigarette.

He made two more flights. Each with a different pilot but the speeches and the maneuvers were the same. By the end of the third flight he did not need the help of the ground crew to release all the connections and get out of the aircraft.

When the flight had finished all of its orientation flights the parachutes were returned. The flight members looked like dogs that had been in the rain and put to bed wet. The march to the barracks was sloppy. Sergeant Hamrick, "You have plenty of time, shower, rest and I will see you at the dinner formation." At the dinner formation our flight membership had gone from thirty–nine to twenty-six. Musher thought, we have not even fired one shot from an aircraft.

CHAPTER 30

Shooting At Sleeves

Today we are back on the flight line.

The senior instructor announced, "Today and tomorrow you will be shooting." The aircraft in which you flew yesterday has been equipped with a caliber 30 machine gun. Once again during all flights all cockpits will be open. You will be shooting at sleeve targets being towed by another aircraft. Each of you will make three flights. You will be allowed to fire as long as the ammunition lasts. Score is kept by the number of hits .This time he was in the second group. Those members who would be required to wait their turn were marched to a covered staging area where they were allowed to smoke and drink cool water. The wait was not very long until it became Musher's time to fly.

The ground crew assisted Musher into the cockpit firing position and made sure he was well harnessed and buckled in. They did the same routine as yesterday. They plugged in his helmet headset, made sure his oxygen mask hose was securely connected to the oxygen port and then cleared the aircraft. The engine roared and the pilot said on the intercom, "Time to go." The aircraft taxied towards the runway and as the aircraft turned on the runway apron Musher heard the same call to the tower, "Tower (Flight Control Tower) this is Flight Trainer Two Two Seven ready for take off." Control Tower responds, "You are cleared for takeoff, have a smooth flight." Musher listened to his pilots' same routine, "Flaps twenty-five, engine to one hundred ten percent, brakes released." The aircraft lurched forward. The pilot guided the aircraft onto the runway and was rolling for takeoff. As the aircraft broke ground he heard his pilot again, "Gear up and checked, Flaps up." They climbed to seven thousand feet when Musher heard his pilot again. "This exercise requires that you wear your oxygen mask. Secure your mask. I will try to keep the aircraft at a steady level parallel to your target. Just as you would be with your combat aircraft commander you and I are a team. I can see you in my rear view mirror. Are you ready or do you want to return to base?" Musher nodded his head and gave the thumbs up sign. "Standby for a target coming up on your six." (Six is the position on the clock which indicates someone coming up on your tail) At any time during this flight you want to return to base wave your arms frantically. When you have the target in sight you are free to fire at will.

Remember your axis and azimuth limitations. You would not want to shoot us down."

As the target came into sight it was flying at the same level he was and on a straight and level course. Just as he was about to fire the target dipped down below the elevation limitation of Musher's gun. Then the target came back to straight and level. This time Musher did not wait to fire. After his two short bursts the target climbed upward and again beyond the elevation limitation of his gun. The target continued its erratic movements and Musher fired short bursts every time he thought he could get a hit. The target was at least three hundred yards away. He soon learned about leading the target. Musher continued his firing discipline until he had expended all his ammunition. He heard his pilot, "Target Tow this is Trainer Two Two seven, we are done. Thank you.

Great job. See you in the club." Musher heard Target Tow," Roger that, Roger and out." Musher's pilot headed for base, made a smooth landing and taxied to his ramp position.

On the ramp the ground crew released his harness, unbuckled him, made the equipment disconnections and helped him step out of the cockpit onto the wing. His legs felt strong. He had not gotten sick but had no idea how he may have scored. When he was back in the staging area drinking cool water he lit a Lucky Strike. He knew he was all right.

He made two more flights. Each with a different pilot but the speeches were the same. By the end of the third flight he felt he passed. He doubted if he would be top shooter but he knew he had passed.

When the flight had finished all its shooting the parachutes were returned. Like yesterday the flight members looked like dogs that had been in the rain and put to bed wet. The march to the barracks was even more sloppy. Sergeant Hamrick, "You have plenty of time, shower, rest and I will see you at the dinner formation." At the dinner formation our flight membership was still twenty-six. Musher thought, we get to do the same shooting tomorrow. We will also get our scores.

CHAPTER 31
Shooting At Sleeves Again

We are back on the flight line again today.

The senior instructor announced," Just as yesterday you will be shooting at target sleeves. These are the same aircraft in which you flew yesterday .Once again during all flights all cockpits will be open. Each of you will make three flights. Score is counted by the number of target hits. The wait was not very long until it became Musher's time to fly.

The ground crew watched as Musher climbed into the cockpit, harnessed and buckled himself in. He plugged in his helmet headset, made sure his oxygen mask hose was securely connected to the oxygen port. At that point the ground crew cleared the aircraft. The engine roared and the pilot said on the intercom, "Let's get it on !" The aircraft taxied towards the runway and as the aircraft turned on the runway apron Musher heard the same call to the tower. "Tower (Flight Control Tower) this is Flight Trainer Three Three Six ready for take off." Control Tower responds, "You are cleared for takeoff." Musher listened to his pilots' same routine, "Flaps twenty-five, engine to one hundred ten percent, brakes released." The aircraft lurched forward. The pilot guided the aircraft onto the runway and was rolling for takeoff. As the aircraft broke ground he heard his pilot again, "Gear up and checked, Flaps up." A couple of more flights and Musher would know the routine. Not how to do the routine but at least recite it. They climbed to seven thousand feet when Musher heard his pilot again. "This exercise requires that you wear your oxygen mask. Secure your mask. Are you ready or do you want to return to base?" Musher nodded his head and gave the thumbs up sign. "Standby for a target. At any time during this flight you want to return to base wave your arms frantically. When you have the target in sight you are free to fire at will."

As the target came into view like the first one yesterday it was flying at the same level he was and on a straight and level course. Musher did not wait to fire. After his two short bursts the target climbed upward and again beyond the elevation limitation of his gun. The target continued its erratic movements and Musher fired short bursts every time he thought he could get a hit. Musher continued his firing discipline until he had expended all his ammunition. He heard his pilot,"Target Tow this is Trainer Three Six, we are done. Thank you." Musher heard Target Tow," Roger and out." Musher's aircraft made a smooth landing and taxied to its ramp position.

On the ramp the ground crew released his harness, unbuckled him, made the equipment disconnections and helped him step out of the cockpit onto the wing. His legs felt strong. He had not gotten sick but had no idea how he may have scored. When he was back in the staging area drinking cool water he lit a Lucky Strike. He knew he was all right. He made two more flights. Each with a different pilot but the speech was the same. By the end of the third flight he felt he passed.

When the flight had finished all its shooting the parachutes were returned. Like yesterday the flight members looked like dogs which had been in the rain and put to bed wet. The march to the barracks could just barely be called marching. Sergeant Hamrick, "Like yesterday you have plenty of time, shower, rest and I will see you at the dinner formation." At the dinner formation our flight membership was now nineteen. You could almost read every flight member's mind, when do we get our scores? Hamrick went on, "After dinner consider yourselves released from duty until reveille tomorrow morning. We will not form after dinner, make your own way to wherever you are going. I will tell you this, I have your scores. Obviously those of you standing here passed."

Despite the fact that they were free to roam everyone headed back to the barracks. They were tired and wound as tight as generator wirings. Even though there were only nineteen left in the flight they still had bunks on the first and second floor. On either floor all the conversations were about their two days in the air. Morning could not come quick enough.

CHAPTER 32

We Are Aerial Gunners

It was Saturday morning and most unusually at 0530 hours Sgt Hamrick had turned on the lights and was rousting people out of bed. "Get cleaned up, look your best pretty because after breakfast we are going to a parade."

Musher had been directed to march as guidon bearer despite the fact that the flight did not have a guidon.

Every squadron was represented on the parade ground. When all were in place the Group Commander and his aide left the platform and headed for Musher's flight. The Group Adjutant General's (GAG) voice came over the loud speakers. "Attention to Orders. Whereas the following named airmen have successfully completed training as Aerial Gunners, they are hereby awarded the silver breast badge declaring them an Aerial Gunner." As the GAG read the names, BG Martin was moving through the flight pinning the aerial gunner badge on each member of the flight. Again, the GAG's voice came over the loud speakers," Airman Saverio Muscarello front and center."

Musher stood in front of BG Martin while the Group Adjutant General went on, "Whereas Airman Muscarello distinguished himself achieving the top academic grades of his flight; and whereas Airman Muscarello distinguished himself as the Top Shooter in his flight, as an acknowledgement of his efforts, by the authorities given to Brigadier General Martin, Commanding Officer, 3910th Aerial Gunners Flying Training Group, Airman Muscarello is hereby promoted to the grade of Airman Second Class." The BG handed Musher a set of A2C stripes. Musher saluted the BG and the BG motioned Musher to stand beside him on the reviewing stand. The GAG gave the order, "Pass in Review". When each squadron passed the reviewing stand Musher saluted whenever the BG did. The parade ended. BG Martin turned to Musher, "My congratulations, make us proud as you go through your career."

Musher rejoined his flight for the march back to the barracks. Sergeant Hamrick, "Fall out. Everyone stay on the first floor."

Sergeant Hamrick again, "Your moving target shooting scores are posted on the bulletin board. Along with them is your cumulative shooting scores for both stationary and moving target shootings as well as your overall academic standings. You gentlemen did very well this morning and I am proud to claim you as my students. Since we were not able to on the parade ground let's give Airman Second Class Muscarello a loud round of applause. Might I remind you that you and I are Subject to the Articles of War and therefore BG Martin can promote or demote any enlisted personnel in his command. This afternoon we will go to Group Personnel. There you will receive your reassignment orders to the Advanced School for Remote Control Gunnery, Lowry Air Force Base, Denver, Colorado, travel vouchers and since Monday is payday, you will be paid all pay due you as of Monday. You will receive one month's flying pay for the rank in which you performed the flying duty. After Group Personnel you will have the rest of today and tomorrow to pack and be ready to leave at 0800 hours Monday.

Lunch at the dining hall was beautiful. Steamed hot dogs, baked beans, cole slaw, chocolate cake for dessert and iced tea. Do you think we will get this type of good food and service at Lowry?

At Group Personnel Musher once again signed a bunch of papers, half-ass read his travel orders, took a small sum for travel meal money and then signed for his back pay: Three hundred eighty-five dollars and twenty-eight cents. Added to his Army poker winnings, his travel money, what little he had left from when he went into the Army Musher had Five Hundred Ninety-eight dollars and change. He had not had that much money at one time since he and Freddie had done some action. When the personnel requirements were over Sergeant Hamrick dismissed the flight at Group Personnel Headquarters. "You are on your own. The Good Lord Willing and the Crick Don't Rise, I will be with you Monday morning."

Musher headed for the Base Exchange (in the Army the Post Exchange). Most of the flight was headed that same way. In the small cafeteria adjoining the BX Musher sat with a coke and smoked a couple of Luckies. As he entered the BX he took a grocery cart. Quickly in the cart went four cartons of Luckies, at fifty cents a carton he could splurge. For laughs he put in a ninety-six cent twenty-four count package of Bull Durham makings. Next went a B-4 bag, the U S Air Force version of a suitcase. Then an actual shaving kit with all the amenities included. A sewing kit, four more sets of A2C stripes, a six pack of coca cola and six candy bars. Even though at that time military personnel could not wear civilian clothes Musher bought a sweat shirt for wearing in the barracks. At checkout Musher had spent less than thirty-five dollars. Outside the BX he took the Base Bus to his barracks area.

Musher questioned his flight, "Does anybody know how to sew? I will pay fifty cents for each set of stripes sewn on my uniforms." He had just finished trying to sew the stripes on himself and all he had to show for it were a bunch of needle pricks in his fingers. There were two takers. Musher gave them his sewing kit, the stripes, one shirt and his battle jacket. He laid out on the empty bunk next to him all the things he would pack and take when they left. The amount of stuff, shoes, uniforms, etc look as if he would need two bags. He began to wonder what he could do without. To be on the safe side he started packing now. As the amount on the bunk bed dwindled there were no serious effects on the B-4 Bag. He knew how the B-4 Bag got its name: "B-4 you discard anything, try to pack it."

Sunday was a leisure breakfast with some of the members of the flight. Lucky Strikes and coffee followed by a walk to the BX. Musher wanted a wallet, a Zippo cigarette lighter and a small satchel type bag to carry emergency supplies. You know, emergency supplies, a carton of cigarettes, a change of underwear, a change of socks, his shaving kit, a deck of playing cards, some food snacks and a couple of bottles of soda. He found just such a bag emblazoned with the words United States Air Force on one side and the USAF emblem on the other. He picked up some more "goodies" and this time the checkout was almost twenty-five dollars. Still he felt rich and shrugged off the cost with an "Oh Well". Rather than walk, outside the BX he took the Base Bus to his barracks area.

It was too early for lunch. Musher scouted the barracks with does anyone have a piece of stationery and an envelope to spare? I also need a stamp and the use of a fountain pen. I will pay and return the pen. One airman gave him a sheet of paper and an envelope, another loaned him a pen and he paid a fifteen cent premium (actual cost was only eight cents) for the stamp.

Back at his bunk it was time to choose to whom he would write a letter the choice was Emily Bilderbook.

"Dear Emily,

It has been some months since we last saw each other. During that time I have often thought about you and could clearly see your lovely, smiling face. Unfortunately we are very far apart and the probability of us meeting again is very remote. I thank you and your parents for a most happy experience.

Sincerely, Saverio Muscarello, Airman Second Class, United States Air Force"

Suddenly it dawned on him that he did not have a return address. There is an outside possibility that she may want to write to him He settled on A2C Muscarello, Remote Control Gunnery School, Lowry AFB, Denver, Colorado. Had he looked at his travel orders the mailing address was clearly stated. He lay down to take a nap. Mex shook his shoulder. Musher opened his eyes. Mex said, "We are going to dinner and then to the base movie. Do you want to join us?" Musher washed his face and the usual five walked to the dining hall. The movie was long and not too good. The popcorn and the soda were. As they left the movie one of the guys said, "There is a pizza place just down the block, let's go have pizza." The pizzeria was not like the one in his Boston neighborhood but it was pizza. They ate pizza and drank three point two beer until they were stuffed and felt as if they were going to burst. Outside the pizzeria they took the Base Bus to the barracks area. Everyone was tired and sleepy. All dropped into the sack.

CHAPTER 33

To School For Remote Control
Gunnery Training

Everyone was up and about at 0530 hours. The flight was impatient to get on its way. They made their area look presentable and carried their suitcases and duffels to the barracks front door. At 0600 hours they made a loose formation and marched even more loosely to the dining hall. Breakfast today was known as a G.I. Special, most customarily referred to by all military personnel as "SOS. Shit on a Shingle". Actually it was shredded fried ground beef (hamburger meat) placed on top of toast and covered with a white gravy. It was known as a "stick to your ribs" meal. The flight ate slowly and individually drifted back to the barracks. Sergeant Hamrick was not expected until 0730 hours. Musher smoked and like every one else paced within the barracks. At promptly 0730 hours Sergeant Hamrick called "Fall-In". Outside the barracks was a six-by, "Have you forgotten anything you have in the barracks. Good . Load your baggage and yourselves into the truck." As the truck pulled through the gate leaving Piute AFB Musher thought it had been a pretty good stay there.

They unloaded their baggage at the bus station. Sergeant Hamrick went into the bus station with them. He pointed to baggage checking, "Put your receipt somewhere secure. You will not need it again until Denver. Your bus leaves at 1200 hours. It is about nine hundred twenty five miles and sixteen hours to Denver. You should arrive in Denver about 0400 hours. Look for the transport buses to Lowry. The bus driver will guide you on the air base. We have said our goodbyes, once again, do well, make us all proud of you." He left the station and climbed into the six-by as the driver headed back to Piute.

In what seemed like five minutes the loud speaker announced, "The Denver Express on Gate 5 is ready for boarding." It was a very large bus, air conditioned and even had a latrine on board, The passenger capacity was forty-four. With the exception of eight men in civilian clothes everyone else was in uniform. Musher hustled to get in line to have better pickings of his seat. He chose a window seat midway on the chassis. Mex slid in beside him. The driver walked the aisle counting heads. Forty-four is correct. The door closing gave a whooshing sound of air, the brake release gave another whooshing sound of air, the bus was backed out of the gate and positioned towards Denver. The driver was equipped with a microphone. "Gentlemen right now I am very busy getting this bus and you all safely on the road to Denver. Very soon I will speak to you again,"

Less than ten minutes later the driver came on again, "If you must use the latrine use as little water as possible, be sure to flush the toilet and do not stay any longer than necessary. There are forty-four passengers on the bus. For you smokers, you may smoke on the bus. The air conditioning should vent the smoke from the bus. We ask that you keep your smoking to a minimum. For you snack and food eaters, please do not throw any paper or bottles on the floor of the bus. Keep them in your possession until you can properly dispose of them. We will make our first break stop in about two hundred fifty miles. Try to relax and enjoy the ride."

Musher stared out the window at the countryside. He was amazed how the terrain changed from the flat dry geography of Piute to the lush greenery as the bus headed north. In the serenity of the ride and the constant hum of the bus he fell asleep. He awoke to find Mex was not sitting along side him. He stepped into the aisle to make a full stretch and saw that at the back of the bus there were people in a huddle. Being nosy he walked to the back of the bus and nudged his way in until he could see what was going on. Lo and behold, they were playing poker. Mex, some other airmen and two of the men in civilian clothes were playing twenty-five and fifty-cent five card stud. Musher looked closely. He could not detect any cheating by either civilian but it was quite obvious the two civilians were playing as a team. He stood patiently and took in every trait of every player sitting in the game. He did see that the two civilians were playing "coin placement "on their cards. This is a quite unnoticeable technique used by partners to identify the strength of the hand. Shortly thereafter he noticed that the way either one of the civilians looked at his hole card he signaled his partner whether or not he wanted a raise in the pot. In Boston these two were so amateurish that they would have been stripped of their money, had both hands broken and tossed into the street with the warning that should they ever return the visit would not have a ticket out. Musher watched for about another hour. The bus driver alerted his passengers, "First bus stop in ten minutes. We will be there about twenty minutes, there is food and latrines available inside the station. Be ready to go when called, I'd hate to leave any of you all here. The next bus won't come through for twelve hours."

At the rest stop Musher smoked cigarettes and took Mex aside. "Mex, do me a favor. Let me sit in the game in your place. How much have you lost? I will pay you your losses and give you ten percent of my winnings." There was no way Mex could refuse.

When the bus was on its way again Mex brought Musher to the game and announced, "I don't feel well, my friend here is going to take my place. Does anyone have a problem with that?" Certainly none of the airmen would complain because they either knew Musher or knew of his reputation. To the civilians this was just another G.I. with money in his pockets to lose. Musher played very conservatively. Dodging the apparent civilian winners and occasionally winning a pot of his own. This game had at least five hours before the next rest area. A couple of times during the play he folded winning hands to let one of the civilians win. During that same time he burned the civilians with hands he knew either one of them could beat.

By the time the bus was approaching the next rest stop three airmen had gone broke and were replaced by three other airmen. Musher had won most of that money. The two civilians had won a small taste

The game began as soon as everyone was on the bus and the bus began to roll. Musher continued his conservative play and steadily kept winning small amounts. From the time he sat in the game he neither smoked one cigarette in the game nor ate one snack. To most players this game would be considered fun. To the two civilians and Musher it was work.

One of the civilians suggested, "Why don't we change to Draw Poker, Jacks or better. We've been playing Stud for a long time now; and why don't we raise the limits to Two Dollars and Five?" It took all of Musher's training to keep his eyes from showing their joy. Two of the airmen dropped out with "Too rich for my blood." That left one airman, two civilians and Musher. None of the kibitzers made any move to join the game.

When Musher estimated that there was less than one hour to the next rest stop he began to play "mechanic". A card mechanic is someone who can control the flow of the cards so that each player will receive whatever hand the mechanic wants him to have. Thanks to his Uncle Marino (street name Fanucci) and the many hours of practice Musher was a good mechanic. Certainly not in the class of the Great Mechanics like Fanucci but more than effective with these two- bit cheap hustlers. Two times within the next hour Musher dealt one civilian a power house hand, the other two players neutrals; and to himself a loser. He called bets and came up second best. This time the Powerhouse opened for five, the airman folded, Civilian 2 called and raised five, Musher called. Powerhouse re-raised, Musher called again and Civilian 2 said, Last raise is mine and I will take it." Powerhouse and Musher called. "Cards" asked Musher. "I'll play these", said Powerhouse. One card for Civilian 2. Musher mimicked with, "The dealer takes one." Powerhouse," I had the best hand going in, five." Civilian 2, I got a little help, call and raise five." Musher,"Call." Powerhouse, "That's my bet, I can't let you buy it, call and raise. five." Civilian 2, "You convinced me, I am out." He quickly discarded his hand into the unused pile of cards. It was now Musher's turn, "I call and raise five." The shocked look on Powerhouse's face clearly told the story, they had been had. He must call but he knew he could not win. Musher's small straight flush clearly won the pot. The civilians were red with anger. When they looked around at all the airmen, Powerhouse spoke, "Can't win them all, but that is enough for me." The two civilians left for their non-adjoining seats.

"OK folks, twenty minutes. Don't get left behind."

As the passengers were milling about waiting to load, Musher went to the two civilian card players and said, "Listen, can we have a minute. I don't want the rest of these people to hear me." As they turned the corner of the building Musher whirled around and kicked both of them in the balls. He followed with kicks to the face and dragged them so that they lie side by side. Kneeling on their chests he told them, "You two assholes aren't even good hustlers. If you make your living riding buses and hustling the ignorant I suggest you give it up now. If we run into each other again this will seem like a walk in the park." He opened their billfolds and took all the money. Surprise, in their billfolds he found a three day pass from Piute identifying these assholes as Staff Sergeant England and Airman First Class Trudy. He felt like he had slain two monsters. "Sorry you will miss the bus but we will make your excuses."

Getting on the bus Musher noticed a new driver. In low tones he said, "Two of the passengers are staying here. Seems a friend in a car is coming to pick them up."

CHAPTER 34
Classes, Maintenance and Very Little Flying

Musher said to Mex, "We should be in Denver in a couple of hours. I want you to do something for me." With that he handed Mex a stack of money. "I want you to go to each airman in that poker game, find out how much he lost and refund his losses from that money. You are not to mention me. You are to tell them that those civilians felt badly for taking money from men who serve their country and they want them to have it back. Use your skills and judgment on whom to pay and how much. Include your self in this distribution." It didn't take long for Mex to return with a portion of the money still in his hands. "I took care of me." Musher counted how much Mex gave him, did a quick calculation in his head and hand Mex thirty-six dollars. "This is your share of the net winnings."

The passengers unloaded and grabbed their luggage. The military guys loaded on the bus marked "Lowry Air Force Base." The driver spoke," Judging by the nice bright shining wings on your chest you must be the class from Piute. I am going to take you to the dining hall, wait for you and then take you to your barracks, first floor, building 621. Later your new flight instructor will join you and fill you in on the details."

The size of the dining hall building was gargantuan. Driver, "Ain't she a beauty? In there three thousand men, both students and permanent party (the people who were stationed at Lowry all the time) eat three meals a day. When you pull your first KP you will get the full briefing. Go in through Door 6 and come out the same way. With that much food being consumed every day the cost of wasted food is down right sickening. You will see the signs, "Take all you want but you must eat all you take." That statement sent a chill straight through to Musher's bones. When they actually got in the dining hall it was still a long way to the serving line. There were at least fifteen serving lines spread throughout the dining hall. The food was placed on indented metal trays. This morning's breakfast was SOS, mashed potatoes, lemon sheet cake (not to be confused with shit cake) for dessert , milk or coffee. There were no table cloths, condiments and four place table settings. You gathered your own utensils and found a seat where you could at the long tables which held fifteen airmen on each side of the table. There were mess sergeants and KP Pushers all over the place encouraging the airmen to eat diligently and make room for the next man. It was the furthest thing from Piute and even the Army mess halls had not been quite like this.

Musher wolfed his food, rinsed his tray in the boiling hot water laden with G.I. lye soap, put his glass and cup in the wooden carrier and his utensils in a large container. He could not get out of Door 6 quick enough and into the haven of the bus.

He took a Lucky from his pocket and was about to strike the Zippo when the driver interrupted. "There is no smoking in any bus on this air base. You may step outside but you run the risk of being confronted by some of the meanest officers in all of the United States Air Force. Take me for instance, three months ago I was an Airman Second Class driving a bus. One day on one of my routes I had no passengers and was running a little early. I pulled over, stepped off the bus and lit a cigarette about that time a Captain drove by. He stopped and asked me what was wrong with my bus. I figured I would be better off if I didn't lie so I told him the truth. The next day I was reduced to Airman nothing and sent back to do the same job I did as an Airman Second Class. If you think the cigarette is worth it far from me to try to stop you."

One by one the rest of the guys came out of the mess hall and onto the bus. The driver quickly told them that smoking was not allowed on any bus on the air base. He spared them the rest of his story.

In front of their new home, first floor barracks 621, the driver told them "There are eighteen single bunks on the first floor. There are no bunk assignments, just pick one and make your self at home. Your beds are already made and a foot locker has been provided. You will use your personal lock on the footlocker. Check the BUTT Cans mounted in the bay. If they need water and you put water in them then it is OK for you to smoke. Unpack and if you like SSS while you wait for your Flight Instructor. Good luck and I hope to see you around."

Musher put water in all of the six butt cans. After that he sat on his foot locker and had a couple of Luckies. Musher knew how serious an offense it was if you were caught lying or sitting down on your bunk while smoking a cigarette. He unpacked, squared away his area and headed for the shower. Just as he was about to turn on the water he heard a very, very loud," Ten Hut. Fall-in beside your bunk." Musher grabbed his shaving kit and ran to his bunk. He noticed that he was wrapped in a towel, barefoot and the rest of the flight was dressed to some degree in a uniform. The loud voice began, "My name is Master Sergeant Charles Willings. I am your Senior Flight Instructor (SFI). He was a tall man whose uniform chest was covered with ribbons, a Paratrooper Badge and an Aerial Gunner Badge. So that you all understand, all my World War II combat time was in a B-24 with open air turrets. During duty times wherever you are so shall I be. For the next four weeks I shall reside in this barracks with you. I am not sure whether my wife is pleased about that or not. In about fifteen minutes a personnel clerk from Wing Headquarters will be here to process you in. Until then continue what you were doing while Lord Godiva finishes his shower and gets dressed. Another nick name. Nicknames are the Italian way, if you do not have a nickname by which you are commonly known you are a social outcast.

The personnel sergeant came and very efficiently did his job.

The SFI brought the flight close as a group. His loud voice mellowed as he began, "There are certain things which I am going to tell you which if you pay attention and do them your next four weeks here will be more pleasant. Lowry AFB is the single largest training facility in the Air Training Command. There is generally twenty-five hundred to three thousand airmen here for technical training. Your look at the dining hall should have told you that virtually everything here is scheduled and the schedules must be met. Since you are only here for four weeks if your flight is lucky you most probably will not pull KP. Being late for scheduled formations causing the flight to be late for class is a serious issue. Roughly thirty men will have been put off schedule and time is one of the intangibles that cannot be recovered. The classes and the practical exercises are difficult and those who do not and cannot keep up will be filtered from the program. Wakeup will be at 0500 hours, breakfast at 0545 hours and classes begin at 0700 hours. Your day will consist of technical training and physical training. All movements by the flight outside the barracks will be in a marching formation. The daily barracks inspections will not be severe but filth and an unkempt area will not be tolerated. We will have one G.I. Party per week the first of which will be after dinner tonight. Every Saturday morning you will participate in the Base Parade. There will be no three day passes while you are in this school. Unless you fuck up and are given extra detail you can expect to be on free time from after the parade on Saturday to 2100 hours on Sunday. During that time you may visit Denver if you wish. There are regularly scheduled buses from Lowry to Denver and return. You are obligated to march with the flight to the dining hall, but you are not obligated to eat. You gentlemen have more service than most of the students on Lowry. I want to treat you like grown competent airmen. I will treat you like grown competent airmen until you give me a reason to do otherwise. You are expected to set the example for all students. Let's fall out and go to lunch."

The detail of eighteen airmen looked lost among the large trainee squadrons all marching to the dining hall. The flight took its place in the line. Musher hardly paid attention to what was being served once he knew it was not liver. Getting all the utensils, drinks and finding a place to sit was amid a high noise level and airmen going in all directions. Again the mess sergeants and KP Pushers roamed urging airmen to finish and make room for the next guy. Eighty-three more meals like this? He did his policing duty and headed out into the fresh air. In the barracks the consensus was that nobody enjoyed the meal. Even those members of the flight who lived to eat.

The SFI called them together in the barracks. "For orientation purposes when you exit the front door of the barracks you are facing east. About two blocks south of here (to your right) there is an Airmen's Club. It is open to any airmen below the grade of Staff Sergeant. It opens at 1800 hours and closes at 2130 hours Monday through Friday. The hours on the weekend are longer. They serve sandwiches, hot dogs, hamburgers, pizza, soda, candy bars and goodies for a minimal price. The club has pool tables, dart boards, ping pong, non gambling card playing and dancing. Dancing with whom? Dancing with members of the Woman's Air Force (WAF's). For today we will fall out for evening meal at 1630 hours. The G.I. Party will begin at 1930 hours. For the rest of the afternoon finish your unpacking and whatever else you care to do in the barracks. A word of caution, incidents which occur in the Airmen's Club are not supposed to be reported outside the Airmen's Club. Don't you believe it! See you at dinner formation."

Musher spoke out, "Can you see what he has done. He knows we are unhappy with the dining hall and he has given us a time frame which allows us to use the Airmen' Club. If we march to the dining hall, fall-in line but never go through a serving line we will be back here to go to the Airmen's Club to get something to eat and relax before the G.I. Party."

A couple of the airmen said, "That's all right but we lost all our money in the poker game on the bus." Even though he believed these airmen had had they losses returned Musher was caught without an answer. Mex chimed in, "Do you guys want to tell me that story or should I tell my story to the flight." Any disagreement ended right there. At 1630 hours the SFI marched the flight to the dining hall. The flight got into the chow line but immediately upon entering the dining hall each did a u-turn and formed outside. The SFI marched them back to the barracks. "Remember G.I. Party at 1930 hours. I'll be watching because I live here." Since the walk to the Airmen's Club would be less than five minutes the flight took the time to position all the tools necessary for the G.I. Party. At precisely 1750 hours the flight was in line waiting for the Airmen's Club to open. While waiting in line Musher went to each member of the flight. "No drinking beer. I don't care if it is three point two. We don't want the SFI to smell beer on our breath and think we are taking advantage of his good nature. If you decide to drink beer, you will answer to me." There was no beer drunk that night.

With smiles on their faces the flight sauntered back to the barracks. They presumed the SFI was there because they could hear music coming out of his room. The G.I. Party was done quickly and well. Everyone showered and did something personal until lights out at 2200 hours.

MUSHER THOUGHT, FREDDIE I THINK YOU WERE WRONG.

CHAPTER 35

The Remote Control Gun Sight

At 0500 hours the lights went on in the bay. The SFI was coaxing the flight out of the sack. "The Denver altitude is five thousand feet (The Mile High City). Until the sun comes up it is darn cold. Put your leather jacket over your flying suit and your field jacket over that. Later today I will get you all to Base Supply for sweaters, gloves, and woolen caps. For now, tough it out." Musher smiled inside, the sweat shirt would be a welcome addition to his attire.

The breakfast formation and the march to the dining hall had just about everybody's teeth chattering. Only the street lights along the marching route proved that beneath the exhaled vapor there existed some human beings. Inside the dining hall it was hot. Airmen were unbuttoning and taking off outer garments. Musher and the flight had conceded that they really did not have a choice. They must learn to enjoy the dining hall as much as possible or perhaps starve to death. The coffee was hot and strong. The breakfast palatable. The flight ate slowly and stalled to remain inside for as long as possible. The mess sergeants and the KP Pushers were not thrilled with the behavior of the flight.

The march to the classroom was long and cold. The flight arrived on time, entered the classroom and was permitted to disrobe whatever garments they chose. Suddenly seated in the classroom were eighteen airmen wearing B-2 leather jackets with white scarves wrapped around their necks. They looked like aerial gunners. When the instructor came into the classroom the flight rose to attention. He went to the blackboard and wrote, SSgt Michael Lesser. As he turned to the class he began," I am not a World War II combat veteran. I am an electronics specialist whose specialty is the electronically controlled remote control firing gun sight. For this entire week we shall study the gun sight. At the end of the week you must be able to disassemble the gun sight, analyze any malfunction, repair the malfunction and have successfully calibrated the gun sight. You will learn about reticles and their relationship to the gun sight." He grabbed a bunch of leaf notebooks, went to the first seat in each row and said, "Take One and Pass them back. This will be your bible for this week. If you open the notebook you will see highly definitive drawings of the gun sight, its electronic diagrams and the nomenclature for each component in the gun sight. Here is where you will take your notes and use it for any other study purposes. By the end of the week you must be able to recite the notebook's contents. We will have daily quizzes as learning tools. Your end of week examination will be the only one which counts for score. The end of week examination will be taken from information you should have learned in the notebook. Unfortunately the Air Training Command does not give "Mulligans". If you do not pass the end of week examination the first time, there is no second time. When you finish this school you will be allowed to take your notebook with you. You gentlemen are the first RCS (Remote Control System) gunners to be trained here at Lowry. Your next assignment will be as an RCS Gunner in one of the USAF combat Wings. We shall have three classes each morning with a ten minute latrine break between classes. You may smoke during that break but remember the consequences if you leave a butt on the grounds. Let's begin. Open your notebook and fill in the ownership page. If somehow you lose your notebook you will be expelled from class. If you choose for one dollar you can buy in the BX a book carrier which has a closing flap and shoulder strap arrangement. If you do buy such an item I strongly suggest you stencil your name and serial number on the outside. When everyone is finished with the ownership page we will take a ten minute break."

The rest of the morning was spent discussing the gun sight. Sergeant Lesser used viewgraphs in his presentations. He cautioned, "Do not try to make too many notes. Your notebook contains the same graphics that I am using on the viewgraph." By the end of the classroom day, the flight was ready to break. Waiting outside the classroom was the SFI. The day had warmed considerably and the march to the dining hall was actually quite comfortable. Musher could not say the dining room was comfortable but it was a necessary evil.

True to his word the SFI brought the flight to base supply. Each airman was issued a sweater, a wool cap which could pull down over the ears, a pair of gloves with glove liners, and a G.I. overcoat. The overcoat was almost ankle length, heavy as a bear but Musher knew that it would be warm. If he never had another use for it, it would make a great comforter on his bunk. Last night was cold. The rest of the afternoon was Community Study and Reference (CSR). Among the airmen what was known as CSR meant "Cokes, Smokes and Relax."

After the evening meal the SFI told them, "You are free until lights out. Tomorrow after class I will take any of you who care to go to the BX. If it were I, this evening I would be devoting as much time as I could studying today's work. Sergeant Lesser referred to "mulligans". A mulligan is a golf term meaning a second try. Just so you know, here at Lowry most students who fail a technical training course are kept at Lowry on permanent KP."

CHAPTER 36
More Learning of the RCS Gun Sight

With one exception, the next three days were the same as the first. Sergeant Lesser continuously pounded on the nomenclature of items making up the gun sight. There were new terms associated with the gun sight. First it was what is a reticle? A reticle is a small circle of light which appears in the gun sight. When the reticle is placed on the target the gun sight compensates for the target distance and speed. It takes away what we learned in open air shooting about leading the target and instinctively adjusting for target speed and distance, otherwise known as shooting with Kentucky Windage. What is a selsyn? Selsyns are electronic tubes which power the gun sight. Each airman had been issued a "Jewelers Kit", a series of small screwdrivers and other small tools. They were the only tools necessary for the care and maintenance of an RCS Gun Sight. When the selsyns were properly calibrated and zeroed they coordinated with the reticle for effective shooting. Not only did Sergeant Lesser introduce new terms (all of which were in the notebook and explained) but he reemphasized what had been covered many times before

On the second afternoon the SFI marched the flight to the BX. Everyone bought a book carry bag and some other small items. Back at the barracks the SFI told them that there would be no PT today. He said that he had put a stencil kit in the latrine and he encouraged the flight to stencil their bags today. Dinner formation would be at 1700 hours.

Tomorrow, Friday, would be the gun sight examination. Despite how confidant he felt Musher had a lingering fear the he would be over-confidant and blow this school. What a horrible picture, almost three years of KP in the Lowry "mess hall".

The next morning Sergeant Lesser instructed them to fill out the cover of the blank test booklet. "This examination would not be multiple guess (multiple choice) or true or false. It would be essay. You must make at least seventy percent to pass. You will write your answers in narrative form. You will have two and one half hours to complete the exam. If you finish sooner put your test questions and answers on my desk and leave the room. You may wait in the class room next door. Later today your SFI will receive the grades and he will post them in your barracks. It is 0830 hours now, you have until 1100 hours. Good Luck. Be brief but exacting with your answers."

Lunch was once again a chore. The food was good but the atmosphere was really bad. The day had chilled and the flight was not properly dressed for the temperature. As a flight, the flight wanted to show off to the other trainees. As a result they wore their flying suits, leather jackets and white scarves. The SFI would not let them wear sunglasses.

The SFI released them at the barracks to await the examination scores.

The air in the barracks was so tense. When the SFI posted a sheet on the bulletin board the rush to get to the board was as if someone was giving away hundred dollar bills. To no one's surprise Musher was high scorer with ninety-eight percent. The vast majority of the grades were spread between the eighties and the low nineties. There were four others whose grade was seventy. Still everyone passed and that was as good a reason as any to celebrate. Look out tonight at the Airmen's Club.

CHAPTER 37
Meet the B-29 Bomber

When the flight came out of the dining hall Monday morning it was loaded on a bus. The bus took the group to the flight line. Parked there was a huge aircraft. The unknown sergeant who had been sitting directly behind the driver rose to speak, "Gentlemen that lovely aircraft is the B-29 Bomber. The exact type delivery vehicle used for the drops of atomic bombs which ended World War II. We will get off the bus and do a walk around the aircraft. The walk around is so that you can appreciate her size and beauty. Later today we will return here and do a much closer orientation of the B-29. Please board the bus so that we may go to the classroom." The classroom walls were covered with various pictures, models and cut-outs of the B-29.

Hanging from the front blackboard was a sign which said, "Master Sergeant Clyde Walker."

"Gentlemen I am Clyde Walker. During World War II I was a member of the 509th Bomb Group, the group which dropped the first atomic bomb on Japan. I was the senior gunner on my crew and responsible for what from this moment on you will refer to as the Central Fire Control System (CFCS).

Using the wall pictures and cut-outs he noted the B-29 was the first combat bomber to have in-flight pressurization. Her service ceiling is thirty-three thousand six hundred feet. Her conventional bomb load is twenty-thousand pounds. You know she can carry and deliver atomic bombs. In our main area of concern, aerial gunnery, she has four gun turrets, one upper forward, one upper aft, one lower forward and one lower aft. Those four turrets are remote controlled. As you learn about crew coordination for the CFCS you will better understand how the turrets are controlled. The tail mount is singularly controlled by the tail gunner. Each shooting position is equipped with two caliber 50 machine guns. The guns are fed with belted ammunition from two cans from each of the five shooting position. Each can holds twenty-five hundred rounds. There are six positions from which firing can be done. The Tail Gunner who shoots independently, the Bombardier nose position who can only fire if authorized by the senior CFCS controller, the left and right waist gunner positions who can only fire if authorized by the senior CFSC controller. Who is the CFSC controller? The ring gunner is the senior gunner. He is called a ring gunner because he sits in a high chair (lovingly called the barber chair) looking out of a bubble and is able to

110

rotate a full three hundred sixty degrees to see all activity coming towards the aircraft. Again, as you learn about crew coordination for the CFCS you will better understand how the turrets are controlled. Let's break for lunch."

Lunch was in a dining hall comparable to Piute. The atmosphere, the gentleness of the conversations and the delicious aroma of the meal made Musher want to scream for joy. There is much more to being a flyboy than the Lowry Mess. In the serving line there was a choice of three entrees. Roast beef au jus, grilled steak with bearnaise sauce or super salads with cottage cheese and fresh rolls. Musher would not care if they didn't give him anything as long as he could sit and relax in this beautiful place. He opted for the grilled steak with sauce, a small baked potato, a small salad and fresh rolls with butter. One of those quietly moving people came to the table to serve coffee, tea or milk. At the table for four there was very little talking just simply joyous eating. Another one of those quiet moving people came to the table to remove the used items, asked if anyone wanted more coffee and would this table need an ash tray. You could have knocked Musher over with a feather. He almost did not get out a yes please. Musher noted how many people were smoking and enjoying coffee. The Dining Room Supervisor announced there are many desserts here, please help yourself. Some went for dessert but Musher just lit another Lucky and sipped his coffee. Before the flight left the classroom Sergeant Walker told them that after they finished eating remain in the dining room and he would tell them when to fall-in. One of the airmen at his table had a watch and remarked that it had been over one hour since they were in the serving line. Musher made a special note to himself, "I must have a watch."

Back in the classroom the familiarization with the B-29 continued. Sergeant Walker expounded the combat history and honors earned by the B-29 in South Pacific Operations. He told of high level and low level bombing missions. What life was life on Tinian and Guam in the Mariana Islands. He told of R and R (Rest and Relaxation) periods on the island of Paulu where the women did not wear tops and sex was considered a daily need.

"Let's get on the bus and go back to the flight line." On the ride to the flight line he advised, "When you climb aboard the aircraft enter through the front ladder. You may look at anything you wish but do not touch. When you exit the aircraft exit through the rear hatch. I told you that this was the first of the combat bombers to be pressurized so that when it was necessary to go from the forward compartment to the rear gunner's compartment it had be done without depressurizing the aircraft. To solve that situation the aircraft designers added a tunnel above the bomb bays which would be pressurized and could be used to crawl between the two compartments. I want you to crawl through the tunnel to the gunner's compartment to exit the aircraft. If you think you have too much clothes on to make it through the tunnel you may take some off. Remember the aircrews did it with their flight gear on and a chest pack parachute harness. I don't need to tell you to watch out for each other." When all the flight had been in the aircraft, exited through the tunnel and were on the bus Sergeant Walker said, "The bus will take you to your barracks. I want you to study the handouts you received today and I shall see you here tomorrow."

CHAPTER 38
Feeling and Firing At the Bandits

The flight was eager to get back to the flight line. The bus passed the B-29 and drove into a hangar. The airmen off loaded and were staring at a number of gun turrets placed around the hangar. The center of the hangar had classroom seating for eighteen persons.

A very small fellow, no more than five foot one stood before them. He was covered with enough stripes to the point that with a color change he could have passed for a zebra colt. "My name is Master Sergeant Joseph Abranson, known here as Sergeant JA. I am the NCOIC (Non-Commissioned Officer-in-Charge) of this training facility. During World War II I was a ball gunner on a B-17. That's the guy who crawled into the little bubble on the underbelly of the fuselage and from there managed two caliber 50 machine guns. I flew one hundred missions, many of them deep into the heart of Germany. Was I a good gunner? Maybe, but I sure was a lucky one based on the premise that ball gunners never made it past ten missions.

Today you will be shooting from a B-29 waist position at incoming enemy fighters, also known as "bandits". Naturally you will not be firing ammo. You will instead fire gun camera film. Please notice that in front of every turret is mounted a large movie screen. There is where you will see the bandits. To add to the high adreline level of a bandit encounter every time you close the gun sight action switch (the trigger for the machine guns) and as long as it closed you will hear simulated gun fire through your helmet headset. You are not obligated to fire at every bandit which appears on your screen. On occasion conversation will be intermingled during the encounter and you will hear an instruction from your ring gunner. Each encounter will last approximately six minutes. If you exhaust your ammunition your exercise will stop there. Your score for each encounter is based on the number of bandit hits. You will have eight encounters during today's training. We have twelve turret stations. There will be one training instructor for each turret station. He is your ring gunner and will interject whatever other disruptions he chooses. He will also rate your physical behavior during the exercise. Using the first letter of your last name the first twelve men step forward."

Musher was number twelve in the first group. He wondered if this was like some of those electronic rifle games he had played on Revere Beach.

You know, the ones where you try to keep the bear reversing direction. At station twelve stood a staff sergeant displaying his name and an aerial gunner's badge on his flying suit. "Let's not waste time. Around here I am known as Squeaker because of my high gentle voice. Put on your helmet, goggles, climb into the turret, plug in your headset, secure your harness and talk to me when you are ready." In a moment from Squeaker, "Number twelve I read you cloud and clear. How do you read me?" Musher answered, "Loud and clear."

"OK, as they say in the movies let the games begin. Your clock is now running." With that two black and silver bandits were on the screen headed straight towards Musher. He was so caught up with surprise he could not even get his hands onto the gun sight before they were gone. Just seconds later another bandit was crossing the screen on a course parallel to Musher and climbing. His left hand closed the ready switch, the reticle appeared, he framed the bandit in the reticle and closed the action switch. He fired three short bursts all the time keeping the reticle on the target. The simulated gunfire in his helmet was loud, very, very loud. With almost no hesitation a bandit appeared on the screen climbing towards the underbelly of the B-29. He heard the ring gunner, "Navigator he is yours lower forward. Waist standby to pick him up as he crosses over us. You have upper forward and upper aft." Musher anticipated the target coming into his view. When he did, Musher's shooting procedure was becoming standard, Close the ready switch, Put the reticle on the target, Fire three short bursts. If the target is still in sight keep the reticle on the target and fire three more short bursts. It seemed as if there was a never ending stream of bandits coming at Musher from all directions. Finally Squeaker said, "Time's up. Secure from the turret and join me." Musher felt somewhat as he did on the first day of T-6 flying when he stepped out of the cockpit and his legs were like jelly. No matter how he feels when he climbs down from the cockpit today he will never show it. His clothes were totally soaked and he was dying for a cool dink.

Squeaker told him his film would be processed and before his next turn in the turret this turn would be critiqued. "It's much cooler in the locker room. There are towels there if you wish to shower and smoking is allowed. Be back in your seat in thirty minutes." Musher thought, "Damned if I don't need a watch." The shower was almost as welcome as the two Lucky Strikes. He had learned his lesson about cigarettes and wet clothes. During one of his BX trips he had picked up a light metal cigarette pack holder, couple that with the Zippo (with the extra flint stuck under the cotton) and you are always ready. He was back in his seat well before his thirty minutes was up.

Squeaker motioned Musher into a small, shaded room. "First let's look at your film". The film showed many hits. "You scored eight hundred seventy-four hits out of a possible fourteen hundred. That's a ratio of six and one half hits for every ten rounds fired. Most gunners would love to shoot that ratio. As for your conduct in the turret, you moved the gun sight well and with the exception of the first bandit approach stayed calm during the entire encounter. I am confidant that if you score as well or better in the next two rounds Sergeant Adamowicz will excuse you from the other sessions." Musher didn't tell him that the encounter had been fun and he necessarily did not want to be excused.

Musher's next two rounds went almost about the same but were slightly lower. When all the flight had finished three rounds Sergeant JA declared time for lunch. The bus drove them to the dining hall where they had an almost two hour delicious pork strip meal, lots of desserts, coffee and cigarettes. Back in the hangar Musher approached Squeaker. "Sergeant I don't want to seem impertinent but on my last two turns I felt I shot better but scored lower. With your permission I would like to adjust the selsyns to the reticle. It will coordinate them better within the gun sight."

"I cannot give you such permission but I will ask Sergeant JA."

"Your request was approved but you must record the selsyn settings before you begin and when you are completed." Musher did as he was told, gave the results to Squeaker and climbed into the turret for his fourth turn. The exercise went smoothly. The film went to processing, Musher went to shower, returned to his seat and waited to be beckoned by Squeaker.

When Squeaker beckoned and Musher entered the room he was surprised to see Sergeant JA sitting there. Sergeant JA, "Squeaker tells me you are the best student he has ever had. He reports your conduct in the turret was outstanding. Certainly shooting sixty-two and one half percent, fifty-nine percent, sixty percent and then a dramatic rise to eighty-nine percent after you adjusted the gun sight yourself places you among the very top shooters in this command. Gun sight maintenance is a job for the boys in the Armament and Electronics Squadron. Did you learn that skill here at Lowry?"

"Yes sergeant, from Staff Sergeant Michael Lesser the instructor for the gun sight and gun sight maintenance."

"He did his job well. You are excused from any further exercises here today. It is very long walk to your barracks and the base buses do not run on the flight line. The best I can offer you is a ride close to your barracks but if you choose you can wait here for the rest of your flight. In any case tomorrow we will take a ride in a B-29."

Musher chose the ride close to his barracks. Squeaker instructed the bus driver and the bus departed with only one passenger. Along the way Musher convinced the bus driver to drop him off at the BX. He looked at many watches and finally decided on a second hand movement indicator, self-winding, glow in the dark, masculine looking watch with a wide leather wrist band. Cost: Twenty-two dollars fifty cents. He went into the BX cafeteria had a chocolate shake and two cigarettes, then the base bus to his barracks. He thought he would march in the dinner formation but not eat in the mess hall. If his time was free he could afford the Airmen's Club.

It was 1830 hours when Musher walked in to the Airmen's Club. He bought a cheeseburger, french fries and a coke. He found an empty table and was just about to take his first bite when Mex slipped into the seat next to him. Almost unable to contain himself, "Musher there is a crap game going on in the latrine. Lots of paper money on the floor." Musher thanked him and went back to eating his dinner. Mex left and Musher was sure he had gone back to spectate the crap game. After he finished a couple of Luckies and his coke, he wandered into the latrine. Sure enough there was an old fashioned down on your knees crap game. The shooter was wearing army type corporal stripes and made two elevens and two tens before failing to make a point therefore relinquishing the dice. Musher spoke to the guy next to him," He sure is lucky, who is he?" The airman looked shocked, "That's Corporal (Cpl) Geary, the duty sergeant for the squadron. He decides who will pull KP, stand guard duty, stand fire watch or any other detail the squadron wants done."

Geary announced to the game, "Guys I need to take a piss. I will be right back." He was standing in the middle of an otherwise empty piss trough. Musher stood right next to him. As he unzipped his fly he spoke to Geary, "Nice action the swooshing of the dice at your mouth. Is that a Florida Five which you put in the game while keeping the real die in your mouth?" Geary started to say something but Musher put his hand on Geary's mouth. "Listen to me, where I come from no one rats on a thief. Instead they join him and share in the profits." He removed his hand and continued, "I will not spoil your action, I will also make a little money on the side. Not so much as to keep them from coming back to your game again, but enough so that you know I am there. There is also another small favor you can do for me. I am a member of the new gunnery students flight from Piute. All the time that we are here, probably about three more weeks, no one, I repeat, no one in my flight is to be assigned to any detail. Do we have an accommodation partner?" Geary nodded yes. "Good partner, let's get back to the game before all the money gets away."

CHAPTER 39
Come Fly With Me

This morning the bus stopped by the B-29 and the flight walked into the hangar behind it. Inside the hangar there was a small seating area. A major in a flight suit, two other Captains and three Master Sergeants stood before them. "I am Major Brandon. Today I will be your aircraft commander. This is Captain Anderson my co-pilot, Captain Zachery our third pilot who is also a qualified co-pilot, Master Sergeant Bordeaux our flight engineer, Master Sergeant Gross our forward compartment training NCO and Master Sergeant Baker, our aft compartment training NCO

This aircraft has been modified with intercom speakers. It would be a sight to have you all in headsets at one time. Only the crew and the two trainees in the waist positions will be able to speak to other members of the crew. During takeoff the training NCOs will act as the waist gunners. They will demonstrate one of the jobs of a waist gunner during takeoff. They will also demonstrate how to turn off the Auxillary Power Unit when directed by the Flight Engineer. The flight today is scheduled to last four hours. If for some reason we have to cut it short and bail out you will hear one continuous bell ringing. Tighten you chute, get to the hatch and bail out. No one on board will wait to take you by the hand. One of the peculiarities of this aircraft is that the fuel tanks are in the wings right behind the engines mounted on the wings. If there is an engine fire which we cannot put out there is very little time before the fire gets to the fuel tanks. If we are not out by then, there will be nothing left to get out of. I am sure most, if not all, other than your short hops in the T-6 at Piute have ever flown in an aircraft, especially one like this. There is an intimidation in the thought of multi-engine aircraft flying. After all, if God wanted man to fly he would have given him wings. Most everyone has jitters and maybe air sickness in the beginning. Since you were able to overcome air sickness and fear of flying at Piute, this aircraft compared to the T-6 rides like the Queen Elizabeth. You will become accustomed to the strange noises which occur in flight. Think of the aircraft as if it were a car. As long as the engine is running smoothly, the car runs smoothly. We have tremendous concern for the quality of our aircraft and in your combat unit you will meet aircraft crew chiefs whose whole life centers around the well being of their aircraft. If anyone wishes to withdraw now is the time to do it." One member of the flight stood. Major Brandon directed him to a small room. "There is no shame in not wanting to fly. In your unit you can expect to fly long missions every three days. After all it is a voluntary assignment. The aircraft has been pre-flighted (all the ground checks to verify the safety of the aircraft have been done), our flight plan (tells Base Operations where we are going and what we are going to do when we get there) is filed and we are ready to go He pointed to another room on the hangar perimeter. There is a latrine, coffee and donuts there and smoking is allowed. Enjoy the next thirty minutes."

The NCOs divided the flight into six for the forward compartment and eleven for the aft compartment. There were parachutes and seat belts at each of the passenger positions. The two NCOs manned the waist positions. With their parachutes, helmets and goggles on either one looked like a Hollywood poster. The Right Waist Gunner (RWG) was heard on the speaker, "Number 3 engine (engines are counted left to right with number 3 being the inboard engine on the right wing) is clear." From the flight engineer,"Starting 3." The engine coughed black smoke and then turned over smoothly. The propeller blades cut large circles in the air. The process was repeated from RWG for number 4 engine. The next voice was that of the Left Waist Gunner (LWG) repeating the process for engines 1 and 2. RWG," Right side clear". From the LWG, "Left side is clear."

On the speaker, "Lowry tower this is B-29 student orientation flight ready to taxi."

"You are cleared to taxi to revetment 24."

In the revetment the flight engineer began revving the engines to check the available power. He reported to the Aircraft Commander (AC) the aircraft engines are ready for takeoff.

"Lowry tower this B-29 student orientation flight ready for takeoff."

"You are cleared for takeoff on runway 9 Right. There is no other traffic in the area."

"Roger Lowry tower, 9 Right for takeoff."

Just as the pilots had done in the smaller aircraft Major Brandon rolled the B-29 turning onto Runway 9 and continued to roll for take off.

LWG," Number 1 and 2 look good." RWG, "Number 3 and 4 look good." Flight engineer, "All dials in the zone." These reports continued throughout the takeoff roll.

LWG,"Left flap coming up." RWG, "Right flap coming up."

LWG, Left flap full up and number 1 and 2 look OK." The RWG repeated the report for flap up and number 3 and 4 engines.

From the AC, "Climbing to eight thousand feet."

From the flight engineer,"Take the Auxillary Power Unit (APU) off line."

Sergeant Gross came out of the LWG position and headed into the tunnel to go forward. Sergeant Baker went through the pressurization hatch and was at the APU when he called for the first six airmen. He demonstrated the use of the APU and when he finished with those six he repeated the whole process for the remaining five flight members. Back in the aft compartment Sergeant Baker reported to the AC that the compartment was secure and ready for pressurization. He then turned to the gunnery trainees. "We are flying to a wide open mountain range gunnery area. Each of you will take a turn in a waist position. The LWG position will fire the lower forward and lower aft guns, The RWG position will fire the upper forward and upper aft guns. The turrets have been locked so that they can only fire in a straight line perpendicular to the aircraft. The ammunition which is loaded is training ammunition. The only difference between it and combat ammunition is that the projectile is not heavy metal. The change is made as a cost saving step. You will be saddled into that position wearing your oxygen mask just as you would be on a combat mission. I will direct when to fire. Are there any questions?"

Aft training NCO to AC,"Sir we are ready to commence shooting training at your command."

From the AC. "Commence training."

"You left waist, you right waist. Saddle up. Be sure to plug in your headset and oxygen mask. Raise your hand when you are ready." In just a few minutes both airmen raised a hand.

"On my command, close action switch, fire."

There was very little sound from the firing inside the aircraft but there was a lot of shaking. None of the trainees was braced for such vibration and one of the waist positions actually fired another short burst.

"OK up and out." The waist positions emptied. One of the students was so embarrassed he looked as if he wanted to cry.

"Next two, you left, you right." Musher was still waiting. This time the vibration caused by the simultaneous firing of all four turrets was expected. The vibration was easily handled. Musher was in the next firing. All went routinely well.

"You five go forward through the tunnel and send the other six back here. Pointing to the remaining airmen, you left, you right. By now you should know the drill. Any questions. Good. Saddle up" Meanwhile the five airmen were trying to enter the tunnel and make their way forward. It seemed to Musher as if the NCO speeded up the shooting process trying to catch the airmen while they were still in the tunnel. Again the shooting exercise went without incident. The six airmen who had been in the forward compartment made their way through the tunnel. Musher was sent forward. While crawling through the tunnel one of the firing exercises was done. The tunnel shook and bounced Musher around. When he got out of the tunnel he took a seat next to the flight engineer and put on a headset. The rest of the flight was devoted to shooting and demonstrations of some of the air maneuvers a B-29 will do in a combat situation.

The AC said, "We are going back to base now. NCOs assume the waist positions." When the wheels touched the ground the AC said, "Four hours one minute. Trainees, you earned your flying pay for this month." Back inside the hangar the AC said, "The personnel from the dining hall knew we would be airborne at lunch so they have set up a light buffet in the same room where you awaited takeoff. Help yourselves. We will take a one hour break."

Musher had a couple of Luckies, showered and then looked for something to eat. The buffet was tasty sandwiches, raw vegetables, coffee and milk. These flyboys know how to live. Following the food break the two NCOs critiqued the firing exercises. No one was chastised but there were a few laughs about some of the trainee behavior and looks when the aircraft was doing maneuvers. Sergeant Gross said in a most confident manner, "You will do all right in any combat unit." Sergeant Baker nodded his head in concurrence. Major Brandon came by and said, "I hope you enjoyed today. There is no life better than that of a combat crew airman in the United States Air Force."

The flight boarded the bus and headed back to the barracks.

The SFI awaited them in the barracks. "You have had a rough day today. There will be no evening dining formation. Any of you who wish to go to the dinner meal may walk independently. Rest and I will see you tomorrow morning." Only after the SFI left did the flight notice that their number had been reduced to sixteen.

CHAPTER 40

The Last Week AT Lowry AFB

Today is the last day of training at Lowry AFB.

Following breakfast the flight was taken to the flight line again. The bus passed the B-29 on which they had flown yesterday stopping at a different hangar. Inside the hangar were some chairs assembled in classroom style. More interesting though were the ten simulated aft gunnery compartments complete with waist shooting positions and a barber chair for the ring gunner. Facing the shooting compartment was an extra large movie screen.

Coming towards the flight was this man in Class A uniform (the uniform worn for parades, when not on the air base and other distinguished reasons). His walking looked slightly shaky as if he had already had a couple of pops. When he got closer the flight rose to attention and the man said, "At ease, sit." On his left arm were ten hash bars (each hash bar represented six months service in a combat area), six hash marks (each hash mark represented three years service in the military) but there was only one ribbon on his chest under his gunner's badge. The ribbon was a field of blue sprinkled with white stars. Musher thought, "My God, he is a winner of the Congressional Medal of Honor." The man in the Class A uniform began, "My name is Master Sergeant Dunford Donovan. Throughout the US Air Force I am known as "Duffy". You may refer to me as either Sergeant Donovan or Sergeant Duffy. During World War II I was a gunner on a B-24 Liberator. I saw my share of action and have been awarded two Purple Hearts, one Legion of Merit, three Air Medals, one Distinguished Flying Cross, and a number of other decorations including some from foreign governments. You will notice I wear only one decoration ribbon.

Your purpose here today is to become very familiar with CFCS gunnery coordination. You will be divided into three teams. Your odd number member will work with two permanent party instructors. Each team will have a permanent party instructor monitoring the team's operations. Team structure and team positions will be rotated throughout the day. Each of you will be given the chance to perform in each position. Your permanent party instructor (PPI) is in charge of your team and he will be obeyed unquestionably. We will take a thirty minute break." Pointing to a room he said, "There is coffee and donuts and smoking is allowed. We will call you to reassemble."

The flight had coffee and donuts. Musher had coffee and Lucky Strike cigarettes. The conversation centered around Sergeant Duffy's Medal of Honor. "Wonder what he did to get it?" "How about those two purple hearts?" Curiosity was plaguing the flight. The flight was called to assemble in the hangar, split into three man teams and directed to each team's shooting station. There the PPI gave his speech. He pointed to the team and said, "You are Number 1, LWG, you are Number 2 RWG and that leaves you as Number 3, ring gunner. The big screen in front of the station will display bandits coming from all directions. At first visual or notification of the bandit the ring gunner must decide who will be the primary shooters. Will he keep the upper forward for himself and give the lower forward to the LWG. Maybe he will give the upper forward to the Bombardier and the lower forward to the LWG. At the closing speed of the bandit there is not much time for that decision. The ring gunner transmits his decisions to the Bombardier by voice and to the two waist gunners by using his feet to tap them on the shoulders. In case he cannot reach the waist gunners' shoulders he can always transmit by voice. Other than an emergency all crewmen stay off the intercom during a bandit attack. Go into the compartment and make ready for combat. Chutes on, helmets, goggles and oxygen masks plugged in. Your oxygen mask has a built in microphone which is on whenever the mask is plugged in. Make sure your harness is as secure as your seat belt. I will be listening and I may break in with a message. Each of you raise your hand when he is ready. The team took a few minutes before each raised his hand. Before Musher raised his hand he told himself to be ready for a quick strike by a bandit.

As if he had been given a game plan the first bandit came diving down towards the B-29 instantly after the PPI said, "We are on." Musher was ready, he kept both upper turrets for himself and voice alerted the LWG if he passes below both lower turrets are yours. Tail, standby if the bastard passes your way. For some indeterminable length of time bandits kept coming and Musher did his best to effectively us the CFCS.

The PPI terminated the exercise. "Make your area ready for the next exercise, go into the coffee room and relax. We will return here for the next exercise. I will come to get you."

The team didn't have to be told twice. Musher lit cigarettes while the other two showered. He then showered, lit another Lucky Strike and drank some cool water before having any coffee. The PPI came in and asked them to bring their coffee into an adjoining room. "The exercise you just finished is not a scored exercise. Your rating is what I believe it should be as a team. I think you have done well." The team beamed with pride. "We are now going back and do the exercise again, except he that was number 1 is now number 2, he that was number 2 is number 3 and he that was number 3 is now number 1. Any questions before we go? None! Good. Let's go."

At the shooting station the PPI could not resist a small summary of his instructions from the first exercise. The second exercise paralleled the first exercise. To Musher it did not seem as long or as draining as the first. He was not involved with every move of every bandit. The PPI terminated the exercise. "Make your area ready for the next exercise, go into the coffee room and relax. We will return here for the next exercise. I will come to get you." Even the routine in the coffee room was almost the same. Musher smoked, the other two showered. Musher showered the other two ate.

The PPI took the team into the adjoining room. "The exercise was not that bad. We will rotate positions again. Any questions? None! Let's go do it."

Once again, at the shooting station the PPI gave a small summary of his instructions from the first two exercises. Once again this exercise paralleled the first two. The PPI terminated the exercise. "Police your area, get all your personal gear then go into the coffee room and relax. We will call you to the classroom area when we want you." The routine in the coffee room was the same. It wasn't long before they were called to the classroom area.

The flight was seated when Sergeant Duffy addressed the flight," The PPI"s tell me that you all did well in every position. When you reach your combat wing and are assigned to a crew I am sure CFSC coordination will get better and better. My experience tells me that your first assignment will be as a Tail Gunner and you will be there a while before getting into the gunner's compartment. Remember, All Things Come To Him Who Waits, Providing He Works His Ass Off While He Is Waiting. We enjoyed having you here and wish you the best of luck in your Air Force career. The bus will take us to the dining hall. Have an enjoyable lunch and the bus will take you to your barracks." Musher thought, "We must have done well, the afternoon training is cancelled. Either that or the permanent party enjoys Friday afternoon off."

In the dining hall Musher was the first person at his table. SSgt Hamrick, the gun sight instructor set his meal along side Musher. The rest of the flight seeing that sat at other tables leaving Musher alone with Sergeant Lesser. Sergeant Lesser began, "I want to thank you and your flight for the generous words you told the flight line people about what you learned and from whom you learned it. Flyboys tend to look down their noses at us technical people. I received a very nice letter from the Wing Commander regarding your gun sight training. That letter will go in my permanent personnel file and is a major boost towards my promotion. I know you finish here today and will be on your way to another assignment. I also know that your travel orders will contain an authorization for a ten day delay in reporting to your next assignment. I don't know if you will take leave or where you will go if you do take it. On this piece of paper is the base operations telephone number and name of my friend who works in base operations. If you decide that you are going to take the leave and you need to travel a long way, I suggest you call my friend and ask him if there are any aircraft going in that direction. There may be none and then again you might get lucky." The rest of the meal was quiet until SSgt Lesser got up to leave. He stuck out his right hand to shake and said, "Again thank you, I wish you the best of luck." With that he was gone. Musher could hardly wait to get to a base telephone. He approached the Dining Hall Supervisor and asked if he could make an on base telephone call. "Sorry, trainees are not allowed to use our telephone."

CHAPTER 41

The US Air Force Airline

Musher was the last one on the bus. The SFI greeted him with, "We thought you went AWOL. Driver to the barracks." Musher asked, "Sergeant can we go by the BX? There are some things I need to pack for reassignment." "Driver to the BX." Musher just knew there had to be a base telephone there. He found a base telephone in the BX lobby which said for "On Base Calls Only." Nervously he dug out the paper with the name and telephone number of Sergeant Hamrick's friend. He dialed and the phone was ringing. When answered the voice said, "Base Operations, Technical Sergeant Collins." That was the name on the paper.

"This is A2C Muscarello. Sgt Lesser suggested I call you about getting a ride on a military aircraft that might be going near Boston, Massachusetts."

"Are you his student called Musher? If you are I have been expecting your call."

"Yes Sergeant, I am Musher."

"You want to get to Boston?"

"Yes Sergeant I do."

"Do you have certification of completion of the altitude program?"

"Yes Sergeant, I have my certification card."

"Are you checked out in the use of an oxygen mask and a parachute?"

"Yes Sergeant I am."

"Do you have travel orders?"

"Yes Sergeant I do."

"Can you leave on Sunday at noon?"

"Yes Sergeant I can."

"I have a B-25 leaving for Pease AFB, New Hampshire Sunday at noon. Will that help you?"

"Yes Sergeant that is only about two hours by bus from Boston."

"All right Musher you be here not later than 1030 hours Sunday and I will get you on that aircraft. Make sure you bring the paperwork."

"Thank you Sergeant Collins I will be there with bells on."

Musher went into the BX and picked up two cartons of Luckies and a small pocket knife. No self-respecting gentleman would ever be caught without a pocketknife.

At the barracks the SFI announced, "You are done with duty for today. There will be no dinner formation. This flight is excused from the Saturday morning base parade. The clerks from Wing Personnel will be here at 0900 hours tomorrow to complete your out processing. At approximately noon tomorrow you will be free to travel. Before you leave you must report to Wing Headquarters to sign out from Lowry AFB. When you sign out the travel time to get to your next duty station begins. If you pack and lock in your foot locker all the things which you are not going to carry, you will receive a receipt for your foot locker. Your foot locker will be loaded, taken to Base Transportation and forwarded to your next duty station. It may take as many as eleven days for your foot locker to reach your new duty station. Pack with that thought in mind. Good day gentlemen, I will see you at breakfast formation."

Musher was amazed at how few items he would really pack in his B-4 bag. He made sure that his sweat shirt, sweater, leather jacket, wool hat, gloves and field jacket would be readily accessible during flight. Who knows how cold the aft compartment of a B-25 can get. There is no tunnel with which you could go to the forward compartment. He doubled checked that his emergency bag contained goodies and soda. He had no idea how long the flight would be or if there would be any stops scheduled along the way. He was confidant that the contents of his B-4 bag and his emergency bag would take him through an eleven day absence from the military.

He was ready to leave. He took a shower and laid down for a nap. When he awoke is was 1730 hours. The Airmen's Club would be open now. Most of the other trainees would be at chow. This was a good time to go get something to eat. At the club he had a large omelet, home fries, sausage, rye toast and coffee. After a couple of Lucky Strikes he went back into the pool table area and found an empty one. He started racking the balls and trying to make some shots. A dark haired WAF approached him and said," How about a little nine ball. Ten cents on the five and a quarter on the nine." Musher figured he could not lose a lot of money even a hundred dollars would not be much to a guy who has almost fifteen hundred in his stash.

Musher said, "Toss for break?" She looked at him as if he were a dummy and said, "Lag." She won the lag. Musher racked the balls. She made two balls on the break, the five ball in combination and the nine on a bank shot. "Thirty-five cents Sweetheart."..... Musher, "Put it on my tab." Musher's turn to break. The five ball went in on the break and he played a billiard shot to make the nine. "I guess we are even Sweetheart." They played for almost an hour and he owed her ten cents. Musher mocked, "Winners buy the drinks." They got two cokes and sat at a table. Musher was going to light a cigarette when she said, "Can you spare one?" He put the pack on the table and said, "Help yourself." He lit her cigarette and his own.

He continued, "My name is Saverio Muscarello, my friends call me Musher. I am from Boston." She chimed in with, "My name is Lucy Gallo. My friends call me Lucy and I am from Brooklyn."

"You are a hell of a pool player Miss Gallo."

"You are not so bad yourself Mr. Muscarello."

"How long have you been at Lowry and why are you here?"

"Been here for four months. I am training to be a flight tower operator."

"How much longer do you have?"

"One month twenty-two days. How about you?"

"Been here almost a month training for Remote Control Gunnery."

"How soon to you finish?"

"I am finished I depart Sunday for a ten day leave on the way to my first combat wing."

"That's a bitch, I find someone I like and he is gone in forty-eight hours. Come with me." She tried leading him out of the Airmen's Club.

"Can't do it babe, must get back to my barracks now." Musher could sense a set-up and he had all his cash in his pockets.

"Then fuck you asshole. Go to your barracks and jack off." With that in his ears Musher left the club.

Back in his barracks he took a shower and shaved. He ate some candy bars and smoked some cigarettes. He crawled in his sack trying to go to sleep. All he could think about was Lucy Gallo.

CHAPTER 42
Goodbye Lowry Air Force Base

Today's morning formation will be the last at Lowry Air Force Base. Per usual the morning chow was good, but the Mess Hall was still the mess hall. Musher wondered where he would be assigned and if the eating facility would be like the mess hall here or a dining facility like Piute. Back in the barracks there was very little cleaning. 0900 hours could not come quick enough.

At precisely 0900 hours two clerks from the Wing Personnel Department arrived. They assembled the flight and began to read each airman's new assignment. The flight was scattered throughout the United States. Musher and another airman named Philip Dexter were going to the 301st Bomb Wing, Smoky Hill Air Force Base, Salina, Kansas. When the list was read and a copy posted on the bulletin board the two clerks set up two processing stations. When Musher was being processed the clerk asked him if he were going to take a delay in route (leave). After establishing that he was and he had a foot locker to be shipped the clerk asked him if he wanted a cash advance. Musher grinned as if to say I am well heeled. The clerk interpreted the grin correctly. "You know airman it is not wise to travel with a lot of cash. I don't know how much you have and I don't want to know. You should seriously consider keeping around one hundred dollars in small bills on your person, and the rest be carried in American Express Traveler Checks. These checks are cashable almost anywhere. If you should lose them or if they were stolen American Express replaces them at no charge to you. You can get traveler checks at the American Express Office next to the BX. American Express does not charge you any fees to issue or to cash any of their traveler checks. One last reminder, you must go to Wing Headquarters and sign out of Lowry when you depart the airbase. With that the clerk wrapped up the processing, gave Musher an envelope full of papers to be given to his next wing personnel department and checked to see if his partner had also finished. In less than two hours they were done. The foot lockers for shipment were loaded on a six-by and the clerks and six-by truck left.

Since the afternoon was free Musher decided he would take the base bus to the BX and have lunch in the BX cafeteria. Lunch would wait while he went to the American Express office. He had fifteen hundred seventeen dollars in paper money. He figured he would keep the hundred seventeen in his pocket and convert the fourteen hundred to traveler checks. It took a lot more time in American Express than he expected. It was almost 1400 hours. He was famished and dying for a cigarette. He took all his time eating and smoking before catching the base bus to his barracks area. He did his SSS and it was near 1700 hours when he was dressed. Might just as well go to the Airmen's Club rather than hang around here.

Musher picked up a coke and walked into the pool table area. There practicing was Lucy Gallo. Musher was embarrassed but he walked up to her and said, "How about some straight pool. Twenty-five points, ten cents a point differential? Lag for break." Lucy lost and walked to the table to break. So far she had not said one word to him. Her break was not gentle and she left two open balls adjacent to the rack. Musher called the six ball in the corner and with that made the six and broke open the rack. He continued to call shots and he ran the twenty-five points before Lucy could even get another turn at the table. Looks like two dollars fifty cents to me Sweetheart." Lucy racked the balls and it was Musher's turn to break. He played the cue ball two rails coming into the rack from the rear. One ball popped loose and as it touched the rail the cue ball nestled up to the rear of the rack. Even Willie Mosconi could not make a shot out of that leave. With no shot available Lucy tried to play a safety. She played a little heavy handed and one of the lead balls strayed from the rack while the cue ball moved free of the rear of the rack. Musher studied the table. He envisioned a dead combination if he played a billard using the loose ball. He called, "The thirteen in the side." Lucy was astonished, the thirteen was in the middle of the rack. Impossible. Musher played the billard, the thirteen went into the side and the rack was open. Once again Musher called shots and ran the twenty-five points before Lucy got another turn. "Looks like five dollars to me Sweetheart." Musher put his cue stick in the rack and went to Lucy. "I behaved badly last night and I apologize. Let me make it up to you at dinner." Lucy laid her cue stick on the table and they walked out of the pool area together. They found a small table in a quiet corner. He offered a cigarette, took one himself, lit both and they just stared each other without speaking.

While Lucy waited Musher went to the food line and got two cheese omelets with hash browns and country ham. He added two large coffees and two slices of blueberry pie. They ate dinner slowly. Lucy talked about her family and her beloved Brooklyn. Musher listened attentively but did not contribute much to the conversation. While smoking their after dinner cigarette the jukebox began playing slow dancing music. Musher thought, "Thank God his mother Filomena insisted all the boys become good dancers." His old man's saying was that the shortest way to the bedroom is across the dance floor. They must have danced for an hour. Being careful to not be too cuddly else the Club Chaperones would break them up. Musher whispered, "Would you like to show me now what it is you wanted to show me last night?" Lucy's head bobbed yes. "We cannot leave together, I will meet you outside."

They walked towards the WAF Billeting area. All the WAF barracks had dark window shades and the space between the barracks was exceptionally dark. Lucy pulled him into one of those spaces and stopped at the midway point of the barracks. She grabbed him and started to viciously kiss him. She was busily unbuttoning his trousers and pulling down his shorts. He was opening her blouse and taking off her underpants. She straddled him as an ice skater would when her partner was going to put her in a suicide spin. She reached down and put his prick in her pussy. This experience was so new to him that in just a few strokes he came. She could feel it and consoled him not to worry. She would fix that. She went down on her knees and began licking and sucking his dick. The sensation was unlike any he had ever had. Without warning his sperm rushed into Lucy's mouth. She swallowed and kept right on sucking. In only a matter of a couple of minutes he was hard again. She helped him enter and this time he was not quite so quick. Again she went down to her knees and brought him back to life. The third time lasted a lot longer. Lucy made soft noises as she curled more tightly around him. Suddenly she bit his shoulder and she shook all over. He kept stroking until he felt his own relief.

As they dressed and became more presentable Musher asked, "Would you like a cigarette? I am going to have one."

They walked back to the Airmen's Club and entered separately. Musher got cokes, they sat and just sheepishly grinned at each other. "Time for me to leave. I need to finish packing. My flight is at 1000 hours tomorrow. You are a sweetheart."

"Will you write me" asked Lucy. "Can I write you?"

Musher, purely lying through his teeth said, "I'll be in touch." When he got back to the barracks he took a twenty minute shower. He had had his first piece of ass and a blow job. Her bite of his shoulder did not bring blood but it left a real good black and blue bruise. It was worth taking the bite. Tonight I should sleep like a baby.

CHAPTER 43

The Ten Day Leave

Musher was up early Sunday morning. He skipped breakfast, grabbed his luggage and boarded the base bus to Wing Headquarters. He entered the building and went to the reception desk where a sign said Master Sergeant Nicolas Purtupis, Charge of Quarters. Musher said, "Sergeant I need to sign out. I am leaving Lowry AFB."

"Let me see your orders. I will take a copy and you fill in the register blanks and sign your full name and serial number."

Musher dutifully complied. "Sergeant Purtupis I need to get to Base Operations to catch a flight. Can you tell me how I can do that?"

"Unfortunately there are no base buses allowed on the flight line. How soon do you need to be there?"

"0900 hours."

The O.D. (Officer of the Day) will be leaving for breakfast very soon you can ask him for a ride." About that time a Captain came from the adjoining room wearing a sidearm and an arm band which said,"O.D."

Musher approached him. "Excuse me Sir I am trying to get to Base Operations for a flight. Sergeant Purtupis tells me that you are going to breakfast at the flight line dining hall. Sir, may I hitch a ride with you?"

"Of course airman. Put your gear in the O.D.'s Jeep outside. I will be with you in a minute or so."

When the Captain came out Musher was standing at attention on the passenger side of the jeep and holding a salute.

The Captain returned his salute and said, "Get on Board."

The ride to the flight line was short but the Captain asked many questions about Musher's presence on Lowy and what did he think of the place overall. "Sir it is a large training facility with thousands of students. I think the permanent party does very well considering the schedules they must meet,"

"Here you are airman. The jeep was parked in front of Base Operations. You have almost an hour and a half before you are scheduled to be here. Good Luck."

Musher responded with a hand salute and, "Thank you Sir."

Inside Base Operations Musher went to the flight passenger desk and told the airman on duty that Sergeant Collins had scheduled him to ride on the B-25 going to Pease AFB. The airman took a bunch of documents from

Musher, verified them and returned them. "You are officially on the Form 1. (The Form 1 listed all the SOB's (Souls on Board) for the flight. The crew will not be here for at least another hour and it will be at least two hours before you can board. Find a comfortable chair and rest. You can smoke here as long as you obey the smoking rules. Sergeant Collins will be here in about an hour." Musher found an unobtrusive chair and settled in. He must have dozed.

He was shaken awake by Technical Sergeant whose name tag said Collins. "It's time for you to board. Walk out to that B-25 and stow your gear in the aft compartment. Report to the senior gunner and he will take care of you from there. I am glad to help anyone who has respect for Sergeant Lesser." Musher thanked him profusely and shook his hand vigorously. At the B-25 with baggage in hand Musher started up the aft compartment ladder. From inside the compartment a voice asked, "Who's out there?"

"A2C Muscarello, I am scheduled to fly as a passenger on your trip to Pease AFB." There was no sound from inside the compartment. All Musher could think was that there had been a fuck-up and he really wasn't going to fly to Pease. The silence broke and he was instructed to come aboard. He was met at the top of the ladder by a staff sergeant in a flying suit with a gunner's badge embroidered into the breast space. He took Musher's luggage and offered a hand to boost him aboard.

"My name is Sam Lollipop. My fiends call me Sugar. That lazy bum decked out at the end of the compartment is our other waist gunner Corporal Angel Angee. He is known as Angel to every hooker in every town in which we have ever landed. That name is a real misnomer."

"My name is Saverio Muscarello commonly known as Musher. Friday I completed training as an aerial gunner for the remote turrets of the B-29 Central Fire Control System. I have only been in the USAF for four months. Prior to my transfer to the USAF I was in the Army infantry for three months. I am on a ten day leave to Boston before heading for my first combat assignment in the 301st Bomb Group, Smoky Hill AFB, Salina, Kansas."

"All right Musher pick out a parachute and a place to sit. Leave your gear there and come with us to the AC's preflight briefing. Wake up Snow White before the Wicked Witch of the Cockpit gets you."

The crew was in a line with the pecking order going from right to left. They were standing in a half attention position. The AC's flying suit had a name embroided over the left breast pocket. Major Fred Tillman The AC looked at Musher and asked Sugar, "Who is this airman?" Sugar explained that Musher was a trainee student who graduated and is trying to get home for a leave in Boston. "This will be an almost seven hour flight. Did anyone think to get rations for this airman? Sugar, break out a few IFR's (In Flight Rations)." (IFR's are to a fly boy as a C Ration is to a foot soldier) "Saddle up and let's get gone."

Aboard the aircraft Sugar told Musher, "There are extra headsets in the box near the parachutes. You can use one to listen but you will not be able to speak on the intercom." Musher picked out a headset, plugged it into the intercom jack, put on his parachute, got seated and buckled in. Once the engines were running the noise level in the compartment sounded pretty much like the mess hall at Lowry. The AC talked to Lowry Tower just as the B-29 pilot had. Cleared to taxi and take off the AC wheeled the B-25 as if it were a T-6. Takeoff was uneventful. Musher wished that he had been able to see outside the aircraft. As if he was a mind reader Sugar came from his waist position and waived Musher into his seat. There was no gun sight or gunner's bubble like in the B-29 but there was a removable glass panel. Aerial gunnery on the B-25 was just a major upgrade from gunnery in the T-6. Musher stared at Denver and the surrounding majestic Rocky Mountains. Someday I will come here as a tourist.

The aft compartment although pressurized and heated was very cold for Musher. Sugar came to Musher's seating area and dropped three blankets in his lap. Musher looked at him gratefully and thought, "Before I cover up let me get my hat, my sweater and field jacket from my B-4 bag." There were still over five hours to Pease. Bundled up like a baby in a carriage in Boston in December he relaxed and was soon fast asleep. When he awakened and looked at his watch more than two hours had passed since he fell asleep. Sugar tossed him a box wrapped in heavy wax paper. The label said IFR Number 2. Musher unwrapped the box and inside was a can labeled ham and eggs; another can labeled crackers, another can labeled peaches and another can labeled chocolate. Nowhere inside the box was there a can opener. Sugar could see the bewilderment on Musher's face as he came over and knelt beside Musher. From around his neck he pulled out his dog tags. On the short chain along with a dog tag hung a rectangular shaped metal object not more than one and one half inches long and one half inches wide. One edge of the rectangle was notched. The other edge had a hinge mounted on it with a one inch scimitar blade attached to it. The blade folded onto the rectangle to keep the wearer from being cut when the object was not in use. "Pay attention boy and see one of the wonders of man's brilliance." Sugar unfolded the blade from the rectangle, picked up the ham and eggs can, placed the notched side of the rectangle on the rim of the can, pushed the scimitar blade into the can and started rotating the blade around the rim of the can. Each movement of the blade made a short cut in the top of the can until the top could be removed. "The most dangerous part of this move is cutting yourself on the edge of the can. This tool's strict nomenclature is "field can opener. Throughout the military services it is known as a P-38 It should be available at your Base Supply, Squadron Supply and if worse comes to worse can be bought in the BX." Sugar took the dog tags off his neck, grasped the P-38, pushed it towards Musher and said, "Use it. I know your not going anywhere with it."

Embarrasingly Musher asked, "Do we have forks, spoons or knives?" "Sorry kid, all flyboys carry their own. We don't have any spares. Some people think the arm pockets in a flying suit are for pencils etc. We know they are for forks, knives and spoons.

Musher didn't answer, he knew he would get by. He was a gentleman and no self-respecting gentleman would ever be caught without a pocket knife. After eating most of his IFR Musher settled down and went back to sleep. Again Sugar awakened him. "We are about thirty minutes from Pease. Police up and square away your area. When we land after putting this baby to bed the crew, including you, will be taken to Base Ops. The officers will stay at Base Ops to do paperwork and we enlisted will be taken to our barracks. We will get the driver to drop you off by the main gate where you can catch the air base bus to Nashua and from there your bus to Boston. Any questions? I didn't think so."

The landing was so smooth Musher hardly felt the touchdown. When Sugar told him to get out Musher went down and his baggage was tossed to him. He did as he done before, lined up under the wing for the AC's post-flight briefing. "Crew, as usual you did a fine job. Airman, did you enjoy the ride?"

"Sir I thank you and your crew for the lift, the meal, the company and the education I received on this flight. Again Sir, Thank you all."

The AC to the Flight Engineer, "Are we ready to go?"

Flight Engineer, "Yes Sir"

The AC, "Let's board the bus."

The bus stopped at Base Ops to let the officers get off. When they were off the bus pulled away. Sugar said to the driver, "Swing by the front gate so we can let this airman off."

Within ten minutes Musher was sitting at the bus stop smoking Lucky Strikes. There was no charge to ride the bus and there were a number of other airmen on the bus heading for town. It's still just early Sunday night.

CHAPTER 44
The Old Neighborhood

It was 2230 hours when Musher arrived in Boston. He dashed for the subway and entered "The Bucket" shortly after 2300 hours. At the door he was greeted by old friends and the bucket regulars. There was much back patting and handshaking. Questions were fired at him from all directions. "How long are you here for?" "Are you out now?" Among the questions was the sixty-four dollar question. "I thought you went into the Army. Why all the air corps uniform stuff?"

Musher was ready with his story. "You're right. I enlisted in the US Army. I finished US Army basic training and even went to Advanced Infantry School. While at that school the government put on a recruiting drive for young soldiers with a high school diploma to transfer to the new United States Air Force and become Aerial Gunners. I figured flying was better than walking so I transferred. This badge here, pointing to his wings, says that I am a qualified aerial gunner in the United States Air Force." The questioning stopped and the various welcome homes continued for a while longer.

Musher went to the Keeper of The Bucket. He knew everything that went on in the neighborhood and to a great extent what the neighborhood people were involved in outside the neighborhood. "Have you seen Freddie lately? Is he still in jail?" The Keeper laughed, "He only did forty days of that three month sentence before they early-released him." What's he doing? "You know Freddie he is still the best at finding small scores which fall off trucks. He has learned two lessons well, one, there are no trucks which have any products fall off in the neighborhood, and two, how to pay tribute to Fanucci" Fanucci was Big Charlie Sorrento, the godfather of the Sorrento Family. "Where can you find Freddie?" "He has a small flat uptown. If he isn't there or at some cathouse he most probably is at Nino's pizzeria on Atlantic Ave." Musher thanked him and asked, "Can I leave my gear here for a while I hate to wake the folks at this hour."

" No problem, remember I close at three and won't open again until ten in the morning."

Musher decided to try Nino's first. Nino's was not just a pizza joint. It was a full service bar small restaurant with a limited dining menu. There was plenty of action for takeout pizza. The place was a favorite hangout of the wise guys and the wanna bees. There were usually card games and crap games in the rooms beyond the kitchen. Among the off color element in Boston it was known as "Boston's Caesar's Palace." He spotted Freddie sitting with a couple of guys drinking beer. When Freddie saw him he jumped out of his chair came to Musher almost shouting, "You look great", as he hugged Musher. At the table Freddie introduced Musher to the Scaparetti brothers. The brothers shook hands with Musher and said,"We have to go," and left. As the brothers were leaving Musher thought I remember them, they were hit men for Caesar.

Musher and Freddie sat down, Freddie called for two cold beers and a couple of slices of pizza for Musher.

"You're looking good guy. You muscled up a little and your face is fuller. Are they treating you OK? When did you get here and how long are you going to be here?"

"Just got in town, went to the Bucket looking for you and The Keeper suggested I try here. You look well. Is everything good for you? It looks like you are moving in some pretty fast company."

"Not me kid, we are just social acquaintances. Not that I would not like to be a member of that crowd but so far it just doesn't seem possible. Your getting here at this time must be destiny. Later tonight some very expensive jewelry is going to "drop off a truck" while unloading in an uptown classy jewelry exchange. I have been studying the routine for over a month. There is an easy alarm system and only one "rent-a-cop" security guard. Our score could be in the five to eight grand each."

Musher asked, "What about the security guard?"

Freddie pulled back his jacket and exposed a shoulder holster with a pistol in it. "This will take care of him. I have another for you. We put you in different clothes and we are back in business."

Musher was shaking inside his body. They had never done anything with guns. He didn't want any part of this job and he didn't know how to tell Freddie. He didn't want the rep of a pussy, but he did not want to be a real gangster. Finally he said to Freddie, "I cannot do this job. It is over my head and I would not be any good for you. Forgive me but I must leave now."

As he left the pizzeria he could hear Freddie, "Pussy, the Army made a pussy out of you."

Musher made it back to The Bucket, picked up his gear and went downtown to rent a room. Lying in his unlit hotel room bed he was trying to understand why something like Freddie's gig would have been routine and now he wanted no part of it. Especially if it involved guns. Was it possible he was growing up?

In the morning he did his SSS, told the hotel clerk he would be staying another night and headed out to find breakfast. Near the hotel there was a small diner type restaurant. He sat at the counter and the waitress asked if he wanted coffee. She brought him a cup and took his breakfast order. She asked, "Do you want to look at the Record?" The Record was the early morning Record American which contained all the sports scores and most importantly the back page showed the US Treasury numbers from the night before. It was easy to read the treasury numbers selecting one from each position in each row. Those four numbers made up the winning number for the "Number Pool". (In those days in a far less sophisticated society the Number Pool was generally called the "nigger pool"). It was probably the most sought after data the newspaper published. Even though he had no bets Musher made sure he still knew how to interpret the four lines of numbers used to establish the winning number in the Numbers Pool. As he turned the paper over to the front page the main headline read, "SECURITY GUARD KILLED IN FOILED ATTEMPTED ROBBERY." A picture of Freddie was an insert and the caption read, "Killer in Custody". Musher read the story which followed. He hardly ate any breakfast.

CHAPTER 45
Paying Respects

The subway ride to his neighborhood was short as was the walk to his Mother's home. He climbed the familiar flights, knocked on the door and when his mother answered her eyes filled with tears as she hugged and kissed him. "Come_ina, come_ina Mia Bambino, I get you someding to eat." Despite Musher's objections she put coffee and Italian pastry on the table. Her eyes were as bright as automobile headlights and her smile as wide as her face. She could not stop asking him questions about where he had been, how was his health and how long would he be here. "Tonight for supper we will have ravioli and meatballs and fresh bread." This time it was Musher's turn to smile widely.

"Saverio I need ricotta and a couple of things from the Gloria Chain. Will you go get them for me? Tell Signore Catalucci to put it in the book." She recited a list and Musher told her he would be right back. Signore Catalucci knew Musher, made some small talk and filled the order before asking, "On the book?" Musher asked him what was on the book and with today's order what would the book total be. Signore Catalucci, "One hundred seven dollars forty-six cents." Musher took five hundred dollars worth of traveler checks from his pocket, signed them and gave them to the storekeeper. "This should square the book and leave Mrs.Muscarello with a very good credit rating. You are not to tell her how this happened. If it doesn't happen I shall come to see you."

"Si, Signore. I will personally take care of it." Musher brought the groceries to his mother, told her he had some people he needed to see but he would be back for supper. "Remember Saverio, your father eats at five o'clock sharpa."

First stop on his list was Uncle Fanucci. He took the subway to Maverick Station, a street car to Revere and got off the street car on Revere Street close to the grade school. Fanucci's operation was a block and one half from the school. His front was a small ice cream stand and candy store. Behind the store front was a pool room and a couple of card tables. If you were a permitted person you passed through a heavy metal door, down a short flight of steps and when recognized passed through another heavy metal door into the horse betting parlor, the heavy card games and the crap table. In addition there were two rooms, one was the money room which had armed guards outside and inside the room, and Fanucci's office which was a fortress in itself. Fanucci was one of Caesar's subordinates but he had stature. He was the number 1 bookmaker for all the east coast north shore from Revere to New Hampshire. Musher had been passed through and was greeted by Fanucci with hugs and kisses.

Fanucci had Musher relay his gambling experiences while he was away. Musher told him the ease which he could win playing cards, the crooked dice spitter and how he had broken the two hustlers on the bus. He credited all his success to Fanucci. His uncle was about to burst with pride. "Can you stay for supper?"

"Most regrettably no. Momma is fixing ravioli and meatballs."

"Have you seen your father since you came home?"

"No, I will see him at supper."

"Don't hang around until he gets drunk. If you do there is no telling how you will react. He has been a worse son-of-a-bitch than when you were kids." Musher's father was Fanucci's brother.

"Uncle I have to go. It's a long ride back to the flat. Momma was emphatic that the old man insisted on supper at five o'clock sharp."

Fanucci got up and gave Musher hugs. When they shook hands goodbye Fanucci slipped some paper in Musher's hands. "I don't need it Uncle, I am financially fine."

"Take it, enjoy it and think of me. I love you and look forward to when you come home to join my team."

The heavy door opened and Musher made his way upstairs and back to the street. On the long ride to his mother's flat he dreamed of the day he would be on Fanucci's team. The supper meal was as excellent as he remembered. The table conversation was as bad as he remembered. After a cigarette he said he had to leave. His mother strongly objected but his father simply sat and drank wine. Musher went into his mother's bedroom found an envelope and put five hundred dollars in the envelope. On the outside he wrote, "Mamma I love you, spend this on you please." and tucked the envelope under her pillow. The parting with his mother was tearful. The old man never got out of his chair. He just sat and drank wine. Uncle Fanucci was right, if he did not go now there is no telling what might happen.

If you want to go you will need to be here at 0600 hours tomorrow. Where are you now?"

"In the Boston city library."

"You are quite close to the base but the public transportation is awful. Do you have anyone who can give you a ride here? A taxicab would probably cost you fifty dollars. In any case I come on duty tomorrow at 0500 hours. If you are here by 0600 hours and have all the right papers I will get you aboard. My name is Master Sergeant Wilcox. What is your name, your rank and your serial number?"

Musher answered his questions and thanked him again and again. He joked with Sergeant Wilcox, "As I heard it said in West Texas, "God Willing and the Crick Don't Rise, I will be there at 0500 hours. Goodnight and thank you again." He walked out of the library looking for a cab stand.

The first cabby he came upon he asked, "Do you know where Base Operations is at Hanscom AFB?" He got a nodded yes. "How much will you charge to take me there at 4 A.M. tomorrow. I need to be standing inside Base Ops not later than 5 A.M."

The cabby thought and said, "Thirty-five dollars and five dollars for luggage plus tolls. I want at least twenty up front."

Musher said to him, "My uncle is Caesar. Do you know who Caesar is? There are no tolls between here and Hanscom (purely a guess on Musher's part). If you try to hustle me I will tell my uncle and you will look very funny trying to hack with broken legs and one arm missing. Do I make myself clear? I have memorized your hack license."

"Yes Sir."

"Very good, here is my hotel and room number. If you are there on time and ready to go all will be well. If you are not then you will jeopardize my future and Caesar will be very disappointed with you. When you drop me off at Base Operations I will pay you the thirty-five dollars and a fifteen dollar tip. Is that a fair deal?"

Musher went to his hotel, paid his bill, packed and tried to go to sleep. At 0400 hours there was a knock on the door. His cabby took the luggage and they left. At 0455 Musher was inside Base Operations and a contented but scared cabbie headed back to the city. "Happy Hanscom" was funny. No gate guards, no vehicle restrictions on the flight line and very few actual active duty air force personnel. These kinds of units were known as "the titless WAFs."

CHAPTER 46

Making My Way To Smoky Hill Air Force Base

Musher carried his baggage out to the C-47. (In the military the C-47 was known as the Gooney Bird). He climbed up the short ladder and faced a wide open compartment with bench seats on both sides, parachutes at each sitting position with a lap safety belt. Not the harness like his other two airplane rides but instead a wide, heavy duty safety latch lock belt. There was no one else on board. .He took a seat halfway up the compartment and put his baggage by his feet. Soon after he was settled three officers, second lieutenants, boarded and took seats on the opposite side of the compartment. Two Captains and a Technical Sergeant followed the officers,. The sergeant pulled in the boarding ladder and secured the entry hatch. As he walked forward to the cockpit he continuously instructed "Buckle In and Standby for takeoff."

The engines came to life and the aircraft began to move. Musher felt his stomach muscles tighten. He could not hear what was going on in the aircraft and he could not see outside the fuselage. It seemed the aircraft taxied a long way before stopping. Each engine was run up and Musher figured it was for a power check. A heavy squealing noise caused him to believe the flaps were coming down. The aircraft taxied a little more, came to a complete stop, and seconds later the engines went to full power and the aircraft started to roll. It had to be trying to takeoff. He could feel the aircraft lift off, he could hear the gear coming up and finally the heavy squealing of the flaps going to the shut position. The Gooney Bird did not climb at the same rate as the T-6 at Piute.

The Tech Sergeant came out of the compartment, told them he was the crew chief and addressed the passengers. "Look at those light signs with the white glass cover. When the sign is off you may ride without your seat belt. When the Captain wants you to put on your seat belt those signs will light up, flash and say seat belts. You may take off your parachutes. If it becomes necessary to use them I will come back here to assist you. Remember, regardless of rank this is my airplane. Next to the aircraft commander I am the authority, especially in this compartment. There is a piss can aft in this compartment. Rule: The first person to use it will clean it when the aircraft lands. We have no food on board. Mounted on the forward bulkhead are two water cans. There are some paper cups there. If you use a paper cup be sure to use the same one during the entire flight. See the signs with the blue glass front. When smoking is authorized they will light up with the word smoking. There are no butt cans on this airplane so if you do smoke you are personally responsible for properly getting rid of the butt remnants. Dirty my airplane and you can bet your sweet ass you will clean it. We will cruise at eight thousand feet so there is no worry about the use of oxygen. The enroute flying time to Offut is about nine plus hours. We will make the flight direct. We do not have any scheduled stops. We will try to keep the temperature in this compartment at a comfortable level. If you are too cold or too hot catch me on one of my walk-throughs. Any questions? Relax and try to enjoy the flight. Console yourselves with the fact that the ride is free." With that he went back into the cockpit.

Musher had not had breakfast. He dug into his "emergency kit", grabbed some goodies and two cokes. He gulped all but the last inch of the first coke, it was after all was to be his ash tray. The smoking light was lit. He had a couple of Luckies before starting to have his breakfast. After his breakfast he had a couple of more Luckies. He put all his trash in his "emergency" bag took a sheet of paper from his orders envelope, rolled it into a plug for the ash tray and placed it in the "emergency" bag. The seats along the fuselage were one continuous bench separated by seat belts and parachutes. With slight rearrangement of the parachutes Musher was able to make a comfortable parachute pillow. He stretched out and before long was sound asleep. When he awoke and looked at his watch he had been asleep for almost four hours. He wondered, "Do I have an affinity for airplanes?"

One of the three officers in the compartment was beckoning Musher to come forward. As he got there the one who beckoned asked," Are you a card player?" He nodded yes. "Do you play whist?" He nodded yes. "Do you play bridge?" He nodded yes again. "How well do you play bridge?" His reply, I am not a life master but I can play. "Would you like to play rubber bridge with us for a tenth of a cent a point?" He nodded yes. "We will deal up and the first two jacks are partners. We will play two rubbers and rotate partners until each of us has played with each person. Does that sound fair?" He nodded yes again. One of the other lieutenants scrambled around the aft section of the compartment until he was able to come up with a semblance of a table and four seats around it.

His first partner asked him, "What conventions do you play?" He replied, "Most all, you feel free to use any you choose. If I use one you do not understand just tell me and I will bid the hand differently." The first rubber was a blitz rubber. (Where you score all the points and your opponents do not score at all) His partner drew the most fantastic cards and was an above average bidder and player. The second rubber was almost the

143

same. Each time they rotated partners Musher's partner would suddenly become loaded with "No Brainers". They played three sets and not in any one rubber in any set was Musher on the losing team. He did not turn one single off-beat card. Rarely was he declarer. These three lieutenants were excellent bridge players. Must be from their college days.

The crew chief came in and announced ,"Offut in one hour."

The lead lieutenant said, "Time to settle up. I lost fifty-two dollars and each of you two, pointing to his two buddies, lost twenty-eight dollars. Airman you win one hu ndred ten dollars." With that they all paid up. The lead lieutenant asked Musher," Where did you learn to play bridge like that?"

Musher grinned sheepishly, you three beat each other.

The landing was smooth and there was a bus waiting on the ramp to take the crew and passengers to Base Operations. Musher thanked the pilots and the crew chief. He nodded his goodbyes to the three lieutenants. They never mentioned their names and neither did he. He asked the passenger services sergeant where he could get a bus into Omaha so he could get a bus to Smoky Hill AFB. The sergeant suggested he stay the night at Offut. "The base bus comes by here and it will drop you at the VAQ (Visiting Airman's Quarters). The rooms are private with a shower. A few yards away is the Base Bowling Alley. You can get something to eat there until midnight. In the morning there is a G.I. bus which goes to Omaha at 1000 hours."

Musher considered, "I have only used three days leave. I am in no big hurry." He went outside to wait for the base bus.

BOOK 3

WE'RE WITH THE REAL
UNITED STATES
AIR FORCE

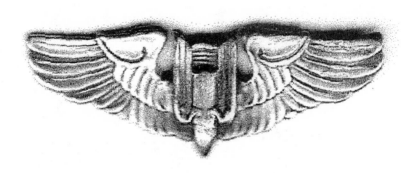

BUT WE WON'T
BE HERE VERY LONG

CHAPTER 47
Combat Living Conditions At Smoky Hill

Morning came and Musher did his SSS. The VAQ was every bit as good as the hotel room he rented in Boston. As he signed out from the VAQ he thanked everybody he ran into in the facility not knowing whether they were VAQ staff or not. Breakfast at the Bowling Alley was good and inexpensive. By the time he finished breakfast and cigarettes it was time to board the bus to Omaha. The ride to Salina would be about four hours with no rest stops on the way and no smoking on the bus. This bus did not have a latrine. Musher thought "no problem I will need to control my bladder for a much longer time as a tail gunner." As the bus rolled south Musher watched the green of Nebraska turn to the brown and barren terrain of west Kansas. Finally they pulled in to the Salina bus station. Musher grabbed his baggage and headed for the latrine. The next important thing was a couple of Luckies.

The ticket salesman told him there were no scheduled buses which came from Smoky Hill to Salina and round robin-ed to Smoky Hill. There was a commercial bus which passed the main gate at Smoky Hill and usually let the military personnel off there. The bus leaves here in two hours. Your ticket is three dollars. Musher debated staying in Salina overnight and getting to Smoky early tomorrow. The only hotel in Salina was full so he really didn't have a choice but to report in later tonight.

He stepped off the bus with luggage in hand. Walked to the main gate where he was approached by an Air Policeman wearing a silver helmet, and white web belt with sidearm. The sight of the silver helmet and white web belt brought back unpleasant memories. "A2C Muscarello reporting for duty." The AP, "Standby while I get the Sergeant of the Guard."

The guard gatehouse was in dire need of repair and painting. The buildings which Musher could see looked in the same state of disrepair. The Sergeant of the Guard pulled up in his jeep and instructed Musher to get in. "I will take you to Wing Headquarters where you can sign in and they will take care of you from there." During the ride to wing headquarters Musher could not help but notice most every building, walk way and open space looked as if it were on its dying leg. "Here we are. Take your stuff in and report to the NCO Charge of Quarters. Welcome to Smoky Hole."

The NCOCQ took his folder of papers, rummaged through them and copied some data from some of the papers into his log. He told Musher to

147

complete the register sign in. "Not very much we can do tonight. The VAQ is next door. Pick an empty room for the night. The latrine is out the back door about fifty yards along the path. The dining hall is closed but the BX cafeteria is about a ten minute walk from here and is open to 2300 hours. Tomorrow morning we will get you to Wing Personnel and they will take you from there. Come in after breakfast but not too early. Wing personnel does not open until 0900 hours. Welcome to the 301st Bomb Wing."

The VAQ was an elevated one story building constructed in a rectangular shape. The roof was tar paper without shingles. The windows were not glass but were heavy celluloid which could either be removed or closed. There was no such thing as a partially opened window. Mounted outside each window was a shutter. The shutter was held open by two struts. It was closed by removing the struts. The shutter wood was failing and peeling as a result of the hot Kansas sun. The bunk was not made although all the ingredients were stacked on the bunk. There was no butt can and Musher had to turn to his soda bottle once again. For dinner he ate what goodies were left in his emergency bag. The room was getting cold. Nobody at Offutt would believe this place. He struggled through the night, smoking, pacing and generally trying to keep warm and his nerves in tact.

At 0700 hours the base bus came by and Musher was getting aboard when he asked the driver, "Do you go by the Dining Hall?" The driver replied, "There is no main dining hall. Each squadron has its own. Are you new and not assigned to a squadron?" Musher nodded yes. "About three minute walk down that way will bring you to the Wing Headquarters staff dining room. Eat there until you are assigned to a squadron."

The outside of the dining hall looked in the same condition as every other building he had seen since his arrival. The most notable exception was that this building had windows that actually opened and closed. As he entered the building he thought, Shades of Piute. The dining room was considerably smaller but set up the same way. The serving line, dishes and normal utensils and a tray to carry everything. "How would you like your eggs airman?" Sunny side please. "Two or three?" Two please. "Help yourself to everything else and if there is something you do not see then just ask." There were no silently moving people as at Piute and the Lowry flight line dining room, there were airmen KPs. He sat alone and ate while always watching who came for breakfast or just coffee and toast. He felt better about Smoky Hill AFB.

He gathered his belongings and headed next door. The sergeant at the reception desk was not the sergeant who had been there the night before. Musher relayed his story and the sergeant told him to take a seat. He heard the telephone being dialed and then "I need a taxi for one airman from Wing Headquarters to Wing Personnel. Ten minutes, OK."

At Wing Personnel the driver said turn left through the doors and go up the stairs. They will take care of you from there. "Welcome to the 301st Bomb Wing." Musher did as he was told and was greeted by a Tech Sergeant who took his papers and told him to have a seat. He kept checking his watch. He had been sitting there almost an hour when the Tech said, "Follow me, Major Armstrong will see you now."

The Major must have been in his late, late thirties. His uniform bore Senior Pilot Wings and an endless number of ribbons above both breast pockets attesting to an active career. Musher gave his best salute and said, "Airman Second Class Saverio Muscarello reporting for duty." The major returned the salute and motioned Musher into a chair.

"Muscarello I am going to be honest with you. Surely you noticed the condition of the air base. The air base is scheduled to close in seven months. There is no money being provided for any upkeep maintenance only maintenance which is necessary for the safety and welfare of the troops. Even that is very limited. This wing has three combat squadrons, the 351st, the 352nd and the 353rd. Our aircraft are well maintained. We have more aerial gunners than we have need for on our crews. Most of the current gunners are WWII veterans who fired from open positions using their personal skills to make hits.

"I'll bet that in three squadrons, twenty-two aircraft per squadron, four gunners per crew, that no more than sixty of the two hundred sixty plus can fire gun film with fifty percent hits. It's not the aircraft, it's not the turrets, it's not a lack of desire it is a lack of knowledge of the CFCS. When we heard that we were getting the top scorer of the RCS training program from Lowry we just knew our wing shooting would improve. That was before we actually knew of the base closing and when it would happen.

I have already told you that we have more gunners than we need. You will not be assigned to a crew. You will fly enough to get your flying pay. You will be assigned to the 351st's Squadron Gunnery Officer. Another WW II veteran with more heart and combat experience than any other gunner in the wing. Unfortunately he does not have the skill to improve the squadron's shooting scores. When your other classmate signs in he will be assigned to the 353rd with the same goal. When they do close this base and our aircraft and crews go to other wings I want their new commanders to be pleased with the crews he gets. Do you have questions or anything you would like to say?"

Musher thought of The Monster, "When you don't know what to say, keep your fucking mouthed closed." No, sir. "You may wait outside, they will finish your paperwork and your new first sergeant will come to get you."

CHAPTER 48
My New Squadron

Musher sat inside waiting for his new "daddy". A jeep drove up with a Master Sergeant driver so Musher took his gear and went outside. The Master Sergeant called, "You Muscarello?" Musher nodded his head yes. "Get your gear and get aboard". The only words the Master Sergeant spoke during the ride to the squadron were," I am your first sergeant. My name is Alba. We are glad to have you here." At the barracks, "Go pick a bunk, take a little time to get settled and then come to the squadron orderly room."

The barracks was the same as the VAQ. Tattered, torn and looked like it would fall apart at any moment. Inside there were two major differences. The barracks did not have rooms, an open bay, and it had two pot belly stoves which were its source of heat for the cold weather. The "windows" were all closed and the air in the barracks was at best stuffy. Again no latrine in the barracks. The latrine was a good fifty to seventy-five yards from the back door of the barracks. Musher counted the bunks which appeared occupied. There were twenty-two single bunks. He took the one vacant bunk and made the barracks complement twenty-three. He did the best he could to unpack and square away his area. There was no foot locker for him but the barracks did have the red cans marked "Butts". He stepped out to the back steps and lit a Lucky. Then another Lucky. Then another Lucky. He walked to the latrine to take a piss and it was as if he was back at Fort Benning. One row of commodes on one side, a piss trough on the other. Ten shower positions, rickety clothes benches, small chipped and tattered sinks and one twelve inch shelf and metal mirror both of which extended the full length of the sinks. Totally depressed he walked towards the squadron orderly room. The rocks which outlined the foot path had not been whitewashed and the surrounding grounds had not been raked. It looks like the whole wing has submitted to its fate of the base closing and adopted Rod's attitude, "Fuck em and feed em frijoles."

When he walked into the squadron orderly room he was greeted by the first sergeant. The first sergeant made cursory introductions of the orderly room staff. "OK Muscarello, what are you called, Muscarello?"

"No sergeant, I am generally called Musher."

"OK then Musher let's go to lunch. Today is most probably the only day you will ever eat lunch with the first sergeant. We will be joined by three of the most senior NCOs in the squadron. Most probably the only day you will ever eat with them."

The dining hall was a picture of the Wing Headquarters dining hall including the KPs who had replaced the silently moving people. One of the two NCOs who joined them was the NCOIC of squadron supply and the other was the NCOIC of squadron operations. The first sergeant directed his comments to Musher. "If these two like you and you treat them well, your life here in the 351st will be much, much easier. After lunch you and I will finish our business and then you can go to squadron supply for whatever they have that you think you need. Tomorrow morning you will report to squadron operations at 0700 hours. There you will be given guidance and instruction Any questions? No, that is a good sign." During the rest of the lunch the three NCOs made small talk and Musher wisely did not interject any comments. Again from the teachings of The Monster, "The Wise Old Bird did not speak, he firmly closed his shiny beak. The Wise Old Bird did not get burned, he simply sat, listened and learned." A few cigarettes and coffee. As they were getting up to leave, Musher acknowledged the two other most powerful sergeants in the squadron and he and the first sergeant went to the squadron orderly room.

In the orderly room the first sergeant named the squadron commander, Lieutenant Colonel Clifford Nelson. He .gave him his canned speech on just who ran this squadron and how every enlisted man was owing to him. He explained the Class A pass rule. If you did not have duty you could do as you pleased including going into Salina just as long you reported to your duty station when required. Barracks inspections were almost non existent and there was a G.I. party every three months or so. As an A2C he would be required to pull KP in the squadron dining hall. He would find that KP in the squadron dining hall was very unlike KP in the Lowry mess. He would take his turn as fire watch in the barracks when the stoves were lit. He would take his turn in the latrine cleaning. All detail assignments were posted well in advance on the bulletin board outside the squadron orderly room. It was his responsibility to check the board every day and to notify his supervisor when he would be somewhere else on a detail assignment. If there was a conflict between a detail assignment and flying with his crew, as soon as he became aware of the conflict he would see the duty sergeant in the orderly room and the necessary changes would be made. Flying always takes priority. Any questions? No, very good. Go to squadron supply and take care of your business."

At squadron supply Master Sergeant Dooley, with whom he had lunch, was at the counter. "What can I do for you airman?"

"Sergeant I need a foot locker, another blanket and I could use another flying suit." The items appeared on the counter.

"Sign the receipt. Did anyone tell you change sheets and pillow cases day was every Tuesday. You bring them here and we give you nice clean ones in exchange. Do you have sun glasses? Here's a pair of aviators. You need not sign for them. If you are going to be a fly boy you should at least look like one."

Musher muscled the stuff back to his bunk and sat on his new foot locker while he smoked. About 1630 hours his barracks-mates began filing in. Some came over to greet him, introduce themselves and offer any assistance. After getting out of their working flying suits and into their "dress" flying suits Musher noticed that of the twenty-two members living in this barracks most were either Staff or Technical Sergeant. The rest were Airmen First Class. He was the lowest ranking as an A2C.

About 1730 hours one of the Tech Sergeants came to Musher and said, "My name is Bob Halloran. I am the ring gunner on Crew R-34. We are going to dinner, want to join us?"

"My name is Saverio Muscarello but I am called Musher. I would be most happy to join you at dinner."

At the dining hall the tables were set for four. Halloran quickly turned one into a table for five. In those years there were not very many married airmen living off base. While eating the conversation quickly turned to aerial gunnery. Musher must have been asked a hundred questions. To each question he gave the same reply,"I don't know what the game plan is yet but tomorrow will be my first time at squadron operations. I know I am to be assigned to the Squadron Gunnery Officer but at this point that is all I know."

Having exhausted that subject the conversation went to the base closing, how will the personnel be assigned and to where. Lots of different points of view but nobody really knew anything about the future.

Back at the barracks Halloran said, "Do you play cards? Have you ever played double deck pinochle? That's OK, come be our fourth and we will teach you the game." For Musher it was not difficult to learn. There are eighty cards in the deck, each player is dealt twenty. There are in hand point count techniques. One queen of spades and one jack of diamonds is called a pinochle and is worth four in hand points. Two queens of spades and two jacks of diamonds are called a double pinochle and are worth thirty in hand points. One ace of each suit is worth ten in hand points, two of each suit is worth one hundred in hand points. There are a great many other combinations which are worth various in hand points. Musher's mind quickly absorbed all that he was told and saw. In hand points are known as "meld". The bidding begins at fifty and goes around the table until one of the pairs has "won" the bid for a given amount of playing score. The last person to bid gets to name the trump. For example the partnership which won the bid has won it for an anticipated playing score of two hundred sixty. Between the partners their meld (the in hand points which are shown on the table before the first card is played) is three hundred. The opponents meld is ninety. The trick play is quite simple. If you can you must present a card higher in value than the value of the one played before you, you must follow suit when you can and you must trump when you cannot follow suit. The playing value of your tricks taken is an ace is two points and a king is one point. If you do not garner a minimum of twenty trick points you cannot score your meld. On rare occasion the bid winner will not score twenty trick points and no matter how much their meld may be they cannot score and it is called "a set". By the end of the evening Musher pretty much had absorbed the game, its bidding techniques, its rules and its playing techniques. He was congratulated on how quickly he had picked up the game and was assured they play an awful lot of double deck pinochle in the United States Air Force.

There was no such thing as lights out in this or any other squadron in the combat wing. One of the things the infantry had reinforced was his ability to sleep irrespective of any lights or noises around him. He grabbed his toiletry kit and headed for SSS. He must look good at Squadron Operations tomorrow.

A couple of cigarettes back in the barracks and off to beddy-bye. His last thoughts before falling asleep were of Lucy Gallo and Emily Bilderbook.

CHAPTER 49

B-29s, Here I Come

He was up, dressed, had his area squared away (another military term for looking neat and clean) and in the dining hall at 0530 hours. He had a great breakfast and was sipping coffee and smoking when his card playing guys joined him at his table. "What are you doing in the dining hall this early?"

I must report to squadron operations at 0700 hours.

"So do the rest of us. Roll call is at 0700 hours in the briefing room. At roll call you sit with your crew in the seat which marks your crew position. One of the aircraft commanders goes to the podium and looks at the crew rows. The aircraft commander of each row where a crew position is vacant will, without standing up, explain the absence."

"My instructions were to report to the NCOIC for squadron ops."

Outside the dining hall were buses with lighted signs 351st, 352nd and 353rd. They were at the briefing room at 0645 hours, fifteen minutes early. Musher walked into the squadron operations "shack". The ops NCOIC was a Tech Sergeant named Wooly. He wore a gunner's badge but because of injuries from a B-29 bailout he was permanently DNIF (Duties Not Involving Flying). He asked Musher to take a seat because they were waiting for another person. Shortly the other person walked in and Sergeant Wooly escorted him and Musher into the Chief of Squadron Operations (CSOps) office.

The officer behind the desk waived them into chairs. "Airman my name is Major Cotter. This is Chief Warrant Officer (CWO) Leary. Mister (the normal reference to a warrant officer) Leary is the squadron gunnery officer. I am told that you will work for him and together you will improve the shooting scores of our navigators and aerial gunners. I don't really know how you are going to do that but I expect that within the next seventy-two hours I will see a written plan to accomplish that goal. You can expect all the support that I and every other person in this squadron can give. Seventy-two hours is not much time, you better get started." Musher and CWO Leary rose, saluted and left his office.

When they were out of the "shack" Mister Leary said, "Let's go to our office. I could use a cigarette and some coffee." The office was not very big but it adjoined a classroom with twenty student seats surrounded by blackboards. It looked like it had not been used in a year and needed a good scrubbing down. He closed the door and thought, "Right now we need a plan."

"Mister Leary if we could sit and talk I have some ideas that I would want your opinion on. There is no doubt that our crews are honorable men whose valor has been tested and found to be solid. Our equipment on board the 29 is good equipment. If it is not the crew members and not the aircraft then we must look elsewhere to find the problem. We cannot solve any problem which we cannot identify. In RCS at airborne training at Lowry my class shot tremendous film scores. Why, because the gun sight and turrets were coordinated and the gunners were disciplined." With that Musher told Mister Leary about his notebook and Sergeant Michael Lesser. We can either go to my barracks to get the notebook or I will bring it back after lunch. Mister Leary had told Musher that when they were alone he was Leary. So typical of a CWO. He cannot command, he is tolerated at the Officers Club and not welcomed at the NCO Club. CWO's are never sure if they are senior sergeants or cadet second lieutenants. Leary was eager to see the notebook.

"I'll borrow the CSOps jeep and we will go get it now. Besides you will be having lunch at the flight line dining hall not at the squadron dining hall."

When they got back to the office Musher went over the notebook with Leary. "We know the gunners can take care of the 50's, belt and load ammo We need to teach the gun sight, its proper care and maintenance and effective firing techniques. At Lowry we had almost forty hours training on the gun sight. I don't believe we want to be so concentrated with our gunners. Give me this afternoon and tonight and at 0700 hours tomorrow I will bring you a draft plan for comments and hopefully your approval."

"Can we go to lunch, I am starving."

CHAPTER 50
The Plan To Make Buffalo Bills

After lunch Musher was sitting at Leary's desk with a yellow pad, a pencil and an eraser. Leary was pacing the office. Musher,"Why don't you go somewhere. You are as valuable here as tits on a boar hog. If you are not back by quitting time I will lock up and see you in the morning." He wrote, erased, wrote again, erased again and it seemed continual until it was time to leave to catch the bus back to the squadron area. Leary had not returned but as some of his hillbilly classmates used to say in Piute, "It ain't no never mind." He took his notebook and his writing stuff and got on the bus. He was so absorbed in his project he hardly heard the polite conversations about his first day in the squadron.

Back at the barracks he openly solicited anyone who would listen. "Where is the Base Library? Is it open tonight? How can I get there?" Armed with the answers he went to dinner as early as possible. Caught the base bus which dropped him off at the library. There were not many people using the library at dinner time. He approached the young lady at the desk and asked, "Are there typewriters available here?" Yes. "Is there anyone I can pay to type one page for me?" Well it is very quiet now and since it is only one page I could do it for you. I will not accept payment. "Could you do a draft copy now?" She took the yellow page and very quickly typed it.

Musher did some editing and asked her, "Could you do it again and make it in three copies?" Very few minutes later he had the copies in his hand, thanked her over and over again and went to a table to digest the plan. The plan read:

MAKING 351ST GUNNERS SHOOT LIKE BUFFALO BILL
- Training Period: Six work days, 0800 hours to 1630 hours
- Trainees: Ten gunners from two crews which crews are unlikely to fly during the six day training period.
- Instructors: CWO Leary, A2C Muscarello
- Training Locations: Classroom adjacent to the squadron gunnery officer's office; and the flight line.
- Materials Required: One gun sight from an active B-29
   Ten "Jewelers" cases with tools.
   Twelve copies of the study handbook.
- To Measure Effectiveness: Two flights where each student will be able to demonstrate his skills in a film shooting bandit attack.

- Evaluation and Critique: Viewing the gun camera films and discussing the individual shooter tendencies.
- Proposed Starting Date: With all needed materials in hand, three working days following the Chief of Squadron Operations approval.
- Submitted by: CWO Leary, Squadron Gunnery Officer

CHAPTER 51
Let the Leadership Grow

Musher entered the squadron gunnery office at 0645 hours the next morning. To his surprise sitting behind his desk was Leary. "Do you have it?" Musher nodded yes. "Let me see it. This looks pretty good. Go over it with me."

Musher explained that the only things he might have a problem with is getting the teaching materials. The paper copying machines used an "onion skin" paper which was not always clearly legible. If twelve copies could be made at the photo lab he could three hole punch them and put them in notebooks. The photo lab could also make the slides for the vu-graph. Major Cotter had promised full support so getting the use of a gun sight might not be a problem. I have no idea where we could get the jeweler's cases but one phone call to Lowry may well provide the answer. Everything else in the plan is controlled by the squadron.

As Musher spoke Leary had been steadily making notes. "OK Musher, you wait here while I go see Sergeant Wooly and see if he can get us into see Major Cotter early this morning."

"Get us in to see Major Cotter". It was apparent that Leary had taken those notes and will use them to present the plan. I, as an airman nothing, will stand there and watch the phony dip into the trough of recognition. Oh well, it must be true that rank has its privelges.

"We are scheduled with Cotter at 1030 hours." At the precise moment they entered the CSOps office. They sat and Leary handed a copy of the plan to the CSOps. Both Leary and Musher were silent while the CSOps studied the plan.

"Done and presented in less than twenty-four hours. It looks feasible but fill me in on any hitches you might foresee." With the aid of his notes Leary completed the briefing.

"Sounds good. You have my tentative approval. Start collecting the materials and make the teaching facility ready. I will get with my staff and we will decide which two crews will be your first students. Chief you have been around a long time. Use that experience to procure the materials as quickly as possible. I want the first class to begin seven days from today. Airman Muscarello you have done a fine job. Not only can I see your efforts in the plan but you have shown great respect for your superior officer."

Back at the gunnery office Leary told Musher he would get him clearance to call Lowry. "Put that on the top of your list of things to do." Musher boo-booed and spat some venom, "You are the holdup. You get the clearance and I will make the calls. Mister Leary is it OK with you if I go back to the squadron area now?" Why? "I have some business with squadron supply. I will lunch there and then will come back here.

"If I get the clearance for you to call Lowry I will find you. If you are delayed don't hurry back and I will see you in the morning".

Do you think it's possible he is feeling badly for not giving Musher any credit when they were in the CSOps office? Of course it is always possible he is lazy and doesn't realize how short a time seven days really is. At squadron supply Musher asked to see Master Sergeant Dooley. Dooley came out with, "What do you need young man?"

Musher listed his needs, "Blackboard chalk, blackboard erasers, a ream of lined pads of yellow eight by eleven paper, two dozen number two pencils, a pencil sharpener some rags, a push broom, a bucket, a mop, three bars of lye soap, two five inch paint brushes and two gallons of white paint. Then the coup de gras, some good B-29 action gunnery pictures. If possible three dozen."

"What is all this about?" Musher showed him the plan. He told him that Major Cotter had given his tentative approval for the first class to begin in seven days. Certainly there is no rush for these items. With a chuckle, this afternoon or tomorrow morning is soon enough. At least could I get the cleaning supplies today?

"Go to an early lunch. Come back here around 1330 hours and we shall see what we shall see."

It didn't take any coaxing for Musher to go to lunch. The dining hall had just opened and there were very few people there. He got his food and was alone when CWO Leary came in to the dining hall. He went through the serving line and joined Musher at the table.

"I have your authorization to make six calls to Lowry AFB. He produced a piece of paper, these six numbers are your authorization codes. You can make the call from any base Class A telephone. I suggest you do it from the squadron orderly room. If they are not able to get whomever it is you are calling you can always leave the orderly room number for a return call. If the return call comes after normal duty hours the CQ or the CQ Runner can get you to the phone"

Musher told him of his visit with Master Sergeant Dooley and the wish list he gave to Dooley. He was to go back to squadron supply at 1330 hours.

"Right now I am going to the squadron orderly room to ask permission from the first sergeant to use one of his phones.". He rose and said, "If you should happen do be at squadron supply at that time I sure could use a hand schlepping the goodies back to our office."

After showing the first sergeant the training plan and telling him of Major Cotter's tentative approval, he asked if he could use one of the Class A telephones to call Lowry AFB. He showed the first sergeant his authorization codes. Tell me who it is you are trying to reach at Lowry and where does he work. Musher scribbled the answers to those questions on a piece of paper. The first sergeant picked up a Class A telephone and spoke to an operator. "This is the First Sergeant of the 351st Bomb Squadron. I want you to contact SSgt Michael Lesser of the 3910th Aerial Gunnery Training Group at Lowry AFB. Yes, I will wait." In very few minutes the first sergeant spoke into the phone, standby you have a call from A2C Muscarello and he handed the Musher the phone. A few pleasantries were exchanged and then Musher told him of the plan. My basic problem is that I don't know where you got the jeweler's case, what they cost and how long it will take to get them. Our first class is in seven days. Lesser's answers were not encouraging in any of the three categories. "It would take about a month to order and receive them. Tell you what, today I will send you six of mine special delivery with the understanding that you will replace them when your order is delivered. I will put all the ordering information and costs in the package with the cases. Give me the exact address for delivery. You realize you can always ask the Air Training Command to send a field team to teach those classes. With your CO's request I could be there in about four days."

"Sergeant Lesser I am in your debt again. I will watch for your package. As for you coming here to teach this subject I will keep you as my ace in the hole just in case I fail. Again thank you. I will keep you posted about our results. Without you none of this would be possible."

Precisely 1330 hours he was at squadron supply. On the counter were two boxes with lids closed. Sergeant Dooley told him his order was filled with the exception of the aircraft pictures. Those he would have by lunch tomorrow. There is nothing to sign for because everything in those boxes is expendable. CWO Leary showed up in the CSOps' jeep. The boxes were loaded and Musher was still thanking Dooley when the jeep headed for the office.

At the office Musher told Leary about the success of his phone call to Lowry. The information they wanted was coming in a special delivery package containing six jeweler cases on a loan basis. It was being sent to the squadron orderly room. Musher went on, "You need to take the notebook to the photo lab and see if you can get them started. We would like the finished work in forty-eight hours or less. You must stress upon them the value of this notebook. It is one of a kind without which our plan could not succeed. Can you do that now while I remain here to start the preparation of the classroom?"

Leary took the notebook and went out the door. Musher went into the classroom to evaluate how much work it would take to make it a learning environment.

CHAPTER 52
Implement the Plan

Musher knew what he must do. He peeled off his clothes down to his underwear. With cleaning supplies in hand and a bucket of water he entered the classroom and began his own G.I. party. After dusting the ceiling and the four walls he washed them down with lye soap and water .The room was so dirty he constantly changed water and washed out rags. Then he washed and dried every stick of furniture in the room. With the exception of the floor every square inch of the room had been scrubbed clean.

Smoke Break.

He returned to the classroom this time armed with paint, paint brushes and an invigorated motivation. He painted every inch of the ceiling and walls. The lights in the room looked brighter. He looked at his watch and it was 0445 hours.

He had missed dinner and was dragging. The flight line dining hall would be open in fifteen minutes. He cleaned himself as best he could and dressed in the clothes he had set aside to do his classroom work He walked to the dining hall and enjoyed a huge breakfast and a large amount of coffee. The Lucky Strikes settled him even more.

When CWO Leary entered his office at 0655 hours he found Musher sound asleep in his chair. Musher awakened at Leary's entry. "Did you spend the night here?" Yes Sir. "Why?" Take a look in the classroom.

Leary opened the classroom door and was astonished at the transformation the room had undergone. While Leary was staring Musher added, "I am not done yet but hopefully by tomorrow morning the physical plant will be ready for students. Unless you have other plans for me I would like to get back at it."

"Carry On"

Armed with a mop, lye soap and a bucket of water Musher attacked the floor of the classroom. He actually had to do the floor three times before it even closely resembled clean.

He came into the office and spoke to Leary. "The front entrance door to the classroom is really beat and about to fall apart. Do you think you could find a replacement door that we could install today? How did it go at the photo lab yesterday afternoon?"

"The OIC was not exactly thrilled with the project or its priority. I mentioned a few facts and some impressive names and he agreed to do the job. Everything is supposed to be ready by 1400 hours today. He is supposed to call me when the materials are ready for pickup. If I don't hear from him by 1415 hours I will go to the photo lab and rest assured I will come back with our materials."

Musher chimed in, "Sergeant Dooley is supposed to have some decorative B-29 combat pictures for me after lunch. Do you know anybody in the field maintenance squadron? I have a small request of them. Do you think we could go there while the classroom is drying?"

"Saddle up and let's ride Tonto." CWO Leary introduced Musher to CWO Maxwell Driver, the OIC of the sheet metal shop. Leary explained their project and told Driver Musher had a small request.

"Mister Driver could you take two pieces of sheet metal twenty-four inches by eight inches, smooth the edges and paint them white. Puncture two holes equidistant from the ends. The holes are for hanging the sign. He handed CWO Driver a paper on which he had printed his rank and name and Leary's rank and name. If each sign had one name stenciled on it in air force blue naturally, that would be the whole project. Not to seem bold but do you have any hanging hooks?"

"We can certainly do the project and we will provide the hanging hooks, naturally painted in air force blue. Come back around 1600 hours and everything should be ready for you."

CWO Leary thanked him, Musher thanked him, they all shook hands and parted. "What now, asked Leary?"

"Why don't you drop me at the office and begin your procurement task for a new front entryway classroom door."

So Be It.

Musher was back in the classroom and had arranged ten desk chairs in a semi-circle. You know the type that looks like a sturdy chair but has a extra wide space on the right side for writing or whatever else use. If you were left handed you had a problem. You had to write across your body. He took the small table and placed it behind the semi-circle. He was lucky there was a power outlet close by which would be the power source for the vu-graph. If needed a simple extension cord could be used. He placed the actual small desk and two chairs behind the view graph. That corner would be reserved for instructors. He added three other chairs behind the vu-graph for any visitors.

Each class would be fifty minutes long followed by a ten minute break. Eating, drinking and smoking would not be allowed in the classroom. He would need to figure a way to have drinking water available at each break. For the smokers he would put two butt cans outside the front entry door. He was getting ready to leave the classroom when he concluded the blackboards needed washing again.

He was outside smoking when Leary drove up. "Check these, a screen door and a solid front door. Neither one needs painting. Give me a hand and we will quickly swap the doors." True to his words he had a tool bag with right tools and in a matter of minutes the doors were swapped. He took a can of oil and applied it heavily to the hinges. He tested the doors, there were no squeaks and latched as they should. "Let's put the old doors in the jeep and drop them off and we can then go to lunch." He drove to the Base Carpenter Shop, they unloaded the old doors and were greeted by the NCOIC of the shop. "Thank you Wally, I owe you one." Off to the squadron dining hall for lunch.

After lunch they hung around and went to the squadron orderly room. No package for Musher. They had stalled long enough to go to squadron supply. Dooley presented Musher with fifteen B-29 combat film prints. Included was an original of the recruiting poster which enticed Musher to transfer out of the Army. Musher apologized to Dooley, "Do you have any small tacks and a small hammer I could borrow?" Dooley looked at him in disgust, walked into the storeroom and returned with a box of tacks and a small hammer. Musher said, "There is one other thing. It would be really outstanding if we had captions for these pictures. Do you know anyone who can identify them?" This time Dooley beamed with pride, "I can. I have a second set of these pictures give me this afternoon and I will do it." Musher,"Could you put it on poster board with each caption an eight by four inch area?"

"Can do, see you at 1600 hours. If I finish sooner I will bring them to Mister Leary's office.

Leary dropped Musher off at the office and headed for the photo lab. He knew he was early but what the hell. To his surprise the OIC had the completed project boxed and ready for Leary. Following a sincere set of thank you's Leary headed back to the office. On the way he stopped at the field metal sheet metal shop and CWO Driver gave him the completed project. Again, following a sincere set of thank you's Leary headed back to the office. He brought the projects into the office and found Musher in the classroom.

Within fifteen minutes MSgt Dooley entered into the empty office and yelled, "Anybody here?" As he entered the classroom and saw his pictures and posters displayed throughout the classroom he almost burst with pride. He had done good work on the captions. The lettering was in air force blue and very well done. Dooley worked with Musher to make sure the right caption was mounted with its corresponding picture. As he was leaving Musher said," I need a stand for the gun sight. Do you think you could find a four by six flat top table about thirty inches high with lockable casters?"

"Let me see what I can do. I will see you after breakfast tomorrow."

"Gee Sergeant Dooley as long as you are being so helpful I need a drinking water device and some Dixie cups that I can put in the classroom."

"Let me see what I can do. I will see you after breakfast tomorrow."

"Sergeant Dooley, I need one last item, a screen to display the vugraphs. It would be great if it were a least four feet by four feet in a roll up container so that it could be mounted on the front wall and rolled down for use."

"Let me see what I can do. I will see you after breakfast tomorrow."

Leary and Musher finished mounting their name tags at the front of the room. Leary, "That's enough for today. Let me drop you off at the squadron orderly room and I will see you at 0700 hours tomorrow."

It had been three days since Major Cotter told them to be ready in seven days. Unless something went screwy Musher felt they would be ready in six.

CHAPTER 53
Can We Be Totally Ready Today?

Musher was back in the squadron gunnery office at 0645 hours the next morning. He was disappointed that yesterday the jeweler cases had not arrived from Lowry. No panic, they still had three days. If they don't get here today he will call Lesser for an update.

He had taken two bright red butt cans from the vacant barracks nest door. He also had taken the nails from which they were hung. He mounted them on each side of the classroom front entryway.

He sat in the classroom to compose the

TRAINING SYLLABUS.
DAY 1   Introduction to the Training Program and Its GuidelinesA Cursory Review of the Training NotebookThe RCS CFSC Gun Sight
DAY 2   The RCS CFCS Gun Sight
DAY 3 The Jewelers Case, Its Tools and UsesThe Care and Maintenance of the RCS CFCS Gun Sight
DAY 4   Flight Line Exercise Calibrating the RCS CFSC Gun sight
DAY 5   A B-29 Film Shooting Flight with Bandits Attacking
DAY 6   Review of the Gun Camera Film and Critique of the MissionUnsigned Student Evaluation of the Course and Instructors

The next thing he needed was an insert cover for the outside face of the notebook

351st Bomb Squadron Aerial Gunners
Training Course for the RCS CFSC Gun Sight

This notebook was used by:

DATE   RANK   NAME   CREW NUMBER

Musher was starting to feel depressed. He was at the mercy of others. Sergeant Dooley was trying for a water cooler and cups, a work table for the gun sight and a screen for display from the vu-graph. The jeweler cases from Lesser at Lowry AFB had not arrived. He needed to get the notebooks from central supply. The notebook materials needed punching and placing in the notebook. The training syllabus and notebook cover sheets need printing and insertion in the notebook. The prime item, an actual gun sight from an active aircraft had not been provided. Three days is not a very long time.

Leary waltzed in whistling a happy time as if he did not have a care in the world.

Musher took Leary aside and told him what he had done today and all the other things that needed to be done. Musher suggested they take the list of things that need to be ready and spend the day trying to get them done. Musher loaded the notebook materials into the jeep and Leary said, "Saddle up Tonto, let's ride."

The first stop was at wing central supply. Leary went in alone and shortly thereafter came out with two dozen three ring notebooks. He explained," The unit count is twelve so I had to take twenty-four". Musher smiled.

The next stop was the base newspaper. Again Leary went in alone and very shortly came out telling Musher, "grab the notebook inserts, the right number of notebooks, the notebook insert cover sheet and the training syllabus." Our friends inside will do all the work and we will have fifteen completed notebooks for pickup by noon." Musher smiled inside while thinking, "Five of the nine items should be done by noon."

They were met by Dooley at squadron supply. Dooley told Leary to park the jeep and for him and Musher to get aboard the weapons carried. Dooley drove to Base Supply and backed into the loading dock. Dooley went in alone. A civilian worker rolled out a dolly cart containing a water dispensing unit, ten five gallon bottles of water and sixty dozen paper cups (the unit pack was twenty dozen). He unloaded them on the dock. The worker rolled his dolly cart back inside. Before you could recite even the smallest limerick the worker reappeared with his dolly cart holding the work table. Dooley came out and while shaking hands with the civilian placed a paper in the civilian's hands. With a loaded weapons carrier they headed for the training classroom. On the way Musher asked Dooley, "Did you bribe that man?"

"Of course not, just a little something to show my appreciation for his help."

The three of them quickly unloaded the weapons carrier. Leary suggested they go to the squadron dining hall for coffee and cigarettes before continuing the scavenger hunt.

Dooly drove straight to squadron supply. He turned to Leary and Musher, "It has been fun. Kinda like the old days in WWII. I'd like to stay with you but I have some paperwork I need to generate. Thank you for letting me help, I will see you at the facility before you have the first class. Leary and Musher dam near fell over themselves trying to thank Dooley for his help.

Sitting in the dining hall drinking coffee and eating coffee cake Leary said to Musher," Tonto you are doing a hell of a job." They drank more coffee and smoked more cigarettes.

Musher, "Can we stop by the orderly room on the off chance our package is here from Denver?" This time Musher went in alone and when he came out his face showed that he had struck gold. Leary,"Is that what we were waiting for?"

"Sure is Lone Ranger."

Leary, "Musher I am going to drop you off on my way to see Major Cotter. I have written a request to Sergeant Driver. Tell him there is no hurry, two hours from now would be fine." Leary dropped him at the Field Maintenance Sheet Metal Shop. He approached the NCOIC Master Sergeant Driver. Ten seconds of pleasantries and Musher handed him the note. Driver looked at him and laughed, "Tell Leary not to bother coming to pick it up. Me and a couple of my boys will deliver it to you at the classroom not later than 1330 hours."

With his package from Lesser tucked firmly under his arm he walked to the office.

CWO Leary was with CSOps. "Sir, it is time for you to authorize the removal of one gun sight from a combat ready aircraft."

"Just how close to ready are you?"

"With the gun sight in the classroom we could begin within two hours after setting up the classroom."

"Given you get the gun sight by 1300 hours when could the first students start training?"

"1600 hours today."

"All right Mister Leary wait about a half an hour and then see the line chief. He will have made arrangements for the Armament and Electronics people to remove the gun sight."

"Sir, if it's all the same to you, Airman Muscarello and I would prefer to remove the gun sight ourselves."

"Anything else Leary?"

"Yes sir, if you could schedule the first class for Monday, August 3rd and provide an advance list of the names of the attendees it would be greatly appreciated."

"I thought you said you would be ready today."

"Yes sir, starting on a Monday gives a smooth flow to the four day classroom curriculum, one day for the flight line hands on training and then the airborne bandit attack. The gun film from the airborne attack will show you whether or not the program should be continued."

"Sounds like you guys know what you are doing. How's my Airman Muscarello doing?"

"Sir he is one of the best airmen I have ever known. He is bright, intelligent, a good planner, an aggressive worker and his shooting scores from Lowry speak for themselves. He could be a Staff Sergeant and never skip a heart beat."

"Thank you Mister Leary, I shall visit your facility at 1630 hours today. You are excused."

Leary drove to the office to pick up Musher. "Bring all the tools you need to remove a gun sight. First, we go get our printing work, then we find the line chief and he tells us which aircraft and which gun sight we are authorized to temporarily remove. To top it all off, the CSOps will visit us at 1600 hours. As they were getting ready to leave Sergeant Driver and his troops showed up. Without conversation Driver and his boys took the sign from the vehicle, two ladders and heavy duty screws. Above the entryway in air force blue the sign read

301ST BOMB WING

351ST BOMB SQUADRON

AERIAL GUNNERS RCS CFSC TRAINING ROOM

Musher almost wanted to cry.

CHAPTER 54
The Visit

Leary and Musher picked up their materials, found the line chief and in just minutes Musher had the gun sight removed. He cradled it in his arms like a new born baby. In the classroom he put it on the work table and moved the table out of the way. Nothing must happen to this gun sight.

For the next hour Leary and Musher made sure all the right things were in the right places in the classroom. The box of vu-graphs were by the vu-graph. The viewing screen had been pulled down. Each student chair had a notebook, pencil and a lined paper pad. The jeweler cases were laid out on the work table. The water dispenser worked and there were cups available. There was a trash basket for the disposal of water cups. The instructor's corner was neat and had extra copies of the class materials. There was chalk in the chalk board tray and the blackboards were clean.

The final prep step: The gun sight was centered on the work table and the work table was centered at the front of the classroom. There was nothing else to do except wait. Musher thought of The Monster, "When you think you have it all covered look again, there will be something you wish to improve."

Time moved slowly as Leary and Musher sat in the office smoking cigarettes. Musher said to Leary, "This office is a mess. Let's control his entry. You tell me he is a very precise person. At 1625 hours we will go stand in front of the classroom entry door. When he arrives we will salute and I shall go up the stairs to hold the door open for him and whomever he brings."

"Sounds like a plan."

At precisely 1630 hours the CSOps pulled up in his jeep accompanied by the Squadron Commander (whom Musher had never met), the Squadron Adjutant (another officer whom Musher had never met) and the First Sergeant. When all had entered Musher went to the instructor's corner and stood at parade rest. He was so proud of the way the classroom looked. He could not tell what the visitors were thinking. They asked questions about the course and its materials. Leary handled them all well. He could see they were getting ready to leave so he broke for the door. As they exited the Squadron Commander said to him, "Looks terrific. Remember the proof of the pudding is in the eating." The Squadron Adjutant," It certainly shows what can be done with hard work and motivation." (If he only knew). The

CSOps, "ll this in only four days. If your students gunnery scores parallel your efforts we will have the finest shooters in the Wing." The first sergeant winked as he walked by.

What a relief. Leary and Musher went into the office to sit and smoke.

Leary said, "It is Thursday, we have no pressure until 0700 hours Monday morning. You may do whatever you choose between now and then. If you would like a three day pass (better than a Class A pass because of the greater mileage radius one could travel) I am sure I can get the first sergeant to give you one."

"No thank you I think I will hang around here."

CHAPTER 55
A Three Day Break

Back at the barracks Musher grabbed his toiletry kit and head for his SSS. In clean clothes he felt far less tired. He knew he needed rest. He lay down on his bunk when the most horrible thought hit him. There are no locks on either the office or classroom doors. It was most probably all right during the day light hours but what about tonight, tomorrow night, Saturday night and Sunday night when the flight line would be deserted. With no locks entry could be most silent and all his work could go up in smoke. He trembled at the thought

He jumped from his bunk grabbed his B-4 bag and started packing. His pillow, two blankets, his sweat shirt and his field jacket were packed along with his "emergency" kit. He took the base bus to the BX. Inside he purchased a small alarm clock, a small desk lamp, an inexpensive radio, two flashlights with batteries, a carton of Luckies, two handfuls of candy bars and other goodies, two six packs of coco-cola, an A2C miniature pin, and a red baseball cap embroidered 351st Bomb Squadron. He went next door to the BX cafeteria and ate. He took two cheeseburgers and a large order of french fries to go. He took the base bus to the nearest point to the office. He walked the rest of the way wondering if he was just foolish or did a real threat exist.

At the office he propped a chair against the entry door. It probably would not keep anybody out but it might give him warning if someone was trying to enter. He made sure the door between the office and the classroom would remain open. In the classroom instructor corner he laid out the blankets and the pillow as a bunk. Put on his sweat shirt over his flying suit. Draped his field jacket over the back of a chair and used the instructor desk as a table top for the radio and his goodies. One of the flashlights was placed by the bunk and the other on the desk top. He used a chair to brace the classroom front door. He had done all the preparation he could do. It had gotten dark. He turned on the desk lamp. The classroom became full of eerie shadows. The radio playing softly helped ease his tensions.

He lay down on his home made bed and dozed off only to be awakened by a loud banging at the classroom front door. He looked out and there stood a Captain with a sidearm and an arm band which said OD. Musher moved the chair and opened the door.

The Captain came in, looked around and snapped on the overhead fluorescent lights. "Who are you and what are you doing here?"

Musher identified himself, showed his Class A pass and gave him the full explanation concentrating on his fear of a break-in since there were no locks on either entry door.

The OD seemed satisfied with the explanation. "Who is your supervisor?"

"Sir, CWO Leary, the 351st Bomb Squadron Gunnery Officer."

"I will note this in my log and talk to Mister Leary in the morning. Good night."

The rest of the night was uneventful. He slept for an hour or two. Musher spent most of his time working on his card dealing skill and card memorization ability.

He shuffled the deck and practiced for various games and various numbers of players. As the night went on his proficiency level escalated. Within three hours he felt he could play "mechanic" in most any game. During his practice he always recalled Fanucci, "You cannot afford a mistake. Once all your fingers have been broken you can never regain the feel and smoothness of a great mechanic."

The card memorization ability required that he shuffle the deck noting the position of each card during the shuffle. Then placing the deck, card face down, predict the suit and the value of each card as it was individually turned. Two hours of practice and he was confident that he had it again. The real benefit of this skill came when he played poker. When folded players tossed their cards into the dead card pile very often he got a quick glance of their discards. Eliminating those cards from his opponent's hands gave him a much stronger mathematical advantage of their hand possibilities. There was no risk in using this skill in any poker game, either a legitimate game or an illegitimate game.

He squared away the classroom and walked to the flight line dining hall for breakfast. He was wearing his new red hat with its A2C rank pin attached on the crown. There were very few people at breakfast, none of whom Musher knew. He leisured through breakfast not wanting to call Leary until at least 0900 hours.

Back in the office at precisely 0900 hours he called Leary. The phone was answered with Mr. Leary. Musher relayed all of yesterday evening happenings including the visit from the OD. He gave Leary a heads up that the OD would also be calling him. Leary told him to stay put and he would be there shortly.

Leary drove his personal car to the front door of the office. He mounted a hasp on each door and secured a lock on each male half of the hasp. He produced two keys for each lock. "I shall keep one set and you the other. I suggest you put them on your dog tags." Musher immediately complied. "Gather the things you want to take back to the barracks and put them in the car." Again Musher immediately complied. At Musher's barracks he said, "Put your stuff by your bunk, pick up a clean flying suit and come back here. By the way, that is a great hat you are wearing." Musher was back in the car and Leary drove to the BX Tailor Shop. He parked and pulled four items from his pocket. "Have them sew this on your left breast, it was a leather square emblazoned with the badge of an aerial gunner; next was another leather rectangle emblazoned with Muscarello, this one goes on your right breast; this one is the 15th air force patch which goes on your left shoulder; and this final one is the 351st Bomb Squadron Emblem. It goes on your right shoulder. Notice the three eagles have a spear piercing through their breasts. Among us 351st members we call it "the three shafted shitbirds". The tailor shop will sew them on for you at a minimum cost. Do you have any money?"

"Yes sir."

"OK then, get it done, enjoy the rest of the weekend and I shall see you Monday." Before Musher could thank him he was gone.

CHAPTER 56

The NCO Club

His barracks room mates started filing in from their work day around 1530 hours. Most took the SSS route as quickly as possible. Around 1715 hours Bob Halloran, one of the guys who had been most nice to Musher told him, "It is Friday steak night at the NCO Club. Bar-B-Qued rib eye steaks, beans, corn on the cob and cold draft beer, all for one dollar. Musher why do you look so puzzled? You are an NCO. An A2c in the air force is a Corporal in the Army. Come with us and join. Membership is one dollar a month. Wait until you see all the things that happen at the NCO Club and we will probably have a tough time keeping you away from there. We ride over to the Club in my car. Sometimes the car stays overnight. Be ready at 1730 hours."

At 1730 hours Musher was standing in front of the barracks. Bob and the other three guys with whom Musher had dinner were also in Bob's 1942 Packard Clipper. It was a big as a hearse. The time to get to the Club and park was less than ten minutes. As the five of them entered the club Bob and his buddies flashed their membership cards. Bob said to the doorman, "This is A2C Muscarello a new gunner in our squadron. Can he pay his first month's dues now and come back over the weekend for the paperwork?" The doorman had Musher write his name, rank and serial number on a piece of paper. Took his dollar and gave him a yellow card marked, Temporary Member.

They found an empty table for six. The waitress came toting three large pitchers of beer and six glasses. They drank beer until bob whispered,"Squeet." (translates to "Let's us go eat"). The food was good and you could have seconds on anything. The food and the beer were well worth more than the dollar plus fifty cents from each as the tip for the waitress. Musher had had all the beer he could handle.

Bob said, "Come, I will show you around. Remember each active part of the Club has its own Sergeant-At-Arms while the room is active. We just came from the main eating area, the door on the right leads to the main bar. Two complete bars with stools and tables, a jukebox and a small dance floor for the cuddly dancing.

Down the hall in front of us are the men's and ladies' rest rooms. The door on the left leads to the grand ballroom. Here they show movies nightly, hold formal and informal dances and play the old standby, Bingo.

176

The hallway between the one in front of us and the grand ballroom door leads us to the stag part of the club. Women and children are not allowed past the entry door to the Stag Bar.When they entered the stag bar they were standing in front of a lengthy full bar. Bar stools yes, tables no. Behind the bar there were three doors.

They took the door on the left into the pool hall. Two billard tables, six pocket pool tables. Bob highlighted that there was action there every hour the club was open and maybe some even when the club was not open.

The center door led them to two crap tables. One was a fifty dollar limit table and the other was a no limit table. The table covers, the stick men, the croupier and the pit boss looked like characters from a Class B gangster movie. Also in the room were five poker tables. All tables played table stakes dealer's choice either five card draw jacks or better or five card stud.

Table 1: Buy-in $50, $1 to $2, three raise limit.

Table 2: Buy-in $75, $2 to $5, three raise limit.

Table 3: Buy-in $100, $5 to $10, three raise limit.

Table 4: Buy-in $200, $10 to $20, three raise limit.

Table 5: Buy-in $500, _ pot limit, no limited number of raises.

If you wanted to play you sign up with the room sergeant–at–arms. He transitions the players smoothly and tries to keep the game "friendly".

The final door on the right led them to a high stakes poker room decorated like many of the Mississippi riverboat family. Big Easy poker chairs, a hand made table covering and crystal ash trays. Here they played either five card stud or five card draw. Not jacks or better, it was called "guts". If it gets to your turn and the pot has not been opened you may open irrespective of the cards you are holding.

The Buy-in is $1,500. It is table stakes; however, if you should lose your original buy-in your seat will be held open for thirty minutes if you choose to reenter with an additional $1,500 buy-in.

Bob and Musher walked back to the Stag Room Main Bar. Bob had a beer and Musher had a coke. Bob started the conversation, "With all those gambling temptations you can easily see how guys get in over their heads. You picked up pinochle very quickly, are you a card player?"

"At times." To himself he said not tonight Cleo, not tonight.

From there they went to the pool table room. Bob showed Musher a room off the pool table room that contained six tables. There were chairs all over the room. Bob offered,"This room is for people who like to play cards but do not want to gamble. The discarded decks from the poker games end up here."

Musher said, "Bob I am beat. I am going back to the barracks. I thank you for being a friend." Bob tried to coax Musher into staying but his mind was made up. He thanked Bob and said good-night. The other three guys were involved in an activity somewhere in the club so he just slipped out the front door. He caught the base bus back to the barracks area.

CHAPTER 57
The NCO Club Again

Musher walked to the Orderly Room Bulletin Board to make sure he was not scheduled for any duties in the next seventy-two hours. None. A casual walk to the dining hall, an excellent breakfast, lots of coffee and cigarettes. He caught the base bus to go to the NCO Club. He was directed through a door which opened to an administrative office. There was only one lady working in the office. He approached her and showed his Temporary Member paper. She asked him to sit while she loaded a form in her typewriter. He showed his Class A pass. She asked and he answered an endless number of silly questions. When she finished typing a lot of other forms she handed him a card testifying that he was a member of this NCO Club. He thanked her and went off to find some coffee. With coffee in hand he went into the pool room and took a kibitzer seat. There were four tables active with nine ball. Of the eight players only one looked like he had sufficient skill to be a hustler. Musher nicknamed him "GrabIt". Musher did not count how many games he had won but they were plentiful before GrabIt's pigeon acknowledged that he could not beat GrabIt, hung up his cue and left the room.

GrabIt asked Musher if he were a pool player. "Somewhat but not in your class." Have you played nine ball?" Yes. "Tell you what, One dollar on the nine but you win if you make the three, five or nine. I will give you the first break." Let me see if I have this straight. You can only win by making the nine ball but I win if I make either three ball, the five ball or the nine ball. Am I right? "Yes you are, I will rack them for your break."

Musher made small pretense of selecting a cue, banged the chalk heavily on the cue tip and lined up the cue ball for the break. The one ball went in the side pocket, the three ball was hanging on the edge of the corner pocket and the two ball was straight in front of it. This simple combination would be made by any novice. Musher made the combination. GrabIt pointed to the overhead scoring rack used to keep points scored in a straight pool game. "This side is you, that side is me. You have one marker. You are one dollar up. In this game the winner breaks. I'll rack em up."

Musher went through his chalking routine and then broke the balls. The four ball went into the side pocket. The one ball was clear along the side rail, the nine ball was hanging at the pocket on the opposite end of the same rail. The cue ball was in the open. Musher made a shot that would appear he was trying to cross bank the one but instead after contact with the one the cue ball traveled three rails to tap in the nine. He tried to look lucky but it was difficult.

Another Fanucci classic, "The most important thing you can do when playing a hustler is get ahead in the money. Make him chase you just to try to get his own money back. Most hustlers have the fear that the pigeon will quit and take their money and run."

Two more times Musher broke and got lucky and made a money ball. On the fifth rack he intentionally missed an easy shot. GrabIt stepped up, ran the rack, broke the next rack and ran it too. After the second rack run he said to Musher, "How about we change the stakes. Say five dollars for the nine?"

Do I still win on the three ball, the five ball or the nine ball? "Yes you do".

Do I still get to break first? If you break I may never get another shot. "O.K., you will break first."

Musher decided it was time to put GrabIt in his place. Musher broke and won the next ten games without GrabIt even getting out of his chair except to rack the balls. Prior to breaking for the eleventh game Musher said to GrabIt" loud enough for everyone in the pool room to hear, " I can do this all day. Be smart, take your licking, pay your debt and be super careful whom you try to hustle next time. What will it be?" GrabIt passed fifty-two dollars to Musher. Musher folded it, put it in his pocket and headed out to find more coffee. The tale of GrabIt's being hustled in the pool room floated throughout the club like the smell of a fart in a windowless room.

Sitting drinking coffee and smoking cigarettes Musher was joined by Bob Halloran and his buddies. The first thing out of Bob's mouth was about the nine ball game with the best pool shooter in the club, Master Sergeant Crowley. "You never said you were a pool player."

"I never said I wasn't. Do you think it is possible Crowley was just over-rated when compared to real pool shooters?" The four of them sat silently and stared at Musher.

Musher, "Did you have a good time last night. I never heard you come into the barracks."

Bob, "My car stayed over night. We are not sure when or how we got to the barracks but we took the base bus to get here this morning. What are your plans for the rest of today?"

"Thought I might play a little poker since it is Crowley's fifty-two dollars that will be at risk." He got up, gave them a short wave and headed for the poker room. To the room's sergeant at arms, "Please sign me up for the $1 to $2 table. No sense calling me for any other table the $1 to $2 table is currently my limit."

He drifted to the crap table while waiting for his call. He bet one dollar on the does pass and lost; and then one dollar on the does not pass and lost it also. He turned away from the table and became a kibitizer. In about thirty minutes the sergeant-at-arms escorted him to a seat at the $1 and $2 table. Of the other six players at the table there was only one who had card sense. At this low stakes level you could not bluff and buy a pot and most everyone stayed in every hand in the hope of catching the magic cards. Musher played conservatively and within two hours his poke had grown to over two hundred fifty dollars. "Thank you gentlemen I enjoyed your company." He went to the sergeant-at-arms and said, "I am ready for the $10 to $20 dollar table." A seat at that table did not come available for over two hours. The sergeant-at-arms escorted him to his seat. He placed two hundred fifty dollars on the table. This game was also table stakes. Two of the players announced that they called all bets and raises. With that gesture came the risk that if you were not able to call you automatically lost the pot. A heroic gesture but certainly not smart.

Again the game was five card stud. These were a better caliber of poker player. Here you could bluff and maybe buy a pot. Musher stuck to his conservative way. His ears ringing with Fanuccis axiom, "If your hole card will not beat all the up cards, get out of the hand. There will be lots more hands." He was not getting favorable cards and he was spending his money on the ante. As always, the cards turned for the better. With wired queens he was able to stay in the hand. At all costs he must avoid an expensive "second-best". There were two other players and him left in the hand when the fifth card was dealt. He caught a third queen and that made him high on the board and first bettor. This is where the card memorization paid off. His best estimate of the hand on his left was three tens. His best estimate of the other hand was three deuces (the card game name for two pair, aces and kings). Obviously he could not be sure so his bet was "check". His left hand player bet twenty dollars. The two pair guy folded. Musher called. His three queens beat the three tens. The obvious question was how his left hand opponent could not see three queens. If he could see the probability of three queens why bet? At that point you are not going to buy the pot from the first bettor who checked and was left alone to keep you honest.

He won a few more hands including a couple of big ones. His poke was now almost eighteen hundred dollars. He told himself, enough, squeet and relax. He did his polite goodbyes and headed for the restaurant. As he passed the bar there sat Bob and his three friends. Musher went in to talk to them and told the bartender whatever they are drinking give them one on me. I will take a coco cola. "Have you guys eaten yet? Take your drinks and come with me, I am buying." A good tip for the bartender and into the dining room.

"How did the poker go?"

"Quite well thank you, let's eat."

"How did Crowley's fifty-two dollars do?"

"It grew to about eighteen hundred."

"Dollars?"

"Can we eat? I am so tired that I am going back to the barracks right after dinner, SSS and be in the sack very early."

"Aren't you staying for the dance tonight?"

Musher thought of Lucy. "I'd like to but as they say, I am plumb tuckered."

CHAPTER 58
The NCO Club One More Time

He started his day with a casual walk to the dining hall, an excellent breakfast, lots of coffee and cigarettes. He caught the base bus to the NCO Club

With hot coffee in hand he entered the pool room. All six tables were in use except that at one table Sergeant Crowley was practicing by himself. No sooner had Musher taken a kibitzer seat than Crowley was in his face. The entire room went quiet.

"I'm not sure you are a better player than I am. Yesterday you had a number of lucky balls fall for you. In straight pool you must call every shot for it to count for score. I think I am better at that than you are. Why don't we play a fifty pointer and find out who is the better player?"

"How much are we going to play for?"

"You name it!"

Musher took a roll of bills from his pocket, counted out one thousand dollars and held it up to Crowley's face. "First to fifty takes it all."

"I don't have that much money on me."

"I'll give you until 1100 hours to find it. Maybe all these other people who think you're such a great shooter would want to buy a piece of the bet. Either be here at 1100 hours or it is two thousand when you do get the cash. Meanwhile get out of my face."

As he was leaving the room Crowley said, "I'll be back here before 1100 hours."

Suddenly Musher was hungry. He went back in the restaurant for more coffee, toast and Lucky Strikes. True to his word Crowley had returned and sent one of his cronies into the restaurant to tell Musher he was waiting. Musher told himself this scenario would not even make a descent Class B western movie.

The pool room was crowded. Crowley was at the end table practicing cue ball direction off the rails. Musher said, "Let's play on this center table so your gallery won't be so jammed on one side of the room." The real reason was that he was sure Crowley played most of the time on that table and knew the table's peculiarities and roll. Crowley could not object without looking like a whiner.

When the crowd was settled and the stakes had been placed in the hands of the room sergeant-at arms, they lagged for break. Musher lost. He did the same two rails from the rear break that he had done with Lucy. Crowley was left with absolutely no shot and a very difficult play for a safety. Musher wasn't sure if he did not know how to play a safety from there or his nerves got to him. In either case he freed the cue ball and left two balls in the open. Musher was hell bent on taking the advantage. He called, "Six in the corner." A sure shot with high left English on the cue ball sunk the six and opened the rack. From there Musher was like a machine, calling and making shots. The shots were all easy because he was such a good position player. At the end of the first rack the score was Musher 14, Crowley 0. Musher made a random selection of a spectator and asked,"Are you any good at racking the balls?" His answer was a nodded yes. "That's your job and I will pay twenty dollars for you to do it well."

The next two racks went the same way. Score, Musher 42, Crowley 0. Before the start of the fourth and what seemed to be the inevitable winner for Musher, Musher said to Crowley, "Tell you what. I will let you buy out of this bet for five hundred dollars and the promise that you will never bug me again. Are you interested?"

Crowley looked at the sergeant-at-arms and said, "Give me five hundred and the rest to him." Musher took the money, paid the racker twenty dollars, gave the sergeant-at arms a forty dollar tip, and headed for lunch. He was hungry again. The pool room talking was at a low buzz level as Musher left.

No sooner than he had ordered lunch Bob and his buddies joined him. "You are quite the celebrity in this club. Good poker player, good pool shooter and big tipper. We saw the match. You were great but why did you let him off the hook?"

"Do you think I really let him off the hook? The most I could win would be five hundred dollars more. His submission will bother him for a long, long time and I have put the fear of God in him for every time he picks up a cue for money. Not to mention you tell me I am now a celebrity." A2C Muscarello a celebrity. No one in the old neighborhood would believe that. Especially Freddie.

"What's on tap for the rest of the day?"

"I think I will live off my laurels. The matinee movie, an early dinner and early to bed. After all my big moment is in the morning. School begins for two combat crews of the aerial gunners. I am sure they would not be impressed with my celebrity status

CHAPTER 59

School Begins

Musher was up early and dressed in his newly emblazoned flying suit. He had shined his brogans (a heavy duty ankle high work shoe) to a high gloss polish. Lastly, he put on his 351st hat and walked to the dining hall. When Bob Halloran came in he joined Musher's table.

"Don't you look pretty this morning. Are you ready for the WWII veterans to attack the young whipper-snapper?"

"About as ready as I can get."

Musher did not need to unlock the doors. They were already unlocked. It was only 0645 hours but Leary must be inside. Any other reason for unlocked doors would cripple him. Leary was sitting at his desk studying some papers. His nervousness showed. "Here's the game plan. I will call the roll, make a few welcoming remarks stressing the importance of the need for this program to be successful for the future USAF aircraft and the aerial gunners who would come after them. Then I will introduce you and you can take it from there."

"Mister Leary I did not get to thank you for the flying suit items you gave me. I hope somehow I can repay you."

"Don't mention it Musher, just do us proud with these students."

About 0745 the students began filling the classroom. They milled around looking at the pictures and the captions. The huge recruiting poster brought chuckles from its viewers. CWO Leary spoke. "Gentlemen please take a seat. We don't have coat racks yet so drape it on the back of your chair." There were two captains, four master sergeants and four technical sergeants in the class. You will attend class here for the next three days. The fourth day will be practical training on the ramp and the fifth day will be airborne film shooting against a bandit attack. The last day will be reviewing your gun film and a critique of the shooting mission. Our squadron reputation as airborne shooters is certainly less than something to be proud of. We hope you will pay close attention in this class and when you do your airborne film shooting the results will make each of us proud. This young gentleman is A2C Muscarello, known to all of us as Musher. He will do most of the teaching. Musher they are all yours."

"Good morning gentlemen. For purposes of this class you call me Musher and with your permission I will call you by your last name. No disrespect is intended, I believe it will make the class less restrictive and

185

improve learning. Does anyone not wish to be called without his proper rank? Hearing no objection that is how we will do it. Class will begin promptly at 0800 hours. There will be four fifty minute classes each morning and beginning at 1330 hours there will be three in the afternoon session. In between classes you will get a get ten minute break. No smoking in the classroom. I am sure you saw the butt cans outside the classroom entry door. There is water and paper cups at the back of the classroom. On your desk is a training notebook. There is also a pencil and a yellow pad. Take any notes you wish on the pad but you will find just about everything we discuss is in your notebook .Please do not make any markings in the notebook. Your markings may confuse the next student who uses the notebook. Your notebook contains a training syllabus for this class. Therein is an outline of what we will do over the next six class training days. The first hour of each classroom day will be devoted to discussing the previous days teachings. The final item on your desk is an insert cover for your notebook. Please let's take a look at it. It is very straightforward. Since you are the first user please clearly print the information requested then slide the sheet into the cover's insert pocket."

He watched closely until everyone was finished and notebooks were closed. "Let me take a minute to tell you about me. I was at advanced infantry training and from the first day of basic training to advanced I was a discipline case. The platoon sergeant did his best but you might say I was incorrigible. One typical late afternoon the platoon sergeant had me double timing on the company street with full field pack and my nine pound Garand rifle at high port. When he was sure the mess hall was closed he dismissed me. I went to the PX and there was displayed the poster you see on the side wall. The next day I went through the chain of command to request transfer to the new United States Air Force. That was about 1000 hours. By 1600 hours I had been discharged from the Army, sworn into the USAF and at 1800 hours was on a bus heading for the air force aerial gunnery school at Piute AFB, Texas. My stay in the Army was about eleven weeks. I completed flexible gunnery in a T-6 at Piute AFB. I completed the aerial gunner remote control training course for the central fire control system at Lowry AFB, have had one ride in a B-29 and been here almost two weeks. Total B-29 flying time four hours, total time in the USAF is sixteen weeks. My total service is twenty-seven weeks, just barely over six months. I was promoted to A2C as a result of my performance at Lowry. I tell you my life history only to show you I am a raw recruit gunner. I assure you I know this RCS system in and out and if you help me at the end of this week you will too. It is 0850 take ten. Back in your seat at 0900 hours."

During the break he was approached by a few members of the class. "Are you the Musher who broke Crowley's ass and spirit and picked up two thousand dollars at the poker tables?"

"Yes and no. I did not win two thousand dollars."

The rest of the morning was devoted to disassembly and assembly of the gun sight. In the process the students were exposed to the contents of the jeweler's case and how important it is for successful RCS gunnery. The vu-graphs were used to show the gun sight cut outs and the steps to disassembly and assembly.

At 1150 hours Musher asked that individual areas be squared away, He announced class would reconvene at 1330 hours.

Mister Leary suggested they go to the squadron dining room rather than the flight line dining room. "This way you will get a little break. In the flight line dining room you would be attacked by some students looking for a play by play description of your weekend in the NCO Club. By the way, if you didn't win two thousand dollars how much did you win?"

"Sorry Mister Leary, that's classified."

All the students were in their seats at 1330 hours. At the back of the classroom sat the CSOps and the Squadron CO. The CSOps said, "Musher don't mind us we just want to watch and listen."

Musher began again with gun sight. He apologized to the CSOps and CO for bringing the class around the work table. This time he had two crew members do the actual disassembly reciting the nomenclature of each part as it was disassembled. He changed crew members for the assembly requiring they name each part as it was replaced in the gun sight. Each crew averaged thirty minutes for its part in the exercise. "Let's do it again" He named a different crew for the disassembly. When they finished he named a different crew for the assembly. Their time was about five minutes better than the first crews. When he looked at the back of the classroom the CSOps and CO were gone.

"Let's do it again" He named a different crew for the disassembly. When they finished he named a different crew for the assembly. Their time was about the same as the first crews.

The class ran a little longer than fifty minutes. "Take a break. Back in your seat at 1425." A strange thing happened, no one left the work table. They all stayed there and talked about the gun sight and the problems of disassembly and assembly. A couple drifted outside for a smoke. Musher was with them.

The rest of the day was spent disassembling and assembling the gun sight.

At 1630 hours Musher told them if they wanted to they could take their notebooks and pads home with them for study. It was not an obligation, just an option. The class was dismissed. Leary told Musher, "Good job. Let's get out of here." "You go ahead sir, I want to set up for tomorrow."

With the morning arrangements complete and the building securely locked Musher starting walking to the base bus line stop. During the walk he evaluated the day. Things didn't go too badly, one might even say they went fairly well. Let's see how the next couple of days go, remember, "Every new project is it own motivation."

He didn't go to the barracks rather he went to the dining hall. Alone at a table he was quickly joined by two others wearing 351st hats and staff sergeant rank pins on the hat. They did not have trays so it was obvious they had not joined him to eat. They introduced themselves by first name. The one called Lonnie began, "We have not seen you shoot pool but from all the stories you are the second coming of Willie Mosconi. The squadron enters a team in the base straight pool league. The season begins in two weeks. We would like you to be on our team. Can we count on you?"

"I am afraid you cannot. Those types of games do not interest me. Besides with all the propagandizing about my ability I could not get a side bet. I appreciate you asking me but I must decline." The two of them stood up and without a so much as a kiss my ass left. He wondered if he should have just stalled and put them off temporarily. He believed those two would spread a different story about him. Oh well, in the words of Rod from Chelsea, fuck 'em and feed 'em frijoles.

It was a quiet night in the barracks. He played a little pinochle with the guys, did his SSS and hit the sack. Just before falling asleep he thought, we need a clock in the classroom.

CHAPTER 60
The Training Progresses

The next day of classroom training was in the same vane as the first. There were three major differences. The morning discussions of the previous day became deeper and more technical, the class was given a short non-graded essay quiz which was critiqued after the class completed the quiz and just about every conversation was about the gun sight.

Musher noticed another significant fact about his students. There was the free interchange of opinions, beliefs and disbeliefs among the students. One of the peculiarities of the United States Air Force is that the commissioned members and the enlisted members of a combat crew are less formal in their speech and conduct. Anyone measuring fraternization between officers and enlisted men would have a heart attack. Such accepted camaderie did not exist in any other job anywhere in the USAF.

The end of Day 1 proved that these students could individually disassemble and assemble the gun sight without help in less than three minutes. Without realizing it they had established the acceptable standard for future classes

They are ready for "selsyns and reticles". Leary had an AC Power Transformer rigged to the gun sight to give it the effect of an aircraft mount. The sight was positioned on the work table so that a student could sit in a chair activate the gun sight and see the reticle at work. The gun sight is active as long as the action switch is closed.

The rest of the morning was devoted to the importance of a happy marriage between the selsyns and the reticle. Without any technical explanation of "the hows" relating to the selsyns and reticle, using vu-graphs, Musher demonstrated the use of the jewelers case tool to access the selsyns without disassembly of the gun sight. The next vu-graph showed a reticle with the target dot at the 1800 hours position. (Pretty close to divorce) The next showed a small left adjustment of the right selsyn, the result, the target dot was now at the 2000 position. Next a small right adjustment of the same selsyn, the result, the target dot was now at the 0900 position. The vu-graphs continued showing minor adjustments to the right selsyn until the target dot was dead center in the reticle. The view graphs showed the initial position of the target dot in the left selsyn. The following vu-graphs showed adjustment changes until the target dot was in the center of the reticle. The gun sight was fully calibrated for effective shooting.

With only one gun sight and ten students the rest of the day would be devoted to each taking turns to "zero" one of the selsyns. (Zero has the target dot in the center of the reticle). After each two successful calibrations, one left, one right, Musher distorted the target dot for the next two students.

During the breaks and at lunch time not all the students left the classroom. Some stayed to get more practice doing adjustments. Leary smiled from ear to ear. "When the students leave you need to show me the smooth technique. I watched all the vu-graphs."

"As we leave today each crew will be given two jewelers cases. One for the bombardier compartment and one for the main gunnery compartment. The CSOps has made an active aircraft available to us from 0900 to 1600 hours tomorrow. You will meet with Mister Leary at 0800 hours at the shack. I will be out earlier playing devil's advocate. We will have box lunches at the aircraft. We shall not leave until either our time is up or we are satisfied that Friday's airborne bandit shoot will be highly successful. Any questions?"

"How will we tell our individual score. What with all of us using the same gun sights."

"For tomorrow you need not worry about that. Tomorrow we concentrate on a perfect marriage of reticle and gun sight. Before the flight Friday you will understand and be confidant that no one will steal your one hundred per cent hits." That brought a chuckle from the class.

"Do you have any objection to us forming a pool for our best shooter on Friday?"

"As my Irish friends say, "What the eyes don't see the heart can't grieve." Let's call it a day. Pickup your jeweler cases and I will see you at the aircraft tomorrow morning."

"Mister Leary I am more than happy to work with you on selsyns and reticles. I need you to do something for us. Use your influence to get box lunches, coffee and water for sixteen. We must remember the crew chief and his crew."

For a big man Leary's hands were very dexterous. It took about one hour for him to master the calibration of the gun sight. Leary helped Musher clean up, disconnect all electrical hookups and empty the trash. Musher grabbed his book carrier from Lowry and made sure it contained all the things he needed. They locked up and Leary dropped Musher at the squadron orderly room.

A review of the bulletin board showed he was scheduled for KP on the Tuesday following the last class day.

CHAPTER 61

Flight Line Exercises

Musher ate breakfast very early, caught the base bus to the flight line and walked to the shack. Every thinking moment was "Did I forget something, how do I make the crew chief like me, will Leary get the lunches, coffee and water, will he get enough?" Before he could drive himself well over the edge he entered the shack. The place was empty. He noticed an aircraft status board which showed "B-29 Number 121, P Patch, Crew training, 0900 – 1600." He left the shack and hailed the first vehicle that came by. As luck would have it, it was the A1C of the Guard. Musher told him his need. He was dropped off at the P Patch. He walked the row of parked B-29s until he saw the tail number 121. Sitting about a hundred yards off in the grass there was someone smoking. As Musher approached him he stood and when within range, "Are you Musher, the guy who wrecked hell in the Club last weekend?"....Yes Sir.…."Musher, I am not a sir. I am Master Sergeant Herbie Long crew chief for 121. To you it's Herbie or Long, your choice. Beating Crowley's ass puts you high up in my book. My crew will be here later but rumor told me you were always early. What do you want to do while we wait for your class?"

"Could I get some aircraft power so I can fuckup your gun sights?"

Long powered up the external APU, went to the engineer's station, threw some switches and climbed down the forward ladder. Walked to Musher," It's all yours. Do you want me with you?"

"No but I would appreciate it if the rear hatch was opened and the ladder put in place."

"Consider it done."

Musher climbed the forward ladder and distorted the gun sight. Then he crawled through the tunnel and did the same thing to the gun sight in the waist positions To Long, "When my class gets here would you make the intercom active?"

"Anything for my hero."

With that they went back to the grass area and smoked cigarettes. It would be more than an hour before the class got here. Long wanted a word by word description of his two encounters with Crowley. When Musher finished Long exclaimed, "I would have paid fifty dollars to see that." Two cigarettes later a flight line bus stopped in front of 121. The ground crew got off and headed for Long. Mister Leary formed the class under the left wing.

191

Musher's greeting was simple, "I trust you are ready. Mister Leary please brief the crew chief regarding lunches etc. We will divide our personnel into two teams. Three members for the bombardier compartment and seven members for the aft compartment. There is no scoring for this exercise. When you think your calibration is at zero either I or Mr. Leary will validate your belief. Your effort result will be measured either in/off time and yes or no. The listings are simply so we evaluate ourselves at the end of the day. When we ask the crew chief will put power to the aircraft and activate the intercom system. There are headsets at each shooting position and both Mister Leary and I will be listening and able to speak. You cannot speak but you will hear all activity while you have the headset on. How many times will we do this exercise and from which shooting positions? We will rotate you among the shooting positions and we will be here as long as it takes unless we run out of time or as a class we are confident that individually we will shoot at least eighty percent tomorrow. The crew chief has power on the aircraft and the intercom active. Neither Mister Leary nor I will select who goes where. You do that among yourselves making sure that each person partakes in one exercise. When all have completed one exercise you can notify Mister Leary and me by using the intercom headset in the wheel well. It is now 0900 hours. Mister Leary and I are going aboard. Everything is ready. Any questions? You can start anytime. Remember when you raise your trigger hand to show you have finished keep the Action switch closed or you will lose the result of your calibration."

Musher was in the aft compartment and had no sooner put on his headset when two of the class entered and took seating in the waist positions. On the intercom, "Forward ready? If so double click your intercom transmitter." All positions heard the double click. It is 0914. Begin"

Their calibration efforts were validated and they were instructed to leave and tell the next group to wait three minutes before boarding the aircraft. Musher noted that the left waist took longer than the right waist because he waited for the jeweler's case. He noted that with the next group he would give one of them his jeweler's case to use. He and Mister Leary distorted the gun sights.

Two more of the class entered the compartment. Musher, "Who has the jeweler's case?" He gave his to the one who did not. On the intercom, "Forward ready? If so double click your intercom transmitter." All positions heard the double click. It is 0925. Begin" Their calibration efforts were validated and they were instructed to leave and tell the next group to wait three minutes before boarding the aircraft. Musher recovered his jeweler's case. He and Mister Leary distorted the gun sights.

Two more of the class entered the compartment. Musher, "Who has the jeweler's case?" He gave his to the one who did not. On the intercom, "Forward ready? If so double click your intercom transmitter." All positions heard the double click. "It is 0940. Begin" Their calibration efforts were validated and they were instructed to leave and tell the next group to wait three minutes before boarding the aircraft. Musher recovered his jeweler's case. He and Mister Leary distorted the gun sights. Two more of the class entered the compartment. They were both the officers.

"We only had one person who had not done the exercise so we decided we would take another turn. We both did our first exercise from the forward compartment. Remember Musher, waste not, want not."

Musher, "Who has the jeweler's case?" He gave his to the one who did not. On the intercom, "Forward ready? If so double click your intercom transmitter." All positions heard the double click. "It is 0955. Begin" Their calibration efforts were validated and they were instructed to leave and tell the next group to standby there. Musher recovered his jeweler's case. He and Mister Leary distorted the gun sights before leaving the aircraft.

He spoke to the class, "We completed a full rotation plus a couple in just about one hour. See the crew chief for water or coffee. Mister Leary and I are going off to compare notes."

They headed off to the grassy area so they could smoke. Sergeant Long had put two tables for eight in the grassy area. From somewhere he had garnered sixteen folding chairs. As Musher and Leary sat down an airman came to them with hot coffee and cold water. He could hear Sergeant Long yelling from the tarmac, "Nothing too good for my hero."

Leary, "What is that all about?"

"I'll tell you later, let consolidate our notes. None of mine was beyond the standard time. As a matter of fact I had some with super calibration times."

"Leary echoed I didn't have any beyond the time and I too had some super calibration times."

"At this point all we can tell them is they were well within the calibration standards. I am afraid to tell me how much we are impressed. Still we need to remember this is static position. Tomorrow before takeoff I am sure they will zero at all five positions. What will they do when we distort the gun sights after the first bandit encounter?"

"We shall bring them here for a critique of the first rotation. I will bald face and tell them they have met the acceptable standard. Would you do that while I consolidate our notes?"

The class was listening intently when Musher described what he and Mister Leary thought of the first rotation exercises and the individual performances. Throughout his presentation he constantly reminded them that here in a static aircraft was not much different than in a classroom. The difference comes with moving aircraft targets. True the first two gunners will start with a well calibrated shooting gun sight. Obviously the first two shooters would be Mr. Leary and himself. We'll talk more about tomorrow later today. Never forget, the gun sight can lead you to the target but you must keep the reticle on target while smoothly closing the firing switch. Would a couple of you gentlemen get the lunches, coffee and water from the aircraft. Don't forget to bring the crew chief and his crew."

The two commissioned officers were first out of their chairs and on the way to the aircraft. When they returned they were not carrying anything. The airmen crew placed everything on the table while Musher introduced Master Sergeant Long to everyone. Long introduced his crew by name and specialty to Musher's crowd. Lunch was long and pleasant. Lots of coffee and cigarettes. When it was obvious that it was time to go back to work the airmen rose to police the area. The class told them to sit and relax, they would take of the policing. The airmen were so surprised to see officers and senior sergeants carrying trash, folding tables and stacking chairs. Sergeant Long and his crew went back to their duties and Musher and Mister Leary went back to theirs.

In the next two hours the class continued the exercises. The results were pleasing to Musher and he declared they go back to the classroom for final critique of today's exercises.

Sergeant Long had his flight line pickup and he drove them to the classroom. As everyone was getting out Long summoned Musher. "I used a little clout with squadron ops and your shooting exercise will be in my aircraft, good old reliable 121. Anything for my hero." With that he headed for the P Patch.

Inside Musher made a pretense of a shooting critique. You all did very well and there is no doubt in my mind if you concentrate you will individually shoot eighty percent or better. "Let's talk about tomorrow. Station time is 0800 hours. The crew bus will be at the shack at 0600 hours. The flight will last four hours. Our maximum altitude will be eight thousand feet. The bandits will be from the 405th Fighter Wing out of England AFB in Louisiana. They will be flying the newest jet aircraft the Star F-80. The cruising speed of the F-80 is five hundred knots per hour. Very few people have encountered jet fighters before. Don't let that distress you. Your aircraft, your gun sight and you are capable of shooting down any aircraft in anybody's air force.

Individual bandit attacks will last three minutes with a five minute break between attacks. The five minute break is so you can zero your sight after Mister Leary and I fuck it up. We will only use three shooting positions, the forward compartment and the two waist positions. Mister Leary and I will record who the shooter is in each position by position, time in the position, bandit attack number and time shooter ends exercise. If the bandits have not broken off, each shooter will be stopped as he reaches three minutes of bandit attack. When the film is shown we can identify each shooter. No one will steal anyone else's one hundred percent hits." Again the chuckle from the class. "If you do as you did today you will score well and be the talk of the 351st. If you score miserably I will most probably be an airman nothing doing KP for the rest of my enlistment

When you get to the shack at 0600 hours make sure you have everything you will need. I want you to bring your A-3 bag with your full cold weather flying gear. We will have lunch after the mission. There will be no coffee on board, just water. The ground crew is taking care of that. You will be happy to know this mission will be flown in 121, Sergeant Long's aircraft. Are there any questions or comments?".............. None.

"Gentlemen about tomorrow this is what the Wing Commander whispered in my ear as he was leaving from his visit, "Looks pretty but the proof of the pudding is in the eating." As my French friends say, "Bon Appetit."

CHAPTER 62

The Proof of the Pudding Is in the Eating

Musher was at the shack at 0545 hours. Leary was already there.

"We have two clipboards. The paper on the clipboards showed the headings to keep track of who was shooting, from which position and when. You will take the forward compartment and I shall take the rear.

Everyone was on the bus at 0600 hours. First stop the Parachute Shop to pick up chutes. Next stop the P Patch and 121. The bus was greeted by Crew Chief Long. The aircrew arrived moments later. Leary and his detail lined up under the left wing. The aircrew lined up in front of them. The AC spoke, "While we do our pre-flight inspections please brief Clinker of the details of this mission. You may put your gear aboard whenever you are free."

The flight engineer went directly to Mister Leary. Sir did you want Musher to brief me. This old sarge knew who ran the railroad. When Leary was gone Clinker said, "Long tells me you're kicking ass at the club. Musher briefed Clinker and headed into the aircraft to make sure the gun sights were zeroed.

The class division and the rules were the same as yesterday. The AC gathered everybody under the left wing. The aircrew verified its aircraft checks. Mister Leary told him his class was ready. The AC instructed all to get aboard.

When Musher entered the aft compartment sitting there was Master Sergeant Long. Musher just looked at him. Long, "I told you I would be here. My hero doesn't go without the worlds most skilled aircraft mechanic on board. I will take care of the ladder, the hatch and the putt-putt (the on board APU)"

The takeoff and climb out to eight thousand feet was without incident. The two regular gunners found space and stretched out to sleep. "On the intercom, Sir, class instructor to AC."...Go ahead..... "Permission to poll the class to insure all are on active intercom." Go ahead. Musher called the roll and each answered with Roger, five square. "Musher to Mister Leary, "Man your shooting position, the bandits should arrive any time now."

On the intercom he heard the AC, "Bandit Leader this 351st Training Fight AG, we are on a racetrack course, 30 miles west of the airbase at eight thousand feet. Do you copy?"

"Copy 351 we are you ready when you are.?"

"Roger Bandit Leader. Bring it on."

Musher remembered how last flight he avoided being caught off guard On the intercom, gunners be ready they will be here in five seconds. He closed the action switch. The reticle looked good. He made small vertical and horizontal testing movements and the reticle followed. The intercom came alive, Bandit at 11 o'clock high. Bandit at 3 o'clock level. Musher trained his gun sight to the approaching bandit. He fired three short bursts. Who knows what happened with the other bandit. Before he could finish the thought he saw a bandit diving towards him from the 2 o'clock high position. He patiently waited until the reticle had the bandit framed. This time he fired five short bursts as the bandit went by in flashing speed. Bandit at 9 o'clock level. There was no way to train his gun on this bandit unless the bandit dove under or climbed over the B-29. The bandit chose under. As he went by Musher the reticle picked him up and Musher fired five bursts.

"351 this is Bandit Leader. We are breaking off. See you again shortly."

"Roger Bandit Leader, 351 Out.

Musher got out of the shooting position and he was soaking wet. Long offered him some water which he gulped. On the intercom, "Musher to Mister Leary. They won't be gone long. Get your shooter in position and make sure your record paper is complete. Thank you, we will do the same here." You two, left and right waist. Get set quickly. Fighter jocks live for this."

The voice on the intercom," 351 this is Bandit Leader are you ready for company?"

"Roger Bandit Leader." The AC made the. "As Shakespeare said, "Lay on MacDuff and damned be he who first cries hold enough."

The bandits attacked mercilessly. The gunners got a good workout. Lots of gun film was expended. Similar attacks took place four more times. To maintain the accuracy of the exercise in the fourth attack the final shooter was the only active gun sight. The entire time for the rotation was slightly over two hours.

On the intercom, "351 this is Bandit Leader. We cannot stay any longer must get fuel. The ETA (estimated time of arrival) for replacement bandits is 1100 hours. Thank you for the show. Take care."

"Roger Bandit Leader we thank you."

To make sure every student clearly heard him Musher spoke on the intercom, "With the exception of your oxygen mask I want you do the next rotation in full cold weather high altitude clothing. Again, I don't care about the sequence of the shooters. I care about your best efforts as an RCS CFCS aerial gunner. Let's take this opportunity to change compartments. Mister Leary please send your students aft. Be sure they bring their A-3 Bags." As the three students dropped out of the tunnel, three entered the tunnel to go forward.

"Musher to Clinker."

"Can you lower the temperature in the aircraft? You heard how we intend to do the next rotation."

"Anything for the Crowley cruncher. You are my hero too."

The voice on the intercom," 351 this is Bandit Leader 2 with three bandits. We are ready at your command."

"Roger Bandit Leader, another one from the US Navy, "You may fire when ready Quigley."

The intercom spoke, "Here they come, two from 10 o'clock. Two more from 7 o'clock.

The waist gunners despite the heavy clothing responded like the veteran gunners they are. .Left waist, "I'm on the 10 o'clock, watch for the 7 o'clock at 2 o'clock. " The bombardier, "I got him in the reticle and I am firing." The right waist, "I got the 10 o'clock. I'm on him. He's framed and I am firing." The next two passes were from different directions. The gunners handled it well.

"351 this is Bandit Leader 2. We are breaking off. We will be in the area. Call us when you are ready."

"Roger Bandit Leader 2. We will lounge around and cut more racetracks in the sky. 351 Out."

The class helped the waist gunners out of their heavy winter clothing. They were soaking wet down to the skin. With some help from their classmates they peeled off everything down to the bare ass level. Each reached into his A-3 bag and came out with clean underwear and a clean flying suit. The class knew the exercise altitude was eight thousand feet. Why else would he have wanted cold weather gear other than to do an exercise in the most uncomfortable circumstances. Musher, not having combat experience could not realize that in a battle individual comfort is not a consideration. These were aerial gunners who had fought bandits from an open waist position with no jacket or sweater to restrict their movements.

"Musher to Leary. Is your next shooter in position?"... "OK." His two shooters were in position and anxiously awaiting the thrill of combat. Even though his aircraft and the fighters were only firing gun film. Over the intercom:

"351 to Bandit Leader 2."

"This is Bandit Leader 2 go ahead."

"The turkey is on the table and we are waiting for you to be the squash."

"Very cute 351 but don't look now, we are sitting on your head ready to clear the table." With that the intercom was filled with transmissions locating incoming bandits. The veteran gunners coped very well with the jet aircraft and its speed.

"351 this is Bandit Leader 2. We are breaking off. We have fuel for maybe two more exercises. I will keep you posted."

"Roger Bandit Leader 2…351 out."

Only six of the ten had done the heavy clothing exercise. Sixty percent is not a great sample but it would have to do. Musher wanted to get at least one more shooting before the day ended. "Musher to Lowry. Would you take care of that front gun sight I think it may need calibration. Thank you." Musher climbed into each waist position and deftly fucked-up the gun sight calibration.

"Class, it seems this may be our last shooting rotation today. We know that in one attack we can shoot and score three gunners. I am putting ten numbers in my hat and I shall draw three. Those three will shoot and the rest of us will pray. Is that clear?"

"Why not ask for volunteers?"

"To shoot?"

"No, to not shoot." Everyone including the aircrew heard all this on the intercom and chuckled.

"As a class is that how you would like to do it?" Eight of the ten spoke an affirmative. Musher asked for volunteer non-shooters. Not one person on the intercom volunteered.

"Ain't this something, I propose a selection method which you did not like, you propose a selection method which I do not like and despite my acceptance of your proposal none of you accept it. It's time for the Machiavellian method (a baby dictatorship), I will appoint and you will accept. He read aloud three names, one for the forward compartment and two for the aft compartment. You sir may make your way forward and send those two here."

Musher to the AC," Sir we are ready when you are."

"351 to Bandit Leader 2"

"Go ahead 351"

"We are ready when you are."

Before the AC even heard a roger the intercom started chirping. "Bandits, two at 2 o'clock high". "Bandits, two at 4 o'clock low." The gunners did their best as the bandits continuously changed attacking points and altitudes.

"Bandit Leader 2 to 351."

"Go ahead Bandit Leader 2"

"We enjoyed the encounter. Hope your squash plate cooked well. See you again. Bandit Leader 2 out." He left no room for a smart retort from 351.

AC to aft instructor, "Please put my people back in their seats. Your people are going through the tunnel now. We will make a straight in approach to Smoky and be on the blocks in thirty-five minutes or less.Musher and all the class were exhausted. There was no chatter. In twenty-nine minutes 121 was parked in the P Patch, on the blocks and its engines shut down. Long scrambled out of the aircraft to go forward to meet with Clinker and hear about any problems. He also wanted to make sure there were no "red crosses" (a red cross is a major flying safety problem and the aircraft is grounded until the problem is fixed).

Everyone except Long's airmen ground crew got on the bus to the shack. The two air crew officers got off there and the remaining fourteen went to the squadron dining hall. The official serving hours of the dining room had ended; however, set in an inverted T shape arrangement there were places and chairs for fourteen people. Mister Leary and Musher sat at the top of the T and each side of its leg has places for six. There was no serving line. Cooks and KPs brought platters of roast beef, baked potatoes, whole kernel corn, gravy and muffins out to the table. It was like an English movie where the servers pass behind the diners and offer the food. It even went so far as to have the servers put your choices on your plate.

Mister Leary stood. "You gentlemen behaved admirably today. Musher and I thank you." The rest of the meal was fairly silent as each ate and ate. The dessert was chocolate fudge brownie covered with French vanilla ice cream. The servers made sure there was plenty of coffee and the coffee was hot. The final step would have been a brandy and a fine cigar. Since both of those are prohibited the group settled for coffee and a cigarette. Musher slipped away from the table and took the Dining Hall Supervisor to one side. Musher placed two hundred dollars in his hand, "Do something nice for your staff and your KPs. Please include yourself in the something nice." He turned and walked away.

Outside the dining hall after all the goodbyes and the we will see you Monday morning, Musher asked, "Leary is your car in this area?"

"Yes I had an early breakfast here this morning. Why?"

"Can you take me to the office so we can store all this stuff away?"

"Of course"

"Can you go to the photo lab and get our films later today or tomorrow? Can you also get a projector? Do you know how to splice film, if you do please get whatever we need to do it. I will be in the office tomorrow morning. Can you call and tell me how you made out?"

"Let's unload and I will take you back to the squadron orderly room. From there I will go straight to the photo lab. They don't exactly love me there but the OIC does have a little fear of me."

He did his SSS and then lay on his bunk until he fell asleep. He was awakened by Bob Halloran. "Aren't you coming to the club tonight? It's Friday, this week it's Italian night, meatballs and macaroni, garlic bread, salad and all the draft beer you want for the low, low price of one dollar. If you don't have a dollar I will loan you one."

"Let me wake up and I will be right out." To himself, "Don't bring a lot of money, you cannot afford a late night. Tomorrow you may have to work a miracle".

CHAPTER 63
A Quiet Weekend

Something caused Musher to awaken. His watch showed 1100 hours. He had been asleep for thirteen hours. No wonder he was sluggish. The cure is a couple of Luckies and a shower. Fifteen minutes later he felt wide awake. First stop, the phone in the orderly room. Mister Leary answered his phone. "Sorry sir I just got up. I haven't slept that long at one time since I came into the military. Sir, did you have any luck?"

"Well yes, a little luck and a little intimidation. All that you asked for will be ready at 1300 hours. I will meet you at the office after I pick up our goodies. See you then" and his phone clicked off.

Lunch was eaten slowly, the bus ride to flight line went quickly, he walked slowly to the office and it was still only1230 hours. At least forty-five minutes before he could expect Leary. He continued to do meaningless things while waiting. At least three smoke breaks and one time just sitting and staring at the aerial gunner recruiting poster. Finally Leary drove up. They unloaded two film cans each the size of a blueberry pie, a projector with extension cord and a small box containing a manual film splicer and the tape for rejoining the spliced film.

They swapped the vu-graph space for the projector. The vu-graph was placed out of the way. Maybe they would need to use it again. Leary plugged in the projector and loaded the first can of film. Musher took the gun sight off the work table, wrapped it in a blanket and stored in a safe spot in the room.

Leary, "I think we are ready. I had some briefings at the lab and I believe I have it right. Please turn out the lights and we will give it a shot. No pun intended."

When the first frame came up Leary put the film on pause. Imprinted on the bottom of the frame are the date, the time, and the position from which the shooting was done. Leary released the pause and the frames rolled with the bottom information displayed on each frame until a summary screen appeared. Leary put the film on pause. "The summary screen shows the cumulative result of the shooting segment. The date, the total time of the shooting, the position from which the shooting originated, the number of rounds expended, the total measurable hits on target and the percentage of hits per round fired. It is amazing what the A&E boys and the photo lab techs can do when properly motivated. I believe this type of gun film interpretation will quickly become the standard for this Wing and maybe for all of 15th Air Force. I am sure you know whose film this is since you and I were the first shooters. Musher, your cumulative hit percentage for rounds fired is 98.7 percent. That's hotter than your normal body temperature. Did you shoot this well in gunnery school? I'll bet you did."

The film rolled again. This time it was Leary's gun film. His summary sheet showed an 88.3 cumulative hit percentage for rounds fired. The film was stopped. Musher needed some time to compose recording sheets to summarize the class's shooting. He also wanted Leary to cut his and Leary's film from the reel. After a short discussion he conceded to Leary that he could splice their film onto the end of the second can. "If you can, put some blank screens between the actual end of the second can and our film."

When his composition was finished the recording sheet had all the summary headings plus a line for the shooter's name and whether this shooting was in high altitude cold weather clothing or not. When Leary was ready they restarted the modified first can and Leary paused the projector at each summary sheet. Musher diligently recorded the information on his lined pad. It was getting late and Leary should be home with his family. "Why don't you take off? You have shown me enough to run the projector and I don't intend to do any splicing. I have some compilations to do and you can't help me. It's a one man job."

Leary didn't raise much of an argument. "I want it clear that you can call me at any time for any thing. Give me a call tomorrow morning and let me know how we are doing. Good night Musher."

Both cans of summary information were recorded on his log. To be sure he had correctly recorded the information he went through both cans again. From his and Mister Leary's notes he determined the six cold weather shooters and appropriately marked his pad. It was now 2000 hours.

The Lowry carry bag was emptied and its contents replaced by a box of unframed vu-graphs and his note pads. The lights out and the building secured he walk to the base bus line. So far he was so proud of today he would sing if he could. Instead he smoked as he walked until he took the base bus to the NCO Club.

His hat went into the carry bag and he checked them with the pretty little worker. "Make sure nothing happens to this and you will be rewarded."...."Certainly Musher." How does she know who I am? Musher's not the name on my flying suit. Maybe I am a celebrity here. In the dining room he ordered a rare T-bone with a garden salad and some coco-cola. No, he did not want any rolls or veggies. He ate slowly savoring the steak. Coffee and a couple of Luckies later he asked for the check. Total eleven two cents. He left fifteen on the table and walked back to kibitz The Big Game.

The room sergeant-at-arms approached him with, "Musher we normally don't allow more than four kibitzers at one time. In your case I feel we could make an exception. " Musher thanked him and put a ten dollar bill in his hand. The table was surrounded by a heavy velvet rope with two entry and exit openings. Kibitzers must stay behind the rope. From there he studied the players. Three of them were in the game the last time he visited this room. Were they a team? From this distance it was hard to tell.

It was late and he had a full day tomorrow. He recovered his carry bag, gave the young lady a five dollar tip and went outside to catch the base bus to his barracks. By time he climbed into bed it was almost midnight.

CHAPTER 64

The Base Library Has It All

It was Sunday. No church bells rang on the base but one could almost feel the lay back attitude of the day. There was nothing new on the squadron bulletin board. Nothing remarkable to say about breakfast. Since he was eating early, by the Saturday night revelers standard, the dining hall was sparsely populated. While enjoying a Lucky and coffee the Dining Hall Supervisor sat down at his table. " Musher, if I may call you that, last night me, my wife, our three cooks and their wives and the two KPs went to Salina. They know me in Salina because I have helped them out a few times. We ate their best, drank a little grape juice (wine) and finished with "holy water." (Holy water was really Anisette served in a cup because in Eddie County no form of liquor could be sold in a restaurant or any other facility. Customers could bring their own and they would be provided setups at an extravagant cost). When it was time for the bill the owners would not accept any payment. I want you to take back your two hundred dollars."

"You didn't get your respect from the owners because they knew of the two hundred dollars, you got their respect because of who you are and what you are. You must keep the money and try spending it well again. Listen I would like to stay and chat but I have something I must do at the Base Library".

"I was about to leave for my quarters, can I give you a lift?"

He was dropped off, he said goodbye and realized that he still did not know the Dining Hall Supervisor's rank or name. Inside, there she was. Looking as good as ever. "Excuse me M'am, do you remember me?"

"Certainly, you're the airman with the major program which took all of five minutes to type. You even offered to pay me. Yes I remember you. What is it this time?"

"It's still part of the same project but a lot more typing. He showed the blank vu-graph pages and his compositions. He asked if each composition could be recorded verbatim with the spacing shown on the composition."

"Yes but it will take about half an hour or more. I cannot have you standing at the reception desk all that time. If you would go sit inconspicuously I will do my best. When I am finished I will find you."

"I will be quiet as a church mouse." In forty-five minutes he was getting impatient and wanted to walk to the desk to see what was going on. Fortunately he restrained himself and continued looking at the WW II

205

picture book. Staring right at him was a crew picture posing in front of a B-29 named "Dirty Dollar". The caption identified the crew by crew position, rank and name. The bottom of the caption read "Crew R-3, 509th Bomb Group (Composite), Tinian , Marianna Islands, January 1945." The aircraft commander Lieutenant Colonel Morehouse was the same Brigadier General Morehouse who now commanded the 301st BombWing. Musher was flipping pages to see if there were any others he could recognize. He had just recognized one of his students, now Master Sergeant Tom Parsons. At that moment a sweet voice said, "You can come to the desk now." He replaced the book in the rack and almost ran to catch up with her.

From behind her desk she placed her work and his notes side by side. "Please check and see if I did it correctly."

"Perfectly. You will not let me pay you, how can I ever repay you? Would you consider dinner with me at the NCO Club followed by a movie?"

"Yes"

"When?"

"When did you have in mind?"

"Tonight at 1800 hours. My problem is I don't have a car to pick you up."

"That is no problem. My Dad belongs to the NCO Club. He would drop me off and you tell me what time I should tell him to pick me up at the movie."

"I hate to run but I must finish the project with the great work you did. What is your name? My name is Saverio."

"Hannah, I will meet you at 1800."

At the office he was busy with the masking tape mounting vu-graphs on view graph frames. While he was in the shack yesterday he saw a roll of masking tape which "had fallen off the desk" Strangely enough a pair of scissors fell right beside the tape. He arranged them in the order he wished to present them. After viewing them he rearranged the sequence. He did such rearrangement until he was satisfied that it was the order he wanted. He broke out the marker he used on his clothes and numbered the vu-graphs 1 to 8 consecutively. In the left hand margin he printed 'THIS SIDE DOWN". In the right margin he drew a bold arrow facing towards the screen and wrote "POINT THE ARROW TO THE SCREEN". To have the wrong side up and the arrow pointing in the right direction is mutually exclusive. He tested and tried every configuration. The only one that worked was, "This Side Down" with the Arrow pointing to the screen. He marked all the vu-graphs the same way.

His watch said it was 1630 hours. He must leave now to clean up and be on time to meet Hannah.

At 1800 hours he was standing in the NCO Club foyer. There was a small florist shop on base. He paid a taxi to go and pickup one long stem red rose which he now held behind his back. As she started up the stairs he went forward and held the door open for her. Still with his hand behind his back. At the cloakroom he handed the attendant Hannah's wrap. Still with his hand behind his back. The Maitre D'Etre escorted them to their table. The Maitre D held Hannah's chair as she sat. When Musher sat the Maitre D placed menus and a wine list on the table. He drifted away from the couple.

Musher brandished the rose. "I am so happy you came." Hannah blushed.

A spiffy waiter came to the table. "May I take your orders? Do you want to order anything to drink while waiting for dinner?"

"Hannah, is there something special you would like to drink?"

"I don't really drink."

"Bring us a split of a very light white wine. We'll order when you return. Tell me Hannah, where were you born and raised?"

"I was born on an airbase in Maine and we were stationed there until I was about ten. We left there and transferred to Smoky Hill. Been here ever since. Graduated from Salina High School. I had been a volunteer worker at the library for about five years. In my graduation week one of library clerks died. I took the civil service tests and have been in the library for a good number of years. Tell me about you."

The waiter appeared with wine. A split is about six ounces. Three ounces hardly dirties a glass.

The waiter stood by Musher with pencil poised to strike. "Your orders sir?"

"Hannah do you like baked stuffed lobster? They tell me it is excellent here."

Hannah nodded yes.

To the waiter, "We will have baked stuffed lobster, minimum one and half pounds, baked potato with sour cream and Caesar salad . No appetizer, serve the salad and some hot rolls while we wait for dinner."

The waiter crouched towards Musher, in a non-whispering tone, "Sir those lobsters are at market price. Your dinners could be very, very expensive." The look that Musher gave that waiter would have melted the balls on a brass monkey. He lowered his hand and pinched the waiter's calf as hard as he could. The waiter limped towards the kitchen.

Hannah smiled and said, "You were going to tell me about yourself. I am waiting..."

"There's not much to tell. I was born in the North End of Boston. If you didn't have three vowels in your last name you weren't really welcome to live there. I graduated high school at age fifteen. I joined the Army finished basic training and I was at Advanced Infantry School when I asked to be transferred to the new United States Air Force gunnery school in Texas. More gunnery school in Colorado. Now here in the 351st Bomb Squadron. Don't drink much, smoke heavily and like to play cards and other gambling games. Don't have any concrete future plans. Know for sure that my future does not include any reenlistment. I am scheduled to be discharged in July 1950."

The waiter placed the salads and hot rolls on the table. Musher asked Hannah if she liked her iced tea sweetened or unsweetened. She answered by bobbing her head in favor of the unsweetened. "Please take the wine and the water glasses. Bring a pitcher of iced tea without any ice in the pitcher." The waiter noticeably limped as he went to the kitchen.

The dinner went well. Hannah asked to be excused. Musher rose to hold her chair as she rose. When she was out of earshot Musher motioned the waiter to come to him. He stood very close to the waiter and told him, "If you ever embarrass me again I will cut your heart out and suck the blood dry. Do you understand me?"

"Yes sir. Forgive me. Nobody told me who you are."

"When you bring my check make sure it is concealed in a folder."

Hannah returned and the waiter was right there to hold her chair. "What a nice polite waiter."

They passed on dessert and coffee. The waiter brought the check and Musher told him to wait there. He looked at the check and put bills in the folder. To the waiter," No need for change." When the waiter opened the folder to submit his payment for the table, he was dumbfounded to realize he had gotten an almost fifty-one dollar tip. He had never had such a tip, especially from a customer who would cut his heart out and suck the blood.

Musher looked starry-eyed at Hannah, "Would you be very upset if we skipped the movie? Why don't we go in the main bar, have a soda and dance a while? I have a heck of day tomorrow and I need to hit the sack early."

They sat at a table for two. He ordered from the waitress a coca cola for me and Hannah what for you? The same. Almost every other time the waitress would not be happy but she knew this was Musher and he takes care of the employees. The music was soft and slow. They danced on "the cuddly floor." After an hour of dancing Musher whispered to Hannah, "Why don't you call your dad to come for you? I am sorry I am such a drag but I promise to do better next time. There will be a next time won't there?"

"There will be if you want it to be." She went to call her dad. "He will be here in ten minutes. I want to thank you for a very, very wonderful evening. I look forward to our next date." She leaned forward and kissed him gently. They picked up her wrap and waited in the foyer. She recognized the family car and left for it. Musher could not see the driver and she blocked the driver from seeing him.

He had a very large dinner but was suddenly very hungry. He went back to the table where they had been. The same waiter came to him asking what he could do for him. "I'd like rye toast, well buttered and a pot of hot tea." The waiter stayed there and said, "I want to thank you for the gratuity. Again I apologize for earlier this evening." Musher nodded and the waiter left. The toast and tea satisfied his hunger but the way he felt about Hannah was puzzling. He didn't think of her as he does Lucy. Got to put those thoughts away. Get to bed and be razor sharp in the morning.

CHAPTER 65

The Last Day of School

Musher walked into the office shortly after 0600. He checked and rechecked the classroom setup to make sure everything was in its proper place. The work table was behind the student seating. The projector was on the table with the first can of film positioned to start. The second can was waiting under the table. The vu-graph was positioned next to the projector. The necessary vu-graphs were stacked in their order of appearance. Both units were tested to insure they were in good working order. Everything was ready.

Musher was outside smoking Luckies when Mister Leary approached and said, "Inside, we need to talk."

"Just before I left my house I got a call from the first sergeant. The Wing Commander, our Squadron Commander and the CSOps will be here to observe the gun film and the mission results. Are we ready for them?"

"We are as ready as any two guys with an impossible project to do in a limited amount of time can possibly be. If you cooperate with me and let me do all the talking unless a question is directly asked of you we will be fine. I need your help. I cannot do all the support things myself and you have not had enough time to study the mission results. Do we have a deal?"

The students started coming in at 0755. Please take your seat and we shall have a little discussion before our guests arrive to watch the gun film with us. The guests are the Wing CO, our Squadron CO and of course our CSOps. I tell you in advance none of you has anything to fear. Your combat reputation will remain in tact and your status among your peers will be severely elevated. The classroom door opened and three guests entered. Leary spoke a soft "Ten Hut" (In English, "Attention")

The Wing CO said, "As you were, Musher are you ready?"

"Yes Sir."

"Carry on and run your critique as if we were not here."

Musher explained to the class what they could expect to see for each shooting exercise. "Because of the records Mister Leary and I kept Friday I am able to tell you whoever the shooter is at the start of every new segment. At the end of each segment there is a summary of the particular shooting exercise just shown. We apologize for the fact that your crew coordination audio efforts were not recorded. Despite the fact that we mixed you up you functioned well as a shooting team. Mister Leary, Please turn off the lights and roll the film"

As the first film appeared on the screen Musher announced the shooter was Master Sergeant Lewis. He repeated his role until the film from the first can had finished. "Lights please. It will take a few minutes to load the second can. Please remain at your seat." It took three minutes to rewind, remove it from the projector and load the film into the first can. It took almost two minutes to have the second film in place. "Lights please, roll the film." The routine for the second film was the same as the first. Following what he knew to be the last summary screen Leary turned off the project and turned on the lights.

The Wing CO again, "Musher, did you and Mister Leary take a shooting turn?

"Yes sir."

"Is that film available for viewing?"

"Yes sir."

"Why have we not seen it?"

"Mister Leary and I did not believe it would make a meaningful contribution to the class."

"May I see it now?"

"Certainly sir. Lights please, roll the film. This first segment is my one bandit attack participation. The next segment will be Mister Leary's. He shot from a different firing position in the same bandit attack."

The film ended with Mister Leary's shooter summary. The Wing CO said, "Very impressive Musher, 98.7 percent hits per rounds fired. Mister Leary you did very well, 88.3 percent hits per rounds fired. Mister Leary has any gunner in this squadron shot equal to or better than 98.7 percent?" No Sir. "Has any gunner in the wing shot that well?" Some have shot in the high 80's and a few in the low 90's but no one ever shot 98 plus percent. "Musher did anyone of your students shoot better than you did?"

"Sir, If you can give us ten minutes we have some vu-graphs which statistically tell a story about each student. We have a compilation graph which shows the effectiveness of the mission."

"I would enjoy seeing and discussing those vu-graphs. First, do you mind if we take a twenty-minute break?"

When the three senior officers returned Musher put up the first vu-graph data sheet. They reviewed each shooters effort. The class average was 86.8 percent hits per rounds fired. Well over the current squadron average of 56.7 percent hits per round fired.

The next vu-graph showed the names of the shooters and the results of two bandit attacks. He advised the three guests that during these attacks the shooters were fully dressed in high altitude cold weather flying gear. There were only six such episodes. Musher explained, "The average for the six shooters was 80.1 percent hits per rounds fired."

The Wing CO spoke, "Gentlemen I am truly impressed. Your ground support, specifically the conversion of this room to a healthy learning environment, the acquisition of all the things you needed with the budget so tight and the impending closure of this base less than six months away makes your results even more impressive.

Your students, all veterans of the Army Air Corps and now the USAF have represented us old codgers with great enthusiasm and courage. Musher I want you to get with the AV (audio visual) people and design a certificate of completion for this training course. I and your squadron commander will authenticate the certificate by our signatures. That's it gentlemen, thank you for a great morning." As he headed for the door followed by the other two officers Mister Leary barked, "Ten Hut". When the Wing Commander passed by Musher he whispered, "The pudding certainly tasted good."

No sooner had the classroom door closed the class members were congratulating each other. The winner of the shooting pool was announced and he was given his one hundred dollars prize. "What say guys, squeet."

As usual the dining hall was clean and quiet. The class occupied three tables adjacent to each other. Musher was bombarded with questions like, "If you don't type where did you get the help on a weekend?" "Is there a pretty girl involved?" Unlike yesterday, everyone went through the serving line to select his lunch.

"Yes there is girl involved. A sweet lady I met at the base library "

"What's her name?"

"I don't her last name right now, but last night we had dinner at the Club. Her dad brought her to meet me for dinner and picked her up when she called. Her first name is Hannah."

The dining room became so quiet you could hear a bubble burst in a pan. "Do you want know who she is? Let's just say her last name is Crowley." Musher blanched

At closing of lunch the Dining Hall Supervisor was making his round asking about the food and the service. At Musher's table he asked the same questions and then spoke to Musher, "I am eager to hear your version of the Club confrontation.

"Right now I cannot stay, I must finish our last school day. Maybe tomorrow when I am here on KP we could find some time to talk?"

Leary darn near exploded. "Why didn't you tell me, you stay here while I will make a couple of phone calls. We will have that roster changed and maybe even permanently."

"Mister Leary please don't make any calls. Let me satisfy my obligations. To avoid a detail at the expense of a fellow airman would not sit well with me." Everyone in the dining room who had heard him, including those airmen on the serving line, rose and applauded him.

The bus returned them to the classroom. They just milled around doing nothing. Musher spoke, "It has been a fun week but now it is over. Leave all of our things on your desk and we will check them. If anything is not in the pile, you will hear from us. Meanwhile back to your crew and the real world. Again, thank you for being such good students." The students left and Musher, with Leary's help, inventoried the classroom supplies and placed them on the desks as if another class would begin tomorrow."

"I am going to call it a day. Do you want me to drop you at the squadron area?"

"I would much prefer you drop me at the club." Leary did just that.

Straight into the bar. "Double Jack with water back." He had heard someone else order that. He downed the whisky like they do in the cowboy movies and ordered, "Do it again." Between the time he finished the first drank and the second one came Musher could feel the effects of the first drink He headed for the latrine where he prayed to the porcelain god. Back in the bar he paid for his two drinks, one untouched, and left a good size tip for the bartender. The Club NCOIC recognized his unsteadiness and escorted him to a small room off the NCOIC's office. He laid Musher on the cot and Musher was gone. He knew he wasn't dead because of the moaning and groaning associated with the porcelain god.

Sometime later the NCOIC nudged him awake. "It's almost 1800 hours. You have been out for almost five hours. Some food will make you feel a lot better. They are bringing you toast and hot oriental tea."

"How did I get here? Where am I? Who are you?"

"All that in due time. Right now we must get you cleaned up and ready to play poker." There was a shower that went with the room. Musher felt better after the shower and the clean flying suit and undergarments which the NCOIC said were only on loan to him.

He was eating toast and drinking hot tea when the NCOIC said, "First, how did you get here. With some help I brought you to this room. You were so smashed you could hardly stand never mind walk. Second where are you? You are in the NCO Club in a very, very private room. The room is in my custody and control. Lastly who am I? My name is John Brewer. That is Master Sergeant John Brewer. I run this club, I am the NCOIC.

You didn't ask the most important question. Why would I do all this for you? I have one big reason. I want you to do something for me. There are two guys playing in the big game who I am sure are playing as partners. I can feel it, I can see the results of it. What I cannot do is prove it. I want you to sit in the game and prove it for me. Either an out-an-out confrontation where they vow never to play in any game in this club for ever and ever or, as an alternative you win all their money and all they come back with. You can rest assured what they may lose in one game is not the extent of their available cash. I will front two thousand dollars. If you lose it, my tough luck. If you win my share is twenty-five percent of the net winnings. Any questions?"

"Just a couple. What makes you so certain I can do this; and if I do, how long will you hold it over my head?"

"Musher I am one of the most influential enlisted men on this airbase. I live by my word. It would never be held over your head and if you choose not to do it there will never be another word from my lips regarding my offer to you."

"I'll do it. Meanwhile can I have something more to eat? "

"The restaurant is all yours but you must stay out of the bar for other than soda."

CHAPTER 66
The Game

Musher walked into the room, went straight to the Sergeant-At-Arms (SAA) and asked for a seat in the game. SAA recited the basic rules of the game. Musher didn't hear a word. He was looking for hidden cameras, clearly disguised mirrors or any strategically placed one sided reflective glass. He would have bet a hundred dollars that Brewer had some way to "spy" on the room's activities. The SAA escorted him to the table and introduced him to the other players as Airman Muscarello. It was obvious they knew he was Musher.

Everything on the table was cash. No chips, no checks, just good old American cash. Musher added his two thousand to the visible cash. This game is pot limit and no one has declared any more money in the game other than what one could see on the table. Of the six other players two looked like they were hanging on, two looked like they may be a little ahead if they bought in at the minimum and his two targets looked really flushed. The next two hours were for Musher ante, ante, win a small pot, ante, ante, and win a small pot. None of the pots he won were won when he was dealer.

"It's time to put some spice into the game. Five card stud gentlemen." He dealt each of the two weak sisters an ace in the hole and an ace up. One of his targets had King up, King in the hole. Musher and two of the other four players folded. Musher knew that the second target's hand would not beat a pair. First ace, small bet and he had three callers. Third card was no apparent help to anyone. This time first ace made a larger bet. Not so large as to intimidate another player. All called and the hand went on. Fourth card, no apparent help to the aces but Target 1 caught a king. Aces check, King bets half the pot. Target two folds, Aces call. Fifth and last card. Aces pair up on the board. Target 1 catches another king. Aces check to the bettor. First ace calls. Second ace folds. Target 1 shows three kings and draws down a healthy pot. Musher knew, he must first get Target 2 out of the game. Next time Musher dealt Target 2 was tapped out by Target 1 and went out of the game. It worked out well, none of the money left the game and was located exactly where Musher wanted it to be.

Two more hours passed and Musher was up by about two thousand dollars. Target 1 was steadily winning but the pots were small. Musher needed another pot or two to get his table money higher than Target 1. In about another hour Musher estimated he had about five hundred dollars more than Target 1. His next deal would be the time!!

Two hands later it was Musher's time to deal. "Five card stud". Four playable hands, one folder, Target 1 and Musher. First playable hand bet half the pot. Everyone called.

Third card paired the first playable hand, he bet half the pot again. Two hands folded, Target 1 called so did Musher.

Fourth card made playable's on board hand into three of a kind. Target 1 caught a queen to give him three queens on the board. Musher caught the deuce of diamonds. Playable went into the pot with all his money. Target 1 called the first bet and raised the rest of his money on the side. Much to his dismay, Musher called all the bets. Table stakes, there was no more money to raise.

Since there could be no more betting on this hand, Musher said, "Turn 'em up and let's look together."

Playable should have been out of this hand a long time ago. His last card gave him four of a kind on the board. Albeit a small four of a kind, it was four of a kind.

Target 1's last card was a Queen for four Queens.

Musher's last card was the five of diamonds. For a low straight flush in diamonds. He had done all could do tonight. He gathered up all his money and on his way out gave the SSA a hundred dollar bill.

He went to Brewer's office without speaking to anyone on the way.

"How did we do?"

"You know exactly how we did. I haven't spotted your spy method but before long I will. I take it as a personal insult that you feel you need to watch me as I work for me and you."

"Yes there is an observation method but it was used not because I don't trust you but because I don't trust the other players in the game. You have my word it will never be used for any game in which you play."

"Brewer, my modus operandi has no room for second chances. In this case I will make an exception. When I figure out how you do it and if I catch me being observed you would have wished you had retired the day before. Because the day I catch you will be your last day on this planet. I hope you believe me because it's the gospel truth. Let's divvy the cash."

The net profit was eight thousand seventy six dollars.

"You have your two thousand back plus your share of the net winnings which is two thousand nineteen dollars. Not a bad return, 100% in less than eight hours. Brewer, if you can, there are two somethings you might do for me. Something Number 1 - Let me store my cash in your safe. It is counted to seventy-five hundred dollars.

"Something Number 2 - Help me find a car that I can buy without being taken. My knowledge of cars is zero. Can you do these things for me?"

Brewer brought forth a bank deposit bag, counted the cash and traveler's checks and marked the bag, "Special Holdings". Made a receipt for Musher and asked when he wanted the car.

"ASAP"

"Is it about Crowley's daughter Hannah?"

"Yes."

"Let's get you the car and then we will take care of Crowley."

CHAPTER 67

My First KP Is a Pleasant Day

He couldn't shut off his small alarm quick enough. At 0400 hours your bunkmates would not be thrilled with the ringing. Still most of them had come in at awkward times and did not hesitate to turn on the barracks overhead lights. He dressed quickly, brushed his teeth and stepped into the night. The Lucky settled him down some. He went into the dining hall and reported to the Chief Cook.

"See that airman over there, he will be your partner today. Get your self some breakfast. You know how early we open for the squadron personnel."

As he approached the table the airman stood, stuck out his hand and announced that he was Airman Second Class (A2C) Thomas J. Flaherty, Son of the Leprechauns. My friends call me TJ, please do so."

Musher started to introduce himself but TJ interrupted. "I know you, you're the guy they call Musher. Is this your first KP here? It is really quite easy. In the Army KP was at least fourteen hours with almost no breaks and a bunch of pain in the ass permanent party personnel trying to hurry everybody along."

Not to be undone, Musher, "I spent sixteen weeks in the Army. I was in advanced infantry training when this opportunity came along. I was honorably discharged from the US Army and sworn in as an airman one minute later. I've done my sixteen hour KP duty cleaning sixty-four, not sixty-six grease traps."

They finished breakfast and Musher lit a smoke. TJ said he never smoked so Musher had a second Lucky for TJ and all the TJs in the world.

The Chief Cook briefed them on their duties in the dining room. TJ had done KP here before so he talked to Musher like the all time expert on KP. Musher had just become one of the silently moving people.

The serving line shut down at 0730 hours. Musher and TJ policed the dining room and reset the condiments for each table. The Chief Cook said, "Good work airmen. You are relieved but you must be back here at 1045 hours. Lunch is served from 1100 hours to 1330 hours."

TJ, "What do we do now? Maybe you could show me how to play some card games?"

Musher took out a deck of cards and showed TJ how to play friendly solitaire. "You practice that while I try to take a nap. Don't let me sleep later than 1030 hours." He dozed off while TJ talked to himself while playing solitaire.

During his serving "customers" in the dining room the first sergeant came to him. "I have already cleared it with the Dining Hall Sergeant for you to leave now. Get to your barracks SSS and be ready in my orderly room at 1250 hours. Our Squadron Commander, Mister Leary and you have been summoned to the Wing Commander's office for 1315 hours."

At 1315 hours sharply, the three entered the Wing Commanders office. Our squadron commander did the reporting. The summoned three, the Wing Commander (WCO) and his two senior officers sat at a large conference table. The WCO began, "There is no hiding how pleased I am with the results from the first class. Musher if you could teach ten in one class, could you teach fifteen in one class? Before you answer I want you to cut the course by one day if that will not ruin the plan and the results. If gun sights are a critical factor we could add another one to your resources. Lastly, another gunner came here with you from Lowry. We will reassign him to Mister Leary. Give me an answer."

"Sir we could do it. We may need a little more support."

"I don't recall you and Mister Leary asking for support help. Can you do it?"

"Yes sir."

"Good, do it. The next class will begin this coming Monday. I am glad this is settled. The 305th Bomb Wing will long be remembered for the quality of its aerial and navigator gunners. There is one last detail to do. Colonel Allison is the Wing Personnel Officer. Please let's all stand."

"Attention to orders. Effective this date Airman Second Class Saverio Muscarello, AF Serial Number 11186274 is hereby promoted to the grade of Staff Sergeant. Signed Brigadier General Alan Moore, US Air Force, Wing Commander, 305th Bomb Group."

The WCO, "Musher keep me proud of you. Bon Appetit."

Mister Leary dropped the squadron commanding officer at the orderly room and then he and Musher headed for the BX for new stripes and hat pin. Musher told him, "I can take it from here. Thank you for everything."

He pinned his new rank pin on his hat and headed for the NCO Club. Sergeant Brewer would not be in for at least one hour. Musher went into the bar and ate a club sandwich washed down with coco cola. Brewer found him in the bar listening to sad songs on the juke box and drinking coco cola as if it were bonded whisky.

"Are you ready for your car?"

"No, I don't have a driver's license. As matter of fact I don't know how to drive a car. Where I come from everyone uses the subway, street cars, busses or walks."

"OK that won't stop us from getting your car. We will teach you how do drive in your own car. Right now let's get you in some khaki's and go to town in my car so you can see if the one I chose is the one you want."

Musher took one look and was in love. It was a two door convertible, sky blue with white wall tires and a rumble seat.

"We will pick it up first chance we get."

"What did it cost me?"

"Right now automobiles are very scarce and the new ones are bringing a price far greater than seems logical. Your car was built in 1942. The owner was drafted into the Army about two weeks after he bought the car. He put the car in the family garage and it has been there ever since. When I put the word out that I was looking for a car, another friend knew of your car and bought it from the mother for six hundred dollars. It is on a car lot because car lot owners have repair license tags they can put on a car and the police will not stop the car for anything minor. It will cost you seven hundred dollars. The extra hundred is split between the guy who bought the car and this car lot owner. I could have gotten out of the extra hundred but it seemed like a low price to keep these contacts in your favorable listing."

"So when do I get my car?"

"As soon as I get a person with a drivers' license to go with me to pick it up. We will park it in the NCO Club parking lot in the reserved spot next to my reserved spot. Every evening after dinner while it is still daylight I will teach you how to drive and the rules of the road. Right now let's go back to the club for an early dinner so you can get back to making us some money."

CHAPTER 68

Hannah My Love

It took one long session for Musher to learn the clutch gas pedal relationship and the clutch gear shift relationship so that he could change gears without the transmission sounding as if it were going to grind the teeth from the gears. By the end of the first week Musher had the driving system down pat and was doing a good job when driving. Brewer took him to Salina in Musher's car for his State of Kansas driving license test. He passed the eye test, maxed the written test and the driving test went well enough to pass. Fortunately for Musher in small towns most parking is pull in diagonal. No telling how well he would have done with parallel parking. Price of the license: Two dollars for one year. Renewable without retesting.

Two steps left: Get insurance coverage and license tags. The State Farm agent was very helpful. He laid out a policy that would protect Musher from any catastrophic incidents. Cost: forty-five dollars a year. Next door was the State of Kansas car license plate office. Cost fifteen dollars a year. The car lot where the car had been was on the way to the airbase. A short stop to swap the dealer plates for his new Kansas plates. Brewer led the way to the airbase while Musher with the top down and the radio blasting cruised as if he were on a vacation. His final stop was at Pass and Registration at the Main Gate entrance. Here they would record his data in the base automobile log and place a sticker on his windshield which would allow the car to pass in and out of the main gate without vehicle inspection. He was also issued an airbase book of vehicle rules.

For about a half hour Musher, being very careful not to exceed the speed limits which could get your car banned from the airbase, simply drove around the air base showing off his new car. He parked in the reserved spot at the NCO Club. He was ready for some food and the game.

In Brewer's office he retrieved his cash stash, paid Brewer for his out laid cash and kept three hundred for pocket change. He consumed a T Bone, smoked a couple of Luckies and headed for The Game Room. Sergeant-at-Arms told him he was second on the waiting list but he would find him in the club when a seat was available to him. Musher went to the kibitizer's rope and studied the players. Over two hours went by before Musher was seated at the table. As he sat down three of the players rose and left. The SSA said he had no players on the waiting list. Did these four players want to continue the game? "Very well, if anyone comes to join I shall bring him here immediately."

These were good poker players. There was no semblance of any unethical behavior. There were no partners. No other players joined the game. Around midnight Musher was up in the six hundred dollar range. "Sorry gentlemen, I must go. Busy day tomorrow. Hope we can do this again some time soon." He skipped going to Brewer's office, got in his car and headed for the barracks vehicle parking lot. The barracks was dark. He went into the latrine to count and separate the cash. He put all the cash in his foot locker and crawled into the sack. Sleep did not come easy thinking of his car and Hannah

CHAPTER 69

Prepare For Fifteen

Musher was at the office at 0700 hours. Mister Leary came in just after 0700 hours. His first question, "Has anybody seen your new stripes?"

"Not yet but they will. Mister Leary the first thing we need to do is figure out how much more of what will we need. Also the syllabus must be changed to reflect it will be a five day course not six. Do you think you could get us a typewriter with a good ribbon, bond paper, carbon paper and plenty of white out to correct our mistakes?"

"Trust me Sergeant Muscarello I will succeed." Did that sound funny? Sergeant Muscarello.

"One of us must talk with CSOps for a second gun sight. You would do better at that than I would. I hope your friends in the photo lab kept the negatives because we need seventeen more notebook fillers. Then you will need to impose on your printing friends to punch and fill the notebooks. I will speak to Sgt Dooley about getting us eighteen jeweler's cases. We can handle the class with the six we have but if we have priority now let's make our wish list long. With the exception of yellow pads and the notebooks our consumables are good for the next class. I need to take my instructor sign to Sergeant Driver to have it changed and a new one made for A2C Philip Dexter who will join us today. He was in my class at Lowry. He was a good student We will see how good he is at training other gunners. Unless you have something else you must do now would be a good time to get started on your scavenger hunt. Remember, the typewriter et al is the most important item to get as quickly as possible."

A voice from the office, "Is anyone here?"

"We are in the classroom."

"I am A2C Phillip Dexter. I have been reassigned to the 351st Squadron Gunner. Are you CWO Leary?"

"I am. This is Staff Sergeant Muscarello known to all of us as Musher."

Dexter blurted, "Staff Sergeant?" "Yes staff sergeant and he is your immediate supervisor."

Musher, in his most severe tone, "Phillip, do you have a problem with that?"

Dexter remembered Piute and Lowry, "No sergeant, no problem at all."

Leary went on his way. "Phil, do you smoke?"

"No sergeant."

"Come sit with me while I smoke." They went out and sat on the classroom steps. "Phil, do you type?"

"Yes sergeant."

"Are you any good?"

"Yes sergeant."

"That's very good. When Mister Leary comes back with the typewriter and supplies we will fix you a place in the office and in addition to being a gunnery instructor you will be our clerk. Our next class begins next Monday. For that class you will take all the training the students take; however, you will not be listed as a student. You will be an observer. You will not do classroom instruction until you and I believe you are ready. We will make sure you get enough flying time to get your flight pay. Do you have a G.I. driver license for government vehicles? Do you have any problem with any of what I have said?"

"No problem sergeant. Yes I do have a license to drive government vehicles up to the size of a six–by and forty-four passenger bus."

"Let's go back in and work on making a presentable classroom for fifteen students." The student chairs were arranged in three rows of five. It suddenly hit Musher, "Where's your gear?"

"I stopped by the barracks and dropped it off on an empty bunk". Musher thought, that's a good sign he can think beyond one step. They juggled the office furniture until there was a desk for Mister Leary and a desk which Musher and Dexter would share. The two phones had one placed on each desk. There were only three chairs in the office. Musher was sure Leary could solve that problem and if not Sergeant Dooley could. The single closet held the one file cabinet and places to hang clothes. There was so much junk in the closet but Musher was hesitant to discard it until Mister Leary gave his approval.

"What say Phil are you hungry? We can easily walk to the flight line dining hall. Bye the way Phil, everyone including the Wing Commander calls me Musher in a most respectful manner."

In the dining hall they were joined by Mister Leary and Musher's friend Staff Sergeant Halloran. Halloran looked at the staff sergeant pin on Musher's hat and softly exclaimed, "Seven months in the military and promoted from Airman nothing to Staff Sergeant. How many blow jobs and to whom did you give them, or did you just simply beat them up until they promoted you?"

Mister Leary took offense and started to rise from his chair. Musher's hand settled him back into his chair.

During the exchange Phil sat simply staring. All he had heard about Musher since they both came to Smoky Hill was that Musher was a hell of pool player and one hell of a card player. He knew nothing of the aerial gunner training program and the magnitude of its success. He did not know that from the Wing Commander down everyone knew that Mister Leary had the rank but Musher had the skills and personality to be a leader.

"Bob I want you to meet the newest member of our squadron, Phil Dexter, Bob Halloran. He will be working with Mister Leary and me. He's already staked a claim for a bunk in the barracks."

In the hopes of ending Halloran's speech, Musher laughed, "I can't help it if the brass recognizes a born leader and an excellent member of the USAF. Sorry Bob, eat your heart out." To himself echoed Rob, "Fuck 'em and feed 'em frijoles."

Mister Leary lightened the conversation. "I had a great morning. We now have a Royal Typewriter, lots of bond paper, carbon paper and a particularly large amount of mistake correcting whiteout."

Musher looked at Phil and Mister Leary, "I'm done. If you are let's go see Sergeant Dooley."

"Sergeant Dooley this is A2C Phillip Dexter. He is the newest member of our squadron working with Mister Leary and me. Musher lied, "It's important to me that you know that when we were in the Wing Commander's office being praised we told him of your major contribution to the success of the first training class. I have another short list of things we need. The class size has been raised to fifteen and the number of days in the training course reduced to five. Can you help us out again?"

"Come see me in the morning. Bring some kind of transport."

Riding to the office Musher asked Mister Leary, "Do you think we have enough clout to get a weaps from the motor pool for the training program? Dexter has a G.I .license for up to a six-by and a 44 person bus."

After the goodies were unloaded into the office and the closet materials re-arranged or discarded Mister Leary picked up the phone to make a call. He motioned to Musher and Dexter to listen on the other phone. The phone was answered with "305th Bomb Wing Motor Pool, you call, we haul, we got two bys, four bys, six bys and them big mothers which go shoo-shoo-shoo and bend in the middle, Technical Sergeant Jefferson Carter here, may I help you?"

"Jefferson (he liked being called Jefferson) this is CWO Leary. Have you heard about the aerial gunnery training program we are running here?"

"Yes Sir."

"Jefferson, I need the full time use of a weapons carrier for the next eighteen days. Can you help me out?"

"Mister Leary, does that fellow called Musher work for you?"

"Yes he does."

"Here's my deal, Musher plays me a one hundred point straight pool game at 1400 hours this coming Saturday afternoon. No bags, no intentional misses, his best talent. The stakes, twenty-five dollars. If it looks to me that he is bagging the game, I take back my vehicle."

"Sergeant Musher will be there. I will be over shortly with a licensed vehicle driver to sign the papers. Look for me in thirty minutes."

Leary told Musher the deal. He took Dexter and off they went to the motor pool. They were back in less than thirty minutes. Leary, "Here are the rules. The vehicle stays parked here at the office. When we use it will be for an official purpose and the vehicle log will be maintained. Dexter this vehicle is to be washed every day. Nothing is to be left in the vehicle overnight. The keys will remain in the center draw of my desk. Any questions? Good. I am going to the shack to see the CSOps. Most probably we shall get the second gun sight tomorrow. From the CSOps I am going to the photo lab and then to the printing shop. From the printing shop I am going home, I will see you in the morning."

"What say Phil, enough for you for today? It is for me. Let's button up and go to the squadron. We'll skip the wash of the weaps today. After we clean up I will take you to your old squadron so you can check your mail. It will give me a chance to use my car."

"You have a car? With you on the airbase?"

"Yes my car is not a new car but my license plate is a new State of Kansas license plate" They cleaned up and decided that after checking Dexter's mail they would go to the NCO Club for dinner. Musher made it clear, "There is no check it is already taken care of."

Musher ordered his usual but this time for two. T-Bone steaks, medium rare, small baked potato, salad and two dinner rolls. Tonight was square dancing night at the club. Musher had only seen it in the movies and wanted to see it for real. With the coffee he lit a Lucky Strike and said, "Dexter, tell me about yourself."

"I am from a small town in Utah. Couldn't afford to go to college so I thought I would join the Army and at the end of my hitch I would be eligible for the G.I. bill. Always thought I wanted to be a veterinarian. I have a girl back in Utah I hope to marry. I am of the Mormon faith. The Army was tragic. Grabbed the first opportunity to get away from the Army and that was to transfer to the new US Air Force. That's when I first saw you at

Piute. At both Piute and Lowry you were what I wanted to be, smart, tough and fearless. I went to Utah on my leave and that is why you got to Smoky a week before I did. I've been the flunky gunner in the 353rd while the senior gunners could not hit their ass with both hands. When I was reassigned to Mister Leary I never suspected that I would be working for Staff Sergeant Saverio Muscarello, the Musher. That sums up my nineteen years" Musher realized Dexter was almost two years older than he was.

Musher noticed that every dancer had on a costume. Most men and women were wearing cowboy hats ranging from low cost straw to high cost Stetsons. The music was interesting and the Dance Caller sounded like something out of a Tom Mix movie. A full hour went by before Musher and Dexter were ready to leave. Musher noticed one of the dancers was Master Sergeant Crowley. He did not see Hannah.

In the car headed for the barracks Musher asked if Dexter had seen the posters in the latrine telling of Saturday's straight pool match.

"I don't see how anyone could miss them. No telling how many more places in the club where they are posted."

They sat in the car in the barracks parking lot. Musher explained, "In the days of dueling each duel participant had what was called "a second." The second was someone charged to insure the dueling weapons were of the type agreed by the participants, look out for his dueler's welfare and if there was a breach of conduct by his dueler's opponent he stepped in and took over for his dueler. For this Saturday's match I need a second. There will be no weapons to check and surely you will not be expected to take over for me. Do you play pool? Good, then you can see when the racked balls are not on the correct spot or not tightly positioned when the rack is removed. Your most important job as my second will be to make the betting slips by which we keep track of my bets and give the SSA enough money to cover the bets. We will offer me as an eight to one favorite. If there are no takers at that price you may go to ten to one, and as a last resort twelve to one. Take any bet of one dollar of more. All bets must be in even dollars. I will give you seventy-five hundred dollars to cover bets. You must keep the money in a box along with the betting slips. We will pick up a cash box at the BX tomorrow. Do not accept bets where you do not receive the bettor's cash before issuing a bettor's receipt. Betting will stop five minutes before the break of the first rack. The SSA will sit beside you and accumulate the betting slips and the cash. If you run out of money to cover bets just announce that the bank has been tapped. Did you follow all that? Is there anything you want me to go over again? Yes, No, I knew you were bright.

What say we go SSS and get some rest. Tomorrow is Wednesday and we must be totally ready by the end of Friday."

CHAPTER 70
It's So Much Better the Second Time Around

The training syllabus must be adjusted for the new schedule.

ADJUSTED TRAINING SYLLABUS

DAY 1 -   Introduction to the Training Program and Its Guidelines A
           Cursory Review of the Training NotebookThe RCS CFSC
           Gun Sight
DAY 2 -   The RCS CFCS Gun Sight
DAY 3 -   MorningThe Jewelers Case, Its Tools and UsesThe Care
           and Maint of the RCS CFCS Gun SightAfternoonFlight
           Line Exercise Calibrating the
           RCS CFSC Gun Sight
DAY 4 -   A B-29 Film Shooting Flight with Bandits Attacking
DAY 5 - Review of the Gun Camera Film and Critique of the
Mission, Unsigned Student Evaluation of the Course and Instructors

There was no need to change the outside cover of the notebook. He
would need eight more. He gave Dexter copies of the old syllabus and the
old notebook cover page. He told him that he wanted them all as originals.
Dexter set up at the type writer and started banging away. By 1000 hours
Dexter was finished and the work looked good. Somehow or other he would
have preferred to watch Hannah do the typing. He must find out what is
going on with her.

Mister Leary had come in while Dexter was typing and he had all the
additional consumables that were needed. The notebook insert pages would
be finished by 1500 hours. If he could get them to the printing shop they
would be ready by 1000 hours tomorrow. This afternoon Musher and Dexter
could take the weaps and go get the additional gun sight. Everything was
falling in place. It was time to see Sergeant Dooley.

Leary and Musher took the weaps and went to squadron supply. Musher
told Dexter to look for things that could make the place look cleaner and
better. Dooley helped loading the items that he was asked for. Sergeant
Dooley, "We are two student chairs short for the class. Can you help us
out?" Dooley told them to standby he would be right back. He returned with
a paper in his hand. "Go to this building, see this man and he will take care
of you. I trust this is the end."

"One last thing, could you spare three bed sheets so we can protect the gun sights when not in use?" He returned and threw them on the weaps. Leary and Musher profusely thanked him as he turned and walked back into squadron supply.

"How did you make out at the sheet metal shop?"

"Driver said they would be ready this morning. Let's stop there on the way to the office."

Driver's second in command said, "He took them to your place less than five minutes ago."

To no one's surprise they were hung in the front of the classroom. Driver was sitting in a chair in the back of the classroom admiring his work. Musher went to thank him and all he had to say was, "I always wanted to be a fly boy, at least this way I can contribute to those who fly." Only heaven knows how many fly boy lives he saved with the sheet metal quality work his shop provided.

The weaps was unloaded. The materials were placed in their proper place. The classroom looked very, very good. "Let's squeet". At the lunch table the three went over, and over, and over all the things which were done or had to be done for Monday morning class.

Dexter drove and waited in the weaps while Musher went into the shack to get the aircraft designation and its parking place. The board showed aircraft 120, parked in the P Patch, Remarks: Removal of one gun sight. As he started to leave he was hailed by Sergeant Wooly. "Congratulations on your promotion. Your first class has spoken so well of you every gunner in the squadron feels you deserve it. When your program slows come work with me. You would probably make one hell of chief operations clerk. Good luck with new class. If I can help, please ask."

"Thank you Sergeant Wooly, you are very kind."

Back in the weaps he guided Dexter to the P Patch until they found 120. Standing at the nose were two men, one of whom was Master Sergeant Long, Crew Chief of 121. They dismounted and went to the two men.

Sergeant Long was the first to speak, "This is the Crew Chief for 120 and one of my closest friends, Master Sergeant Theodore Ferrante. Teddy this is Staff Sergeant Saverio Muscarello, better known as Musher" Musher spoke, "Sergeant Long, Sergeant Ferrante this is A2C Phillip Dexter. We came from the Army at the same time, went to both gunnery schools at the same time and he is now in the same squadron as I." There was a lot of hand shaking going on.

"Sergeant Long, Why are you here?"

"One, it gives me the chance to congratulate you on your promotion; two, I am right next door and you don't think I would let my hero come near without trying to be some help. Teddy and I have the APU running and the air conditioning blowers on. Maybe it will make it cooler for you and your partner. The hatch is open, the ladder is in place and there is a jug of ice water and some cups in the compartment."

"Thank you both very much, is it OK if we get started now?" With that they went after the gun sight. Musher let Dexter remove the gun sight while he watched. Dexter did very well, wrapped the gun sight in a sheet and they left the compartment. At the hatch Musher climbed down and Dexter passed him the gun sight and then the water and cups.

"We appreciate your help."

Sergeant Long, "Musher can't you stay for a Lucky Strike or two and tell us about the pool match on Saturday."

"As soon as you do what you have to do with this aircraft and we get this gun sight secure in the weaps we will meet you out on the grass." Those two Master Sergeants moved like greased lightning. All four were sitting in the grass and Teddy was the first to speak. "I am not a member of the Crowley fan club. He is a vindictive, arrogant son-of-a-bitch. Rumor says you and his daughter Hannah had a dinner date for which he drove her to the NCO Club without knowing who her date was. Have you spoken to her since and has he spoken to you since he found out who her date was?"

"No and no."

Sergeant Long, "Tell us about the pool match."

Musher told them the deal on their promise of absolute silence until the match is over.

"The stake is twenty-five dollars?"

"Jefferson set the stake."

"How about side bets?"

"Dexter will handle the money with the SSA. We are offering eight to one but will go as high as twelve to one. We are presenting seventy-five hundred dollars. That's the sum and substance of the pool match. We must get back to the office."

In the office the new gun sight was placed on the work bench. Dexter was to disassemble, check the parts and reassemble. He did it smoothly and without hesitation. He's a doer let's hope he is a teacher.

Musher used one of his Lowry authorizations to get Lesser on the phone. "This is Sergeant Lesser."

"This is Staff Sergeant Muscarello."

"There was a pause and then, "Say again, who is this?"

"Thanks to you this is Staff Sergeant Muscarello. Our first training class was such a success. The individual average hits per round before the class was fifty plus percent and after the class rose to an individual hits per round of eighty plus percent. We are increasing our student class size from ten to fifteen and shortening the class by one full day. The next class begins Monday with five gunners from each of the three bomb squadrons in the wing. A2C Dexter who was with us in your class is now a member of our staff in the training program. We ordered jeweler's cases but as you know they will be slow coming." He lied with a straight face, "I am working with my superiors to have you recognized as the impetus for this program. How is it with you?"

"I am now a tech sergeant and doing well in our school. If one of those 29's is coming to Lowry jump on and we will celebrate your promotion and mine. Been on long time must get off. Good luck, keep me posted."

"Dex, there's not much more we can do here today. Why don't you go gas up and wash the weaps. I will wrap it up and we will call it a day. We still have Thursday and Friday for the final touches"

Dexter returned, they secured the area and headed for the base bus. At the barracks Musher got in his car. "Dex, I am going to the club. Want to come?" "Hop in." At the club they ate and again Musher paid the check. "Dex I need to talk to the club NCOIC. I won't be long. Wait for me in the pool room."

"Well hello Sergeant Brewer. Long time no see. Listen I am sure you know about the pool match Saturday. I will need seventy-five hundred dollars as bet money. I am about fifteen hundred short. Advance me the money and you get your usual cut after expenses."

"Done. When do you want it?"

"Noon Saturday. See you later."

In the pool room all the tables were full. Musher walked to the center table, "I need to practice would you mind letting me use this table?"

"Please."

"Is that a house cue?"

"Yes"

"Mind if I use it?" Thank you.

For the next hour Musher practiced rail banks, kick shots, billards and high powered English. Most of the play in the pool room had stopped to watch him practice. He played rotation and practiced position on a ball other than the next one in the rotation. Some of the spectators made a slight noise when he missed or his position from the ball he needed to make was terrible. He and Dexter walked out of the club and he pointed his car towards the dining hall for dinner. After dinner he played pinochle for about three hours. Throughout the games he was bombarded with questions about Hannah and the pool match. He just ignored them all. SSS and off to bed

CHAPTER 71
We're Ready For the Fifteen

Today is Thursday and the class does not begin until Monday. When the notebooks are completed today everything that is needed will be on hand. It has been checked and doubled checked. Certainly Mister Leary and Dexter can finish those tasks. "Mister Leary, can I have today off?"

"Anything special Musher?"

"Today is the first day we can wear civilian clothes providing we do not mix them with our uniform garments. Uniform shoes are OK to use but that is about all. I would like to go buy some civilian clothes and play civilian all day. I have a Class A pass. I will be here at 0700 hours tomorrow."

"All right Musher. If you get hung up somewhere just be sure to be here by 1600 hours tomorrow afternoon. The barracks G.I. party begins at 1900 hours and there is a squadron inspection and parade Saturday morning. I am sure Dexter and I can hold down the fort. Be careful out there. I need to go see Sergeant Dooley. I will give you a ride to the squadron area."

He picked up his "emergency" bag and decided to stop at the BX to fill it. As he stopped at the front gate for the Air Policeman (AP) to check his pass and dog tags, the AP warned him, "There are state troopers on the road to town looking for speeders." As he passed the two sate troopers sitting on their motorcycles on the side of the road he waved a hello.

In the general mercantile store he bought a shirt with pearl buttons, a pair of Levis, a tooled belt with a fancy buckle, a pair of socks, a straw cowboy hat and a pair of stovepipe boots with walking heels. Total cost was fifty-six dollars. He paid and asked if there was a place he could change clothes. The storekeeper pointed to a curtained area. When Musher came out he looked like a different man. I doubt if anyone would take him for a cowboy but in a group he could meld. In his car to add to his cowboy image he put a Bull Durham makings in his breast pocket with the string hanging out. He checked his cash, he was all right, he still had over two hundred dollars. He topped his tank at the local station (fourteen cents a gallon) and bought a state atlas. He would head east to Topeka.

He gawked at all the different looks along the highway. He stopped in Junction City to find some sun glasses, bad enough cowboys rarely wore sun glasses much less alone metal framed aviator glasses. He put his clothes, his sun glasses and his emergency bag in the rumble seat and locked it closed.

No telling who might wander by and like what he saw. He was sure that some of these people specialized in items which fell off trucks.

In the drug store he bought a three dollar fifty cent pair of the darkest glasses he could find Outside the drug store he saw a window painted brightly with "Snooker, Dominoes, Sandwiches and Beer". There were no parking meters on the street so he sauntered into the emporium. The place was a beehive. Four tables of Dominoes, two snooker tables and a lunch bar with about eight seats. An older man came up to him, "Something I can help you with son?"

"I'd like to get a sandwich and a coke and I'd like to watch the domino players if that's all right."

"What kind of sandwich? It's fine if you watch but do not speak. These boys get sensitive over losing fifty cents. Do you play dominoes?"

"No I don't."

"I will explain the game while you eat your sandwich."

The explanation of the rules of the game took about two minutes and in five minutes more Musher had heard the basic playing techniques. He had just finished eating when a player at one of the tables left. One of the three remaining players asked him if he wanted to join. "Yes I would but I am just learning."

"That's OK, we play as individuals and if you can afford to lose the money you'll never get cheaper lessons." Musher sat down. "You settle up when you leave." They played and played and played. Musher lost virtually every game. He looked at his watch and it was almost five in the afternoon. (Military time is on vacation). He had enough dominoes lessons for one day. "Gentlemen I must leave. Where is the hotel? How much do I owe?"

"Well son there ain't no hotel in this town. You owe a total of twenty-one dollars and twenty-five cents. There is a boarding house where you can get a room for the night and darn good supper and breakfast." He wrote the name of the place and the street address on a piece of paper. "Tell her the domino players vouch for you." Musher put twenty-two dollars on the table and he got back three quarters. "Thank you guys, I hope we can do it again sometime."

A young woman answered the door. Musher explained his needs and she told him two dollars for the room, one dollar fifty cents for supper whether you eat or not and one dollar for breakfast whether you eat or not. If that's you car park it around back, I'll wait for you here." He did as he was told. She was waiting at the door. "Four dollars fifty cents in advance.

She showed him to a room. The toilet is at the end of the hall. You can come to the kitchen if you want to fill your wash basin pitcher. The key is in the lock. When you leave the room carry your key. We are not responsible for any missing items. Supper is at six thirty."

There were five other people seated at the table. No one paid much attention to him. Supper was glorious, fried chicken, mashed potatoes, corn on the cob and apple pie with coffee for dessert. Most stayed to smoke cigarettes and have more coffee. One of the persons who stayed asked Musher if he was a poker player. "I am but I am not sure I play very well."

"We play five card draw jacks or better. No wild cards. Ante five cents, open for ten cents, three raise limit. Each player deals a hand in his turn. You would be the sixth player in the game. We deal last round at 10:30. Are you interested in joining us?"

"I am most interested and appreciate you offering me the chance to play the game. As I said I don't play well but I enjoy the game immensely."

A quip came from the adjoining room, "For your sake, sure hope you play better poker than you play dominoes." As the last round started Musher calculated he was two dollars thirty-five cents ahead. During the final round he managed to lose four dollars thirty-five cents. Everyone was getting up to leave and one of the players remarked to Musher, "With some help and experience you could become a decent poker player."

The bed was not the greatest but as tired as Musher was it felt wonderful.

It was not even light when a loud knock came on his door. "Breakfast in thirty minutes. One sitting. Miss breakfast and all you can get is coffee."

He dressed, hit the toilet and went down for breakfast. The same five men were sitting at the table. Breakfast was more like a dinner than a breakfast. Chicken fried steak, mashed potatoes, gravy, home made biscuits and butter. There were large pots of coffee sitting on the table. Without realizing it he ate like a man who was going out to do ten hours physical labor. All the other diners were dressed to go out and do ten hours of physical labor. Each one made a complementing remark as he left the table, "Great breakfast Miss Priscilla; Ain't had nothing so good in years, thank you Miss Priscilla" and so on.

At least he now knew her name. She was in her early twenties with a pretty face and an even prettier body. He sat and smoked as she cleaned the table. He was tempted to help but he knew that would not be very cowboyish. He gathered his things, came down and called "Miss Priscilla". She answered, "I am in the kitchen."

"I didn't want to leave without telling you how much I enjoyed my stay at your place. If you hadn't guessed I am stationed at Smoky Hill AFB. From time to time I get a three day pass and I am so content with my less than twenty–four hour stay I would like to come back and stay longer. Do you have a business card with your name and telephone number so I could call ahead to make sure you had room for me."

"No business cards but let me write the information on a piece of paper." She handed the paper, stuck out her hand, "We enjoyed having you. I hope you do come back again." The pressure of her hand shake and the glimmer in her eyes told him he would be coming back again.

He drove cautiously to Smoky. The AP checked his car sticker, his Class A pass and his dog tags before letting him through the gate. He parked in the squadron lot and walked to the barracks. He didn't pass anyone he knew. When he entered the barracks the cat calls began, "Howdy Tex Musher", "Where are your six guns Tex", "Can you really roll that Bull Durham hanging from your pocket" and there were more. Musher ignored them all. He stripped and hung his new clothes and placed his boots properly in the row beneath his bunk. With towel and shaving kit he headed for the latrine for his SSS. When he returned to the barracks (remember the latrine is about fifty yards from the barracks) the cat calls began again. He ignored them again. He set his alarm clock for 1600 hours, crawled into his sack and went soundly to sleep.

The alarm clock caused him to jump. Like all nicotine addicts before anything else he lit a cigarette and sat on his foot locker while he gained his composure. The bay was busy with individuals preparing for dinner or the 1900 hours G.I. party. He dressed and was walking to the mess hall when he was joined by Airman Dexter. "Dex, how are you here so early today?"

"Mister Leary let me go at 1400 hours."

"Is everything done that needed doing?" Yes sergeant.

There was no conversation between them until they had taken their food and unloaded it onto a table. Like a hound after the fox, within thirty seconds Sergeant Halloran joined them. To Musher, "Where did you go? Where did you stay overnight? Was there a woman involved?"

"Please Bob give me a break. I hardly slept at all last night."

"So there was a woman."

Since everyone was present and the two barracks airmen volunteered to do the latrine with four other airmen from other barracks, our barracks chief suggested the G.I. Party begin early. When the first sergeant came by to see how things were going the G.I. Party was just about finished. He did a walk through inspection and declared the barracks passed. Get a good nights sleep this place must be A-OK for the group inspectors tomorrow. We fall in for the parade at 0800 hours. Goodnight gentlemen."

Musher worked on his personal belongings making sure that no inspector would write him up for any reason.

CHAPTER 72
Two Parades

Breakfast in the dining hall, squared away his barracks area and went outside to smoke cigarettes until it was time to fall in. In no way was he going to dirty the butt cans before inspection. The squadron formed and the first sergeant carried the guidon. The squadron marching skills did not in any way frighten the base drill team, but for fly boys they were in step and pretty good. The number of speeches was few and it seemed in thirty minutes or less he heard *"Pass In Review."* After passing the reviewing stand and General Morehouse the squadron headed back to it area. The squadron commander who had led the squadron through the parade, "You men did a good job. Dismissed."

Musher grabbed Dexter and in Musher's car they went to the NCO Club. Musher's staff sergeant stripes stuck out like a fluorescent colored light. He left Dexter in the bar while he visited the Club NCOIC. Brewer handed him an envelope containing seventy-five hundred dollars. Another envelope containing four inch by four inch blank white papers. Musher counted the fading money and sealed the envelope. Brewer handed him a cash box. The tray on top had two stacks of betting slips. The bottom was reserved for accepting the Musher copy of the betting slips and the cash received from the bettors. The seventy-five hundred dollars fading money was in a sealed envelope was also in the bottom of the cash box. Yesterday Musher had shown Dexter how to keep cumulative score of their exposure on a yellow pad. He did not think the side bets would be that high but one never knows. This was a mutually exclusive contest, either you win or you lose. There is no tie.

The NCOIC, Musher and Dexter went into the pool room. There was hardly any room to stand much less alone sit. The NCOIC spoke, "Gentlemen this is the first of this kind of head-to-head match we have had in this club. The referee for this match will be Master Sergeant Crowley. He will also double as the racker. The game is straight pool and all the rules and ethics of straight pool shall apply. Sergeant Crowley is authorized to disqualify either player for a valid reason. Each ball called and made is one point. The first player to reach one hundred points is the winner. The players will lag for break. The worse of the two lags will be the breaker. We have about fifteen minutes before the match begins. A2C Dexter sitting at the table next to the shooting table will accept bets for the next ten minutes."

"Staff Sergeant Muscarello is offering eight to one to anyone who thinks he will not win." Very few bettors came forward to bet against Musher. Dexter, "We will now offer ten to one to any one who thinks Staff Sergeant Musher will not win." A few dribbles. Dexter again, "We will now offer twelve to one to anyone who thinks Musher will not win. Final offer, this book closes in three minutes." There were no takers.

A voice came from the audience, what kind of odds do you want to say you will beat him by fifty points?"

"How much money are you willing to bet?"

"Five thousand dollars."

"I will take that bet at even money. Put your money where your mouth is. He turned to Dexter, "Take five thousand and give it to the NCOIC after you see big mouth give the same amount to the NCOIC." The room was so quiet you could have heard a fart. Dexter looked to Musher and nodded his head. The bet was down.

The players lagged for break and Musher lost. He made his standard break which left Jefferson without a shot. Jefferson played an excellent safety. Musher could not see a shot so he too played a safety. Jefferson could not see a shot so he played another safety. This tactic went on until Jefferson's tenth attempt at a safety. He made a tiny error but it was enough to free two balls and leave the cue ball in the open. Musher walked around the table studying the open balls and the rack. Neither open ball offered a shot which could be made and open the rack at the same time. Musher announced, "Thirteen in the side off a billard from the twelve." The thirteen was on the far side of the rack from the twelve ball and the cue ball. Musher made his stroke and sure enough the thirteen ball rolled into the side pocket. A large burst of applause, even Jefferson was tapping his cue for an excellent shot.

Musher went to work. Seven straight racks for a total of ninety-eight points and Jefferson could do no more than watch. On the eighth rack Musher made the object ball and broke the rack open as he had been doing. There were two balls almost in one corner pocket. He made one and the other hung on the edge. He thought, "Maybe I should end this with class and kick it in off three rails?" The voice inside was Fanucci's, "Remember why you are playing this game. For the money. Not to prove what a great player you are. Never risk the most important thing, the money." Musher called the easy shot and sunk it without fanfare.

The applause began and Crowley called, "The winner is Staff Sergeant Muscarello. Final score, Muscarello one hundred, Technical Sergeant Carter zero." Jefferson came to Musher, "It was worth the twenty-five dollars to see you work. I doubt that I could ever beat any man who can take advantage of one mistake and run the game. That is the finest shooting I have seen in all my life and I have spent a lot of my life in pool rooms." Next came Crowley with his hand extended to shake. "Musher, I hope you can overlook our previous meetings and start again from here. I can certainly understand how a shooter who is as good as you are could be upset with my level shooter who thinks he is better than he really is. Can we be friends?"

"You know I had one dinner date with your daughter and I am extremely interested in her. I believe she is interested in me. Are you telling me I may call her and you will not interfere?" Crowley nodded Yes. "In that case how about you, Mrs. Crowley and Hannah be my guests for dinner tonight? Say 1700."

Musher took the box from Dexter and asked him to wait for him while he settled with the NCOIC. Brewer, "That was one hell of a performance. You must be a professional."

"Truth Brewer is I was about the fourth or fifth caliber player in my home pool hall. I figure you have twelve hundred fifty from the side bet and two hundred from the non-believer bettors, total fourteen hundred fifty. I will take care of Dexter from my share. Add three thousand to my bag. That puts my bag at five thousand and gives me eleven hundred plus in my pocket. I want to thank you for putting Crowley in a highly visible position. We have buried the hatchet although I am not sure he buried the handle. He, Mrs. Crowley, Hannah and I are having dinner here tonight. I would appreciate it if you would have four of the best lobsters set aside. Right now I got to run. Need to buy some civvies for tonight. "

He picked up Dexter on his way out and they headed for the BX. Musher gave Dexter two hundred dollars, "This is for your work today." At the BX he bought a suit which only required cuffing, a coordinated French cuff shirt and tie, cuff links, dapper suspenders, high shine cordovan wing tip shoes, socks to match the tie and an inexpensive US Air Force ring with a blue glass stone. He waved to Dexter, "Be right back."

At the tailor shop he put on the suit so it could be checked and the trousers cuffed. The tailor said, "It will be ready Monday. I close in fifteen minutes." Musher held out a twenty dollar bill, the tailor blinked. Musher added another ten. "It will be ready in ten minutes. I will press the suit."

"Don't close until I come back." He gathered up Dexter and they waited inside the tailor shop. True to his word a grateful tailor had pressed his suit and put it in a garment bag.

To the barracks for SSS and some Luckies.

CHAPTER 73

Close To Being a Civilian

Musher went to the club early and found the waiter who would serve their table. "We shall have four for dinner, baked stuff lobster, baked potato with sour cream, creamed broccoli, hot rolls. Salad served before the lobster. A chilled bottle of a light white wine served when you serve the salad. Do not bring a check to the table I will catch you privately. Take this fifty for you, the other two fifties are one for the bartender and the other for the waitress who serves our table in the ballroom. Tell the bartender to run a tab and I will settle with him privately. Can you do this for me?"

"Yes sir"

It was about time for Crowley to arrive. Musher was waiting in the foyer. He stood there looking like the typical North End Boston "wanna be". A quick pass to the cloak room and into the dining room. The waiter came to assist the ladies seating. Musher said, "I took the liberty of ordering dinner since I know you are from New England." The waiter showed the wine bottle to Musher and popped the cork. When he finished pouring Musher raised his glass, "To long enduring friendships." The dinner conversation was light and mostly about families and backgrounds. Musher wasn't much of a contributor but as usual was an attentive listener.

Crowley," Do you smoke cigars Musher?"

"No, I am hooked on Lucky Strikes."

"The club does not look kindly on cigar smoking, why don't you and I go to the veranda for a smoke while the ladies refresh themselves." Everyone moved as if an order had been given. Five minutes later they were escorting the ladies to the ballroom. A waitress greeted them as they entered, "I have your table." A well placed table, not so close to the band that you could not hold a conversation but not so far away as to feel as if you were not in the same room as the others. Crowley, "A pitcher of draft for me and the missus." Hannah, "A tall coke." Musher, "The same for me."

"Musher don't you drink other than wine?"

"I have but the two times I did I was miserable praying to the porcelain god."

"If you would excuse us, Hannah will you dance with me?" She almost bounded out of her chair. They snuggled closely and glided across the floor.

Mrs. Crowley, "Come on Sarge, she's your daughter but she is a grown woman."

Musher danced with Mrs. Crowley. It was easy to see where Hannah came by her good looks.

About 2200 hours Crowley said, "If you two don't mind we are going home. It's getting late for us. Musher, thank you for everything, take care of my baby. Goodnight."I didn't get a chance to tell you how handsome you looked No one would take you for a G.I. in those clothes. Is that the way they dress in your home town?"

"Pretty much when they have a date with a gorgeous woman. He drew her more closely. He recalled the older guys talking in the Bucket about the dancing under the stars at the Oceanview Ballroom in Revere. "You could tell by the way the woman was dancing whether or not there would be any loving tonight." Right this minute he would have given odds about what was ahead for him tonight. He whispered in Hannah's ear, "Had enough? Why don't we leave?" She squeezed his back and hand. She picked up her purse and he suggested she go freshen up while he took care of a little business. He paid his tab at the bar and added another ten dollar tip for the bartender. He caught his waiter, paid the check and added another twenty dollar tip for the waiter. They retrieved Hannah's coat and of course Musher gave the attendant a five dollar tip.

The night was cool but not cold. In Musher's car the first thing they did was engage in a long, passionate kiss. "I don't know this airbase very well, why don't we take the scenic route?" He got on the perimeter road and as soon as he spotted a secluded, dark area he pulled in and shut off the car. The passionate kissing went to groping, he had her breasts bare and was kissing them. She had her hand on his crotch and was rubbing. He raised her skirt and starting rubbing her crotch. When he tried to pull down her panties she broke away and said, "I don't do that." She pulled away, put her head in his lap, pulled out his penis and gave him a blow job. "I am a virgin and I will be until I marry." She continued to play with his penis. "I like doing this." When he was erect again, she gave him another blow job. After a lot of hugging and half-ass kissing Musher said, "Time to go. Tomorrow is a busy day."

In front of her house he gave her a ginger kiss and said I will call you. He walked her to the door, waited until she opened it and said, "I had a wonderful time. I hope we can do it again."

"Any time, any time."

He drove back to the NCO Club, went to the bar and had two stingers on ice.

CHAPTER 74
The New Fifteen

The students filled the classroom ten minutes before class time. They looked and talked about the pictures and the captions. CWO Leary spoke. "Gentlemen please take a seat. Drape your coat on the back of your chair." There were three captains, ten master sergeants and two technical sergeants in the class. You will attend class here for the next two and one half days. The second half of the third day will be practical training on the ramp and the fourth day will be airborne film shooting against a bandit attack. The final day will be reviewing your gun film and a critique of the shooting mission. Our wing reputation as airborne shooters is not something we would want published in the newspaper. If you will pay close attention in this class, when you do your airborne film shooting the results will make each of you proud. This young gentleman is Staff Sergeant Muscarello, known to all of us as Musher. Sitting in the back of the class is A2C Phillip Dexter, another one of our teaching staff. Musher will do most of the teaching. Musher they are all yours."

He repeated the same caveat as he did with the first class. ""Good morning gentlemen. For purposes of this class you call me Musher and with your permission I will call you by your last name. No disrespect is intended, I believe it will make the class less restrictive and improve learning. Does anyone not wish to be called without his proper rank? Hearing no objection that is how we will do it."

He covered the completion of the notebook insert noting that for some they will be the first to use that notebook, for others you can see who used the notebook before you. He concentrated regarding no notes written in the notebook, use the pad provided. Are there any questions? Let's take ten, be back in your seat at 0845 hours. (He made a mental note that the classroom needed a large clock visible to all so that everyone will use the same time)

The morning was spent using the vu-graph for the students to learn the gun sight. The vu–graphs were repeated and repeated until they were shown without any identification of the parts. Musher randomly selected students to give a particular part nomenclature and its function.

Earlier Mister Leary had called Jefferson Carter to ask for the use of a twenty person aircrew bus for the week. After listening to Jefferson's reciting his account of the pool match he was ready to give Leary the entire motor pool. Leary sent Dexter to sign for and get the bus. Dexter had returned and the bus was parked outside the classroom.

By 1150 hours the class was talking about the gun sight as if they had been the designers and builders. Still none of them had yet put a hand on these two gun sights

Musher announced. "There is a bus outside for those of us who wish to go the 351st dining hall. Those who wish to go elsewhere certainly may. Everyone back in his seat at 1330 hours."

Dexter and Musher were joined at lunch by Sergeants Long and Ferrante, the two B-29 Crew Chiefs. They were on a fact finding mission. Neither bothered to have lunch, only cigarettes and coffee. Nothing to interfere with their cross examination.

"So tell me my hero, who was the sucker who lost the five grand. Was it a shill?"

"It was the 509th Bomb Wing Senior Gunner from Walker AFB, Roswell, New Mexico. He came here to look at the personnel records for this base closing. He was heading to Las Vegas from here but his mouth got him short-stopped."

"Did you talk with him?"

"Only long enough to tell him I hoped he would come back this way with a lot more money."

"Our spies say you had dinner with the Crowley family Saturday night. Fill us in."

"There is nothing to fill in. He acted as the racker and referee for the pool match and after the match he came and made a sincere apology for his past behavior. You know how I feel about Hannah. Do you think I would let the opportunity pass? As I told Brewster, NCO Club Brewster, I think we buried the hatchet but I am not sure Crowley didn't keep the handle exposed."

"Well our hero, where do you go from here?"

"After a couple of Luckies and some coffee back to my classroom to do my job."

The students were in their seats at 1315 hours.

Musher gathered the students around the work table. The entire afternoon was spent by Musher and Mister Leary doing and talking through the disassemby and assembly of the gun sight. They did it very, very slowly enunciating every component and its role in the gun sight.

Musher felt that the class had absorbed all it was going to get from this exercise. He had almost an hour and a half left in the classroom day. He jumped ahead and introduced the jeweler's case and its tools. He had tomorrow to measure today's results and act accordingly.

"Its 1615 hours, please police the area and then you may feel free to leave. You may take your notebook and pad with you if you so choose. Class convenes again tomorrow morning at 0800 hours. Gentlemen it has been a good day."

Musher said to Leary, "Dex and I can take it from here. Good night Sir."

Dexter went to the orderly room to see if he had any mail. Musher went to the barracks and then to the shower to get refreshed. One of the things he enjoyed about the military was that there was always a lot of hot water for the showers and lots of showers for the troops. A far cry from the three room cold water walk-up flat in the North End. He needed to get some money to his mother but if he mailed it the old man would get it and surely drink it down. Fanucci maybe? Maybe one of Fanucci's sons?

CHAPTER 75

More Class Work With the Gun Sight

The morning of the second day one member of the class disassembled and another member of the class assembled the gun sights under the watchful eyes of Musher and Mr. Leary. They did a good job. The class average time to disassemble and assemble was just over three minutes. It could only get better with more of the same exercise.

Musher gave the class a short quiz. "I want you to take your pad. I am going to ask you ten questions. The correct answer can be written in one word. Are you ready? First question, What is the name of the lowest part of the gun sight?" He gave seven more questions. " Question nine, What is a selsyn? Question ten, What is a reticle? You score your own answers.

Question one, he called a student's name for the answer. "Base". Correct

Questions two through eight different students the same correct result.

Question nine. No response.

Question ten. No response.

"Two of the most important parts of effective shooting are the selsyns and the reticle. He stressed the role of selsyns and the reticle and how together they calibrated the gun sight with the turrets. When the gun sight is properly calibrated and you can get your target in the reticle and hold the target in the reticle while you fire, you will hit the target. The only tools you need to do the calibration are contained in the jeweler's case." A vu-graph of the case and its components was displayed while Musher walked around in the classroom holding up each tool one at a time. Then came the reinforcement, a vu-graph showing the contents but without identifying each item. A random selected student identified one of the tools. The reinforcement was done again, and again and again.

A vu-graph of the left selsyn was displayed. Shown was the access point to its adjustment screw and the particular tool for the screw. The next vu-graph showed similar information for the right selsyn. The third vu-graph showed the gun sight with the access point for each selsyn and how with the correct tool in each hand the selsyn could be calibrated to zero. When the selsyn was zero only half of the shooting calibration was done.

A new vu-graph showed the gun sight action switch closed and the reticle circle illuminated. "The reticle is only illuminated when the action switch is closed." Within the reticle the target dot was at 5 o'clock. The next vu-graph showed the right selsyn was selected for adjustment. A series of vu-graphs followed showing how the target dot behaved when the selsyn was given a minor adjustment to either left or right of its zero position. The next vu-graph showed the target dot dead center. The action switch was then opened. When it was closed again the reticle appeared with the target dot at 8 o'clock. The left selsyn was selected and the adjustment vu-graphs followed the target dots travels to dead center. The action switch was opened. When the action switch was closed this time, the target dot was dead center in the reticle. The gun sight and the turrets which were either primary or secondarily controlled by this gun sight were calibrated for effective shooting.

The remainder of the morning and the entire afternoon session were devoted to Musher and Mister Leary fucking up the gun sight calibration and the students recalibrating the gun sight. Each student took a turn to calibrate the gun sight while the other students watched and offered help if the student got stuck. By the end of the day each student had at least six turns calibrating a gun sight.

Musher," The classroom day is just about over. We want you to know that your teaching staff is extremely pleased with the way you have grasped the classroom work and your ability to use what you have absorbed. Tomorrow morning we will do more of what we did today. The afternoon will be spent on the ramp using the nose firing position and the two waist positions to calibrate the gun sights. Again, thank you for an excellent day and we will see you in the morning."

Without being told the class policed the area.

"Mister Leary, Dex and I can take it from here."

"Goodnight you two, I too am extremely pleased with the enlisted component of the teaching staff."

Musher and Dexter secured the facility and headed for the base bus and the barracks. As usual Dexter went to the orderly room for mail and Musher to the showers for refreshment.

CHAPTER 76
Class Work and the Flight Line Exercise

At 0600 hours Musher entered the shack. Sergeant Wooly was already there diligently typing. Musher said Good Morning and Wooly nodded his head and said, "What a pain in the ass this is every month making the eligible for flight duty pay roster. Every name, rank and serial number in alphabetical order by last name. With rare exception it is always the same names. Some day the air force will either pay a person for being on flying status or not pay the person for flying status."

He looked at aircraft status board which showed " 121, P Patch, Crew training, 1300 – 1600." That's Sergeant Long again. He said goodbye to Sergeant Wooly. hailed the first vehicle that came by and asked for a ride to the flight line dining hall.

Breakfast was good and he enjoyed the solitude while eating. Mister Leary came in for coffee and toast. There was very little talking. They were in the office at 0700 hours and Dexter was already there waiting.

Dexter spoke, "Musher is it OK if I take the bus to the wash rack and gas station while you hold morning class?"

"That would be fine Dex. You can leave whenever you wish." With that Dexter was out the door.

The class was in position at 0800 hours. The gun sight calibration training resumed with the same format that was used yesterday. You could see the confidence building and the time to calibrate decreasing. The average time to calibrate was now fifty-one seconds.

At 1100 hours Musher asked everyone to get on the bus. We will eat lunch early because we need to be at the training aircraft at 1300 hours. At 1230 hours everyone was back on the bus.

Musher directed Dexter to the P Patch. The bus stopped at B-29 121. Master Sergeant Long greeted Musher and the class and invited them to sit in the shade under the wing. He directed Dexter to where he should park the bus.

"Could I get some aircraft power so we can fuckup your gun sights?"

Long powered up the external APU, went to the engineer's station, threw some switches and climbed down the forward ladder . Walked to Musher," It's all yours. Do you want me with you?"

"No but I would appreciate it if the rear hatch was opened and the ladder put in place."

"It is already done."

Musher told Dexter to take care of the nose position gun sight and he would take care of the waist positions. To Long, "Would you make the intercom active?"

"Already done."

To the class, "We will divide into three teams. Five plus Mister Leary for the bombardier compartment, ten for the aft compartment, five with Airman Dexter and the other five with me. There is no scoring for this exercise. When you think your calibration is at zero your team instructor will validate.

Your effort result will be either be in/off time and yes or no. The listings are simply so we evaluate ourselves at the end of the day. The crew chief has put power to the aircraft and activated the intercom system. There are headsets at each shooting position and both Mister Leary and I will be listening and able to speak. You cannot speak but you will hear all activity while you have the headset on. How many times will we do this exercise and from which shooting positions? We will rotate you among the shooting positions and we will be here as long as it takes unless we run out of time or as a class we are confident that individually we will shoot at least eighty percent tomorrow. Neither Mister Leary nor I will select who goes where. You do that among yourselves making sure that each person partakes in one exercise. When one has completed the exercise he may leave the compartment and wait under the wing until all have finished. When all have completed one exercise you can notify Mister Leary and me by using the intercom headset in the wheel well. It is now 1400 hours. Everything is ready. Any questions? You can board anytime after we three instructors. Remember when you raise your trigger hand to show you have finished keep the Action switch closed or you will lose the result of your calibration."

Musher was in the aft compartment and had no sooner put on his headset when two of the class took seating in the waist positions. On the intercom, "Forward ready? If so double click your intercom transmitter." All positions heard the double click. It is 1405. "Begin"

By 1415 all their calibration efforts had been validated and one of class transmitted, "All the class is done and standing by under the left wing." The instructors distorted the gun sight selsyns and dismounted from the aircraft.

Musher directed, "Mister Leary's group right waist, my group the nose position, Airman Dexter's group the left waist position. Let's get aboard."

On the intercom, "Forward ready? If so double click your intercom transmitter." All positions heard the double click. It is 1428. "Begin" This time it was 1437 when all their calibration efforts had been validated and one of class transmitted, "All the class is done and standing by under the left wing." The instructors distorted the gun sight selsyns and dismounted the aircraft.

Musher directed, "You know which firing position you have not used. Get aboard appropriately." On the intercom, "Forward ready? If so double click your intercom transmitter." All positions heard the double click. " It is 1450. Begin"

This time it was 1500 when all their calibration efforts had been validated and one of class transmitted, "All the class is done and standing by under the left wing." The instructors distorted the gun sight selsyns and dismounted the aircraft.

Sergeant Long had set up a table under the wing with two five gallon jugs of ice water accompanied by oversized drinking cups. No one was drinking the water despite the fact that their flying suits were soaked with sweat. Musher, "Let's have a cool drink and take a break. Get your water and come back here and sit down." He waited until everyone else had filled their cup before getting some water himself. Another of The Monster's axioms rang loudly in his head, "A good leader is first in a fire-fight and last to eat when its over."

"Let's look at how we are doing with this exercise. Besides sweating our balls off, there are some good statistics. Fifteen students, each performing three units of the exercise in a total of twenty nine minutes. Forty-five units of calibration in twenty-nine minutes. Average time per exercise unit is less than forty seconds. I am not sure we can get any better. Your time is far superior to the last class. I want to take a poll. Dexter give each student a piece of paper. If we don't have enough writing tools you all can share. The most you will have to write on the paper is three digits. Here is the poll question. What percentage level do you believe you will shoot eighty percent or better hits tomorrow? Don't show it to anyone, fold it and put your answer in Dexter's hat. Everyone must start at the same time and finish within thirty seconds. Looks like everyone has the paper, go, While Dex is collecting the poll why don't we all have some more water. I know I need some more."

"Dexter will keep track. The first response, 100 percent, the second response, 100 percent. The entire poll responded with 100 percent. Gentlemen I think we can terminate this exercise now. Does anyone object? The other instructors don't have any criticisms of your performance. Dex, crank the bus and get the air conditioning going full blast. Those of us who are smokers are going to retreat to a safe smoking distance. Sergeant Long, again we are in your debt for your aircraft, your support and the cool drinks. Is your aircraft scheduled for tomorrow's flight? If it is will you be aboard?"

"It will be my aircraft and I will be aboard. Anything for my hero."

CHAPTER 77
The Proof of the Pudding Is in the Eating

Musher was at the shack at 0545 hours. Leary was already there.

"We have three clipboards. The paper on the clipboards showed the headings to keep track of who was shooting, from which position and when. You will take the forward compartment, Dexter and I shall take the rear. It's the same as last shooting flight but a lot more important."

Everyone was on the bus at 0600 hours. First stop the Parachute Shop to pick up chutes. Next stop the P Patch and 121. The bus was greeted by Crew Chief Long. The aircrew arrived moments later. Leary and his detail lined up under the left wing. The aircrew lined up in front of them. The Aircraft Commander (AC) was the same AC who had flown the training mission last time. Again he brought his own waist gunners. The AC spoke, "While we do our pre-flight inspections please brief Clinker of the details for this mission. You may put your gear aboard whenever you are free."

The flight engineer went directly to Mister Leary. "Sir, I remember your group, did you want Musher to brief me"? This old sarge knew who ran the railroad.

When Leary was gone Clinker said, "Long tells me you're kicking ass at the club and Crowley approves of you dating his daughter. Be careful, he would love to marry her off."

Musher briefed Clinker and headed into the aircraft to make sure the gun sights were zeroed

The class division and the rules were the same as yesterday. The AC gathered everybody under the left wing. The aircrew verified its aircraft checks. Mister Leary told him his class was ready. The AC instructed for all to get aboard.

When Musher entered the aft compartment sitting there was Master Sergeant Long. Musher just looked at him. Long, "I told you I would be here. My hero doesn't go without the world's most skilled aircraft mechanic on board. I will take care of the ladder, the hatch and the putt-putt (the on board APU)."

The takeoff and climb out to eight thousand feet was without incident. The two regular gunners found space and stretched out to sleep. On the intercom, "Sir, class instructor to AC." Go ahead. "Permission to poll the class to insure all are on active intercom." Go ahead. Musher called the roll and each answered with two clicks. . "Musher to Mister Leary, man your shooting position, the bandits should arrive any time now."

On the intercom he heard the AC, "Bandit Leader this 351st Training Fight AG, we are on a racetrack course, 30 miles west of the airbase at eight thousand feet. Do you copy?"

"Copy 351 we are you ready when you are.?"

"Roger Bandit Leader. Bring it on."

Musher remembered how in the last flight he avoided being caught off guard. On the intercom, "gunners be ready they will be here in five seconds." He closed the action switch. The reticle looked good. He made small vertical and horizontal testing movements and the reticle followed. The intercom came alive, Bandit at 11 o'clock high. Bandit at 3 o'clock level. Musher trained his gun sight to the approaching bandit. He fired three short bursts. As the bandit dove under the B-29 Musher alerted Dexter, "He's coming your way. Who knows what happened with the other bandit." Before he could finish the thought he saw a bandit diving towards him from the 2 o'clock high position. He patiently waited until the reticle had the bandit framed. This time he fired five short bursts as the bandit went by in flashing speed. Bandit at 9 o'clock level. There was no way to train his gun on this bandit unless the bandit dove under or climbed over the B-29. The bandit chose to pass under the B-29. As he went by Musher's reticle picked him up and Musher fired five bursts.

"351 this is Bandit Leader. We are breaking off. See you again shortly."

"Roger Bandit Leader, 351 Out."

Musher got out of the shooting position and he was soaking wet. Long offered him some water which he gulped. On the intercom, "Musher to Mister Leary. They won't be gone long. Get your shooter in position and make sure your record paper is complete. Thank you, we will do the same here. You two, left and right waist. Get set quickly. Fighter jocks live for this."

The voice on the intercom," 351 this is Bandit Leader are you ready for company?"

"Roger Bandit Leader." The AC made the same comment he did last flight. "As Shakespeare said, "Lay on MacDuff and damned be he who first cries hold enough."

The bandits attacked mercilessly. The gunners got a good workout. Lots of gun film was expended. Similar attacks took place four more times. The entire time for the rotation was slightly over two hours.

On the intercom, "351 this is Bandit Leader. We cannot stay any longer must get fuel. The ETA (estimated time of arrival) for replacement bandits is 1100 hours. Thank you for the show. Take care."

"Roger Bandit Leader we thank you."

To make sure every student clearly heard him Musher spoke on the intercom,. "Mister Leary please send your students aft". As the three students dropped out of the tunnel, three entered the tunnel to go forward.

The voice on the intercom," 351 this is Bandit Leader 2 with three bandits. We are ready at your command."

"Roger Bandit Leader 2, another one from the US Navy, "You may fire when ready Quigley."

The intercom spoke, "Here they come, two from 10 o'clock. Two more from 7 o'clock."

The waist gunners responded like the veteran gunners they are. Left waist, "I'm on the 10 o'clock, watch for the 7 o'clock at 2 o'clock. " The bombardier, "I got him in the reticle and I am firing." The right waist, "I got the 10 o'clock. I'm on him. He's framed and I am firing." The next two passes were from different directions. The gunners handled it well.

"351 this is Bandit Leader 2. We are breaking off. We will be in the area. Call us when you are ready."

"Roger Bandit Leader 2. We will prepare for your arrival. 351 Out".

Musher to Leary." Is your next shooter in position?".... "OK." His and Dexter's shooters were in position and anxiously awaiting the thrill of combat. Even though his aircraft and the fighters were only firing gun film. Heard on the intercom:

"351 to Bandit Leader 2."

"This is Bandit Leader 2 go ahead."

"The fox has been given the job of protecting the henhouse."

"Roger 351"

With that the intercom was filled with transmissions locating incoming bandits. The veteran gunners coped very well with the jet aircraft and its speed.

"351 this is Bandit Leader 2. We are breaking off. We have fuel for maybe one more exercise. Don't wait to long to engage. "

"Roger Bandit Leader 2. 351 out."

"AC to Instructor"

"Musher here sir"

"Did you hear that? Get ready quickly we don't want to lose this shooting opportunity."

Musher wanted to get at least one more shooting before the day ended. Musher to Leary.," Would you take care of that front gun sight? I think it may need calibration. Thank you." Musher and Dexter climbed into each waist position and deftly fucked-up the gun sight calibration.

"Class, it seems this may be our last shooting rotation today. We know that in one attack we can shoot and score three gunners. I am putting fifteen numbers in my hat and I shall draw three. Those three will shoot and the rest of us will pray. Is that clear?"

"Why not ask for volunteers?"

"To shoot?"

"No, to not shoot." Everyone including the aircrew heard all this on the intercom and chuckled.

"As a class is that how you would like to do it?" Eight of the ten spoke an affirmative. Musher asked for volunteer non-shooters. Not one person on the intercom volunteered.

"You're no different than the last class. They couldn't handle it either. I will designate the shooters and you will accept. He read aloud three names, one for the forward compartment and two for the aft compartment. You sir may make your way forward and send those three here."

Musher to the AC," Sir we are ready when you are."

"351 to Bandit Leader 2"

"Go ahead 351"

"We are ready when you are."

Before the AC even heard a roger the intercom started chirping. "Bandits, two at 2 o'clock high". "Bandits, two at 4 o'clock low." The gunners did their best as the bandits continuously changed attacking points and altitudes.

"Bandit Leader 2 to 351."

"Go ahead Bandit Leader 2"

"We enjoyed the encounter See you again. Bandit Leader 2 out."

AC to Musher, "Please put my people back in their seats. We will make a straight in approach to Smoky and be on the blocks in thirty-five minutes or less.

Musher and all the class was exhausted. There was no chatter. In thirty-one minutes 121 was parked in the P Patch, on the blocks and its engines shut down.

Everyone except Long's airmen ground crew got on the bus to the shack. The five officers got off there and the remaining fourteen went to the squadron dining hall. The official serving hours of the dining room had ended; however, set in an inverted T shape arrangement there were places and chairs for fourteen people. Like the last time, there was no serving line. Cooks and KPs brought platters of food to the table.

Mister Leary stood. "You gentlemen behaved admirably today. Musher, Dexter and I thank you." The rest of the meal was fairly silent. The servers made sure there was plenty of coffee and the coffee was hot Outside the dining hall came all the goodbyes and the we will see you tomorrow at 1000 hours. To Leary, "Dex and I will take the bus to the office and store all this stuff away? Can you go to the photo lab and get our films back later today? Dexter and I will be in the office waiting. No matter how late you can get them to me."

"From here I will go straight to the photo lab. They know me now. I will get them back ASAP. I will call you when I start for the office."

Dex wasn't thrilled to stay and work but he did the typing Musher asked him to without a complaint. About 2300 hours Mister Leary walked into the office carrying two large cans of film. "I didn't call because I thought you guys might be napping."

CHAPTER 78
Serving the Pudding

They swapped the vu-graph power to the projector. The vu-graph would be needed again. Leary loaded the first can of film. Musher took the gun sights off the work table, wrapped them in the sheets and stored them in a safe spot in the room.

Leary, " Please turn out the lights and we will see what we have."

When the first frame came up followed by another frame until a summary screen appeared. Leary put the film on pause. "The summary screen shows the cumulative result of the shooting segment. I am sure you know whose film this is since you, I and Dex were the first shooters. Musher, your cumulative hit percentage for rounds fired is 98.8 percent." The film rolled again. This time it was Leary's gun film. His summary sheet showed a 91.1 cumulative hit percentage for rounds fired. Dexter's film summary showed 98.4 percent cumulative hit percentage for rounds fired.

He wanted to keep the school staff results first.

When Leary was ready they restarted the first can and Leary paused the projector at each summary sheet. Musher diligently recorded the information on his lined pad. "Mister Leary why don't you go home? Dexter and I can run the projector and we have some compilations to do and you can't help us."

"Call me at any time for any thing. I'll be here about 0900."

Both cans of summary information were recorded on his log. To be sure he had correctly recorded the information they went through both cans again.

Dexter typed the information on the correct vu-graph forms. He and Musher taped the forms to a vu-graph holder. They switched the power from the projector and ran the vu-graphs for visibility and correctness. Musher sequenced the vu-graphs and made the proper placement markings. They switched the power back to the projector, loaded can number 1, and ran a few feet to make sure they had done it right. They were ready for the students and any visitors who may wish to watch the critique.

"It's almost 0600 hours. What do you want to do Dex?"

"Whatever you say."

"Let's go back to the barracks, shower, put on clean clothes, have breakfast and be back here at 0800 hours." With that they walked to the base bus stop.

257

They were back in the office at 0800 hours. They checked and rechecked to make sure everything was in place. Mister Leary came in at 0900 hours.

"For guys who have been up all night you look very fresh. Dex, we'll have to get you a dapper flight suit like Musher's. I'll take care of that. Are we ready?"

"Did you get any notice of any visitors to the critique?"

"No, but don't be surprised if they show up."

The class came and took their seats at 0930. "As of this moment we know of no guests who will be here for the critique. I tell you in advance the same thing I told the last class. None of you has anything to fear. Your combat reputation will remain in tact and your status among your peers will be severely elevated." The classroom door opened and six guests entered. Leary spoke a soft "Ten Hut"

The Wing CO said, "As you were, Musher are you ready?"

"Yes Sir."

"Carry on and run your critique as if we were not here."

Musher and Dexter scrambled into the office to get three chairs for the unexpected guests.

Musher explained to the class what they could expect to see for each shooting exercise. "Because of the records the instruction team kept yesterday we are able to tell you who the shooter is at the start of every new segment. At the end of each segment there is a summary of the particular shooting exercise just shown. Despite the fact that we mixed you up you functioned well as a shooting team. The first three shooting segments are mine, Mister Leary's and Airman Dexter's in that order. Dex, Please turn off the lights and roll the film"

As the film appeared on the screen Musher announced the first thee shooters were him, Mister Leary and Dexter. The first class shooter was Master Sergeant Starling. He repeated his role until the film from the first can had finished. "Lights please. It will take a few minutes to load the second can. Please remain at your seat." It took almost two minutes to have the second film in place. "Lights please, roll the film." The routine for the second film was the same as the first. When the last summary screen appeared Leary turned off the projector and Dexter turned on the lights. "If we may let's take a twenty minute break while we set up for the compilation data."

In less than ten minutes the first vu-graph was positioned on the viewer. When all were seated the first graph of individual scores was shown on the screen. Musher recited each individuals score. The low individual score was 87.6 percent hits per round fired and the high was 98.1 percent hits per round fired. The average for all fifteen shooters for as many rotations as the bandits would allow is 90.1 percent hits per round fired. 90.1 percent hits per round fired is fifty-one percent higher than the wing aggregate average. "Lights please."

The Wing Commander went to the front of the classroom. "You gentlemen are to be commended. Most of you are combat veterans and understand the importance of the aerial gunners protecting the squadron, wing or flight formations. This may be the atomic age but every nation will always have a fighter interception capability. To the school staff my congratulations. Definitely, you have proved the taste of the pudding is in the eating." He came to shake Mister Leary's hand, Airman Dexter's hand and the Musher. "You have justified your promotion. Take care of yourself." When he headed for the door Musher broke out to hold the door open and Leary barked, "Ten Hut." Three of the guests were the bomb squadron commanding officers, the other two were the director of wing personnel and the airbase commanding officer. None of them spoke as they left the building. Musher closed the door and everyone fell silent for a moment.

"Class make sure you have left everything that belongs to the training school. I haven't done it yet but I am charged with designing and preparing a Certificate of Completion from the Wing Commander and my Squadron Commander. I'll get to it soon. Thank you for making us look so good. Have a good day." As they filed out each stopped to shake hands with Mister Leary, Airman Dexter and Musher. Their comments were most flattering. When all were out the door Musher said, "If I were a drinking man I would have one now."

Leary went into his desk and brought out a fifth of Wild Turkey. "I keep it for medicinal purposes." He poured three short shots, raised his glass and said, "To probably two of the best airmen I have ever worked with. Cheers." Dex was a Mormon, he faked drinking the toast. Musher wished he had faked drinking the toast. The Wild Turkey had been rightly named.

CHAPTER 79

Play Cowboy in Junction City

From the pay phone by the dining hall he placed a call to Priscilla. When she answered he said sweetly, "Hi it's Musher, remember me?"

"Yes I do."

"I am off duty until Sunday noon and I thought if you had a vacancy I would come over today and spend a couple of nights in Junction City."

"Yes, I have a room for you for tonight and tomorrow night. What time do you think you will be here? Remember supper is at 6:30."

"I should be there well before that."

"OK, drive carefully."

Musher went to the BX and bought a small, civilian looking suitcase, two pull over, cowboy looking T shirts and a dark blue sport coat with leather patches on the elbows. As he was going to the cashier a medium size cooler was there at a sale price. He took it too. Since he had a place to put them he also picked up two six packs of coco cola bottles and a dozen candy bars. He paid for the items and was taking them to his car when he noticed that just a few stores away from the BX was the Class 6 store. The items in Class 6 stores were limited to beer, wine, booze, cigarettes and party type items such as peanuts, popcorn, paper cups, and bags of ice. One bag of ice would serve his needs. In the BX parking lot he filled the cooler with the ice, added the cokes and the candy bars. Secured the lid and put the cooler on the floor of the rumble seat.

At the barracks he undressed down to naked and put on the white civilian underwear he had bought. Socks, cowboy boots, Levis with the leather belt and fancy buckle and one of the new T shirts topped off his attire. He packed the other T shirt, some civilian underwear, his cowboy shirt, a pair of socks and just in case, his new sport jacket. His emergency bag had the cigarettes and a couple of candy bars in it. He put on his straw hat, grabbed the suitcase, the emergency bag and was on his way out the door. Dexter was coming in as he was going out.

"Where you going Musher?"

"Out of town for a couple of days."

"Do you want me to go with you?"

"Not this trip, maybe next time."

He put everything in the rumble seat then looked at his watch. It was just past 1 P.M. Driving wisely he would be in Junction City before 4 P.M.

He pulled up in front of the mercantile in Junction City just past 3:15. He bought another cowboy shirt, this time plain white without any pearl buttons.

At Priscilla's place he took his suitcase and emergency bag and knocked on her door. She came to the door looking great. Tight jeans, tight blouse, fancy buckle on her belt and alligator boots. "Hi Stranger, come on in." She led him to his room on the upper floor. This time the water pitcher was full and the bed was turned down for sleeping.

"I can't dally right now, I am busy fixing supper and you would only be in my way. Why don't you go down to the emporium and play dominoes or shoot a little pool. Just be sure you are back in time for supper." She kissed him on the cheek and headed down the stairs.

He took his time to unpack and hang his clothes best he could. On his way out he hollered, "See you for supper."

There were some friendly faces and greetings in the emporium. The four domino tables were going hot and heavy. One of the snooker tables was vacant. He told the old man he wanted to use the snooker table. "It's yours for two dollars an hour or any part of an hour." Musher grabbed a cue and started trying to make balls into the pockets. The table was bigger and the balls were smaller. The entry way to the pocket was rounded and it was not easy to make any shot which was not at the right speed when the object ball got to the pocket. He didn't care about the rules of snooker he was simply trying to make balls and play position on the next ball he specified in his head. He had been at it for over an hour and a half and he was mentally exhausted. He knew he was a great pool player but this game of snooker was something totally different. Fanucci popped into his head," If you are a jock with intelligence and great hand-eye coordination, you can master any sport which is not simply beyond your physical capabilities." He patted the table and said to the table, "I'll be back." He settled with the old man and said to the room, "See you all later."

He was back at Priscilla's long before supper. In his room he laid out to rest and dozed off. The knock on the door was loud and the male voice told him supper is on the table. The same five men were already seated. He greeted them with a friendly hello and he got nods and grunts in return. Dinner was lamb and all the trimmings. Priscilla came around with a gravy boat and a ladle. "This is lamb's liver gravy." The word liver conjured such pictures and feelings he had trouble remaining seated. "No thank you, I like my lamb plain." He didn't eat much dinner. The dessert was deep dish apple pie. He had two pieces of that and lots of black coffee. The same fellow as last time asked, "You going to play poker with us tonight?" Priscilla chimed in, "He can't. He promised to take me to the Eddie County Barn Dance tonight." Musher added, "Sure wish I could but you know, a promise is a promise." Her statement explained how she was dressed when she met him at the door earlier in the day.

She sidled up to him and whispered, "Hope you don't mind. I need to clean up the kitchen then me. I'll be ready in about and hour."

Musher went into the living room, lit a Lucky and read the local paper. In less than an hour she stood in the doorway. "I am ready to go. Did you bring any liquor? I should have told you. It's OK I have a couple of pints of vodka. Let me get them."

When she left the room Musher darted upstairs and grabbed five packs of Luckies.

They walked around back to his car he put the vodka and the cigarettes in the glove compartment. As he was moving away from the glove compartment she put her arms around his neck and planted a hot, wet kiss on his mouth. Her tongue darted in his mouth and worked around his tongue. When she let go she said I know you don't know your way around so I will guide you to the dance. It is about thirty to forty minutes from here. The car had a bench seat. As he drove away she pushed her bottom against his thigh.

The place was actually an over-sized barn. She took the vodka and he put an extra pack of cigarettes in his other breast pocket. Admission was five dollars for men, ladies got in free. Inside there was an elevated platform around just about the entire perimeter of the barn. The band was situated at the far end on an elevated portion of the platform. A railing followed the contour of the platform. At intermittent spaces there were openings with rails to protect patrons who took the two steps down to the dance floor. It looked as if three hundred people were either on the platform or on the dance floor. There wasn't a vacant table so Priscilla and he joined another couple. There was no exchange between the couples. A waitress came by and Priscilla ordered two seven-ups with ice. The waitress returned, "Four dollars please." Musher gave her five and thanked her. Priscilla put the bag of vodka on the table, opened one bottle, poured the vodka over the ice until the glass was half full. Did the same for the other glass. Topped the glasses off with seven-up, raised her glass to Musher, "Here's looking at you kid." He sipped his drink and she downed hers in one tip of the glass. She refilled her glass with the same mixture. Some of the ice had melted and therefore there was more vodka in the glass. He topped his drink with seven-up.

He had been watching the dancing and knew he had never done anything like that. When she asked him to dance he panicked. "I've never danced like that."

"It's called the Oklahoma two-step. In five minutes you will be dipping and moving around the floor like you had danced this way all your life. Let's do it." She was right, in very few minutes he was comfortable. It was nothing but close order drill with a two step cadence. The emphasis was on the twirling and moving around the dance floor. They must have danced that way for ten minutes. It certainly was a test of stamina.

She never even took a deep breath. Back at the table she gulped her drink, fixed another and gulped that one too. Musher just kept adding seven-up to his drink. The waitress passed by and Priscilla ordered two seven-ups with ice. Meanwhile she was sipping her last bit of seven-up and vodka. Musher added the rest of his seven-up to her glass. She looked at him curiously and he said, "I prefer my vodka on ice." The waitress returned, "Four dollars please." Musher gave her five and thanked her.

Down on the dance floor were lines of men and women doing a dance step to the tempo of the music. "It's simple, left foot forward, bring up the right. Left foot back, bring back the right. Left foot forward, bring the right to the same position. Clap your hands and do the same steps again. Add any body motion you choose and you are "Line Dancing. Let's do it." They joined the end of the last line. Priscilla spoke the steps as they did them. Very quickly she did not need to speak the steps. She contorted her body while making the steps. He moved somewhat but he was more interested in watching her. The Line Dance went on and on. People dropped out and others dropped in. About eight minutes into the dance Musher motioned to Priscilla that he was going back to the table. She blew him a kiss and kept right on dancing. When she returned once again she gulped her drink, mixed another and gulped it, mixed another and sipped it. They had been there less than two hours and she had drunk almost a full pint of vodka and put a dent in the second pint. He needed a way to get her out of here before he had to carry her out of here.

"What say Priscilla, are you ready to leave. You've danced my legs off and you showed these people what a real dancer looks like."

"OK, let me finish this drink and we will go." One chug-a-lug and she was ready. He picked up the bottle and they went to the car. He put the bottle in the glove compartment. She had closed her eyes and went to sleep. He retraced his steps to Junction City but along the way he was pulled over by a Kansas State Trooper. "Both of you please get out of the car." Musher complied but he couldn't even wake up Priscilla.

"Have you two been drinking? Is she passed out?"

"Officer I believe she is. I have had less than two drinks since eight thirty this evening."

"Is there any liquor in the car?"

"There is a partial pint of vodka in the glove compartment. My license, registration papers and proof of insurance are also in the same glove compartment."

"Put your hands on the car, keep them there while you take a step backward and spread your legs." Musher knew the position from Boston. He was patted down but obviously there was nothing there. The officer put him through a number of roadside tests which Musher easily passed.

"You are not a drunken driver. You can go provided you don't let your friend get anywhere near the steering wheel no matter what she may think she wants to do." He walked over to the passenger side of the car and flashed his light on her face. "Priscilla? How do you know this girl?"

"I am staying at her boarding house."

"She's my ex-wife and a non-drinker. I don't need for you to tell me why you got her drunk. Get out of here before I run you both in."

Musher pulled away slowly and proceeded to Priscilla's house. When he parked in the back he decided to stay with her in the car until she woke up on her own. About three-thirty she moved and moaned. She sat up and asked, "Where are we?"

"Parked in your back yard."

"How long have I been passed out?"

"About five and a half hours."

"What time is it?"

"Three-forty five."

"Thank God it's Saturday and breakfast is not served until eight-thirty. Can we go in the house now?"

"Do you think you can make it or shall I carry you?"

"I'll try." She took four steps and started to collapse. He took her in his arms and as quietly as possible got them to the upstairs. He whispered, "Which room is yours?"

"The last one on the left."

Fortunately the door was unlocked and they entered with almost no noise except the door clicking shut behind them. He deposited his cargo on the bed. He pulled off her boots and socks. Took off her Levi's and blouse. She lay there in her bra and panties.

"Please take off my bra and panties. I always sleep in the nude." He did as she asked and had an immediate erection.

"Would you like to fuck me now?" He pulled off his boots and underwear. Slid between her legs, put her legs on his shoulders and entered the heavenly gate. He fucked until he came, stayed inside until he was hard again, and fucked her once more. She loved it.

He withdrew, took a towel and wiped himself. He tossed her the towel which she put between her legs and crawled under the sheet. "I need to be up at seven-thirty to have breakfast ready. Will you knock on my door at seven?"

He nodded yes, picked up his boots and drawers and went to his room. He undressed and gave himself a field bath as if he were doing it in an infantry helmet. He crawled in bed and slept until 6 A.M.

He gathered his clothes and slipped into Priscilla's room. She was still sound asleep. He licked her breasts and stomach. She awakened and grabbed his head and pushed it towards her pussy. He moved the towel and licked her from end to end of her pussy. She stirred in the bed. He mounted and fucked her as if he had never fucked before. She held on tight and squeezed him closely. When he discharged he lay gently on her.

"I would love to do it again but if I don't serve breakfast my business is gone. Stay here until you come down for breakfast." She put on her bra, panties and a robe. "Lock the door behind me."

At seven forty he dressed and went down for breakfast. It wasn't the usual fanfare. Scrambled eggs, fried potatoes, grits and toast. Lots of hot coffee. No one complained. He went back to his room, undressed, gave himself a whore bath, crawled in bed and fell back to sleep. Last thought before sleep, either I need a watch with an alarm clock or when I go away I must put my alarm clock in my emergency bag. When he awakened his watch said it was almost noon. He dressed and noticed the paper which had been slipped under his door. "I am back in bed to sleep. See you at supper. Love, Prissy Pussy." He finished dressing, gathered his belongings and money and went to the kitchen. Two glasses of milk made him feel much better. Next stop the Emporium.

He acknowledged the domino players and the old man. He sat at the counter and asked if the old man had any chocolate milk. "No, but I can make you some." "Do you have chocolate ice cream?" Yes. "Then make me a chocolate frappe." A what? "A frappe, you know, chocolate milk, chocolate syrup, chocolate ice cream all mixed together in a blender."....You mean a chocolate shake......"Whatever, can you make me a large one?" The old man started gathering the ingredients when he said, "Did you and Priscilla drink too much at the Eddie County?"

Musher just stared at him.

"There isn't much happens to a Junction City citizen without the facts getting back to me. I hear tell you met Priscilla's ex-husband last night while he was on duty and she was stone drunk. Want to talk to me about it?"

"Not on your life old man." With that the old man served his shake in the mixing blend and a tall cold glass. Musher took the container and the glass and went back to the empty snooker table to practice. He devoted the first hour to making red balls in a pocket while positioning the cue ball for the next red ball. The old man came to the table, "Let me help you improve your practice. He took the 4 ball, 5 ball, 6 ball and 7 ball and placed them on their respective spots on the table. The secret to successful snooker playing is to pot (make) a red ball and on the next shot pot one of the numbered balls. You get one point for the red ball and the number of points dependent on which of the numbered balls you pot. The value of the numbered balls is the numeric value on the ball, i.e., the 4 ball is worth 4 points, the 7 ball is worth seven points. Any numbered ball you pot after potting a red ball is retrieved from the pocket in which you made the numbered ball and the numbered ball is replaced on its respective location. The total number of points you make before missing is referred to as the number made on your break. Practice well."

Musher thought about what the old man had said. I need to pot a red ball and each time position the cue ball to pot the black ball. Total 8 points. I must not lose sight of the fact that no matter how well I position the cue ball for the next shot it is meaningless if I don't pot the red ball. He practiced diligently for another two hours before hanging up his cue. On his way out he paid his tab with the old man and added a ten dollar tip. He drove back to Priscilla's, parked his car in the back, opened the rumble seat long enough to get the chest and carried it to his room. He gulped most of a coke so he would have an ash tray. He opened another coke to enjoy and lit a Luckie. He sat contemplating Lucy, Hannah and now Priscilla. He grew hard and started doing math problems to divert his concentration. At 6:25 he went down to dinner. As usual he was hungry.

Dinner was typical Saturday night. Hot dogs and beans. Buns and all the trimmings. It must have been the Saturday night standard. Four of the five regulars had a beer on the table. Musher excused himself, ran upstairs and came back with three cokes. He offered one to the only guy without a beer. He more than happily accepted. Musher ate three hot dogs on a bun, a very large helping of beans and two cokes. If he lived like this as a civilian and didn't work out he would weigh two hundred fifty pounds. There was no dessert or coffee.

"The poker game begins in fifteen minutes. On Saturday night we play dealers choice, Jacks or better, five card stud or seven card stud. Ante ten cents, open for ten cents, raise to twenty cents. The three raise limit is in force. Last round at 10 P.M. Are you in?"

"I am in but you better be careful I feel very, very lucky.

"First Jack deals. Musher your deal."

"Everybody ante up for five card stud." He already knew who would win this hand.

Each player with one card down and then one card up. King, Queen, Ace, Ace, Jack and a seven. First ace bet ten. Everyone calls.

Next card, King, Queen, Ace, Ace, Jack and an eight. First ace pair bets twenty. Everyone calls.

Fourth card, deuce, deuce, seven, eight and ten. All the players notice Musher has three clubs and a possible straight. Second ace pair bets twenty, three players call, Musher raises twenty, first ace pair calls the raise and so do all the others.

Last card, King, Queen, deuce, deuce, Jack, six of clubs. Second ace checks to the raiser, three players also check, Musher bets twenty. King calls, Queen calls, First ace calls, Second ace calls, Jack folds. Musher turns his hole card the six of clubs. A small straight flush. He collects the pot and passes the cards to the next dealer. This pot is big enough for him to play the rest of the night without losing any money. From here he plays conservatively and totally honest.

By the end of the last round Musher is ahead about eighteen dollars. The game breaks and Musher says," I warned you I felt very, very lucky."

"You're still not a good player but being lucky is better than being good."

"Good night all." Priscilla had already gone to bed.

In his room he stripped to his shorts and lay on his bed. He heard his door open and the key turned in the lock. She dropped her nightgown and climbed onto his chest with her pussy in his face. He took the offer and licked it like an ice cream cone. Then with her clit in his mouth he gummed the clit. She climaxed and slid down his chest. He rolled her onto her knees and mounted her dog fashion. He banged away until he popped his load. She flattened out with him on top of her. He whispered, "Go suck my cock."

"I don't do that but you can fuck me in the ass if you want."

That would be new for him. It wasn't easy but he managed to insert his hardened cock. It was so tight that it was a very short time for him to come. When he rolled off she got a wet towel and wiped his private area and handed him the towel for him to do her. They had two more sessions before she said,"Got to go. Must be up early for breakfast." She slipped out as quietly as she came in.

The next morning he packed and took his suitcase, chest and emergency bag to his car. He put them on the rumble seat floor and headed inside for breakfast. He ate lightly and waited until all the other diners had left. He went into the kitchen, came up on Priscilla's back and whispered, "You are something else. I must go to be back at my duty station by noon. I can't tell you how much I enjoyed the weekend. Can I come back again?"

"Any time cowboy, any time."

CHAPTER 80
End the Weekend In Style

Musher was back in his barracks at noon. He unpacked, put his dirty clothes in the second laundry bag and put the bag in his foot locker. He hung his Levi's on the rack next to the suit garment bag and put his boots next to the other shoes under his bed. He wrapped his towel around his waist. Armed with his shaving kit, cigarettes and lighter he headed for the showers. He must have stayed in the latrine for forty-five minutes, thirty of them in the shower. Back at his bunk he dressed in his G.I. attire. He counted his money and he had a little over three hundred in cash. It is time to go play something to build up his cash on hand. At the club he approached the SSA in the poker room and said, "A seat in the 10-20 game."

A seat was not immediately available so he walked back to the crap table where he had last lost two dollars. There was no one there except the table operators. "Musher, would you care to shoot?"

"I seldom win anything in this game but I will waste twenty-dollars."

First roll seven. "Let it ride" Next roll eleven. "Let it ride." Next roll seven. "Let it ride." Next roll eleven. "Let it ride" Next roll seven. "Let it ride" Next roll seven. "Cash me out."

The pit boss counted twelve hundred forty dollars. "For the boys", Musher threw a hundred dollars on the crap table. His pocket cash was now up to fourteen hundred twenty dollars. He said to the SSA, "I have lost interest in playing." He laid a twenty dollar tip on the SSA. He went in the bar and asked the bartender if he could get him some well buttered rye toast and a pot of hot tea.

"Sure I will be right back with your order." The bartender was the same one on duty the night Musher had the Crowleys to dinner.

Musher decided to take a ride into Salina to see if there was a pool hall with snooker tables. He was in luck, there were five pool tables and three snooker tables. Off to one side of the room there were two poker tables and six domino tables. The poker tables were quiet but the domino tables were going hot and heavy. He spoke to the man in the high chair who looked like he was supervising the room. "May I use one of the snooker tables to practice?"

"Two dollars an hour or any part of an hour."

"Can I get a cold coke?"

The coke appeared on the table, the man opened it and Musher said, "Here's five dollars, two hours in advance. Will that cover the coke, although he had already seen the sign saying coke cost twenty-five cents, "If it does, keep the change." He practiced making red balls and predetermining where he wanted the cue ball to be for the next red ball. This table rolled slower than the one in Junction City. Handling the extra length cue stick with a different shape and using the stick bridge became easier as he tried and tried more shots using them. One hour had gone by.

He racked the table to look exactly as the adjoining table and decided he needed to learn how to break. Not break by the snooker definition but by the straight pool definition. He remembered the old man said, "The cue ball must touch the red ball rack and at least one red ball must touch a rail." He tried his two rail straight pool break with a little more energy so that one red ball would reach a rail. Time and time again he either made contact with a number ball before the cue ball could reach the rack, he stroked the cue ball in a neutral location and the cue ball did not have enough impetus to make one red ball reach he rail or even worse, the cue ball had such impetus that it broke open the red ball rack.

Almost two hours practice went by and he was exhausted. He replaced the cue, reset the table and walked towards the door. Stopped to watch one of the nine ball games where the stakes were two for the five and five for the nine.

One of the players said to him, "Do you just play snooker or are you a nine ball player?"

"I am just trying to learn to play snooker and yes, I am a nine ball player."

"Would you like to join us? We're playing two and five."

"I appreciate your asking but I will pass."

"What is it airman, are you too good for us?"

"Yes I am."

The entire hall went quiet. "Just how good are you?"

"As good as I need to be to be a winner. I came to town to practice snooker. I have told you how good I am. If I prove it you will get upset and maybe a group of you will hurt me. Why don't we let it pass and I will go to the airbase?"

"Why don't you give us an exhibition?"

"Other than practice I only put a cue in my hand for significant money."

"Is twenty-five and seventy-five significant?"

"How many players will be on your team?"

"Five."

"Will you give me the first break?"

"Yes."

"Will we play a ten game set?"

Musher's mind calculated, five players, each losing one hundred dollars a rack, total five hundred dollars a rack, ten racks, five thousand dollars profit. "You must promise if I beat you all badly you will not retaliate against me as a group. If one of you five decides he wishes to retaliate that is all right with me."

"Show us your money."

"Musher handed the man in the chair one thousand dollars. If you will rack for me I will pay you. They will pay your fees. Show me your money."

Each put five hundred dollars in the hands of the man in the chair.

"Shall we begin." Musher selected a house cue from the rack, looked at the man in the chair and said, "Rack please."

He rolled the cue ball the length of the table a couple of times and banked the cue ball of a couple of rails just to get the feel of the table. "We begin."

Musher ran ten straight racks, hung up his cue and said to the man in the chair, "Five hundred for you and the rest is for me." Counting his thousand, five thousand five hundred.

His opponents were gripping their cues tightly and he was mentally preparing himself. He wished he had not put his cue back in the rack. The man in the chair was holding a shotgun on Musher's opponents and said, "Part of the deal was no group retaliation."

The guy who had prompted all this said, "One of us is OK" and started towards Musher. Musher made the great street move of falling on his back and kicking the oncoming enemy in the balls. He sprung to his feet, his enemy was bent forward and Musher gave him a vicious punch to the adam's apple, took his cue and beat him on the head with it. Kicked him in the ribs, rolled him onto his stomach and climbed on his back. "That's your one try. He is going to live but the next one or the next group will not." He turned to the man in the chair and handed him another five hundred dollars. "I appreciate your support. I hope I am welcome here again to practice snooker."

"Anytime Airman, Anytime."

CHAPTER 81

Waiting To Be Told

It was 0700 hours, the instructor team was sitting in the office and no one was speaking. Musher broke the silence. "For sure Dexter you must return the bus to the motor pool. Washed, cleaned and fully gassed. Get a signed receipt with the words on it, "no visible damage to the vehicle." Make sure Jefferson signs it. Please go now and we'll see you back here."

"Mister Leary why don't you and I sketch what we would like the certificate of completion to look like."

"I don't have any real artistic talent. You start, I'll watch and maybe I can make some contributions."

"I picture the certificate to be eight by ten on white parchment paper. The four corners of the perimeter would be anchored by a vertical colored picture of an incendiary round for the caliber 20 millimeter cannon. The space between the corners would be filled with vertical colored pictures of caliber .50 linked ammunition. An air force blue outline of the B-29 could fill most of the background. The text would be bold black. The heading would be centered below the border. We could use the same one as the one we used for the notebook cover. We could dress it up a little with wing and squadron emblems on either side of the heading: 301st Bob Wing (SAC), 351st Bomb Squadron, Aerial Gunners Training Course for the Remote Control System for the B-29 Central Fire System Control Gun Sight.

This to certify that (Rank and full name) successfully completed the 301st Bomb Wing Aerial Gunners Training Course for the Remote Control Systems for the Central Fire System Control Gun Sight (Rank and full name) participated in aerial gunnery film combat with the newest jet fighter aircraft in the US Air Force arsenal. His scored exercises confirmed that for every one hundred rounds of gun camera film fired at his target, he scored (Put in the percentage number as a hard number) hits on his target.

Clifford Nelson	Lt. Colonel Alan Morehouse,
Commanding Officer	Brigadier General
351st Bomb Squadron	Commanding Officer
	301st Bomb Wing

Dated	Dated

Leary looked at Musher's sketch done with colored pencils Leary didn't even know he had bought. "Where did you learn to do all that?"

"I am a high school graduate with a vivid imagination."

"You should consider college, there's no telling how far you could get."

Musher thought about his future as a bookie. Good money, fancy clothes, lots of girls, status among his peers, no worries about jail time and since he was Sicilian, maybe becoming a made man. "You're right Mister Leary". In the most frontal part of his mind, "No Way Jose!"

Dexter had returned and was instructed to staff the office while they were gone. With Musher's sketch in hand they headed for the wing audio-visual department. The OIC (Officer-in-Charge) was aware of the wing commander's wishes. He looked at the sketch and commented, "Very well done. I think we can make you happy. Give us a couple of days. We will make one for your approval before making the two masters for printing."

Leary called the office and told Dexter to meet them for lunch at the squadron dining hall. The three of them were eating lunch when they were joined by the first sergeant who simply delivered a message and left. "You two, at the Wing Commander's office at 1000 hours tomorrow."

Since the rest of the day looked dead, Leary was going to the Officer's Club "for a meeting."

Musher was going to Salina to practice his snooker.

Dexter was going to the office to hold down the fort. Musher would call him every hour and a half to see if there were any new developments.

He walked into an almost empty pool hall. Two domino tables were going, no poker and no snooker. The man in the chair greeted him, "Hello Musher."

Musher looked quizzically. "One of the domino players here yesterday is from Smoky Hill. He told everyone in here what your street name is and about your reputation as a.pool shooter, card player and fighter. You know your assailant is still in the hospital. Not too seriously hurt but seriously enough for them to keep. One of the guys you took the money from went to the sheriff to complain. The sheriff came here and I explained the whole situation and he just said to forget it all."

"Seems I am in your debt again. Two things, may I use your phone and can I get a coke?" He dialed Dexter and said, "Talk to me. Good I will talk to you soon."

The opened coke was on the counter and there was no mention of any advanced payment. He went back to the snooker table and resumed his practice. Two hours later he hung up his cue. At the desk waiting to pay he called Dexter. "Call it day. I will see you for dinner."

Some other people came while he stood there and said, "Hello Musher I enjoyed your pool shooting exhibition yesterday. Doubt if you will ever get a bet around here again. I know you won't be attacked by any single person."

The man in the chair said, "Four dollars twenty-five cents." Musher handed him a five. The man in the chair went on, "To be a serious snooker player you must own your own cue, one which will feel the same to you every time you pick it up. Behind me are six excellent quality cues which I have purchased from former snooker players who gave up the game. I will make you a very good price for one or two of your choice. New they originally cost over two hundred dollars each. With them I put in the carrying case. My price to you is what I paid for each cue. Twenty-five dollars per cue."

"I will take two, but not at twenty-five dollars each. My payment price is fifty dollars a cue including a carrying case for each one." He put one hundred dollars on the counter and asked to see all six cues. He chose two, cased them and left. Dinner with Dexter was very quiet. Musher did his SSS and was in his bunk very early.

CHAPTER 82
The General's Plan

Musher and Dexter were in their fanciest flying suits, shiniest boots and their 351st Bomb Squadron hats. It was 0815 hours when Mister Leary came into the office. He looked like death warmed over and as if he had passed out somewhere in his clothes. He had really hung one on. "I think I have a twenty-four hour bug. I am going to sick call. You take Dexter with you to see the wing commander. If he asks you can tell him I have come down with some kind of bug."

There was no comment from either Musher or Dexter. Leary turned and left the office.

"Dex we can do this. You must not speak unless you are asked a direct question. If you do not know the correct answer do not try to make one up and fool your questioner. That is fatal. I know you understand. I will do the talking and take all the heat if any comes our way. Let's walk to the flight line dining hall for coffee. Not later than 0915 we will take the base bus to wing headquarters."

At 0950 they entered the wing commander's waiting room. Musher went to the desk sergeant, "Staff Sergeant Musher and A2C Dexter here at the wing commander's request." "Take a seat and I will call you."

1000 hours came and went, 1030 hours came and went and finally the desk sergeant said, "You may go in now." Musher saluted, "Staff Sergeant Muscarello and A2C Dexter reporting as instructed. Sir, Mister Leary has come down with a bug and is at sick call."

General Morehouse said, "I could see he was coming down with a bug. He was trying to drown it at the club last night. Gentlemen, please sit down. We have less than ten weeks before the base closure and our aircraft and crews will be spread about in the rest of the Strategic Air Command. We have sixty-six fully staffed combat crews a total of one hundred forty-four enlisted aerial gunners. If we drop the commissioned staff from your training we can train eighteen every five days. I am afraid that at such an accelerated schedule you two might not be able to provide the finished product of the quality of the two first classes. Here is what I propose. We will do two more enlisted personnel gunnery training classes of fifteen students each. That will give us fifty highly qualified aerial gunners. From those fifty we will evaluate and select thirty, ten from each combat squadron, whom you will train to teach your course. I want you to provide me with a training program for the next two classes and the instructor course. I will give you four weeks from this coming Monday to finish the program. I want to see the curriculum and operational needs by Thursday. Musher, is Dexter sufficiently qualified to take on such a burden?"

"Sir, you have seen his shooting results. He is well schooled in the material, he is a hard worker and willing to sacrifice for the success of the program ."

"I will rely on your judgment. As usual you can count on the support you have had in the past. One last item. This Saturday morning I am holding a meeting of the combat crews at 1030 hours in the base theatre. I will explain our new enlisted personnel gunnery program. I want you, Leary and Dexter on the stage with me. I also want to award the Certificates of Completion for the first two classes. Will they be ready?"

"Sir, I shall be here not later than Wednesday at 1300 hours with the proposed certificate for your approval."

"Gentlemen I think that wraps it up. Make me proud."

Musher and Dexter rose, saluted and left his office.

On the base bus headed for the squadron dining hall Musher exclaimed, "Dexter, is this a load? If you have any plans for the next four weeks just unmake them. Between me and you, you know how much help Leary will be. No snickers or wise remarks when I ask him to do the menial chores to support this effort. Let's squeet."

They ate like two starved animals. Nerves will do that. Lunch ended, "Dex take the bus back to the office, figure out how we are going to get eighteen chairs in the classroom. Without guest chairs it would probably work. Do you think we need another gun sight? We will need many more notebooks and jeweler's cases when we get to thirty in the instructor class. We need to inventory our consumables for the full program. Don't mind me I am writing these down in my mental notebook. OK, I am going to call Jefferson for some taxi service to audio-visual and then back to the office. Any questions?" A nodded no.

Dexter left and Musher went into the Dining Room Supervisor's office to use his phone. After the typical motor pool greeting, "Jefferson, this is Musher. I am at my squadron dining hall and I need some taxi service to audio-visual and then back to our flight line office. Can you help?"

"Be there in less than five minutes, stand outside." The car pulled up and Jefferson was the driver. "I needed to get out of the office and I figured I would ride with you." He drove excellently, pulled up in front of A-V, "Do you want me to wait here?"

"Park it and come inside where it is cool. I cannot tell how long this may take me."

Musher asked to see the OIC. "Sir, General Morehouse has a different time table than you and I do. I must present him the draft tomorrow, the certificates must be made, dated for August 14, 1949 and lettered by 1200 hours Wednesday. The two authenticators must sign before 1800 hours Thursday. It has been suggested that the awarded to rank and name be done in Old English lettering. The shooting two digit one decimal point hard number be in black bold arial. We are all on the General's schedule. Can I expect to pick up the draft at 0900 hours tomorrow? I will bring the rank, names and shooting score for each certificate recipient." The OIC nodded yes. "Thank you sir, I will be here at 0900 hours."

"Jefferson, I am ready when you are."

On the way back to the office, "Jefferson can you pick me up at the squadron dining hall at 0830 hours tomorrow? Do I need to make a morning request?"

"I will take care of that. See you at 0830 hours tomorrow."

"Dexter, I need three copies of the graduate list showing rank, full name and middle initial and one decimal point hard number shooting percentage without the percentage sign. You know, 86.1, etc. I need it when you come to the barracks tonight. I will get it from you if not tonight at breakfast. We already have the five day course syllabus. I will work on the Instructor Course syllabus this afternoon and hope to finish tomorrow."

Dexter finished at 1800 hours and Musher had made a good dent in his composures. "Let's button up. We'll take the base bus to the NCO Club and I will buy you dinner."

CHAPTER 83

Set Up For Saturday and Monday

Musher and Dex were in the dining hall at 0630. After breakfast Dex went to the office to inventory the supplies needed for two fifteen student classes and one thirty student class. He also had instructions for Mister Leary. Leary came in about 0800 looking very well. He insisted and Dex replayed the meeting in the wing commander's office.

"Where is Musher?"

"He's at the squadron dining hall waiting for taxi service by Jefferson. He will go to A-V to pickup the certificate draft and drop off the names to be put on the certificates. He's supposed to get it at 0900 and if he is satisfied he is going to take it to the wing commander's office for approval before the final two originals are made. He promised it to General Morehouse not later than 1300 hours Wednesday. You know Musher, everything must be done ahead of schedule. Mister Leary Musher made this list of things he would like you to get for the next two classes and the instructor program. He said he would appreciate it if you could get all those things today."

Leary read the list, turned on his heels and went out of the office.

Musher looked at the proposed certificate. The A-V people had captured it all. The OIC had put one in a protective cover. They had made two just in case something happened to the first one. The OIC said, "One of those goes in my office safe. Can we get an approval as quickly as possible? The printing shop will need to make your fifty and we will need time to enter the individual data."

"Is this certificate ready for the printers? If it is approved I will take it to the printing shop for expedited print. I will be back with the blank certificates as soon as I can."

In a voice loud enough to be heard throughout the A-V Shop, "Jefferson, to the Wing Commander's office please."

He walked to the reception desk and said, "Staff Sergeant Muscarello to see the Wing Commander on an urgent item. The Wing Commander asked that I bring this item for review whenever it was ready." The desk sergeant picked up the phone, talked in a very low voice and then said, "You may go right in." Musher knocked, entered, saluted the wing commander and held out the protected certificate.

As the wing commander withdrew the certificate his eyes became bigger and so did his smile. "This captures it all. Who was the concept designer and artist?"

"Sir it was I. The A-V people took my sketch and instructions to make that product."

"Musher, you amaze me. Keep going. You're doing great."

Musher saluted and left the office.

"Jefferson, to the printing shop. You might want to come in. It might get interesting."

"Mister Leary just left here are you sure you need to see the OIC?"

"Yes please, this is a different matter for the same program."

"Musher, what can I do for you?" The OIC was a combat gunner-navigator who because of combat injuries was grounded but stayed in the military.

Musher showed him the certificate. "I need fifty of these in the next two hours."

"This is a three color process. I am not sure we can process fifty in two hours."

"I am due back in General Morehouse's office for his signature at 1400 hours. Do I call and tell his sergeant I cannot make it?"

"Get back here at 1330 and they will be dried and ready. I'll put them in a protective box."

In the car Jefferson said, "Were you a used car salesman before coming in the service?"

"Let's go to the club for lunch , I'll buy and I will shoot you a little one pocket pool. Will anyone report this car at the NCO Club?"

"If they do they will report it to me." Jefferson wolfed his sandwich and drink. He was ready to shoot some pool. All the tables were full. In anticipation of seeing a shooting match one table said, "We're done. You are welcome to this one." No one in the pool hall challenged that. Disappointment befell the pool hall as Jefferson and Musher played friendly one pocket bank pool. Jefferson was very good at that game and actually won more games than Musher.

"It's 1300, we better haul ass."

At the printing shop, true to his word, the OIC was there with fifty beautiful reproductions of the certificate. "We'll make sure General Morehouse knows of your support." To the A-V shop. He had withdrawn twenty-seven certificates from the box giving them two extra for uncorrectable mistakes. "You have twenty-five certificates to complete. It is now 1345 hours, three hours and fifteen minutes left in the work day.

Twenty-five certificates to complete in one hundred ninety five minutes, more than eight minutes for each one. Sir I don't wish to be disrespectful but with your highly competent staff five of them finish the project in less than one hour. I'll be back at 1600 to pick up the finished product. When I pick them up please return the data sheet I gave you for the certificate entries. Thank you very, very much. See you later."

"Musher you must have been a catholic used car salesman the way you lay on the guilt."

"Jefferson, let's go to my office and see what's happening. If you need to get back just drop me off and I will get Leary to take me and Dexter at 1600."

At the office Jefferson said he needed to go back to the motor pool. If Musher needed anything else give him a call. Maybe they could spend some time playing one pocket bank pool. Musher thanked him and asked for a rematch. Jefferson had a story to tell.

To Leary and Dexter, "How's it going. Did we get a lot done today? We pick up the completed certificates a 1600 today. Tomorrow I get our squadron commander to sign them and then deliver them to the Wing Commander for signature."

Dexter, "Look in the classroom. Mister Leary and I have arranged eighteen student chairs and still have the work table and the projector/vu-graph setup in tact. The instructor desk is now in this office it was taking to much space. Besides we didn't recall using it too much."

Leary. "I got all the consumables and the notebook inserts will be printed, punched and the notebooks filled tomorrow."

Musher. "So far one hell of a day. Mister Leary I think we still have time for one trip to base supply. If you drive I will tell you on the way. Dex button up anytime you wish and I will see you in the barracks."

On the way to base supply, "Mister Leary let me tell you what I think would make a real class act. I noticed in the orderly room those light black frames with a glass front. If the General gave out framed certificates that would be classy. We would need eighty-five to carry us through this program."

Musher waited in the car while Leary went into base supply. Soon the same little man who had helped Leary before came out with a cart loaded with little boxes. He put them in the trunk of Leary's car, Leary thanked him, shook hands with him and once again passed him some paper. "The unit pack is twelve. I had to take eight boxes."

"Did you bribe him?"

"That would be dishonest, do I look like a dishonest man to you? Let's go to the A-V Shop."

"It's a little early"

"If I know my man they will be ready. He is from the old school "Never make things look too easy."

He was right again, they were ready and the original data sheet was in the box also.

"Let's go sit in the dining hall and check that each certificate is correct." Each one was. "Tomorrow after breakfast I will take these to the first sergeant for him to get Lt Colonel Nelson's signature. If I can get that done in short time I will take them to the wing commander's office for signature."

"Wait for me in the orderly room and I will go to the Wing Commander's office with you."

CHAPTER 84

Last Minute Do's For Saturday and Monday

Musher waited until 0800 hours before entering the orderly room and approaching the first sergeant. "Sergeant Alba, excuse me. I am sure you are familiar with General Morehouse's program for the enlisted gunners in this wing." He took one certificate and handed it to the first sergeant. "There are twenty-four more of those in this box. I would appreciate it if you could get Lt. Colonel Nelson's signature so that I may take them to General Morehouse's office for his signature."

"When do you want them back?"

"I would like to wait for him to finish so I can take them to General Morehouse for his signature."

"Have a seat." He picked up the box and went into the Commanding Officer's office.

The first sergeant, "Muscarello come in here."

The Commanding Officer," Does General Morehouse intend to distribute these at the aerial gunners meeting on Saturday?"

"Sir that is what he has told me."

"I would like one of these for myself."

"Sir as soon as I get them framed I will deliver one to Sergeant Alba."

It took Lt. Colonel Nelson less than fifteen minutes to sign the certificates.

"Sergeant Alba, Mister Leary directed me to wait for him here because he wants to go to the wing commander's office with me. May I sit here?"

"You know what he wants don't you? He wants on the gravy train and a few points for his OER (Officer Efficiency Report). You can't smoke in here but feel free to wait outside. If he questions why you are outside, send him to see me."

It was 1030 hours before Mister Leary appeared at the squadron orderly room. He looked all right but you could tell he had a heavy drinking night. They drove to wing headquarters and Leary said, "I'll wait here."

Before going into wing headquarters Musher added five certificates to the pile. In the wing commander's waiting room he told the desk sergeant why he was there. The soft voice on the telephone and then, "He said to leave them and come back about 1330 hours and they will be ready."

In the car Musher relayed to Leary what had happened on his delivery.

It's close to lunch why don't we just go to the squadron dining hall to eat. Musher was ready to eat. They were among the first in the serving line. They had corned beef and cabbage, whole white potatoes and corn bread. The air force believes in large lunch, lighter dinner. They had almost an hour and half before they needed to be back at the wing commander's office. One hour and fifteen minutes later they were back in the wing commander's waiting room. The desk receptionist said, "You may go right in."

Mister Leary led and they saluted. General Morehouse waved them into a seat. "Musher how do you propose to set these for distribution."

"Today and tomorrow we will mount them in a frame, separate them by squadron, alphabetize by rank and last name, and make easily handled packages. We will prepare a list of the recipients using the same sort features. Airman Dexter will have the same list we give you. It is our job to make sure you don't call one name and get the certificate for another name. As you read a name and the data, I shall hand you the certificate for that individual. Airman Dexter and I will be in place with all the items at 1000 hours Saturday morning."

"My A-V people will take care of the setup. Behind me on my right will be Airman Dexter, you, Mister Leary, then my senior staff and the three bomb squadron commanders. Do you have anything else?"

"Sir would you consider as part of your closing the naming of the individuals whose outstanding contributions greatly assisted for these two classes to succeed?"

"Have the list in my office tomorrow morning."

They rose, saluted and left his office.

There was still a lot to do. The Musher made sure he had kept five blank certificates with the original wing commander's signature separated from the group. The three of them practiced doing Lt Colonel Nelson's signature. They concluded Mister Leary made the closest resemblance. Musher made sure the certificates with the phony signatures were not for members of the 351st.

While Musher and Dexter worked on the list for the General, Mister Leary signed the blank five for Lt. Colonel Nelson.

"It's getting late. We should call it a day. We have Thursday and Friday to mount the certificates and get everything ready for Saturday. Mister Leary, on your way in tomorrow could you see your little buddy at Base Supply and get four boxes of eight and one half bond paper. Not reams, boxes. We will transport the certificates in them."

Leary, "I'll drop you guys off at the squadron."

CHAPTER 85
Time To Goof Off

While Mister Leary and Dex were mounting certificates in the frames Musher made the list of people without whose support the gunnery program would not have been successful. General Morehouse would identify them, praise them and solicit a major round of applause for them.

"Mister Leary, why don't you take this list to the wing commander's office? Dex and I will finish the framing, sort the certificates and put them into the squadron boxes for Saturday?"

"I should be back in an hour."

"We'll be right here."

Dexter quizzed, "Musher, why did you ask him to go there. You know he is trying to capture the laurels for this program?"

"Dex, he is a lifer. (**One who makes the military a career**). He has a drinking problem. He is not exactly wearing one of General Morehouse's halos. If we can do anything to help him out, let's do it."

True to his word Leary was back in less than an hour. "I gave the reception sergeant the list for the General and he handed me this envelope addressed to you. It almost killed me not to open it."

Musher extracted the paper. It was hand written on the General's note stationary. He read aloud:

"Musher, notify everyone on your list to be at the Saturday meeting in full Class A uniform. They are to sit front row center."

"Mister Leary I think you should be the one to tell them. We know they will be curious. Let's play the military game. Give them this answer, "I don't know any more than you do but when a Brigadier General asks for my presence you can bet your sweet ass I will be wherever and whenever he asks me to." You have the rest of today to personally notify six men. We are ready for Saturday and Monday. We don't want to fool around with our situation you know what they say, "Don't oversell the car."

Mister Leary spoke," Dex give me a copy of the General's list. I promise not to lose it. How about I give you guys a ride to the squadron dining hall and you both take the rest of the day off. We will meet here tomorrow morning." It didn't take any coaxing to square away and lock up.

At the dining table Dex asked Musher, "What are we going to do with the rest of the day?"

"Hadn't given it much thought."

"Maybe we could go to the matinee or you could teach me to play gin rummy."

"I have a better idea, write your girl a nice long letter."

"Boy, I know when I am not wanted." He left the dining hall.

Musher gave him time to get close to the orderly room before leaving for the barracks. He showered and put on his cowboy clothes. Checked the contents of his emergency bag and was satisfied everything was there. He counted his money and with the money from the NCO Club and his most recent scores he had over ninety-five hundred dollars. Next stop the American Express office where he opened an account with eight thousand dollars. Feeling on top of the world he headed for Salina and the Emporium.

He was greeted by the man in the chair. All the pool tables were active, both snooker tables were active, all the domino tables were full but there was one seat open in the two and five poker game. He remarked to the man in the chair, "What are you giving away today. It's only Wednesday. Can I sit in the poker game?"

"I don't see why not, your money is as good as anybody else's. Come let me introduce you."

"Can you take care of my cues?" But of course.

"Guys this gentleman is from Smoky Hill. I know him to be tough but honest. He wants to join your game. Anyone object?"

There was no cash on the table only chips. The apparent banker said, "We play five stud or five draw jacks or better. Nothing wild, dealer's choice. Fifty dollars to buy in."

Musher put a hundred on the table, "a double buy please."

The game was typical small time gamblers, chasing cased cards, trying to buy a pot for five dollars and in five card stud raising the bet because they had an ace up. Musher played his usual conservative game. There was no hanky-panky in this game. Within two hours his hundred dollar investment looked like three hundred dollars. It was almost four-thirty and he was tired of playing this game. It looked like he was the big winner and he didn't need another confrontation in this place. "Guys, I must go. I have duty at Smoky at 7:30 P.M. today. I appreciate you letting me play. I am sure we will do it again some time soon." He picked up his cues from the man in the chair and gave him a twenty-dollar tip.

He headed for the NCO Club.

CHAPTER 86
Two Days Till Saturday

Thursday was a tortuous day. Checking and rechecking the preparations for Saturday and Monday. The three of them did "nothings" to pass away the morning. Mister Leary broke the ice, "I'll drop you guys off at the squadron dining hall. Musher you guard the fort here this afternoon. Dexter I'll see you in the morning.".

At the table Dexter said, "Listen Musher if you have something you want to do today I will go back to guard the fort. I have already written all my letters."

"Thanks Dex but it might be nice to have a few hours of absolute quiet. Maybe I will try to write a letter."

Back at the office he cleared Leary's desk and took out a deck of cards. He hadn't practiced in a long, long time. Don't believe the axiom, practice makes perfect. It does not, practice makes permanent. He spent three hours doing all the things he would do if he were trying to control a game. The easiest of all games to control is Black Jack. As dealer, banker, you don't care what anyone else gets you concentrate on your own hand. If the table bet is so heavy you put all the aces on the bottom of the deck and make sure you have two face cards. Even playing "a push is a push" you must have a better hand than five of the nine hands playing.

It was 1600 hours when the Wing Commander entered the office. Musher stood at attention. " I was on the flight line and I thought I would drop in and see if you all were ready for Saturday. Where are your other two staff people?"

"Sir I believe Mister Leary would be in his quarters by now. Airman Dexter is most probably in the barracks writing letters home."

"Our gunnery training program has attracted a lot of attention outside the 301st Bomb Wing. General Lemay, the SAC commander, called me this morning asking for a personal report after we finish the instructor training program. Within seventy-two hours following the last instructor critique I want you to deliver to my Chief of Wing Operations a completed staff study of the program. I know you don't know how to do one but the library is full of books laying out the who, what, when, where and why. My Chief of Wing Operations will edit your work and make suggestions for you to achieve a report worthy of sending to General Lemay."

The wing commander left as quietly as he came.

I need to at least get some ideas how to do a completed staff study. The library, they must have books that tell how. Besides Hannah might be there. He picked up his car and headed for the library. Hannah was there. He asked her about the books he might need and she led him to a rear section of the library. She was on a step-up stool when he ran his hand under her dress. She lost her balance but he caught her. "What time do you get off?"

"1900 but my dad is coming to pick me up."

"Call him and tell him I am picking you up and we are going to eat and maybe the 2200 movie."

"My mom says OK but I must be home not later than midnight."

"I'll just sit here and read this book until 1900." The book, "How to compose a completed staff study" was not very thick and it was full of exhibits and suggestions. By time 1900 came, he had a proposed table of contents and outline pictured in his head. He took the book to Hannah and she did the mechanics which would allow him to take it from the library. She left the return date open-ended.

They ate in the BX cafeteria. They talked, laughed and he smoked. "What say Hannah, ready for the scenic tour?"

In his car they drove to the same spot they had been the night of the dinner at the club. The activities repeated themselves. It was 2215 when he walked her to her front door, kissed her lightly and promised to call.

CHAPTER 87
Tomorrow Is the Day of Recognition

The three were in the office drinking coffee which Mister Leary had brought. Musher told them of the unannounced visit from the wing commander yesterday afternoon and the context of the wing commander's conversation. He acknowledged that he had never even heard of a completed staff study much less alone written one. He solicited their help in the fact gathering. By Monday morning each of them would have a stenographer notebook and at the end of every day each would write what he believed to be the highlights of the day. The notebook would be for no other purpose.

Mister Leary, "Did he ask why you were here alone?"

"No he asked where you were. I told him you were in your quarters and Dex was in the barracks. He certainly did not look upset. If we goof tomorrow he will remember yesterday afternoon and surely believe we did not do all we should have done in preparation for tomorrow We are not going to goof. Dex and I will be there tomorrow at 0815. Mister Leary please come not later than 0940. Today we will put everything we need for tomorrow in my rumble seat. Dex and I are going to wear our fancy flying suits and 351st hats, Mister Leary it's your choice but I think a combat veteran as highly decorated as you are would come in Class A uniform. I believe we are totally ready except to put the items in my car."

Mister Leary, "Let's put the stuff in my car and I will transport it to your car. Dex this is your day to guard the fort. Stay until 1600 just in case. I will be in my quarters, Musher where will you be?"

"I hope to be in Salina practicing snooker."

He had second thoughts about leaving all the materials in his car. He brought them into his barracks, emptied his foot locker and secured the materials there. He put the contents of the locker on his bed. There really wasn't anything that anyone would want and if they did, it was all replaceable.

There was a snooker table available for practice. Coke in hand and his two cues, he went back to the empty table. He alternated cue sticks and the type of shot he was trying to make. He had been practicing when the two fellows at the next table stopped shooting, shook hands and one left the pool area. The other came to Musher.

"Are you interested in playing a game?

"Yes I am."

"Would you still be interested in a hundred point game at ten dollars a game and time?"

Musher thought, "What can he beat me for at ten dollars a game. Fifty maybe or at worst a hundred. This will give me a chance for some competition. Yes I am."

Fortunately Musher won the lag. He said to his playing partner, My name is Musher." His playing partner said, "They call me Chili. It is my brother you sent to the hospital. If the man in the chair told me the truth as he always does you didn't start it and you warned them you would take all their money. It's closed as far as I am concerned."

Chili made a great break. There was no shot available to Musher. He played a safety and Chili returned the favor. After three more safeties Musher made a mistake. Chili pounced; he ran sixty points before he missed.

Musher believed that if he did not run the game he will not get a second chance in this game. He played his best but on the seventy-sixth point red ball his shot rattled at the top of the pocket but did not drop.

As expected Chili finished the game.

The next four games were close but Chili won them all. Musher handed him fifty dollars and said, "I hate to quit even though you are kicking my ass. Tomorrow is a big day for me."

Chili, "The man in the chair tells me you have been playing snooker for less than three weeks. I don't want to meet you after the next two months. I will, because you are a good competitor and you are good for my reputation."

Musher left ten dollars on the counter and headed back to Smoky. Dining at the squadron, to the barracks and check the foot locker contents, take the items off his bunk, crawl in the bunk and try to sleep. He set his alarm clock for 0530 hours. He would wake up Dex at 0530 and they would head for their first major exposure to their peers.

CHAPTER 88
Maybe This Is a Better Life Than a Bookmaker

"Dex, up, up. Grab your kit. SSS time." Before he put on his best flying suit Musher half-ass made his bunk. He took his gear off the floor to put it on his bunk. He explained to Dex what was in his foot locker and why. They carried the locker to Musher's rumble seat, locked it in and drove the car to the squadron dining hall. Neither ate much breakfast. Musher was almost chain smoking and Dexter kept sipping cold milk. They were at the base theater at 0745. No one else was there and the theater was closed.

The first members of the setup teams showed up at 0800. Musher and Dexter took their locker to the stage. Dexter used the locker as a table top and arranged the certificates in the order they would be awarded. Musher sought out the A-V OIC.

"Sir I don't know if you have the same instructions as I have from General Morehouse but he wants the distinguished honorees to sit in the center of the first row, directly in front of him. Here is a copy of the list. I am so pleased you are on the list. There is no specific seating arrangement for the honorees since none will do more than stand and face the audience when called by the General. The list is arranged alphabetically by rank. As for the certificate awardees, may I suggest you seat them in the first row in accordance with the list sequence to minimize the time to get to the General when the General calls them up to receive the award. Sir that is my understanding of the General's wishes."

"I want to thank you for putting me on the list. I will do the seating as you understand the general's wishes."

A check with Dexter showed everything in place and in the right order. There was nothing to do but wait. Mister Leary came in at 0930 in his full regalia. He could have easily been the poster boy for the adult USAF lifer. At 0959 General Morehouse came on the stage to a "Ten Hut" which brought everyone to his feet.

"Good morning gentlemen, please be seated. Our program this morning will be divided into three parts.

Part One. To talk a little bit about the last two classes of training on the RCS CFSC gun sight; To talk about the two upcoming classes of training on the RCS CFSC gun sight; To talk about the graduates of those classes of training on the RCS CFSC gun sight; and To talk about the selection and training of thirty graduates to become qualified instructors to train other gunners on the RCS CFSC gun sight. He talked in greater detail about the four items in part one.

Part Two. To award a certificate of completion to those who have successfully proven their capability as an aerial gunner using the RCS CFSC system. He read the first statistic on his list. Master Sergeant Alan Ackroyd, 351st Bomb Squadron, Percentage of hits per rounds fired, 89.6. Ackroyd saluted, they shook hands and Ackroyd made his way to his seat exiting the stage from the opposite end from which he came on. He read the next statistic on his list. Master Sergeant Fred Bartholomew, 351st Bomb Squadron, Percentage of hits per rounds fired, 88.4. Bartholomew saluted, they shook hands and Bartholomew made his way to his seat exiting the stage from the opposite end from which he came on. The General repeated this process until all the awardees had received their certificates and were back in the seats. Gentlemen let's stand in applause for their accomplishments.

Part Three. Anyone with one hour of flying time knows that nothing is done well without the support of the people who back up the flight crew. Our training program has been highly successful because of the efforts of these officers and airmen. Please stand and face the audience when I call your name. Major Spunky Dickerson, OIC the Photo Lab. Captain David Wentworth, OIC Audio-Visual, Master Sergeant Dooley, NCOIC 351st Bomb Squadron Unit Supply, Master Sergeant Driver, NCOIC 301st Sheet Metal Shop, Master Sergeant Huey Long, Crew Chief, B-29 Combat Aircraft Number 121, and so on until he completed the list. Gentlemen let's stand in applause for their contributions.

No acknowledgements would be complete without recognizing the three individuals who made the entire training program possible. CWO Leary, 351st Squadron Gunnery Officer, Staff Sergeant Muscarello, Aerial Gunner and Training Instructor, and A2C Dexter, Aerial Gunner and Training Instructor. Gentlemen let's stand in applause for their accomplishments." During the applause the General walked to the three and shook their hands.

"That's it for this morning. I want to thank you for coming. Keep up the good work." At 1154 General Morehouse left the stage to a "Ten Hut" which brought everyone to his feet.

Mister Leary, "Are we eating at the squadron dining hall today?"

"Yes we are."

"Good I will see you there."

They were standing in the serving line when Mister Leary joined them. "When I lived in the BOQ (Bachelor Officers Quarters, you need not be a

291

bachelor to live there) I came here every Saturday night for dinner. Hot dogs and beans. Just love them."

Lunch today was beef stew, gravy, biscuits and salad. Ice cream for dessert. Bob Halloran joined them at their table. "I was there, congratulations to you three."

Musher asked Dex to take his car back to the lot and bring his foot locker into the barracks. He said he needed to make a long distance call and he would be along as soon as it was finished. He dialed Priscilla's number. To the sweet voice, "This is Musher how are you?"

"I thought you had transferred or just dropped me."

"No way, I have been up to my ears in work. I am off now until 4 P.M. tomorrow. Can you stand a guest?"

"Of course, remember supper is at 6:30."

"I thought we might go to Eddie County if you wanted to."

"Great, see you for supper."

At the barracks he changed into his cowboy clothes, packed his small suitcase and headed for the Class Six Store. "Three bottles of Vodka, the weakest proof please." He added, two six packs of seven-up, two bags of ice and a two quart thermos which he filled with water. Back at his car he emptied half of each bottle of vodka and filled it up with water. He put the vodka and the seven-up on ice in his chest and put the chest on the rumble seat floor. She likes to drink vodka with seven-up, she will never know the vodka has been cut.

He was in the Junction City pool hall by quarter to three. Every table pool, snooker, dominoes and poker was full. The man in the chair greeted him warmly. He could see Chili playing snooker. As he watched closely Chili was laying off so as to not make the game too much of a runaway. Chili acknowledged his presence with a slight nod. Chili's partner paid Chili six dollars, they shook hands and his playing partner left. Chili looked at him, "Are you up to a rematch. Same stakes only this time I give you a ten point handicap."

Musher almost told him where he could put the handicap but instead thought of what the aircraft commander had said to the bandit leader, "Lay on MacDuff and damned be he who first cries hold enough."

First game, Musher one hundred with handicap. Second game Chili one hundred Musher thirty-six. Third game, Musher one hundred with handicap, Chili fifty-four. It went that way for almost two hours.

At five o'clock they were even. Musher, "Time for me to go. I'll pay for the time in thanks for the lessons."

"Remember I said how good I thought you would be in two months, make that two days. You are phenomenal for your experience. You staying at Priscilla's? Taking her to Eddie County tonight? Be careful, word on the street is that her ex-husband will be laying for you. Take this paper, it will show you an alternate route back. He won't be looking there. Have a good night."

He parked in the back, took his suitcase and knocked on the front door. She looked fabulous. He gave her a kiss peck and headed for his room. She had put a large ash tray where no ash tray had existed before. His legs wee tired from the afternoon bending and stretching on that oversized snooker table. He rested until 6:25 and then went down for supper. He knew it would be hot dogs and beans and he ate his share plus. As the diners were leaving the table the head of the poker night said, "The way Miss Priscilla is dressed I suppose you are taking her dancing. How are we supposed to get our money back?"

At eight forty they arrived at Eddie County. Musher went into the rumble seat and came back out with a fifth of vodka in a paper bag. He paid his five dollar entry fee and there were no empty tables. They sat at a table which showed there were two others there but they were most probably out dancing. The waitress brought two seven ups and two glasses of ice. He had prepped for this at the Emporium. He traded the man in the chair five twenties for twenty fives. He gave the waitress a five and thanked her. They were line dancing on the floor and he said to Priscilla, "I remember this, let's go do it."

"Not until I have had a couple of drinks."

Musher filled her ice glass more than half full of the vodka and she drank it like a camel on the desert. She held out her glass and he filled it again. She gulped that one and said, "Let's dance." For the rest of the evening she drank the watered-down vodka and it did not seem to have an effect on her. They danced and she was very pleasant. About eleven thirty he coaxed her into leaving. Most of the watered-down vodka was still in the bottle. At the car he put the vodka back in the chest and locked the rumble seat. The man in the chair told him that if you had unopened liquor in your car but it was so positioned that you could not reach it while driving you could not be booked for an open liquor bottle when driving.

She asked why he was taking the back road route. "Scenic, that's all baby, scenic." The road was mostly dirt and without any lights. The scenic route took longer but they were back at her place without incident. Meanwhile sitting out on the highway was a state trooper eagerly awaiting the little yellow convertible so he could cart them off to the county jail for any or no reason.

They kissed lightly in the hall and went into their separate rooms. Before long he heard her enter his room and crawl in bed beside him. It was a sensational night.

Breakfast was at six thirty. He packed, put everything in his car, went into the kitchen for coffee and told Priscilla he had to leave earlier than expected. He had something to do before duty which he had forgotten. He squeezed her, patted her butt, kissed her neck and told her she was just wonderful. He promised to call her this week.

The truth of the matter was he could not wait to get to the snooker table at the Emporium. It was seven thirty when he got there and it was open. It looked like it had been open all night. The poker players were going at it hot and heavy. He went back to the snooker table and began his practice. By ten thirty he was done. He paid the man in the chair, thanked him and promised to return soon.

"Be careful on the highway, Priscilla's ex is till looking for you. I guess you used Chili's return route because her ex was breathing fire when he came in here at two this morning." Musher pulled into the barracks parking lot without incident. Now for SSS and a long nap. Tomorrow begins the eighteen.

CHAPTER 89

Eighteen Students For Each of the Next Two Classes

The instruction staff was in place at 0730 hours, Monday. The students were in place at 0815, Monday. Everything was set to go. Mister Leary made his welcoming speech introducing the other two instructors.

Musher did his introductory presentation.

The day went smoothly. The class went to lunch in the aircrew bus provided by Jefferson Carter. At the 1615 class wrap up the students policed the area and most took their notebooks when they left.

The three instructors sat with their notebooks writing in what they considered the highlights of the day.

Musher was so tired from the day he had dinner in the squadron dining hall and soon thereafter his SSS. Long before 2200 hours Musher was fast asleep . He didn't even bother to set his alarm.

Tuesday and Wednesday morning were copies of Monday. Wednesday afternoon the P Patch was hotter than hell. The class did its gun sight calibration exercises without complaint. The students who were not active in the aircraft sat in the air conditioned bus. The instructor staff spent the entire exercise period aboard the aircraft. At the end of the exercise period the instructor staff looked like they had been standing under the shower.

No one spoke riding back to the classroom. Mister Leary reminded them that tomorrow was the shooting day and station time at the shack was 0700 hours. He dismissed the class while they were still on the bus.

Despite their discomfort the instructor staff went into the office, took their notebooks and made their entries.

Mister Leary dropped them off in front of their barracks. Both could not wait to get their kits and hit the showers. It was going to another early to bed like yesterday.

Everyone was on the bus at 0645 hours. The routine was standard. Pickup parachutes, load the aircraft, listen to the briefing by the aircraft commander, be divided into forward and aft shooting teams and board the aircraft. Routine takeoff and climb out. Contact with the bandits. The instructor team was not shooting today. With eighteen students every minute of attack time must be reserved for them. At the end of the attack period some students had a three time shooting opportunity and some had a two time shooting opportunity. The landing, parking and deplaning was without incident. Musher thanked the AC and his crew for their help. The AC and his crew had their own crew bus. Mister Leary et al were going to return the parachutes and then head for the 351st dining hall. There was lots of chatter on the ride in and it continued in the dining hall. None of these gunners had ever "fought" against a jet aircraft. They marveled with the comparisons of a prop driven fighter to the angles and speed of the jet. "I'll be lucky if I even got a hit".

Musher stood to make an announcement. "Tomorrow is the critique of the class work and today's shooting. There is a lot of data to review and compile so that each of you will know his results from today. Given that we will be very busy tomorrow morning, we cannot get the film until much later today, class will convene at 1300 hours tomorrow. Any questions? From here you may go where you choose or you may ride with us back to the classroom. Remember class convenes at 1300 hours tomorrow."

Despite their discomfort the instructor staff went into the office and made their notebook entries.

Mister Leary told them he would have the film in the office not later than 0800 tomorrow. He dropped them off in front of their barracks. Both could not wait to get their kits and hit the showers. Tomorrow should be an easier day.

As tired as Musher was he had dinner and was in bed early.

Mister Leary brought the film as promised. Musher and Dexter began the note taking while Leary ran the projector. As usual they ran the films twice to be sure they had not made an error. Dexter already knew what the compilation would look like and had made a template of this class. It was merely a matter of filling in the blanks correctly. The three of them masked the vu-graphs to the holders, Musher marked the sequence and the arrows for the correct placement on the vu-graph. They did a walk through and were satisfied they were ready. It was already 1130.

"Dex, why don't you take the bus to the motor pool. Musher and I will meet you there. Give it a quick bath, you know the routine. Go."

By 1200 the three were eating lunch in the squadron dining room. By 1245 hours they were in the office waiting for the students. All the students were in place by 1250 hours. At 1300 the critique began. It followed the same routine as the previous two classes. The highest scorer was 98.1 percent and the lowest was 87.0 percent. The class average for the eighteen students was 92.1 percent. During the results reading there were a number of "I don't believe it", "You must have mistaken my film for someone else's", "I didn't think I even got a hit". There were a number of comments about the way the material was presented and the motivation for good shooting. The classroom was set up for the next class of eighteen students. A lot of hand shaking and thank you's from the students.

Musher had Dexter come in on Saturday to type a report to the wing commander, the 351st squadron commander, the CSOps. and the other two squadron commanders who had students in the class. He would have Leary deliver the reports later today or he would. While Dex was typing he devoted his attention to consolidating the information from the three notebooks. He was sure he would still be doing it tomorrow. There were a few common observations which he knew would appear in the final report.

The second class of eighteen begins on this coming Monday.

The training week was a duplicate of the week of the first eighteen student class. Nothing really changed, the same questions were asked, the same answers were given, the ramp exercises were the same and the fourth day airborne shooting exercise was the same. The critique followed the same routine. The highest scorer was 92.3 percent and the lowest was 85.5 percent. The class average for the eighteen students was 88.6 percent. As expected, during the results reading the students mumbled the same comments, "I don't believe it", "You must have mistaken my film for someone else's", "I didn't think I even got a hit". Even the goodbyes and thank you's were the same.

Dexter had the format for the results report. Musher asked him to have it ready by noon tomorrow. He would accompany Musher when they dropped off the report on Sunday afternoon.

Mister Leary, "Well guys you did excellently again this week. I am leaving."

Before he could get his first step towards the door Musher told him that he and Dex would deliver the reports tomorrow. "You and your family deserve a good Sunday."

CHAPTER 90
Selection and Training of RCS CFCS Instructors

Mister Leary and Dexter were working in the classroom while Musher continued to study the three notebooks of training class highlights. The phone rang and Musher picked it up. "This is Sergeant Wooly. You and Mister Leary will report to the wing personnel officer at 1100 hours. Is Mister Leary available?"

"Yes sergeant, he is here and we will be there. Thank you." He had just barely hung up the phone when Leary and Dex were staring at him. He relayed Sergeant Wooly's instructions. They were at the wing personnel officer's office at 1030. They were escorted to a conference room where there were two other officers also waiting. Colonel MacIntosh, the WPO came in at precisely 1100 hours. All stood.

"Please be seated". The two officers were introduced, Major Denton, OIC, Base Education Office and his assistant Captain Robert Seals. Then Leary and Musher were introduced. "Let me get right to it. First, Mister Leary and your staff have done a superb job training the aerial gunners in the technical use of the gun sight in your program. That is what you and your people did, train the technical use of the gun sight. The shooting scoring results of the sixty-one shooters bear witness to that fact. Now we are faced with the selection of thirty of those to be trained to teach others what they have learned from you. The art of instruction requires special training by personnel who are trained to teach the art of instruction. The responsibility to teach the art of instruction is transferred to the Base Education Office (BEO). Staff Sergeant Muscarello you will sit as an advisor to the BEO selection committee. Major Denton's staff will brief you on the selection procedure and where to be and when. Mister Leary, as for you I have good news and I have bad news. The bad news is that we have received a request for a wing gunnery officer for one of the SAC wings. You meet all the criteria and this week you will be transferred to satisfy the request. The good news is the SAC wing is at McCoy AFB, Orlando, Florida. That's it gentlemen, carry on." They stood and he left the room.

Major Denton stopped Musher, "The selection process begins tomorrow. Please be at my office at 1500 today for your briefing." With that he and his assistant left the room.

Leary and Musher sat down. "I am glad for you. I have never been in Florida have you?"

"Years ago, it is a great place. No sand and you can bet as an active combat wing the best personnel and equipment available in the Strategic Air Command. I need to go home and tell the wife. She will be packing today. She will be thrilled. Next year my only daughter starts college. We will be Florida residents and the tuition will not be too bad. I'll drop you at the dining hall. I will be scarce from here on out."

Musher walked into the dining hall to find Dexter waiting for him. They went through the serving line and Dexter looked as if he was going to burst. At the table Dexter could no longer hold it. "Guess what Mush, the first sergeant called me at the office. He told me he had good news and good news. Effective next week I am an Airman First Class; and, in less than two weeks I am being transferred to McCoy AFB, Orlando, Florida. Is that good and good?"

"That is a good good combo. I am very happy for you, you deserve it." Musher wondered if Dex was being sent to McCoy to protect Leary.

"What happened at personnel?"

Musher relayed what happened at personnel. "We are definitely out of the teaching business and after the selections are made I have no idea what will become of me."

"Maybe you will come to McCoy too."

"We'll see. Right now I need to freshen up, get my car and make sure I am not late at the BEO. I want you to go back to the office and make a list of things that you and Mister Leary should take to McCoy. Be sure to include a jeweler's case for each of you. I intend to take one and return three to Lowry with a note that three were lost in training missions. Lesser will be off the hook for pecuniary liability. If you want to come with me I will drop you at the office on my way to the BEO."

At the office drop off Musher said to Dexter, "Look Leary has transfer orders and just about told me he was done worrying about this place. Don't you go so lax that we could not handle any turn of events. We will have time for breakdown and return of goods before you leave. OK?"

At 1430 hours Musher was in the BEO's waiting room. His secretary, a cute little Mexican girl, led Musher to a conference room. There sat Captain Seals the Assistant BEO Officer. He introduced the NCOIC of the BEO as Master Sergeant Walter Reading. Together they briefed Musher on the procedures which the selection process would follow and what they were looking for in each candidate. Musher's role was to sit and listen. They emphasized sit and listen. When the individual interview was over they would draw a conclusion about the candidate. If he had any reason to disagree with their conclusion he was encouraged to speak it. Did he have any questions?

Captain Seals, "The interviews begin at 0800 hours tomorrow. You are expected to be in the interview room 0730 hours. The interviews will be held in Room 246 in this building. Each interview is scheduled for thirty minutes. If they are done in less so be it. With sixty candidates the program requires thirty interview hours or almost five full work days. Since we are beginning on Tuesday we will go straight through to Sunday if necessary. One more point. During the interviews do not make any paper notes or smiles or grimaces when a candidate answers a question or gives and opinion. Please do not wear a flying suit. Wear khakis. If you have no questions or comments that is it for today. We will see you in the morning."

Next stop the NCO Club. Two cokes and three Luckies later he called Dexter. Button up, see you at the barracks.

He lay on his bunk and concluded I am only window dressing. The BEO wants to say they had a technical adviser to the selection committee who had seen the candidates in the classroom and the airborne shooting environments. In his world he would be labeled a "shill", one who makes the game look good but has no real investment in the outcome.

After dinner he was looking at his khakis and they did not look very good. He had seen a couple of guys who pressed their own khakis and they always looked sharp. He went to the first one with his shirt and pants and said, "Two dollars to press these and make them look like yours."

"Deal."

In fifteen minutes they were returned on a hangar looking beautiful. He put on the brass, his wings and his sharpshooter badge. His garrison cap was brushed, his shoes were at a high gloss and his belt buckle did not show a scratch. They could not complain about those clothes. In the morning he would wear a flying suit to breakfast and come back here to change before going to the BEO.

CHAPTER 91
I Was Not To Speak, Just Be Seen

Musher was up early, did his SSS, squared away his area and had a good breakfast. He came back to the barracks dressed in his khaki's and with his stripes, his aerial gunner badge, sharpshooter medal and his air force blue name tag over his right breast pocket, no one would know he had only been in the military for almost ten months. Yesterday he noticed that the BEO building had a large parking lot. He parked his car in a space without any reserved parking indicators. At 0710 he was in Room 246.

At 0745 Captain Seals and Sergeant Reading came in carry stacks of personnel records. Musher rose, Seals said, "Carry On."

Musher sat and became as comfortable as he could. This was going to be a long day.

The first candidate entered at precisely 0800. Seals began the questioning. Musher listened intently to see what kind of answer he would give before the candidate answered. Sergeant Reading asked the next question. Musher paid close attention. The "good cop, bad cop" routine continued until Seals thanked the candidate and excused him. The candidate rose, saluted and left. Six more candidates were interviewed in the same manner.

At 1130 hours Seals declared there was not enough time before lunch. Reading stepped into the waiting area and told the candidates to break for lunch but be back here not later than 1245. Inside Seals told Musher the same thing. As Musher went out the door, Seals was right behind him locking the entry. Reading joined Seals and they headed off without a single word to Musher.

Sitting in his car smoking a Lucky, Musher felt it would take too much time to go to the squadron dining hall to eat so instead he would go to the Headquarters Squadron dining room. He had been there before so he was not uncomfortable with the almost silence which existed. There were no flying suits in this dining hall and almost no officers. He presumed they ate at the Officers Club. To his surprise Seals and Reading came in together. He ate lunch alone. He studied the people in the dining room while had more coffee and certainly more cigarettes

At 1245 he was sitting in the waiting room along with five candidates. One turned to him and said, "Musher are they interviewing you to be an instructor?"

"No, I am sitting with the interviewers as an advisor."

"Most of us don't take too kindly to this. These two guys have always served on the WAF side of the flight line. We are afraid that is what they are trying to do to us."

"There is nothing that says they are the only ones who can ask questions. You might ask them where selection and training to be an instructor would lead to."

The interviews started again at 1300. It was obvious to Musher and to the interviewers that this combat hardened, crude, cursing master sergeant would not be chosen for the training. As a matter of courtesy, which Musher was happy to see that Seals could be courteous, Seals stopped the interview with a thank you to the sergeant. As he rose to salute Sears and leave, his eyes went to Musher and one winked. In the classroom he had been well spoken.

The next candidate responded to the two prong questioners. After answering a number of questions the candidate asked for permission to speak. It was granted. "I have been a combat gunner since the start of WWII. I have always been on the flight line. If you select me for instructor training will that training lead to an eight to five job off the flight line; and would I be sacrificing my flight pay?"

Seals responded, "The program is designed to keep you on the flight line teaching your peers. I cannot guarantee you will always be an aerial gunner anymore than I can guarantee you will always receive your flight pay."

"Sir, I respectfully request that my name be withdrawn as a candidate for instructor training." He rose, saluted and left the interview room.

From the interview room you could see into the waiting area. The sergeant had stopped and was whispering to the three waiting candidates. Two rose and left the building with him. Seals called for the one remaining candidate.

The interview was much gentler. The questions were the same but the voice inflexion was not the hard military bark. Seals thanked him for coming and excused him. He rose, saluted and left the room.

Seals was not happy. "It is just 1415 and we have no more scheduled candidates to interview. We might just as well call it a day. Sergeant Muscarello please be here at 0745 tomorrow and we shall resume. Today's score is 9 done and presumably 3 withdrawals. It will be interesting to hear what was so upsetting about my answers. The grapevine will tell me. Sergeant Muscarello if you go to the NCO Club please listen and in the morning tell us what you heard. "

Musher stood, saluted and left. Sitting in his car he said to himself, fat fucking chance that wimpy son-of-bitch would ever hear anything from me. If he and his pimpy NCOIC were not titless WAFs he would know, threaten to make a combat veteran a titless WAF and take away his flight pay and you and your program are in his eyes his mortal enemy.

He was in the NCO Club ten minutes when he was paged for a phone call. It was Sergeant Reading, "The BEO wants to see you now."

"I'll be there as quickly as I can." In less than ten minutes he was standing before Major Denton, the BEO. He reported and was waived into a chair. Captain Seals and Sergeant Ready were seated next to him.

"Muscarello, since the first withdrawal we have already had fourteen others. Can you explain why?"

The Monster's axiom, "When you don't know what to say don't say anything."

"Sir, May I hear the two interviewer's reasons why they think this has happened?"

"No, you may not. I have heard them and that is why you are here."

They are trying to figure out some way to blame this on me. Here goes," Sir, consider this, no disrespect intended, when you threaten to make a combat veteran a titless WAF and insinuate there is a possibility he may lose his flight pay, you and your program are in his eyes his mortal enemy."

There was a pregnant pause of silence. "How did you reach that conclusion?"

"Sir, which is why I wanted to hear Captain Seals' and Sergeant Ready's explanations given to you before I offered my uneducated opinion."

Major Denton turned to Seals, "Is there a possibility that your answers could have caused your candidate to reach that conclusion? Sergeant Ready could that interpretation be possible?"

Both responded in the affirmative.

"All right, what do we do now to get this program back on track? Any thoughts Muscarello?"

"No sir, not at this time."

"Seals, Ready, how about you two?" Neither offered a suggestion.

Major Denton, "We are not going to wait for General Morehouse to clean up our mess. Tomorrow morning at 0700 be here with some reasonable alternatives. Dismissed."

Musher headed for the NCO Club. He knew that if he sat at the bar even drinking coke he would be approached by some very pissed off candidates. Eight of the fifteen withdrawals surrounded him. He asked them to join him in the private small room off the bar. Get yourselves a couple of drinks. He spoke to the bartender, "Put them all on my tab."

In the privacy of the closed room Musher detailed the happenings in Major Denton's office. He emphasized how Major Denton had chastised Seals and Ready and of Denton's obvious fear of General Morehouse's dissatisfaction with his personal project. He told them his theory regarding the competence of Captain Seals and the ass kissing of the NCOIC. Tomorrow morning this is what I am going to propose to Major Denton. Listen closely for if you are not unanimously in agreement with me, the proposal will never work. After detailing his suggestion he asked for a vote of confidence. The vote was unanimous. Whoever among you is friendly with the other seven withdrawals get to them tonight. I want all fifteen of you to be here for breakfast at 0630 tomorrow morning. The breakfast is on me. I will be here then because if all fifteen are not in favor of my proposal I shall not make it to Major Denton. Right now let's go to the bar and have another drink."

After all had been served he paid his tab included a nice tip and said, "Hey guys I need to leave. This is my only set of khakis and I need to get one set ready for tomorrow."

Master Sergeant Tom Parsons who had been in the picture book with General Morehouse on Tinian said, "Come home with me for dinner. My wife will wash and iron this set and you can borrow one of my flying suits. "

"Thank you I have a spare flying suit in my car. Not dressy but it is clean."

Musher had his khakis done, an excellent dinner and Mrs. Parsons even put the khakis in a garment bag. They sat in the living room drinking coffee while Musher asked a million questions about Tinian and the 509th. At 2000 hours Musher thanked them for their hospitality and for Mrs. Parson's excellent work. Tomorrow he would send her a dozen roses.

CHAPTER 92
We Can Salvage the General's Program

Musher was in the NCO Club at 0615. He greeted the candidates as they entered. At 0630 all were in agreement to support Musher's proposal to the BEO. He spoke to them and said, "I'm off to see the wizard."

Seated in Major Denton's office with Seals and Ready, they waited for Major Denton. When he entered they all stood and the BEO asked them to please sit.

To Captain Seals, "Do you have a suggestion?" No sir.

To Sergeant Ready, "Do you have a suggestion?" No sir.

"Your turn Muscarello."

"Sir, I have been in contact with all fifteen of the withdrawals. They have made some suggestions which if you care to consider they would withdraw their withdrawals.

Suggestion number 1: That you provide them a statement which in essence says that your program will in no way endanger their aircrew status or flight pay.

Suggestion number 2: That your candidate interviewers will be enlisted members of your staff that have had combat experience.

Suggestion number 3: That you relocate your interview room to a place on the flight line.

Suggestion number 4: That the candidate interviews are scheduled for a given time and the candidates do not report all at once and wait to be called.

Suggestion number 5: That you designate in advance the flight line location where the class will be held. The candidates want it stressed that they normally eat lunch at the flight line dining room without the expense of eating at the NCO Club.

Suggestion number 6: That I, Staff Sergeant Muscarello continue as adviser to the candidate selection committee; and, that I attend the instructor course as a stabilizing influence.

Suggestion number 7: Those candidates who have completed their interview will not be required to be interviewed again."

"Let me have that paper. Seals, do we have two enlisted men with combat experience who could handle the interviews? You don't know? Go get me the answer now."

"Ready, draft the statement assuring the candidates that our program will not result in their view of a punishment. Go do it now."

"Muscarello, locate an interview place on the flight line that we can use starting tomorrow morning. I want to know where by 1100 hours today. You will continue as advisor to the selection committee. When I approve of the interview location you can notify the withdrawn candidates. Seals will have the interview schedule and location posted by noon today."

"Sir, I can tell you now. The classroom in which these candidates trained is available and I will reconfigure it for the interview program."

"You have my approval. Be sure it is ready by 0830 hours tomorrow morning."

Seals came back into the room, "Sir we have four senior sergeants with WWII combat experience who are capable of doing the interviews."

"Seals, I want an interview schedule published and posted in all necessary locations not later than noon today. You might even have one in each dining hall. Schedule each interview for fifteen minutes. Keep your schedule loose enough to keep candidates from an extended wait for their turn for the interview. Make sure you do not re-interview those who have completed one interview. Also make sure when the class convenes Staff Sergeant Muscarello is a member of the class. We have time to locate and equip a proper classroom on the flight line. I am not sure if Ready is writing a novel but the finished product will be in the hands of the assigned interviewer."

Musher rose, saluted and left. He headed straight to the NCO Club. This morning he had given five of the candidates the names of two other candidates. If Denton accepted the proposal he would call them and tell them the where the interviews would be and where the interviewee schedule would be posted before noon. Each would notify the two names on their list. Now all he had to do was go the office and do a little rearranging in the classroom to make it an interview room. When that's done he will just relax and wait for tomorrow.

CHAPTER 93
Interviews and Recommendations for Selection

Musher picked up a copy of the interview schedule in the dining hall. During breakfast he studied today's candidates. He had spoken before to at least three of them. The first candidate was due at 0830 hours. As he was leaving Dex was just entering the dining hall. "Dex you are still a member of our team. Have breakfast and get your butt to the office as quickly as possible." At the office Musher printed a small sign and hung it on the classroom entry door, "Please Use the Office Entryway".

At 0745 the two interviewers from the BEO arrived. She told Musher, "My name is Master Sergeant Jill Hunter. I have been in the military for over seven years. Six of those years were in the Army. I have an undergraduate degree in education and I do have combat experience as a combat photographer. I traveled from Omaha Beach and later to Germany with Patton." All anyone had to do was look at her chest and read the ribbons. The Purple Heart with cluster, the European campaign ribbons with eleven campaign stars and a lot of other decorations." Her partner chimed in, "I am Jack Masters, I was a tank commander in the Army for nine years. If you look at my chest you will see that I have combat experience. I too have a degree in education"

I am Staff Sergeant Muscarello, everyone calls me Musher. They nodded. He thought if they had introduced themselves in reverse order they would be Jack and Jill. To him they are Jack and Jill. Jack handed him a sheet of paper. "These are the ten questions we will ask each candidate. Only one of us will ask the questions for each candidate. Sergeant Hunter and I will grade each candidate on a scale of one to ten with point five increments. At the end of the day we will come to a rated agreement for each candidate and seek your opinion regarding our rating and why. Are you OK with that procedure? Good. Show us where we will do the interviews."

Musher led them into the classroom and turned on the lights. The desk chairs were arranged in an arc with the candidate facing them in the center of the arc. The chairs were spaced so that no one would feel crowded or pressured.

"This will do fine. The atmosphere and familiarity with this room should help us get factual responses to our questions. It is now 0810 and the first candidate is not due until 0830. Where do we go to smoke?"

307

Musher gave Dexter his key and asked him to take the lock off the classroom entry door. They stood on the steps outside the classroom entry way and smoked until 0825. They were seated in the classroom when at 0830 Dexter knocked on the door which adjoined the classroom and announced the rank and name of the first candidate. Jack and Jill were so smooth. Jack asked all the questions of the first candidate. The interview was over in twelve minutes. The next candidate entered and Jill elicited the answers to the ten questions. The interview was over in eleven minutes. The process was repeated until 1000 hours. Jack told Dexter we are taking a break. We will reconvene at 1030 hours.

The three of them went to the steps to smoke. Mister Leary joined them with cups of hot black coffee. Musher introduced him to Jack and Jill and Leary joined them in the coffee and cigarette break. At 1025 the three went into the classroom and Leary into the office. At 1030 Dexter announced the next candidate. Jill handled this interview and Jack handled the next. They alternated until at 1130 hours Jack announced they would break for lunch and reconvene at 1300 hours."

The scheduling had gone well there was no one in the office waiting to be interviewed. Jack and Jill had completed eleven interviews this morning. Dexter joined them for lunch and he locked both doors on his way out. The four of them walked to the flight line dining room. Jack remarked that the conversation level in this dining room was far above that in the headquarters dining room. Musher noted, "One of the differences here on the flight line."

At 1300 Dexter announced the afternoon's first candidate. Jack handled this interview and Jill handled the next. They alternated until at 1615 hours Jack announced that was the schedule for today. Before anyone did anything else Musher looked in the office to be sure there was no candidate waiting.

Jack and Jill had done twenty-two interviews today. When they had an agreed rating for each candidate they showed the list to Musher for his comments. He totally agreed with their ratings. "How did you two get here this morning? The Base Bus! Let me make a phone call I will be right back."

"Jefferson I need a taxi for two people from my office to the BEO. I need it now. Can you help me out? Great, they will be outside waiting in five minutes."

"The base taxi service will pick you up outside in five minutes. I told him you needed to go to the BEO. Only insane persons would not report to the Major and relay the excellent results from today. I will see you here at 0800 tomorrow. Am I right?"

Jack and Jill thanked him and went outside to wait.

He and Dex squared away the office and classroom. Locked the doors and walked to the base bus. It had been a full day. This would be another early dinner, SSS and off to bed. Tomorrow must be easier than today.

CHAPTER 94

Day 3, Interview Wrap-Ups and Recommendations

Jack and Jill were such professionals. The last of the interviews was completed at 0945 on the third day. The three of them took a long smoke break before Jack and Jill went in to finish rating this morning candidates. Musher was invited to listen to their discussion and interject whatever thoughts he might have. Jack had the foresight to add the candidates who were interviewed by Seals and Ready. He and Jill had used Seals and Ready's notes to rate those nine people. Jack and Jill had worked last night to categorize the candidates by their interview rating score. Of the total sixty people who were interviewed forty-seven were master sergeants and the remainder were technical sergeants.

Compounding the decision making was the fact the first thirty-three people scored the maximum and they were all master sergeants.

Musher, "Within the thirty three who scored maximum eleven came from each of the bomb squadrons. The instructor training class was being considered for thirty students plus me. Why not consider the class for thirty-three students plus me. No one would be hurt by not being included. The other candidates are all lifers. They will understand what has happened and most probably would agree."

Jack and Jill bought into that.

Jack, "From here on in you are just another student. Unless the BEO wants something special for you watch for the announcements and we will see you in class. Sergeant Hunter and I will teach the class. We thank you for your support and contributions." In a flash they were both gone.

Musher went into the office. Dexter was there with his new A1C stripes on and a box of materials he wanted to take to McCoy.

"Musher I am leaving this afternoon. I am shipping my stuff to McCoy and taking a fifteen day leave before reporting there. I thank you for all you have taught me and especially for my promotion. Jefferson is getting me a ride to the barracks and then to the bus station. I know you would have taken me but I want this to be our goodbye,"

"Mister Leary is gone and now you. We had a run didn't we? Take care of yourself and take care of Mister Leary. Remember what I told you about him being a lifer."

A horn tooted outside, they shook hands and once again Musher was alone. What the hell, he had been alone before and there is no doubt he would be alone again.

CHAPTER 95
Learning a New Job

Yesterday had been a depressing day. When Dexter left it invoked a series of unpleasant memories about being alone. Today would be better. In the dining hall this morning the first sergeant told him to report to the shack and not to his office. He tried very hard but he could not think of anything he had done wrong which would get him a call to the shack.

Sergeant Wooly was alone in the shack. It would be at least thirty minutes before the morning roll call would be over and the troops would scatter some of whom would come into the shack.

Wooly, "I hear you did a good job with the BEO's people and you are scheduled to attend the instructor certification class. I have a better offer for you. Work with me here in squadron operations. Here you will find out how a squadron operations works, who the real power people are in any squadron not to mention the administrative procedures that go with a combat squadron. You might even learn to type here. It cannot last very long since the base is closing very soon and it will give you a skill to take to your next assignment. You know that in just about every bomb squadron the gunners have two jobs. Since they only fly maybe four or five times a month the Honchos cannot stand to see them doing nothing the rest of the time. Most of them are assigned to their aircraft's crew chief and he keeps them busy cleaning the aircraft, changing spark plugs and other menial tasks. Wherever you go you will be able to offer more to your squadron's chief operations clerk. Your normal day will be 0800 to 1630. We shut down for lunch and in rare circumstance work Saturday or Sunday. You stay on flight pay and do not perform any squadron duties. Learning squadron operations will be far more valuable in your career than a piece of paper which says you can teach a class."

Musher evaluated Wooly's words and concluded that although he is not worried about his air force career, it does sound better than sitting in a classroom all day or sweating his ass off doing crap shit tasks in the P Patch. "When do I start?"

"Right now. In the typewriter I have the flight pay approval list for this month. That particular report must be ready not later than the twentieth of each month for the eligible flyers to receive flight pay on payday, the last day of the month. There are roughly two hundred fifty names, ranks and serial number on the finished product. Today is Monday, the twelfth. I expect you to have it finished by Thursday night. I know you will be a two finger pecker typist but this way you will accustomed to the key board. Later you will type excellently."

Musher sat at the desk with the typewriter, stared at the last month's list with corrections and began.

He banged away at the report, used a gallon of whiteout to correct his mistakes and pressed on diligently. He had lunch with Sergeant Wooly. It was like being in a classroom because all Wooly did was talk about the things which need be done often and effectively to run a good squadron operations. After lunch and for the next two days Musher worked on that report. Finally on Wednesday afternoon he proudly gave the report to Wooly.

Wooly was pleased and said, "Don't worry about being on time here tomorrow. Go to unit supply and ask Dooley for a copy of the blue book called "How to Type." Right now, take off and I will see you tomorrow."

In the morning he was at unit supply and had asked Dooley for a copy of the book. Dooley gave him one and said, "Listen Musher, when they close your classroom I want to get all my stuff back, especially the pictures. Can you take care of that?"

"You have my word."

Back at the shack Wooly gave him instructions. "Take the book and read it. Then sit at the typewriter and practice. When you are tired of practicing then it's time to practice some more. Typing is an acquired skill." Musher typed all day Thursday and Friday. Wooly had given him a key to the shack. He typed all day Saturday and Sunday. Monday morning Wooly handed him some hand written sheets of paper. "Make me a double spaced draft of these so I can edit them before Major Cotter, the CSOps, reviews them."

There were about seven hand written pages. In about fifteen minutes Musher handed them to Wooly. Wooly reviewed them, made some changes and handed them back to Musher. He also handed Musher another paper and said, "This is the format. See what you can do with the report."

Thirty minutes later the finished product was in Wooly's hands. "Very, very good Musher." He made a couple of corrections and format changes. He asked Musher to do it again only this time put in a carbon paper and make two copies.

Thirty minutes later Wooly was looking at the finished product. He congratulated Musher on a job well done and showed Musher how to correlate a document. "Your product is excellent, but it took almost an hour an a half to do it. Fear not, the way I figure it in about a week that same type document of the same size will take you fifteen minutes or so. I have great hopes for you. If you want to practice your typing go ahead. At this moment I am not doing anything which would help you learn ops."

Wooly held class again at lunch. When they were back at the shack Wooly said, "My first name is Tom. I prefer you call me Tom rather than Sergeant Wooly. Do you have a problem with that? No, that's good. You know the flight pay roster you did, often times when I did it I never had time to fully check it and if there is an error regarding any entry for any person, finance will red line that person from the roster and he will not receive his flight pay on payday. I want you to spend the afternoon to do a one hundred percent verification of the roster. Even if it means we may need to retype some pages."

Musher took the current roster and the roster from which the information was copied and methodically checked every entry. There were no differences in the entries. When he finished he thought of The Monster, "Check and double check." It took almost as much time to guarantee the accuracy of the roster than it did to type it. He confirmed to Tom that the roster was accurate.

Tom took the roster and the transmittal letter into Major Cotter. He could hear them talking but he could not understand what was being said. When he came back out he asked Musher if he knew where Base Finance was.....No.... "It is very close to wing headquarters. Take this transmittal envelope which I have marked from the 351st to the Flight Pay Section and hand deliver it to the Flight Pay Section of Base Finance. Inside the transmittal envelope is a receipt for the documents. Be sure to have it signed. From there call it a day."

"Tom, would it be all right if I went by my barracks parking lot and picked up my car first?"…"Thank you. I will be here at 0800 tomorrow."

From Base Finance he headed straight to the NCO Club. "I feel like a little poker."

There was a seat open at the $10-$20 three raise limit table. He placed three hundred dollars on the table Just as he sat here the first time of the six other players three seemed to have card sense and the other three were relying solely on luck. From all appearances there were no partners and the game was honest. Musher played his conservative game more than willing to win a little at a time. Four of five times players left and new blood sat down. By time 2100 hours came around Musher estimated that totaling what he had clandestinely squirreled and what was on the table, deducting his three hundred, he was about eight hundred fifty dollars ahead. That's enough for today. He had not turned a dishonest card.

CHAPTER 96

Lots of Typing, Phone Answering and Errands

He waited until 0830 to call the BEO for Master Sergeant Jack Masters. In his most solicitous voice he told Jack of the opportunity to work in squadron operations until his reassignment comes through. Jack agreed it was a smarter move. After all look at the teaching results he had with the gunnery program. It would be difficult for anyone to say he does not have teaching skills. Jack wished him luck and hoped they would meet again somewhere, sometime. Musher invited Jack and Jill and their guests to dinner at the NCO Club. Jack politely refused without any explanation.

Musher's day was occupied typing documents written by Tom, Major Cotter, the Assistant CSOps and it seemed anyone else who cared to write something. In between typing assignments he answered the phone and took messages. **He certainly felt like a titless WAF. The job was only temporary.** He was learning more about what it takes to keep combat aircraft and aircrews combat ready. The job also had it rewards. Every day, Monday through Friday, at 1630 he could pack it in and not be concerned about any air force issues. Saturday and Sunday made like a three day pass which began on Friday after work and ended at 0800 Monday when he needed to be present for duty at the shack.

It was 1500 and he asked Wooly if he could be excused. He told Tom he wanted to go to the classroom and pack all the things that needed to be returned to Sergeant Dooley. Tomorrow at lunch he would deliver Dooley's things to unit supply. Tom told him he could go and tomorrow he would drive Musher to Dooley's and then they could have lunch in the squadron dining hall.

When he finished in the classroom he headed straight to the NCO Club. He had a sandwich and coke in the bar. He asked the bartender for a ten dollar roll of quarters. Paid his bill with the usual substantial tip and headed for the privacy of the pay phone. "Operator, please get me Atlantic two eight four, four three two seven nine in Peabody Massachusetts? Person to person for Mrs. Joanna Giardelli."

"I have your party on the line. Please deposit two dollars for the first three minutes. You may go ahead sir."

"Hello Sweet Sister." He loved her. She had always tried to protect him.

"Musher is that you? Are you all right? Where are you? Are you in trouble?"

"No trouble, I am in Kansas in the United States Air Force. I need a favor. I know Mama is having a hard financial time with that drunken SOB. Last time I was there I squared the book at Gloria Chain. I intend to do more."

"Mama told me you were here overnight but didn't come to see us!"

"I was on a special job that required I get in and out. I'll see you all next time. Let me finish my reason for calling. Here's the favor I need. In the next two days I am going to send you a registered special delivery letter which will have in it an American Express money order for three thousand dollars. I don't want anyone to know you have it or where it came from. Use it for any purpose which will make Mama happy. You might even get her one of those new things, the television set. Tell any stories you want but keep me out of any story. You can tell your husband, but nobody else. Can you do this for Mama?"

"Of course I can. Tell me about you."

"Not right now. There are others waiting to use this phone. I will write you all the details."

Joanna knew and he knew no such letter would ever be written.

"Sweet Sister, I love you." He hung up the phone

CHAPTER 97

Big News Today

He had returned all Sergeant Dooley items as promised. He purchased an American Express money order for three thousand dollars payable to Sweet Sister and it was on its way. He was forced to use part of his reserve cash but he still had two thousand in his pocket and seven thousand stashed.

The last two weeks in the shack had been quite routine. He had been helping to prepare flight schedules, typing them and posting them inside and outside the shack, in the briefing room and on the squadron orderly room bulletin board.

Today he was going with Tom to a briefing regarding which crews and which aircraft would be transferred to which air bases. The ground crews would accompany their aircraft. The first transfers would be three days from now. Eight of the initial transferees would be from the 351st. There were tons of personnel documents relative to the squadron air crews which would need to be assembled and catalogued for transfer with the aircraft and the crew. All eight of the 351st aircraft with the personnel who keep the aircraft combat ready were transferred to the 98th Bomb Wing at Spokane, Washington. If he thought getting eight aircraft and their personnel ready for transfer was complex imagine what it would be like at the 98th with twenty-four new aircraft arriving with sixteen or more personnel on each aircraft.

Within ten calendar days the remainder of the 351st aircraft and attendant personnel had been transferred from Smoky. The aircraft assignments were scattered throughout the Strategic Air Command. All the non-aircrew officers would be gone within a week. Musher was left in his barracks with two other guys both of whom would be discharged within a week. The orderly room still had the first sergeant and one clerk. Tom was transferring to SAC headquarters at Offutt AFB. Musher wondered where he would be sent.

The Crowley family had transferred to California. The NCO Club was a shadow of itself. No real poker games or pool matches. Everything was closed in the Club except the bar and the restaurant. The restaurant menu could hardly challenge a diner. The first sergeant instructed Musher to report to him every morning at 0800. If no transfer orders had been received he dismissed Musher for the rest of the day.

Just about every day Musher went to the Emporium in Salina. There were still domino games, pool games, one poker table and some use of the snooker tables. The man in the chair suggested to Musher, "Ride around town and watch it die."

BOOK 4

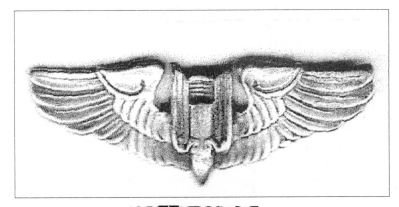

WALKER
AIR FORCE BASE
ROSWELL
NEW MEXICO

I WILL FINISH MY HITCH
RIGHT HERE

CHAPTER 98

My Reassignment Is Here

This morning the first sergeant said, "Be at wing personnel at 0930. Your reassignment is here. That's all I know about it. When you finish there come back to see me."

Musher was in place at 0900. At his scheduled time he was ushered into cubicle. The personnel guy was a master sergeant with lots of ribbons on blouse topped off by an aerial gunner badge. He said his name was Wilfred Beasley but everyone called him Billy.

"So you're the high roller known as Musher. Your records show you came up awfully fast. You will finish your first year in the air force in thirty-two days. I would be interested to hear how you did that but at the moment we do not have the time. We received a by name and serial number special request from the Director of Personnel of the 509th Bomb Wing. That is your next assignment, 509th Bomb Wing, Walker AFB, Roswell, New Mexico. The request did not specify when they wished for you to report so we will treat this as an ordinary transfer. When do you wish to head out?"

"Billy how much travel time and am I allowed to travel POV (privately owned vehicle)?"

"Two days and yes at six cents a mile."

"How about a delay enroute?"

"You have fifteen days accrued, how much do you want?"

"Ten days delay and I will be ready to leave in five days."

"Do you want a cash advance?"

"No thank you."

"Come back here at 0900 four days from now and we will process you out. Do you have any more questions or concerns?" No. "You may go. See you in four days."

Back at the orderly room he told the first sergeant what had happened at personnel and that he was going to the 509th Bomb Wing in Roswell, New Mexico.

Sergeant Alba, "New Mexico is a tough climate. You may want to consider trading your convertible for something more stout."

Musher made tracks to the NCO Club and the Club NCOIC. He told him of his impending transfer and how it had been suggested that a convertible might not be the best vehicle in a New Mexico sand storm. "Could we go to town this afternoon and trade cars?"

321

"The way Salina is dying we might be able to make a very good deal. Let's have a bite to eat and then go."

They cruised by the car dealerships until Musher saw one he liked. He didn't know what make it was or what year it was, he just knew he liked its looks. They drove into the lot and Musher put a zipper on his mouth. They walked over to the car and by time they could get there a salesman was already waiting.

Brewer, "Tell me about this car."

"1942 Pontiac Sedan, eight cylinder, five gear transmission with the stick on the floor, stayed in the owner's garage when he went to WWII. Unfortunately he never returned. There is very low mileage on this car, eighteen thousand four hundred. The car is on the market because his mother cannot drive and she needs some cash. I can make you a very good deal,"

Brewer did a walk around checking the paint job, the tires, opening and closing doors and windows, the condition of the glass windshield and the two spare tires mounted in the front fenders. He sat inside checking the floor mats, upholstery, and the back seat. He opened the trunk. The jack was in its original location. "Hand me the ignition key." He started the engine, watched all the gauges and then opened the hood to see the stability of the idle setting. "It needs some work. Tell me your very good deal."

"Are you trading that little convertible?" Yes. "Here's my deal, your trade plus four thousand dollars."

"Will you take my car and twenty-five hundred?"

"I'll take your car and thirty-five hundred."

"I'll give you my car and three thousand."

"I'll take your car and three thousand two hundred fifty."

"You fill up the tank, do the paperwork now and it's a deal."

"Come to the office with me. Bring all your paper work for your car."

It did not take very long for him to provide a bill of sale, a title to the Pontiac, a change of insurance from the convertible to the Pontiac and the transfer of the license plates from the convertible to the Pontiac. Musher counted him out the cash.

Musher made sure he had everything out of the convertible and in the trunk of his new car. They headed back to Smoky. At Pass and Registration Musher told them he was transferring in five days. They gave him a seven day temporary pass to place in his windshield.

CHAPTER 99

Some Goodbyes

"Sergeant Alba may I have your permission to go to Junction City for a couple of days? I have made some friends there since I came to Smoky and I would like to say goodbye before I head for Roswell. I will be back in plenty of time to meet my obligation at wing personnel."

"All right. You be careful. Don't let her convince you to cut it close and miss your obligation. You would leave me no choice."

He called Priscilla, "I am off tonight and tomorrow night. Do you have a room for me? Great. I will see you in a little while." He changed into his cowboy clothes made sure he was packing for two days and headed for Pricilla's place. It was almost eleven in the morning when he knocked on her door. She didn't look like she was expecting company. "Sorry to catch you while you were working but we need to talk. If you wanted to could you get someone to handle the supper meal and breakfast? If you wanted to and you could, we would drive to Topeka have a very fancy meal in a very fancy dinner club, stay in the fanciest suite in the fanciest hotel, have a fancy breakfast and be back here tomorrow around one in the afternoon. What do you think?"

"Give me ten minutes and I will tell you." She headed for her phone, made some calls and came back saying, "What time do we leave?"

"As soon as you can get your things together."

"I need to shower and fix my face."

"Don't bother, we'll check in the hotel early and do our dinner prepping there."

When she saw the Pontiac, "What happened to the cute convertible?"

The ride to Topeka was mostly silent but a comfortable silence. They checked into a large suite in the Topeka Five Star. Musher had the foresight to put one full bottle of watered down vodka in his emergency bag.

Musher had four large glasses, six bottles of seven-up and a large container of ice brought to the suite. When the bell boy left still thanking him for the tip, Musher poured two vodka seven-up drinks. They perched in the suite sitting area looking at Topeka while they enjoyed the coolness of their drinks. Of course they had a second drink.

"You know Prissy this hotel has a five star restaurant and a lounge for drinking and dancing. Not much sense leaving the hotel to go to a fancy restaurant and then to find a cuddly dance floor. If we decided to have dinner here I could make the reservation for say, seven o'clock. We could take a nice shower together and crawl in that huge bed to nap. When we decided it was time to put on the pretty clothes we could take another shower."

She was standing naked in front of the shower door. "Do I have to come get you?"

The shower and the love making lasted a long time. In their big robes provided by the hotel they went back to the sitting area, her for another drink and him for his Lucky Strikes. It wasn't long before they slipped into the big bed and started the foreplay. He awoke at five thirty and she was not in bed. She had already started getting ready for her big night in Topeka. When she finished she looked stunning. He put on his full North End regalia and they made a fine looking couple.

They stopped at the lounge for a drink before dinner. Fortunately Priscilla excused herself to go to the ladies room. Musher took the bartender aside and handed him a fifty dollar bill. "What ever drink is ordered for her I want you to fake the alcoholic ingredients. You can ring full charge and make yourself a buck there. If you do as I ask there will be another tip waiting for you. Do you support the dining room from this bar?

"I support everything but wine. There is a wine steward who will come to your table. Give him this fifty and tell him to stay away from us. Here's another fifty for you . We will be coming in here to dance after dinner."

It didn't take long for the word to get out that this northern mafia looking guy was a big tipper. The food and the service were spectacular. In the lounge they drank and danced until midnight. Back in the suite they peeled clothes as if the clothes were loaded with ants. Into the bed for a glorious, glorious night. They had sex every way imaginable given her one no-no.

He awoke about eight. The drapes had been drawn by the hotel staff when they prepared the beds for sleeping. He partially opened one to let in some sunshine. He called room service for immediate delivery of coffee and orange juice. Full breakfast would be brought in one hour. He patted Prissy and she awakened smiling. The coffee and juice came and that was the signal for them to take a shower together. Back in those robes they sipped coffee until breakfast came. He told her it wasn't as good as the breakfast she served but look at the bright side, she didn't need to cook it, and she won't need to do the dishes.

"What would you like to do today? Do you know about Topeka?" No. "Let me call the concierge and have him book us on a Topeka Tour. One that lasts no more than three hours."

"They will pick us up here at ten thirty. The tour includes lunch and we should be back here before two." They put on their cowboy clothes and went down stairs to wait. The tour was in a well air conditioned bus so that smoke was not a problem. The driver pointed out various houses and buildings and described what made them significant land structures. Lunch was at a Kansas Steak House. The food was super. There was a very short time left on the tour. True to his word the bus driver dropped them off at the hotel at one-fifty. Getting off the bus Musher gave the driver a fifty dollar tip.

In the lobby they spoke to the concierge. "Last night we dined and danced here and it was fabulous. Tonight we would like to do something less formal but fun."

"You two are already dressed for the party. About three blocks from here is The Honky Tonk. Lots of drinking and dancing. They don't serve liquor but they do provide setups. If you need some liquor I can take care of that for you."

Musher passed him a fifty dollar bill, "Low proof vodka and a cab here at 6:30. Where do we go for an early supper?"

"I would suggest Bonesy's. Catfish and ribs are the specialty. No reservation is required. It's across town so I would not release your cab you might have a hard time finding another."

Musher and Priscilla went to the suite. They had other things to take care of before the next shower.

Bonesy's was a twenty minute ride from the hotel. There he passed the cab driver the toll fare plus and extra twenty so he would wait while they ate. Catfish and ribs were not only the specialty they were the only choices. Musher ordered one of each and a large pitcher filled with ice and seven-up. The only utensils were your hands or if you brought your own. They ate to their heart's content and didn't finish the catfish or the ribs. Wash up was done at trough with paper towels for drying. Musher paid the bill with a healthy tip and they climbed into their cab. "Driver, to The Honky Tonk." At The Honky Tonk he paid the driver, included a substantial tip and asked, "What time do you quick hacking tonight?" Midnight. "Can you be back here for us at eleven ?"

Well aware of the size of the first two tips, "I will be sitting right here."

The entry fee was ten dollars for men nothing for women. Inside The Honky Tonk it was just as its name said. Cowboys dressed like they came from a drugstore and cowboys who looked they had been on the range for a month. The cowgirls were in full color in their squaw dresses and either boots or moccasins. They were seated and Priscilla left for the powder room.

325

Musher ordered two glasses of water and two glasses of seven-up with ice. The waitress came back before Priscilla did. Musher took the vodka and poured half the contents onto the dirt floor. He filled the bottle with the water. What water didn't fit he drank.

They danced and Priscilla drank. At ten forty-five they were both danced out but Priscilla was still sober. They stepped outside to wait for their cab but he was already sitting there. Ten minutes later they were in front of the hotel. Musher paid the toll and added a forty dollar tip. "Goodnight, you did a fine job."

The concierge greeted them. "Was everything all right?"

"Fine, just fine." Musher did not tip him again.

They showered, made love, she was sipping a watered down vodka seven-up and he was smoking a Lucky. "Prissy I need to tell you something and I have been trying to for two days. Here it is in cold facts. Four days from now I am being transferred to Roswell, New Mexico. You knew Smoky was closing and most everyone is gone. I am among the last to go. If I could stay I would."

She never said a word. She just sat in the bed crying. Musher put out his cigarette, put her drink on the end table and crawled in bed beside her. She whispered, "Musher make love to me all night. I know I will never see you again." He wanted to lie to her but the words would not come out of his mouth.

They were up early in the morning. They packed, had some coffee and toast, the bell hop took their bags, Musher paid the bill, tipped the bell hop and they headed for Junction City. There was almost no conversation during the two hour ride. At Priscilla's house he whispered I shall never forget you, we will meet again.

He drove away and headed for the Emporium.

To the man in the chair, "I will be leaving in four days I am being transferred to Roswell, New Mexico. I could not go without thanking you for all your help and support."

To Musher, "That is the reason for getting out of the small convertible. Smart move. Have you told Priscilla yet? You are among the finest pool shooters I have ever seen or heard about. There is no doubt that some day very soon I will be able to say the same thing about your snooker game. Can't say you will ever be really good at dominoes. You need to work on that game. The boys you played poker with tell me you are honest, but very, very smooth. We will miss you around here. I will miss you around here and not because you are a big tipper. You are a gentleman. Not a gentle man, a gentleman."

They shook hands and Musher headed for Smoky Hill.

CHAPTER 100
Farewell To Smoky Hill AFB

It was the morning of the fourth day. He was due at wing personnel at 0900 hours. Yesterday he had gone to the office and taken the recruiting poster which brought him to the US Air Force. He also took two notebooks and a jeweler's case. He had dropped the keys to the office with the Squadron Charge of Quarters. He saw no need to fill out a mailing change of address form since he did not get mail anyhow. Everything was neatly placed in his trunk or in the back seat. He even took his foot locker, a couple of blankets a pillow and two sheets. Never know where you are going to sleep. He had counted his cash position. Three thousand in traveler's checks when he closed his account, twenty-three hundred stashed in various locations in the car and three hundred eighty in his pocket. He often wondered why he never had any change. The base service station mechanic had checked the car overall. He gave the mechanic a ten dollar tip. He had his loaded ice chest in the front seat but the vodkas were in the trunk.

By 1100 hours he was out-processed, signed out and was on the road to Roswell. The whole drive was about six hundred fifty miles. A full day if he so chose but he decided he would just see how the day went. Around 1500 he decided to get off the road and get something to eat. His natural instinct brought him to a pool room. The place was hot and stuffy and everyone stared at him as he walked in. He decided this was no place for him to be. He asked the counter clerk how to get onto the highway. Thanked him and left. Make a special note: "Do not stop in a strange pool room. Nothing but trouble awaits a stranger there."

A few miles down the road there was a cut-out area. He parked the Pontiac, broke open his chest and served himself a lunch of candy bars and coke. As he resumed his ride towards Roswell it was getting dark and there didn't seem to be a town close to the highway. He found a spot off the highway that was fairly secluded, locked his doors, crawled into the back seat and put the pillow and blankets to good use. He couldn't figure out how he could have started this trip without flashlights and lanterns.

It was first light and he was awakened by a heavy tap-tap on his window. Standing beside his car was a New Mexico State Trooper in full uniform including the drawn pistol. "Come on out here with your hands in plain sight."

He did as he was told. Answered a bunch of questions, showed all his identity materials and finally his transfer orders to Roswell.

"You sure picked a hell of a place to park. Look out there, fortunately for you the train is not due through here until about noon. You're parked so close to the track who knows what might have happened to you and your car. You can go now. I suggest you get back on the highway and head for Clovis, New Mexico. It's about fifty miles from here. There's an air base there. It is about one hundred miles north of Roswell. Welcome to New Mexico."

"Thanks officer, I appreciate your help. Just as soon as I can get a cold soda from the chest I will be on my way." During the middle of all his thank you's he was beating himself mentally, how could you not have flashlights and lanterns? At the air base he showed his orders and his I.D. and they gave him a seven day temporary pass for his windshield. At the VAQ (Visiting Airmen's Quarters) he asked to be billeted for two nights. (He could always leave before that if he wished) The VAQ was a standard air force barracks which had been modified to individual rooms with internal locking devices. The latrine was on the first floor. After Smoky this would be called the modern barracks. A long SSS and he fell into the sack. It was 1500 before he awoke. Seems all the excitement of the move and the move itself had taken its toll. The dining halls would not be open for at least two hours. The base map mounted by the front entry way showed the NCO Club.

The NCO Club was not very elaborate but they served breakfast twenty-four hours a day. After a good breakfast and some Luckies he paid his bill, left a conservative tip and explored the club. This was a fighter wing. Rumor had it that in a fighter wing there are more officers than enlisted men. This club would bear out that rumor. Four o'clock in the afternoon and practically nothing going on in the club. The activity scheduled showed that tonight was the monthly pinochle tournament. He drove to the VAQ to rest and wait to go back to the NCO Club later.

The ballroom was set up for forty tables. At the registration desk each pair's name was posted and at which table they would begin. Many of the pairs were either two women or a man and a woman. Each game of two thousand points reduced the number of players by one-half. Winners went on, losers went elsewhere. At the end of six rounds only two pairs would be left for the night's championship match. Whoever wins two out of three two thousand point matches will be recognized as the night's champions. Musher had been watching and listening to the goings-on when he was approached by a man probably twice his age.

"Son, are you a double deck pinochle player?"

"I have played but I am not very good."

"My normal partner is sick. The entry fee is five dollars but I will pay that for you. I would rather play one round for ten dollars than to not play at all. If you want to partner with me tell me your last name so that we can be registered on the board. Play starts in about ten minutes."

Musher and his partner were ousted in the second round.

"You did well for a beginner. You didn't make any playing mistakes but your bidding could have been more aggressive. How long have you been playing? Let's go in the bar and I will buy you a beer. My wife will not be here to pick me up for at least an hour. She would never believe I would not get past the second round."

In the bar he ordered a draft and Musher ordered a coke. "Not a drinker, that's good."

"Not a beer drinker. Totally dislike the porcelain god."

"Tell me, what squadron are you in?"

Musher told him his story about the Smoky Hill AFB closure and his transfer to Roswell."

"How long have you been in the air force?"

Musher modified his military career somewhat. "I have been in the air force for just under a year, I was in the Army before that."

"Too bad you're not assigned here. I could make one hell of a pinochle player out of you." He talked pinochle, pinochle and more pinochle until his wife appeared in the bar. "Thank you son, be safe on the rest of your trip and you can come here to be my pinochle partner any time."

CHAPTER 101

The Longest Last Hundred Miles

He was up early and decided not to stay. He would get his car gassed up, replenish his ice chest, have a light breakfast and be on his way. He passed through the main gate on his way to Roswell at 0745. About two miles out on the highway there was an A2C hitch hiking going south. Musher pulled over, moved the ice chest to the back seat and let the airman come aboard.

"Thank you. My name is Joey Germaine. How far south are you going?"

"I am called Musher. I'm going as far as Roswell. Where are you going?"

"Me, I am headed for Juarez, Mexico. Ever been there?"

"Can't say I have. As a matter of fact I don't even know where it is. I have been assigned to the 509th Bomb Wing at Roswell."

"Man, there is no place like Juarez. Where else can a fellow rent a room, stay five days, drink tequila and beer until he can't walk, have as many senoritas as he can handle and do it all for under fifteen dollars a day? I am on a seven day leave and I am heading for paradise. I spent my last leave there and it was wonderful. I have saved my money for this leave. I have one hundred ten dollars. I am loaded for bear. When are you due to sign in at Roswell?"

"Actually I have fifteen more days delay enroute."

"If you have a few bucks why not come to Juarez with me. I would give you something for the gas. I have some civvies in my small bag. You will never regret going to Juarez."

"How far is it from Roswell?"

"About two hundred miles. I could share the driving with you and we would be there about 1500. Of course we would not go straight to Juarez. Biggs AFB is very close. I would suggest you leave your car at Biggs or else it may disappear while we are in Juarez."

Musher thought about it and could not see any real downside to going. "OK Joey, you have a partner in crime."

They passed through Roswell and about a hundred miles later stopped for gas at a place called High Lonesome. It was a general store and gas station which served the outlying ranch owners and ranch hands. Gasoline was seventeen cents a gallon and they need twelve gallons. Joey was digging for money to pay when Musher put his hand on Joey and said, "Save it, we may need it later." They took a couple of bottles of root beer and some packaged cup cakes. Total bill is two dollars forty nine cents. Musher paid with a twenty while Joey tried to see how much money Musher had in his roll.

After proving who they were they were given a seven day temporary pass to have the car on Biggs AFB. They parked the car in the VAQ lot. They didn't register at the VAQ but they did use the showers. Musher reduced his pocket cash to two hundred dollars. They secured everything in the car, took their "emergency bags", found the base bus stop which took them to the base bus terminal. The schedule said there was a bus to Juarez every hour on the hour. The fare was fifty cents. Joey insisted on paying their fare. Twenty minutes later they had paid their one penny toll and were walking across the bridge into Juarez.

"Musher I don't know what you are going to do but I am going to start this leave with a piece of ass." There were brothel entrances all along the main street of Juarez. Joey stepped inside one. Musher wasn't that eager but he thought he would go in and do some window shopping. Within five minutes the girls had been so all over him he took one to a room. How could he go wrong for one dollar?

Joey led him to the Florida Hotel. They paid for rooms for five days in advance. The total cost was fifteen dollars each. The Florida Hotel hosted one of the most popular night spots and cat houses in all of Juarez. The Florida Bar. Tequila sours cost ten cents each. Bar drinks for the girls were five cents each. The bar girls danced on the bar without any under garments. The quickie rate was one dollar and the overnight hooker rate was three dollars. They hadn't eaten anywhere yet but it was easy to see why Joey figured he could have a hell of a leave for fifteen dollars a day.

For the next three days all Joey did was drink tequila and get laid. By the end of the third day he looked like death warmed over. Musher didn't look a whole lot better. They hadn't shaved or bathed. In a sober moment they decided it was time to leave. They struggled for the strength to walk back into the United States and catch a bus to Biggs AFB.

It was almost 2300 when they walked into the VAQ to register for one night. The CQ said, "You must have had a great time in Juarez. I am going to get you a base taxi to take you to the dispensary for a precautionary penicillin shot. Clean up and come back here. Don't feel exceptional. You are more the rule than the exception."

There were no questions asked at the dispensary. They didn't even want to know their names. It was Musher's first shot of Beeswax Penicillin. His butt felt like it had been struck with a red hot branding iron.

It was well after noon the next day when Joey was knocking on his door. "Are you alive? Let's squeet."

Musher dressed and said, "First, let's go to the BX and buy some fresh clothing. We pretty much beat up what we wore in Juarez. I am buying you this gift for introducing me to a phase of life I had never seen."

They bought new under clothes, new shirts, new Levi's and new socks. Musher even picked out for Joey a new belt with a fancy buckle, a straw hat and a pair of stovepipe boots. "How about we go back to the VAQ, SSS and get into our new duds?" From his car he added the twenty-three hundred to his pocket cash.

They ate in the BX cafeteria. By the time they finished eating it was after 1500. "No sense leaving now. Why don't we spend another night in the VAQ and leave early tomorrow. This is a big SAC bomber wing, the NCO Club ought to be something special." There were two bomber wings and an air division headquarters at Biggs.

They showed their club memberships from another base and were welcomed into the club. The NCO Club was something special. It looked as if it had been built with the same plan as the club at Smoky Hill only larger. He walked directly into the poker room with Joey trailing behind. He went to the second door and sure enough there were ten poker tables. He asked the Sergeant-At-Arms (SAA) about the poker games. It was almost as if he was listening to a record from Smoky Hill. The third door showed a high stakes poker game but the decor looked as if someone had taken a picture of the high stakes poker game at Smoky, enlarged it and this was the building result. He asked the SAA the rules of this game. Once more it was like listening to a recording from Smoky

His curiosity was killing him. He led Joey to where the non-gambling card room should be. When they entered the room it was huge. Individual type games had roped off sections and signs to identify it. Bridge, whist, pinochle, hearts, spades, euchre and a section marked "Optional". Without going there his logic told him there was a large bar area for drinking and dancing; and, the ballroom could only follow the vastness of the rest of the club. His last stop was the pool room. Like the rest of the club it had a large capacity and equipment. Four snooker tables, four billiard tables and twelve pool tables, each with superior lighting above the table. He made a decision. Tomorrow he would buy Joey a ticket to Clovis and he would spend a few days here.

He and Joey racked to play eight ball. Musher played left handed and still had to dog some shots so Joey could win a few games. He didn't feel as if they were being watched.

CHAPTER 102

A Few Days At Biggs

At breakfast he told Joey of his plans. The bus ticket was in appreciation for his company and wisdom. I will be in Roswell by the end of the week. If you are ever there or need to go somewhere for a weekend you can always find me. There won't be too many named Muscarello stationed there. Joey checked out of the VAQ and Musher asked if he could stay a few more nights?

"Seven nights is the limit for transients. You are OK."

The ride to the bus station was filled with reminisences of the days and nights in Juarez. At the terminal the mood became more somber when his bus to Clovis was called. They shook hands and hugged. "I'll give Roswell your regards as we pass by. Take care of yourself. You have been a real pleasure to know. Maybe we can go back to Juarez together some time."

Musher nodded his head yes but he knew it would never happen again. It was noon but he was not hungry. He went to the VAQ and changed into some khaki. He wanted to blend in as much as possible at the NCO Club.

He went into the pool room and practiced bank pool. If he ever played Jefferson Carter again he did not want the same result. He was approached by a sergeant who said, "Would you like to play some competitive bank pool?

"Yes I would."

"My name is Dusty Rhodes. How about we play for twenty-five cents a ball?"

Musher calculated if Dusty made all fifteen balls that would cost him three dollars seventy-five cents. If it's hustle it's not much of a hustle. If it's the base for a bigger hustle it won't take me long to discover that. "Sure, they call me Musher. Lag for break." You don't need to be a good player to know the table lingo.

They played for about an hour plus and Dusty was twenty-five cents ahead. "Musher, do you play snooker?"

"Yes, but not near as well as I play bank pool and you know how well that is."

They had hung up their cues, racked the balls on the table and were about to go to a snooker table when a voice said, "Hi Brother."

"Musher I want you to meet my twin, Muddy Rhodes. He's the pool player in the family. Probably the best player on this air base and in all of El Paso if not all of Texas."

Muddy asked, "Musher do you play straight pool?"

"Sometimes."

"Do you play for money?"

"Sometimes."

"Would you like to play me a one hundred point game for one dollar a ball?

"Maybe."

"What maybe?"

The pool hall had gone quiet and everyone was listening to the exchange between Muddy and Musher.

"You know, not one dollar a ball but five hundred dollars for the first one to reach the one hundred point game."

Muddy smiled, "How about two thousand a game?"

"If you will give me five minutes to add some cash to my pockets, how about five thousand a game?"

"You have a bet. I will need ten minutes to get more cash."

All the playing had stopped and everyone had chosen his best available position to watch the match. Musher was back first and was rolling a cue ball on the most center table. He had laid five thousand cash on the table rail. Within a matter of minutes Muddy showed up and put his five thousand on the same table rail.

Musher to Dusty, "You hold the cash." He turned to one of the spectators he had earlier seen playing straight pool. Can you give us a good rack? Do it well and I will pay you fifty dollars. We need a good, honest player to act as referee." The spectators yelled for McCarthy. "McCarthy, do the job well and whoever wins will pay you one hundred dollars. Muddy, shall we lag for break."

Muddy lost the lag and made a pitiful break. The cue ball and two other balls were free of the rest of the rack. Musher looked over the table and selected his shot. From there he ran one hundred straight points. Muddy never even had a chance to get out of his chair after his bad break. Musher collected from Dusty, paid the racker and the referee. Without another word he went to the bar to drink coke and smoke cigarettes.

He had about five minutes alone before they started with the congratulations and the "I have never seen shooting like that before." Amid the well worshippers an older master sergeant said, "You're Musher from Smoky Hill aren't you? I was there the day you did the same thing to the wing gunnery sergeant from the 509th. I recognized you right away. I am not a friend of the Rhodes and I really wanted to see if you could do it again. You are masterful. If we were civilians I would have you on the road beating all the hustlers out there."

The parade of well wishers continued for another ten minutes. The last in the line were Dusty and Muddy Waters. "You beat us at our own game. Dusty's job is to get you involved in some cheap game so I can evaluate your skills without being seen You did a good job showing good but not great skills. We thought we had you set up. We just a few minutes ago found out that you are Musher from Smoky Hill. We knew you were a transient because we make sure of that before we try to run our game. We paid the price for stupidity. We hope you do not have any hostility against us. We are done with the game and my reputation as a good pool shooter has been relegated to fair."

Musher simply nodded shook their hands and said, "Good Luck."

With things happening so well today maybe he should try for a seat in the big game. After all it wasn't his five thousand he was going to risk. There was no seat open at the moment. As usual he stood at the proper distance and watched the players. The deal changed with each dealer, it could be five card stud or "guts". Three of the players were definitely partners and that explained why they had all the cash. They "tapped out" one player and a seat became open. Musher sat and put five thousand dollars on the table. He needed a couple of quick wins to get some of their money to play with. He won two straight guts hands netting him about fifteen hundred. He was not the dealer for either hand. He tapped out another player netting an eight hundred dollar pot. It should have been obvious to the other players but apparently it was not. The three partners all folded or one folded and one raised the bets until his partner won the pot.

When it was Musher's turn to deal Musher decided this was as good a time as any to confuse the partners. Partner Number 1 was dealt four aces and a kicker. He opened the pot. Partner Number 2 was dealt four kings and a kicker. He called and raised the pot. Partner Number 3 was dealt a straight flush to the eight. He called and raised the pot. Musher just called. Partner Number 1 called and raised the pot again. Partner Number 2 folded. Partner Number 3 called and raised the pot again. Musher called. Musher asked. "Cards gentlemen?" Partner Number 1 took one. Partner Number 3 stood pat. Musher drew one card. Partner Number 1 went all in. Partner Number 3 called as much money as he had left on the table. Musher just called.

Partner Number 1, Laid down "Four Aces". Partner Number 3, Laid down "Straight Flush to the Eight." Musher laid down "Straight Flush to the

336

Ten." Not counting what he had put in, the pot was worth close to five thousand dollars. The only money the partners had left was Partner Number 2 and it was not enough to fight for. Partner Numbers 1 and 3 stood to leave. Musher also stood. Without a word he went to his car. The fifteen thousand was burning a hole in his pocket. What he wouldn't give to be stationed here. It would be like going to the bank for a withdrawal. For sure there would be an American Express office on an installation this large.

CHAPTER 103
509th I Am Here

After what happened at the NCO Club yesterday Musher thought it might be a good idea to leave Biggs. Not that he done anything wrong but who knows how the Rhodes and The Partners may react after the beating they took. He packed his car and stopped at the VAQ office. It was the same sergeant who had been on duty the night he and Joey came from Juarez. Apparently the story from the club had spread base wide.

"They say ten grand in one day at the club. Is it true?"

"Some is some isn't. I kind of left the room in a mess. Would you divide this among the people who maintain the rooms?" He put three twenties on the counter. Then he added another fifty. "This is for you for taking care of me and my friend when we checked in." On his way out he located the American Express Office on the airbase. There he bought ten thousand dollars worth of traveler's checks in fifty dollar units. Secured them in his trunk, put two thousand in his pockets and hid the rest of the cash inside the car. He turned in his temporary access card and asked the Air Policeman if there were any diners or restaurants on the highway to Roswell

"Once you get about ten miles out of town they are all over the place. For breakfast the best place is The Corn Crib. Drive carefully, watch out for the troopers."

He was right. Huge servings at a good price. He left a conservative tip.

About a hundred miles up the road from breakfast he came to the High Lonesome general store. While his car was being serviced he went into the store for a cold drink. In a display case sat two nickel plated six shooters, ivory gripped, caliber .41 pistols mounted on a caliber .45 frame. Also displayed was a two holster gun belt with the ammunition loops fully loaded. He wondered if the pistols were loaded. The owner came in and saw him staring at the display case.

"Aren't they beauties? They don't make those anymore. There are a lot of stories about that rig but who knows if any of them are true."

"Is the rig for sale?"

"Not for less than fifteen hundred dollars."

"Will you take fifteen hundred?"

"Only if it is in cash."

"I'll be right back." He dug in his trunk and was back in a minute with fifteen hundred dollars in traveler checks. "Write me a Bill of Sale. Is there anyone here who could witness the sale? Your wife is here and can she witness the sale? You get her and I will start signing these traveler checks." Ten minutes later all the paperwork was finished. "How much do I owe you for my gas and a soda?"

"It's on the house. Be sure to register these with your Provost Marshal, the Roswell Police Department and the State Highway Patrol. If you don't they will confiscate them. I must send all three of them the notification of sale. Of course as busy as we are it may take as long as nine months for me to do that."

Musher checked the pistols to see if they were loaded. They were. He wanted so badly to put on the gun belt and pistols and play cowboys and indians. That was a tough game to play in the North End of Boston.

The High Lonesome owner saw the happy look on Musher's face. "The law here in New Mexico allows you to have weapons on the inside of you car and within your reach so long as the weapons are properly registered."

Musher put them in the trunk and took off for Roswell. It took almost three hours to cover the last hundred miles. Periodically he would pull off the road on a cattle path and fire his new toys. He did that two times within the hundred miles.

At the main gate he showed his orders, his identification, his dog tags, vehicle registration papers, insurance verification papers and his driver's license. The air policeman put a red temporary tag on the inside mounted in the corner of the driver's side windshield. The air policeman gave him directions to wing headquarters. Report to the Sergeant of the Guard (SOG).

At wing headquarters the SOG reviewed his orders and remarked, "Allowing two days for travel and fifteen as the base leave number you still have eleven days leave. When you sign in your leave ends and you are officially present for duty. Go next door to the VAQ. When you are ready to be present for duty come here at 0800 hours and sign in. He registered at the VAQ and decided to check out the NCO Club.

It was an exact duplicate of the club at Smoky Hill. It was the same in every detail from the interior layout to the furnishings. The pool room was active as were the lesser poker games. The big game was not in play. He wandered around aimlessly until he picked up a club activities schedule for the month. Over toast and coffee he studied the schedule. To him the most attractive activities were the special dinner offerings every Friday night. Nothing else really lit him up.

He took his car to be serviced. From the service station, which also doubled as the Class 6 store, he went on a scenic ride around the air base. There wasn't a lot of greenery. Just a lot of desert sand and open space.

CHAPTER 104
Not A Happy Day

At 0800 Musher was standing in front of the Sergeant of the Guard. He handed the SOG his envelope containing the documents relative to his assignment to the 509th. The SOG said, "If you are signing in off your delay and enroute and you want to be present for duty complete the Sign/Out Register." He handed Musher his assignment documents and instructed that when he finished the register go to the second floor Room 207.

Room 207 was the office of the Wing Director of Personnel (WDP). The WDP's WAF secretary took his papers and directed him to a seat. Almost two hours went by without anyone speaking one word to him. Finally the WAF told him to go to Room 212 on this same floor. He knocked, the voice invited him in. Musher took a deep breath and opened the door. Seated behind the desk was a master sergeant in Class A uniform covered with fruit salad and an Aerial Gunner Badge.

Without a salute, "Staff Sergeant Saverio Muscarello reporting as directed." He was not asked to sit. He extended his personnel envelope which the master sergeant took and pushed it to one side of the desk top.

"We won't need to look at that. We already know all about you. For some time now I have personally monitored your activities at Smoky so we could ask for your by name transfer here and your hero worshippers at Smoky could not stop our request. I think it is important for you to know who I am so you can figure out what is happening to you. My name is Charley Crossbow. You probably have never heard my name but you certainly heard my voice that day in the Smoky NCO club pool hall when you ran one hundred points in straight pool and took my five thousand dollars."

Musher did not recognize the man or his voice but he certainly could feel the wires tightening around his balls.

Crossbow continued, "I am aware of your success with your programs teaching 301st gunners to shoot better and set personal and wing shooting records. You won't need those skills here. We are overstaffed with aerial gunners. Even if we weren't overstaffed I would use the same logic to keep you out aerial gunnery. For me to have you busted and grounded for no apparent reason could raise eyebrows and cause the higher ups to ask embarrassing questions. You will continue to be flight pay eligible but as a Reel Operator in the 509th Air Refueling Squadron. What is a Reel

Operator? SAC is developing an air to air refueling capability between B-29 bombers and B-29 bombers modified to be fuel tankers. The modified version is known as a KB-29. Reel Operators will replace the waist gunners on the modified KB-29. There will be two Reel Operators assigned to each aircrew. The aircrew size is reduced to seven; the AC, Co-pilot, Navigator, Radar Operator, Flight Engineer and two Reel Operators. I will process your papers here in Wing Personnel. You go sit in the waiting room until your new first sergeant comes for you. Just remember I am watching your every move. That's it hot shot."

"Question sergeant? If I returned your five thousand plus two thousand as interest earned, would you make all this go away and let me return to aerial gunnery?"

"Yes I could make it all go away but I don't want to. I have never been hustled the way you did it. I have never been so publicly embarrassed. It is time for my pound of flesh. I want to see you come apart among the other reel operators most of whom are WWII combat gunners. Go downstairs and wait for your new first sergeant. Who by the way I flew combat with in WWII. "

It was almost noon before Master Sergeant Ralph Pippin, his new first sergeant, beeped the horn calling Musher. "Get in son, let's go have lunch and we can talk there." They went to the headquarters dining room. At the table Sergeant Pippin said, "I am going to talk and you keep eating and listening. Crossbow is a tough bird. When he didn't go to Vegas for his last leave and was back here in two days everyone wondered how he could have missed his crusade for the Holy Grail. Rumor led to story, the wing became familiar with the happening at Smoky Hill. Anyone who knew Crossbow knew he would never get a day's rest until he found a way to take revenge on the person who made him the butt of a hundred jokes. I don't know how many asses he kissed or what he promised to get a by name request for you to be transferred to this wing. You're here and no matter how good a gunner you are or how many other skills you may have, he will find a way to keep you from using them or to disrupt them. No one in our squadron knows you other than they will soon know you are the guy from Smoky. It won't take them very long to figure out what is happening with Crossbow. Be careful who you become friendly with in the squadron and don't turn your back if you can help it. Me, I have known Crossbow for a very long time. We are not social friends but I recognize the influence he has in this wing and I don't wish to test it. I am sure you noticed he is a Congressional Medal of Honor winner."

Musher almost dropped his fork. He had not noticed the white stars on the field of blue. Most CMH winners don't wear any other ribbons. True this would have been solitary above the rest of the ribbon racks but he was listening to Crossbow so intently he did not notice. To the first sergeant, "Given that I am fucked, now what do I do?"

He asked Musher to tell him the content of his meeting with Crossbow as best he could remember it. "You finish eating, have a couple of Luckies and I will take you to your car. You follow me to the squadron parking lot we will go into your barracks and see what bunks are available. The gear for the vacant bunks is ready for today. You pick one. You unload your stuff. Smoke some more cigarettes and come to the orderly room to see me."

He followed Pippin's plan. Where does he store his new guns? Would his foot locker be secure? If he left them in his car would Crossbow have his car stolen some night? Musher was not ready to go to the orderly room and begin his time in the 509th Air Refueling Squadron. He knew he had to go there very shortly.

Sergeant Pippin gave him the usual first sergeant speech about who ran the squadron and what role the officers played in running the squadron. He was issued a Class A pass and a mailbox number. He was shown the duty roster. As a staff sergeant he is required to pull Charge of Quarters duty in the squadron and Assistant Charge of Quarters at the wing level. "Do you have any questions?"

Musher told him about his guns and what he had been told about registering them.

"Where are they now?"

"The guns are in my foot locker the gun belt rig is in the trunk of my car."

"I want you to go get them now. Bring them back here for safe keeping."

Pippin locked the guns and the rig in the squadron safe, gave Musher a receipt for them and led him out of the orderly room. "We are going to squadron ops and get you started."

"This is Technical Sergeant Jack Johnson, squadron operations sergeant. Jack this is Staff Sergeant Saverio Muscarello."

Johnson did not reach out a hand to shake instead he said, "You're Musher. From Smoky Hill. Sergeant Crossbow told us you would be coming. Have a seat and when Major Curtis gets unbusy he will see you. Thank you Sergeant Pippin we'll take care of him from here."

Musher sat in that chair for almost two hours before Johnson escorted him into the Squadron Operations Officer's (SOO) office. Musher saluted. The SOO pointed to a chair. "You were Sergeant Crossbow's personal assignment to our Reel Operator Program. The NCOIC of the Reel Operator Section will explain everything about being a reel operator. At the moment our aircrews are fully staffed so you will be assigned to the NCOIC of the Reel Operator Section. Sergeant Crossbow says you are very bright, physically strong and resourceful. I expect that in very short order you will be a fully qualified reel operator. You are dismissed. Sergeant Johnson will take you to the reel operator's shack."

A shack was exactly what it was. The shack was one large room with a latrine, overhead florescent lights, forty-four student chairs, a blackboard along the front wall, one desk, a chair and a file cabinet. Johnson introduced Musher to Master Sergeant Bucky Walter, the NCOIC. Johnson left.

"What do people call you?"

"Sergeant Walter I won't talk to you like you were an idiot if you promise not to talk to me that way. Don't you already know what people call me? Didn't Sergeant Crossbow brief you about me and what his plans are for me?"

"Yes Musher he did. That doesn't mean I am part of his plans and that you will be treated any differently than any other USAF airman sent to me to be a reel operator. I cannot protect you from Crossbow but I can keep from putting you in an untenable position. Give me your best efforts and total honesty and you will be all right in this squadron. Do you believe that?"

"Yes."

"Are you willing to do that?"

"Yes."

"Tomorrow we will start your ground school. Unfortunately we just finished with the last group of reel operator trainees. You will be a class of one. I don't have a syllabus or a training plan. I do it on the blackboard and it may not be exactly the same for every group. I will mentor your training as if you were a full class. That's it for today. Go to your barracks and get settled in. Be here tomorrow at 0730 for roll call. I will introduce you to the other reel operators at roll call. Wear a flying suit. There is a map in ops showing the base bus routes and their schedule."

Back at the barracks, which were the same as Offutt without the private rooms, Musher unpacked, checked the made bunk and sat on his foot locker smoking. A quick trip to the BX was necessary. He would not show up tomorrow morning improperly attired. He debated dinner at the NCO club but instead drove back to the squadron parking lot. The walk to the squadron dining hall was not very long. The dining hall was the same as the one at Smoky. No one joined him at his table. He ate a light dinner and made his

343

way back to the barracks. Not one barracks resident came to him to introduce himself or offer a welcome to the 509th.

The long arrow of the Crossbow.

CHAPTER 105

They All Know Me Now

Musher sat at the front of the shack next to Sergeant Walter He had on his best flying suit, the 301st emblems had been replaced with the 509th emblems, and a 509th ARS (Air Refueling Squadron) baseball cap. The purchases were made at the BX yesterday afternoon while the tailor was taking care of the flying suit. Before the roll call Walter introduced Staff Sergeant Saverio Muscarello. "Because all crews are fully staffed Muscarello will be with me here in the shack." The roll call and a few announcements were made. When the formal session was over Walter and Musher went to the back of the room where there was always coffee and donuts. Neither was for sale you made a donation to the next purchase of donuts. Sergeant Walter's wife made the donuts for every work day and Walter picked up the coffee from the dining hall. Musher found out later that most of the time the donations did not cover the cost of the materials to make the donuts. When he found out Musher thought of Rod, "In that case fuck 'em and feed 'em frijoles."

One of the taller, leaner, meaner looking reel operators in a not too clean flying suit and oily hat touched the leather aerial gunner badge sewn on Musher's flying suit. In probably his most arrogant tone he said, "Where did you get that?"

"The gunnery school at Piute AFB in Texas."

"No, no, I mean where in combat did you earn it?"

"I have never been in combat. I was too young for WWII."

The questioner reached out and tore the leather patch from Musher's flying suit.

Here we go again. Musher feinted left stepped right and did his routine. A kick in the balls, a punch to the Adam's apple followed by knee to the face of his bent over attacker. He finished the job by raising the attacker's head from the floor and slapping his face as you would a misbehaved child. "If there is anyone else who believes he would like to question my background and capability step up now. With the exception of Sergeant Walter you have all behaved as if you were Crossbow's private cocksuckers. Especially you who live in the barracks. Let me tell you this. I am not a lifer and have no intent to be a lifer. If assholes like you can become reel operators I should be the best in this squadron in very short time. Now if you feel insulted and you want satisfaction of your honor just step up. I will

345

end your career as a reel operator and most likely end your military career. It will not be a school yard encounter. If you are thinking about more than one at the same time you had better kill me. If you don't I will surely kill everyone in the group who attacks me." No one stepped up. Musher's attacker started to get up. Musher walked to him, slapped his face twice and banged his head on the shack floor.

Walter barked, "Enough. You men report to your crews or whatever other duties you have today. I expect we have heard the last of this incident."

CHAPTER 106

Reel Operator Ground School

"You certainly gave Crossbow something to nibble on. Fortunately I was there and it happened so fast it was over before I could move. To tell you the truth I enjoyed seeing Tickman getting his clock cleaned. He is a constant troublemaker among the aircrews. He is on his second crew and his aircraft commander has asked me if I could move him and give him a replacement. Maybe when we get you qualified you may be the answer. Do you know how to run a film projector? Good that you do. I am going to set up a fifteen minute film of an air to air, KB-29 to a B-29 air refueling. I want to watch it ten times. Each time you watch make notes of your questions and significant maneuvers of each aircraft. The tanker, our tanker, is identified by the "K" on its vertical stabilizer. You can smoke in here. Make sure you use the butt cans. I have something I must do."

He turned the lights out and Musher rolled the film. It was 1140 when Walter entered the shack. Musher had just finished his tenth review of the film.

Let's break for lunch. You can go wherever you wish to eat just be back here not later than 1315. Me, I go home for lunch. If you want to go to the squadron dining hall I can drop you there it's on my way home. I can pick you up at 1255 and we can return together.

In the dining room he was sitting alone when he was joined by three other residents of his barracks. They introduced themselves and shook hands. He catalogued them as Curly, Moe and Shep. The three made small talk while Musher listened and ate. Finally Moe said, "That was some demonstration of brute power with Tickman. None of us minded, we all think he is an asshole. For sure it will be some time before he lets his mouth overload his ass again." It was Curly's turn, "Crossbow has taken some real ribbing about being hustled by a teenage pool player."

Musher put down his knife and fork. "I am going to tell you the whole story and then you tell me if I hustled Crossbow or if he made a bad bet." He told the story about a one thousand dollar straight pool game in which he let his opponent buy out for five hundred dollars when the score was ninety-six for me and zero for my opponent. Crossbow's voice then came from the spectators, "Would I like to make a two thousand dollar bet spotting my opponent fifty of the one hundred points?" I raised the bet to five thousand and he faded my offer. We lagged for the break I lost and I made a safety

347

break. For whatever reason on his turn my opponent caused two balls to come free from the rack. In the middle of the rack there was a ball dead to the side pocket. It needed impetus. I called that ball in the side pocket. I explained my intended shot before shooting to keep any skeptic from calling it luck. I played a billard off one of the loose balls banging the cue ball into the rack, the ball from the middle of the rack went into the side pocket. I ran the hundred points. I only found out who the five thousand loser was after the game and the 509th and his job had no significant meaning to me. Yesterday I offered to give Crossbow his five thousand back with two thousand interest earnings. He is consumed with the need for revenge for a hustle which never existed. I don't know what story he told here but I will bet it involved some form of cheating on my part."

The three agreed Crossbow instigated the bet right after seeing you run ninety-six points in a one hundred point game. There was no hustle, just a bad bet. Shep spoke, "We will spread the truth. We will tell people about yesterday's offer."

"You cannot do that. It would add fuel to his fire and may cause him to set me up for a general court martial. Any one who hates this much is capable of doing anything and rationalizing its appropriateness. The best thing you can do for me is to keep it to yourselves. If you truly believe me as you say you do then your knowing means that there are four of us in the 509th who know the truth and not just me."

"Can we tell trusted friends?"

Only if you are sure they will not make it a fairy tale version of the truth." He couldn't think of a better way to have the true tale spread throughout the wing. Of course there is some logic to the assumption that someone that intense could resort to a very drastic action. In the words of Rod, "Fuck 'em and feed 'em frijoles."

At 1310 they were back in the shack.

"Go to the blackboard and using stick men techniques draw the initial formation of the tanker and receiver." ....."Yes but which one is the tanker?" ... "That's right. What is that trailing from the receiver's tail?" ..."You don't know, it is a dishpan with a bayonet fitting on the end of a one hundred foot steel cable which is attached to a drum in the receiver. What is that hanging from the tanker?"...."You don't know, it is a one hundred pound conical weight attached to a one hundred foot cable which is attached to a drum in the tanker."

"Draw the second, third and final positions of the aircraft during air to air refueling."..."That's right, the tanker moves forward maintaining altitude separation, crosses over the top of the receiver, reduces power to fall back until the weight from the tanker locks with the dishpan from the receiver. The pilots hold their positions. From here the reel operator takes over to establish the refueling. I leave your drawings on the board for you to memorize the first steps in the air refueling process."

Walter hands Musher a group of eight by eleven black and white photos. "These are pictures of the reel operators working area inside the KB-29. The nomenclature for each component of the area is marked on these photographs. I want you to memorize the name of each component and where it is located in the working area. When I believe you have them totally committed to memory we will discuss the function of each component. Spend the rest of the afternoon studying the photos."

At 1630 Walter told him, Leave things they way they are and take off. I will see you at roll call at 0730 in the morning."

"May I ask you a question before I leave?"

"Shoot."

"What are all these fancy scooters I see running up and down the flight line?"

"The more common one here is the Vesper. It is Italian made, about sixty miles to the gallon and the oil mixes with gasoline. Cost in Italy when new about two hundred dollars American. You see them on the flight line because they are authorized to be ridden on the flight line. They are not authorized to ride off base unless they are properly licensed with the State of New Mexico and properly insured. No special driver license is required. The only requirement to ride the scooter on base and on the flight line is that the scooter is registered with the air police and has a Walker Air Force Base decal."

"Do they sell them in the BX?"

"Not likely. They are flown in here directly by one of our aircraft returning from a temporary duty (TDY) overseas. If they are brought for other than personal use they are turned over to Sergeant Jim Nance in the motor pool and he resells them for one hundred dollars above cost, twenty-five for him and seventy-five for the guy who brought it. It may not be totally legal but no one ever questions what is going on. If you're considering one and cannot afford a new one, there are always some resales listed in the NCO Club. Sergeant Nance always has two or three for sale."

"May I use the shack phone for an on base call?"

"Sergeant Nance's phone number is in the rolodex."

"Sergeant Nance this is Staff Sergeant Muscarello, I am very interested in buying a new Vesper. Do you have any for sale?.......Yes, you were recommended by Master Sergeant Walter of the 509th ARS.......He is here. I will put him on the phone."

"Yes Jim he is my new reel operator trainee....Permanently assigned to my squadron........I will tell him. I will drop him off on my way home.......Thanks Jim. Musher button up and I will drop you at the motor pool."

"Sergeant Nance, I am Staff Sergeant Muscarello, Sergeant Walter spoke to you about me?"

"You're the one they call Musher. Crossbow's boy. Earlier today I heard a different story from the one he told every chance he got. All the Vespers are white with either a black or blue trim. They come with a front head light but you can have the option of three front lights. The main light and one on each side of it, the left one aimed to highlight the road marking and the other to highlight the road shoulder. You can add a two by two by two waterproof storage box mounted behind your riding seat. The box is within the width of the fender. You can upgrade the riding seat to a waterproof slightly larger but considerably more padded one. You can add a windshield. It does not come with windshield wipers. You can upgrade the kick stand to a larger, more durable, easier to use version. You can upgrade the starter kick pedal to a larger, wider version. Let me show you the Vesper and you can tell me if you want any of the upgrades."

There was no hesitancy by Musher. "I'll take the white and blue one with all the upgrades. When will it be ready?"

"You realize it will cost you seven hundred dollars cash?"

"Yes."

"For another fifty dollars I can get it registered on the airbase without you being there. For another hundred I can get you off base insurance without you being there. For another hundred I can get you a State of Mexico registration license plate without you being there. I provide you with a Bill of Sale and Title to the Vesper."

Musher said, "I am not very good at arithmetic but it looks like nine hundred fifty dollars does the deal. Here is one thousand cash. The extra is for you. I expect to pick up the finished product at noon tomorrow. Can you do it?"

"I will deliver it to your shack at 1100 tomorrow. The deal will be done. Can I offer you a ride somewhere? By the way have you ever ridden a motorcycle or a scooter?"..........No..............."Forget what I said you be here after 1100 tomorrow"....."Now where do you want to go?"

Nance dropped him off at the squadron dining hall. Again he was joined at his table by Moe, Curly and Shep. "We know you are a pool shooter, are you a card player? Do you play double deck? How about being our fourth a little later?"

"What are the stakes?"

"Fifty cents a game, twenty-five cents a set. Winners do not pay their sets. If you have a cash shortage you can play jawbone. (Jawbone means you owe until payday) We rotate partners after every game."

CHAPTER 107
More Ground School Plus a New Ride

Musher took the last seat in the shack for roll call. Normal announcements and the gunners were released for their other duties. Musher was first at the coffee and donuts. He moved off to a quiet location where he was joined by some other reel operators. "Did you notice who was not here for roll call this morning?" ......Yes ...... "They kept him in the Base Hospital for observation. That was some beating."

"Actually I would not call that a beating. I only struck him seven times and each of those blows was in self-defense. If it were a beating I would be pleading self-defense to a jury."

"You are kidding aren't you?"

"There are very few things I kid about. Defending myself from arrogant, ill-mannered, ill-equipped assholes is not one of them." Suddenly Musher was standing there by himself. Walter hurried the rest of the donut eaters and coffee drinkers out of the shack.

Walter sat across from Musher and held up pictures as if they were flash cards. At the end of each run of pictures Walter would shuffle them into a different order. Many of the pictures were duplicates of others only portrayed from a different angle. It took Musher nine run throughs before he named each picture without a mistake. Walter made him do it three more times to prove the first all correct effort was not luck.

Walter proceeded to enumerate the function of each component of the reel operator work area and where it fit into the air refueling process. The rest of the morning was devoted to this aspect of ground school.

It was time for lunch. "How did you make out with Nance for your scooter?"

"He was going to deliver it here, ready to ride until he asked me if I had ever ridden a motorcycle or a scooter. When I said no, he told me to come to the motor pool anytime after eleven today. I guess he is going to teach me to ride without killing myself or someone else."

"You are doing exceptionally well with ground school. You may go there and then take the rest of the day off. Would you like me to drop you off on my way home for lunch? ......Yes ....."OK, let's secure this area and go on over."

At the motor pool Walter could not resist the temptation to go in with Musher and see what he had bought. The scooter was beautiful. Nance had added, without charge, streamers which flew from the fuel and transmission control grips on the handle bars when the scooter was in motion. Walter wished Musher good luck and said, "See you in the morning."

Nance took him to the back reaches of the motor pool. Nance used a scooter other than Musher's to demonstrate the kick starter and the need for balance when the scooter is stopped but not on its kick stand. He operated the left handle bar which has a squeeze type clutch and the three gear transmission gear shift. Both of these were incorporated into the left handle bar. The right handle bar incorporated the throttle and a manual brake Nance stressed that the synchronization of the gear change and the accompanying throttle fuel flow was no different than the clutch, gear shift and the accelerator in a car. Just as when you learned to drive a stick transmission car you will need to practice to get the feel of the scooter. Remember, when the scooter is in motion keep your feet on the scooter foot boards, use the hand brake gently and put your feet down when the scooter slows to a stop. Keep your balance and do not try to burn rubber when you take off on your scooter. Nance did a walk-around asking Musher to name the various components and tell him about their use and dangers. The last items are the ignition key and the light control switches. The light control switches need no explanation; however, the ignition lock is modified on your scooter. Next to the ignition key slot is a small black button. Normal starting is key on and the kick starter. On your scooter the small black button is a "kill switch" When you turn the ignition off and press the black button two times, all sources which could provide power for ignition are interrupted. When you start the scooter you must turn on the ignition and press the button three times to reenergize the ignition circuitry. That is a gift from me. Are you ready to try riding the scooter. With the exceptions of the upgrades and the condition this Vesper is the same as yours."

Musher's first attempts were not perfect. For example, he tried to start the scooter with the transmission in gear. It will start that way but it will buck like a rodeo horse. One time he drove around the open space and when he came to a stop did not have his feet down and the scooter toppled with him on it. Within two hours he was riding well, making good gear transitions, stopping with a high degree of smoothness and able to maneuver between the cones Nance had set up as a driving course.

"You're ready. Let's go to your scooter." Nance gave him a set of ignition keys and all the properly executed scooter papers. He locked one key and the scooter papers n the carry box.

"Drive it around here for a little bit so I can know you will not kill yourself or somebody else. If you zero and watch the trip odometer and fill the three gallon tank with the right oil mixture you are good for a minimum one hundred fifty miles. Your tank is properly filled and your trip odometer now reads zero."

Musher made a few passes in and around the motor pool. He stopped in front of Nance. "Thank you for everything." As he shook hands with Nance he pressed another hundred into Nance's hand.

It was still early afternoon. Musher put on his sun glasses, felt regal and started an orientation ride of Walker AFB, Roswell, New Mexico. He rode most everywhere and ended up at the NCO Club. He had not had lunch so he settled for rye toast and a coke. The most enjoyable part was the Lucky Strikes with the coke. The scooter windshield was fairly protective. He would need to try smoking while riding. Most of the airbase speed limits were either twenty-five miles per hour or less. Before he takes his scooter on the flight line he must make sure he knows and obeys flight line rules. He took another short orientation ride and ended up in the squadron parking lot. He parked the scooter next to his car and pressed the black button two times.

Most of his barracks mates were already in and a number of them were playing various card games. Basically they were killing time until dinner. He washed, sat on his foot locker smoking and when the crowd headed for the dining hall he walked with them. He was sitting with three others than Curly, Moe and Shep. They asked him how ground school was going and when would he finish it?

"It must be OK Walter gave me the afternoon off."

"For what reason? Did he need to go somewhere?"

"He didn't I did. I picked up my new Vesper today. Finished all the paperwork and went riding around the air base this afternoon. It is in the squadron parking lot, it is blue and white with every imaginable accessory that can be sold."

"How about showing us after dinner? .....Sure..... "Maybe even let us ride it?"

Musher guessed what was happening. "You can look but cannot ride. My insurance only covers me on the scooter. Sorry but unfortunately that is the way it is."

CHAPTER 108
The Ground School Simulator

Musher parked his scooter along with all the other scooters outside the shack. A number of personnel who saw him ride up asked him where he got such a fancy Vesper and how much did it cost? He was willing to give Jim Nance a strong testimonial but was totally unwilling to discuss cost.

When the shack cleared Walter began again with testing all the cogent items of the reel operator's work area. Some questions were oral and some were responses to a picture. When he was satisfied that Musher could hold an intelligent conversation regarding the work area they got in Walter's car for a ride to a stand alone building at the far end of the runway. On the way Walter took the scenic route through the P Patch. Musher had his first real look at a KB-29. He was in total awe the way the tail mount area had been converted to an aerodynamic cone to reduce drag on the aircraft. Even more astounding was the fact that the under fuselage had been cut away and strengthened to accommodate the installation of the reel operators work area.

"Just thought you might like to see a real tanker."

Musher was once more astonished. The building contained a full model of the reel operator's work area.

"We left the blackboard in the shack with both the tanker and receiver in proper position for fuel transfer. We said that at that point the reel operator became the most important part of the air to air refueling. I will demonstrate in abbreviated form the next steps for the air refueling process. As I go through the exercise I will tell you what I am going to do and you tell me which of the work area components I should use for that function. Then tell me exactly what to do.Step 1, I need to bring in my weighted line which would also bring the receivers trail line. ...."Use the clutch motor on the left side of the platform. Holding the control knob to the left will retract you weighted line."............That is correct.

Step 2, The size and configuration of the cutaway do not permit the tanker line weight and the receivers dishpan to be fully brought into the work area..............."Since I am harnessed into the work area and cannot fall out of the aircraft, I take the two hay hooks, lay them under my tanker line and draw the two items the last two feet into the reel operator's work area. Secure the tanker line to the inboard holding vice. Bring additional receiver line into the aircraft and secure it to the outboard holding vice. Remove the tanker weight, store it and rewind all the tanker cable wire to its drum and secure the wire drum. Remove the dishpan from the receiver line, extract the bayonet fitting, run the receiver wire under the platform and marry the receiver bayonet fitting to the hose nozzle."........Very well spoken and totally technically correct. Now what?............."Notify the flight engineer that the hose is ready for release and listen to him confirm with the receiver flight engineer that we are releasing the hose. Stand clear of the receiver cable vice for release. Release the hose drum brake and release the receiver cable vice. Gravity will unravel the hose and the receiver operator will use his clutch motor to retrieve his cable and with it the hose. When the hose is engaged in the receiver we should hear the confirmation from the receiver flight engineer. Our flight engineer will open the fuel tanks which have been installed in the bomb bay and gravity will cause the fuel to flow into the receiver.".......Very good description. The fuel transfer may take as long as twenty-five minutes. Most air refueling will be done above ten thousand feet so the reel operator is back at his platform does his work with his oxygen mask on. The work is so strenuous most reel operators take off their heavy flight jacket because they need the mobility to do their job. During the transfer period the reel operator tries to warm up and sucks a lot of one hundred percent oxygen.

What comes next?......."Our flight engineer will broadcast when the transfer is complete and how many pounds of fuel were transferred. The two aircraft commanders will agree on breakaway with the receiver counting down from ten to zero. The receiver gunner with primary responsibility for air refueling will extract the receiver bayonet fitting from the hose. When he has done that the count down would begin. At zero the hose holding clamps in the receiver would be released and the aircraft commander would increase power to move forward, the tanker aircraft commander would reduce power to increase the separation between the receiver and the tanker. The free swinging hose would dance in the sky like a cobra snake searching for its prey. It will settle some as the aircraft increases speed. Using the hose clutch motor the hose is brought back to the aircraft. The reel operator must watch and insure the drum wrap is smooth. Very easily a hose could get caught between the hose drum and the fuselage. When all the hose is in place, the nozzle has been securely locked in place and the area policed the reel operator will go forward to the "Gunner's Compartment" so the aircraft could be pressurized"

"Musher you did very, very well. Ground school is finished for you. As soon as I can I will schedule you with one of the crews for a familiarization mission. If you cannot guess what a familiarization mission is, it simply means watch but keep your mouth shut. Are you ready for lunch?"

"If you don't mind I am going to tour the base on my scooter. I am not even sure if I will have lunch."

"OK, be back at the shack at 1315."

It was great fun riding his scooter on the flight line, into the P Patch and out around the GCA (Ground Controlled Approach) trailer. He was shocked to see two WAFs sitting outside the trailer smoking cigarettes. He waved as he went by and they waved back vigorously. Gotta check that out later. As he rode he found out that with the windshield and the slow speed he could enjoy a cigarette. He hadn't figured out how to field the strip the cigarette until he learns how to ride no hands on the scooter. His watch told him it was time to get back to the shack.

Walter was already waiting in the shack. "I have arranged for you to take a familiarization ride tomorrow. Station time is 0900. The mission will probably be about six hours long they are planning two refueling exercises. For each one you will lie on the top of the hose drum container. The aircraft is modified with a two step staircase and a flat finished top surface over the width and length of the hose drum. There is an oxygen outlet on either side of the platform. The reel operator has his two oxygen outlets on the kneeling edge of his work area. Do you have an A-3 Bag, helmet, oxygen mask, throat mike and cold weather flying gear?" ....Yes to the A-3, helmet, oxygen mask and cold weather gear. I do not have a throat mike...........Walter walked to his desk and returned with a throat mike. "Remember your oxygen mask has a built in mike. The aircrew will board the bus at squadron ops at 0730. A flight lunch has been ordered for you. You can get your chute when the crew gets theirs. Under no circumstances will you participate in the refueling exercise, I repeat, under no circumstances will you participate in the refueling exercise. Is all this clear to you?"..... Yes ....."OK we will call it a day. I will be waiting to critique you after tomorrow's mission. "

Fully knowing that even as only an observer his presence would be evaluated and he would work hard to blend into the mission without causing any disruption. He checked his A-3 bag to make sure all the flight gear he might need was there. He remembered how much his students had perspired in the heavy cold weather flight gear and he added spare undergarments, a flying suit and a blanket to his A-3 bag.

Better safe than sorry.

CHAPTER 109

Airborne Watching of a Real Refueling

Musher was in the dining hall for breakfast at 0545. The independence of his scooter allowed him to set his own time schedule. He lashed his A-3 bag on the scooter and was sitting in front of squadron ops smoking Luckies at 0700. Some other scooter riders pulled along side him. The tall one came to him and asked if he was Muscarello......Yes....."Grab your bag and come with me." The bags were left in front of ops. Inside the introductions began. "I am Master Sergeant Steve Sanchez flight engineer, these are the two reel operators, Master Sergeant Tony Lima and Master Sergeant Bubba Weakley. Air refueling crew sizes have just been increased to eight to add a radio operator. This is our new radio operator Staff Sergeant Charley James. Gentleman this is our observer for today, Staff Sergeant Saverio Muscarello better known as Musher." There were handshakes all around. The aircraft commander, Captain William Lonigan entered with the other officers. Sanchez, "Let's get all the gear on the bus."

Everyone checked the release pins on his chute and signed for it. Musher noticed there were none of the joking signs on the walls as there were at the parachute shop at Smoky Hill. He wondered if there was any significance to that.

Musher loaded the gear into the right compartments while the aircrew did its pre-take off safety checks. The crew and Musher stood under the left wing while the aircraft commander re-briefed the mission and recognized Musher's presence as an observer. The taxi, the engine run-up checks, tower takeoff approval, takeoff and the climb out were the same as his flights at Smoky. He certainly could handle that part of the reel operator job description.

Tony Lima came to Musher. "I will be the primary operator on our first refueling. It will be done at eighteen thousand feet. Do you know how to use the six minute walk around bottle? ....No...... Lima showed him the simple hookup and the flow control valve. "You will need to use this when we depressurize and you and I go aft while the aircraft is re-pressurized. Six minutes is a very long time but don't waste any of it. Hookup to the oxygen outlet on the reel platform as quickly as you can. Sanchez, the flight engineer will tell us when to suit up. We will check our oxygen masks and their built in mikes before the aircraft is depressurized There is no reason you should need to do anything or say anything other than Observer OK when Sanchez runs his crew checks. The aircraft is going to bump more than any roller coaster you have ever been on. Have you been air sick on any craft?" ....No....."That's good. If you do raise your mask and blow it out. Do not take off your mask until we are back in a pressurized cabin. Any questions?" .....No..... "Standby for dressing instructions."

Musher sat nervously and contemplated every thing Lima had said. He sure hoped he did not need to do anything especially after Walter's instructions.

"OK guys get into the heavy clothing. Tell me when you are ready."

While he was dressing he heard the aircraft commander, "830th Warrior 6 this is Tanker 102. Do you copy?"

"Roger 102"

"Warrior 6 I have you in sight. I am above you and six to eight minutes away from my position. Will contact you when I am in position."

"Roger 102 Warrior 6 out."

Musher was clothed, Lima told him to do the oxygen mask checks. "Flight engineer primary operator. we are ready to go into position."

"Roger Tony, crew stand by for depressurization. Flight engineer to crew tell me when you are ready for depressurization." One by one the crew acknowledged ready. A soft hissing came throughout the aircraft. "OK Tony unseal the hatch and go to your position. With a soft chuckle, don't forget to take Musher. Call me when you are both in position with good oxygen flow."

Musher followed Tony out of the compartment and as soon as they were out the hatch closed. Tony went up and over the platform top to his position on the working area platform. Musher laid down on the top of the platform and immediately hooked into the oxygen system. The safety belt was a harness which was mounted to the strong support beams of the platform and engaged off center of his front. That allowed him to lie on his stomach without the security buckle pressing on his belly button. Lima gave him the OK sign and Musher returned it. "Flight Engineer, reel operator and observer are secure in position and are ready for air refueling."

"Warrior 6 we are in position one. Are you ready to start fuel transfer operations? You may trail your dishpan. We are ready here.'

"102, we have begun dishpan trailing operations."

Musher listened to the coordination messages voiced between the receiver and his tanker. True to Walter's prediction Lima had shed some of the heavy clothing. He performed the entire operation without a hitch.

"102 to Warrior Six. We have given you all we can afford. On your count let us disconnect." The disconnect went without incident. Lima finished the cleanup steps to an air refueling, made sure all the equipment was good and in place for the next air refueling.

"Lima to flight engineer. Can we come in now and can you turn up the heat please?"

"Roger Tony, crew stand by for depressurization. Flight engineer to crew tell me when you are ready for depressurization." One by one the crew acknowledged ready. That soft hissing came. "OK Tony the hatch is unsealed, you and Musher stay on oxygen until we pressurize."

Musher unlocked his harness, hooked up his walk around bottle and headed for the aft compartment. Lima was right on his heels. Lima shut the hatch the other reel operator gave him an OK signal and the aircraft was pressurized to eight thousand feet.

Flight engineer to crew, "You may remove your oxygen masks." Lima was stripping from his wet clothes and putting on clean clothes from his A-3 bag. Musher took off his heavy clothing but he was dry underneath. Why not, he hadn't done anything but watch. Again from the flight engineer, "Total refueling time one hour eleven minutes, fuel transferred one complete dreamboat tank, eighty thousand pounds."

"Navigator to AC. Climb to fifteen thousand feet, steer course 290 degrees. Our next rendezvous should be in twenty-five minutes. Our receiver should be flying at eleven thousand feet."

"Thank you Navigator. Crew we have about a twenty minute period before the next contact. Let's squeet."

Lima called Musher to sit between him and Bubba Weakley. Lima critiqued his performance. He noted things which he thought he did not do well and the couple he thought he did do well. Musher thought he did everything well. The in-flight box lunches were the same as Smoky. They were good but they could skip the pickles. After eating lunch the three of them smoked cigarettes and generally relaxed. The KB-29 Radar Operator's position was in the aft compartment with the reel operators. This particular radar operator never spoke unless required on the intercom.

He heard the aircraft commander, "830th Warrior 8 this is Tanker 102. Do you copy?"

"Roger 102"

"Warrior 8 I have you in sight. I am above you and six to eight minutes away from my position. Will contact you when I am in position."

"Roger 102 Warrior 8 out." From this point on the refueling mission was a carbon copy of the refueling with Warrior 6. Bubba was very efficient, stronger than Lima and seemed to be finishing every task as if he were in the simulator not at fifteen thousand feet in a very cold, very bumpy tanker.

When they were back in the pressurized compartment Bubba said to Musher, "What did you think of that kid? Am I good or what?"

The Radar Operator, Captain Matthew "Spike" Jones broke in," Don't listen to him Musher he just had a very good day today. We could talk of some other days." The compartment went quiet and its silence was broken by the flight engineers report of the fuel transfer.

"AC to crew, you did excellent work today. I am sure you impressed our observer because I know you impressed the hell out of me. Navigator, take us home."

Musher offered to help police the aircraft but Lima told him the ground crew would take care of that. On the aircrew bus the AC invited Musher to attend debriefing interrogation with the crew. He was pleased to go. In true tradition of the air force each aircrew member was given a one ounce shot of Wild Turkey. Musher had his experience with Wild Turkey so he slipped his medicinal allocation to Lima. He didn't speak at the debriefing but he felt like he was part of a combat crew.

How do I keep that son-of-a-bitch Crossbow from depriving me of this feeling?

CHAPTER 110
The Critique

Roll call the next morning was very friendly. Lima and Weakley were telling how I observed them, didn't get sick when it was really bumpy and I even looked like I understood everything they did for the fuel transfer.

When the shack was empty Walter questioned Musher about every aspect from getting on the aircrew bus in the morning to the debriefing after the mission. You could tell Walter was pleased. "Musher I am going to give you a certification ride. As soon as I can set something up you and I will go along on a multiple refueling mission and you will perform one of the refuelings with me as your evaluator."

Musher was thrilled. He could not wait. Walter went to squadron ops. When he returned he said, "Seven days from today. You may have the rest of the day off."

Musher thought that is like aircrew. Not scheduled to fly or any detail, you are off. That certainly sounds good. He jumped on his scooter and headed for the NCO Club. He was hungry. After a large cheese omelet, lots of hot tea and Lucky Strikes he was ready for a nap. The Big Game room had some couches maybe he could relax on one of those.

The room was exactly like every other big game room in SAC. Sitting at the table was Crossbow. He had a very large stack of cash in front of him. Thank goodness there were no open seats. Instead Musher watched the players as he looked for tells. He watched for almost two hours. He committed the faces of the players to his memory. He did not need to commit Crossbow's face it was already burned in his mind. He found a very nice padded wing chair and took a nap. He was awakened by Crossbow. "What are you doing here in the middle of the day?"

"I am excused from duty and I came here to have something to eat. I was tired and thought I could relax in here where it is so quiet."

"Are you a poker player?"

"I play some."

"Do you play poker as well as you play pool?"

"I don't do anything as well as I play pool."

Crossbow left and Musher headed to the bar for a coke. He sat there sipping and was joined by Bubba Weakley.

"Musher did you notice the ease which I handled the dishpan and the weight and how Tony struggled some with both of them? The answer is shoulder and arm strength. You're fairly well built and I am told you are as tough as nails. You lack muscle definition and maximum strength. I work out in the base gym not to look like a Mr. America but to have the strength to be the best at my job. If I am not flying I am there every Monday, Wednesday and Thursday at 1715. The whole workout is less than one hour. I eat after my workout. Join me and I will bulk you up. If you do decide to come bring a towel and a change of clothes."

"I will. I will be there the next Monday, Wednesday or Thursday which I am not committed to something else. Thank you."

CHAPTER 111

To Win Some You Must Lose Some

Life in the shack was boring. He studied the blackboard until he could close his eyes and see all the details written there. Walter quizzed him about procedures. He preached to Musher the things which could go wrong during a refueling and how to overcome them. He gave him a key and let him go to the simulator to practice.

At the simulator Musher did very little reel operator practice he spent most of his time practicing his card mechanic trade. During his practice he formed a plan which he hoped would get Crossbow off his back once and for all time.

That afternoon, more specifically around 1730, he was at the Base Gymnasium with Bubba. He got the full lecture on how to build strength. The workout may have been less than an hour but it strained his muscles. His first concern was would this strength building interfere with his card dealing. He would not run the risk. No more strength building until Operation Crossbow has been successfully executed.

Friday night after another boring day at the shack Musher headed for the NCO Club and the game. Sure enough Crossbow was sitting with most of the cash on the table. No one had ever explained the theory of diminishing returns if you are the big winner in a table stakes game. Musher thought "This is good. He is not only a son-of-a-bitch, he is a greedy son-of-a-bitch." Musher sat as soon as he could and played to lose about eleven hundred dollars to Crossbow. When he had accomplished that he said to the table, "Good night gentlemen, I guess this is just not my night."

Crossbow could not resist the temptation. "Saturday night is the night all the big players come. Why don't you come and bring all your money. We would be more than glad to have you."

"I'll come but only if I can sit next to you where some of your good luck might jump over to me."

"It's a deal. I will keep the seat on my left open waiting for you."

Musher wondered why the seat on the left. Crossbow is not left handed. Of course in normal betting he would bet before Musher and maybe he thought he could intimidate the game with money. Musher couldn't be any happier with the seating arrangement.

CHAPTER 112
Revenge Is Best Served Cold

He needed to pass time until tonight. When he and Freddie had something planned for the night the day was interminably long. Inside he felt the butterflies he had not felt since his first couple of scams with Freddie. It was kind of like a football player who is nervous until his first hit. After that he was settled in the game and ready for war. Musher had been through the butterfly routine and knew it would pass when he touched his first card. He didn't believe he would be back at the barracks before the game so he assembled all his cash. He would not take it all. He decided eight thousand would be more than enough for show and no matter how much money Crossbow lost his attitude towards Musher would not change.

I'll spend the day sightseeing. He had not been off the base since his arrival. He passed through the main gate and immediately saw a diner, a pawn shop, a grocery store and a liquor store. New Mexico was not a dry state. There were no houses but there were three small living type trailers with a woman sitting under a large umbrella outside each trailer. "Gee, I wonder what those trailers were for?"

There were no other facilities of any type until he came to a "Y" junction in the road. North led almost immediately into Roswell and South led to Carlsbad and ultimately to El Paso, Texas and Juarez, Mexico. He drove up the main street of Roswell and it struck him as slightly larger than Salina and a lot drier climate. It certainly was not liquor dry he counted at least four bars on the main street. He passed over a culvert bridge and on his left was the New Mexico Military Institute (NMMI). All the grasses were green, the display cannons brightly painted black, the flagpole with the US flag on top, the State of New Mexico below and the NMMI flag below that. (Later he learned the slang expression for NMMI was Numerous Maniacs and Many Idiots) NMMI was considered the Citadel of the west. The direction signs showed the next town to be Portales, ninety miles north. He had driven through Portales coming south to Walker AFB. It was time to find some lunch and then somewhere to rest.

The sign said, "Sonny's Bar-B-Q, All you can eat with iced tea $2.50" He filled a good size plate took a large iced tea and settled into a picnic type table. Two young men about his age settled in the seats across him. "Gunslinger" as Musher named him asked, "You from the air base?" ......Yes..... "Been here before? .....No....."We think you should enjoy your lunch and never come back in here again." .....OK, but would you tell me why?....."You and your types want to chase our waitresses. Our Roswell girls are definitely not your type." .....If I told you I would not chase your girls would I then be allowed to come here to eat? ....."You airbase guys are all the same, you lie through your teeth." ..... I do not lie but today I do not have time to prove that. I must be somewhere else very shortly; however, one day soon I will come here to eat and it will not be to ogle or make a pass at your waitresses. If at that time you still do not believe me I will happily prove it to either one or both of you. For now, if you will excuse me I must pay my bill and leave. ....As Musher went to the register to pay his bill and leave a conservative tip, Gunslinger and his buddy sat there unable to figure out what to do.

It was still too early for the NCO Club and he did not want to go back to his barracks. He drove until he found a shady spot, parked and fell asleep His watch said it was 2000. He could now go to the NCO Club. True to his word Crossbow had saved the seat on his left for Musher. Musher put his eight thousand on the table and took the seat. The SSA announced "Either five card stud or "guts" are the only two games allowed. Nothing wild. Dealer's choice. Crossbow, deal for first jack."

As if he had an invisible partner the first jack fell to Crossbow. "Guts, ten dollar ante." It wasn't a particularly large pot but again with the help of his invisible partner Crossbow won the pot.

For the next couple of hours nobody made a shark like kill. The money moved around but Crossbow seemed to be the only one gaining. Musher lost a couple of pots to him which he knew he could have won but greed must be fed.

It came time for Musher to deal. "Guts, twenty dollar ante." This is it. Fanucci used to say, "You can shear a sheep many times but you can only skin him once." He dealt six players, two bad hands, two good hands, a better than good hand to Crossbow and a potentially good hand for himself. The betting was heavy. Before the draw there was still one of the good hand players in the pot, Crossbow who had been the big raiser and Musher. After the draw Crossbow bet nine thousand, Musher called what he could and the good hand folded.

Crossbow "Four Aces and laid his cards on the table. Musher reached over to spread Crossbow's cards so that he could read them. The Good Hand player said, "Wait a minute Crossbow, you have six cards!" Crossbow reached in and sure enough there were six cards. He blanched and could not speak. Good Hand player carried on, "No wonder this cocksucker wins all the time. He's a fucking cheat. He's been cheating us all along and we

366

thought he was a good player with a lot of luck. He's nothing but a cocksucking, fucking cheater!" Crossbow could not speak one word in his own defense. Good Hand said, "Tell you what cocksucking cheater, Musher wins that pot because he played it to the end. We other five who have been playing with you for a long time will take whatever is in front of you, plus you empty your pockets and we will divide it among us. Is that OK with you Musher?"

"Yes, I think each of you should get out of this pot what he put in, is that OK with you?"

"That's good. As for you, you cocksucking cheater we will spread the word how you were a winner for all these years and make sure you never play in another NCO Club in the United States Air Force and any other military club we can reach. Don't ever show your face in this NCO Club again and if I were you I would try to get out of this wing as quickly as possible."

Each took his money from the pot and the others divided what ever Crossbow had left. Nobody was happy but they were glad to have recovered something. Moreover they had discovered they were not really bad or unlucky players they just could not win against a cheater.

Good Hand suggested they adjourn to the bar for a drink. Musher declared that he was the big winner thanks to Good Hand he should be allowed to buy. No one argued with him. These men did not drink while they played but they made up for it after the game.

Musher slipped the bartender a hundred fifty with the understanding that whatever they don't drink was his tip. Musher said his goodnights and thank you's and headed for the barracks. He sat in his car and counted. Total in hand, fifteen thousand five hundred. Eight was his so the profit was seventy-five hundred. Ninety-six percent return on the investment. To think it was for just the right placement of the right card at the right time.

It was a good win but it was not the most important win. His mouth watered with the sweet flavor of revenge. Crossbow will not bother him again.

CHAPTER 113

Can I Qualify As a Reel Operator

Sunday was an absolutely do nothing day. Lots of naps, eating and playing cards with guys in the barracks. Monday morning roll call put a jump in the day. Walter took the roll and then announced, "At 0300 hours this morning the Medical Response Team entered the home of Master Sergeant Crossbow to find him dead of a suicide caliber .45 bullet taken in his mouth. His family had gone to visit relatives the day before. There was a note which said, "I am not a cocksucking fucking cheater." Memorial services times will be announced later. You are dismissed."

The chatter was loud about Saturday night. "Musher you were in that game. What happened?" Musher relayed the story as best he could emphasizing who had discovered the playing card differential and who had placed the fucking cocksucker label on Crossbow. He stressed that as the newest kid in the game he was no more than a bystander to all the ballyhoo.

The consensus was that Crossbow was always a hardass, a non-forgiving individual who could not live with being found out. Not too many were surprised with his choice of suicide.

Once more Musher thought of Rod, "Fuck 'em and feed 'em frijoles." He's better off than if I had to bring Bruno down from the North.

The shack had emptied and Walter began his pre-certification flight review again. Question after question on how to cope with an unexpected incident on the reel operator's platform. Repeat of the checklist of items which Musher must be sure to take with him in his A-3 bag.

Walter released him for the day. After all they still had all day Tuesday for more review.

Musher steered his scooter directly to his car, picked up his snooker cues and headed for the NCO Club. Snooker was not the most popular game and generally one of the two tables was open. Today was no different. He went to the table most farther away from the pool tables and began his practice routine. About an hour into his practice he was approached by a master sergeant who introduced himself as Mosconi Taft. "The Mosconi is a nick name this wing has given me because I am the best straight pool and snooker player on this airbase. How about a snooker training session?"

"How much is it going to cost me?"

"Free, compliments of Mosconi Taft."

"No thank you, I don't play pool for free and I only take lessons from anyone who is now or was a professional snooker player."

"In that case how about a twenty dollar one hundred point game winner take all."

'Do we lag or do you let me be first in the half circle?"

"I'll rack, you can have the half circle."

Musher had a break (what we call a run) of thirty-eight points. Mosconi stepped up and had a break of fifty-four points. Musher's next break was for forty-eight bringing his total to eighty six. Mosconi's next break was for forty-three points bringing his total to ninety-seven points. Musher needed just fourteen points to win. The Fanucci classic, "The most important thing you can do when playing a hustler is get ahead in the money. Make him chase you just to try to get his own money back. Most hustlers have the fear that the pigeon will quit and take their money and run." All doubt left his mind. He made the next fourteen points without making any difficult shots.

"Well played. Want to do it again?"

"Same bet? The worst I could do would be to break even. It's your turn to be first in the half circle."

By this time the audience had grown quite large and most of the pool playing stopped. They whispered among themselves about the result of the first game. Their very best had been bested.

Mosconi could hear the undertones and he became more determined to win. His desire to win pumped so much adrenalin that his hand bridge quaked slightly and his stroke suddenly had a small dip just prior to contact with the cue ball. As a result his first break was eighteen.

Musher deliberately moved slowly ever conscious of the penalty if more than sixty seconds lapsed between shots. His mental clock would alarm at forty seconds. He was well within the time limit for each shot. His first break was sixty-four.

Mosconi had calmed down and had a shot of whiskey while waiting for his turn. When it came he looked like the Mosconi of the first game. His break was forty-two. That total made him only four points behind Musher.

Musher attacked the table setup as if the cue was part of his arms and the table top was his body with pockets for collecting money. At one hundred points he walked from the table to shake Mosconi's hand. Mosconi handed him forty dollars. There was a loud applause from the spectators as Musher packed his cue and left the room.

CHAPTER 114

Today Is My Day To Stand Tall

All day and I mean all day Walter harped on the same procedures and corrections to malfunctions that he had preached for two full days. The last words out of his mouth were, "Station time at squadron ops is 0730. Be sure you bring all your gear and don't be late."

It is now 0700 Wednesday and I am sitting outside squadron ops smoking cigarettes and waiting for Sergeant Walter and the aircrew. This crew was the same crew he had taken his observation ride with. Early morning greetings are short and simple. By 0715 Sergeant Walter and all the crew and their gear was aboard the aircrew bus. First stop the parachute shop for a pick-up, field check and a sign out of the parachute. The procedures at the aircraft were the same as his last mission with this crew. His confidence level increased greatly when he saw the crew.

Everything went along just as he remembered it. From engine start on the P Patch through to climb out after takeoff. Everything was running through his head. The six minute walk around bottle. Hookup to the oxygen outlet on the reel platform as quickly as you can. The flight engineer will tell him when to suit up. Check his oxygen mask and its built in mike before the aircraft is depressurized The aircraft is going to bounce up and down. If you get sick raise your mask and blow it out. Do not take off your mask.

."OK guys get into the heavy clothing. Tell me when you are ready."

While he was dressing he heard the aircraft commander, "830th Warrior 12 this is Tanker 102. Do you copy?"

"Roger 102"

"Warrior 12 I have you in sight. I am above you and six to eight minutes away from my first position. Will contact you when I am in position."

"Roger 102 Warrior 12 out."

Musher and Walter were clothed. They did the oxygen mask checks. Musher called, "Flight engineer primary operator. I am ready to go into position."

"Roger Musher, all personnel stand by for depressurization. Flight engineer to crew tell me when you are ready for depressurization." One by one the crew acknowledged ready. A soft hissing came throughout the aircraft. "OK Musher unseal the hatch and go to your position. Call me when you are in position with good oxygen flow."

Musher led Walter out of compartment and as soon as they were out the hatch closed. Musher went up and over the platform top to his position on the working area platform. Walter gave him the OK sign and Musher returned it. "Flight Engineer, reel operator and evaluator are secure in position and are ready for air refueling."

"Warrior 12 we are in position one. Are you ready to start fuel transfer operations? You may trail your dishpan."

"We are ready here 102, we have begun dishpan trailing operations."

Musher listened to the coordination messages voiced between the receiver and his tanker. Musher had shed some of the heavy clothing. He performed the entire operation without a hitch.

"102 to Warrior 12. We have given you all we can. On your count let us disconnect." The disconnect went without incident. Musher finished the cleanup steps to an air refueling, made sure all the equipment was good and in place for the next air refueling. He followed Walter into the compartment, secured the hatch and in one minute the aircraft was pressurized to six thousand feet.

AC to crew,"Musher did an excellent job. I don't know what Sergeant Walter's evaluation will say but I say let's welcome our newest certified reel operator to the squadron." Sergeant Walter broke in. "Let me be the first, Here, here." One by one the crew echoed "Here, here." Musher was flattered as he was peeling off his soaking wet clothes and getting into the dry ones from his A-3 bag. He was so hungry. Thank goodness they are going to eat.

Weakley did the next refueling. When it finished the navigator gave a course for home. Lima got out of his seat and directed Musher in his place. Musher made all the correct observations during the landing process and the taxiing to the P Patch. When the aircraft was parked, chocked and all the engines shut down the crew and its baggage lined up under the wing. The AC, Captain Lonigan, talked about how pleased he was with the mission and again congratulated Musher. They took their baggage and boarded the aircrew bus. This time was a little different, at the briefing room airmen took their chutes for return to the parachute shop and their A-3 bags which they would leave at squadron ops.

At briefing the usual Wild Turkey was given to each person with the crew. Musher passed his off to Sergeant Sanchez. He said nothing during the debriefing. He listened very closely to the questions asked by the interviewers and they seemed to be the same as the last flight. He paid very close attention to Lima and Weakley's contributions. He would be expected to contribute if he were ever a regular crew member.

At squadron ops he lashed his A-3 bag to his scooter. Walter, "I need to see the squadron operations officer before I can leave. You may take the rest of the day off and rest. I will see you at roll call in the morning."

It didn't take much encouragement for Musher to leave for the barracks and a long SSS, clean clothes, a couple more Luckies and then lay on the bunk to rest. It was 2300 when he awoke. Some more Luckies, some goodies from his emergency bag, a couple of cokes, a couple more Luckies and he was back in the bunk asleep. His last thoughts, "I may not be as good as the best today but I will be better than the best in good time." His chest was bursting with pride.

CHAPTER 115
Heading For Juarez

Thursday morning's roll call had interesting announcements. Walter began with, "Staff Sergeant Muscarello completed his training as a reel operator and to prove that we issue him the same accreditation certificate each of you got when you completed your certification as a reel operator. Musher come get this. The squadron commander and the squadron operations officer have made a few changes. Effective today, Sergeant Tickman will transfer to the 715th Bomb Squadron as an Aerial Gunner. Tickman, wishes do come true. (Most everyone in the room knew it was a move just to get rid of this constant whiner and dissenter).

Effective today, Sergeant Weakley will take Tickman's crew place and become the primary reel operator on that crew. Effective today, Sergeant Muscarello will take Weakley's crew place and become the junior reel operator on that crew. The powers to be in this squadron believe Sergeants Lima and Sanchez along with aircraft commander Captain Lonigan will mold Muscarello into an outstanding aircrew member.

One last thing, this coming Monday is a federal holiday and the wing is standing down. The wing commander has decreed that anyone who does not have a scheduled duty between noon today and Tuesday roll call is free to do whatever he chooses. He emphasizes he will deal harshly with anyone who takes advantage of his good nature and abuses this holiday. You are dismissed."

Musher asked for quiet. "At noon today I am taking my car and heading for Juarez. I have room for three more people. First preference will be given to reel operators who live in the barracks with me." At least seven people came forward wanting to go. Musher put their names in a hat and had Walter draw the winners. "Those of you whose names were not drawn are primary for my next trip. Believe me, I have only been to Juarez once and I know there will be more trips after this one. You three lucky winners be ready to leave the barracks at 1145."

Musher hurried back to the barracks, gathered all his cash and headed for the American Express Office. Taking his cash from all sources he had over nineteen thousand dollars. "I want to open an account with fourteen thousand, I need a two thousand dollar money order payable to Joanna Giardelli and two thousand in twenty dollar traveler checks.

He put his bankbook and the money order in his foot locker. He would stash the traveler checks in his car and keep a thousand in his pocket. He packed his suitcase for the trunk along with the chest. He had enough time to gas up the car, fill his goodie bag with candies and cookies and fill the chest with ice and cokes.

He pulled his car in front of the barracks at 1130. His passengers stepped out and put their small suitcases in the trunk. After making sure everything was secure he said, "Mount up rough riders, we are going to climb some hills and plunge into some valleys. Before we go, tell me your cash status."

Vladju from Pennsylvania, " One hundred eight cash."

Anthony from East Boston, " Two hundred cash."

Miguel from San Antonio, "Eighty-three cash."

"Each of you has more than enough for two nights and three days. We will return on Sunday in the early afternoon. We will establish a meeting place for Sunday when we get there. If for some reason any of us gets in trouble contact one of the other three and we will all get together to solve the problem. Have all of you been to Juarez before? All right, you are veterans of the hills to climb and the plunges into the valleys. We're off like a herd of turtles. Driving time to Juarez is about two and one half hours." At one minute past noon they passed through the main gate heading to the "Y" and then south.

They made one piss stop and each had one or two cokes and some candy. As hot as the temperature was even with all the windows down and the wind coming into the car, Musher would not allow smoking in his car. They sat beside the highway. There were no shady spots and smoked until Musher declared it time to go.

As they came closer to the bridge to cross to Juarez Musher spotted what he had been looking for. The sign read, "Bruno Bottecelli's Car Repairs and Storage." Musher pulled up in front of the open garage door. He walked in and said in a fairly loud voice, " Is Caesar here?"

He was joined by a big man who asked, "Caesar who?"

"You know, Caesar from Boston."

"Who are you?"

"I am Saverio Muscarello formerly of the North End of Boston currently in the Air Force in Roswell, New Mexico. Me and my buddies are going to Juarez for a couple of days and I would like to know that when I come back my car will here and untouched."

"Mister Bottecelli's employees would watch over your car, wash it, gas it up and get it ready for your ride back to Roswell. Do you plan to head back to Roswell on Sunday? See if you do it is a little more costly. Such services would be three hundred dollars."

Musher counted out three hundred dollars. "Tell Mister Bottecelli how grateful I am and I will be sure Caesar hears of his accommodation." Musher and company gathered their things from his car and walked to the bridge leading into Juarez.

He turned his head to see his car being driven into the garage.

CHAPTER 116

Forty-Two Glorious Hours

"Guys our first stop is the Florida Hotel. We book four rooms for two nights and it costs us six dollars each. Not to fancy but secure. Highlight to the hotel, it has the Florida Club the hottest bar in Juarez. Tequila sours ten cents, drinks for the bar girls five cents and a quickie for one dollar. Let's get the rooms, unpack and head for the bar. Who knows what happens there. Who am I kidding?"

The bar was bubbling. In less than five minutes all three of his buddies were in one of the back rooms spending a dollar. He held off until he recognized one of the girls he had been with when he was here last time. Whether she remembered him or not she made a great pretense of remembering. He took her to one of the back rooms to spend a dollar.

Musher asked where they should go to eat. Miguel from San Antonio was fluent in Spanish and he made the inquiries. They were offered two choices. One if they wanted Mexican food the other if they wanted American food. The consensus was American. Basically everything in Juarez was in walking distance.

The front window of the restaurant was painted, "The Cattle Barn. Bulls, Studs, Happy Cows and Heifers." The menu was elaborate and the prices were a little higher than in most other restaurants in Juarez. The drinks were basically five cents higher. The bulls, studs, happy cows and heifers paraded throughout the restaurant showing their wares. The meal was good, the service was good and the drinks were also good. Musher paid the twelve dollar bill and left a one dollar tip. They were sitting sipping coffee and the corral residents hovered over them enticing them for their any wishes. Vladju and Anthony could not resist the temptation. They went off with two happy cows. Miguel said something to the rest of the corral residents in Spanish and they scurried away from the table.

"What did you say?"

"I just told them you were my lover."

Musher did not know what to say so he just laughed. He told himself that he had just eaten his last meal in the Cattle Barn. Vladju and Anthony returned from the pasture and the four of them headed back to the Florida Club. They were greeted as if they had been away for a year.

After too many tequila sours and too many one dollar escapades Musher told the group he was off to bed. "Tomorrow I am going to rent a car with driver and sightsee Juarez. Anyone who wishes to go with me be in the breakfast joint next door at 1100. Good night all."

He did not know how long he had been asleep when he was awakened to his penis being fondled. He made no effort to resist. The fondler then began licking and sucking until he could no longer hold it and he ejected shamelessly. The fondler stayed in place and continued her efforts until he was hard again. She mounted and fucked him until he came again. She took a wet towel and wiped him clean. He found his money, gave her three dollars and rolled over to sleep.

Breakfast in the "Egg Nest" was typically American. Miguel and Anthony joined him. No one had seen Vladju since the night before in the bar. At Musher's request Miguel asked about a car and driver rental for the day. It was available but it cost twelve dollars a day plus any tip. Miguel ordered the car.

The driver passed through the congested streets of Juarez and headed for the less densely populated small towns in the low hills which surrounded the Juarez area. He frequently stopped and let them get out to enjoy the view. The next stop was in a little village called El Pinto. They went into the cantina and had mescal.

The driver looked at his watch and asked Miguel, "Do you want to go to the bull fights in Juarez?" With that they left the cantina and headed back to Juarez.

At the Plaza de Toros Musher asked Miguel to get four of the best seats and to invite the driver to join us. Inside Musher was enraptured with the Traje de luces and the stature of the Matador. As the corrida progressed and the bull was almost covered with barbed sticks and heavily bleeding Musher lost his taste to watch the end. He excused himself and went out to the car to await the return of his group. He chained smoked Luckies to get the pictures from his mind. As soon as all were in the car Musher barked, "Back to the hotel." There he thanked the driver, paid him with a generous tip and took his business card promising to recommend him to any friend who came to Juarez.

The first thing Musher did in the bar was gulp two tequila sours. Thank goodness there are no bull fights in the United States. Vladju was sitting at the bar surrounded by senoritas. He looked terrible but he had a smile that spread all other his face. This evening was like last evening. Tequila sours and sex were the two factors until bed time. Musher wondered if tonight would be like last night. When he said goodnight to his trio he reminded them we go back to Roswell tomorrow at noon. Be ready or be left here. I will be next door for breakfast around 1000.

This night was the same as last night. The mysterious visitor drained him until he felt like a limp rag. He gave her some money and she exited as quietly as she came in.

At 1000 he was eating breakfast when his cronies showed carrying their suitcases and not wanting breakfast. At 1130 hours they stepped out of the restaurant to walk across the bridge. There standing beside Musher's car was the big man from Bottecelli's garage. "Mr. Bottecelli has spoken to Caesar and you have received most glowing reports. You will not have any trouble driving into the United States. Mr. Bottecelli says that if you ever come this way again feel free to leave your car in his garage." He told Vladju, Anthony and Miguel to get in the car. "Mister Bottecelli would be most appreciative if you would drop this package in the US Mail at a remote box in Texas." Musher never even looked at the address. Along with the package he handed Musher an envelope containing two thousand dollars.

"I would certainly do that for Mr. Bottecelli. The envelope is not necessary."

"Mr. Bottecelli wants you to have it. That ends all discussion. Drive safely."

Musher crossed into the United States without incident and headed for the Biggs AFB dispensary. He explained to his passengers why they were going to Biggs. The people at the Biggs dispensary were as polite and gracious as they were the last time he was there.

Heading North somewhere between El Paso and Roswell they detoured to the small town of Dry Gulch, Texas. Musher spotted the flag pole by the US Post Office and dropped the package in the mail box outside the building. It was Sunday and not a soul could be seen around the post office. Back on the highway fifty miles north of Dry Gulch they made a piss stop. The sodas in the chest had been re-iced and there were fresh candy bars. Popsicles had been added and they were still fairly hard. They rested and smoked for half an hour.

Vladju asked, "Musher if we do not need to be back at Walker before tomorrow morning why are going back today? We could have stayed another night."

"If we did we probably would have had to bury you. Don't look in a mirror until you SSS. You look like hell."

Everyone except Musher slept until they reached the main gate at Walker. The AP's checked them through without a problem. One AP remarked, "How much blood did you leave in Juarez?" Musher drove away without comment.

CHAPTER 117

I May Not Be a Gunner But I Am On an Aircrew

Musher spent Monday between the barracks and the dining hall. When he wasn't eating he was showering or sleeping. By dinner time Monday he felt he was going to live and his energy was coming back. He assembled his cash. With the contribution by Bottecelli minus what he spent at the garage and in Juarez he gained twelve hundred dollars. His cash looked good. His goal was to have fifty thousand by the time he was discharged from the air force. He had a little over twenty-four months left on his hitch. He would need to squirrel another fifteen hundred every month. Not much of a goal but certainly attainable. He must put all cash in his American Express account except for the three thousand pocket money he needs to gamble.

His first roll call with a crew. He was in the shack long before anyone other than Walter. He took his seat in his crew row next to Sergeant Lima's seat. On his left would be James the radio operator and next to Lima would be Sanchez the flight engineer. Ever since he parted from Freddie he felt alone. Sitting here in the row with his crew he felt part of a team. He felt even better when Walter called his name as part of his crew. No gang can give this feeling. The bondage in gangs is not based on trust and loyalty as it is in the air force

The crew did not stay for coffee. Instead they went to the flight line dining hall to drink coffee and talk about crew expectations. Since he and James were new the discussion and questions lasted for over two hours. From there they went to the P Patch and talked about their assigned KB-29 aircraft, their duties during pre-flight inspections, post flight inspections and airborne crew coordination. They were introduced to the aircraft crew chief, Master Sergeant Nicolas Sperios and his crew. That took them to lunch at the flight line dining hall. Lunch was more of the same about crew coordination. At the table it was established that the names they would use for each other were Steve, Tony, Musher and Shaky, Charley James now called Shaky because his right hand fingers always seem to tapping out Morse code messages,

The afternoon is clear. We have no scheduled activity for tomorrow so we might just as well go to the NCO Club and pass the afternoon. In the non-gambling card room they were playing bridge. They were one player short of completing eight tables. Musher offered to fill that vacancy and for a partner he had the wife of the NCOIC of the Wing Directorate of

Personnel. He introduced himself as Staff Sergeant Muscarello. They played duplicate style and they finished second East-West. She was ecstatic. Could he come all the time? No, his crew was not flying today so they had part of the day off.

He joined the others in the pool room said his goodnights and proudly said, "See you at morning roll call."

CHAPTER 118

Preflight Today, Fly Tomorrow

At roll call Tony asked him if he had seen tomorrow's mission board. He had not. Tony reminded him that the next full week's missions are posted there and updated daily. "You are responsible to know your flight schedule all the time. On the days we do not fly we take our instructions from Steve. Today we will be at our aircraft checking the equipment, doing a lengthy preflight inspection and helping the ground crew any way we can. Aircrew is not all glamour. Most of the time it is just plain hard work."

He certainly wasn't kidding about the hard work. When all the reel operator equipment was checked and rechecked Nicolas, the aircraft crew chief, taught him how to open and close Zeus fasteners with a screw driver He showed him how to remove engine cowling for access to the engine itself. Musher learned the theory of fuel injection rocker boxes and how vital it was that one did not leak. Nicolas intentionally removed the safety wire from the holding bolts so he could teach Musher how to properly do the safety wire installation.

Nicolas, "Musher I want you to personally check each rocker box on each engine. If you find one you think needs safety wire replacement you come get me and I will supervise you doing it." The rest of his crew had gone back to the flight line dining room for coffee. Musher had replaced seven safety wires. It was lunch time before he finished. Nicolas congratulated him on his job well done and showed him a notebook which had printed on the cover "Staff Sergeant Saverio Musher Muscarello, Task Completion Log." Nicolas opened it to show forms with his name on them and a column listing all the tasks Musher would learn. Nicolas checked off those Musher had demonstrated capability today and signed his name authenticating the sign-off.

The rest of his crew was still in the dining hall when he showed up. They had waited just to talk with him. Steve,"Tell us what you did with Nicolas." Musher relayed what he had learned, what he had done and his surprise at the Task Completion Log. They congratulated him.

Steve again, "Normally the day before a mission we do what we did this morning and then take the rest of the day off for the express purpose of resting for the next day's mission. Instead of us coming here we would have all gone our separate ways except for you. You would have gone to the In Flight Kitchen and placed the lunch box orders for the mission. Tomorrow's

382

takeoff is at 1040 which means we would be airborne for lunch. The mission is six hours which means we would be back on the airbase in plenty of time to have dinner in the dining hall. We are a crew of eight so you request four three gallon jugs, two with coffee and two with water. The flight kitchen will automatically provide the cups, milk and sugar. Station time at squadron ops is two hours earlier than takeoff. Both you and the aircrew bus will be at squadron ops at 0740 three hours before station time. You will put your gear on the bus and the bus driver will take you to the In Flight Kitchen to pick up the lunches and drinks. Then you will swing by the Parachute Shop and pick up nine parachutes. By time you get back the rest of us should be ready to board the bus and go to our aircraft. This will be your responsibility every time this crew flies.

Tony was right, "It seems most of the time aircrew life at his level is just plain hard work." I'll bet being the junior reel operator will get a lot easier with familiarity and practice. When the crew left he jumped on his Vesper and headed for the In Flight Kitchen. Surprise, Surprise, Surprise! Who is the NCOIC? Nobody but the best straight pool and snooker player in the wing, Master Sergeant Mosconi Taft. He greeted Musher respectfully and took his order. "Your order will be ready at 0730 hours tomorrow."

"Mosconi I am leaving here for NCO Club to practice my snooker. If you can get away come on over and we will practice together. Heaven knows we might meet in the Club or Base snooker tournaments."

He practiced for almost three hours before Mosconi came into the room. His eyes were almost glazed with anger. He walked straight to Musher and put three hundred dollars on the rail. "One game, three hundred points, winner takes all. Do I have a bet?"

"You got a bet, let me put my cash with yours and we will use the SSA as the bank. We lag for first in the half circle" Musher lost the lag.

Mosconi came to play. His first break was sixty-six. Musher had told himself the three hundred dollars was meaningless his reputation was at stake. To lose to this guy would severely damage his image. After the first few shots he was in his zone. One hundred thirty-four points later he made his first miss.

When Mosconi stepped to the table his first shot made him look a little off balance. It was almost as if his mind were a billboard visible to everyone in the room. His billboard repeatedly flashed, "I can't let this guy beat me again, I cannot let this guy beat me again." Over and over the billboard flashed until the distraction caused him to miss at his fifty-eight break. His new total was one hundred twenty-four, ten less than Musher's first break and he had to give Musher the table.

Musher could hear Mosconi's death knoll. Don't get ahead of your self, get back into your zone. The zone came and Musher had a break of one hundred forty-one. His new total was two hundred seventy-five.

Mosconi went to the table telling himself I need a break of one hundred-seventy six. The best break he had ever had in all of his snooker life was one hundred-fourteen. He played extremely well but his break was ninety-three, for a new total of two hundred seventeen.

Musher was ready for the kill. He potted a red ball then a black seven, another red ball and another black seven, another red ball and another black seven. The last red ball potted made three hundred. The audience broke out in a loud applause.

He was putting his cue in its case when he turned to Mosconi. "You played very well, just not well enough. I will give you a choice. Tell me your Christan name. So your name is really Joesph Taft. You can either keep your three hundred dollars and from this moment on shun the nickname Mosconi and be known simply as Joe Taft, or you accept the second choice where I will use your three hundred dollars to publicize the best pool and snooker player in this wing is a staff sergeant called Musher. To publicize that option I will be forced to tell the airbase just how badly you got your ass kicked. Don't hurry you have fifteen seconds to make your choice."

Joe Taft walked towards Musher with his hand out and said,"My name is Joe Taft, very happy to meet you." Musher clasped his hand and said, "Let's go into the bar for a drink on me." He gave Joe his three hundred and the SSA a twenty dollar tip. The room was buzzing as they left.

In the bar both ordered cokes. Joe asked Musher,"Just where did you learn to play snooker like that."

"About four months ago in Junction City, Kansas in a place called the Emporium I had heavily kicked ass to the locals in a nine ball game. The next weekend I was off I was back at the Emporium. Between me and you I was really back in Junction City for a woman I know there. Anyhow that weekend I took on their best straight pool shooter in a two hundred point game for one thousand dollars. I shut him out two hundred to zero. From there on I couldn't play pool in that place and it was the only place in town. They had two snooker tables one was not in use so I tried to just make balls in a pocket of my choice and played mental position for the next shot. The owner of the Emporium gave me snooker tips and watched me practice whenever I was in Junction City. He sold me a couple of snooker cues that he had bought from some snooker players who had given up the game. When I couldn't get to Junction City I went to the pool room in Salina, the town closest to the air base and did disciplined practice. I shot my first snooker shot less than four months ago. Are you duly impressed?"

CHAPTER 119

My First Mission As a Certified Reel Operator

Musher was at squadron ops at 0700 hours. The aircrew bus showed at 0710. They were at the In Flight Kitchen at 0720. The counter man was Joe Taft.

"Good morning Musher you are early but we are ready. Those two boxes are your lunches and the four jugs are yours, two coffees and two water. The small thermos box marked Musher is for you as a surprise. Have a good flight. Let me know if you think I run a better kitchen than I play snooker." They both laughed

Musher and the driver put the mission foods and drinks on the bus. Musher put his separate thermos box so that it would be taken off last. The parachute shop was slow because Musher had to inspect the release pin condition on each chute and the date it was last packed. He actually rejected one chute for a bent release pin. The shop NCOIC looked at the pin and thanked Musher for being so precise. He helped Musher and the driver load the chutes into the bus. Musher knew today that some packer was going to catch Holy Hell and it would spill over to everyone in the shop.

They were back at squadron ops at 0820. The full crew was waiting and Musher was formerly introduced to the officers. He had already met the Aircraft Commander Captain Lonigan. The co-pilot was Captain Rusty Barton. Barton had been a navigator throughout WWII but had a passion to be a pilot. He took an in-grade reduction from Lieutenant Colonel to Captain so he could go to pilot training. The navigator was Captain Thomas Clapton. He had been a member of the RAF during WWII. He transferred to the USAF when the war was over. He still had his English accent and wore a monocle like a Nazi Officer or a member of the British Royalty. Musher had not formally met the radar operator but he was aboard on Musher's accreditation flight. His name was Stanley Jones but everyone called him Spike. The AC called for all aboard.

The bus was met by crew chief Nicolas and his ground crew. Everyone went off to check the aircraft. Musher and Shaky were left to unload the bus and get the equipment and lunches on board. They were helped by the ground crew unloading the bus. The ground crew spread nine parachutes under the left wing. They knew where the A-3 bags went and placed them in the proper compartment. They took two jugs forward and two jugs aft and mounted them in their designated locations. Musher split the lunches for five forward and three aft. The ground crew took them on board. Musher made sure that the airman taking the lunches aft put the thermos box marked Musher in the right waist position.

The crew lined up under the left wing, checked the parachutes and put them on. The AC rebriefed the mission. This was to be a high altitude refueling over the Gulf of Mexico. We do it well and then head for home.

Musher stored his surprise thermos box where it would not fly free. Nestled himself into his position, put on his headset over his base ball cap, his sunglasses and throat mike. God did he feel good. His first intercom crew check with his response of right waist roger almost made him come in his pants.

He took his leads from Tony, for instance while the aircraft was taxiing Tony would say over the intercom, left wing clear. Musher would assess the conditions on his side of the aircraft and say over the intercom, right wing clear. After the engine checks and the aircraft was taxiied to the pre-takeoff position Musher stared for something that could hurt his side of the aircraft

He heard the Tower clear 102 for takeoff. The flaps squealed and Tony reported, "Left flap down twenty-five degrees." Musher made the same call for the right flap. He was thankful the flap was painted to show the number of degrees down. The aircraft lunged forward and Lonnigan made a rolling takeoff. Tony's voice broke in, "One and Two OK." Musher repeated the same transmission in relation to the number three and four engines. Each of them made four more such reports during the takeoff roll. Tony, "Left flap full up." Musher made the same call for the right flap

"Navigator to AC. Steer heading one three five degrees. ETA for rendezvous contact forty-six minutes"

"Roger Navigator."

Musher laid out his cold weather refueling gear and checked the walk around bottles and his oxygen mask. Tony watched closely and gave his nod of approval. "Relax Musher it will be a piece of cake."

"Radar to AC. I have him on my screen we are about one hundred miles out."

"Roger Radar, Navigator time to target please."

"Fifteen to twenty-five minutes"

"Tanker 102 to Spearhead 5 do you copy?"

"Roger 102 Spearhead 5 reads you loud and clear. Over"

"Spearhead 5 I am coming up on your six at sixteen thousand feet. I shall be in my Position 1 in ten minutes. You may trail your dishpan whenever you are ready. Over"

Flight engineer to reel operator and crew,"Reel dress out. Call when you are completed. Crew prepare for depressurization."

"Reel to flight engineer. I am ready."

"Everyone on oxygen, standby for depressurization. Depressurization complete. Reel you may go to your position." With that Tony opened the hatch leading aft. Musher scrambled through and onto the reel operator's platform. He was off the oxygen walk around bottle, on the main oxygen system and plugged into the intercom in less than ninety seconds.

"Reel to flight engineer, I am in position and ready to begin air refueling procedure."

He heard, "Spearhead 5 this 102. We are ready to begin when you are. Over."

"Spearhead 5 to 102. Roger that. I will hold this altitude and course. Over."

Every step of the procedure went smoothly including the disconnect. Musher realized that Bubba Weakley was right he needed to build his arm and shoulder strength.

As the hose was coming back into the aircraft one of the coils overlapped another coil near the side of the hose drum hose jammed and the drum stopped.

"Reel to flight engineer", he explained what had happened and he was ready to take corrective action.

"Go ahead reel do you need help?"

"Not at the moment." Walter had discussed this type situation and had given him one way to possibly relieve the jamming. Musher took the heavy weight rubber hammer and pounded on the jammed coil until the jam coil came loose. He pounded it in place and began bringing in the rest of the hose.

"Reel to flight engineer, Problem corrected." The rest of the wrap up went smoothly but the pounding with the big rubber hammer reinforced his need for greater arm and shoulder strength.

"Reel to flight engineer, I am ready to come back to you all."

In less than two minutes the aircraft was depressurized, Musher was in the aft compartment and the aircraft was pressurized to eight thousand feet. Before he did anything else Musher drank two very large cups of water followed by a cup of coffee. Off came the very wet clothes and from his A-3 bag dry, fresh underwear and a flying suit. A couple of Luckies and more water and he was ready to do another refueling. At least that was the front he showed. At that point his arms and shoulders could not hold a deck of cards.

AC to Musher, "Whatever you did you did it right. We will be interested in hearing the whole story at debriefing. Meanwhile crew we have a couple of hours back to Walker let's eat and try to relax. Navigator give me a course."

Musher picked through his flight lunch unable to wait to open his surprise. Inside the thermos box were half a dozen chocolate Dixie cups, two coco colas, some sliced cantaloupe wedges and a note, "For the best pool and snooker play at Walker AFB, Sincerely, Joe Taft." Musher shared the ice cream cups in the compartment but not the cokes or the note.

On the ground at Walker and parked in the P Patch it was time to unload the aircraft and police its interior. Musher figured he would need to do it alone. But he was wrong each crew member carried his parachute and his A-3 bag out of the aircraft and onto the aircrew bus. The ground crew took all the trash and the items to be returned to the In Flight Kitchen. The bus driver would return the parachutes. Musher stuck his thermos box surprise in his A-3 Bag. Captain Lonnigan thanked the crew chief for the wonderful shape of the aircraft. The bus headed for debriefing. The bus driver would drop the A-3 Bags at squadron ops before returning the parachutes. Musher felt he should tip the bus driver and the ground crew for such tremendous support. He was sure tipping was not allowed, he would find another way.

At debriefing he passed his medicinal whiskey to Tony. Each crew position was asked specific questions. When it came Musher's time he relayed the entire story about the jammed hose and how he freed it. He gave all the credit to Master Sergeant Walter who had anticipated his need to know how to solve circumstances which had occurred during other refueling operations. The debriefing officer had been very busy writing. "I'll submit this to your Squadron Commander and the Squadron Operations Officer."

Musher could hardly wait to get to the barracks and the showers. In clean underwear he smoked Luckies and noticed the twinge of pain when he raised his cigarette to his lips. I don't care if it is only 1815 I am going to bed. It has been a hell of day.

CHAPTER 120

I Am Not An Inventor But

Roll call the next morning was a pleasant experience. Walter told of Musher's experience with his first solo refueling operation and the correct, appropriate actions which he took. There was a round of applause in the shack.

When the crew was together outside squadron ops, Steve announced that there was no scheduled activity today. Steve directed Shaky to take Musher to the radio operators training room and teach Musher how to do Morse. The standard for aircrew other than the radio operator was to send fifteen words a minute and to receive ten words a minute. Steve told Shaky if he doesn't have it by lunch send him home for the rest of the day. We don't want to scramble his head. There is no deadline for him to qualify but we do want him qualified. Tomorrow is Friday and we are not scheduled to fly until next Tuesday. We will meet after roll call tomorrow and set our weekend plan. Right now I am going with Tony to talk with our AC. Have a good day."

Shaky sat Musher at a seven inch reel tape player. He put a large ear cup headset on him and plugged the headset into the tape player. "This is a two hour reel. From it you are expected to be able to recognize the sound of a dot from the sound of a dash. There is some help on the tape. A voice will tell you things like "a dot dash dot dash" combination is coming up, this is the sound of the letter Q. These hints will be interspersed throughout the tape. There is no way I can help you with this exercise except to sit and wish you well. You can only be qualified when you are tested and certified by the wing radio operator."

Musher listened to the full two hours and at the end the dots and dashes sounded the same. He told Shaky of his dilemma. Shaky suggested they call it day and pick it up tomorrow. Shaky also had a Vesper, not as fancy as Musher's but it ran well and he never would take it off base. They arrived at the squadron dining hall like the Lone Ranger and Tonto.

After lunch Shaky went to the barracks and Musher to the BX. He filled his shopping cart with a twelve and an eighteen inch ruler, a protractor with pencil, a twelve inch by eighteen inch drawing pad, a soft gum eraser, some geometric shape items such as triangles, circles, rectangles, squares, and cylinders, two dozen soft lead pencils and a pencil sharpener. The next stop was the Base Library for its peace and quiet. He found the most deserted library table and emptied his shopping bag on the table.

He could see what he wanted to draw in his head but he did not know how to start.

He took the pencil in hand and sketched a hose drum filled with hose and the hose nozzle in its correct position on the drum. To make the hose coil lines more prominent he darkened the outline of each coil and he darkened the outline of the hose nozzle.

To the hose drum he added the side panels to which the drum was fastened. He didn't know how to make the drum mounting bolts visible in his sketch. As it was he was thanking Mister O'Malley his high school teacher for the training he received in his junior year in Mechanical Drawing.

It was a much easier task to add the top to the drum containment structure. He didn't worry about the ladder coming onto the platform from the aft compartment of the tanker. It would not be in play from this angle.

The next step was to add the reel operator's platform. That too was not too difficult it was rectangle mounted on the fuselage floor and bolted onto the side panels of the hose drum housing.

For purposes of this sketch he needed to add the two vices on the platform. They would come in use after the disconnect. Also he needed to add the clutch motor used to retract the tanker weight with tanker wire line and with them the hose.

Why must there be an improvement? Walter had said hose jams occurred when a hose coil failed to fall in place during the hose rewind. The failure to fall in place caused the hose to jam against the hose drum container on the starboard side of the aircraft. Sometimes the reel operator was lucky as Musher was. Other times it is necessary to chop the hose from its jam until the jammed piece is ready to fall free of the aircraft. The reel operator must foresee the hose break and free fall and be sure to release the weight and wire from the vice or the aircraft could be pulled into a non-recoverable spin. When the cut hose falls the remaining hose is no longer reparable, the very expensive nozzle goes with the hose as do the weight and the tanker cross over connect wire with bayonet fitting. Another significant damage that could occur when the cut hose falls away, the remaining hose might whip snap and either hit the reel operator or damage the aircraft.

Musher knew he was not an inventor but if he could put his suggestion across well enough to interest Walter maybe Walter could get the powers to be to listen. Here goes nothing.

There are four new pieces of equipment to add to the current system. An automobile type jack with handle; a one inch steel bar with ratchet grooves from the left end of the bar to the center of the bar; a spring loaded cylinder two inches in diameter three quarters the length of the one inch steel bar and an eight by eleven by one inch rectangle made from the same steel as the bar.

The proposed installation of the new components for the modification.

The jack needs to be attached to the reel operator's platform. The clutch motor for the trailing weight release and take in might need to be repositioned so the jack would be directly in line with the outer wall of the hose drum container. It may also require cutting a hole in the platform for the jack arm to pass through to be secured on the external wall of the container. The jack handle is a separate piece of the jack assembly.

The spring loaded cylinder is to be mounted flush on the outer wall of the container. The base of the cylinder and is to be welded to the jack lifting arm so that the cylinder can be raised and lowered by using the jack.

The steel rectangle is to be welded to the steel bar.

The steel bar is to be inserted in the cylinder.

Prior to beginning hose recovery, since the hose is coiled from left to right, the steel rectangle would be positioned at the three coil wrapping point on the first coil row. It would withdraw into the cylinder as the coils fill the row. When it is evident that a coiling problem would not exist for that row the reel operator would crank the jack higher to be in position for the next row. The spring loaded rectangular coiling guide would be clear and spring into its three coil wrapping point position for the next coiling row. If the coiling process went without incident the coiling protective system would be at the highest point of the hose container and would remain there until the next mission.

If a coiling incident were to happen the reel operator would see it happening and discontinue reeling in the hose until he can cure the coiling problem. Solving the problem would be simpler because the coiling problem would be on the drum itself and not jammed between the drum and the hose drum container.

Hopefully, this modification would eliminate the need to chop away hoses.

Musher went over his sketch. He realized his limitations and he needed help to make the sketch more professional. He had time to go to the Audio –Visual shop and seek a professional illustrator. He asked to see an illustrator and a young airman, A2C Mickey Ventola came forward. Musher showed him his sketch and asked, "Can you do this in color to scale?"...... Yes..... "Can you do it so I can have it tonight?" .....I don't think so....."If I paid you two hundred dollars cash to do it on a poster board could you then do it tonight?"......Yes, but you would have to be here with me to answer any illustration questions which came up. I could not begin until after the regular duty day."

"I will be back at 1630. Thanks Mickey, I'll see you then."

Musher went back to the squadron and traded his scooter for his car. He put all his sketches and materials in the back seat. Drove to the BX and filled the ice chest with cold cokes, sandwiches and goodies. At 1630 the A-V staff had left so he was able to park right outside the front door. He gathered his sketches and notes and went inside looking for Mickey. They went into a small cubicle and Mickey starting outlining the sketch. He selected a scale which would almost fill the poster but leave more than enough room for a border and any notes they may want to add to the poster. Musher sat in awe. Within an hour Mickey had a full sketch and he was ready to add the color. Musher selected which color he wanted on which item in the sketch. Musher had never seen air brush techniques. It took Mickey more than an hour to color the sketch.

While they wee waiting for the sketch to dry Musher brought in the ice chest and they had dinner. Smoking was not allowed in the A-V. Mickey wanted to know if they could take a fifteen minute smoke break. It gave Musher the chance to put his chest back in his car and have a few Luckies.

The work was beautiful. Musher only hoped the proposed modifications would be so beautiful. Mickey added an air force blue border and signed his name on the poster. When the poster was totally dry Mickey put it in a transport container.

Musher gave him the two hundred dollars which he did not want to take. Drove him to his barracks, thanked him again and again. From there to his barracks, SSS and be ready for tomorrow.

CHAPTER 121
My Presentation To Modify the
Hose Compartment

After roll call and announcements Musher asked Walter if he could remain in the shack when all the others leave. ......Yes.

Musher asked Tony if he could get Steve and Shaky and bring them here?...Yes

At the same time everyone was leaving Tony was just returning with Steve and Shaky. Musher asked Walter to take a seat. He went to the back of the shack and took his poster from its protective folder.

He mounted it in the blackboard tray.

"Gentlemen you will recall on my first mission I had a hose jam between the hose housing and the drum reel. We were fortunate that we were able to overcome the problem by using the heavy rubber hammer. Sergeant Walter tells me that hose jams in that configuration are not uncommon. This proposal recommends modification of the reel operator's area to hopefully eliminate the hose jam problem."

From there he used the poster to show the new components to add to the reel operator's area, their installation and their operation. When he finished he turned to Walter, "What do you think?"

"First off you did a great presentation. Your visual aid is very well done. If I were not a reel operator I would still understand the problem and your recommendation to hopefully eliminate the problem. As a reel operator I think the suggestion has great potential. I don't know what the powers that be might think of it but I am sufficiently impressed to show it to them after you and I tweak your presentation. For now leave the poster here so you and I can discuss it more deeply."

His crew congratulated him on a job well done.

Steve, "Yesterday I had a talk with the AC. He is most interested in Musher being certified for Morse. So Shaky, take him back to your radio operators training room and work with him again today. Musher how did you do yesterday?"

"By noon my head was one big dot or dash. I slept last night with dots and dashes. There are only a couple of things I can recognize and send, SOS and the letter Q. Trust me Steve I will get certified very soon."

Steve," The rest of us are off until Monday morning. Shaky when you think he has had all he can absorb today you are both off until Monday morning. Let's break."

"Walter, when can we get together?"

"Talk to me Monday." Sure sounded like a brush off.

He and Shaky went to the training room and Musher studied again. Today he concentrated on alphabet recognition. If Q, "Pay day to day" had a rhythm they must all have a rhythm. Listen for the music. By noon he had picked up the rhythm for most of the alphabet. He asked Shaky," Is this room open all the time".....0800 to 1700, seven days a week......" Can I come in here without you?" ....Yes ...."Let's squeet and I will come back to practice on my own."

It took him the rest of the day to hear the rhythm of the entire alphabet. When he thought he had it cold he called it a day. Tomorrow he will have Shaky give him a message tape to decipher where the messages come at different speeds. After the message the tape voice announces the correct interpretation. He wanted to be certified Monday.

He and Shaky went to the training room Saturday at 1000. Shaky set up a two hour message interpretation tape. He also laid aside a two hour transmittal tape. The transmittal tape asked for various length messages be transmitted via Morse. Musher was so into it he sat and practiced for six straight hours. Tomorrow he would ask Shaky to play evaluator and to give him simulated certification tests.

They were at the training room at 1030 Sunday morning. Shaky sent him live messages to translate in English. The first was the minimum standard certification level of receiving ten words per minute. Musher waltzed through that and subsequent tests until he failed at twenty-six words per minute. Four more times he failed at twenty-six words per minute. Shaky was happy he far exceeded the minimum for certification.

The second half of the exercise was the transmittal twelve words per minute criteria. Shaky gave him some sheets of prepared text to transmit. Without error, his first attempt yielded a thirty word per minute transmittal rate. The next five messages were at a thirty-one words per minute low and a forty-two words per minute high. Shaky declared he was ready for certification.

Shaky emphasized to him that the goal was certification and not to see how high he could score for certification. "Take it slower and make sure of your accuracy. If you ever need to do this in real combat you will probably only get one chance."

CHAPTER 122
Preflight and Morse Certification

The crew met at squadron ops. Steve announced takeoff tomorrow is at 1100. The mission is two air refuelings over the Gulf of Mexico at fifteen thousand feet. Total flight time is eight plus hours. Stations here are at 0900. Musher you know your job for the flight. The aircrew bus will be here at 0800 tomorrow. Let's go preflight.

When the preflight was over Shaky announced that Musher was scheduled for Morse certification at 1400 today at the radio operator training facility. Steve was concerned that his training period just began last Thursday afternoon and even though the AC wanted him Morse certified he might not be ready. Shaky told how Musher had spent twenty-two hours in the training center and yesterday he had given Musher many pre-evaluation tests. Musher averaged twenty-nine words per minute receiving Morse and thirty-nine minutes transmitting Morse. His error rate was less than one percent. "He is ready."

"OK Musher you go make the arrangements at the In Flight Kitchen and then take your certification examination. Shaky be with him at the exam and call me at my house when you have the results. Let's break."

On the counter at the In Flight Kitchen was Joe Taft. Musher's opening remarks were, "You certainly are a better NCOIC than a snooker player." He returned the thermos box and thanked Joe for the surprise contents. "Joe, I need to pick up the in flight stuff at 0800 tomorrow for a standard crew of eight with an 1100 takeoff on an eight plus hour mission."

"It will be ready. I will be here. When are we going to practice our snooker?"

"If nothing goes wrong I should be there about 1530." He had told Shaky he would meet him at the squadron dining hall for lunch. They had lunch and just generally killed time in the dining hall waiting to go to the radio training facility for his accreditation test. When it was time to go they mounted their Vespers and rode off like the Lone Ranger and Tonto.

Shaky introduced him to Technical Sergeant Robert Doyle the wing radio operator. They went into a small room where Musher would sit facing a blank wall at a table with a Morse key mounted on it, a headset and a pad and pencil next to his Morse key. Behind him Doyle sat with a Morse key and a note pad beside it. Above Musher's head Doyle could see an oversized clock with a large second sweep hand. Shaky also sat behind Musher with a headset to listen to the transmissions and responses.

For the next half hour the only noises in the room were the clicking of the Morse keys. Shaky heard Doyle transmit, "We are done. You may disconnect."

They left the small room. Doyle went into his office while Shaky and Musher smoked cigarettes. Another fifteen minutes went by before Doyle came out of his office with his hand extended.

"Sergeant Muscarello for someone who just started to learn Morse four days ago you did very, very well. I can only hope you will continue practicing and maybe pass the radio operators accreditation tests. Here is your framed accreditation certificate." My congratulations as he shook Musher's hand. Musher thanked him and turned to Shaky. "Much of my success belongs to Sergeant James."

Shaky went to the phone to call Steve and tell him the news. The Lone Ranger and Tonto left the training facility mounted on their Vesper steeds headed for the NCO Club. In the bar with a cold draft they toasted the Musher's success and Shaky's major training contribution. Shaky left for the BX and Musher for the snooker table.

Joe Taft came and he and Musher played snooker for a couple of hours. Joe was more relaxed and played a lot better. Musher was trying to make the most difficult shots on the table and was missing. Joe was playing as if it were for his life. Consequently he won a few games and he felt much better about himself. True, he knew Musher was only practicing.

"Sorry Joe but I have to go. Flying in the morning and I need to prepare and get my rest."

"OK pro, I'll see you at the kitchen."

CHAPTER 123
Missions and a Trip To Boston

The next day mission went as smooth as clockwork. For the next four months all the missions went like clockwork. Musher spent his free time working on his poker to build his cash to the fifty thousand dollar level he wanted at his time of discharge. During those same four months there was a change of wing commanders. The new general was from the Boston area. His elderly mother was sick and at his last assignment he took every opportunity to visit her. At crew roll call it was announced that the general was going to make a Thursday morning takeoff for an air refueling mission and then land at Logan Airport in Boston. The aircraft would leave on Sunday noon and make another air refueling mission then land back at Roswell Sunday night. He needed a volunteer crew which he hoped would be made up of all Massachusetts residents who came from close to Boston. Anyone who was not otherwise committed to a duty during that period may apply. Lucky Musher, no duty commitments. Unlucky Musher, his name was not one of those picked in the lottery. He sought out one of the reel operators who had been chosen and offered five hundred dollars for his seat. Both he and the second reel operators refused. At eight hundred the third reel operator relinquished his seat.

His AC and Steve approved of his going on the mission. He would be the most junior reel operator and probably would not get to participate in the actual air refueling. That did not really bother him. He had lost interest in the refueling exercises when they became boring and nothing more than cold, hard work. The aircrew glamour was slowly slipping away.

The flight to Boston and the air refueling were routine. They landed at Logan airport at 1435 hours. The aircraft was parked there among the Air Force Reserve Fighter Jets. The ground crew put the aircraft to bed while the others unloaded the baggage. The general left in a staff car and the AC briefed the crew. "Stay out of trouble or you may queer all future deals of this type. Be here ready to preflight and fly Sunday at 0900 hours. We start engines as the general steps aboard. Anyone not here by 1000 hours Sunday will be barred from all future flights of this type flight and most probably will be left behind. Dismissed."

Before anything else Musher went to pay his respects to Caesar. He thanked him for his support in the Juarez parking affair. Caesar told him

Bottelucci respected him and maybe we would want you to spend another great weekend in Juarez. At our expense of course.

"Godfather you know I would do anything you ask."

Caesar came to him and gave him a hug. Musher bent and kissed Caesar's ring.

Next stop was to rent a hotel room and change into civilian clothes. At the Bucket he asked for Freddie. "He's in Walpole still waiting for trial of the rent-a-cop killing. He was denied bail but he is allowed visitors."

Third on the list was his Mother. When she saw him it was as if someone had turned on Niagara Falls. She saw the civilian clothes and asked if he was now home for good.

"Not yet but soon. Now I must go see some people I will be here tomorrow night for supper. Macaroni and meatballs sounds good. Do you need anything from the Gloria Chain?"

She mumbled a few items and clearly said, "I don't understand it. They tell me I have a credit balance on my book. I don't understand it but it is OK with me."

"I will talk with Signore Catalucci when I am there."

He went to the cab stand where he had once hired a cab to take him to Hanscom AFB. Sure enough the cab driver he had hired before was there and idle. Musher greeted him with," Do you remember me?"..... Who could forget....."I need to go to Peabody and I will want you to wait for me while I am there. Can you do that?" ... Yes...."Good let's go."

In Peabody the cab driver asked how to get to a certain address and very shortly parked in front of the house. "I'll be here until you come out."

Sweet Sister answered the doorbell and almost fainted. "Musher, my baby, come in here and give me a hug." Her husband and two sons came running to the front door. He shook hands with her husband Humberto and she told the boys "This is your uncle Musher. Shake hands and give him a kiss." The boys were eight and ten. They were all right with the hand shake and hug but were not sure about the kiss. "We are having an early dinner. We are going to Josephine's for her girl's birthday party. Come eat with us and we will all go."

"I am not sure if my going would be a good idea. I will eat with you cause something smells so good." It was sausage, peppers, onions and oven baked potatoes.

"You are in civilian clothes are you out?"

"No. I still have less then two years to go." Musher told her the story about the general's mother and the flight here and that they leave Saturday back to Roswell, New Mexico. She had so much food that he fixed a plate for the cab driver and had the boys bring it to him with a large glass or orange soda. While the boys were gone he asked about the Gloria Chain and Momma's finances. He also handed her the two thousand dollar money order to be used for Momma.

"I suppose I shouldn't ask where you get this money so I won't. The old man has not seen a penny and I still have a small amount left."

"Use what you have left on yourself or the boys. I am going to the Gloria Chain tomorrow to pick up a few things for Momma and I will take care of the book plus. Right now I must go. I have the cab waiting and tomorrow I am also going to Walpole to see Freddie." He shook hands with Humberto, hugged the boys, kissed Sweet Sister and headed for the door. The elder boy came to the cab to get the dishes and the glass. As he stepped into the cab he said to his family, "I'll be in touch."

He told the driver where the Gloria Chain was. They would look and see if by chance it would still be open. Signore Catalucci was behind the counter. Musher went in while the cab waited. Signore Catalucci recognized him and greeted him in a most friendly manner. Musher asked him to write down these items for Mrs. Muscarello. "Could he have them delivered first thing in the morning?"

"Of course he would."

"Add those items to her book and tell me the book balance."

"After this order she would still have a credit balance of eighty-four dollars seventeen cents. A lady, whom I think is her daughter came in one day and put a five hundred dollar credit into Mrs. Muscarello's book."

Musher counted out money and handed it to Signore Catalucci. "This makes her credit balance One thousand eighty four dollars and seventeen cents. Don't you agree?"

"Si, Signore, I shall take good care of Mrs. Muscarello and no one will ever know of your role."

Musher got in the cab and they headed for his hotel. Musher handed the cabbie two hundred dollars. "Is that fair for today?"....."Good. I will need you all day tomorrow. Are you available?" ..... Yes......"Pick me up at the diner across the street at eight-thirty in the morning." He turned and went into his hotel. SSS and off to sleep. The next day he visited Freddie and then spent the time in the Bucket.

CHAPTER 124
Temporary Duty To the United Kingdom

Back at Roswell Walter still avoided me. My crew told me to write it off. One of two things had happened, your proposal was rejected by the powers that be or Walter has scarfed it up as his own. It would be a great step for him on his quest for Warrant Officer.

The wing commander called for a meeting of all 509th aircrews. There he announced that the wing would be going TDY (Temporary Duty) for one hundred nineteen days to the United Kingdom. The 715th and the 830th Bomb Squadrons would be at Lakenheath Air Base; and the 905th Bomb Squadron and the 509th Air Refueling Squadron would be at RAF Station Wyton.

The first echelon of the 715th and the 830th will launch in thirteen days. The second echelon will launch two days later. The crossing will made in three stops. The first stop will be at Barksdale AFB, Louisiana. The second stop is Kindley AFB, Bermuda. The third stop is Lages AB, Azores. The fourth stop is your designated airbase. Takeoffs will be scheduled so that landings will be made in the daylight.

Each aircraft will carry in addition to its aircrew and ground crew three flight line support personnel. Our aircraft will be rigged with additional safety belts for the passengers. Each bomber will hang cargo racks on its bomb racks. Since the Air Refueling Squadron cannot remove its fuel tanks the bomb squadrons must allocate space on their cargo racks for the tanker's equipment and other necessities.

The Wing will stand down in preparation for its move.

The high point to Musher was that when the wing returned he would have less than five months to discharge. He most probably would not meet his cash goal but he would still be well off.

Captain Lonnigan made arrangements with the 905th for his and three other Vespers belonging to his aircrew would be transported by the 905th. In addition there would be some mechanics' tool boxes and some B-4 bags. All items to be transported by the 905th must be properly labeled and delivered to the 905th five days before launch. Our tanker was crowded but there were still some spots where people could lay out and rest.

Musher made a deal with Sergeant Jim Nance to store his car in the motor pool and look over its welfare. Musher gave him two hundred fifty dollars in case there was something that needed to be done on the car.

He was fully packed except for the items he would need until the launch. An orderly room clerk came into the barracks with a note for Musher. "Please call this number ASAP". The exchange was the Boston area.

As quickly as he could he called the number. The voice said, "Can you get away for a day and night in Juarez? Call this number and tell us if you can and if so when." The phone went dead.

He found Steve at the NCO Club playing ten cent Booray. He asked if he could speak to him for a moment privately. "I am packed and ready to go, I will deliver my B-4 Bag to the 905th today, may I take the next two days off the base to visit a girl before we leave?"

"Never knew you had a girl. Where?"

"She lives in Junction City, Kansas but if you let me go she will take a bus and we will meet half way. By car it is eight hours to Junction City. I cannot do the return trip and have any time with her in two days if I had to drive both ways."

"Take three days but don't drive both ways. The bus plan sounds best. You be careful, today is Tuesday, be back here by 1600 Friday and check in with me so I know you are back and OK. Drive carefully and have a good time."

"I will leave early tomorrow morning. Steve I thank you."

He found a pay phone and called the number. When it answered he said, "Yes I can get away. I will leave here early tomorrow morning." The phone went dead. He picked up his B-4 bag and delivered it to the 905th. From there to the BX to fill his ice chest for the drive down.

To the barracks for his SSS before dinner. He was in bed not too long after dinner.

CHAPTER 125

My Three Day Errand

Musher was in the dining room for breakfast at 0600. He was on the road at 0645. At the "Y" he turned south for Juarez. Three hours later he pulled into Bottecelli's garage. He was greeted by the big man. "When are you returning?"

"Tomorrow around eleven in the morning."

Musher made no attempt to pay for the overnight storage, took his "emergency bag" and headed for the Florida Hotel. He paid for one night. He did a wash up in his room and headed for the Florida Bar. Most of the girls there recognized him and the game was on. During the course of the afternoon he drank a few tequila sours and spent a couple of dollars in the back room with the ladies. He ate a Mexican dinner in the bar and switched to coco cola. He danced and fooled around with the girls but he did not make any more trips to the back room. As soon as it got dark he excused himself saying he was tired and was going to bed.

He undressed and laid spread eagle on the bed. The room was dark but he heard the door quietly open. His mysterious visitor appeared again, dropped her clothing and began the fondling, sucking process. After almost two hours of sex he gave her some money and she left as quietly as she came. He closed his eyes and slept until 0630. He took a long time doing an SSS in a Mexican hotel room. He smoked Luckies until he went to the Nest Egg for breakfast at 1000. At 1100 he paid his bill, left a good tip and walked out the front door. Sure as God made little green apples his car was waiting and the big man was standing by the driver's door.

"Good morning Musher. I trust you enjoyed your overnight. Mr. Bottecelli would be most appreciative if you could mail this package in a small Texas town other than the town you used last time." He handed Musher the package and an envelope full of money. "For your troubles. Drive safely." Musher knew better than to say anything. He shook hands with the big man and went on his way.

His next stop was the Biggs AFB dispensary. After his shot he went to the BX to buy fresh underwear and a new shirt. With clean clothes in hand he registered at the VAQ simply to use the showers. Refreshed he stopped at the Base Gas Station to fill up and add ice to his chest. Back on the highway he set a mental speed well within the speed limit and began his cruise north. About seventy miles north of Dry Gulch, Texas he turned off the highway and into Sutters Creek, Texas. It was a small town and he had no trouble dropping the package in the mail box outside the post office. This time he made the mistake of looking at the mailing and return addresses. They meant nothing to him but he knew he should not have looked.

He quietly drove out of town. Just before turning onto the highway he saw the blue and red lights of a police vehicle behind him. He heard the loudspeaker, "Pull off the road and stop." He did what he was told.

A Texas State Trooper spoke via of his loudspeaker, "Please get out of the car and keep your hands where I can see them." Musher obeyed. The trooper asked for his license and registration.

"They are in the glove compartment."

"Walk to the passenger side to get them. I will be behind you so don't make any sudden or ridiculous moves." The trooper withdrew his pistol from its holster. Musher retrieved the papers and handed them to the trooper. He showed identification and his dog tags.

"What are you doing off the highway?"

"I am an air force sergeant. I had been visiting friends at Biggs AFB in El Paso. On my drive back to Roswell, Walker AFB, I decided I would like a closer look at a small Texas town. I had time to spare and I randomly selected Sutters Creek."

"What were you doing at the mail box outside the post office?"

"Dropping some postcards to friends and relatives in Boston."

"In any case you were speeding when you left town." Oh, oh, here it comes, the shakedown. He knew he had not been speeding. He was the perfect target, out of state license plates and a big shiny car.

"I am sorry officer I guess I just wasn't paying enough attention,"

"Unfortunately I am required to write you a ticket and to take you to the Magistrate to settle the ticket."

"Officer if you do that I will be late returning to my duty station and I would be considered AWOL (Absent Without Leave). That could have serious effects on my career. Is there another way we can do this?"

"Well I know what the fine would be. I suppose if you had the cash you could give me the fine and I would settle it with the Magistrate. The fine is one hundred dollars."

"Officer I would appreciate it very much if you could do that for me." He counted out one hundred dollars and gave it to the trooper.

"What's in the chest?"

Musher opened the chest, "Cold cokes and candy bars. How about a cold coke on this hot day?"

404

The officer reached in and took two cokes and two candy bars. "You can go but watch your speed and drive safely."

"Thank you officer I appreciate your consideration." He knew his home town was full of shakedown artists but those boys could take a lesson from the Texas state troopers.

It was dinner time when he passed through the main gate at Walker. He headed for the dining hall. He joined Shaky who asked him where he had been. He perpetuated his lie about the girl and gave himself a good way out when he told Shaky she dumped him because of the TDY and he was an airman.

Back at the barracks he did another SSS and went to bed early.

CHAPTER 126
Finally the Launch for England

The time had come. They were third in line for takeoff in a flight of three. This was the first time for the extra passengers to fly in a B-29 of any type. They were without headsets and not sure what was going on. When the AC starting rolling the aircraft to the runway for takeoff you could see the tenseness in their faces and their grips on their parachutes. The strange noises of flaps, gear going up and the engine roar added to their concern. Tony kept giving them thumbs up signs in the hopes of getting them to relax. There were a lot of takeoffs and landings before they landed in England. As the flight progressed the passengers seemed to be calmer. When the descent to land at Barksdale AFB began the passengers seemed to be having trouble clearing their ears. Tony gave them some bubble gum. Apparently it worked quickly because they gave Tony a look of gratitude as if he were a saint. The noises were not so frightening because now they had some understanding where they came from and they were not noises of distress. Captain Lonnigan greased the landing. The fuel trucks were waiting to top off the tanks.

The AC formed everyone under the left wing. "Remember the game plan. We wash up, we get something to eat, we sleep, we wake up to get something to eat and we are at the aircraft at 2000 for a 2300 takeoff. Time to Kindley AB, Bermuda is roughly nine hours depending upon the wind. Steve, they are yours." The officers got on a bus and left. Steve hustled all the enlisted men onto a bus and they went to the dining hall. When everyone had finished eating once again Steve hustled them back on the bus and they were taken to their sleeping area for today. "Take this time to sleep. Be outside at 1800 for dinner. If you don't want to eat you must still be part of our formation. I don't want to lose someone in the crowd."

The second hop to Kindley AB went very smoothly. The on the ground routine was the same as it was at Barksdale.

At 2300 hours Tanker 102 rolled down the runway. Lonnigan maneuvered the aircraft to join the other two members of the flight. The three aircraft flight was separated by five hundred feet vertically and three miles horizontally. It was the job of everyone who had visibility outside the aircraft to monitor the formation. As the dawn came the AC asked the navigator, "What is our ETA for the Azores?"

"Two hours forty-six minutes." The time went by very slowly. About one hundred miles before reaching Lages in the Azores, the AC broke in and told everybody to listen up.

"Tanker Leader to tanker flight, do you copy?" Both tanker aircraft responded positively.

"Tanker flight there is ground clutter at Lages. We will set up a race track pattern and await landing instructions. It seems one of the earlier 915th aircraft lost two engines turning onto landing final and slipped off the landing glide path and a wing tip struck one of the mountains very close to the runway. We will get more details on the ground. Meanwhile Tankers 1 and 2 move into a safe trail position for the race track pattern. Lages tower estimates it may take as long as two hours before we can land. We have plenty of fuel and daylight remaining. Did you copy?"

Both tankers acknowledged five square. The AC came on the intercom, "I want this explained to the passengers as calmly as possible. Emphasize we are in no danger we will just be in the air longer. Crew acknowledge." All positions acknowledged. The probability of such an accident had never entered Musher's mind. He felt funny inside, he didn't know if he was scared or maybe growing up just a little bit more. Almost three hours later Lonnigan set the bird down most gracefully.

Once more, the AC formed everyone under the left wing. He restated the game plan. "We wash up, we get something to eat, we sleep, we wake up to get something to eat and we are at the aircraft at 1900 for a 2200 takeoff. Time to Wyton is roughly nine hours depending upon the wind. Steve, they are yours." Steve hustled all the enlisted men onto a bus and they went to the dining hall. When everyone had finished eating as before Steve hustled them back on the bus and they were taken to their sleeping area for today. "Take this time to sleep. Be outside at 1630 for dinner. If you don't want to eat you must still be part of our formation. I don't want to leave someone behind."

At 2200 they rolled down the runway to take their position in the flight of three. Except for the crew checks and the navigator giving ETA updates the flight went smoothly. The weather at Wyton was foggy which was never a surprise to anyone. The USAF GCA (Ground Controlled Approach) Team guided the aircraft to a dead center, first two hundred feet landing. Lonnigan thanked the GCA team and taxiied to his parking spot. The aircraft was chocked and blocked. There was a Lorry (a six by to you and me) to unload the gear and an aircrew bus for the personnel. The ground crew stayed with the aircraft to get it ready to fly while the aircrew went to debriefing. There was lots of chatter going on about the 915th aircraft. The medicinal whiskey seemed to be more than one ounce. Musher gave his to Tony. His crew had no special contributions to the debriefing. As they were leaving, the officers headed for their BOQ and the enlisted for their RAF barracks, the AC said, "Wing briefing for all aircrews at 1900 hours in the RAF combat briefing room. Don't be late."

The RAF barracks was not bad. Double decked bunks, a clothes rack and a foot locker. The barracks latrines, the showers were not very large and the hot water was not very hot. Still Musher unpacked and did a SSS along with most everybody else. If this is going to be home for the next few months he had better make the best of it.

The mess hall was just across from the barracks. Everyone was ravenous and quick to get to dinner. Dinner was SOS on heavy English toasted bread and strong black coffee. He ate like horse. Steve gathered his brood and they were sitting in the RAF combat briefing room at 1830 hours. Shortly thereafter they were joined by their officers.

There was a loud "Ten Hut" when the 509th Deputy Wing Commander came to the podium. "This is not easy for me and for you. Yesterday we lost one of our crews at Lages. Today one of our crews did not make it to Lakenheath. His initial radio transmission said he was having multi-engine trouble and he was diverting to land at Sidi Slimane, North Africa. There were two follow-up position reports. The last position report came from about one hundred fifty miles from Sidi well over the water. There have been no signals since then. It's too late and too dark to search today; however, our search will begin before first light to take us to the main search area by dawn. After we break up AC's Navigators and Radar Operators will attend specialized briefings outlining the search area and each crew's zone. According to staff we should launch at 0430. One last thought there will be a lot of B-29's in the search flying at about five hundred feet above the water. Stay alert we cannot afford to lose two more aircraft. Dismissed."

In addition to the regular crew the aircraft crew chief and two of his airmen were aboard the aircraft. Enroute to the search area there was very little silence between the individual B-29s and the search coordinator who was in a B-29 flying a wide loop race track pattern at twenty-thousand feet. The navigator was very busy keeping the aircraft well within its search zone. The radar operator was glued to his scope watching the airborne traffic making sure we stayed our proper distance from the adjacent cell searchers. Lonnigan and Barton were engrossed in flying the correct search pattern at from three hundred to five hundred feet above the water. Musher had been warned not to get an eye fixation on the white caps on the water. Despite the warning he became fixed upon the waves and ultimately became very, very vomiting air sick. One of the ground crew took his position in the waist while he vomited and dry vomited until he actually passed out. The search was still going on when he awakened. Tony told him to eat a dry sandwich and get back into his position. Despite the weariness and soreness in his chest Musher sat back in his position looking for survivors. He had learned his lesson about fixation with the white caps and vowed he would never be air sick again.

One by one the search coordinator called individual B-29s off the search. He gave them an altitude and a heading to their respective air bases. Because they had plenty of fuel the tankers were the last to be released from the search. There would be 0030 specialized staff briefings for a 0430 launch. Search zones would be assigned at the specialized briefing.

The search day was the same as yesterday. There were no positive sightings for survivors. Again, one by one the search coordinator called individual B-29s off the search. He gave them an altitude and a heading to their respective air bases. The difference was there was no mention of a briefing for a third day's search.

CHAPTER 127
Welcome To England

All roll calls were held in the RAF combat briefing room. The AC answered for his crew. There were only three announcements. Because of the heavy flying on the aircraft the wing would stand down for two days. A memorial service would be held for the lost and killed airmen in the Base Chapel at 1000 hours. When the AC determines his aircraft is ready for flight his air crew may be dismissed from duty until 1600 tomorrow at which time there will be briefing of the flying schedule for the third day. Attendance at this briefing is mandatory for all air crews. There were no individual aircrew busses but there was a steady stream of base busses which could be used to get to the flight line. RAF Wyton did not have a P Patch.

They were greeted by Nicolas and his ground crew. Nicolas told the AC that his bird is ready to fly right now. Tanker crew 102 did a full preflight anyhow.

The AC told the crew that if Steve concurred they were free to do as they please until the 1600 briefing tomorrow; however, they are restricted to the air base. Steve added that he had no pressing details today but the enlisted crew would meet in the mess hall for lunch tomorrow. The officers went their separate ways.

Musher and the enlisted crew went to the 915th aircraft which had transported Tanker 102 personal belongings. Everything had been downloaded and was sitting under the left wing. Steve hustled a lorry to take the items to the barracks. Musher rode his Vesper to the barracks and Steve rode Lonnigan's Vesper to the BOQ.

At the barracks everyone unpacked and squared away his area. Musher had Shaky in the top bunk and Tony in the lower on his left. Before shipping his Vesper Musher had Nance take off the carrier and install a second seat with foot rests. He had the front left and right lights changed to yellow bulbs and redirected for "wrong side" driving. Also Nance had shortened their range to give better road discrimination for traveling in a fog. One last gift from Nance was a pair of orange tinted sun glasses which he said would also help when driving in a fog.

To kill the afternoon Musher rode to the RAF Airman's Mess. The RAF Airmen's Mess was to the RAF what an airmen's club was to the USAF. Anyone was welcome provided he was below the grade of USAF Master Sergeant which was the British equivalent of Full Sergeant. The club had snooker tables, dart boards and cribbage tables. Musher was the only American in the place. One of the airmen came stuck out his hand and said, "Welcome Yank, I am called Dukie."

"Thank you, I am called Musher."

Dukie took him around introducing him to other airmen. "What's your pleasure, snooker, darts or cribbage?"

"I have never played darts or cribbage but I am willing to learn."

"You're a snooker player then are you?"

"Not very good but I truly enjoy the game."

"Right then, you and I will play fifty points for six pence. You are first in the circle." (Six pence was the equivalent of seven cents)

Musher lost five straight games, thirty-five cents. Four of those five he felt he could have run from his first shot to victory. Dukie said, "Let's have a pint." Musher could not beg off but he discreetly managed to only take a sip or two while getting rid of the rest in someone else's glass.

"Thank you for your hospitality. Maybe you will let me come again some time?"

"Any time Yank, any time."

Musher joined Shaky for dinner and told him about the RAF club. "Shaky do you play darts or cribbage?"

"I've played a little cribbage but not in a very long time."

"That's good maybe we can go there tomorrow and lose fifty cents or so."

CHAPTER 128
Briefing At 1600

The first few minutes were devoted to the excellent efforts of the aircrews and ground crews to find any survivors of our missing aircraft. As far as the squadron ops officer was concerned the issue was closed.

To the business at hand, tomorrow we shall fly six refueling missions and we will fly six refueling missions for the two days following tomorrow. He listed the primary aircraft and crews for the next three days. Musher's crew was not among the entire list. The supernumerary crews and aircraft (crews and aircraft ready to fill in for any reason) for the next three days was announced. Again Musher's crew was not on the list. The crews not on the primary or supernumerary lists would be free from duty for ninety-six hours beginning tomorrow right after roll call.

What do you do with four full days? The consensus was "Go to London". The grapevine said if you put four cartons of Pall Mall and two fifths of Johnny Walker Black or Red in your B-4 bag you would be greeted at the railroad station by persons who deal in the black market. Your two dollar investment (four cartons of cigarettes) and your two dollars fifty cents investment (two fifths of scotch) would turn into sixteen pounds sterling (forty-eight dollars eighty cents American) A seven hundred percent return on investment.

With sixteen pounds you could stay in the best hotel in Piccadilly Circus, drink the extra fifth you brought for yourself, smoke your own cigarettes, take sightseeing trips, go to the tea dances and choose your own room mate for two nights. After taxi fares and train fares (first class of course) you would still get back to Wyton with four pounds. You could expand that by selling your personal scotch and cigarettes at the train station when you were leaving.

It wasn't Juarez, it was a lot more classy. The thrills were the same they just cost a little more.

Back at RAF Station Wyton he still had a free day before the next morning roll call. He went back to the RAF Airmen's Mess. Dukie was there and invited him to play snooker. This time Musher won the first game and stayed one game up until they quit playing. Musher said he got lucky but Dukie was not buying it. Musher insisted on buying Dukie a pint while he himself had an orange crush.

"Would you like to learn how to play darts?"

"Very much so."

"We play as a team and the losing team buys a pint for the winners."

Let me explain the game.

The board is divided into twenty segments and each segment is its basic point count. Plus the outer bullseye ring counts for twenty-five points and the inner bullseye ring is fifty points. There are two wire rings surrounding the perimeter of the board. A dart between the wires of the outer ring doubles the point count for that segment. Towards the center there are two more wire rings and any dart in between those wires counts for triple points for that segment.

In a normal doubles game each team begins at numerical five hundred one, thereby the game is named 501. Each team must begin by scoring a double count before they can start to subtract the dart total from 501. To win the game a team must finish with a one dart double which brings the score to zero. Not very complicated eh what?

The reason most British boys are so good at arithmetic is because of darts. See the gentleman at the chalk board subtracting each teams total as they go and telling them what is left of the 501. You can rest assured each team member knows but it is a courtesy of the game.

A pair stakes its claim to the next game by "taking the chalk" and being score keeper for the current game.

Watch the way these boys hold the darts. They are not slinging arrows they are purposefully pushing the dart to the board. Notice that some have long darts some have short darts, some have light darts and some have heavy darts. Most everyone carries his own darts. It is rather like bringing your own snooker cue."

Dukie took the chalk and very quickly the 501 game was over. Challengers are first to the board. Dukie had told Musher to aim for the right side of the doubles wire. There was more room for a mistake. Musher did as he was told and his aim was so poor he put his first dart in the double twenty, or in British slang, double tah. Everyone knew this was Musher's first game but they teased him as "ringer", "yank slick" and a few other names. Dukie was a good player but in essence it was three against one.

Musher contributed his one shilling for the beer (fourteen cents American) and waited for another turn. He asked Dukie if he could take the chalk. He knew his arithmetic was strong enough to keep up with the game, and it did.

Dukie and Musher lost four more times before they gave it up. Musher promised Dukie he would practice and they would rise like the Phoenix.

The US NCO Club had dart boards and Musher practiced with the best players in the club every chance he got. Losing there was considerably more expensive than losing with Dukie. Every time they flew a day time mission they flew over a castle. The story was that the royalty who lived there was the Duke of Gloucester. The castle had beautiful grounds including horse stables and a massive swimming pool.

With his flying schedule and duties he did not get a chance to return to the RAF Airmen's Mess for almost three weeks. Of course Dukie was there. Musher said, "How about if I take the chalk. I have been practicing every chance I could. I even have my own darts."

Challengers first up. Musher hit a double tah and two triple tahs for one hundred sixty points. At his turn Dukie hit three triple nineteens. Total one hundred seventy-one points At Musher's next turn he and Dukie had one hundred seventy remaining. Musher prone to brag in front of all the RAF said, "Dukie they can't get out and I will leave you your favorite double nineteen." Triple eighteen, triple eighteen and double twelve, one hundred thirty-two points leaving thirty-eight for winner double nineteen. The other team shot well but was too far behind to get out and win the game. Dukie stepped up and with the first dart scored double nineteen for the winner.

Musher's braggadacio cost him the respect of many in the club and their leaning towards friendship for him. The undertones were, "typical show off yank", "the sportsmanship of a goat" and who knows what else. Dukie took him off to the side and gave him a long talk about the error of his ways. All was not lost even British airmen respect great skill particularly after having seen him in his first dart efforts.

CHAPTER 129

Life At the Castle

The next time Musher visited the RAF Airmen's Club he made a full, public apology for his rudeness and poor sportsmanship He tried to explain the he does not win many things very often and is not good in any other sports and he got carried away winning in another country in a game he just learned to play. He promised to be a better sportsman and a gentleman.

Dukie asked him if he was scheduled for any three or four day breaks from duty.

"As a matter of fact yes, next week my crew will receive a three day pass beginning on Friday at noon and I must be signed in to the squadron not later than 1800 on Sunday."

"Have you made any plans for that time off?"

"I guess like everyone else I will stuff my B-4 bag with tradeables and head for London. Why do you ask, why don't you come to London with me? We would have a great time. Money would not be one of your problems. I have enough tradeables for you, me and two other guys."

"I was thinking more on the line that you come home with me for that weekend. See some real British living and generally have a jolly good time."

"Would there be room at your house for me?"

"We would happily squeeze you in. I will pick you up Friday at noon. Don't worry about what to bring you and I are about the same size and I have enough for you and me and those other two mythical guys you mentioned."

The week dragged on. It gave Musher time to get six cartons of Pall Mall, two fifths of Johnny Walker Black Label Scotch and two fifths of Johnny Walker Red Label scotch. For Dukie's mother he bought a five pound box of chocolates and three pair of nylons. He packed his "wanna bee" suit with all the trimmings and three hundred pounds sterling.

When Dukie picked him up in his little sports car convertible Dukie looked like something out of magazine. Matching cap, scarf and gloves, all of which matched the convertible top.

Musher mocked, "I say old boy you look absolutely sterling. Do we have very far to go?"

"Less than thirty minutes." The convertible was so noisy there was no way to talk. In less than thirty minutes they passed through a very fancy wrought iron gate which sealed the eight foot wall which extended as far in either direction as the eye could see. They traveled on a well maintained road lined with very high, full trees. At the end of the almost two kilometers (one and one quarter miles) road they stopped on a massive circular drive in front of a castle.

"We're here." They were greeted by two servants who took the luggage and the staff chauffeur who took Dukie's car for cleaning and servicing.

"Welcome home Master Richard. Your family is waiting for you in the library."

"Thank you Hereford, we shall have a wash and change of clothes before seeing them. Please take Mr. Muscarello to his room. Musher I will come and get you when I am ready. Relax."

The room was larger than the flat in Boston where he was raised. Hereford explained, "I have drawn you a bath and placed towels and robe there for you. While you are bathing I shall lay out your clothes."

How long since Musher had sat in a bathtub. It felt so good he almost fell asleep. Clothed in his robe and slippers he entered the bedroom. Hereford was standing at attention and Musher's full attire was laid out on the bed. Against Hereford's insistence he put on his underclothes. Hereford took over from there. He dressed him in high quality stockings, riding pants and boots which were as soft as cloth. He finished with a white shirt with Ascot and jacket to match the breeches. He paraded Musher to the full length tri panel mirror. "I must say Mr. Muscarello you were born to wear those clothes. You could easily be one of the Duke's sons."

Musher was saved further embarrassment by the knock on the door. Hereford opened it for Dukie.

It was Dukie's turn, "I say old boy you look absolutely sterling". They were identically dressed. They made the long walk to the library where Dukie's family was waiting.

As they entered the library looking like the Bobsey Twins, Dukie went to place a kiss on his mother's cheeks, and a kiss on each of the two young girls who were Dukie's sisters. His father rose from his chair and Dukie spoke. "Father this Staff Sergeant Saverio Muscarello of the United States Air Force. Musher, as we all call him, my father Richard Gloucester The Ninth, Duke of Gloucester, Knight of the Round Table and Sworn Loyalist to the King. God Save the King."

The Duke came to Musher, "Do you mind if I call you Musher, Richard has told us so much about you. I am most happy to meet you. I want you to enjoy yourself here. If there is anything, anything we can do to make your stay more pleasant please do not be bashful just ask." With that he returned to his chair and motioned Dukie and Musher into the chairs next to him.

416

Dukie's mother and sisters quietly left the room. The Duke lit a cigar which was Musher's OK to light a Lucky. Dukie also lit a cigar. He was trained and being trained to be the next Duke of Gloucester.

"Richard tells me you are an excellent snooker player. Why don't we go into the game room and play a little snooker. I am sure Richard won't mind. Not many of my peers can beat me. Remember Musher, no holding back just to make me feel good."

The Duke was first in the half circle. His initial break was forty-nine. Very good by most standards. They had settled on a game of two hundred points. Musher just ran out the two hundred points. Dukie said to his father, "I told you he was good. You should feel proud Dad. Musher generally refuses to play without sufficient stakes to make it worthwhile. As his host you received special consideration."

"Musher in a single game of snooker what is the most you have ever played for?"

"Five thousand dollars American."

"How would you feel about playing for fifty thousand pounds?"

"That's only five thousand with another zero added. If I am not mistaken that is one hundred forty thousand dollars American. Sorry Sir, I do not have that kind of cash."

"The Duke of Willingham and his family are invited here tonight for dinner. Willy as we call him is the only snooker player in our group who beats me regularly. I will front the fifty thousand pounds if I can get him into a snooker game to three hundred points. He is a sixty point break shooter. I figure being the gentleman that he is he will let you have the half circle first. With his skill level you will get the opening and a least three more turns at the table. It would be a quick way for you to earn forty thousand dollars American." Musher thought about getting discharged just about four months after his return from this TDY and what forty thousand dollars added to his stash would do for him in his first venture into civilian bookmaking

Musher wanted to address the Duke but he did not know what to call him. He thought of The Monster, "It is always safe to call someone you don't know Sir."

"Sir if you have the confidence I will win for you and me. Do you want me to beat him as badly as I can?"

"Musher this will be a one time game so you win as strongly as you can and let him think about this beating for as long as he lives. Right now why don't we rest and wait for dinner."

"Dad I want to show Musher the stables. He has never touched a horse and I would like him to ride at least once while he is here." The stable amazed Musher. It was as clean and bright as any house he had ever been in. With Dukie's coaching he patted the horse's face. Dukie brought the horse out of the stable. The more Musher patted the horse on his face, then his neck, then his flank and very soon he was talking to the horse in a calming voice. His bravery extended to the point where he actually let the horse take an apple from the palm of his hand.

Dukie said, "Musher would you believe that horse is worth ten million dollars American?" That didn't surprise him. Often Fanucci had talked about the thoroughbreds and the millions of dollars they were worth. Dukie stabled the horse and brought Musher into the tack room. Musher knew from the cowboy movies that this saddle was without the horn or size to make it comfortable for long periods. Dukie discussed some other items in the tack room. "Musher, tomorrow we will ride. Not long and not far, but we will ride. Let's go rest before dinner."

Hereford was waiting in his room to help him undress. "Shall I draw your bath or do you wish to wait awhile?"

"Hereford, would it be gauche if I showered rather than bathed?"

"Sir, Sir, please wake up it is six o'clock. We must dress and join the family." With Hereford's help Musher was in his black tie formal attire. He joined the family in the main drawing room. Dukie and Musher looked so much alike they could easily have been brothers. The Duke of Willingham and his family were already there.

Dukie made the introductions. "Staff Sergeant Saverio Muscarello of the United States Air Force may I present William Willingham The Tenth, Duke of Willingham, Knight of the Round Table and Sworn Loyalist to the King. God Save the King."

Willy came to Musher with hand extended, "I will call you Musher if you will call me Willy. I am very pleased to meet you. Young Richard speaks most highly of you."

"Sergeant Muscarello, Musher, the Duchess of Willingham and her two daughters, Ann and Mary". Musher did what Hereford had told him. A slight nod of his head to the three ladies. The Duchess nodded back and the girls did a slight curtsy. There was a short period of light conversation before the announcement, Dinner is Served.

Dukie escorted Mary and Musher escorted Ann. The boys were seated next to the girls. Mary stared at Dukie like "when are we going to marry?" Ann batted her eyes to Musher sending the "I am interested message."

Dinner was uneventful. The main conversation consisted of questions to Musher about Boston and the United States Air Force. "Did he intend to make it a career?"

"No, as a matter of fact when I finish my temporary duty here I shall have only four months left before becoming a civilian."

Dinner finished. The ladies went one way and the men went into the game room for cigars and brandy. Willy picked up a snooker cue and began playing shots on the table. Musher watched intently to learn the table peculiarities. Willy asked Musher, "Do you understand this game?" ..... Yes Sir .... "Do you play the game?" .....Yes Sir ...."How well do you play?" .... Sir, I believe I am unbeatable....."Really, step up here and show me.".....Sir I don't play for fun, only for money..... "How about we play a three hundred point game for five thousand dollars American?" ....How about we play for fifty thousand pounds sterling? ....."I doubt if you have that kind of money."

The Duke of Gloucester interrupted, "He is my house guest and I will not have you question his honor. I shall stand for the fifty thousand pounds."

"Musher, I shall set the table and you may be first in the half circle."

Musher's first break was two hundred nine. Willy's first break was seventy three. Musher ended the game making ninety one points on his second break. He put up the cue and said to Willy, "Sir, I do not wish to be disrespectful but I warned you that I was unbeatable." To the Duke of Gloucester, "Thank you for coming to my rescue. I knew I would not need the money but Willy did not. Gentlemen may I be excused unless Willy you would like to try to regain your losses." Musher and Dukie went to join the ladies.

Outside Musher said to Dukie, "Your Dad is a hustler. True he is royalty but he is still a hustler."

"You have made him very. very happy. When I take you to your barracks you will have forty thousand American dollars in your pocket. Now, forget that I want to get in Mary's pants. Good luck with Ann."

They danced and danced and suddenly Musher realized Dukie and Mary had disappeared. Musher danced Ann out of the room to the terrace. He kissed her and she returned the kiss passionately. She asked Musher if he had ever seen the gazebo. They walked to the gazebo. There they continued the love making until he had climaxed three times. They heard the soft sound of the hunt bugle.

"Dad is ready to leave. We must go in." They walked back into the drawing room looking just as prim and proper as they did at dinner.

When the Willingham family was gone Musher said goodnight and headed for his room. Hereford had been there. Pajamas lay out and the bed turned down. In bed Musher had two thoughts, "I could easily get accustomed to this life; and, Freddie, jail could never be like this."

CHAPTER 130
A Day In the Life of Royalty

Hereford knocked gently and came in. He was surprised to see Musher sitting in his robe smoking cigarettes. "Master Richard says he will meet you for breakfast in twenty minutes. You two are going riding." With that he began laying clothes on the bed. "Master Richard says you must dress identically."

Musher was more accustomed to Hereford and went along without a fuss. He was amazed at the softness of the stovepipe in the boots and the firmness of the arch, sole and heel. "Hereford, how old are these boots?"

"At least forty years old. They are some of the newer ones in the family. The boot maker who made those is long gone to his rewards. Don't forget to take your head protector and riding crop."

Breakfast was a family gathering. Musher was the last to enter. He received friendly greetings from everyone. The Duke was beaming. As if on cue the ladies excused themselves and went off to do whatever it is ladies do.

"Musher I have never enjoyed myself as much as I did last night. My only regret is that we do not have a movie of Willy watching you kick his ass. His expressions would have made a great advertisement for disbelief. For your information I am going to donate my share in your name to the American Serviceman's Hospital in Cambridge. I thank you for a most pleasurable evening. Did you two have a good evening?"

"Yes Dad and it is time for us to go if I am ever going to get this Yank on a horse and riding."

The stable hands had saddled the most gentle mare in the stable. Musher walked the horse named Sally May into the practice ring. Dukie explained the use of the reins, the knees and the gentle urging with the heels of his boots. Musher had seen many, many cowboys mount a horse. They mounted using one hand to hold the mane and the other hand holding the saddle horn so that when the cowboy put a foot in the stirrup the cowboy could launch himself into the saddle without the horse moving away from him. It was a little different here, there was a mane, there was a stirrup but there was no horn to grasp. Dukie showed him how to put his hand on the saddle and use it in lieu of a saddle horn. Musher was sitting in the saddle but he was not feeling very comfortable.

Dukie took a bridle lead and walked Musher around the practice ring. Without Musher noticing Dukie had dropped the bridle lead and Musher was walking the horse around by himself. After thirty minutes of walking Musher could feel the horse's motion and he started moving in conjunction so that he was not coming down when the horse was going up. A lot easier on his ass. Dukie called to him to get down. ....."How" .....Pull back slightly on the reins and tell him to "Whoa." Sally May behaved beautifully. Musher got down and could feel the thirty minutes in the saddle. Dukie took the bridle and saddle off Sally May. Sally May went to a feeding trough

"Come on Musher, you did well. Let's go in and have a snack and a cigarette." The luncheon area in the stable was air conditioned and better then any diner or restaurant Musher had ever seen. The cook brought tea and rye toast. There was a package of Lucky Strikes on the table and a book of matches. "Compliments of Hereford who knew you left the room without cigarettes."

"When we finish you can bridle and saddle Sally May while I get my horse. We will ride one of the bridle paths. We will stop anytime you say."

Musher struggled but he finally got Sally May ready to ride. As they headed onto the bridle path Dukie told Musher to give Sally May a little nudge with both his boots. Sally May stepped up her stride and speed of stride. Musher took a few bumps on his butt even though he was in pretty good rhythm with the ups and downs of Sally May. Dukie told him Sally May's stride and speed was called a "canter." Dukie said if Musher gave Sally May another two boot nudge she would break into a slow run. Musher did and so did Sally May. Musher got quite a few more bumps on his ass during the run. It lessened as he became more synchronized with Sally May. Dukie pulled up along side him and said, "Let's stop and stretch our legs." They reined in along the banks of one of the many small lakes on the estate, tethered the horses, loosened the saddle cinch and walked to one of the permanent picnic tables. Musher had just barely lit a Lucky when Ann and Mary rode up. They were riding side saddle and were dressed to fit their position as daughters of a duke. Come to find out the other side of the lake was Willingham property. Dukie and Mary disappeared into the thick woods along the bank. Musher and Ann did likewise. At least two hours passed before all four were back at the picnic table enjoying the lunches that the Willingham Kitchen had packed.

There were tender kisses all around as the ladies mounted and headed to Willingham Castle. The gentlemen mounted and headed to Gloucester Castle. Musher was in a groove with his horse and the ride was smooth. The dismounted at the stable and the grooms were there to care for the horses. "See you at five-thirty cocktails."

Hereford was waiting in the room for Musher. He had drawn a bath in anticipation of Musher's sore bones and sore ass from his ride. Musher accepted all the help he could get until he was in the bed and fast asleep. He knew of no special occasion this evening but Hereford had him dressed in black tie and tuxedo. Dukie poured two very light gin and lemon crush drinks, one for himself and the other for Musher. The conversation centered around Musher's experience with the horses. He admitted as sore as he was, "I hope we can do that again tomorrow."

In the game room after dinner smoking cigars and cigarettes and sipping brandy the Duke said, "Richard tells me you are an accomplished dart player. Why don't you and I give it a 301 go, or is this like your snooker where you only play for money?"

"Sir I do not have my darts with me. (Of course they were in his room in his emergency bag) I am afraid I may not be able to give you much of a run."

Dukie led him to a box filled with all types of dart. Musher found three that felt like his own. "You first Musher, you are the guest." The old British gentleman.

Musher's first three darts were double tah and two triple tah. Score 160, balance for 301, 141.

The Duke made a very good showing, double tah and two triple nineteen.

Score 97, balance for 301, 204.

It didn't really matter what the Duke scored it was Musher's turn again. Triple nineteen and triple tah, (117), balance twenty-four, double twelve (24), game over.

"Where did you learn to play like that?"

"From Dukie, I beg your pardon from Richard."

"When?"

"About four weeks ago."

"That is incredible. How did you learn so quickly and so well?"

"Once you know the rules of the game and you are capable of "taking the chalk" it is then only a matter of hand eye coordination. It is the same as snooker, straight pool or any other table game except you shoot from a fully vertical position. Sir I hope you are not offended I did not think you would have wanted me to sandbag for your ego."

"No, of course not. I am off to bed. I will see you at breakfast."

"Goodnight sir, it is too early for me. I had a great nap this afternoon."

"So did I" said Dukie, "How about I show you some card tricks? Are you familiar with prestidigitation?" He did ten or twelve different tricks while Musher sat in amazement. He would be good at a young child's birthday party but in the card playing world he would not survive a day.

They sat and talked about Mary and Ann until Dukie finally said, "That's it for me. See you at breakfast."

CHAPTER 131
A Weekend To Remember

Musher had Hereford help him carry his gift boxes down to breakfast. As usual all the family was assembled for breakfast. Musher spoke, "I am very embarrassed. When Dukie invited me to come home with him I never imagined that he was the son of royalty. In my misconception I thought only what my limited experience in England had shown me. That translated into black market cigarettes, whiskey and chocolates. As an ignorant Yank I gathered some of these as gifts for Dukie's parents. Please forgive me but try to remember it was done from ignorance and not disrespect." He presented the chocolates to the Duchess and the cigarettes and whiskey to the Duke.

The Duchess was covering tears. The Duke, "Musher, we completely understand and we share the fault for your embarrassment. Richard should have done something to prepare you for your first experience with us and our life style. We want you to know and believe that your gift gesture could not be more warmly received if you had brought chests of gold and silver. We have enjoyed meeting you and hope that you will visit with us again. If we could have a brother for Richard, it would be you."

Like all tough guys Musher took his handkerchief to sneeze and cover the water which filled his eyes.

After breakfast Musher took Dukie aside. "The staff, especially Hereford has been so good to me how do I repay them?"

"Actually it is their job. My father pays them well and treats them well. Most have been with the family all their adult life. You probably noticed most all smoke and they definitely all eat chocolates. If you wanted to send them a thank you note attached to a package they would be more thrilled that you remembered than receiving the gift. I planned for us to return to Wyton at 1500. Is that all right with you?" ....Fine...... "In a couple of hours Willy and his family are coming for brunch. My mother and father are crazy about playing bridge would you mind playing for a couple of hours?"

On the card cut Musher drew the Duchess as his partner. "Musher, what conventions do you play?"

"You tell me what you play and we will play those."

She looked at him with that "I don't believe what I just heard" but she rattled off her favorite conventions. Not only was the Duchess a good player she continuously held great cards. As a result of the Duchess' luck and skill they tromped the Duke and son for three straight rubbers.

They changed partners. This time he had the Duke. It was as if an angel sat on the Duke's shoulders. He was a quality player but now that he was drawing cards he became the dominant force. They tromped Dukie and his mother for three straight rubbers.

They were preparing for the next set. Dukie and Musher would be partners. The butler announced, "Sir, the Duke of Willingham and his family are arriving now." Thank God that ended the bridge.

"Musher you are an excellent player." Jokingly," when did you learn last week?"

"Sir I have been a card player since I was five. I have been trained by the very best the United States has to offer. True most of my trainers came from the old country but have been American citizens for years."

Brunch was very light hearted. Much to everyone's surprise Willy joked about his beating at snooker. I am sure his wife did not know it cost him one hundred forty thousand dollars. He asked if Musher played any other gambling games.

Musher told him the story of his school years memorizing poetry when one of his uncles who lived with Musher's family asked him what he was doing. He answered his uncle, "I am learning poetry." His uncle told him there is only one poem you need to know, "I will play any man, from any land, for any amount, he can count. When you can recite that and back it up, you will have all the education you will ever need."

Time was running short. Dukie asked that they be excused and the four of them went into the garden. Dukie and Mary disappeared. Ann took Musher to the gazebo. They could only stay an hour since the boys had to get ready to leave at 1500. Willy and his family were staying for the day. The girls would entertain Dukie's sisters.

Hereford had Musher's clothes packed and the clothes he came in were washed, ironed and laid out on the bed. Musher rushed his SSS.

Dukie's car had been serviced and was parked in front of the main entryway. There were a lot of thank you's, come back soon's, hugs, tender kisses and goodbyes. As the car headed down the drive way the families were still waving.

On the way back to Wyton Musher continually thanked Dukie for the weekend. At the moment he did not know it but there was forty thousand dollars American in his emergency bag.

CHAPTER 132

The TDY Ends, We Soon Return To Roswell

Monday morning's briefing brought some definite news. The squadron would leave for Roswell on the last day of the month, just twenty-two days from today. The flight routes, the enroute landing and refueling stations were the same ones used coming over. The night take-off, day landing schedule would be in effect. There would be refueling missions for the next ten days. Musher's crew had been tagged for two of those missions. One of the missions would be a short six hour mission the other would be a USCM (Unit Simulated Combat Mission) which would be for sixteen hours. His crew was still being lucky. They would fly the USCM first and the short one later. A USCM is a career maker or breaker for a lifer. I doubt if the AC would let me do the refueling operation on the USCM mission.

After the morning roll call Captain Lonnigan held a crew meeting. "Today is Monday. We fly our USCM with a 2300 takeoff Friday. We should be in our refueling area shortly after dawn. Steve, I am very happy with our crew. We don't need to do anything differently than we have been doing for quite some time. Let each of us use today to plan for his rotation to Roswell. As of Wednesday at 1600 we shall restrict ourselves to the air base, and no drinking until we share the after mission whiskey. Any comments or questions? Hearing none I will see you all at roll call tomorrow morning."

Musher's mental list of important things to do began with rounding up twenty cartons of Pall Mall and twenty pounds of chocolated eight ration stamps but he needed twelve more ration stamps to get twenty cartons. They were easily available for a price. He will need to locate a lorry with a trustworthy driver to deliver the packages to Gloucester Castle. He will need to write a short thank you note

He will go to the American Express office with thirty-eight thousand of his weekend earnings. He would have AMEX transfer the thirty-eight thousand to his AMEX account at Walker AFB, Roswell. Let's go to AMEX and do the plan. He went and the transfer was done. After the transfer to his Roswell account the balance in his Roswell account is sixty-eight thousand two hundred dollars (American).

Next priority, garner the cigarette ration coupons. He would not be able to buy them all at one time. The single purchase limit was six cartons. He will get the first six now. There is no limit on the amount of chocolates which can be bought at any one time. He will get four five pound boxes now. Back at the barracks he emptied his foot locker to make room for the cigarettes and candy.

It was time to go to the RAF Airmen Club to see if Dukie is there or if anyone knew whether or not he would be there later. It was no surprise to find him there playing cribbage. When he saw Musher he forfeited the game and paid the six pence (seven cents) loss. Musher told him of his need for a trustworthy lorry driver and lorry to deliver a package to Gloucester Castle.

"Where and when do you want them?"

"The USAF NCO Club parking lot at 1630. What do you think I should pay him?"

"Normally two pounds. In your case two when he takes it and you tell him three more when he brings Hereford's receipt."

"Thank you Dukie. We were told today that we leave for the states twenty-two days from today. We have a couple of heavy missions between now and then. I will see you before I leave. Again, thanks for everything."

After dinner he wrote his note to Hereford. "In my short life I have never experienced the support from any individuals which compares with the support you and the Gloucester staff gave me during my stay. It is not possible for me to express my feelings towards you. I hope that you and the staff will enjoy this slight token of appreciation. Lovingly, Musher. P.S. Please sign the driver's delivery slip. Without it he cannot be paid. If you do not get to read this note, his life is in extreme peril." He addressed the envelope with the simple name Hereford.

He noticed there was a two and five poker game going on. Cigarette ration stamps were used as currency worth one dollar American. Musher offered two dollars American for each stamp. He bought fourteen (decided he might want a couple of cartons for himself.) He offered fifteen dollars (only need three for the cigarettes) in advance for anyone who would get six cartons of Pall Mall and have them in the barracks by 1300 tomorrow. He quickly got two takers. "Let me leave you gentlemen with one final thought, if for whatever reason I am waiting in the barracks and either one or both of you do not show up with the cigarettes, the person or persons who does not keep the commitment might not be ready to fly in twenty-two days. If you doubt my sincerity think about what you know about me. Enjoy your game, goodnight."

CHAPTER 133
Time Drags When You Are Waiting

The morning roll call was over and Captain Lonnigan had the crew together once again. "Other than buying to take home, packing and getting our scooters and luggage to the 915th for transport home, what specific things must you do before the rotation? Fill me in."

None of the enlisted men had anything to add. None of the officers had anything to add. "Captain Barton will coordinate with 915th setting a schedule to bring our stuff to the 915th and which aircraft. Steve you work with our ground crew and bring them into the picture. Is it now safe for me to believe that with the exception of the few things we talked about this morning the aircrew and the ground crew will be ready to launch seventy-two hours before launch, seventeen days from today, four days before the launch?"

The crew answered in unison, "Yes Sir."

"Let's talk about the upcoming USCM. This morning I want you all to go out to our aircraft and see if you can be of any help to the ground crew. When you finish there you may take off for the rest of today and I will see you all at roll call in the morning." With that he popped on his Vesper and left.

There was really nothing to do at the aircraft. We all checked our duty positions and equipment. The crew chief assured Steve the aircraft is in mint condition. Steve said all the enlisted men were dismissed. Tony jumped on the back seat with Musher. Musher headed for his barracks to wait. His two purchasers entered right after noon with their items. He thanked them and gave them and extra twenty dollars each for their services. He stashed the cigarettes and went to the dining hall for lunch.

He wrapped his gifts in plain paper and marked on the outside of each, HEREFORD, 1 OF 2; and HEREFORD 2 OF 2. Still almost two hours before his rendezvous. He forgot to tell Dukie how his man would recognize Musher. As an assist he parked at the far end of the empty parking lot. To kill some time he went into the Club for some pool room practice. All the tables were full except for the billard table. He had not played billards in such a long time this practice would be good. As usual when his practice session was being watched by an audience he played his own billard game. He attempted to see how close he could come to making a billard yet not touching the object ball in the scheme. He realized he was doing quite well by the noises in the audience. He decided he would try to miss by an inch.

He stood beside his Vesper waiting for the pickup. At a couple of minutes before 1630 a small lorry driven by a big man stopped beside him. "My name is Falzone. Dukie said you need a package delivered."

"Actually two packages and a letter. Inside the letter is a delivery receipt which you will bring back to me. I will pay you two pounds now and three pounds when you bring me the delivery receipt. Do you know the Duke of Gloucester's place?"...Yes.

"That is the delivery address, either to Hereford personally or to the Duke himself. I will allow you one and one half hours to get there, it should take you no more than forty-five minutes, ten minutes to do business, and one and one half hours to return to this spot. You should be here no later than seven fifty in the evening. I am sure Dukie told you about me and what happens to people who try to screw me. If you have no questions be on your way." Musher sat awaiting Falzone's return. He was gone and back in less than two hours. He looked at Hereford's receipt and gave the driver his three pounds plus a bonus of two pounds for doing such a good job. Content with the result he headed to the barracks for a good night's sleep.

It wasn't easy getting to sleep thinking of Lucy, Priscilla, Juarez, London and Ann.

CHAPTER 134
Another New Experience

The USCM was eighteen hours long but everything went to perfection. The rendezvous at the precise time, a good fuel transfer and every last drop we could spare went to the bomber/receiver. The "lifers" were ecstatic. Debriefing was fun.

Musher was the primary operator for the short mission. Everything went perfect. Once again "the lifers" were ecstatic. Musher actually took a sip of the Wild Turkey at debriefing. Now he knew for sure why he didn't like it, it tasted awful. Paul finished it for him.

The next morning after roll call Captain Lonnigan reminded everyone that there were only ten days until launch to Roswell. He had been given permission that if he, his crew and their equipment were ready they could have a five day pass. Unheard of, a full crew five day pass. Part of those five days was a four day R&R (Rest and Relaxation) trip to Hitler's summer home Kehlsteinhaus in Berchtsgaden, Germany. It was more than Hitler's place, Berchtsgaden was famous for spring skiing, luxury hotels and all types of entertainment. This crew had been allocated four seats if anyone wanted to go. Does anyone want to go?" Everybody raised his hand. "OK, two officers and two enlisted. How do we decide?"

Steve, "Cut cards two low go." He took a deck from his flying suit and tossed it to Musher. "Shuffle." In the process of shuffling Musher palmed a deuce and a three. Steve took the deck and took charge.

"Paul, you first." Nine"Shakey, now you." King"Musher." Three

"Now me." Seven. "There you are Captain, me and Musher." He passed the deck to Captain Lonnigan who shuffled and the officers did their cut. No one would notice one missing deuce until Steven went to use the deck for some game and hopefully by then Musher would have the last deuce in the deck.

Captain Lonnigan again, "Station time for the flight is 0700 hours tomorrow at Squadron Ops. No flight suits, no civilian clothes. Maximum luggage, your B-4 Bag. You might want to consider bring some tradeables. Unless someone has a question or a comment I will see you in the morning. Remember they will not wait on you. Dismissed."

Musher made a bee line for the BX. Garnered all the Pall Mall's he could, scotch whiskey, tooth paste and soap. As he was leaving the parade of eager shoppers was just entering.

Musher was waiting at squadron ops at 0640 hours. At 0700 the C-47 aircraft Commander took a roll call. Everyone was present with one B-4 bag. The Loadmaster walked his passengers to the aircraft. The C-47 AC, Co-pilot and crew chief boarded. The Loadmaster boarded the passengers. Baggage was stored in the aft section of the aircraft. There were canvass bench seats and a parachute for every seat. When everyone was aboard and the Loadmaster checked they were properly in their parachutes and buckled into their seats the Loadmaster brought in the ladder and secured the hatch. He stood midway to the cockpit and roared, "Engine start in about two minutes, take off in less than ten, about three hours in the air. Please stay in your seats and buckled in place. I will come back to tell you when you can unbuckle, move around and smoke."

Having ridden a C-47 once before Musher knew there was its tendency to be rough riding. Just like the last time it was free and going where he wanted go.

"Steve, want to play a little gin rummy? Break out the cards." He never expected to be able to put back the deuce this quickly. They played for over an hour at a tenth of a cent a point. Musher lost almost two dollars. Steve wanted to close his eyes and relax. He thought "two dollars is pretty darn cheap for this round trip ticket."

The Loadmaster appeared. "Starting our descent for landing. Everyone please put out all smoking materials, please get back in your seats and please buckle up. We should be on the ground in less than fifteen minutes. When you leave the aircraft form a line to the truck so we can pass the luggage onto the truck. There will be a bus for us. We are all staying at the same hotel so we will get the luggage in the correct owner's hands there. One last thing, please police your area. Take any trash with you. Thank you."

Touchdown, taxi, parking and on the blocks was smooth. In very short order the luggage was on the truck and the passengers on the bus headed for the hotel. At the hotel there were many bellboys to take the luggage into the lobby. When you registered and were given your room number and key a bell boy took your luggage. You waited for the next registrant so the bag boy could handle two at once. Because of the order in which they registered Steve and Musher were in adjoining rooms. Steve had spoken to his friends who had been here before so he tipped the bell boy two dimes. Musher looked shocked.

Steve, "Remember the daily rate in this hotel is thirty-five cents and that includes hot and cold running maids."

CHAPTER 135
Better Than Juarez

A soft knock on the door. When Musher opened it there stood a tall well-dressed man who announced, "My name is Fritz. I specialize in tradeables. May I come in?"

"Certainly." Thank goodness for the adjoining door, "Steve would you come in here please?"

Fritz waited for Steve to enter the room, "I deal in tradeables. I pay top dollar and can arrange anything for you that you may want while you are here. Do you have any tradeables?"

"Steve, why don't you bring yours in here while I spread mine on the bed?" To Musher's six cartons of cigarettes, two fifths of Johnny Walker, twelve bars of soap and twelve tubes of tooth paste, Steve added six cartons of cigarettes, two fifths of Johnny Walker, two one pound cans of ground coffee and one fifteen pound smoked ham.

"Fritz, can you handle all this?"

"My offer, twenty dollars a carton for cigarettes, fifty dollars a bottle for the scotch, five dollars a bar for the soap, five dollars a tube for the toothpaste, seventy five dollars for can of coffee and thirty dollars a pound for the ham. My count is a total eleven hundred sixty dollars but I round if off to twelve hundred dollars American."

Musher thought this guy is good. "Fritz could you wait outside for a minute." Fritz obliged. "Well Steve what do you think?"

"Shit I don't know but we aren't going to shop our black market goods. The sooner they are out of my hands the better I will feel. Take a weak shot to see if you can crank him but don't lose him."

"Fritz would you come back in here please?" As the door closed Musher said,"Before we came we talked to some of our friends who made us think they did a lot better. Is this the best you can do? If it is we may want to shop around."

"Let me sweeten the pot." He knew the slang all right. "I will raise to fourteen hundred plus I will pick up both your tabs for whatever you spend in the hotel, room, meals, beer, soda, no whiskey drinks and make sure you have free frauleins who work this hotel."

"We want to learn basic skiing. What can you do there?"

"I will arrange for instruction, lift tickets, rental clothes and rental skis at no cost to either of you. I will be at your beck and call while you are here."

433

Musher looked at Steve who nodded. "Deal. When do you move this stuff?"

"Just as soon as I can count out your money. I have help waiting outside in the hall."

"We won't know if you have kept your word until we try to use these benefits. We are going down to lunch now. It is only fair for me to tell you that if you welsh on your promises I will find you and cut your heart out and feed it to the snow dogs. Do you understand, capisce, wakalimasu, comprendez, comprendi, verstehen?"

We had the cash and Fritz was gone in less than five minutes. The cash was divided according to contribution, four hundred sixty for Musher and nine hundred forty for Steve.

The dining room menu was weak but we had sauerkraut, sausage, heavy dark bread and beer. When you are hungry it all tastes good. Steve was going out sightseeing. Musher was going back to the room to sample an available fraulein. She was good. He tipped her twenty-five cents American. He never knew when she left.

Steve gave him a shake, "What say buddy are you ready for dinner. I know of a restaurant where they serve an American menu. A little pricey but we can handle it. There was no shower and Musher was not in the mood for a bath. He did a wash up and dressed. While walking to the restaurant Steve told him he had seen Fritz. Skiing lessons were at ten tomorrow morning. The bus goes to the mountain at 0830. Dinner was meatloaf, mashed potatoes, beets, bread and beer. Including tip twelve dollars each.

Next stop "das Lokal bar". Sad music, slow dancing, lots of booze and lots of working frauleins. It was easy to see Steve believed in R&R and not I&I (Intercourse and Intoxication). A couple of beers later they headed for the hotel. Musher was not accustomed to drinking beer and actually felt whoozy. At the hotel Steve closed the adjoining door while Musher undressed and fell into bed. He needed to sleep the spinning was getting to him. A couple of hours he awakened and took a full bath. In fresh clothes he felt so good he went down to the restaurant for tea and toast. The bar was full of working frauleins. He picked one and upstairs they went. . She was good. He tipped her twenty-five cents American. He never knew when she left.

FREDDIE YOU MUST BE MAD. THIS IS A GREAT LIFE.

They had heavy toasted black bread with margarine and hot tea for breakfast. They were waiting in the lobby for the bus. There were others also waiting for the bus but they were fully dressed for skiing. Even to the point where they were carrying skis. The bus ride lasted about forty-five minutes over a small curling road. Musher quit looking out the window because the higher they went the more narrow the road appeared and the cliff drop even steeper. He was certainly happy to get out of that bus and into the lodge. They were expected and outfitted with all the ski apparel of a pro. They certainly looked the part.

Their instructor, a young woman named Frieda, talked about balance and equipment. For some time they did crouching exercises and knee lateral movement exercises. On came the skis. They were short beginner's skis with easy buckle-in and release features. Balancing on skis is far different from balancing on your ski boots. Both fell a few times just simply standing and trying to do the crouch and lateral knee movement exercises. Before adding ski poles Frieda explained and demonstrated how you could make yourself fall by changing your balance with implement of one or both ski poles. You could also make your self fall by radically changing the positions of your arms and poles. The weight of just one pole could distort your balance.

"We have been out here for almost two hours what say we go to the lodge for a little snack?"

When they were seated a waitress brought a large tray of very small sandwiches and a very large pot of hot tea. It was not possible to determine what was in the sandwiches but they tasted good. What more information is necessary? There were more than enough sandwiches for them. Lunch conversation was at a minimum. Musher brought out his Lucky Strikes and offered one to Frieda. "Yes please." Musher lit both their cigarettes. Frieda puffed like it would be her last cigarette. Musher finished his and offered her another. "Yes please." She seemed to enjoy that one even more than the first.

Back at the slope Frieda led them to an almost flat slope. She demonstrated how to stop by doing a "snow plow". Done by spreading your legs and making the tip of each ski meet in the middle and actually plow the snow. She said to them, "You know how to bend at your knees, laterally move your knees to change and when you change directions, how to use your ski poles and how to stop when you want to. You are ready. The three of us will go down this beginner's slope with me in the middle. I know you can do it."

They lined up across the top of the slope and Frieda said, "Light push with both poles. A light push." The full length of the slope was only about three hundred yards before it flattened and the arc went uphill to make sure the skiers stopped. Steve and Musher made it all the way to the end without falling. They were so proud.

Frieda led them to the side of the slope where there was a pulley rope to bring them back to the top. Frieda cautioned, "Keep your weight on the inside of your skis and the skis parrell to each other. If they cross you will fall." Both made the climb without incident.

Frieda had them do it two more times. Both were done without difficulty. She led them to a steeper slope. "Everything is the same as the other slope only since it is longer and since it is steeper you will go faster. Whether you ski at one kilometer an hour or one hundred kilometers an hour, skiing is skiing. You have the skill you must now sharpen it. I will be behind you."

They made it through the first run without a fall and successfully used the rope pulley to come back to the top.

Musher said, "Could we take a smoke break?" He pulled out his Luckies and lit two. One for him and one for her. One was not enough, he lit two more.

They did two more runs. Both successfully without incident. She led them to a steeper slope and repeated her speech, "Everything is the same as the other two slopes only since it is longer and since it is steeper you will go faster. Whether you ski at one kilometer an hour or one hundred kilometers an hour, skiing is skiing. You have the skill you must now sharpen it. I will be behind you."

They made it through the first run without a fall and successfully used the rope pulley to come back to the top "There is nothing more I can teach you today. You should practice this run until you are tired. I will be here with you until you stop for the day."

They made the run three more times and looked at each other with the "That's enough". At the lodge they were asked if they were coming back tomorrow. They agreed they would if they could have the same instructor. She would be their instructor. "Since you are coming back keep the clothes and the skis. We will wash and iron yours and keep them here."

At the table there were more little sandwiches and hot tea. They took the edge off the hunger. Musher lit two Luckies and passed one to Frieda. "You gentlemen did very well today. Tomorrow we will go play with the big boys. We will start with the half mile run and work our way up from there. The trails will not get much steeper until you get to the Advanced and Expert levels. I doubt if we will get there tomorrow."

Musher lit two Luckies and passed one to Frieda. It was time to catch the bus. Musher took his full spare pack of Luckies and gave it to Frieda. "This should last you until tomorrow. We appreciate your help. We will see you tomorrow."

"If you have dinner at the hotel and a beer or two in the bar, don't be surprised if you see me there. It's my second job, I work there nights."

Musher had Steve sit by the bus window. He could not bring himself to watch the descent on that narrow winding road. In the lobby Musher asked the concierge if he could get a heavy bath robe and slippers for each of them. He also asked for housekeeping to bring four extra bath towels. Less than five minutes after they entered their rooms housekeeping was there with the robes, slippers and towels. Musher gave a twenty-five cent tip. The hot bath and the two hour nap made him feel like a new man. His own fresh clothing felt good too.

Dinner was lamb, potatoes, lamb gray, beets, dark bread and beer. If he ate like this every day he would weigh two hundred fifty pounds. The bar was not really crowded. There were more working girls than the total male population in the bar. Moments after Musher and Steve sat down they were joined by Frieda and another attractive young lady.

"Are you surprised to see me? This is my friend Hilda." The waitress brought drinks for the ladies. The couples went to the dance floor. Steve looked as if he might be warming up to Hilda. He had his hand on her ass and was gently squeezing. Hilda had her lips on Steve's neck and was whispering something. Musher could guess what it was. Frieda was hanging onto Musher for dear life. She managed to gently rub her knee in his crotch while her left hand kept pulling him closer to her thigh. The music stopped. The couples returned to their table.

Steve and Hilda never said a word. They just simply rose and walked out of the bar. Musher wondered if Steve just switched from R&R to I&I.

Musher lit two Luckies and passed one to Frieda "After this cigarette we go to my room and you can continue with the skiing lessons."

The room was dimly lit but when Frieda undressed Musher could see the body development of muscles as part of a perfectly proportioned body. She walked to where he was standing and knelt before him. "This is called "examining the pole". With that she took his penis gently stroking it and rubbing it across her lips. When she took it in her mouth he almost screamed with pleasure. She sucked a little then stopped while she rolled her tongue around the head of his dick. Finally he grabbed her by the back of her hair and pushed his dick further into her mouth and shot his load. She never let a drop get away.

Frieda went to the bed and lay spread eagle on her back. "Your turn." Musher responded immediately. He lay between her legs and sucked her pussy. She guided his tongue to where it felt best for her. He was sucking and licking while reaching up and playing with her breasts and nipples. She arched her back and he held her ass in the air while he sucked the pussy and she climaxed. He had hardened again.

She sensed his eagerness and took his dick into her pussy. They were locked in the missionary position with her powerful legs holding him while they bounced and turned all over the bed. He could feel her fingers tightening on his back while the heat was building inside him. Together they both squeezed viciously and climaxed.

They lay on the bed smoking Lucky Strikes. She told him she must be out of the hotel not later than four o'clock. They still had three and one half hours. At the moment neither knew what they could do with it. Musher suggested they share a bath.

They sat in the tub smoking Luckies and playing footsies. He could feel himself hardening and her pushing her pussy against him. Before long he was inside her and they were drowning the bathroom.

The extra bath towels got their use as they dried each other off. The drying was interspersed with kisses and licks. He put on his fancy robe and slippers while he watched her dress in a much brighter light than when she undressed. Her body was beautiful. As she was leaving Musher gave her two packs of cigarettes and five American dollars. She thanked him, kissed him on the cheek and whispered, "See you on the slopes."

Musher crawled in bed and fell asleep thinking of Lucy, Priscilla, Juarez, London, Ann and Frieda.

FREDDIE YOU ARE REALLY MISSING SOMETHING !

438

CHAPTER 136
Another Day of Skiing

Steve banged on the adjoining door until Musher opened it. "Come on buddy it is almost 0800. Get in your pretty ski clothes and let's squeet. Don't I look pretty? We must get a couple of pictures before we go back to Wyton."

"Go on down I will be right there. Do me a favor and take my skis too." Steve grabbed the skis and headed for the dining room. Musher was drained. All he could do was mentally relive last night. What he would have given for a cup of real coffee. He dressed, loaded his pockets with his stuff and went to join Steve.

The special this morning was scrambled eggs, fried potatoes, heavy white toast and hot tea. Musher ordered a double breakfast. He never mentioned last night. If Steve wanted to talk about it he would bring it up. He asked the waiter to send for the concierge.

"Sir, how may I help you?"

"Can you get Fritz here in a hurry?"

"Yes Sir I will." Musher put an American dollar in his hand. He walked briskly out of the dining room. Within ten minutes Fritz was at their table.

"Fritz I need a good German camera, the film and the accessories for it. I need it by nine forty-five this morning. Can you do that?"

"I can but it will cost somewhere between two and three hundred American dollars."

"We will be here in the hotel lobby until nine forty-five. If you are not here by then we shall presume you could not make the deal." Fritz left.

At nine fifteen Fritz asked the boys to step into a private room. "I have for you a probably the best camera in the world, a Leica. The film is loaded you have twenty-three pictures. The light setting is for a clear day. He demonstrated how to focus by turning the lens wheel. As you focus it will automatically adjust the range to your subject for the best picture. The F Stop is set for a clear day. Push this button to activate shutter opening and closing, actually taking the picture. Use this lever to move the film to the next available position for another picture. Wait until you get back to England to have the film removed and developed. Your cost is one hundred pounds for the camera and accessories and five pounds for my handling fee, or two hundred ninety-four American."

"Fritz you did a good job. Here is three hundred American you may keep the change. Time for us to get on the bus."

Frieda greeted them as they got off the bus. "Let the eager beavers go first. We will have toast and tea before we go. Lunch may be late." The waitress came and took their order while Frieda lit two Luckies and passed one to Musher. Steve was getting antsy and you could tell he either wanted to go ski or go back to the hotel. It did not matter to him as long as we did one or the other now. Musher told Frieda to lead they were ready now.

The three of them went down the half mile track without incident. Steve and Musher were introduced to the chair lift. Much better than holding on to a rope. One more run then on to the one mile track. Three runs on the one mile track without incident. On to the three mile track.

After the second three mile run both Steve and Musher were ready to call it day. Back at the lodge Musher had Freida take a bunch of shots of Steve and himself. There were no girls anywhere in any picture which showed Steve. Musher had a few taken with Freida. They swapped their ski togs for their own clothes and made a quick change. Musher asked the billing manager how much did he owe for himself and Steve. "There is no charge for you two gentlemen. It has already been taken care of."

Sitting in the lodge dining room eating those little sandwiches and drinking hot tea Steve reminded him the next bus to the hotel was in ten minutes. They thanked Frieda and Musher gave her a twenty dollar tip. There were kisses on the cheek and handshakes on the way to the bus. Frieda asked, "Will we see you tonight?" Musher caught the we as Steve answered, "I certainly hope so."

At the hotel Steve announced he was going to take a nap and he would like to eat dinner at the American restaurant. Musher was going to walk the town and take pictures.

Small steak smothered with fried onions, French Fries, apple pie and one cup each of real coffee. Cost for two including gratuity thirty-four dollars. Wonder what they pay to Fritz and the other "tradeable dealers"?" Back at the hotel bar they were joined by Freida and Hilda. Steve and Hilda vanished like The Phantom. It wasn't long before Musher and Frieda were in his room getting ready for a big night.

It was a night comparable to last night in every respect but one. They talked less. The highlight was the bath and after bath playing. As she was leaving Musher gave her two packs of cigarettes and twenty American dollars. She thanked him, kissed him on the cheek and whispered, "I will never forget my great American student."

Musher crawled in bed and once again fell asleep thinking of Lucy, Priscilla, Juarez, London, Ann and Frieda.

FREDDIE YOU ARE REALLY MISSING SOMETHING!

CHAPTER 137

Back To Royal Air Force Station Wyton

Steve and Musher both slept late. Late being 0800. Baggage must be in the lobby not later than 1000, check out must be completed by 1045, the bus to the aircraft will board at 1100. At 1010 their luggage was in the lobby and checkout was simple. All their expenditures in the hotel and its other attractions not advertised had been taken care of by Fritz.

They were sitting in the lobby waiting to go to the aircraft. Fritz and Frieda sat down beside them. Fritz, "My daughter and I wanted to catch you and thank you for being such excellent persons. We have enjoyed being with you and hope that maybe someday you will come back again." There were handshakes and tender kisses. Frieda exited with "Auf Wiedersehen".

Two hours later they were cruising to RAF Wyton. Steve turned to Musher, "That Hilda is something else. I haven't had sex like that since my honeymoon; and two nights in a row. I am not sure I could have withstood three nights like that. I take it Frieda was good? If she was as good at sex as she was as a ski instructor she has to be one of a kind."

Musher grinned at Steve. I&I had taken hold. He would never be the same man again. Musher thought "Maybe if I go to Juarez again I will just take him with me."

The Loadmaster announced, "Fifteen minutes to touchdown. You all know the drill. No smoking and stay buckled in your seats until the engines are shut down." The baggage was unloaded onto the ramp. Each man picked up his own luggage and boarded the bus. The bus went to the Officer BOQ first, 915th BS second, the 509th ARS third and then took the non aircrew personnel to their quarters. There is a clear picture of the difference between aircrew members and non-aircrew members.

It was just about 1600 when he was unpacked and his gear stowed. That gave him plenty of time to SSS before dinner. In a freshly washed and ironed flying suit (the laundry support on this base was superb and not expensive) he sat and had a few Luckies before dinner. Steve came and asked if he was ready for the dining hall. Musher became worried. Because he knew Steve had fucked his brains out during the I&I are they now buddies? Steve was older, higher in rank, lower in finances and a lifer. Musher needed a way to stop this friendship before it starts. How without making your NCOIC angry and willing to make your next few months miserable? "Sure Steve, let's squeet."

They sat with two other 509th ARS airmen who did not make the trip. Steve talked incessantly about his sightseeing and how he and Musher learned to ski. These airmen wanted to know about pussy not skiing. There was no pussy discussion.

CHAPTER 138
We Head For Roswell

Four days before launch of the first step towards Roswell the crew reported everything was ready. Scooters were at the designated 915th aircraft. B-4 bags would go the day before the 915th launches. The ground crew was fully briefed and ready. Everything had been checked and double checked.

Captain Lonnigan, "We will meet every morning at roll call and decide what we will do for the day. Today we will take off but will not leave the airbase. The next two days were the same as today. The fourth day, launch day was busy with an early pre-flight for a 2206 launch.

During the do nothing days Musher spent a good bit of time with Dukie. They drank cokes and talked about nothing. The final goodbye was a sad, tearful separation. Neither one believed they would ever see each other again.

As Tanker 102 took off every light in the Duke's castle was on. Musher's throat dried as they climbed and the lights from the castle faded from his view.

As dawn broke the intercom spoke. AC to crew, "We are about one hour from Lages, Azores. Everything looks good." In fifty-three minutes they were on the ground and parked on the ramp. No one said anything but everyone gave a deep sigh of relief. The AC gave the same speech, "Eat, sleep, rest and station time is 2000. Dismissed."

At 2206 Tanker 102 took off headed for Kindley AB, Bermuda. The flight was uneventful. As dawn broke the intercom spoke. AC to crew, "We are about two hours from Kindley." In two hours ten minutes they were on the ground and parked on the ramp. The AC gave the same under the wing speech, "Eat, sleep, rest and station time is 2000. Dismissed."

Tanker 102 was at its prescribed altitude and in formation with the other two tankers. Two hours into the flight the AC spoke to the crew, "We have received a change to our orders. We will not accompany the wing to Roswell. We will land at Barksdale AFB, Louisiana to top off our tanks. We will receive a flight plan there. We are going to do a refueling somewhere over the Gulf of Mexico. Navigator give me course for Barksdale and an ETA."

Navigator to AC, "Course for Barksdale 200 degrees. ETA five hours twenty-three minutes."

AC to Flight Engineer," Do we have enough fuel for Barksdale plus the mandatory reserve for an alternate?"

"Yes sir."

AC to Shakey, "Send a report to SAC Headquarters. Give them our current position, our course and ETA for Barksdale."

"Roger Sir."

AC to Navigator, "Break out the charts and make a plan for an alternate landing site."

"Roger Sir."

AC to crew, "Tell our passengers what is going on and above all relax. This is a piece of cake for this crew."

Tanker 102 landed at Barksdale four minutes earlier than its ETA. The ground crew immediately started repair of any minor non-safety discrepancies and topping off all the fuel tanks. The aircrew went to briefing. Debriefing may or may not come later. There were sandwiches and hot coffee waiting for the crew. There was a low Ten Hut as the Commander of the Strategic Air Command walked to the podium.

"Please be seated. Let me tell you what is going on. A B-29 carrying a simulated atomic bomb four hours ago left a SAC base in the most northern part of the United States. The aircraft will fly its USCM profile. That profile will put the aircraft over the Gulf of Mexico in three and one half hours from now. In our simulated test your tanker was the only one which could land here, top off tanks and rendezvous with our bomber. To make the rendezvous before the bomber runs out of fuel you will need to be off the ground in less than two hours, make great navigation moves, your radar must pick him up as quickly as possible and your crew must transfer all the fuel he can take and leave yourself enough fuel to reach a safe landing site. Your briefing data will tell you what the minimum amount of fuel the bomber must receive in order to complete his USCM. I tell you this, if there is a choice between him getting enough fuel to complete his mission and your aircraft getting safely back to a landing site, you are ordered to give him the fuel and you ditch or bail out at your discretion. *Let me repeat that:* Your briefing data will tell you what the minimum amount of fuel the bomber must receive in order to complete his USCM. I tell you this, if there is a choice between him getting enough fuel to complete his mission and your aircraft getting safely back to a landing site, you are ordered to give him the fuel and you ditch or bail out at your discretion. Is that clear?

Our capability to retaliate under adverse circumstances is being watched by the President and Congress. I have asked you to do the most difficult. I know you can do it. Your aircraft is being supplied with food and beverages.

Specialized briefings will be held next door. I expect your engines to be turning in one hour and your aircraft airborne in one hour fifteen minutes. Gentlemen, good luck."

Steve and the guys went to the aircraft and made sure when the officers stepped on board engines three and four would be running and engines one and two would be started in less than a minute. He explained to the passengers why they could not ride on this mission. Tower gave them full clearance to taxi and take off. Captain Lonnigan rolled his aircraft onto the ten thousand foot runway and pushed the throttles as far forward as they would go. Take off was smooth as was the climb out to fifteen thousand feet. The aircraft was on its prescribed course. Radar constantly swept the sky until he called, "Radar to AC. I have him on my scope. He is transmitting the correct IFF code. (IFF is a predetermined airborne radar transmission which Identifies the aircraft as Friend or Foe). You may want to try him on voice. At the same time have Shakey Morse your message to his radio operator."

"Tanker 102 to Hawker 24. Do you copy?"

"Roger Tanker 102, I read you five square."

"Hawker 24 we are coming up on your six. What is your course and altitude?"

"Tanker 102 we are a two three thousand feet on course two four zero degrees."

"Roger Hawker 24 we have you visual. We will call you when we are ready in Position 1. You may trail your dishpan whenever you are ready."

AC to crew,"Prepare for decompression. Dress out for high altitude refueling. Call when your position is ready." One by one the crew acknowledged ready for high altitude refueling. The aircraft was decompressed and Paul went back to the reel operator's platform. Paul acknowledged in position and ready. The aircraft was pressurized and the heat turned up. The refueling went smoothly. Engineer to AC, "Hawker 24 has received his needed amount plus an additional two thousand pounds. We have enough fuel to make any of our landing sites."

"Hawker 24 your tanks should be full. Please acknowledge."

"Roger Tanker 102 we are in great shape. Thank you, we owe you one. I will disconnect on my count of three; three, two, one, disconnect."

AC to Reel, "Wrap it up and get back in here. Crew standby to depressurize. Reel tell me when you are ready."

"Reel ready."

The aircraft decompresses and Paul gets into the aft compartment. The aircraft is pressurized to eight thousand feet. As usual Paul was soaking wet and changed into dry clothes as quickly as possible.

"Navigator give me course to Roswell and an ETA."

Navigator to AC, "Course 270. ETA two hours thirty minutes."

Everyone felt good, tired but good. They devoured the food and beverages Paul took a nap and he deserved it.

There was minimum conversation enroute to Roswell.

Tanker 102 aircrew was truly surprised at debriefing. The Commander of the Strategic Air Command individually greeted them with his congratulations. He toasted them with his Wild Turkey. Musher thought he could not afford to not drink it so he did. Awful stuff. The rest of debriefing did not have any luster. Musher went to his barracks and everyone else to their home.

He showered and lay in bed telling himself only forty-one days to discharge. The drive out the front gate as Mister Muscarello was only forty-one days away. Discharged and out the gate on July 3, 1950.

THE BEST
LAID
PLANS OF
MICE AND

BOOK 5

CHAPTER 139
Forty-One Days To Discharge

The wing stood down for the next three days. Musher took care of personal stuff, getting his car back from Nance at the motor pool, getting his scooter and B-4 from the 915th, and transferring his funds to a bank in Boston.

In between doing his personal stuff he made a telephone call to a number in South Texas. When the voice answered he merely said, "I am back. I will be discharged in thirty-eight days." The phone line went dead.

He had seventy-one thousand in his new Shawmut Bank account with Sweet Sister named as a co-owner of the account. He mailed Sweet Sister a simple note: "You are co-owner of account number 3087912 at the Shawmut Bank branch in Peabody. If anything should happen to me be sure to claim it. Meanwhile go there to establish your signature verification. Please feel free to use any part of it to take care of Mama. My discharge date from the USAF is this coming July 3rd."

Thirty-eight days to discharge.

At roll call this morning Walter announced, "Six aircraft and crews will go thirty days TDY to Ramey AFB, Puerto Rico to participate in a SAC exercise." He read the list of crews and one of them was Captain Lonnigan's crew, his crew. "The aircraft and crews will leave in four days. Since Sergeant Muscarello is scheduled for out-processing and discharge he is replaced on his crew by Technical Sergeant John Gandy. This personnel action is effective with this roll call. Until out-processing begins Sergeant Muscarello is assigned to squadron ops. Dismissed."

Musher attended his last crew meeting with Captain Lonnigan. Everyone told him what a good crew member he had been and how he would be missed. All he could think of was, "I will never forget old what's his name?" Captain Lonnigan and crew, including Musher's replacement, went to Tanker 102. Musher went to squadron operations. **Twenty-eight calendar days before out-processing.**

His welcome to squadron ops was not a very warm welcome. He immediately realized he was in with a group of lifers who did not really want this short-timer around. His first assignment proved he was right: Make the squadron flight pay roster. It is due in three days. For the next two and one-half days he fooled with the roster. He probably could have done it in two or three hours but what was the sense. When he finished this assignment they would give him some other menial tasks to do. No one fucked with the person doing the flight pay roster.

Musher became more and more lax. What tasks he did he did poorly and they needed to be redone. Late for duty in the morning, late coming back from lunch, leaving early every chance he could sneak out but worst of all he constantly bitched and made derogatory remarks about the office staff, the squadron operations officer, the squadron commander and the United States Air Force in general. To say the least everyone was pissed at him. Fortunately for him the Uniform Code of Military Justice governed the air force so he could not simply be busted like it was in the old Articles of War.

OUT-PROCESSING BEGINS TOMORROW
JUNE 24, 1950

There were seventeen people registered for out-processing. They were all anxiously waiting at the Separation Center. Two warrant officers, seven Master Sergeants (two of whom were WAF) and two Technical Sergeants who will process for retirement. Musher and the other five were first-hitchers eager to get out and be civilians.

The NCOIC Master Sergeant addressed the group. "Here is your schedule for the next ten days." He detailed what we could expect and just how much free time we would have. With the exception of the hospital physical and the dental physical it was all paper work until the morning of the discharge at which time finance would make final payment to each individual. Each person was given a pre-examination form to fill out for the medical and dental examinations. "When I have checked your forms you may go. Be sure to be at the hospital not later than 0800 tomorrow and at the dental clinic not later than 0800 the next day."

Musher headed for the NCO Club to play poker in whichever game there was an available seat. Every game except the big game had an available seat. Musher sat in the ten to twenty game. Ten hours later he was over one thousand dollars ahead and realized he was tired and hungry. On his way out he gave the SSA a fifty dollar tip. The dining room was about to close when his favorite waiter told him he could have anything he wanted. "Medium size, medium rare filet mignon with bearnaise, iceberg lettuce with Russian dressing and lots of hot tea."

To the barracks and to bed. Certainly don't want to be late at the hospital.

CHAPTER 140
Out-Processing "You Can't Do This To Me"

The medical examination took all morning. Musher had no signals that he might have any problems. He knew he was physically fit with no ailments. He was not restricted to the airbase so he headed to Roswell to pass the afternoon. He actually ended up in Carlsbad just south of Roswell. He visited the Carlsbad Caverns and the bat colonies therein. By time he got back to Walker AFB it was time for dinner. He had a night of playing pinochle and early to bed. Can't be late at the dental clinic.

They took the retirement candidates first. Only one dentist had been assigned to do the examinations. After the retirement candidates they took them by rank. Musher was all right there. It still took three hours before he was out of the chair with an OK.

The dining hall lunch conversation was about the North Korea attack on South Korea. "Where is South Korea?" "What do we have to do with South Korea?" "For sure there would be no need for tankers since I understand it is close to Japan and Okinawa." These were the questions of the younger members of the 509th. The veterans who had been at Tinian, Kwajalein and the Marianna Islands knew exactly where Korea was located.

It was the consensus that refueling tankers would not be stationed in the Far East. Maybe stationed in California or Hawaii to fuel the bombers during their transition to the Far East. It was all guesswork by the amateur logisticians.

NOT TO WORRY, HE WOULD BE OUT IN EIGHT DAYS.

The next morning when everyone was seated the NCOIC Master Sergeant once again addressed the group. "I have here an Executive Order from the Office of the President of the United States. It is applicable to all branches of the military service.

DUE TO THE ATTACK OF NORTH KOREA UPON SOUTH KOREA, AN ALLY OF THE UNITED STATES, THE UNITED STATES MUST HONOR ITS TREATY TO SUPPORT THE FREEDOM OF SOUTH KOREA AND ITS CITIZENS. IT IS IMPERATIVE THAT OUR MILITARY FORCES REMAIN AT THEIR PRESENT STRENGTH WHILE WE BOLSTER THEM AROUND THE WORLD. THEREFORE IT IS DECREED THAT ALL MILITARY PERSONNEL SCHEDULED FOR SEPARATION FROM ACTIVE DUTY ON OR BEFORE

DECEMBER 31, 1950 WILL HAVE SUCH SEPARATION DATE
EXTENDED ONE YEAR.

SIGNED, HARRY S. TRUMAN, COMMANDER-IN-CHIEF,
PRESIDENT OF THE UNITED STATES OF AMERICA

There were a bunch of "you must be shitting me sarge", "they cannot do
this to me. I have plans" and many more just like them. The NCOIC
instructed them to leave all their paperwork here and report to their
squadron immediately. Musher contemplated going out the gate and never
coming back. How long could he live in Mexico on seventy-thousand
dollars? When they caught him he would be like Freddie only for a much
longer term.

YOU KNOW WHAT FREDDIE, YOU MIGHT HAVE BEEN RIGHT !

He went directly to the first sergeant and asked for permission to see the
squadron commander. "Strangely enough Musher he is with the squadron
operations officer waiting for you. Get your ass down there now."

Musher entered the squadron operations officer's office and sure enough
the squadron commander was sitting there smoking a big cigar and drinking
coffee. Musher saluted and spoke, "Sir, permission to request a transfer to
another squadron."

Both officers broke out laughing. The squadron ops officer quit
laughing. "Musher let's review your military history. You joined the Army
to keep from going to jail. You couldn't hack the Army so you bailed out
into my air force. You were transferred here by someone you grossly
embarrassed at Smoky Hill. He wanted revenge so he kept you from being a
great gunner and made you a reel operator instead. Then he kept you from
being assigned to a crew. Later he committed suicide and the rumor is you
did something to cause it. You designed an improvement to the refueling
hose component and it is still being studied. You hob-nobbed with royalty
while at Wyton but never made noise about it or used it for your personal
benefit. You performed excellently until you were assigned to work in my
office. We all knew you would never be a lifer. You had us all fooled. You
showed your true colors by your behavior and disparaging remarks about
me, your squadron commander and our air force. Now you have the balls to
ask us for a favor. We are going to grant your request. Not to another
squadron, but to another wing. Our wing personnel has received a request

from the 98th Bomb Wing at Spokane, Washington for qualified B-29 RCS CFSC gunners. You certainly are that. The 98th is scheduled to leave for Okinawa and combat duty in ten days. Your orders are being cut so that you may board a transport at base operations tomorrow afternoon at 1700 bound for the 98th Bomb Wing. I would wish you luck but I would want it to be bad luck and I don't care to jinx a crew just to get your ass. Now, get the fuck out of here and don't let me see you again."

He had less than twenty-eight hours to get ready for the change of plans. He loaded his car with everything except his B-4 bag, A-3 bag and his emergency bag. He packed all the clothes he could fit in his B-4 and A-3 bags. He kept his SSS kit for his emergency bag. Everything else he loaded in his foot locker and in his car. He jumped on his scooter and headed for the motor pool. He told Nance about the changes in his plans. "Do something for me Jim get one of your guys to give us a ride to my barracks. I will explain there."

"Sell the Vesper. Take the car and sell it and everything in it. All the necessary papers are in the glove compartment. Keep your commissions and send the rest and the proceeds from the Vesper sale as an American Express money order payable to this person at this address. Can you do that for me?"

"Consider it done."

One more stop to pick up his pistols, ammunition and gun belt. It was not his intention to take them to Spokane. He would package them and mail them to Sweet Sister. He would enclose a note simply saying hold these for me. It took a while to get them from the orderly room and time to package them but with the help of a BX box and packaging service he had the package in the post office by 1700 hours. He insured the package for one thousand dollars.

Nothing left to do now but wait until the 1700 takeoff time to Spokane.

He made a phone call to South Texas. "There has been a change in plans. Because of the Koran War I am not being discharged for at least another year. I am going to a bomb group in the State of Washington and from there to combat service from Okinawa."

Time to go to the NCO Club and a few Tequila Sours.

CHAPTER 141

Goodbye 509th, Hello 98th

Waiting for 1700 hours made for a very long day. Musher went to the NCO Club to kill the day. He dabbled with pool, snooker, darts and coffee drinking. Lunch broke the monotony after which he found a big comfy chair and took a nap. He dozed and dozed until 1400. He called the motor pool and asked Jim for taxi service from the NCO Club to his orderly room to sign out and pickup paperwork, to his barracks to pick up luggage and from there to Base Operations.

"It might take thirty minutes but someone will be there for you in thirty minutes or less. Is that OK?"

"Jim thank you for everything. Maybe we will meet again some time."

In less than thirty minutes the taxi arrived. They made the prescribed trip and Musher and his luggage were standing outside Base Operations at 1615 hours. He approached the passenger service desk and presented a copy of his orders. The clerk did whatever it is clerks do. He told Musher it was a C-121 aircraft, known as the Constellation and is comparable to the civilian commercial airlines version. He instructed him to put his luggage on the cart located just through the entrance to the flight line. Musher kept his emergency bag and took a seat in the waiting area. Behold, who enters the waiting room? Technical Sergeant Melvin Tickman. Tickman came to Musher with his hand extended. "I want to apologize for my past behavior. Whatever I got I asked for. We are going the same place for the same reason. I am not sure we can ever be friends but I would like to believe we are not enemies."

Musher wondered if this is the first sign of foxhole religion. Musher rose and held out his hand. "Why not? One never knows when one needs a friend."

Until the passengers were called for boarding the two of them discussed how life had been after their incident in the ARS. On board the aircraft they sat together.

This aircraft was fully equipped for passengers. The voice system spoke, "Good evening. Welcome to MAC (Military Air Command) Flight 806 from Walker AFB to Fairchild AFB. This is Major John Walsh your Aircraft Commander. The Co-pilot is Captain Thomas Lennon, the Navigator is Captain Baxter Brewer, the Flight Engineer is Master Sergeant Thomas Zachary and the two stewardesses are Staff Sergeants Ava Guardino and

Lillian Massey. Our flight time is four hours nine minutes at an altitude of twenty-eight thousand feet. Please obey the smoking and seat belt signs. We suggest that when you are in your seat you are buckled in. Dinner will be served very shortly. Enjoy your flight." Dinner was roast beef in gravy with mashed potatoes and buttered corn kernels. The stewardesses provided coffee, tea, milk or soft drink. All this for free. Touchdown was smooth. There were two busses were waiting on the ramp, "VOQ and VAQ". "Your luggage will be delivered to your quarters."

WHAT AWAITS US AT THE 98TH?

The bus pulled up in front of a barracks. The NCO escorting the new personnel spoke, "This gentlemen will be your home while you are here. The bunks were freshly made for your arrival. There are foot lockers and butt cans in place. If you cannot lock your foot locker do not put any valuables in it. For those of you who forgot to bring a towel you many get one from the barrack chief on a loan basis. I suggest you get to sleep as quickly as you can. Wake-up tomorrow will be at 0500. We will form outside the barracks at 0530. The dining hall is a relatively short march from here. At 0635 the bus will take you to the base theatre. The Wing Commander will arrive at 0715. Goodnight gentlemen, Welcome to the 98th Bomb Wing."

Musher set his alarm for 0445 and crawled into the sack.

CHAPTER 142
Orientation, Crew Selection and Training

When the lights went on in the barracks Musher was already up, dressed and on his way to brush his teeth. Two NCO's went through the barracks gently awakening those who did not respond to the lights. Everyone was dressed and in "formation" by the designated time. The "march" was at best sloppy. Cadence was in a low voice in order to keep from disturbing the other barracks. The dining hall was typical of the dining hall in Roswell. Here they had those silently moving people who made dining a pleasure. One thing Musher noticed was that the tables were arranged to seat six, the number of enlisted men on a B-29 bomber crew. With slight modification seating could be rearranged to ten, the number of personnel on a B-29 bomber crew.

At precisely 0715 there was the command Ten Hut. A tall, skinny Brigadier General strutted to the podium. "Please be seated. My name is Zack Bryan I am the Commanding Officer of the 98th Bomb Wing. I welcome you to the wing. What we are going to do here would make any Personnel Officer cry and pull out his hair. In the front of the stage there are seven boxes or as I like to call them Grab Bags. They are marked by B-29 bomber crew position. There are thirty rows of the center section of this theatre marked with crew numbers beginning with 98-S01 and ending with 98-S30. The "S" in the crew number is because we think you are Special. On the screen behind me we shall project the in the row crew seating sequence. Since we have only one Grab Bag for gunners the Aircraft Commander and his crew will decide which gunner will take which position. Before I go any further let's do the Grab Bag and become B-29 aircrews." He walked off the stage and the crew seating sequence diagram was on the screen.

There was no control over who went to the Grab Bags first except for the people sitting in the center section who went first. When it came time for Musher to take one from the gunner's Grab Bag he pulled and looked at it. His new crew is known as 98-S22. He was the first gunner for that row. The aircraft commander and radar operator were already there. He was shocked to see Tickman enter his row and sit next to him. Neither of them spoke a word. In a matter of minutes the last two officers, the two additional gunners, the radio operator and the flight engineer were seated. Ten warm bodies will now be known as 98-S22.

A soft but distinctive Ten Hut.

BG Zack Bryan never gave a carry-on or at ease or rest. He picked up where he left off and never missed a beat. "I salute the newest thirty crews as members of the 98th Bomb Wing." He snapped a West Point salute. "Gentlemen between today and tomorrow we shall receive fifteen additional combat ready B-29s. Our newest thirty crews will be divided into fifteen units of two aircrews for each unit. Each unit will be a team taking turns to fly the aircraft. How will we determine which two teams will make a unit? The Grab Bag personnel management system worked so well we will do the same type selection process for making the two crew unit. Aircraft commanders come up and draw the number of your new team partner.

In nine days we leave for Okinawa. When we get to Okinawa we will fly a combat mission every other day for as long as the aircraft are combat ready.

Crew A flies the Day 1 mission and Crew B has a non-flying duty day.

Day 2 is non-flying duty day for both unit crews.

Crew B flies the Day 3 mission and Crew A has a non-flying duty day.

Day 4 is non-flying duty day for both unit crews.

Crew A flies the Day 5 mission and Crew B has a non-flying duty day.

Day 6 is non-flying duty day for both unit crews

The cycle is repetitive. On a thirty day schedule Crew A will fly eight times and Crew B will fly seven. Crew A will have twenty-two non-flying duty days and Crew B will have twenty-three. It will balance itself out in the next thirty day schedule.

Mind you, no crew will lose its crew integrity. It's kinda like a tag team wrestling match. Keep a rested wrestler in the ring all the time. What will we do on the non-flying duty days? I am sure there will be lots to do. I want each crew to spend the rest of the day getting to know its members. The dining halls will be open around the clock and the tables are set for ten.

Before we break up I need to tell you that it is true that some of you were not necessarily selected for this assignment because of your superior skills. I know and you know that you pissed someone off to the extent that they took the opportunity to get rid of you. Me, I am not going to lose any sleep over that. If you are smart you won't lose any sleep over it either. A lot of you are WWII combat veterans and that is enough endorsement to know that you are reliable and good at what you do. You younger guys going to combat for the first time might sound glamorous but I tell you it isn't. Learn from the guys who have been there. Pay close attention to the next statement: You have a clean slate here. I may sound like I am a forgive and forget commander but I am not. You fuckup in my wing and I will have you in the fucking stockade forever. Those of you who were close to discharge if you fuckup in the hope of being discharged your discharge will come only after you have served a good sentence in a stockade or federal prison. I am glad to have you in my wing and you have my full respect." He turned to walk off and the soft refrain of Ten Hut accompanied him followed by the command Dismissed.

My new aircraft commander gave his name as Patrick Puckett. "My friends call me Papu. It is a little early for lunch but I suggest we take advantage of the dining hall arrangement. There is a base bus stop just outside. This may not be the right route to get to a dining hall but if it isn't the route must go very close to a dining hall. We will save the "get acquainted" until we get there.

So far, so good. The new aircraft commander's first leadership act worked. The base bus stopped at a dining hall. The driver gave each of them a base bus schedule. Without his scooter and car Musher and everybody else would be dependent on the base bus service.

The dining hall was set up as General Bryan had said. Funny thing the crew members seated themselves in the order they sat in the theater. Musher told himself the ash trays on the table meant that it was OK to smoke. He lit a Luckie and left his cigarettes and Zippo on the table in front of him. From his cue others lit theirs. One of those precious silent people brought large pots of coffee and pitchers of ice water.

Captain Puckett began, "You already know my name. My nickname is Papu. I think we should have some rules for this soul bearing session. First you can tell where you call home, where your last assignment was, but it is not necessary to tell why you were selected for this assignment. It would be nice if we knew how much military service each of us has and if any of that service was in combat. I implore you to tell us what words upset you and anything else that we can do to avoid friction within the crew.

Since I am already talking I will continue. My home of record is Austin, Texas. I have been in the air force since I graduated from West Point nine years ago. During WWII I flew as a B-29 co-pilot in the Far East. I have been married but no longer am. We never had children. After the divorce I began drinking too much. I was a checked out B-29 Aircraft Commander. My flying skills began to fade because of my drinking and my crew was hesitant to fly with me. I was brought into squadron operations with some shit title job just to get me off the flight line and protect me. I know you have heard the axiom about the Long Grey Line takes care of it members. All that was three years ago. I have not had an alcoholic drink since then. You will find I am an excellent pilot and a considerate aircraft commander.

My former wing commander saw the chance to transfer me gloriously and just maybe, just maybe I would do the job well."

Next to speak was the First Lieutenant co-pilot. "My name is Charles Rowe, I am generally called Charlie. My hometown is Caribou, Maine. I was at Biggs AFB in El Paso before coming here. I have been a B-29 co-pilot for two years. I was scheduled for discharge before Truman's executive order. As of today my total military service is three years, five months and twenty-one days. I have no combat experience and certainly am not eager to get any. I was selected for this assignment because as a bachelor who absolutely loved pussy of any kind. I found some on forbidden ground. I serviced the division commander's wife. Need I say more?"

"It must be my turn. My name is Captain Winston Wong. My friends call me Wong. Yes I do like Chinese food. My hometown is San Francisco, California. I am a navigator because I flunked out of pilot school. This is my tenth year in the military. In WWII I did sixty missions as a navigator on a B-17 out of England. I am not a bad aerial gunner with the old B-17 nose mount. I have been married twice but I am not now. I have two daughters living in San Francisco. I came here from Carswell AFB, Fort Worth. Actually I volunteered to come here. I love to gamble and I had such debt among the sharks I couldn't get out of Fort Worth fast enough."

"My name is Captain Han Stein, I am known as Stiney. I am married with one son and we call our hometown Seacock, New Jersey. I was Infantry for two years and Army Air Corp for ten years and the last three in the USAF. I have more than six years combat experience. I agree with Charley I neither need nor want any more. In my wing there were six radar operators equally qualified for this assignment. The wing commander decided it would be most fair if we all cut cards and the low person would volunteer. I cut the low card. I should have told him to stick it up his ass."

"My story is not very interesting said Flight Engineer Master Sergeant Terrence Cairns. I will answer to most anything but I definitely answer to Terry. My hometown is Brize-Norton, England, United Kingdom. During WWII I was a Spitfire fighter pilot in the RAF. I am a double ace. I have much more combat experience than any one individual should have. I don't need any more but I will not run from it. I came from England and enlisted in the Army Air Corps in 1946. I was flight engineer on a B-29 crew which generally could not do something right. All the enlisted men on our crew are here. I guess the squadron felt it cleared house."

"This will be different. I am Master Sergeant Thomas Turner, most people call me Tommy. I have been in the military as an aerial gunner since February 1942. I have a home of record for record purposes only. I don't have a home town. I am not now and never have been married. I am here because I volunteered. Peacetime boredom had set in and I was going crazy with meaningless missions against phantom enemies."

"My story is not much more interesting. My name is Master Sergeant Steve Poe and I am called either Steve or Poe. I prefer Poe. There are so many things that light me up we would be here all day if I started reciting them. Let's just say I am not easy to get along with but I will certainly try. I have no combat experience. I have been in the Army Air Corps and the USAF since 1943. For all that time I have been an aerial gunner. How did I get so lucky as to get this assignment? I am a heavy card player and a damn good one. There was so much money owed to me on that air base that if I collected it all at once I would be sitting pretty. One of my leading debtors worked in wing personnel. My orders were cut and I was enroute here in less than six hours. While I was at personnel I confronted him and he responded, "All debts and friendships cancel on transfer."

"I am Technical Sergeant Melvin Tickman, most people call me Tick Tick. They say it is because they never know when I am going to explode. I come from New York City, New York. I have ten years military service as an aerial gunner, five years as a B-17 aerial gunner and five years as a B-29 waist gunner. My last assignment was a B-29 Bomb Squadron at Walker AFB, New Mexico. I was sent here because I had such a bad reputation as a griper, whiner and just a general pain in the ass. Despite my efforts to demonstrate the new me, they shipped me anyhow. As my nickname applies everything used to bother me. I have changed and rarely do I get upset."

"I am Staff Sergeant Carrington Worcester, better known as Carry. I am a great radio operator. I can send and receive over one hundred words a minute with absolute accuracy. My problem is I am clumsy. I came from a northern B-29 wing where it seemed no matter what I tried to do I fucked it up by being clumsy. My home is in Bumpass, Tennessee. This is my eighth year in the military and I do not have any combat experience. My last crew used to tease me to stay away from the gunsights before you shoot us down. I am loyal, cooperative and a team player. I ask that you help me not fuck up this team. You can guess why I was sent on this assignment."

"Last but not least. Staff Sergeant Saverio Muscarello, better known as Musher. Hometown is Boston, Massachusetts. Total military service is less than four years and no combat experience. Like Tick Tick I came from Walker AFB, New Mexico. Because of a vendetta with the wing gunnery sergeant, who I am happy to report committed suicide, I was not assigned to a bomb squadron but instead to an air refueling squadron. Since then I have been a reel operator and have not flown as an aerial gunner. The reason I am here is because from the day I started out processing for discharge I told everyone in the USAF what I thought of their service and their skills. I am one of those Hairy Ass Truman extended discharge people General Bryan was talking about earlier today."

Papu, "Those are some stories. I know this crew will get along well. Let's have lunch and we will decide what to do after that."

Lunch was eaten slowly amid innocuous conversation.

Papu began with a question, "How are we going to settle which gunner will fly in which position?" First response came from Tommy Turner, "That's easy, the most junior gunner always won the tail." The silence was tacit approval of his suggested methodology.

Musher must not let that happen. What idiot would want to be alone in that cramped space for God knows how long each mission. There was not enough room to fully stand and stretch much less alone move around. "Gentlemen I offer this for your consideration. I finished RCS CFCS school number one in my class in both shooting and gun sight maintenance. At Smoky Hill I taught classes to other gunners, both enlisted and commissioned officers on the care and maintenance of the B-29 gun sight. My squadron gunners went from an average fifty-six percent target hits per number of rounds fired to an average just under ninety percent based on the same criteria. I was promoted from airman second class to staff sergeant because of my teachings throughout all the bomb squadrons in the wing. Trust me I can make our crew's shooting results cause every other crew to take notice. Take into account where the gun sights are in our B-29. If one was to malfunction and I am in the tail there is no way I can fix it in flight. Do we put me in the tail to adhere to military tradition or do we put me in the aft compartment where I can be readily available to all gun sights except the tail. We have five firing turrets controlled by gun sights, with me available we can count on least four always working."

Tick Tick spoke up, " When Musher came to Roswell his reputation and how he made staff sergeant preceded him. I am convinced he would best serve this crew being in the aft compartment. I am not saying he should be the ring gunner because I don't know anything about that. What I am saying if you all concur I will be the tail gunner for this crew."

Papu, "Let me say this about that. Musher your logic is good providing you are what you say you are. If it turns out that you are not there is a lot of water between Okinawa and North Korea and all I can say to you is "How long can you tread water ?" As for you Tick Tick that is true crew spirit. I and the rest of the crew appreciate it. Tommy, Stovepipe, who has the most experience as a ring gunner?"

Stovepipe, "I have none."

Tommy, "I have a little over two years."

Papu, "That's settled. Easy wasn't it? It has been a long day. I am going to the Q to nap before dinner. You all might consider doing the same. We will meet here for breakfast at 0615. Enjoy the rest of the day."

What a crew. A reformed drunk called Papu. A co-pilot named Charlie whose goal in life was to fuck every skirt he ever came across. A navigator known as Wong who is a frustrated pilot with a losing gambling habit so strong he volunteers to go to combat to get away from the sharks he owed his soul to. A radar operator called Stiney not Stoney who was conned by his wing commander to volunteer for this assignment. A flight engineer called Terry who was here because he was on a fuckup crew on his last base. He is a cross over from the RAF where he was a double ace fighter pilot in the Battle of Britain. A radio operator called Carry who couldn't carry a bucket half full of sand without spilling the entire bucket. One gunner called Tommy who actually volunteered because he likes combat duty, Another gunner name Poe who devotes his life to winning at gambling games. He was shanghaied here by a personnel sergeant who owed him a lot, of money. A third gunner called Tick Tick. He is a Born Again Christian who was sent to this assignment because before he became a Born Again he was the biggest whiner, complainer and pain-in-the-ass in his previous wing. The fourth gunner is called Musher. He is here only because of an executive order.

Musher took the first letter of each crew member's calling name: PCWSTCTPTM. Not one single vowel. That definitely is not a good sign.

CHAPTER 143
The Other Member of Our Team

Musher had a terrible time sleeping last night. The first letter of the calling name for each of the crew members haunted the deep recesses of his mind. PCWSTCTPTM, not a single vowel, which was not a good sign. There must be a way to describe this crew using those letters and turn it into a truthful, good sign. He tried many scrambled versions of PCWSTCTPTM until it fell into place. He juggled the letters to *PTWCMCTPS*. The description followed:

*P*ROBABLY *T*HE *W*ORST *C*OMPLETELY *M*ESSED-UP *C*REW *T*RYING HARD AND *P*RAYING FOR *S*URVIVAL.

Musher went to the dining hall feeling much better than the night before. Wing Commander Bryan outdid himself again. The tables were set for twenty, the team crew numbers were displayed on the tables and the chairs were marked so that each crew member sat next to his counterpart on the other crew of the team. Again the Wing Commander showed one of the signs of great leadership, none of the seat markings said "Crew A" or "Crew B" in reference to the two crews. They were marked Papu or Mickey, the other crew's aircraft commander. When all the team members were seated Musher was pleased to see Papu take the lead. "Let's go once around the table with each of giving his rank and name and what name he would like to be called. Certainly none of us will remember them all but it will help until we spend more time together." Breakfast was a lot of gabbing about sports, home towns, past times and of course women and girls. Charlie reminded them all that there is a major difference between women and girls.

As the crews filed into the base theatre for briefing Musher realized that there was probably no end to the wisdom of this wing commander. At each crew position there was a brand new flying suit with the trimmings of Musher's fancy flying suit. The leather patch with the aviation badge, the leather rank and name tag on the left breast side, the SAC emblem on the right shoulder and the 98th Bomb Wing emblem on the left shoulder. For the creme de la creme, sitting on top of the flying suit was a scarlet red hat with 98-S22, his crew number, embroidered on the crown.

Moments later, to a soft Ten-Hut, in walked Brigardier General Zack Bryan. Musher's vote for President of the United States. "I trust you are more relaxed today than yesterday. Don't get too relaxed we are only eight days away from our launch to Okinawa. Gentlemen I would appreciate it if when we leave this theatre each of you changes into his newest flying suit and hat. It is my wish that whenever you are on the ground you will wear what I call a dress flying suit and your crew designator hat. I am sure you noticed in the dining hall this morning we did not attempt to designate a crew identifier for each crew of its team. When you are dismissed from here today I expect each aircraft commander and his crew to use whatever method they choose to identify Crew A from Crew B. I am sure you understand that we have named the crew teams from one to fifteen. We need the A and B for scheduling and we need it by the end of the day. Our Wing Logistics Officer's staff will contact you today for your decisions.

This morning and from just about now on I expect the two crews to be like Siamese twins. We will not change billeting here because of the short time we will be here. Each aircraft commander must know what is happening with his counterpart on the team. A listing of the team matchups, team designators and team personnel will be given to you as you leave the theatre. All fifteen of the newest B-29 additions to the wing have arrived. Each team's primary aircraft assignment will also be shown on that same list. I suggest (in the military that is the same as an order) that when we leave we take the busses that are outside and go to visit our primary aircraft and meet the crew chief and his ground crew. The aircraft call signs are "NEWGUY SUGAR 01" thru "NEWGUY SUGAR 15". That along with the crew chief's name will also be shown on that same list.

There will not be a morning meeting tomorrow. Instead we shall meet at 1330 here. I suggest your team spend the morning with the crew chief." As he walked away came the gentle "Ten Hut" followed by "Dismissed."

The list was most comprehensive. Aboard the bus Mickey said, "Why don't we get our A and B designation now?"

Poe popped in, "Cut the cards, high card chooses A or B." With that he pulled a deck from his flying suit. One of Mickey's gunners named Flip said, "If my aircraft commander agrees we will cut but we will use my deck. Let your junior gunner shuffle and cut for you and I will cut for us. Is that agreeable to all?" No one spoke against it.

Musher took the cards and they were marked by a real amateur. It is important that Flip cut first. Musher placed two Aces, a King, and a Queen where he could easily find them. As an additional safety precaution he palmed another Ace. Flip spread the cards Las Vegas style. It allowed him to read his amateur markings. He slipped a card out and it was a King. He smiled broadly and thought to himself the odds against this boob are seven

466

to one for a win or tie, and thirteen to one for a win. Musher could not risk misreading the amateur markings so he took his security blanket palmed Ace, made the motions of a pick from the cards and turned the Ace up. "It's your choice Captain Puckett."

Grinning inside and not wanting to be a smart-ass, he calmly said, "We'll take A."

The bus pulled up to aircraft "New Guy 13". BG Bryan's ops people named the aircraft the same way they named the teams. Add the last two digits of the two crew numbers and divide by two. Crew 98-S04 and Crew 98-S22 became Team 13 ergo the aircraft call sign NEW GUY 13. Not very scientific but for a special bunch of aircraft it was novel.

The crew chief, Master Sergeant Arthur Rizzuto and his ground crew of eight were lined up under the left wing. One by one both aircrews went down the line introducing themselves to Rizzuto and Company. The flight engineers went with Rizzuto to check the Form F and all the maintenance records. Rizzuto told the aircraft commanders that sometime today a paint crew was coming out to paint a large "S" on the vertical stabilizer. The other crew members checked their individual battle stations and every other aspect of the physical aircraft. It became evident why the wing commander scheduled tomorrow's crew meeting at 1330. The morning would be spent ground checking the aircraft. The last thing Rizzuto said to the crews as they were loading the bus to go back in, "See you at 0730 tomorrow."

After dinner Musher was sitting on the barracks steps when Poe sidled up. "Got a spare smoke and light?" Musher handed him both. "You're pretty good Musher. I can't swear that you had that ace palmed but if the truth were known I am sure I would be right. Do you want to share a confidence with me? Together we could clean out Okinawa."

"Poe, I wish I had that kind of talent. Unfortunately I do not."

CHAPTER 144
The Gunners Have An Agreement of Their Own

While shaving Musher positioned himself beside Tommy. "Tommy may I offer a suggestion?"

"Feel free Musher."

"Today when we are checking out the aircraft to have eight gunners checking the gun sights would be a cluster fuck. You might consider appointing one of your gunners, namely me, and they appoint one of theirs then the two of us could check out the gun sights and each others capability. Granted we would always calibrate ours before a mission but we want them to shoot well so the team is respected."

"Let me think about that."

At breakfast the two air crews were at the same table sitting in the same chairs. Tommy, Papu's ring gunner rose to speak. "Having eight gunners aboard the aircraft checking the gun sights would be a cluster fuck. I suggest each aircraft commander appoint one gunner from his crew to check and calibrate the gun sights. On our scheduled day to fly each crew will check the sights during its normal preflight."

Both aircraft commanders concurred. Papu designated Musher and Mickey designated Flip. Both aircraft commanders thanked Tommy for his good idea.

At the aircraft the other position players checked out their equipment. The engineers were busy with their extensive pre-takeoff check lists. While the engines were running the other gunners and the navigator/bombardier checked the bomb bays and the bomb racks. Musher and Flip started with the tail mount. Flip went first. He calibrated without a jeweler's case. His work was pathetically off. After his calibration Musher invited him to see the reticle follow the gun sight with the action switch closed. Flip made no comment as they went into the aft compartment

"Where did you get those fancy tools?"

"It's called a jeweler's case and has delicate screwdrivers and smaller wrenches which allow much more precise calibration than the bare hands. Try the left waist with your hands and take a good look at your reticle. Then I will use the fancy tools and we both will look at the reticle position and behavior."

Flip was impressed with the difference in their results. Musher suggested Flip watch over his shoulder as he did the right waist. Musher talked through every step as if he were back in the classroom teaching the gun sight. The calibration was flawless. Musher suggested Flip do the Ring position. He did a fair job but his hands were not accustomed to the small soft turns which affected the reticle. Musher finished the calibration and posed a move thru the tunnel to the forward gun sight.

It had been some time since Musher crawled through the tunnel. Without a chute it was a piece of cake. Flip went first on the gun sight and he had improved since his last adjustment. Musher put the gun sight at zero and ready to accurately fire at bandits.

They wouldn't be able to leave the aircraft until all the engines were shut down so they crawled aft through the tunnel. Sitting by the back hatch Flip said to Musher," Let's make a deal. Until I can get my own you lend me your jeweler's case. You monitor my pre-flight of the sights to zero until you are confident that I can do it alone. This must be a deal between you and me not to be shared with anyone else. If you agree in return I shall teach you many, many things about playing winning cards. You out drew me on a thirteen to one odds bet. Luck is fine except that some time it is too critical to leave to chance. Do we have a deal?"

"We do if you promise not to use any of your winning ways when you play poker or any other card games with Poe, Wang or any other member of my crew, including me."

They shook hands for the deal. Musher no more believed this cheap hustler would keep his word than the man in the moon is made of cheese. Still if he didn't keep his word Musher would break him of playing cards ever again. From Fanucci, "You can fool me once, shame on you, if you fool me twice, shame on me."

Engine shutdown came and everyone piled out of the aircraft to assemble under the left wing. Each pair reported their findings during the inspections. No one reported anything significantly wrong.

Time for lunch and the wing commander's meeting at 1330.

At precisely 1330 hours General Bryan walked on the stage to the quiet Ten-Hut. He walked to the podium and said, "You gentlemen are a beautiful sight. Thirty of the finest B-29 combat crews in the Strategic Air Command. Please be seated and report."

From the first row we could hear, "Sir Aircraft Commander, Flight A, Team 9. There are no difficulties with New Guy 09 and Crew 98-S1 is ready and standing by for your orders." "Sir Aircraft Commander, Flight B, Team 9. There are no difficulties with New Guy 09 and Crew 98-S17 is ready and standing by for your orders." With the exception of one aircraft which had a safety of flight item all the reports from the floor were the same.

"Gentlemen I am so pleased. Tomorrow we shall fly a two hour sortie with each crew handling the aircraft for one hour. The aircraft commanders shall control who flies the first hour and who flies the second. You are a team and so far you have resolved any questions among yourselves without any interference from me or any member of my staff. Each crew will do two touchdown go arounds. Which ever crew makes the take off the other shall make the last landing. Navigators and Radar Operators will enter simulated course changes in their flight log, and insure the IFF is squawking correctly. Radio you will make traffic with the airbase ground station. We shall load the gun turrets with four hundred rounds of caliber 50 ammunition for short burst firing by each of the gunners. There is going to be a lot of traffic in the local area so everyone keep on your toes, stay on your prescribed course and above all listen to the tower. Takeoffs will begin at 1200 hours. I know you will do a good job." He exited to the soft Ten Hut followed by "Dismissed."

Before they left their row Papu said to Terry, "I want an A-3 Bag check and make sure everyone has everything. Do that when we part today."

Outside Mickey said, "Breakfast at 0530. Any questions? See you all at breakfast."

At the barracks Terry did his A-3 Bag inspection. Everyone was properly equipped.

Dinner, rest and sleep. 0430 will come early.

CHAPTER 145

Our First Flight As a Crew and a Team

Thanks to Musher's alarm he was up, dressed, had his A-3 Bag on the crew bus and had finished breakfast by 0530. While the others came in and ate he drank coffee, smoked Lucky Strikes and listened to the table talk. At 0600 Mickey spoke,"Papu and I have agreed the two radio operators will be responsible for getting and checking the parachutes If they want you to sign for them, sign for them. If we use all the chutes your signature won't mean much; and, if we don't use them they will be returned. The ground crew has put some coffee and water aboard the aircraft. Musher thought to himself I am glad my emergency bag with cookies, candy and coke is in my A-3 bag. The preflight was thorough especially since there was two of each position making the pre-flight checks.

"Tower 98 to B-29 S-13."

"S-13 Go ahead Tower."

"You are cleared to take position number four for takeoff. Hold just short of the runway until Tower gives the roll clearance." Papu Puckett's crew perked up and their intercom reports and discipline was exemplary.

"Roger Tower standing by for roll instruction." Puckett had made the take-off which means Mickey would make the landing. Puckett came on the intercom "This flight will be at eight thousand five hundred feet. Oxygen will not be required but we will do an oxygen drill prior to landing. When we reach our altitude we will let the gunners fire three short test bursts. Navigator, Radar and Radio you may begin your logs and activities now." Tick Tick had turned off the APU and was settled in the tail mount. Tommy was in the barber chair.

AC to crew,"Combat check." One by one the crew responded "Ready Sir." At eighty five hundred feet the AC gave the gunners permission to fire three short bursts using the RCS CFSC. All turrets fired without incident. AC to crew, "Time to transition to Mickey's crew."

It didn't take long for Mickey's crew to get in position and report combat ready. Mickey gave the gunners permission to fire three short bursts using the RCS CFSC. The lower aft turret jammed and would not fire. AC to crew, "Time to transition to Papu's crew."

"AC to Navigator give me a course for a straight in approach to home. The active runway is 9R. Crew pay extra attention there is lots of traffic up here so keep your eyes moving. We are going to make two touchdown go arounds before Mickey and his bunch make their two and they will do the final landing, The touch and go landings went very, very smoothly. The crew coordination was as if they had been flying together for years.

Mickey's last phase of the mission went just as smoothly. If you did not know better you would swear there was only one crew on that aircraft. At the blocks both flight engineers went to see the crew chief about some red diagonals (things which need repair but do not jeopardize safety of flight). All the gunners headed for the jammed turret. When the aerodynamic cover was removed it was found that a cartridge belt link had traveled in a direction not prescribed and caused the turret to jam. Nothing could be done in the aircraft to prevent this mishap or fix it. The link may have been out of alignment when the ammo was loaded into the can. The loaders will need to pay more attention to this possibility.

Debriefing was followed by lunch and a meeting with the Wing Commander at 1330 hours. The usual soft Ten Hut as BG Bryan walked to the podium. "Seems everything went well this morning we didn't shoot down any of our aircraft and no one made a crash landing. Again I am pleased. Tomorrow we will do some formation flying. The first group of fifteen will takeoff at 0800 tomorrow for a two hour sortie. The second group will go 1200 hours. As usual you decide who will fly first and who will fly second. All I know is that at 0500 there will be fifteen crews in the briefing room ready to fly. I will lead the formation myself." The usual soft Ten-Hut as he left the stage followed by "Dismissed".

Papu said to Mickey, "Should we take the guys and go pre-flight now?"

"That won't be necessary After all Papu formation flying is singularly a test of pilot skills. We just got off a good aircraft. Let's enjoy the afternoon and you guys can sleep in tomorrow morning."

CHAPTER 146

We Are Ready For a Bomb Run

Mickey and Papu did well in their formation flying exercise. Of course no formation leader would ever not repeatedly say to the aircraft commanders, "Bring it in. The strength of our guns lies with the tightness of our formation. Bring it in, bring it in." Debriefing was for the crew but only the aircraft commander had anything to say. Privately Papu would speak to his crew about being part of the formation flying.

At debriefing the crews were told to meet with the wing commander at 0900 tomorrow.

At 0900 BG Bryan began. "Yesterdays's formation flying was fairly good. My deputy led the second element and he pretty much felt the way I did. In combat it is most important because without the protection of our guns we are unprotected. Hopefully we would have fighter escort to and from the target but I would not bet on it.

Today we will stand down. Tomorrow we are going to make a bomb run on a bombing practice range in Montana. The range is situated in a valley and the two observation posts are well out of the way for even the worst bomb releases. They are high above the valley sitting on a mountain top. Each aircraft will be loaded with two two hundred fifty pound practice smoke bombs. Each crew will make two passes at two different targets on the range. Flight leaders will be designated at full briefing. The aircraft will go across the target in trail. Spacing will be three minutes apart. The first run will be visual Bomb/Nav from eighteen thousand feet. The IP (Initial Point to begin the attack) and both visual and radar pictures will be given at today's briefing. The second run will be Radar from twenty-two thousand feet. These scores coupled with all your other exercises will determine which crews are combat ready and which crews are not.

As for the crews which will not fly on Day 1 they will spend the day in the classroom learning as much about the North Korean culture and language as possible. On Day 2 day the crew which had flown on Day 1 would devote its day in a classroom learning as much as possible about the North Korean culture and language as possible. The crew which will fly on Day 3 will devote its morning to North Korean culture and language class and its afternoon to pre-flight. Day 4 when neither of the crews is flying the crews will devote themselves to learning the North Korean culture and language. Does this sound like the every other day team flying concept we

473

will employ in Okinawa? Now those crews which are going to fly on Day 1 get yourselves off to briefing. Those crews which are not flying on Day 1 stay put and you will receive further instructions." To the soft Ten-Hut he left the stage.

The audio-visual people moved everyone to the center section, started a slide projector and for the next hour talked about North Korea.

CHAPTER 147

We Are Ready For Combat,
Okinawa Here We Come

It has been three days since the bombing runs. Just about everybody is absolutely full of North Korean culture and language. Most of us aren't sure if we learned anything. We are all sure we don't want to have to use the language. Maybe General Bryan will have something interesting today. The soft Ten Hut sounded and the General appeared.

"I know you all have been anxiously waiting for the bomb run results. At the end of this meeting each aircraft commander will be given the results for his crew and every other crew which participated. Let me just brag about you all. Thirty visual drops, twenty-six shacks (a shack is a dead on bullseye). The four measured CEP were 0, 0, 2 and 3. (CEP = Circular Error of Probability. It is expressed as a number from zero to one hundred. Zero means the bomb just barely missed a shack and one hundred means the bomb should not have left the aircraft. Any score below 5 is considered excellent bombing.) The thirty radar drops were all shacks. I challenge any thirty B-29s to meet those results. You are entitled to burst with pride.

Gentlemen you are ready. Three days from today our fifteen aircraft and thirty crews will leave for Okinawa. We will stop at Hickam AFB, Hawaii just long enough to top the tanks and bring on fresh coffee and water. The next stop will be Anderson AFB, Guam in the Marianna Islands. We will only be there long enough to top the tanks and take on fresh coffee and water. Our final stop will be Kadena Air Base, Okinawa. With two crews aboard there is no reason we cannot do this with little or no difficulty. By the end of the day give my Chief of Operations which crew of each team will make the takeoffs and landings. We will combat load each turret. One never knows. In addition to the two crews you will have the crew chief and four of his mechanics on board.

Today is Thursday. We launch on Sunday. We will launch in three flights. Launch times will be posted later today. As of now everyone is restricted to the air base. No alcohol beverages until we reach Okinawa. General mission briefing is at 1300 tomorrow. The Specialized mission briefing will be immediately following the general briefing. Take the rest of today and until the general briefing tomorrow to make sure your crew including your ground crew is totally ready for this move. Saturday we preflight, load the aircraft and catch up on the things we may have to finish. Sunday's first station time for launch will be 0500

The Team assembled in the dining hall. "Here's the setup" said Mickey. "Papu and crew will make the takeoff from here. Me and mine will make the landing at Hickam. We will also make the takeoff from there. Half way to Guam we will change crews and Papu and his crew will finish the leg and make the landing at Anderson. They will also make the final stage takeoff to Okinawa. Me and mine will make the landing at Kadena."

Papu added, "Mickey and I shall want the gun positions manned at all times. This may be another faint sign that Papu Puckett is the Alpha dog on this team. "We don't care how often you all change gunners but the guns must be manned at all times Here's another thought for you guys with a tape worm. Stock up your A-3 Bag with goodies for the flight. You heard the old man, top off the tanks and go. Let's be sharp all the way."

Sunday came and Musher's crew was scheduled as the first aircraft in the last flight of five with a takeoff time of 1222 hours. Another good sign. His crew number was 98-S22 and the take off was 22 minutes after 12 noon. It is often said among flyboys that the two most dangerous times in any aircraft are the take off and the landing. This takeoff was great. Cruising altitude was eight thousand five hundred feet. They were the low flight in the formation. If bandits did attack they would mostly likely come from above and his crew would have some warning.

Midway between Fairchild and Hickam Mickey's crew took control of the aircraft. Papu's gunners who had just been relieved found a vacant spot, stretched out and went to sleep. As far as he could tell the ground crew had been asleep since the aircraft leveled off. Mickey made a "glass of water" landing. (Pilots would place a full glass of water on the console by the throttles and bet whether it would be spilled at touchdown) By the time the last aircraft in the fifteen aircraft flight was parked and chocked the refueling tankers were just about finishing the first five B-29s to land. People were scurrying in every direction to get ready to launch. General Bryan wanted these aircraft enroute to Guam in less than two hours after the last of the fifteen made touchdown. The slowest part of the whole exercise was the number of guys who ran to the edge of the grass to piss, officers and airmen alike.

The aircraft and the crews were ready in one hour ten minutes. The real thanks goes to the refueling truckers and the ground crew for each aircraft. An orange flare burst overhead. Papu, "Saddle up. It's time to ride". They boarded and were positioned in record time. Most of Papu's crew was without a headset so Flip relayed the messages from Mickey to Tower and

476

the Tower to Mickey. Everything went off without incident. When NEW GUY 13 was in its formation position it was time for some nourishment. Most everybody had taken Papu's advice on the goodies in the A-3 Bag. A couple of the ground crew airmen did not have any goodies so Musher gave them each a couple of candy bars and a coke. Two Lucky Strikes after the caloric intake Musher was sound asleep only to be awakened with "time for a crew change." As they say in the medical field "the transition was unremarkable."

Papu's landing at Anderson AFB, Guam was every bit as good as Mickey's in Hawaii. A sort of pride filled Musher's chest. The same hustle and bustle energies existed on Guam just as they did in Hawaii. The orange flare burst overhead. Papu again, "Saddle up. It's time to ride". They boarded and were positioned even quicker than Hawaii. Most of Mickey's crew was without a headset so Tommy relayed the messages from Papu to Tower and the Tower to Papu.

About three hours into the flight the intercom came alive, "Left waist to AC and Flight Engineer. Sir Number 2 engine is belching black smoke and fire from the nacelles."

Papu, "What do you think Terry?"

"Feather number 2 and I will expend the fire bottles."

AC, "Feathering Number 2."

Terry, "Fire bottles expended. Gauges show no fire in the engine. Left waist is it clearing up?"

"Roger the propeller is feathered and there is no sign of fire from the engine."

Flight engineer to AC, "I have balanced the power on the remaining three engines. This baby will do well in flight on just three engines. She can do well in flight on just two engines."

The intercom went silent but there was a lot of chattering in both the forward and aft compartments. Papu spoke to Mickey. "Tell me my man, how much three engine time do you have and how many three maybe two engine landings?"

"About five hours three engine time when I was a co-pilot. No three engine or two engine landings."

"Mick, I have at least twenty three engine landings and I too have no two engine landings. I know that in transition training everyone practices three engine landings but the difference is the fourth engine is available if the landing does not seem right. Here we do not have such a luxury. One shot, no go around power, land or crash. I ask that you let me and my crew finish this leg into Okinawa. I would ask you to sit as co-pilot but as you know the duties are no different than for a regular landing except the AC gets more gauge readings about the aircraft."

"You need not ask. Once I knew of your experience background I probably would have suggested such action myself. I will tell my crew individually. When I am finished I will come back here and if you don't object I will ride the idiot seat (a small seat mounted just aft between the AC and Co-pilot which can be activated for an observer.)"

Papu to crew, listen in, "New Guy 13 to formation leader."

"Go ahead New Guy 13. I read you five square."

"We have lost number 2 engine to a possible fire. It is feathered and shut down. There is no indication that the fire was not extinguished using the engine mounted fire bottles. We are able to maintain our air speed and altitude without difficulty. Over."

"New Guy 13 I want SAC and the 98th advised of your status and I want position reports to SAC and the 98th every fifteen minutes. I want oral reports from you every fifteen minutes. Do you copy?"

"Copy. One last thing, we were to have changed crews for the last leg and landing in Okinawa. Captain O'Ryan and I compared experience with three engines and concluded that I and my crew will fly the entire leg and make the landing at Kadena. Over"

"Be sure to include that in your initial report to SAC and the 98th. Do you copy?"

"Copied, Roger and Out."

AC to crew,"You heard, we shall not make a crew change on this leg. We will stay until the aircraft is on the blocks at Kadena. For those of you who have never made a B-29 three engine landing the procedures are basically the same as any other B-29 landing except it puts a greater test on the AC's skill. I have made at least twenty three engine landings during my B-29 career. When we first met I told you I was a good pilot. Today I shall prove that to you. Stay as calm as possible and try to keep others that same way." No doubt, Papu is the Alpha Dog on this team.

As they approached Kadena Papu declared an emergency. Kadena already knew of our situation. Papu wanted a straight in approach off the ocean. Tower agreed and gave all the particulars regarding the landing runway, the weather, wind and would have all the crash equipment in position. The day could not have been more clear if it had been painted by Norman Rockwell. The wings rocked a little bit during descent but other than that Papu's landing might have spilled a drop or two from the glass but certainly not the whole glass.

As quickly as the aircraft could stop on the runway the Fire Department attacked the number 2 engine to be sure no fire ignited again. The crews and passengers left the aircraft quickly and boarded waiting trucks. The trucks pulled away to a safe distance. Musher could not wait to light up a Lucky. The first one tasted so good he had another.

When all the crash crews were confident that no danger existed New Guy 13 was hooked to a tow vehicle and parked in a revetment at the far end of the parking area. The crews followed and unloaded the aircraft onto waiting six-by's. The crew chief and his guys stayed with New Guy 13 to totally assess the damage and make sure he was treated right after a very long haul to this strange air base.

At debriefing a double ration of Wild Turkey was presented to each crew member. As usual Musher gave his to the other gunners. Papu gave his to the other officers on our crew. Amazingly enough both crews were behaving like the fire and the three engine episode was like an every day occurrence. They were the last to finish debriefing and the last to be seated in the general briefing room. There was that soft distinctive Ten Hut and General Bryan walked to the podium.

"You are to be congratulated. You have set a new record for ferrying combat aircraft and combat crews for a distance more than ten thousand miles. Right now the Director of Maintenance and his staff are selecting which aircraft could be ready to fly a combat mission tomorrow. We want to put up eight, two flights of four. We know that any crew in this room could fly the mission. Tomorrow is the final step to this move. A combat mission putting live bombs on enemy targets

It is 1040 hours local time. Right now get to the dining hall and eat. Your luggage will be at your living quarters. Each "hooch" will quarter the enlisted men of the team and another "hooch" will quarter the officers. The two living quarters will be side by side in the aircrew area. After eating I want each of you to get a minimum ten hours rest whether it be all sleep or a combination of loafing and sleeping. Ten hours rest. We will meet here again at 0100 hours. Come ready to fly if your aircraft is selected for the mission.

One last item, a special congratulations to Team 13 for the demonstration of flying it gave us all today." There was that soft distinctive Ten Hut as General Bryan walked off the stage. As usual it was followed by "Dismissed."

CHAPTER 148

We Are At War and Today Proves It

A midnight snack and in your seat at 0045 hours. The soft Ten-Hut accompanied General Bryan on to the stage. "Gentlemen please be seated. You all are looking fresh as a daisy. Our maintenance people are able to put thirteen of the fifteen aircraft in our unit available for combat duty today. My Director of Operations Colonel Vincent Jackson will read the list of aircraft selected the crews to fly them and the take-off time. All the gunners on one of the teams seems to have a stomach virus worst than malaria."

Before the General could say any more Master Sergeant Tommy Turner was on his feet speaking loudly enough for everyone to hear him. "Sir, my crew is not listed to fly this mission. I am the senior gunner of Crew 98-S13 and we would consider it an honor if me and the gunners from my crew could fill those vacancies for this mission."

"Great spirit Master Sergeant Turner. You and your gunners get with the aircraft commander of Unit A for New Guy 6. We will break for the general and specialized briefings." He left to the soft Ten-Hut.

Tommy, Poe, Tick Tick and Musher filled the row of Crew 98-S05. The aircraft commander said, "Let's listen and we will do the intros later."

The general briefing began.

"This mission will be the first to strike the North Koreans in their own back yard. The primary target is a fuel storage facility named "*Tuel Olc Tuel.*" It is written in Korean phonetics and means 252.

The secondary target is another fuel storage facility named "*Ahope Tuel Tuel.*" It is written in Korean phonetics and means 922.

The total time to target and return is approximately eleven hours.

Navigators/Bombardiers and Radar will get better information at their specialized briefings. Bombing will not be a "toggle drop." In a toggle drop the lead bombardier calls all the moves and all the aircraft release on his command. Of the four aircraft in each flight two will be loaded with five hundred pound general purpose bombs and two will be loaded with incendiary bombs.

Radio verify your code pad for today.

Gunners you can expect to see Russian MIG-17's flown by Russian pilots.

The weather is good both ways. Let's break for specialized briefings."

The officers went to specialized briefings and the enlisted men to the aircraft New Guy 06. Musher zeroed all the gun sights. Tommy, Poe and Tick Tick made sure the A&E (Armament and Electronics) people had properly filled and properly loaded the ammo cans in the turrets. The ground crew assisted in loading the A-3 Bags at the correct positions. Water and food was aboard and checked to make sure there was enough for a full crew on this long a mission. Musher still had his emergency bag in his A-3 Bag. The parachutes were lined up under the left wing awaiting the rest of Crew 98-S05. So far it was no different than any other training mission.

The crew arrived and the aircraft commander spoke. "Today is a historic day for us. Not only will we make the first strike in the enemy's homeland but we have been designated as the formation leader for the two flights. I know we are up to it. Our thanks to the gentlemen who are filling for our sick gunners today. As you can guess I am the aircraft commander Major Alan Hammer and called "Red Ryder". The co-pilot is Captain Bobby Joe Williams and called "Wampum". The navigator/bombardier is Captain Steven Libertore called "Stargazer". The radar operator is Captain Dean Withers called "Lookng Glass". The flight engineer is Master Sergeant Fritz Gunther called "Firemaker". The radio operator is Technical Sergeant T.J. Gaff called "Smokemaker". Gentlemen please introduce yourselves." The four temporary gunners went through the same individual definition as the aircraft commander.

"Firemaker" reported everything was ready. The group stepped away for a smoke and very shortly the orange flare lit up the sky.

"New Guy 06 to sortie special. Confirm when ready for taxi and takeoff." One by one the individual readiness was confirmed. "Tower this is New Guy 06 with a flight of eight ready to roll."

"Roger New Guy 06 and Tower gave all the takeoff data. You and your flight are cleared to proceed as numbers 1 through 8 for taxi and takeoff. Good luck New Guy."

"Roger Tower. New Guy leader to New Guy flight. I am rolling keep your interval." With that the brakes were released and New Guy 06 rolled and made its takeoff. The flight followed at correct interval. When the last of the eight had joined the formation the formation took its course to the target. Enroute the guns were test fired without difficulty from any formation member. So far it was still just like a training exercise.

About five hours into the flight Red Ryder broke the silence. "New Guy Leader to formation. Get alert, we are entering the fighter aircraft coverage zone. Let's tighten up the formation, bring it in, bring it in."

Musher still remembered being caught off guard once before and swore it would never happen again. He closed the action switch and watched the sky. From somewhere in the formation, "bandits at one o'clock high and diving". From the barber chair Tommy took the upper forward turret and gave Musher the upper aft. Musher kept the reticle on his attacker and finally fired three short bursts. Before his very eyes the fighter aircraft disintegrated. There was no possibility that the pilot got out. Tommy cheered, "Scratch one for Musher." The chatter from the flight aircraft, "I got that one", "Watch your six. Watch your six" and "My God New Guy 03 is smoking and on fire. I see chutes opening but I can't count them, Oh My God she blew up."

Red Ryder's soothing voice came into play, "Settle down, settle down, tighten the formation, bring it in, bring it in." Just as suddenly as the bandit attack began it ended. Red Ryder again, "Be alert we are in the flak zone. First flight climb five hundred feet, second flight drop five hundred feet. Alternate from climb to drop and we learned in evasive action formation flying. Repeat this pattern until I give you new orders. Stargazer how far to target?"

"Fifty-five seconds to IP, one minute twelve seconds to target."

New Guy Leader to New Guys, "It will be all over in less than a minute and a half. Be sure of your target before release."

New Guy 08 to New Guy Leader,"I'm hit and having aircraft control. Permission to break off."

"Negative New Guy 08 there are less than twenty-five seconds to bomb release. If your aircraft is not steady for release do a toggle release with my bombardier. Do you copy? Stargazer oral count your release sequence for those who may need to toggle."

"Bomb bay doors open. Release on one. Begin the count down now. Three, two, bombs away. Close bomb bay doors. Red Ryder let's hit the trail for the reservation."

There would be no more combat on the ride back to Okinawa. With the exception of Smokemaker who after filing strike reports became violently ill the lunches were consumed like no one had ever eaten before.

The airwaves suddenly became full of inter-aircraft chatter about the strike. Red Ryder again, "Gentlemen please, no conversations until debriefing. Thank you."

Musher wasn't sure how he felt. He didn't recall being scared during the bandit attack. Was it because he was too busy fighting bandits? After all he did get one confirmed kill. During the flak attack he could hardly bring himself to look out his blister to monitor his side of the aircraft. Definitely during the bomb run being totally inactive brought on the internal tremors of fear. Now that it was over and he had eaten a good lunch and smoked four Lucky Strikes he felt calm but not necessarily ready to go through this again. The worst part was that he knew he would go through it again and again if he stayed lucky

General Bryan was waiting at debriefing. He was showing strike photos taken by a reconnaissance fighter aircraft just following the attack. The target was obliterated. He stood in the middle of the room and said, "Gentlemen you did a spectacular job. The North Koreans now know we can come anywhere where they are and blow them to kingdom come. We also have nine confirmed kills of MIG aircraft. Our losses were one B-29 and ten personnel. No loss is ever good but unfortunately that is the price of war. Tomorrow we shall do a five aircraft strike against another target in North Korea. The crews and aircraft have already been selected. You may sleep until noon if you wish. There will be a roll call at 1330 tomorrow." No one ever calls Ten Hut in a debriefing room.

Musher went to get some more to eat, then SSS and in the sack. It was a long day.

CHAPTER 149

My First B-29 Test Flight

It was 0600 and Terry was shaking him awake. He was doing the same to Tick Tick. "When at debriefing the Old Man said everyone could sleep until noon that did not include you two heroes. Our crew has work to do this morning and we fly a combat strike tomorrow. Get dressed and get to the dining hall. I will tell you about it there."

When an aircraft has a major flight component change and in our case an engine change, despite all the ground checks the aircraft must have a test flight. Test flights are done in the local area and do not require a full crew. The crew requirement is an aircraft commander, a co-pilot, a flight engineer and two scanners, in this case the two gunners are scanners. The flight will not last more than forty-five minutes and will include some maneuvers to prove the aircraft air worthy. We will preflight at 0900, takeoff about 0930, land at about 1030 and then preflight for tomorrows mission. Our other crew members will be at New Guy 13 when we finish the test flight."

The takeoff and subsequent flight checks went without comment. AC to crew, "Buckle in snugly. Here we go." With that the engines went to maximum power and the aircraft started to climb. The co-pilot read the gauges. "Eighteen thousand, nineteen thousand, twenty thousand, twenty-one thousand, twenty-two thousand" and the engines just quit turning. The aircraft fell nose forward headed straight for the ground. At about eleven thousand feet the aircraft commander had recovered the aircraft and it was flying straight and level. The AC,"Power stall OK. Recovery OK." Musher felt like his stomach was above his eyes and his asshole was tighter than a virgin's pussy. Everyone except Musher had experienced these test flights before and they thought it would be a good laugh to excite the unexcitable Musher.

If your first high altitude power on stall in a B-29 is not a memorable moment I don't know what would be.

CHAPTER 150
My Last Combat Strike

As promised the rest of the crew was waiting for us to return from the test flight. After all the stories of the power on stall were told and laughed about Papu brought a serious note to the lineup.

"Tomorrow we shall fly our first combat mission as a crew. We will preflight just as if it were no more than a long training mission. It's not as long as any USCM any of us has flown and with the exception of maybe two hours maximum there will be no unusual activity. General briefing for all crews will be at 1330 with specialized following immediately after. When our preflight is done we will have no need to come back to the aircraft until station time tomorrow. Let's do the preflight and have lunch. We would not want to be late to the 1330."

The Director of Operations started the briefing naming the five crews which would fly the mission, the aircraft call sign for each aircraft and the take-off times. Captain Puckett with Crew 98-S13 would be the flight leader. The target is the port of Hing Kow along the North Korean coast. Total flight time a little over ten hours. Bomb release would be a toggle drop. The DO gave the usual reminders about the mission. He closed by saying General Bryan had returned to the states to schedule and execute the move of the remainder of the 98th Bomb Group to Okinawa. Until the General's return he would be the DO and the acting Commanding Officer." He left to the soft "Ten Hut" followed by "Dismissed."

Papu told them, "Our takeoff is at 0800 so stations at 0600. Rest and unless something goes awry I shall see you in the morning. Terry they are all yours."

Terry and the boys went to the hooch to rest and sleep until dinner. Then after dinner back to the hooch to rest and sleep until 0430 hours.

Musher's interest in the general briefing was not as keen as it had been the first couple of times. They would bomb somewhere in North Korea. There would be fighters and flak along the in-route and maybe the ex-route. He knew he would hold up.

The next day they flew the mission. When the mission was over, debriefing finished and the crew dismissed Musher thought "That mission was just like the bombing training sortie to Montana." They did not see any fighters and were not chased by flak. They just simply cruised in, released their bombs and turned for home. It was OK with him if all the missions were that way. The next two were that way.

His fifth was another story. They had been jumped by bandits but managed to get through unscathed. They took flak hits but none of them were serious. After bomb release on the target while making the turn to get the hell out of there Number 2 engine just simply quit. Moments later Number 2 broke out in fire. The nacelle engine fire bottles did not put out the fire. The feared sound of the alarm bell rang throughout the aircraft. On the intercom,"Time to go. Get out. Good luck."

CHAPTER 151
A Whole New Way of Life

Sometimes at night when he lay in bed trying to fall asleep his mind would continuously show him the picture of that B-29 disintegrating before his whole crew could bail out. He couldn't imagine how many times he had seen that picture in his dreams. When he was awake and it visited him he told himself, "When you hear the bailout bell get your ass out regardless of anything else." The bell was ringing and he pulled the groin straps and headed for the aft hatch. Tick Tick had already opened the hatch and was motioning Musher to go. Musher stood in the door and seemed to be welded to the fuselage. Suddenly he was hurtling through open air. Tick Tick had loaned him a boot.

What little parachute training he had said, "Count to ten before pulling the parachute release handle so that you are sure you are clear of the aircraft." Musher gave the ten count of a man in fear, "One, Two, Ten." He yanked the release handle and suddenly he felt like he had been kicked in the balls and turned upside down. The chute had opened and filled with air. His falling speed felt as if it had stopped. He was coming down but drifting towards a body of water. That same limited parachute training had said, "If you want to go left give a slight pull to the left riser, if you want to right give a slight pull to the right riser, but in either case be careful not to pull too hard because you may spill the chute and plummet to the ground." He thought about that and folded his arms across his chest. "Go where you want to go, I can swim and tread water." As it was he did not land in the water, he landed in an open field across the water.

Again he thought of his limited parachute training. The instructor said, "When you are going to land bend your knees, keep your elbows close to your body and roll upon impact." Did he do those things? Who knows, all he knew he was safely on the ground, nothing felt broken and he was getting out of his chute. When he stood up less than one hundred yards away from him were at least twenty-five people. It looked like some had farm tools and the others were uniformed soldiers with rifles and bayonets attached. He thought about the caliber .45 automatic hanging in a holster on his chest. If he made any move towards it even to throw it away they would shoot him right there. He put his hands in the air and stood silently. The uniformed soldiers approached him and indelicately took the .45 and holster off his shoulder. They tied his hands in front of him and spoke loudly to him. He wished he had paid more attention in the language classes but he got their message when they began prodding him with bayonets.

In the village they took him into a house before a man with a much fancier uniform. Musher figured he must be an officer of some type. He questioned Musher in Korean. Musher could not understand so he tried to answer in some form of American. All that got him was a slap in the face. They emptied all the pockets of his flying suit but were only rewarded with Luckies, his Zippo and the dog tags from around his neck. He was sat down in a corner while the one in the fancy uniform made a field phone call.

It was much later when a new man entered the room. His uniform was even more decorative than the one already here. He had to be a senior officer. Everyone jumped to their feet until he said something which made them all relax. He spoke more words and they stood Musher up, untied his hands and brought him to a chair to sit down. He sat across from Musher. They brought a pitcher of what looked like water and two glasses. The senior officer poured some of the contents into each glass. In perfect English, "Are you thirsty? Would you like some water?" He picked up one glass and motioned to Musher to pick up the other. "To your health" as he swallowed the contents. Musher picked up the other glass "To your health" swallowed and held out the glass for more. His glass was filled and he sipped it slowly.

"I am Lieutenant Colonel Soo Kim of the Army of the Republic of North Korea. I was educated at Ohio State and I am an engineer by profession. At the moment I am serving as a senior officer in the intelligence department of the Army of the Republic of North Korea. (ARNK). We know you are an American from the B-29 group that has been bombing our citizens and hospitals. I am here to take you to a detention center. I can do that one of two ways. You can cooperate with me and ride along in my car, or you can not cooperate and walk hands bound through the villages where you will most likely be beaten as you walk. It is just about one hundred miles to the detention center. Take a minute and tell me your choice."

"What exactly do you mean when you say cooperate?"

"Answer a few simple questions. From your dog tags we know you are not a person of rank. Since we know you are not an officer we know that you must either be the flight engineer, the radio operator or one of the gunners. We know all we will ever need to know about the Far East and enough of us were educated in the United States to have all that information. We would just like to know more about you personally."

Musher thought how much this sounded like a hustler's pitch. Too often the good hustler will get too smooth. I think Colonel Soo is too smooth. Still

488

if I walk to the detention center from the way his original captors behaved he would probably never live through a one hundred mile walk. "Sir, I will ride with you." The Sir was a small display ploy of subservience.

Neither one spoke throughout the entire ride to the detention center.

Musher was given a hot meal, a shower, clean clothes and a light for one of his Lucky Strikes. Colonel Soo walked him to a freshly made bunk and said, "Get a good night's sleep and we will talk tomorrow." The heavy sound of the door lock and bolt made him think of Freddie. If he could get used to it so can I.

CHAPTER 152

I Could Only Dance For Two Days

Musher was already awake and dressed when he heard the door bolt slide and the door lock move to open. Colonel Soo walked into the room smiling asking how Musher had slept. " Are you ready for breakfast?" Breakfast was in a small room with tablecloth and full condiments. Breakfast itself was what the North Koreans believed to be standard American, sunny side eggs, home fries, sausage, toast and coffee. Colonel Soo also provided a Lucky Strike and a light.

"Saverio, you won't mind if I call you Musher will you? Last night our people on Okinawa sent us your complete service record and a synopsis of your relationships with other people there. The information shows that you are credited with one MIG kill. Is that true?"

Musher had been warned in survival training that as a Prisoner of War you must not engage in casual conversation. It will only lead to more definitive questions. "Yes."

"How long have you been known as Musher?"

"Ever since I can remember."

"Is it a derivative of Muscarello?"

"I guess, I did not give myself the handle."

"Why are you here bombing innocent civilians and hospitals?"

"Colonel let's understand each other. You know my status in the pecking order so you know I don't choose the targets. To the best of my knowledge no civilian population or hospital was targeted on any strike."

Colonel Soo let that pass and followed up with, "Musher you don't strike me as a lifer. What are you doing over here anyhow?"

"That's easy. President Hairy Ass Truman executive order added a one year hitch extension four days before I was scheduled to be discharged and be a civilian. Do you really think I would be doing this if I had a choice?"

"Our information shows that extension happened while you were stationed in New Mexico. How did you get to Spokane?"

"My superior officers saw a chance to fuck me and fuck up my life. They knew the Spokane wing was going to Okinawa to fly combat missions."

"Is it fair to say you took two fuckings in the same twenty-four hours?"

"It certainly is."

Colonel Soo recognized that he had made major in-roads with this dumb asshole. He did not want to spook him so he said, "Musher, let's take a walk and have a smoke or two."

The outdoors felt good and so did the cigarettes. They walked without talking. Under a shade tree they relaxed while Musher smoked another cigarette. Colonel Soo made the mental note that this guy is really addicted. It might be a good tool later.

"We need to go back now. I have a meeting very soon. You will be fed lunch and then you can rest until I return. We will talk again later."

Musher had lunch and a Lucky. He was escorted back to his sleeping room. The sound of the door lock and bolt was even louder now than last night.

In their later meeting Colonel Soo asked Musher "If he wouldn't like to take a smack at the people who put him here when he should be a civilian. Take a look at this paper and tell me what you think."

"My name is Staff Sergeant Saverio "Musher" Muscarello, United States Air Force. I am an aerial gunner on a B-29 bomber flight crew stationed with the 98th Bomb Group Special Targets Unit flying from Kadena Air Force Base in Okinawa. I was scheduled for an Honorable Discharge but my superiors colluded to use me as an instrument of their war.

I have been on bombing flights where civilians have been killed and hospitals have been destroyed. On my last mission my aircraft was shot down and I am a captive Prisoner of War of the Army of the Republic of North Korea.

There is no doubt that this war is being fought for imperialistic gains and a way for the military-industrial complex to line the pockets of the war mongers with gold.

I am being treated well and have written this letter of my own volition without any promises from my captors.

Saverio "Musher" Muscarello, SSgt, USAF   AF 40656121"

"Well Musher just sign and you will be off to a less restrictive detention camp."

"There are some expressions with which I have a little trouble buying. Let me take it and sleep on it overnight. We will talk again in the morning." Musher was escorted to his sleeping room and the door lock and bolt were exceptional loud. No one came to take him to dinner.

Colonel Soo came early the next morning. "How about breakfast?"

Breakfast for Musher was tea and toast. There was no offer of a cigarette.

"I have brought a copy of the letter for you to sign." He pushed the letter and a pen to Musher.

"Let's discuss a couple of points." The discussion went on for almost two hours. Colonel Soo knew the letter was never going to be signed. He would send him to one of the prison camps in China and let them try to get it signed. The other advantage is that they can tell the international press that there are no American prisoners in North Korea.

Later that morning Musher was loaded onto a covered truck and driven north until the truck crossed the border into China. He was transferred to another truck which drove until night fall. In Chinese the sign said, Prisoner of War Camp # 9. Because he had been traveling north he knew he was some where in China but where? They pulled him down out of the truck and he fell to the ground. In English one of the uniformed guards said, "Up, up" while prodding him with his rifle butt. It was dark so they directed his march with the butts of their rifles. They literally kicked him into a building. A voice whispered, "There's an empty bunk here." He crawled to the voice and climbed into the lower bunk.

He was tired and hungry but he fell immediately into a deep sleep.

CHAPTER 153

How To Survive In a Prison Camp

"Come on son you must get up. Very soon they will fall us out for chow. If you are not there you will not get to eat. To survive in this place you must eat everything you can whenever you can."

There were only eighteen prisoners including himself standing there waiting for food. Every prisoner except him had a bowl, cup and wooden spoon. When it came his turn to get food he was given a bowl, a cup, a wooden spoon and what looked like a piece of wash towel twelve inches square. This morning's breakfast was a bowl of who knows what and a cup of hot green tea. Without a sound everyone sat at the outdoor table and ate. Musher sidled in next to the man who woke him up. He started to ask a question and when his first words came out of his mouth he felt a severe smack across his shoulders. The guard had struck him with a short bamboo pole and kept saying, "No talk, eat. No talk, eat." Musher did not try to talk again. After breakfast the prisoners "washed" their utensils in a water barrel and headed back into their living quarters.

Lesson Number 1 in Survival: Do not miss a chance to eat and eat anything you can get. Lesson Number 2 in Survival: Do not voluntarily speak unless there is no one close enough to hit you with a bamboo pole.

Inside the hooch they came one by one to introduce themselves to Musher. Not one mentioned his rank when telling his name and the name he is generally known as. The one who had already befriended Musher twice gave his name as Shaun Mulroney. They were all US Army and had been captured just hours after the North Koreans invaded South Korea. They were all members of the same US Army ELINT listening station (ELINT = Electronic Intelligence) located just south of the North Korea border. They were smack dab in the middle of harm's way. They believed they were of special interest to the North Koreans because they knew the ELINT equipment and procedures. Shaun said, "To now they had not been severely questioned and only mildly mistreated. If you consider a straw bunk, no sheets, a pillow, one blanket, a meal when they were in the mood to give them one and raps with the bamboo pole as mildly mistreated. What's your story?"

Musher gave them the short story ending up with Number 2 engine on his B-29 catching fire and the need to bail out. He told how he was treated well by a Colonel Soo Kim until Soo became convinced that he was not going to sign any letter which made America and Americans out to be bad people. Next stop here.

"That Colonel Soo Kim was here a few weeks ago. The uniform he was wearing was not a Chinese uniform. He spoke perfect English. He didn't ask us for anything said it was just a social visit. Came here so he could see first hand how we were being treated."

"He is smooth, far too smooth. He has all the trademarks of a hustler. Either these people here will get the answers to the questions he left them or he will be back to get the answers himself. His visit was an investment and he will be looking for a return on his investment."

Lesson Number 3 in Survival: There are no sweet captors. Anytime they give you what looks like a break beware it is nothing more than a Trojan Horse.

"So what do we do all day?"

"Twice a day they take us into the yard for one and one half hours exercise. During one of those periods one of us will have a smoke. They give us one cigarette per person per month. We cut them so that the seventeen cigarettes are fairly distributed to each person and only one person may smoke on any given day. We used to have some non-smokers but that is a thing of the past.

We also have in-house training classes. Of the seventeen guys in this hooch we have two who have a masters degree in mathematics, one with an undergraduate degree in literature and the other with an undergraduate degree in political science. Two who have a doctorate in mathematics. We have four who have a masters degree in electronic communications and among them undergraduate degrees in geology and biology. There are four who are culinary arts specialists (cooks and bakers to you) and five of us grunts to take care of these geniuses. Musher figured at least eight or nine of them had to be officers."

"What is the current curriculum?"

"The daytime subject is Calculus I. This week the evenings are devoted to the writings of William Shakespeare. There is no tuition charge or book purchasing requirements. As a matter of fact everyone is enrolled whether they want to be or not. We do not have any requirement that the students pay attention and there are no pop quizzes or examinations. This is learning for the sake of learning and passing away the hours in this miserable place. You are now enrolled."

The one nicknamed Einstein said, "Since we have had only one small session for this subject I wish to begin again for the benefit of our newest member." Musher had had a brush with calculus in high school. Einstein was good, very, very good. Unlike his high school teacher Einstein made you want to learn so you would not miss any part of life. The lesson lasted a little over an hour before the guards had them falling out for exercise.

Musher noticed there had been no food at lunch time.

Lesson Number 4 in Survival: Do not exercise too heavily. Without calories to burn your body will eat itself.

Musher limited his exercise to slow walking and when stared at running in place without raising his feet too high. The exercise period ended, the troops went back into the hooch and the Calculus class resumed. Class ended for chow call and Musher realized that he had learned more about the theories and applications of calculus than he did in his entire high school class.

Dinner was a bowl of rice and who knows what, a chunk of dark bread and hot tea. When they were back in the hooch Shaun told Musher the twelve inch cloth was his latrine cloth to be used in lieu of toilet paper.

The lights in the hooch were turned off at 2000. When all were settled a voice began, "Again tonight we hear about William Shakespeare's Macbeth. He wrote this tragedy of regicide and its aftermath in 1606 A.D. We pick up the story with the king's visit to Macbeth's Elsinore castle. He told the story for about another hour and ended the lesson with Shakespeare's "Good night princes, parting is such sweet sorrow."

CHAPTER 154
Our Captors Start Using Our Bodies

A new activity was added to the prison life of a resident of POW Camp #6. All POWs are required to attend three hour daily classes where the true nature of the American imperialistic state would be discussed.

The first day the course syllabus was discussed. The instructors were all fluent in American. It was highlighted that at the end of each day's class there would be an essay examination regarding the day's contents. Since all Americans seem adverse to signing their name they would not be required to sign the examination paper. Everyone is expected to score one hundred percent correct. To keep the student seating chart each class day you will sit in the same seat. The class was no more than the expounding of the virtues of communism and the depredation of a capitalistic society. The test was a simple two or three word essay answer. One instructor would read the question which was also printed on the paper handout, and another instructor would dictate the correct answer. The papers were collected in a sequence which matched the seating chart. The two instructors "graded" the papers and then announced. "You Feinstein, come to the front of the classroom."

They lashed him bent over a chair and each instructor took a turn hitting Feinstein in the kidneys with a short bamboo pole. One banged the left kidney the other banged the right kidney. When each had administered ten blows to each kidney they unleashed him and told him to take his seat. He made it but only just so.

The instructor began, "What you just saw was an attempt to cause Feinstein to pay closer attention in class. That special study period will be given to any student who for his first time incorrectly answers all or just one of the daily examination questions. For that student to make subsequent examination errors or even just one error the special study classes will be longer and hopefully more effective. Do I make myself clear?" The class answered HAO Long (pinjin for Yes Sir).

"You may leave now. It is almost time for lunch. We shall meet again here tomorrow. Remember, sit where you sat today."

Feinstein was in no shape to stand in line for lunch. The chow rule was if you are not in line you do not get to eat. Lunch was the same rice and who knows what else concoction, dark bread and hot tea. No one washed their bowl or cup. Each had saved a little to make a lunch for Feinstein.

Do you think you would find that consideration anywhere else but in the US military?

One night two guards came to the hooch and took Musher to the Camp Headquarters Building. He was sent into the shower with a razor, soap and a wash cloth. His instruction was to get clean and pretty. The first thing that struck Musher was "These bastards are going to butt fuck me and at five to one there isn't going to be much I can do about it." When he stepped out of the shower he had the towel wrapped around his mid section. Two guards led him into a room with a heavy carpet and two full walls of glass. He had seen those kind of glass walls before. They just cried out that they were really one way mirrors. Whoever was on the other side of the glass wall could see what was happening on the inside without being seen himself. In the middle of the room in full view of the two glass walls was a wooden cross. He told himself Jesus handled his crucifixion and so would he. Another surprise there were no nails. Only ropes which secured him in a vertical spread eagle. His legs and arms were stretched to their limit. He was left alone and was so nervous he involuntarily urinated. He could picture whoever the sick bastards watching were laughing their ass off. Entering from the same door Musher had entered were three totally naked North Korean girls. They could have been anywhere from thirteen to thirty-three. Their busts were the size of grapefruits which had been left in the sun too long. There was no real hair around their crotch. They began a sexy looking dance lightly brushing against him. No matter how hard he tried he could not keep his prick from swelling and hardening. When it was standing straight out and begging for relief one of the young girls smashed a short bamboo pole twice across his prick. All the sexual orientation drained from his body and he screamed in pain. The women left the room only to return again in ten minutes. They repeated their arousal techniques. Musher tried with every nerve in his brain to ignore the fondling and kissing of his prick until it arose to the temptation. The short bamboo pole treatment was repeated. Later the game was repeated at his expense. He did not know when he passed out tied to that wooden cross. The guards released him from the cross, dressed him in his old clothes and practically carried him to his hooch. They opened the door and rolled him in on the floor. He doesn't remember anymore about that night.

The hooch training classes had been going for over six months. Musher was amazed at what he had learned from his fellow POW's. Einstein told him that in those six months he had been taught what a college student would take two calendar years to learn. Einstein explained to him that when he was released from here (they were all sure they would be) he should take the College GED Examination (General Education Development). If his stanine results were good enough he could be awarded as many as sixty college credit hours. On his record it would be the same as having completed two years of college. Einstein assured him that the hooch training classes would continue as long as they were held captive.

We had been in Educational Classes for over four months. No one had made the mistake of making a mistake on the daily examinations. They were still not being asked to sign their examination papers. During these past months the food had gotten better and more regular. The rule that you must be in line to get food had been repealed. The cigarette ration had gone from one per month to two per month. The prisoners had stopped losing weight and were actually gaining very small amounts.

He brought to mind: Lesson Number 3 in Survival: There are no sweet captors. Anytime they give you what looks like a break beware it is nothing more than a Trojan Horse.

Sure enough the lesson was true. At the end of the class the instructor announced that the POWs would receive a shower, shave and new clean clothes. This was being done because the POWs were going to be part of a medical training program. The local hospital's nursing training school needed its students to practice withdrawing blood. Five days a week eighteen student nurses will come to the camp and draw blood from the POWs. It will be a very low cubic centimeter drawing. "We will not have class this coming Sunday. That will be your bath and cleanup day. Starting this coming Monday when you are dismissed from here you will report to the camp dispensary. After each first drawing you will be given four ounces of orange juice with your lunch. You may have as many as two or three drawings each day. Do I make myself clear?" The class answered HAO Long.

This blood draw thing could be a two edge sword. The trainees will get their practice but twenty ounces of orange juice could go a long way to keeping the POWs healthy.

There had been another significant change for POW behavior. Talking during the exercise period was allowed as long as no more than three POWs were talking together. Something was in the wind. The Sunday breakfast, shower, shave and clean clothes, including sox and shoes felt wonderful. He had not had a shower since his stay with Colonel Soo. He wondered if Soo was behind all this. After feeling so clean and fresh the School Instructor told them to strip and put on their old clothes. These new clothes would be left at the dispensary and used from Monday to Friday. They were to be worn only while the nursing trainees were in the camp.

It was a Trojan Colt.

It was 1030 hours Monday morning and our POWs were in their new clothes sitting in a large room in two rows of nine. At the front of the room there were nine blood drawing stations each equipped so that two arms could be attacked for the blood drawing. The trainees came at 1045. They were all either young girls or young women or matured women. Chinese women like most Oriental women look the same from age thirteen to age thirty-three. They were accompanied by three older nurses. There were four unarmed Chinese guards in the room.

One of the nurses motioned for the first row to take a seat at the work stations. There was a lot of chatter among the students and the trainees. None of the POWs could understand a word. The trainees worked in rhythm together as if they were doing close order drill. "Hut, Put squeeze ball in patient's hand, Two, Tie tourniquet, Three Feel for a good vein, Four Insert needle and draw blood." "Hut, remove tourniquet and recover ball, Two withdraw needle, Three, apply gauze pressure to stop bleeding, Four Put band-aid over needle input point and make sure band-aid sticks." "Release patient".

Not all sticks were successful but the training moved as if they were. At this point Musher began to worry. The sterilization process after the first patient consisted of wiping the needle with what he hoped was at least alcohol. One of the nurses motioned for the second row to take a seat at the work stations. The process was repeated as it was for the first row.

The Chinese instructor told the POWs to follow him. They went into a small room where lunch was served. It began with four cold ounces of orange juice. The lunch was actual meat and rice, heavy white bread and unlimited hot tea. It tasted so good he wondered if they had made a devil's bargain.

The Chinese instructor told them to wait here until called. If you wish to talk keep your voices low. The POWs whispered their opinions of the setup and the training program. Musher wasn't the only one who noticed the non-sterilization of the needles before reuse.

The POWs were back in their seats. The Chinese nurse made a statement which the Chinese guard interpreted. "You did very well this morning and we appreciate your cooperation. Not many men would volunteer for this type of training project. You can be proud that you will have been part of saving lives. When you come to the work stations this time please seat yourself at the opposite end from this morning. I have rotated the trainees so that the middle patient will not have the same trainee. May we begin?" With that she motioned the second row to come forward.

Both the second and first row underwent the blood withdrawal. It appeared the syringe had been changed but the needle sterilization between groups one and two had not changed. When the blood drawing was finished the Chinese guard brought them into the room where they had had lunch. Their old clothes were waiting there along with eighteen four ounce glasses of orange juice. "A reward because you did so well." Their new clothes went into marked bags and they went out the door along a route to their hooch which made sure the nurse trainees or nurses did not see them.

It was yard exercise time but they were excused so they could rest. Remember this is only four of the twenty sticks to come this week. Musher wondered if in a month would there be any places left on his arms where he had not been stuck. Eight ounces of orange juice at his body weight left him tired and sleepy. He rested until meal time and then begged off any hooch classroom training. He was asleep very early.

CHAPTER 155

The Games Our Captors Play

It was just about one year since Musher came to POW Camp #6. He had had lots of hooch training and seven months of arm sticking to draw blood five days a week. Despite all that the POWs just seem to exist and wait for repatriation. There was no word how the war was going in Korea. Their Chinese captors had not eased off.

For an infraction of the rules or just for the sport of the guards they would select one POW and put him "in the box". The box was five hundred meters outside the perimeter of the camp. The box was made of iron and shaped like a casket. There were holes drilled in the cover to let in air. Of course those same holes let in the cold or rain. At its most narrow point it was two feet wide and at its broadest point is was four and one half feet wide. The depth of the box was two and one half feet. Someone confined in the box could only urinate by lying on his side and pissing against the box. If he were forced to defecate he would need to lie in it until he was released from the box. The hot sun could bring the temperature in the box to over one hundred degrees and the night temperature could drop into the fifties. The smell emanating from the box was so pungent that sometimes it reached the camp. The prisoner was given water by pouring the water in thru the ventilation holes. The prisoner received no food while in the box. The amount of time a prisoner stayed in the box was arbitrary.

There were no fences around the camp. There was just a two foot ditch along the perimeter which defined the inward dimensions of the camp. The prisoners were not locked up at night or chained together to keep them from trying to escape. Every prisoner in POW Camp # 6 knew the rule. Anytime a prisoner wanted to leave there was nothing to stop him. Just step over the two foot ditch and be on his way. Like everything else there was a catch. Once both the prisoner's feet had crossed the ditch he would be hunted as an escapee and brought back to the compound dead. There was no coming back into camp alive. Since Musher's time at POW Camp #6 no one had crossed the ditch.

There was lots of talk about escape among the eighteen prisoners but when confronted with the realities no one ever tried. Crossing the ditch would be easy but when you get on the other side where are you? You are somewhere in China. Your allies and friends are somewhere south but where? How far would you need to travel to safety? Do you think you could pass for a Chinese citizen? Could you speak the Chinese language? If you needed money where would you get it?

The guards knew escape plagued the minds of their prisoners. They would select one and prod him to the edge of the ditch. The few who spoke English would egg him on. "You can do it?" "I promise to give you a full day's start before we come to look for you." Many, many more taunts until the prisoner broke down and fell to his knees. Then they would berate him for being a cowardly American, killer of women and children.

One day during the trainee nurses blood drawing The Camp Commander Lieutenant Colonel Cha Pyong came into the training room and sat down to watch. He was not looking at the procedures or at the females in the room he was looking at the nice clean American POWs. Pyong was a small man on a small frame, slick hair and a moustache. Musher watched Pyong's eyes. He had seen that look many times in Scolley Square when the fags were cruising for a partner. Pyong had zeroed in on Percy Hollingsworth the other mathematics PHD besides Einstein. As the POWs were leaving Pyong said to the guard, "See that fellow over there, the one with the blond hair and blue eyes, bring him to my office I want to personally critique this program. Send his old clothes with him." Apparently it was a long critique because Percy didn't get back to the hooch until well after lunch. When questioned he told how he and Pyong had a common love for mathematics. With him he brought a carton of American cigarettes, two number ten cans of peaches and a can opener. Today was his first of three months of many mathematics discussion sessions with Pyong. From one of his visits he brought three unopened decks of cards.

The blood drawing program ended and POW life went back to Chinese Educational Classes and perfect quiz answer sheets.

CHAPTER 156

Are We Changing Camps Or What?

About 0230 hours one morning the lights went on in the hooch. Five armed guards came in with the one who spoke English "Out of bed, take your blanket and get into the truck. All except you" as he pointed to Hollingsworth. Two of the guards went to stand beside Hollingsworth. When all were aboard the truck rolled out of the camp and headed south. When the POWs started talking to each other neither of the two guards riding in the back with them objected.

"What do think this is all about? Better try to rest you don't know what awaits us." The truck rolled for the longest time and suddenly came to a stop.

"Everybody out, take your clean clothes bag with you. There are razors, shaving cream, soap and shampoo in the latrine. There are plenty of towels outside the showers."

The POWs were skeptical. Is this how the Nazi's lured the Jews into the gas showers? The guard could sense their skepticism and he went into the latrine and turned on all the showers. The POWs were convinced that the delousing was poisonous. When all had SSS they were led into a dining hall with a table set for seventeen. Roast beef, mashed potatoes, green beans, hot rolls, butter and cold milk.

"Don't wolf it down your stomach is not used to such rich food." Coffee and cigarettes came after lunch. Almost two hours had passed since they got off the truck and the Chinese guard was now saying, "Time to roll, we have a long way to go today. Your old clothes have been burned."

Much later they made another stop and once again went through the delousing and SSS routine before putting on a pair of new pajamas. The dinner was as good as the lunch. They were escorted to a sleeping room with bunks that had fresh sheets and pillowcases.

They were awakened early and served breakfast. They were back on the truck for another long ride. The truck stopped and Musher stole a glance at the guard's watch. It was 1100 hours. "Everybody out of the truck and form a single line."

As they stood there they were approached by Lieutenant Colonel Soo Kim, ARNK. "Gentlemen in less than one hour you will be repatriated. The war continues between North and South Korea or more appropriately I should say between North Korea and the United States of America. In exchange for our delivery of you all we will get one of our more prominent spies who had been working in the United States. As the old Texas saying goes, "A fair trade is no robbery." I trust I shall never see you again in this part of the world. I wish you good luck."

The day was not too clear and the POWs were convinced that halfway to the other side they would be shot in the back for attempting an escape. At the same time one of their snipers would execute the spy to avoid the embarrassment of his capture.

Fortunately none of that happened. The seventeen POWs passed the North Korean spy with a slight nod of the head. They were warmly greeted by personnel from the United Nations, the United States and many other countries which were participating in the war. They were told that they would be taken to the nearest military air base in South Korea which was in Soeul (Sole). From there to a better life at Tachikawa (Tatch-E-Cow-Ah) Air Base just outside of Tokyo, Japan.

CHAPTER 157
Becoming A Person Again

It seemed they had just boarded the bus at the exchange point and now the WAF stewardesses were policing trash and making their little speeches in preparation for landing at Tachikawa Air Base, more lovingly known as Tachi. The Ex-POWs were quietly whisked away from the flight line and deposited in a ward in the Tachi Hospital. The ward door was guarded by an armed air policeman standing beside a sign which read, "Admittance Only with Proper Credentials Authorized by the Hospital Commander" There were seventeen freshly made bunks with new pajamas, large bathrobes and shower slippers resting on them. The ward latrine had been stocked with individual shaving kits containing razors, tooth brushes, tooth paste, shampoo, soap and cologne. There was a large towel warmer loaded with bath towels. Wash cloths and hand towels were stacked along side the towel warmer. The shower room had been equipped with sitting benches.

From one side of the ward you entered a room adjoining the ward. In there a dining area had been established. To say the least it was better looking than any dining hall Musher had ever seen.

On the same side of the ward you entered a hall which had six rooms as off-shoots to the hall. The rooms were eight feet by eight feet and furnished with cushy chairs, a sofa and a sitting table.

From the other side of the ward heavy double doors led to a very large room. One part of the room had a podium and 20 cushy chairs. It was segregated from the other part by heavy duty standing floor dividers. Using large floor privacy dividers the remainder of the room was equipped as a primary medical care unit. In addition to the medical furniture and equipment used for primary care it housed a dental clinic.

At the end of the ward was the entry to the latrine and shower area.

The ward entry door swung open and in walked a full colonel and a captain. The colonel politely asked, "Would you gentlemen please go to our meeting area." The captain led the way. At the podium, "My name is Colonel Frank Cramer, I am the Hospital Commander. This is Captain Martin Melke, my Special Liaison Officer for what we are calling Project Make Right. We named this project fully knowing that no matter what we are able to do for you we shall never be able to make it fully right for you. Believe me gentlemen we will do our damn best. Captain Melke is a voice straight to me. If you wonder about the armed air policeman at your door it is not to keep you in it is to keep the nosy and not necessary people out. True your movements will be limited to this area for a while but that is for your health. We want to know, as I am sure you do, that you are physically fit and only need to put some meat on those bones. Speaking of meat, your dining room will serve you just about anything you ask for at any time. The dining room is open to any of you twenty-four hours a day. Of course you can always go in and help yourself.

Your families have been notified of your repatriation. They do not know where you are they simply know you are in good health. If you choose we will place a telephone call for you and you can take it in our private room. I must tell you in advance that the call would be monitored and on a five second delay to make sure our intelligence people feel you have not slipped and said something they would just as soon not be common knowledge at this time. Who among you would like us to place such a call?"

Everyone raised his hand except Musher.

"We want you to rest and sleep as much as possible. We will not wake you unless it is something which cannot wait. We will try to make your stay here as pleasant as possible. Every night when the clinical part of this ward is finished we will run movies of your choice. Captain Melke will provide you with a list of the available movies and we will show them here. Most of the movies will be the latest releases that are currently showing in the base theatres. Not today but very soon we will give you the full picture of Tachikawa. I am sure I have talked too long. May I suggest that at this time you do whatever you please."

"Question colonel? May we have some regular playing cards, some pinochle cards and some of the works of William Shakespeare?"

Captain Melke spoke, "Consider it done."

"Again gentlemen good night. I will see you often because I am extremely interested in your health." As in every hospital there was no Ten Hut as he left.

Almost if there was a plan the seventeen Ex-POWs headed for the dining room. The first in line asked for a bowl of chocolate ice cream, chocolate sauce and whipped cream. The rest of the order was sixteen more.

Before bedtime it was showers and eating. For the first time for as far back as he could remember he thought of Lucy, Priscilla and Hannah. He took that as a sign of going to normalcy.

CHAPTER 158
The Recovery Routine

Musher could not believe how much better he was feeling just after one night's sleep and some great food. The hospital people had brought him a carton of Luckies and he had smoked to his heart's content. Every morning was spent taking care of either medical or dental items. Then at least two hours with the psychologist. The afternoons were spent in one of the cozy rooms with debriefing personnel. Two weeks of this routine established that the only thing wrong with Musher was that he was underweight and riding the edge of a deep cliff. Heaven knows how many times a day he was eating and slowly gaining weight. His nervous system and temper were a different story. Most all the times he was very calm but certain things would trigger him and he would go off screaming at the object of his wrath.

One morning he and the other Ex-POWs were summoned to the office of the Wing Commander. When they reported in they were introduced to Major General Thomas Whitney, Commander FEAF (Far East Air Forces).

"Please stand at ease." The FEAF Director of Personnel read, "By authority of the President of the United States the following named personnel are hereby promoted as follows, each of the Ex's who were officers were promoted one grade, effective the date of capture by the enemy." MG Whitney approached each of them with their new rank insignia in hand.

The FEAF DP began again, "By authority of the President of the United States the following named enlisted personnel are hereby promoted to the grade of Master Sergeant effective the date of capture by the enemy." That declaration only benefited the ELINT enlisted men who were already Technical Sergeants. The others were already Master Sergeants. The greatest benefactor was Musher. That order promoted him from Staff Sergeant to Master Sergeant "in accordance with AF regulations which specified if an aircrew airman's aircraft is shot down and the airman is taken POW he may be promoted two grades but is limited to the number of promotional grades which will establish his rank as Master Sergeant." MG Whitney approached each enlisted man with their new rank insignia in his hand. He told those who were not eligible for additional promotions that he would surely entertain their application for promotion to the grade of warrant officer.

The FEAF DP began again. "By authority of the President of the United States the following named officers are awarded the following medals and service ribbons for recognition of their service to the United States Air Force and the United States of America." He enumerated the medals and service ribbons. He repeated the same discourse for the enlisted men. The only difference was that the enlisted men received a good conduct medal or a cluster to their already existing good conduct medals. Officers cannot earn a GCM.

That concluded the ceremonies. BG Whitney, "I have reserved a special room at the Officers Club where we will have photo opportunities and later we will have lunch." The photographers were every where taking pictures of everything that moved. There were no reporters looking for statements.

BG Whitney spoke to Musher. "I am told you are a superior card and pool player. Have you ever tried golf? We do not have a golf course here at Tachi but there is an excellent facility at Yokota AB which is only twelve miles away. There would no charge to you and your compatriots for use of the equipment and the course. If you wish I will make sure the Tachi motor pool responds well to any request from any of you to go to Yokota. At the same time I will make sure the Yokota motor pool is so advised. I have been playing for many years and to this day I am just a mediocre amateur. It is a game of strength, determination and a cool disposition. I find that when I play regardless of the score or whether I lose four or five dollars it is an enjoyable time. Try it, I am sure you will adapt and learn to love the game."

Lunch was festive. Musher thought it was not hard to see how these guys can enjoy being a lifer especially if you are a general.

At the ward Musher took a survey of the Ex's regarding their either being golfers or wanting to learn the game. He told them of General Whitney's transportation commitment. That also did not spark much interest.

It was 1400 hours and Musher was scheduled for a meeting with one of the wing personnel sergeants and a wing finance sergeant. The personnel sergeant spoke first. "These are your service records. We will concentrate on the period of your capture to your first night here at the hospital. Let's see if we can agree on the dates."

Musher agreed with the entries. The finance sergeant took over. "We were confidant that that the dates were correct so we computed what pay you are due from the last time you were paid before capture until your first night at the hospital. The items are broken into three categories, Category 1: Pre-Capture as a Staff sergeant entitled to flying pay. Category 2: Internment as a Master Sergeant entitled to flying pay inclusive from the date of your capture to the first night you stayed at the hospital here at Tachi. Category 3: To Date as a Master Sergeant entitled to flying pay residing in the Base Hospital. You can see the titled and sub-titled entries for each category. Please review them and the value we have placed beside each one. The value calculations are shown on the pages attached to the summary. Why don't we take a coffee and smoke break while you review this very important document."

Musher took the finance pages and they all went to the dining room for coffee and cigarettes. Not having any source data to compare for individual unit rates all he could do was verify the arithmetic. It was a pretty number sixty-eight thousand four hundred thirty dollars and nineteen cents. He was done checking in a matter of minutes but he made it appear he was having trouble doing the arithmetic. He simply wanted to have a piece of pie, more coffee and some cigarettes.

Back in the room the finance sergeant asked Musher if everything was all right. He slid a paper to Musher which in essence said he had reviewed the documents and the payment was correct. Between the last line and his signature he added, "To the best of my knowledge but I reserve the right for me or my agent to further examine these documents for their accuracy." He slid the paper back to the finance sergeant to initial the addition and sign the document. When he got the paper back he did he same but held on to the paper. He asked the following question: When do I get my money and how?"

"We can do it most anyway you want except we are limited to how much American money we can disburse at any one time. Green money here far exceeds the power of the yen. The legal yen trades at three hundred sixty to the dollar. A one hundred dollar American bill traded on the black market will bring six hundred yen to the dollar. Six thousand yen versus thirty-six hundred yen, you can see why we must keep American Green off the market." Musher thought if these US military people are the same as the US citizens you won't have much luck stopping that profit margin.

"Here in Japan for purchases at US facilities we use what is called script. It is paper currency which replaces American green in all the denominations from a nickel to twenty dollars. Anyone accepting American green for any transaction on a US facility faces severe consequences. Off the US facilities most Japanese purchases of any kind the proprietor gladly accepts script. To offset that we periodically change the script without notice and give those personnel who normally would use script an opportunity to exchange their script on a dollar for dollar basis. This is a very short explanation and I would be very happy to come back and go into greater detail with you."

"For the moment I think I understand enough to stay out of trouble. This is how I would like to be paid." He gave his American Express account number in the states to the finance sergeant. "Please transfer sixty thousand dollars and nineteen cents to that account and get me confirmation of the transfer and what the new balance is. I would like a check of American value in the amount of six thousand dollars to open an American Express checking account here at Tachi. I will take the remaining two thousand in various script denominations and four hundred thirty dollars in yen."

"Four Hundred Thirty Dollars American at the yen legal rate is One Hundred Fifty-Four Thousand Eight Hundred Yen." The highest yen note is currently ten thousand yen."

"Here's how you do it. 10 @ 10,000; 4 @ 5,000; 4 @ 3,000; 11 @ 1,000 and 118 @ 100 yen. I believe that is 154,800 yen. When can we do this?"

"I will bring the money and the paper work tomorrow. If you fill it all out I can open your American Express account but I will need to make another trip to bring you some blank checks."

"Thank you gentlemen I will see you after lunch tomorrow".

Tonight's movie featured Doris Day. "I've got to get out and do something."

CHAPTER 159
What Is This Game Called Golf?

Yesterday had been a typical day. Medical, dental and psychiatry filled the morning. As promised the finance sergeant brought the transfer receipt with his new balance in the states, his cash and the forms necessary to open his checking account. The sergeant made a special second trip to bring him some blank checks and identity cards. He went into one of the private rooms where he asked the telephone operator to get Captain Melke on the phone. Very shortly the phone rang and it was Melke returning his call. "Captain I have a request. I know I have not been off the base yet but I would like to go to Yokota tomorrow morning and start to learn how to play golf. Is that possible?"

"It certainly is. General Whitney told us about his suggestion of golf to you and how the motor pools would treat you. I would make the arrangements for you but we want to test the system to insure you don't have any problems. When we finish call extension 470, tell them who you are and that you would like transportation to the Yokota golf course and at what time you want to be picked up. If you get any trouble just say thank you and call me at extension 245. I will follow-up and call you back. Rest assured it will work as planned." Musher had the same trouble and called Melke to tell him.

True to his word he called back in less than five minutes. "I want you to call extension 470 and make your same request. If you get guff again call me at extension 245. If I don't hear from you in ten minutes I will figure all went well. If there is any trouble with Yokota motor pool call. Keep my extension number handy. Enjoy your day." The rest of the day passed slowly. He read Shakespeare until he fell asleep after dinner.

His pickup was scheduled for 0800 hours. He was ready long before then and was sitting outside the hospital when the motor pool car showed up. The driver was an "oh joe san" (phonetic Japanese for a young woman). The twelve mile ride from Tachi to Yokota was scenic. It was also a little scary. This American Chevrolet using the same road as was built for two smaller cars caused some distress to Musher every time a car passed them going in the opposite direction. The countryside was pretty. It was bright green and little houses were interspersed along the route. When they pulled up in front of the Yokota Golf Pro Shop the driver said, "Yokota Motor Pool telephone extension same as Tachi, 470. Enjoy day." Musher felt like he should be giving her a tip.

He wanted to see what golf was all about but he knew that if he liked it and wanted to get better it would consume his life. The step to the front door was hesitant but he took it, walked into the Golf Pro Shop and entered into a new world. The place was filled with fancy clothes, shoes, golf clubs and who knows how many other things. A man with his right arm amputated at the elbow walked to him with his left hand extended and said, "I am Timmy Buckles, the Club Professional. Let's go sit and talk about golf."

They drank a lot of coffee and talked about the rules and etiquette of golf. He talked about the language of golf and how like any other foreign language there was a lot of memorization necessary until he became a frequent player. Timmy explained the fourteen club rule which constituted the maximum number of clubs any player could have in his bag while playing for score. His suggestion to Musher was that he buy some golf shoes, a golf glove and a baseball type hat. In the beginning Timmy would supply everything else. For at least the next thirteen days Musher's golf activities would be limited to the driving range. The basic plan was that each day Musher would receive a lesson with a different club from 0900 to 1000, practice that lesson from 1000 to 1200 and break for lunch. He would be back on the range practicing with same club from 1300 to 1600. Timmy would often drift to the range during the day to watch his practice and tweak his swing as needed. By the end of the thirteenth day his swing was looking pretty good but he had not gained consistency in his swing

Just as the snooker had and everything else in his life except being an infantry man Musher was consumed by the desire to be one of the best at everything he tried. Timmy gave him a putting lesson. Musher found putting to be like shooting pool, a smooth stroke with an intensive mental picture of the target. He was so intent that after his range practice he would devote another two hours practice putting.

It had been twenty-two days since Musher began his quest to be a good golfer. He had not missed a day of practice and not one day had been shorter than eight hours. His hands had blistered, recovered and blistered again. When he was not at the golf course he was in hospital ward practicing his golf grip with a training device Timmy had loaned him. The device allowed him to practice finger placement and grip intensity. It reminded him of when he was first learning to be a card mechanic and Uncle Fanucci would say, *"Practice does not make perfect, it makes permanent."* Musher noticed when practicing on the range he thought less and less about his grip and more and more about making a consistent swing.

If all of the elements of a golf game were measured in relationship to individual difficulty for Musher the most difficult element was playing from a sand trap. Timmy and he spent three hours in the two sand traps at the driving range. He spent the next three full days practicing the long sand shot, the short sand shot and the "fried egg" sand shot. This part of the game will require many more hours of training and practice before he would gain any confidence.

What is called "the short game" came easily to Musher. His sense of touch developed by years of playing cards and pool made it easy for him to control the amount of energy he transferred from the golf club to the golf ball. He became extremely accurate with the "scoring clubs" particularly the wedge. He enjoyed practicing with the wedge. He was amazed when the golf ball would fly high to land on the practice green surface and spin back towards him. Timmy told him that such spin shots could only be effective when he became good enough to know how much energy to transmit to the golf ball and at what angle the ball should be struck.

The golf course was closed on Monday for weekly maintenance. Today was Sunday and Musher had just finished practice and was sitting in the "19th Hole." The "19th Hole" was the nickname for the small and limited food service area and the bar that adjoined it. Timmy came and sat with Musher to drink coffee.

"I don't know if I have ever seen anyone work at hard trying to learn this game. When you finish eating we are going to take a cart and ride around the golf course. I want you to see it before you play it tomorrow. Musher's face showed the surprise and he smiled broadly. "Let's see if all the training and practicing has been to no avail."

Musher took this opportunity. "Timmy you have never mentioned my cost for all your time and the golf course equipment. I see the price of a bucket of range balls is twenty-five cents and in the last month I wouldn't even want to guess how many hours you have spent with me and how many buckets I have hit. When are you going to tell me?"

"Let me remind you that my instructions were you would only pay for personal purchases. I am paid by the United States Air Force. You are rehabilitating after a tragic episode. We cannot do enough for you. I have said enough about that. You paid for your shoes, hat and gloves. Have you bought anything else that you did not pay for? You will have an additional expense tomorrow morning. We are going to select a set of golf clubs for you, a golf bag, a couple of new gloves, new shoes, socks, maybe a couple of sweaters, maybe a couple of shirts, a couple of pair of pants and a hat to replace that sweaty collapsed one you are now wearing. All together that may run as high as five hundred dollars. If you are not in position to spend that much tell me and we will do whatever your budget will allow. By the way, I will give you two dozen golf balls and tees from my personal stock. I do not pay for my personal stock it comes from the manufacturers so don't think I am doing you a big favor. Now can you afford five hundred dollars?" ..Yes…"Good. Let's go look at the golf course."

Musher spent a restless night worrying about his first venture on a golf course.

CHAPTER 160
Golf Is Not a Game of Fun

Musher had a visitor at breakfast. It was the Hospital Commander. "Musher I have been monitoring your progress and I am really quite pleased. You have put on some weight, your general body health is good and I understand you are engrossed with the game of golf. Do you agree with my assessment? If you do I think you should move to a regular Bachelor Airman Quarters and you can continue to see your psychologist once weekly on an out-patient basis."

"Sir I believe you are right."

"Your BAQ is a good size room with a private bath. You are permitted electric cooking facilities if you wish. For a very minimum amount you can have full time maid service. It is located quite near the NCO Club and the base bus line runs in front of the BAQ. Would you like to see it before you move?"

"Sir that is not necessary. It is just that I cannot do the move this morning. Would tomorrow morning be all right?"

"You know Musher I play golf and Timmy told me you were on the course for a playing lesson today. Captain Melke will contact you about the move and provide any assistance you may need. Play well, swing easy with all your might."

Swing easy with all your might. Is that an oxymoron?

Musher was greeted in the pro shop by an "oh joe san" whose name tag said "Nite-tie". "Pro Timmy tell me dress you like a professional." They began with matching shirts, socks and pants with a universal belt. Everything fit well. From there they added matching shoes, hat and golf gloves. Musher modeled the complete outfit and Nite-tie said, "Boot-E-Full." She took him to a collection of golf bags but made no suggestion. He should pick the one he likes since they are all about the same size and do the same thing. He decided to wait for Timmy to see the golf clubs. Nite-tie added a matching cardigan sweater to his attire. She put all the clothes he came in with in a bag to hold for him. He paid sixty-three dollars in script. Nite-tie told him that he was only charged the actual costs of the clothes. And anything he purchased would be at cost. He had brought seven hundred dollars so as not to be embarrassed.

Timmy came into the coffee shop where Musher had been waiting. "Stand up and let me see you. If I didn't know better I would say we had a visiting pro. Let me have a cup of coffee and we will get you clubs and a bag."

At Timmy's suggestion Musher bought a set of MacGregor copper faced irons, MacGregor woods with head covers and a Bullseye putter. They went to the range where Musher hit some balls to loosen up and try to feel his new clubs. Amazingly enough they were a new model of the clubs he had been practicing with. Timmy took the driver in his only hand, his left hand, teed up a ball and made a full swing. He hit a severe hook. (A hook is where the ball starts out straight but takes a left turn part way through its flight) He turned to Musher and said, "Be careful that's what happens when you use too much right hand." Musher didn't know what to do or say finally he chuckled as Timmy walked to the cart.

On the first tee Musher hit one of those dreaded hooks. It went outside the golf course boundry. (Known as "out of bounds")

"Tee it up you are now hitting three. Think practice tee." The out of bounds penalty was loss of distance and stroke.

This time Musher hit a viscous slice which went out of bounds. (A slice is where the ball starts out straight but takes a right turn part way through its flight)

"Tee it up you are now hitting five. Think practice tee"

The next ball was in play. The rest of the round (they only played half a round, nine holes) it was hit another, good shot, read the putting line, notice how the putting grass is leaning, etc, etc, etc.

Back at the golf cart barn they were greeted by two Japanese workers. One took Musher's bag and the other headed for the wash rack with the cart. Timmy spoke in Japanese to the one holding Musher's bag. "Make him a name tag with the word Musher". He spelled it while the attendant wrote it down on a piece of paper. What stall will his clubs be stored in?" The attendant stepped into the cart barn and quickly returned with a piece of paper with the number 147 written on it. Timmy turned to Musher and told him he could tip provided the tip was not more than fifteen yen (just about five cents).

Musher was in trouble. He did not have any yen with him and to use script is a punishable offense. He told Timmy of his plight and Timmy gave him fifteen yen to use. "You owe me, I have you written in my book." It took Musher a few seconds to realize he was joking. As they were walking to the 19th Hole Timmy said "Don't normally walk. Take the cart to the barn and one of them will get on the cart and return it when you get out wherever you are going. Let's go critique today." Musher blushed.

"You didn't do that badly. You wanted to do so well at times you lost your concentration. Your swing is solid and with more use in playing conditions it will become more reliable. You hit a number of excellent wedges. From one hundred yards from the stick your wedge must be within eight feet. Your putting stroke is solid and as you learn to read greens you will be an excellent putter. At the rate you have learned and your dedication to practice I believe in a short time you will be a low handicap golfer. Right now you need a little more beef on your frame. Do not play or practice tomorrow.

"I'll be right back." He went into the pro shop for just a minute or so and returned with, "Come let me show you the locker room." Timmy led him to his assigned locker, number 286 with the name of "Musher" painted on the front door. He handed him the key along with ten one hundred yen notes and twenty five yen notes. "Now you really owe me."

The locker room was fully equipped including an attendant. The attendant's name tag said "Nite-tie 2". (Got to see what this Nite-Tie is all about)

"I am at your disposal. I can arrange for anything. May I call you Musher-san?"

"Please do."

"Musher-san you look very tired. May I suggest nice hot bath and massage. We have both those as a service of this locker room. Cost very low and satisfaction guaranteed."

"How much?"

"Do not worry. Inexpensive. If when you finish you not happy do not pay." Musher disrobed and Nite-Tie 2 gave him a large towel to cover his body. He then led Musher through a double door which had four private rooms opening from each side of a hallway. The door to his room locked behind him. There was a small tub full of hot water, a small wooden stool, a massage table and a bare breasted oh-joe-san.

She spoke, "Your first time here?"

"Yes"

"My name Nite-Tie 6" Here we are with the Nite-Tie again.

"Your name please."

"Musher-san"

"Please come sit on stool." When he did she took soap and a sponge and started washing his body. "Japanese clean before entering hot bath tub. Water seems very hot but you will get used to it." She continued washing and then handed him the sponge. "You wash there please." Musher washed his balls and his dick and actually started to harden. Boy is that a good sign.

Nite-Tie 6 washed his hair and then used a small bucket to rinse him off. The rinse water came from the hot tub and his body actually started to feel as if that hot water were normal. "You get in tub please."

It took Musher a long time to lower his full body in the tub. Once it was done he felt as if he could go to sleep there. "You want cigarette and beer or soda?"

"Cigarette and soda please."

Nite-Tie 6 pulled two separate long silk hangers. In a minute there was a knock at the door and a tray handed in. His Lucky Strikes and a coke. He sat in the tub and soaked while she lit a cigarette and handed him the coke.

FREDDIE, I KNOW THEY DON'T DO THIS IN PRISON.

"You get out now please." She wrapped the towel around him to dry him off and then said, "You get on stomach on table please." She took the towel away and started lightly massaging his body. "You turn over please." The massaging continued but as she neared his thighs and groin his dick began to rise. She leaned her head forward with her mouth positioned at the end of his dick. "You want?" He murmured, "Please."

She was good at sucking cock. He had not had any kind of sex in so long it was almost instantaneously for him to climax. She took it all but did not swallow. She went to a bucket and rinsed her mouth. Took a damp cloth and wiped him clean. Her drying and rubbing with the towel caused him to harden. She took hold of his dick and said, "Again?" He responded. "Yes Please." The second time took longer but felt better. She alternated from sucking his dick to licking his balls. He could feel the rising in his crotch as he held her head in place while he spurted semen into her mouth. He felt good but not finished.

She had taken it all in her mouth but did not swallow. She went back to the bucket and rinsed her mouth. Again she took a damp cloth and wiped him clean. Again her drying and rubbing with the towel caused him to harden. She looked at his dick standing tall and said, "You want more?"

He motioned to her to come up on the table and straddle his dick. Inside her pussy it was warm and moist. He started the motions but she took over. She fucked him until he grabbed her shoulders to come hard into her pussy. He knew he was finished now. More importantly to him was that despite the prison camp episode he could still appreciate a good blow job and a good piece of ass. He knew he was finished for today.

Wrapped in his towel he turned to Nite-Tie 6 and tried to use one of the Japanese expressions he learned while in the hospital. "Dough-Mo-Ah-Ree-Gat-Toe" (Thank you)

"She nodded and said,"Dough-E-Marshy-Aash-Tah" (You are welcome) Later he learned that the slang was "Don't touch my moustache".

Nite-Tie 2 helped him get dressed. Without asking he told Musher, "If you are satisfied with all our services your fee is fourteen hundred forty hundred yen." (Four dollars American)

Musher did not have fourteen hundred forty yen. He had one thousand from Timmy. He was thirteen hundred forty yen short. Three script dollars equates to one thousand eighty yen. Together they pay the bill and leave a tip of over five hundred yen. Musher said to Nite-Tie 2, "You can see I do not have enough yen would you accept some script to make up the difference?"

"I am not supposed to but we will add it to our list of confidences. Most members here have confidences with me."

It was his way of saying most any kind of money is acceptable. Musher learned that he needed to carry three kinds of money.

TODAY'S GOLF WAS NOT A GAME OF FUN BUT YOU SURE COULD NOT BEAT THE 20TH HOLE.

CHAPTER 161

Moving Day

Musher could not remember the last time he slept so well. He had a late breakfast and called Captain Melke. "Is there a chance I could see my new permanent temporary living quarters at the BAQ?"

"I'll pick you up in thirty minutes."

Musher field stripped his Lucky Strike, remembrances of The Monster, as he stepped into the car.

Let's drive around so that you can see where all the support facilities are in relation to your "permanent temporary" living quarters. Everything was pretty much as the hospital commander described it. The room in the BAQ was a large first floor end room which could easily be accessed from the rear entrance. There was a vehicle parking lot adjoining the rear of the building. The furnishings were barracks style. Musher asked Melke. "If I discarded all these furnishings and bought my own would that be all right?"

"It's your money. I would certainly support you. You know you will probably lose all your investment when you transfer. Of course on a PCS (Permanent Change of Station) you have enough rank for the government to ship it to your next station at no charge to you."

"If you could make a call for everything including the overhead fluorescent light to be removed, I will paint it and move in as soon as possible."

"I can do that. I will have it painted. What colors would you like?"

"Paint soft blue on the walls and put a wall-to-wall soft blue shag rug on the floor. Paint the windows and trim in dark blue. Paint the bathroom in bright white. Could you also get the electricians to put four double outlets on each wall and another outlet in the bathroom? If you could give me a date when it would be finished I could tell the BX when to deliver."

"Today is Tuesday it will be finished by noon tomorrow. If for some reason it cannot be done, first I will know why and you will know immediately after I do. Is there anything else?"

"Sir there is one last thing. Is it at all possible for me to get a base telephone in my room? Naturally I will pay all the installation expenses and any other costs associated with the telephone. That's it, I am trying not to be a pig. I am so close to the BX why don't I go there and you go wherever it is you need to go. I truly appreciate your help and understanding. Forgive me if I am overbearing and demanding."

"Remember Musher, 245 for anything. Good luck shopping."

The Base Exchange at Tachikawa was so large it was housed in an aircraft hangar. Musher sought out one of the facility managers and explained his situation. He was assured his purchases would be accumulated and if he paid for them before leaving the purchases would definitely be delivered tomorrow between 1500 and 1600 hours. If he calls this number, the manager gave a card with his phone number and name on it, by 1330 hours the delivery could be rescheduled. The BX would provide help to off load and place the items in the BAQ.

Musher bought everything from a small refrigerator with ice maker, a queen size bed, a mattress, four sets of matching sheets and pillow cases, three pillows and a down bed comforter. One end table, a small eating table with two chairs, one floor lamp, one end table lamp, china for four and stainless steel table settings for four. He added two table cloths with matching napkins and the accompanying salt and pepper shakers. His next three two purchases were a two burner hot plate cooking stove, an eight cup electric coffee pot and two alarm clocks. He finished his purchasing for today with a combination high-fi multi record player and a short wave radio.

He would have five thousand transferred here from the states. The manager with whom he had been speaking did the accounting gave him the same type discount he had received at the pro shop. He renewed his delivery promises. Seems Captain Melke had called the BX and spoken to this manager. He wrote a check for the purchases. It put a major dent in his local American Express account. He would have five thousand transferred here from the states.

He would practice or play golf early in the morning, get his few belongings from the hospital and be waiting for delivery in the BAQ by 1500 hours. If he cut his practice short by two hours he might even get a bath and a massage.

He made one more stop, the Base Housing Office. The staff was aware of his situation and they would schedule five house maids for him to interview to see if any of them would be his choice. He would pay their monthly fee along with his minimum residence fee directly to the housing office. After he has selected one he would receive a full briefing on what he could expect from his maid service and what he could not expect. "When and where would he want to do the interview? We would prefer it be done here."

"How soon would they be available for the interview?"

"Within the next ten minutes."

"Is my maid shared with any other resident of the BAQ?"

"It depends, for one dollar a day she is shared, for two dollars a day she is your exclusive maid. The exclusivity choice must be made at the time of hiring."

They all looked alike, dressed alike and behaved alike. One was more fluent in English than all the others. She gave her name as Yoko. She had been the exclusive maid for a Warrant Officer at Yokota Air Base. He had rotated back to the states. He was married and faithful to his wife. They had never had sexual relations. She was not married and lived in nearby Fussa City, just outside of Yokota Air Base. She was his choice. He gave her best "Domoahregatto." She bowed and gave him a "DoughEMashaAshTah".

He advised the housing staff of his choice and they said she would have been their choice for him. Your monthly fee is sixty dollars for maid service, five dollars housing fee and three dollars a month for telephone service. Monthly total is sixty-eight dollars. Your base telephone number is extension 4726. All fees are payable in advance.

Musher gave them two hundred four dollars in script for the next three months.

Back at the hospital Musher made currency packages for tomorrow. One thousand American, thirty-six thousand yen, one thousand script, and one thousand forty yen for Timmy.

CHAPTER 162
Golf Plus

At 0700 hours Musher was eating breakfast at the 19th Hole. He had already bought three new shirts, matching pants, sox and two white golf gloves. His basic color scheme would be air force blue accessorized with white shoes, etc.

He had the cart boys bring his bag to the driving range. For the first half hour on the range he was trying to extend the distance he could hit the ball with his driver. Timmy came by to watch and made a slight grip adjustment for use with woods. Musher noticed he was hitting the driver from fifteen to thirty yards longer. Timmy worked with him on how to hit a draw (not a hook but the same flight pattern only more controlled as to how far left the ball turned in flight) He worked at hitting a slight draw to hitting a violent draw almost like a hook. Timmy worked with him how to hit a fade (not a slice but the same flight pattern only more controlled as to how far right the ball turned in flight) The new practice exercise was hit a draw, hit a fade, hit a straight shot. Musher practiced these shots with great success using all four woods in his bag. The big question is would he be able to do it tomorrow, the day after tomorrow and any time he needed to use such a shot. Only time will tell.

Before Timmy could leave Musher repaid him the one thousand forty yen he had borrowed yesterday.

"Don't mean to run but I thought I would get a quick massage. I need to be back at Tachi to move to my new quarters." Musher emptied his pockets into his secure locker except for five hundred yen which he put in the waist band of his towel He approached Nite-Tie 2 and asked, "Is Nite-Tie 6 available?" She was, Nite-Tie 2 took his dirty clothes and led him through the doors.

"Nite-Tie, I am not going to be here very long can you get my clothes done quickly?"

"Very, very quickly."

Musher explained to Nite-Tie 6 that he needed to be back at Tachikawa very soon. She washed and rinsed him diligently. He was in the hot tub for just a few minutes when Nite-Tie 6 had him out, dried and laying on the massage table. She massaged for a few minutes before she had her head with mouth open in front of his dick. "You want?"

"Yes but only until I bring you up here to fuck me." She licked and sucked until the sensations were driving him crazy. He grasped her hair and motioned for her to come mount his dick. The pussy was so warm and moist. She fucked him slowly until he burst from inside. He could feel the hot semen charging into her pussy. His dick was still hard. She started on him again only this time not moving so slowly. It was a magnificent fuck. He climaxed again and felt drained.

She cleaned him and wrapped him in his towel. He gave her a hand shake with five hundred yen enclosed in his hand. He made the "Sh-sh-sh" motion with his finger over his mouth. "Between you and me."

Nite-Tie 2 handed him his freshly done clothes. When he came back to pay Nite-Tie 2 he was dressed in his air force uniform complete with badges and decorations. He paid the bill in yen with a tip beyond what was the norm. Nite-Tie 2 was tongue tied with admiration.

Musher went into the pro shop to use the phone and Timmy stood as if he were frozen while he admired Musher in the splendor of his uniform. "My God boy, you are the hero they made you out to be."

Musher's ride came and he said to Timmy, "Can I play on the course tomorrow? I'll be here by 0830."

It was 1230 hours when they reached the hospital at Tachi. He garnered his few belongings said his goodbyes to whoever was there and headed for his new quarters. All his belongings were in his new quarters by 1300 hours. Also in his quarters was the new maid Yoko. As they were hanging up his clothes he realized that he had not bought a clothes dresser and at least half of this closet space was unusable.

He explained to Yoko about the impending delivery. She could either go or stay. Whichever she chose to do. The delivery was on time and the two delivery agents brought everything in and set it up. Musher gave each a one hundred yen tip. They were astonished and thanked him over and over agin. Yoko said, "Too much tip. Spoil economy." Musher ignored her. Musher had arranged the room to allow for the purchase of a dresser. Yoko made the bed but other than that was no help. He told her to go home and come back the day after tomorrow. She didn't understand that but she did as she was told.

Musher used his new telephone to dial Melke. "I hate to be a pain in the ass but could I get some assistance from the carpentry shop?"

"What do you need?"

"My closet needs redesign and modification. I can do the design but I need a good finish carpenter to do the work. I also need some shelves in the

524

room. Again I can do the design and placement but I need a good finish carpenter to make them and mount them."

"How soon will you have the designs?"

"I can do them tonight."

"At 1400 tomorrow be at the carpentry shop and ask for Master Sergeant Chuck Wood, affectionately called Wood Chuck. He will take care of your needs. Do you have anything else at the moment?"

"Nothing but my sincere thanks. The telephone is a real blessing. God Bless you and Colonel Cramer."

He still had time to get to the BX and buy a small dresser to match his other furniture. He selected the one he wanted and also bought a new jack knife, a sketch pad, a ruler, a protractor, a gum eraser and some drawing pencils of various colors. He was checked out by the same manager who had checked him out before. The cost of the dresser and other items was fifty-three dollars. He paid in script. "Would you like it delivered now? You could ride back to your quarters with our guys."

He was on the truck with the same guys who made the earlier delivery. They carried it into his room and he gave them each a fifty yen tip. It fit into the place Musher had allocated.

He was hungry and the NCO Club was just a few minutes walk away. When he walked in he realized that he had nothing to prove who he was and what his rank was. Fortunately no one questioned him. He walked into the dining room and had dinner. He ate, paid his bill and tipped the waiter. He was back in his room sitting at his table to design the closet and the shelves. He finished late in the night and set his alarm clock for 0600 hours.

This had been a really full day

CHAPTER 163

Another Golf Day Plus

Musher was at the golf course at 0630 hitting warm up balls on the range. After forty-five minutes he went to the putting green to practice his stroke. Timmy came to him and said, "I can't teach you any more about putting. You know the concepts. Your tee time is 0820. I have put you with three of the better golfers stationed at Tachi. Come inside and meet them. At the table Timmy began, "This young gentleman has a long fancy Italian name but we all call him Musher. Musher this Fernando, this is Augustus and the big guy is Big John. You have fifteen minutes before you are on the tee. Musher your stuff is in the cart with Big John."

Big John asked the question that was bugging all three playmates. "What's your handicap?"

"I don't have one. I haven't played enough rounds to have a handicap. As a matter of fact this is my first round ever."

"You mean your first round at Yokota. Right?"

"No, I mean my first round ever. Timmy just started teaching me the game about three weeks ago."

An unequalled look of despair came over the faces of his three playmates. It could not be heard but they were saying to themselves, "A hacker." "This round may take six hours." "Wish there was a way I could get called out for an emergency." Like true gentlemen they were committed and they headed for the first tee.

The beginning hole was a Par 5. The first three drove their balls into the middle of the fairway. Musher hit a low climbing draw which ended up in the fairway twenty yards ahead of the other three. Each of them hit a fairway wood to a good position. Musher hit a two iron which left him one hundred yards short of the green. Their three approaches all went onto the green the best of which was twelve feet from the hole. Musher hit a towering wedge past the hole and it spun back to within three feet of the hole. They two putted while Musher one putted for a Birdie.

The next hole was a one hundred seventy-four yard Par 3 with the pin on the right side of the green just over a sand trap. To Musher, "Your honor." He chose a six iron, made a silk smooth swing and watched as the ball started towards the left side of the green, faded and landed with the fade left to right spin which took him closer to the hole. He was eighteen feet away and looked disappointed. All four players made par.

There was delay on the next tee box and Big John asked," Do you think we are going to buy that cock and bull story about first round ever? You are probably not a hustler because no good hustler would show such skill in the first two holes. What's the deal?"

Musher told them the whole truth. He wasn't sure if they believed it or not. As the round continued he made an occasional error and at the end of eighteen he had a score of seventy-six. Four over par. His playing companions had seventy-four and two seventy-fives.

They were in the bar having a beer while Musher had a coke. Timmy joined them and said to no one in particular, "Is he something else of what? Give him two more months and he will beat anyone at Tachi. Maybe even anyone at Yokota." It was flattering sitting there listening to everyone talk well about you. "Gentlemen I have a 1400 hour appointment at Tachi. It was really enjoyable to play with you and I hope we can do it again sometime."

Big John, "We have 0900 tee times for Saturday and Sunday we would certainly enjoy your company as our fourth."

"I'll be there. Thanks again."

At the Tachi wood working shop he asked for Master Sergeant Chuck Wood. A slight fellow stuck out his hand, "I am Wood Chuck you must be Musher. Captain Melke called me. Did you bring your designs?"

They laid the designs out on a table where Wood Chuck inspected them. These are doable. Painted air force blue like the walls in your room? The closet looks a little more tricky. We may not be able to pre-cut and paint the pieces. That depends on how accurate your measurements are. No sweat, we will get it done. Can you be in your room at 1500 tomorrow so we can install the shelves and do the closet?"

"I will be waiting. If there is a change of plans you can always call me at my room, Extension 4726. Thank you again."

I need my own transportation. This calling the Motor Pools every time I need to go somewhere is for the birds. He made it to the American Express office and did the paperwork for a ten thousand dollar transfer from his stateside account to his Tachi account. He was told it would be in place tomorrow. It was still early enough to go to the BX and see if they sold cars and if so what kind.

The BX sold every kind of American car but the catch was they were sold only for pickup in the United States. On one wall there were a number of advertisements for used car sales. Mostly the owners were rotating to the states and the cars were not valuable enough to take home. Musher's eye caught an ad for a British TR-6 convertible. The picture almost looked like Dukie's little sports car. The steering column was on the right side of the vehicle and not the standard American left. He would need to learn a new driving technique. The owner was a RAF Squadron Leader Rossman who lived in Tachi base housing. Musher called and had the motor pool take him to see the car.

Cosmetically the car was in excellent shape. The convertible top was almost new and so were the tires. It was seven years old. It had two different owners in its seven years. The asking price was two thousand dollars American. That amount was just about the cost of the car when the car was new. Musher told the RAF Squadron Leader Rossman that he would like the car checked out mechanically before making the purchase. The owner produced a portfolio of vehicle maintenance records for the past three years and offered to take the car to any location on Tachi which Musher chose. Musher offered one hundred dollars for the right of first refusal pending any actual sale. He took his receipt and said he would be in touch very soon.

Yoko was waiting back his room. She had made the bed and cleaned the room well. The room was still not fully organized. He sent her home and told her to take tomorrow off. When she was out of the room he called Captain Melke to tell him of his plan and once again ask for his help.

"Of course I know Squadron Leader Chesney Rossman. His father is the Duke of Barnsworth in the Surrey area of England. An honorable man. I will call him and tell him when and where to take the car for inspection. Our agent will provide you with a statement or certificate of worthiness. Whatever price he asked for the car don't pay it. You and I will do better when we finalize the deal. You will need an international license to drive off base. It is not a photo identification type so I will take of that and all you will need to do is sign it. The same with your US Government license. When I talk to Chesney I will get all the particulars of the vehicle and have both on and off base insurance papers made which we could put into effect at the point of sale. I will also bring a Tachikawa Air Base windshield sticker which allows free access to any US military installation in Japan. Musher, do you have a clue how to drive a stick shift which is totally opposite from the ones we are accustomed to? Do you have at least two thousand in script available?"

"Sir I have an American Express checking account here on Tachi which will more than cover any expenditures I may make. No I don't have a clue how to drive on the wrong side of the road with the wrong steering and transmission setup. I learned to ride a horse in two days. Learning the TR-6 might be difficult but I will learn."

"OK Musher, I will be at your place around 1000 hours. Have a good night."

It was not good night for Musher. He walked to the NCO Club with the intent of dinner and an early night in his new bed. The first part of his plan went smoothly. He was amazed how good the food and service was and how inexpensive it really was. He figured out why when he saw the room full of slot machines and everyone of them in full use. Tachikawa was the main POE (port of embarkation) for the Far East and these temporary personnel fed the hungry slots. The profit margin is ridiculously high. The NCO Club was not allowed to show a monthly profit greater than two percent of its expenses therefore the costs to customers stayed low.

He went to the office and filled out his membership application, received his NCO Club identification card and a stack of papers explaining the rules of the club, its hours, etc. The monthly membership dues were one dollar. He paid twelve months in advance. As he left the office he passed a door which said "Gentlemen Only". Thinking it was a latrine he pushed the door open only to find it was a very large gambling room. There were people playing poker, playing pool, playing snooker, playing gin rummy, playing darts and even playing snooker. He floated as quietly as he could around the room trying to measure the money action and who the better players were. None of the poker games showed any evidence of foul play. In one alcove there were a number players engaged in a game called "Four-Five- Six." He had never seen the game before and he stood there trying to learn. He compared the game to Blackjack. After considerable time he grasped the concept and execution of the game.

Four-Five-Six, often called Three Dice in a Cup." The "banker" or sometimes called "house" is actually one of the players. How it was determined who would be the banker when the game began he was not exactly sure. The number of players in each betting hand depended on how much money was in the pot and how many players it took to cover (or to use the dice expression

fade) the pot. In some of the lesser pots it may have only been one player whereas in the large pots it may have taken as many as twelve players. When all bets have been made and in some cases the total money to fade the pot is actually less than the amount in the pot, the banker shakes the dice in the cup and rolls them onto the table.

There are four basic options which may occur with the banker's roll.:

Option 1: The natural winners for the banker are, 4-5-6, three of a kind and any pair accompanied by a six. He wins all faded bets.

Option 2: The natural losers for the banker are, 1-2-3 or any pair accompanied by an ace (1). He loses all faded bets.

Option 3: "The Point." The Point is reached when the banker rolls neither a natural winner nor a natural loser but does roll a pair with the third die showing a value from 2 to 5. The value of the third die is "The Point."

Option 4: If none of the above three options occur from the banker's roll is null. The banker then rolls again until one of the three options occurs.

Options 1,2 and 4 are self explanatory. Option 3 works differently. In this instance we will say the banker has established his point as 4. The first fader to his left will now roll the dice with the same options. In the event the fader also makes a point of four, it is a "Push". Neither the fader or banker wins. The faded amount remains in the pot. The dice are passed to the next fader to the left and he plays the same rules as the first fader. Each fader get his turn until all have had an opportunity to win, lose or push

There are few interesting wrinkles to 4-5-6.

Wrinkle 1: After the completion of each roll the banker may either take all the money out of the pot or let it all ride for the next roll. Those are his only choices. There is no "Squirreling part of the pot."

Wrinkle 2: If a fader during his opportunity to beat the banker's point rolls 4-5-6 when all the faders have had their opportunity the first fader to have rolled 4-5-6 has the option to become the banker. If he denies the opportunity and in the course of the roll following him another fader has rolled 4-5-6 then that fader has the option to become banker, if he too denies then wrinkle 3 applies.

Wrinkle 3: If a player is the last person to fade the amount necessary to consider the pot faded and the banker rolls an automatic loser that last person to fade the amount to consider the pot fully faded has the option to become banker. If he denies the option then the dice pass to the first person on the banker's left and he has the option to become the banker. If he also denies the option to be banker then the left moving dice are passed until a player elects to be the banker.

Musher liked the looks of 4-5-6 and was sure that at some point he would try it. Just as soon as he studied the odds and how to get an edge.

CHAPTER 164
I Am Finally Settled In To Tachi

He didn't know anyone in the dining hall so once again he was alone. He conjured the past and remembered what it was like to always be alone. Lately he had some good company but no one he would call a friend. Captain Melke and Timmy came as close to being friends but in reality they were only doing their job as they had been directed. Still he wasn't going to take himself into depression he had a lot to be thankful for. This week he saw his psychiatrist again and that was a depressing two hours. Soon it would be 1000 and Captain Melke would be coming to his room.

Melke was surprised at how the room looked. "You have done a fine job."

"Wood Chuck will be here later with his gang to put the finishing touches on this place. None of this would have been possible without you."

"So much for the flattery. Let's get you ready to drive and hopefully not kill yourself" Musher did a lot of signing and ended up with the two different driver licenses, both types of insurance, a military establishment access sticker to put on his windshield and a letter certifying the condition of the TR-6. "The one thing missing was the Japanese license plate for off base driving. That will be waiting for us at Chesney's house. You owe me a total of seventy-nine dollars that I put out for these documents." Musher handed him an American one hundred dollar bill.

"I cannot change that. Pay me later."

"No such luck partner. You are forced to keep it because I am sure you have spent more than the difference doing things for me."

"What time is Wood Chuck due here? Let's go get your car. You will get Chesney's gas ration card as part of the transaction. We will get you your own later. Are you fixed for cash? Let me call him and tell him we are coming and we will go."

Chesney had everything ready. He had the title and the bill of sale in his hand. Melke spoke, "My man says the car is only worth fourteen hundred. Musher told me you said the sale price was two thousand. Would you like to reconsider that?" As the Yiddish would say "they hondled" until the selling price was sixteen hundred. Musher had already given Chesney one hundred and when he handed the other fifteen hundred dollars in his personal American Express check Chesney looked at it bewildered. Melke said, "I stand behind it."

Melke left and Musher and Chesney went out in the TR-6 for a driving lesson. They were at the far end of an inactive runway when Musher first tried driving. The transmission groaned and the car bucked. It wasn't too long before he adjusted to the clutch gas pedal coordination and the proper time to shift gears. He drove Chesney to his home and went back out to practice some more driving. When he pulled into the lot behind the BAQ he stopped smoothly and parked with the nose towards the building. He would need to practice parrell parking with this little baby. He zipped the cover over the driver and passenger sides securing it on the dash board. It did not look like rain but he needed the practice.

Inside his room Yoko was waiting again. She had made the bed, hung up his clothes, emptied the ash trays and generally cleaned the area. "Yoko what are you doing here. I told you to take today off."

"Cannot afford day off. Must earn full pay every month."

"When I give you time off you are paid just as if you were working. Now go home and don't come back until tomorrow." She smiled, bowed and left.

Musher set his alarm and lay on the bed for a nap. At 1500 Wood Chuck and his boys came in carrying shelves and pre-cut closet pieces. Everything was painted air force blue. With the exception of Wood Chuck all the workers were Japanese. Musher showed Wood Chuck where and how he wanted the shelves mounted and Wood Chuck relayed in fluent Japanese what to do. The closet assembled just as it was designed. He had doubled his clothes handing space and made a special floor area for shoes. It took these pros less than two hours to complete all the tasks. Musher could not thank them enough and Wood Chuck said, "Hey guy you deserve whatever we can give. Call me if you need anything else."

Musher spent the rest of the day organizing and putting things where he wanted them. The room was twenty feet by eighteen feet. The shelf in the bath room accommodated the hot plate, the coffee pot a couple of pans and some cooking utensils. The refrigerator held his cokes and a couple of bottles of wine. He needed to go grocery shopping to fill the refrigerator. It had a freezer section where he could make ice cubes and keep ice cream. One shelf was a pantry shelf cabinet style. It was one of the larger shelves beside the refrigerator and would hold some canned goods, condiments, etc. He looked around his large one room apartment and felt good about it.

He was hungry and had nothing to eat in his room. He walked to the NCO Club for a bite. He was enjoying his club sandwich when a man in civilian clothes sat down beside him. "You're Musher right? I was at Smoky when you were and I was at Roswell when you were. Right now I am at

Kadena and here on R&R. We all heard about your capture and release. You must be one tough guy. I never knew you but I certainly knew of you. Did you really have anything to do with Crossbow's suicide?"

He had been drinking so Musher decided to overlook his arrogance. Instead he said to him, "What's your name?"

"I am Technical Sergeant Gerald Stark, crew chief of a B-29."

"Listen closely Gerald, I am going to overlook you tonight but I don't want you to approach me again. If you do you may be one of the victims of the stories."

As he started to rise from his chair he said, "I don't think you're so tough" Before he was half way up Musher smashed him over the head with the water pitcher. His fall to the floor caused a commotion and the Sergeant–At–Arms came running to the table. Musher said, "I think he has had too much to drink. He fell to the floor and the water pitcher smashed on his head. I am going to pay my bill and leave now. Goodnight." He left fifteen dollars in script and headed back to his room.

Sleep did not come easy.

CHAPTER 165
I Must Balance the Day

Musher awakened to the smell of coffee. Either he did not lock the door or Yoko had a key. "How you like coffee?"

"Black." She appeared from the bath room with a tray holding a mug of black coffee, two cinnamon rolls, an ash tray, Lucky Strikes and matches. As he sat up she puffed the pillows behind him.

"You want play radio?" He nodded and she turned it onto the Armed Forces Network. She had done these things many times before. She was not as good as Hereford but who knows how she may develop. "You go doctor today? What time you go?"

Musher was not thrilled about two hours with the psychiatrist. Especially after last night. When he finished the coffee she had his robe and slippers waiting for him. "I go shower and shave."

"You want I wash back?"

"No thank you." When he came from the shower she had laid clean underwear, clothes, socks and shoes on the bed. She went to clean the shower area while he dressed. She came from the bathroom with his coffee mug in hand, "More coffee?"

"You want I stay and cook Japanese dinner for you?"

"No thank you. If I am not back by 1630 you may go and I will see you tomorrow." With that he went out the door, got into his TR-6 and drove to the hospital. He was not looking forward to his appointment but he was on time for his weekly appointment with Doctor Terence Mulcahy, of the Hyde Park Mulcahys. The session began with the Mulcahy opening speech. "You are looking well. I understand that your golf skills are remarkable for the time you have been learning; and that you have bought yourself a TR-6. Good luck with both. What have you done since last week?"

"I am living in new quarters, have a full time maid and you know about the other things you just mentioned."

"Do you want to tell me about last night? Did you know that Sergeant Stark is in the hospital with a number of stitches in his skull and a slight concussion?"

"No I did not."

"Do you care about him?"

"Not particularly."

"Do you realize you could have killed him?"

"Not me Doc, the pitcher smashed on his head when he fell to the floor. Show me someone who saw it differently."

"There isn't anyone who actually saw the incident."

"Doc is it OK if I ask you a few questions? Thank you. When you were a schoolboy did you ever have a fight in the school yard? No, I am not surprised, how about through high school and college? No again. Did you avoid fights by backing off or apologizing for something that you knew there was no need for you to apologize? Your yes is no surprise either. Have you ever struck a blow in anger? Only against subservient animals. You see Doc in my neighborhood you would have been a wimp and someone's bitch. How could you ever hope to understand someone like me who has been an aggressor all his life starting in his early childhood. In my ethnic background there is nothing more important than your honor and your word. If you fail to defend either you may just as well leave the country. Without knowing I would bet you are a student of the martial arts. There you can strike inert objects or team mates who do not have the intent to kill you. Your favorite movies are either violent war movies or movies where the good guys beat up on the bad guys and the good guys are always the winners. Doc it is summed up in the term "vicarious living." That slob last night invaded my private life without an invitation. I gave him the full opportunity to walk away unharmed. He let his mouth write a check his ass could not cash. People like me anticipate the behavior of people like him and strike first. There are no rules to survival. Don't you believe that this particular trait allowed me to survive when I should have given up? Musher went on to tell him the story of the three Korean girls and the bamboo poles. You are the only person I have ever told about this and if it gets to someone else, somewhere else I will kill you. Fortunately it has not deprived me of a sex life which I am proving just about every day."

Doctor Terence Mulcahy was dumbfounded. Almost unable to speak. "Musher we need to work on your control. When you attack it seems the intent is to kill or severely maim. Right now I don't know how to get you in better control of your instincts. Maybe by next week I will have some idea."

It was obvious to Musher that Doctor Terence Mulcahy wanted to end this session now. Musher would not be surprised if he had shit in his pants. Like most any one who lives "vicariously" they don't want to face the truth of their persona. Musher was almost looking forward to the next session. He had Doctor Terence Mulcahy in his sphere of control. He headed his TR-6 for Yokota feeling much better.

Driving to Yokota Musher was getting the feel of why the Japanese drive as fast as they can and blow the horn at anything. He joined the game and could feel his driving skills getting better. At the golf clubhouse the parking attendant took his car and he walked into the pro shop. He bought another shirt and pants outfit plus sox and an extra belt so that he would always have clean clothes in his locker.

He was going to the sand traps to practice that segment of his game when Timmy called to him. "Musher I want you to meet Major Susan Blanchard. Susan is a three handicap from the Ladies tees and a seven from the deep blue tees. She is looking for a game and I thought you two might enjoy playing together. I have told Susan about your fabulous learning curve and she promised not to beat you too badly." The fire lit in Musher.

"Tell me Timmy is Major Blanchard a gambler?"

"She has been known to play a twenty dollar Nassau with ten dollar bonus points." He had to explain that game to Musher.

"Has she been known to play fifty dollar per stroke differential?"

Susan broke in,"That's all right with me if you think you can afford it."

They chose not to ride a cart. Each had his own caddy. They played from the deep blue tees. Hardly a word was spoken during the round. When it was over and they were in the 19th Hole bar Musher said, "You lose eighty for the twenty dollar Nassau. You lose sixty for my six birdies and you did not have any. You lose forty for my four closest to the pin shots on the Par 3's. You shot seventy-six and I shot sixty-eight. You lose four hundred in stroke differential. You lose a total of five hundred eighty dollars." He did not smile, it was strictly business. " I do accept cash."

"Sorry Musher I don't have that much cash in my pocket but if you will follow me to my BOQ I have it there." Her BOQ room was just about the same as his BAQ. Not nearly as tastily done as his was. In the room she said, "I am going to have a scotch. Can I get you one?" Musher was not a drinker but what could one scotch and water hurt? She brought him his drink and excused herself to get out of the golf clothes and into something more comfortable. When she returned she had just showered had her hair down, was wearing a see though nightgown and robe and smelled good enough to eat. She stood behind the couch and was lightly massaging his neck and shoulders. "You are so tense, the golf must have tensed your body. If you want you can take a quick shower. You will find a kimona (a Japanese bathrobe) you can use."

Musher headed for the shower. When he returned she was prone on the couch and motioned him to lie next to her. He could not resist kissing her neck and shoulders and she did nothing to discourage him. She put her hands on his shoulder and pressed his body downward. As he moved down he massaged and kissed her breast. She kept pushing him down until he was in her crotch. "Oh baby make the pussy smile." He varied his moves from licking her pussy to nibbling on her clitoris to sucking deep inside the pussy. She moaned with joy until she grabbed the hair on his head and pressed his tongue deep into her pussy. She climaxed with the gush of a fountain. She pulled him up to her, stuck her tongue in his mouth and sucked him dry. She liked the taste of pussy. As she relaxed she said,"Oh thank you. I needed that. What can I do for you?" Musher didn't speak he simply climbed on her chest leaned forward and put his dick in her mouth. "Suck it dry bitch." She reacted to his language and the more he spoke the harder she licked and sucked. He was not surprised when she swallowed every drop of his semen.

"Would you like another drink with your Lucky Strikes?" He smoked and drank scotch while they talked about sex and how to best enjoy it. She asked, "Have you had sex with two women?" Musher nodded no. She called, "Misu-san" and her maid appeared. The oh-jo-san was about twenty years old with a tender body. Without direction Misu knelt before Susan and started licking her pussy. After a few minutes they reversed positions and Susan was licking Misu. Watching the two women had brought Musher to full hard. He took a position behind Susan and fucked her doggie style. After the climaxes Susan and Musher lay on Susan's bed while Misu washed them clean. Misu dried Musher so delicately that once more he had a solid hard-on. Misu mounted him and started a slow fuck. Susan sat on his chest while he licked her pussy. Musher could not contain himself. He climaxed inside Misu while Susan climaxed in his mouth. The three of them lay together with their bodies intertwined.

Susan awakened Musher. "Sorry but you cannot stay here overnight. Will you be all right to drive to Tachi or do you want a motor pool driver?"

"A quick shower and I will be fine."

"I'll make you some coffee while you shower."

As Musher was leaving Susan said, "We must play again. You must give me a chance to get even. Good night Good Man. Be careful driving." She kissed him on the cheek.

He was extremely cautious driving back to Tachi. In his room he threw off his clothes and fell into bed. His last thought before sleep overcame him, " I did a pretty good job at balancing the day. My medical visit, my good round of golf and great sex for dessert."

CHAPTER 166

What a Life

Yoko awakened him at 0600. "You have 0900 tee time?" He quickly showered, dressed and was out the door in fifteen minutes. When he reached the driving range to warm up his three playing partners were already there. For the first time Augustus spoke, "We thought we would play ten dollar Sixes if that is all right with you." Musher had no idea what Sixes were but he acknowledged that Sixes were all right with him. "Musher each of us will play with the other three for six holes in the round. It is match play for ten dollars a match. Total exposure is thirty dollars. There are no considerations for handicap in Sixes. Of course individuals can make any additional bets they wish but those bets are outside the scope of Sixes. We also play ten dollars per man for the low handicap round. I repeat the low handicap round. We are all three handicaps and we rate you as a one. Is all this agreeable to you?" Once more Musher nodded agreement.

On the first tee Augustus took a ball from each player and tossed them in the air. The two balls which ended up closest were partners for the first six holes. Each had his own caddy and they had two fore caddies. The job of a fore caddy is to stay ahead of he players on the same hole and ear-mark where the balls stop on any given shot. All four played well.

While sipping a cold drink and waiting for lunch Augustus said, "Musher wins all three Sixes so we lose ten dollars each. We each had a net seventy-one and Musher had a net seventy. We each lose another ten dollars. Musher is the only winner for a total sixty dollars."

Fernando chimed in with,"If we are going to play with him again tomorrow we are going to find a game where we simply do not contribute to the Musher Fund for Wayward Golfers. By the way we heard from Timmy yesterday you beat Sandy Blanchard for over five hundred dollars. Of course she didn't have that much money on her person so you went to her BOQ to collect. We are all married so she doesn't challenge us to a golf match. Did she pay you Musher?"

"When I gamble I pay if I lose but I also collect if I win. She paid handsomely."

With that they all three left for home, he paid the bill and sat smoking his Lucky Strikes. He wondered what he would do with the rest of the day. All the choices were simply great. He could go play another round of golf. He could go spend some time with Nite-Tie 6. He could go to a matinee movie. He could go to the NCO Club and gamble at what ever is available. He could go back to his room and order in a nice oh-joe-san for afternoon pleasure. He opted for the last choice. During the drive to Tachi he wondered how he would order in the delicacy. Maybe Yoko would know although she said her former client was a faithful, married man.

The room was totally cleaned with everything in its proper place. Musher took off his shoes and lay on the bed . "Yoko, if I wanted female companionship for the afternoon how would I get it?""You tell me and I make it happen. I get young, pretty, healthy oh-joe-san. You give me money and I do rest." She had also done this many times before.

"What would it cost?"

"What sex you want?"

"All kinds."

"One thousand yen for her, two hundred yen for taxi. If you want how soon you want?"

"Just as quickly as I can shower."

"I use telephone?" She spoke in Japanese and when she hung up she said, "You shower now. Guest be here twenty minutes. I meet guest outside and bring here."

The guest was beautiful. She disrobed and had the body to match her facial features. Yoko asked,"OK I watch?"

For the next two hours the guest took Musher through every type of male-female sex he could imagine. A few times Musher would glance at Yoko who was sitting with her knees up and her hand vigorously fucking her pussy. Yoko took oh-joe-san into the bathroom and they showered together. He figured Yoko also liked to suck pussy.

They came out of the shower with smiles and looking graceful. Yoko made a phone call and in a very few minutes the guest was gone. Yoko asked, "Yoko do good job. Musher feel better?"

Musher crawled under the sheet and told Yoko she could leave, turn out the lights and lock the door. He would see her tomorrow.

Is this a great life or what? His golf course winnings were sixty dollars and his golf course expenses were eight dollars. He had afternoon sex for under four dollars. His profit so far for today is forty-eight dollars. Is this a great life or what?

He woke up hungry. A quick SSS and into a full uniform. He walked to the NCO Club for dinner. It was Saturday night and the place was packed. Dinner was being served in the main ballroom. There was not an empty table in the place. He was asked if he would object to joining a table of one gentleman and two ladies. The maitre d' brought him to the table and asked if there was any objection from them. The maitre d' left and the gentleman was the first to speak. "I am Tony Russo I am here on a sixty day temporary duty, this is Marcella Paone a teacher in the American School here on Tachi and this is Rita Doss also a teacher at the American School."

"My name is Saverio Muscarello but everyone calls me Musher. I am here recovering from an experience."

Rita blurted, "You're the Ex POW undergoing treatment here."

"Not so much treatment as putting a little meat on these bones. Have you all had dinner?" They had so he ordered his. While waiting for service he asked of the group, "Why does it appear there are so many pretty unescorted ladies in the room?"

This time it was Marcella, "There are approximately five hundred female school teachers living in a Ladies Quarters called "L Block." Most of the men permanently assigned to Tachikawa are married and either have their families here or are faithful to the wives. The ones who are not faithful are generally scum bags. Musher are you married?"

"No I am not and I do not have any intention of getting married anytime soon." His food was served and he ate his dinner. Most of the couples on the dance floor were ladies dancing with ladies. It seemed as if there was an extreme shortage of males. It was not hard to figure out. Why would a guy wanting pussy try to woo a round eye (a Caucasian) when for less than five dollars he could have great sex with the Ohjoesans?

Musher asked Marcella to dance. It was slow moving music and Marcella pressed her body against his. He did not return the pressure. When the next song began he asked Rita to dance. The song finished and they stayed on the floor for another dance. This time Rita whispered in Musher's ear, "My pussy needs exercise. Can you help me?" When the music ended they made no pretense of an unnoticed exit. It was a short walk to Musher's room. Before he had the door locked she was stripping her clothes. Naked on the bed she asked if he had condoms. He did not. She took six from her purse and said, "I hope these are not enough for tonight." At 0300 Musher called her a cab and she quietly left saying, "We can do this anytime you want but you must bring your own condoms."

Is this a great life or what?

540

CHAPTER 167
They Are Getting Wise To Me

The next couple of months were as if they were out of Aladdin's Lamp. He played golf just about every day. In his TR-6 he went to other golf courses in the area and was having sex just about every day. The weakest part of the two months was his visits with his psychiatrist Terence Mulcahy. The doctor kept insisting that he was improving each visit and very soon he could be discharged from this treatment. Musher knew that would mean reassignment

One of the highlights of the two months was the USAF Far East Golf Tournament at Hickam AFB in Hawaii. Musher went as part of the Tachikawa five person golf team. The team was made up of himself, Fernando, Augustus, Big John and a WAF named Captain Jane Purcell a scratch golfer in her own right. Despite the fact that each team had at least one enlisted man all team members including the WAFs were billeted in the lavish BOQ. They played two practice rounds and three tournament rounds. The Tachi team played well but not well enough. They finished second to the Yokota team coached by Timmy. Musher's three rounds were sixty-eight, sixty-eight and sixty-five. He was awarded the low medalist trophy. At the awards dinner Timmy made a big deal of the fact that Musher picked up his first golf club less than six months ago and he is living proof of what dedication, hard work and good instruction can produce. Musher's acceptance speech was "Thank You".

Susan Blanchard spent the night in Musher's room. The next day everyone departed for their home station. Hawaii was quite the place.

Musher returned to his hedonistic life style. He was called for a meeting with Colonel Cramer the Hospital Commander. Also in the room were the Wing Director of Personnel, Doctor Terence Mulcahy and Captain Martin Melke. Cramer began, "We have concluded that your treatment has gone well enough for you to be discharged as a hospital patient and reassigned for further convalescence. Your psychiatric treatment will continue wherever you are for as long as necessary. Do you have a preference where you would like to continue your convalescence?"

Musher thought I don't want to be near to Boston. England would be nice. "Yes sir, I do. I would like to continue my convalescence in England."

The Wing Director of Personnel said, "I am sorry but I am afraid that cannot be done."

Musher went into his screaming act, "Why do you ask me if you don't give a fuck what I want. You are no different than all the bastards who want to control my mind and body." He continuously screamed these two sentences. Doctor Mulcahy tried to calm him down and he gave Mulcahy his "I could kill you if I want" look. Mulcahy backed off. Three times Colonel Cramer yelled, "Musher, I am sure we can arrange England." Captain Melke had a knowing look on his face.

The room was silent when Colonel Cramer asked Captain Melke to take Musher into a separate room to quiet him down. They went into an adjoining smaller conference room where there were water and ash trays. Musher lit up and was sipping water when Melke said, "Caesar would be proud of that act."

"Why would Julius Caesar care about me?"

"Our mutual friend North End Caesar has asked me to look after you. My name before the change was Martino Melchioni, known as "Mallet Hands Martino, former resident of Fleet Street. Thanks to our friend Caesar I am a lawyer from Boston University. The Korean War gave me the choice of being drafted or joining the judge advocate's office in the USAF. Like you I am only here as long as I need be. They will agree to send you to England. At this time Mulcahy wants you anywhere but near him. Whatever you said to him he is absolutely terrified of you."

"I must confess Martino I did not know how you got everything done but now I understand. You will make a great Consigliere."

They were summoned into the meeting room. The Wing Director of Personnel spoke,"We will reassign you to England for further convalescence. You will continue to receive your flight pay and when you get there you will establish a visit schedule for psychiatric assistance. This will take some time to coordinate such a reassignment When we are ready one of my senior sergeants will contact you to make all the arrangements. I wish you the best of luck."

Colonel Cramer, "Musher thank you for coming. I am sure everything will work as you choose. You are excused from any further visits with Doctor Mulcahy. Until you leave Captain Melke and I are here to assist you." Melke lagged behind and whispered to Musher, "Please stay out of trouble until you leave."

Musher went back to living the good life of golf, good food and sex every day. It was getting much cooler at Yokota and Musher was not sure he wanted to handle playing golf in the cold weather.

CHAPTER 168
Sayonara Japan

Over three weeks had passed since Musher's meeting with Colonel Cramer. He was not complaining. He was living the daily routine of golf, good food and sex. At the NCO Club he had tried his hand at 4-5-6. and luck had smiled upon him. He won over three thousand dollars in all kinds of money ranging from the British pound to the American dollar. His plan would require cash availability.

He was visited in his room by Chief Warrant Officer Kevin O'Grady, Special Assistant to the Wing Director of Personnel. His departure date was established and his new assignment location determined. His actual flight time on his departure date was not set in concrete. Out processing would take less than a day.

Musher asked O'Grady a question. "Am I not entitled to a sixty day convalescent leave between here and my next duty station?"

"Yes you are.""Do I not have more than thirty days accrued leave?""Yes you do.""Is it possible for me to get a ninety day delay enroute by combining the two types of leave?""It is possible.""Would any travel days be added to that ninety?""Yes they would.""Would you have my reassignment order cut to show the enroute leave and the allowed travel time?""Yes I will. Will you require a passport during your travel to your next assignment?""I have not figured out a route yet so may I please have a passport."O'Grady took a white sheet from his bag and draped it on the closet door. He had Musher stand in front of it while he took six bust pictures. "I will take care of the passport."O'Grady asked a series of questions. "Will you need a cash advance? Will you ship your car, your furniture, clothes lockers or anything else? Anything you ship will require approximately two months to get to your new assignment. Your goods will be received at the nearest Port Of Entry to your duty assignment."

"Mister O'Grady is it possible for me to leave here on a flight to Hawaii. I want that to be my first step in convalescence."

"I am sure I can arrange that. What luggage will you have?""My B-4 Bag, my Golf Clubs and a small carry on bag.""Thank you Sergeant Muscarello I will see you in two or three days with a solid itinerary for your departure from Tachikawa."

Musher went to Yokota to hit balls for a couple of hours. He needed work with his fairway woods. Hunger overcame him and he ordered a big omelet with lots of home fries, extra rye toast and a large pot of hot black tea. He was joined by a master sergeant in full uniform. "My name is Steve Franklin and I just signed in at Tachi for a two year tour. I have been assigned to Tachi before and today I had the pleasure of seeing your living quarters. You have done an excellent job. How did I get to see your quarters? The base housing people showed it to me because I will get your room when you leave Tachi. Here is my proposition. If you will leave everything there except your personal things I will pay you six thousand American dollars. If you also leave your car I will pay you an additional two thousand American dollars."

"My next duty station is in England. I am shipping my car in the next seven days. You can have all the room furnishings for seven thousand dollars."

"It's a deal." From his pocket he withdrew a roll of American hundred dollar bills. "Here is two thousand in advance. You get the rest when you give me the key to your room."

His car was shipped, his bags were packed, his golf clubs were securely covered and he had said goodbye to Yoko. Tomorrow he was leaving. He made his last trip to Yokota in a motor pool car. Timmy was in his office when Musher walked in. "I thought you would be getting ready to leave"

"I am but I needed to see you before I left." He put two thousand American dollars in the middle of Timmy's desk. "This is not payment for your help it is an early Christmas present. I cannot thank you enough."

Sayanora Tomaduchi (Phonetic Japanese for Goodbye My Friend)

BOOK 6

THE LAST
DAYS
OF JOY

CHAPTER 169

Aloha Hickham AFB

Musher arrived at Hickam on a warm day and he could feel the tropical sea breeze blowing across the island. Base Operations Passenger Services provided him transportation to the Visiting Airmen Quarters (VAQ). He filled out the registration form marking his intended length of stay as thirty days. His daily room fee was one dollar. Musher paid thirty dollars for his anticipated length of stay. His room was in the main building on the first floor. The room was good size, had a private shower, a telephone, a combination alarm clock radio and a refrigerator. The small desk was covered with publications such as the base bus schedule and routes, the location of the NCO Club, the dining hall and the golf course. The base bus stopped in front of the VAQ and stopped at the golf course. The bus ran twenty-four hours a day with less route times between 2300 and 0400.

Musher showered, dressed, grabbed his golf clubs and headed for the course. At the pro shop he paid for a visitor's temporary thirty day membership. The membership allowed for one green fee per day at a reduced rate no matter how many holes played; it allowed for a reduced cart rate although the club recommended use of a caddy; and unlimited range balls for practice. Another advantage of the temporary membership was for a small fee the golf clubs could be stored at the golf course and a temporary locker could be assigned. Musher was quick to notice that the prices in the pro shop were far greater than the prices in Japan. Of course here, he was not buying at cost. All that is all right. He had eight thousand American dollars in his pockets. Only American money was acceptable at Hickam. Before he left the pro shop he asked if they could squeeze him in tomorrow morning.

"Do you have an established handicap?" Musher showed him the handicap card Timmy had given him at Yokota. It showed his handicap as plus one. "If you are ready to play by 0830 I am sure we can work you in."

Musher carried his bag to the range and for the next two hours hit balls. Then he did an hour of putting practice before going back to his room. Musher was not comfortable with all his cash in his pockets. He stashed all but one thousand dollars in the room. He did a SSS and then to the NCO Club for dinner.

It was a nice club and definitely oriented for family use. He doubted if this was the action location at Hickam. Maybe they have an American school and contracted teachers living on Hickam.

His first day at Hickam he ate dinner alone. Fortunately being alone was a personal trait he had learned to live with for many years past.

CHAPTER 170

My Second and Last Day of Leave At Hickam

Musher was eating breakfast at the golf course at 0600. He was on the driving range at 0645. He warmed up on the range and the putting green until 0800. He was drinking hot tea when he was joined by three gentlemen. The spokesman said," My name is Seth Davis and I am the Head Professional here. This is Colonel Carmine Fasano and Colonel David Henne. We will make up the foursome this morning. We don't have any type bets because I am prohibited by my job. You gentlemen can do whatever you please." Colonel Fasano said, "Is a twenty-five dollar Nassau between you and me OK with you."

Musher thought, "Fuck you Colonel. Are you trying to intimidate me with your rank?" He answered with "How about a hundred dollar Nassau? Colonel Henne you can have the same bet."

Colonel Fasano, "Automatic two down presses?"

"You too Colonel Henne?" Henne was not thrilled with the Nassau bet and certainly not the automatic presses but he meekly said it was OK.

The Pro led them to the first tee where the caddies were waiting. Pro tossed a tee to determine the first tee hitting order. Musher was last. The first three hit good drives dead center in the fairway. Musher hit his dead center but thirty yards past the farthest ball. He played like a demon and shot a cool sixty four. Each of the two colonels shot seventy-one but as good a score as that is in the face of sixty-four they both lost the Nassau and four presses. Total loss was eight hundred dollars each.

They had lunch at the golf course and the colonels were given the treatment normally associated with officers of their rank. Pro and Musher were treated equally well but only because they were in the rays of the suns. Colonel Henne, "You played magnificently for someone playing this course for the first time." Colonel Fasanao added, "What is even more amazing is how well you read the greens; and, you read them without the help of your caddy."

Musher made no reply. He caught the slight smile on Pro's face. No one mentioned paying the losses. Pro could read the look in Musher's eyes and excused himself to go to the latrine. Musher said in a very low voice, "Gentlemen there is the matter of your losses of eight hundred dollars each."

Colonel Fasano, "What will you settle for?"

"Eight hundred dollars each! You thought you had another tourist with a phony handicap. It was not my first time to play this course. You did not know that and you did not know that I had been the Medalist in the Far East Tournament held right here. It is not my fault for what you did not know. In my country you win you collect, you lose you pay."

Colonel Fasano again, "You are not aware that I am the commander of Hickam and Colonel Henne is the commander of the support group."

"I wouldn't care if you were disciples of Jesus. When you play you must be prepared to pay. I will take your personal checks."

"And if we refuse to pay on the grounds you hustled us?"

"My stay at Hickam will be short. Your stay on this planet will be even shorter."

"You could get a general court martial for that remark."

"That would be interesting. I can hear the defense's opening statement now. These two senior field grade officers, graduates of West Point, tried to hustle this airman at golf. On his second morning of arrival for a leave at Hickam they played together and they used large bet sums to try to intimidate the airman. You have heard the testimony of the resident golf professional who was part of the foursome where the bets occurred. He testified that the airman neither cheated nor displayed improper etiquette; he simply played very, very well. In the presence of the resident golf professional the two colonels acknowledged their losses were eight hundred dollars each. They later refused to pay their losses. The airman insisted they pay. Again they tried to intimidate him with their positions on the Hickam AFB organizational chart. The airman stressed that their losses were in no way connected to their positional status at Hickman. The airman told them what the consequence of not paying would be. They threatened this court martial. With this court martial they are trying to intimidate him and you. They still owe the debt, maybe not legally but certainly morally."

Each wrote a check in the amount of eight hundred dollars payable to "Cash". Colonel Fasano strongly suggested he end his leave at Hickam and continue it somewhere else. He would leave word at Passenger Service to provide Musher with whatever help he would need to leave the island. The colonels left.

Musher sought out the pro Seth Davis. "What's the deal Pro? You knew me and you certainly knew them. Which of us were you setting up?"

"Not you. There was no doubt in my mind you would win. They are both relative newcomers to the island, good amateur golfers but the biggest pains in the ass. They are arrogant and want to tell me how to run this golf course.

Maybe they will slow down for a while. I will make sure this story spreads around the air base. Did you collect?"

Musher showed him the two checks.

"Let me cash them with club funds. Knowing them they may be thinking of stopping payment. Once I cash them their obligation will be to the USAF." He left and returned with sixteen one hundred dollar bills.

"Pro, Fasano strongly suggested I leave the island now and offered to have Passenger Service go out of its way to help me leave."

"I have a friend in Passenger Service let's give him a call. Sergeant Billingsley please. Hello Bill this is Seth. Bill I have a friend who needs a ride to the states mucho pronto. There is nothing any earlier than the day after tomorrow? You have a SAC B-29 going to McCoy in Florida. Takes off at 0200 tomorrow morning. Does he what? You talk to him."

"Sergeant Muscarello here."

"You can hitch a ride on that B-29 only if you meet certain criteria. You must have an altitude card, oxygen certification card, valid travel orders and money to pay for your on board lunches. Do you have these things?"

"Yes"

"This is a non-stop flight from here to McCoy with air refueling on the way. If you still want to go be at base operations at 2300 hours. What do you have for luggage and what do you weigh?"

"My B-4 Bag, my golf clubs and a small carry bag. I weigh about one hundred sixty five pounds."

"Dress comfortably and if you're late no one will wait."

"Thank you Sergeant Billingsley. I will not be late."

Pro was helpful. They gathered all of Musher's belongings, he waived return of any paid fees and they headed for his BAQ. After unloading his gear into his room and saying goodbye to Pro, he walked into the Base Housing office and announced his surprise departure. They refunded him twenty-two of his thirty dollars. He left ten with the desk clerk for the people who had and who would clean up after him. In the room he assembled his cash. Including today's net gain he had nine thousand eight hundred forty-two dollars American. At the BX he bought an oversized flannel flying suit, an oversized B-15 sheepskin lined jacket, heavy gloves, a heavy scarf and a sheepskin lined helmet type hat with pull down ear flaps. He knew how cold a B-29 can get during refueling. He added to his cart two decks of cards, cookies, candy bars, twinkies, devil dogs, a six pack of coke and two cartons of Lucky Strikes. He needed a larger carry on bag so he bought one. The time was 1800 hours. Back in his room he finished packing. His newly purchase heavier clothing was packed in his newly purchased larger bag. His smaller emergency bag was stuffed with goodies and put in the larger bag with the heavier clothes. His B-4 Bag was packed, his golf clubs and his other bag waited by the door. He called the motor pool for transport to base operations, took his baggage and waited outside. On the third Lucky Strike the motor pool vehicle arrived. He was in Base Operations at 2200 hours. He presented his documents to the Sergeant working Passenger Service and was asked to put his luggage in a certain area. He would load it in the crew bus later on. His paper work was fine and he was now listed as a passenger on the B-29. In the course of conversation during the check-in he found out the B-29 was returning from a ninety day TDY to Kadena AB, Okinawa. The crew had been flying strikes on North Korea. Musher had almost forgotten the Korean War was not over. While he was waiting Musher had slipped his new flying suit over his uniform. One of the officers from the crew came over to him and told him to put his gear on the bus and take a seat. A few minutes later the bus headed out to the B-29. Everything was off loaded and the crew lined up under the left wing.

The Aircraft Commander Captain Goode spoke, "The first order of business is our passenger. Master Sergeant Saverio Muscarello. Sergeant why not take off the suit and remove your blouse. I can understand the flying suit." Musher did and in the bright light his gunner's badge and ribbons stood out to the AC's eyes. "Sergeant may I see your blouse?" He held it up for all the crew to see. "Please tell us a little about these decorations."

Musher went through his training as an RCS CFCS B-29 gunner, a certified air refueling reel operator in the 509th, as a waist gunner in the 98th Bomb wing, how they lost their B-29 aircraft after a strike made on North Korea from Kadena. His fear during the free fall bailout and his capture. He time lined fourteen months in a Chinese prison camp, seven months at Tachikawa, Japan, two days at Hickam before two very senior officers suggested he vacate the island. He is now on convalescent leave. He is hoping to play a lot of golf and enjoy Florida for at least thirty days.

The AC returned Musher's blouse and gave a short recap of the mission. All pre-flights had been done and it was time to board the aircraft. The aft compartment gunners rushed to help Musher get his gear on board, a chute properly fitted, a headset and a throat mike. "We have food and drink on board for you."

The takeoff, climb out to altitude and cruise was smooth. Musher dozed woke up, ate some goodies and dozed off again. As the sun came through the blisters Musher's eyes opened to the glare. One of the gunners held out a pair of sun glasses, "Use these. I can always get more."

Musher was starving. "Is it all right if I eat a lunch now and have some coffee?" Before he finished the question there was a lunch in his lap and a hot, steaming cup of black coffee in his hand. The lunch box cover had been ripped off and the lunch exposed. He devoured everything in the lunch box except the pickle. The coffee went down easy. One of the gunners came and took the trash. Musher took out his Lucky Strikes and made the motions to see if it would be all right if he smoked. On his headset he heard, "AC from Ring. Sir our passenger wants to smoke. Is that OK?"

"You give him anything he wants. Our rendezvous is in about one hour."

Musher practically ate two Luckies and settled back. On his headset he heard "Dolphin 22 this Tanker 102 do you copy?" The voice was familiar and the call sign was his old call sign from Roswell. The conversation between the two aircraft commanders was the same one he had heard many times when he was a 509th ARS Reel Operator. On the intercom he advised the AC of the tanker call sign, its history with him and asked if it would be possible to get the tanker AC's name.

"For you it is possible. Tanker 102 this is Dolphin 22, over."

"This is Tanker 102 go ahead Dolphin 22."

"I have a passenger on board who thinks he may be familiar with your crew. He asks your name, over."

"Lonnigan. Who is your passenger? over."

"Master Sergeant Saverio Muscarello but we all call him Musher, over."

The airwaves went silent. Musher's eyes welled with water.

"Tanker 102 to Dolphin 22 we are in our number one position. Let's get you the gas and later we can chat for a minute or two, over"

Musher did not have an oxygen mask for when they depressurized but once again one of the gunners handed him one. "We keep a couple of extras just in case." Thank goodness for the heavier clothing and the sheepskin jacket. The refueling went smoothly as did the breakaway.

"Tanker 102 to Dolphin 22, over"

"Go ahead Tanker 102."

"Please advise Musher that we too will land at McCoy and RON (Remain Over Night). We have a similar mission tomorrow going the other way. We will get together on the ground. Thank you Dolphin 22, Tanker 102 Out."

"Roger Tanker 102, Dolphin 22 Out."

Musher couldn't get on the ground fast enough. The gunners had insisted he get out of his flying suit and into his blouse. It might be a little warm but you should have them see you as you are not in that ill fitting flannel overcoat. The two aircraft were parked in different locations so the crews would not meet until the aircrew busses dropped them off at Base Operations. On the bus Musher went to each crew member and thanked him for the ride and the courtesies they extended. He particularly emphasized his gratefulness to the AC Captain Felix Goode.

With the exception of his replacement the crew was still intact. There was lots of hugging and handshaking. Musher said to Captain Lonnigan, "Sir I know you all have work to do today and must prepare for tomorrow's mission. Here's my deal. When you finish your work reverse the dropping off order. Come by the BAQ first where I and I am sure your crew will be staying before you go to your BOQ. I will meet your bus at the BAQ and tell you the dinner arrangements. It is my treat for all of you still being alive and well."

Captain Lonnigan, "You still know how to make a deal. We will see you very soon."

Musher hurried to get checked into the BAQ. He asked for the name of the best steak house not too far from the main gate. He was given a name and telephone number. "Do the rooms have a telephone?"

"Yes but only for on base and local calls. You must Dial 9 to get a tone for local calls."

He took his gear to his room and dialed the restaurant. "This is the Cattlemen's Club may I help you?"

This is Lieutenant Colonel Melke (Melke would understand) "Do you have a small private room for a dinner party of ten?"

"Yes we do."

"Is it available for tonight?"

"Yes it is but there is a fee of fifty dollars for using the room."

"Is there a full bar in the room?"

"Yes there is but there is a fee of fifty dollars to set up the bar and drinks are the same price as they are in the restaurant."

"If only one server is assigned to the party I would like two."

"Extra servers are an additional fee of fifty dollars."

"Do you serve Kobe beef?"

"We do but it is very expensive."

"Please make sure you have enough Kobe beef for everyone in the party. I would like a good Burgundy served with dinner. Can you do that?"

"Yes sir we can."

"I will not be there myself. My assistant whose name is Musher will take the lead on this party. There will be nine in the party and we will want dinner at eight. To whom should he speak when the party arrives?"

"The Maitre D' is named Juan."

554

"When Musher arrives he will give Juan one thousand dollars to provide your management comfort that this is not a ruse. If this were not so last minute I would have made the arrangements in person and left good faith money. Is this circumstance all right with you? What is your name?"

"Yes it is all right. I shall personally see to the success of your party. My name is Mrs. Juan."

His next call was to the base taxi service. "This is Master Sergeant Muscarello. I need three taxis at 1800 to take nine people to the Cattlemen's Club in Orlando. I will need those three or another three to pickup those same nine passengers and bring them back to the BOQ and the BAQ. Can you handle that?"

"Sergeant if I may make a suggestion. We have a nine passenger limousine which would keep all your party together and would be less expensive. The rental fee with driver is one hundred dollars plus any tip you may wish. The rental period is ten hours. Do you think that might be a better choice?"

"Yes and I appreciate your help. First pickup will be at the BAQ at 1800 hours, five passengers. The next pickup will be at the BOQ, four passengers. How long to do you think it will take to get to the Cattlemen's Club?"

"Once we clear the main gate, twenty to thirty-five minutes depending upon traffic. Are you one of the passengers, if so in the first pickup or second?"

"Yes, I am in the first."

"Please do not be insulted but could you pay the driver the basic one hundred dollar fee when you get into the limo?"

"I understand. Please tell him that when I pay the basic fee there will be a tip along with it. It will not be his whole tip but a sign of things to come. Thank you and I will see your service at 1800."

When they entered the restaurant they were greeted by Juan who escorted them to the private room. Musher passed him the thousand dollars. The bartender was waiting and the two servers stood along the far wall the way the servants did at Dukie's house. No one drank heavily. It was mostly soda. At 1945 hours one of the servers asked the crew to please take a seat. The table was set as an arc. There were nine place settings. The dinner was shrimp cocktail, Kobe beef fillet cooked to individual taste, baked potato and white asparagus. Red wine was poured but it didn't look like anyone even finished the first glass. Dessert was Baked Alaska and coffee with or without a liqueur. Musher had some holy water in his coffee. Throughout dinner it was laughing and questions to Musher. Paul his senior reel operator had a hard time swallowing that he was still a technical sergeant and Musher only in the air force for less than three years was now a Master. Musher told them how he and Tickman had been on the same crew and how Tickman kicked his ass out of the aircraft when he was holding tightly to the hatch fuselage. He touched lightly on prison camp and his recuperation in Japan. There were many other stories that went around the table. One of the stories that touched Musher was that his nemesis the Air Refueling Squadron Operations Officer had bought Musher's car and Vesper from Nance. The joke was that he would do anything to ride Musher's ass. Captain Lonnigan said he could not wait to get back to Roswell and fill in the squadron about Musher.

Musher had told them that his next duty assignment would be in England. Lonnigan said the rumor at the 509th was the wing would be going TDY to England within six months.

Lonnigan assumed his role as an aircraft commander. "Musher on behalf of the crew we thank you for this outstanding dinner and a most pleasant evening. We are so happy you are doing well and we know you will do better. You know the bed rest rule so I am afraid we are going to have to call it a night. Our station time tomorrow is 1300."

"The limo is waiting outside I will be right with you." Musher went to the servers and the bartender and gave each of them a fifty dollar tip. Juan gave him a bill. It totaled eighteen hundred twelve dollars including fees and gratuities. Musher gave him nineteen one hundred dollar bills. "This too much, after deposit you only owe seventeen hundred twelve dollars." "Juan, the rest is for you and Mrs. Juan."At the BOQ there were hand shakes, thank you's, and we will see you soon moments. At the BAQ it was the same. Musher lagged and gave the driver a fifty dollar tip to go with his first fifty dollar tip. "Sir my name is Peter. I also drive one of the base taxis. Please let me serve you again."

Musher kicked of his shoes, lay down on his bed and almost instantaneously was sound asleep.

CHAPTER 171

Florida, USA

What a good night's sleep can do for a person. He would SSS and go to the golf course for breakfast. He took the time to unpack and evaluate the room. It had a telephone. He was going to need a radio equipped with an alarm clock. He would pickup some goodies for the refrigerator which also had a freezer compartment to make ice cubes. He didn't want to load up until he was sure he would be here for a while.

The golf course 19th hole and pro shop could in no way compare with Tachikawa or Hickam. He reminded himself that this was a SAC Combat Wing and social amenities were not very high on the priority list. After breakfast he found the head professional, David Bull. "I am here on convalescent leave for the next thirty days or so and would like to feel like a member of this club."

"Do you have an established handicap?" Musher showed him the card from Tachikawa. Bull looked at Musher and grinned. "You're the guy that broke it off in those two colonels. Welcome to McCoy."

"I would just as soon that story didn't get around."

"Too late. By now I would guess it is all over the air force and who knows where else. As a visiting airman you are permitted a thirty day membership and it could be renewed one more time."

He paid the fees for temporary membership, club storage and a locker. He bought range ball coupons redeemable at the range. He was set for practice and practice he did. He got the urge to play a round. It was so hot and there were no caddies available so he bought a pull cart and a pair of what they called "Bermuda shorts." In the locker room mirror he looked at himself in the shorts. His legs were so boney he put the shorts in the locker and put his trousers back on. There was no one on the first tee and the course was fairly empty. It was a work day for most and the heat was something else. More often than not he hit far more balls on each hole than was the regular par. He studied the greens trying to learn their peculiarities. On every tee box there were soda machines and large thermos containers of cold water. He did not miss drinking at least three paper cups of water at each tee. By the end of nine holes he was soaking wet and very, very tired. He showed his storage receipt to the cart barn attendant who told him his bag number is 1158. In the pro shop he bought a shirt to go with his Bermuda shorts. With everything secure in his locker, number 216, he spent thirty minutes standing and sitting under the cool spray of the shower. He must remind himself to play early in the day when the heat was tolerable. Right now I just want to get to my room and rest.

CHAPTER 172

Endear Yourself To the Golfers

Musher fell into a real vacation routine. He had bought a small electric coffee maker and two coffee mugs. He programmed the coffee maker to make coffee at 0500 every day the same time for which he had set his alarm. He started every day the same way, a quick SSS, two cups of coffee, two Lucky Strikes and packing a change of clothes in his small bag. He checked in at the pro shop made his desire to play known and then went into breakfast. Most days he was on the first tee with a playing group right around 0700. He played with every range of golfer who came to the McCoy golf course. He was cordial and used the rounds with hackers as practice round. Very soon he was known by just about everyone who played golf at McCoy. Even without any serious bets he was shooting between sixty-eight and seventy-three. His scores did not necessarily reflect it but his ability to create shots had greatly improved.

One day at lunch the Pro, David Bull, sat with him. "Musher do you know there is a ten dollar skins game here every Saturday and Sunday? There are five foursomes who regularly play. One of their group has been transferred so there are now only nineteen players. I have spoken with them and they know your capability as a golfer. This skins game is an eighty percent handicap game. They have asked me to see if you would care to join them while you are here. Are you interested? I could not imagine you not being interested. Here's the setup. You have one hundred eighty dollars at risk if there were a skin on every hole and you did not have any one of them. Hardly unlikely but it is a possibility. Whatever side bets are made are outside the jurisdiction of the skins game. Since this is an eighty percent handicap game and since you must play with a zero handicap you will get eighty percent of nothing. You can rest assured they will be coming at you with side bets. The saving consolation is no one can play in this game whose handicap is more than six so no one can get more than four handicap strokes. The handicaps fall where they are on the card. Most difficult scoring hole is number one handicap, second most difficult etc. The players run and police the game themselves. The two leaders are known as Johnny Appleseed and Grapevine. The first tee time is 0900 and every six minutes thereafter. You must be here at 0800 or earlier for the draw. When you check in at the Pro Shop you will draw a slip which tells you your tee time and ergo then you make an effort to meet your playing partners until you know the group. If you don't show by 0800 or earlier without prior notice of your absence the first time is excused, the second time results in ejection from the group. There are many players at McCoy who will not understand why you, a temporary member, were selected when they have been on a waiting list."

Musher had adopted another item to his daily routine. Before dinner he visited the Base Gymnasium and did a strength work out. One of the air force instructors took him through a forty minute routine every week day. Since he started the routine two weeks ago he could already feel the difference it made in his forearms and shoulders. He was hitting the golf ball farther than before. He looked forward to being able to wear Bermuda shorts without looking like the stick man. The air force instructor recommended certain diet changes and Musher tried very hard to follow them. He just couldn't put down the cigarettes and his early morning black coffee.

CHAPTER 173
A Weekend of Competitive Golf

Musher did not sleep well last night. He was visited by the ghosts of POW Camp #6 and Doctor Terence Mulcahy. But it was morning now and the demons were gone and he was alive sitting on his bed, drinking good coffee and smoking Lucky Strikes. The night visitors had drained his energy. Of all days, today was Saturday and his first time in the Skins Game. He went through his morning routine, gathered his belongings and was at the Pro Shop at 0550.

Today the golf course had caddies, young male dependents of the air force families here at McCoy. Musher was assigned a caddie named Skipper. The rate for the caddy was ten dollars if he carried double or twenty dollars if he carried single. Musher opted for a non-shared caddy. He drew the 0924 tee time, the last tee time. That gave him a little more time on the putting green.

At breakfast he met two of his three playing partners, Appleseed and Grapevine. What a strange coincidence that they should be paired together. Do you think that it is so they can watch his game, etiquette and honesty? Their fourth soon joined them and he had a normal name, Ralph.

On the practice range Skipper was waiting with Musher's clubs, golf balls, drinking water and a spare towel. He was probably fourteen or fifteen years old. He was alert to Musher's movements for club change and cooling water. When Musher went to the putting green to practice Skipper went with him to take the hole poles out and retrieve the balls each time Musher putted. The large clock on the putting green showed 0916. Skipper gathered Musher's equipment and balls and headed for the first tee.

The starter had each player pull a number from a hat which determined the first tee off order. Again Musher drew the last position. The three drives before him were substantial and in the fairway. His drive was in the first cut of rough fifty yards past the longest of the first three drives. All four hit a GIR (Green In Regulation) and two putted for a par. At the fifth tee all four players were still even par. The fifth hole was a Par 5. The hitting order had not changed from the first tee. Again, all three landed in the fairway. Musher was also in the fairway but at least seventy-five yards in front of the longest ball. Following their three lay up shots Musher was contemplating what to do. Skipper whispered, "Faint heart never won Fair Maiden." Musher hit a two iron within two feet of the hole. The fifth hole was not one of the four hardest holes on the course. Musher made six more birdies during the round and ended up with a score of sixty-four.

As they left the eighteenth green Musher gave Skipper forty dollars. "Will I see you again tomorrow morning?"

"Yes Sir. Me and your clubs will be on the range waiting for you."

One of the benefits of being last off the tee is that you do not need to wait for others to finish. Posted in the bar was a board showing each player's name and his hole-by-hole score. The individual hole scores were shown both gross and adjusted for handicap. Appleseed reviewed the board with the group and only on three of the eighteen holes did one player score lower than all the other players. That is the definition of a Skin. Musher had one for his eagle and on two different holes two others had adjusted net eagles. At check-in this morning each player was required to escrow one hundred eighty dollars. Twenty players made a pot of thirty-six hundred dollars. The pot is divided by the number of skins made in the game. In this instance it was three so each skin winner was paid twelve hundred dollars.

When Musher stepped forward to collect his money Appleseed told the group a little about Musher. Until that moment Musher did not know that Captain Goode, the AC of the B-29 that brought him to McCoy had played as a substitute in today's game. Regular group members were allowed to substitute for themselves if it is done three days in advance. That provision allows SAC aircrews a chance to periodically play in the game. Musher was joined for lunch by Captain Goode, Appleseed and Grapevine.

Luncheon conversation revealed that Appleseed and Grapevine were actually two master sergeants who had been aerial gunners and were now permanently DNIF. (Duty Not Involving Flying). Despite his insistence they would not allow him to pay for lunch. It was explained that we do just about everything Dutch (Each person pays for his items).

Grapevine, "What are you doing tonight? Why don't you meet us at the NCO Club for dinner? We are taking our wives. Be there about 1830. OK?"

What the Hell. What else would I do? "Thank you, I shall be there."

Dinner was good and he even danced a few times. It was 2130 when Musher asked to be excused for the night. He had a tough day tomorrow and needed his beauty rest.

Lying in bed trying to fall asleep his thoughts ran to the women he had in his life. "I have got to do something about this very soon. This is stateside and a different kind of life."

CHAPTER 174

Sunday, A Skins Game Plus

Today he had the 0906 tee time with three different players from yesterday. Skipper had been on the range waiting and did an excellent job again today. Musher played what is best described as: Ah..ah..ah.." He had four birdies and no bogeys for a score of sixty-eight. Most every amateur in the world wishes he could play that way but Musher was not happy. In the bar room when the round was finally completed by all and posted on the board Appleseed reviewed the round for skins. Musher had none and there were six total in the round. He had given Skipper another forty dollars so that at worst he was over nine hundred ahead for the weekend.

He spent the afternoon napping. At dinner time he went to the NCO Club and as usual was sitting alone. His waitress was cute and friendly. Historically the NCO Club is very quiet on Sunday as everyone prepares to go back to work on Monday. Finally Musher made a pass at his waitress, "Could I interest you in a drink when you get off?"

"I am not allowed to stay in the club and drink when I am not working. If you like there is a cute place not too far outside the gate where we could go."

"Sounds great but I do not have a car."

"Maybe you don't, but I do. It's the white Chevy coupe in the employees parking area. Wait for me there." He did as he was told.

Twenty minutes later she came towards the car looking even better than she did inside. She opened the driver's door slid in and said, "Are you ready Musher?"

"How do you know my name? What is your name?"

"You can call me Sunshine. I am going to brighten your life and mine. Everyone in the club knows Musher. Here's your choice, we can go to a place outside the gate for a drink I don't want or to your BAQ for some heavy body contact?"

"Let me show you where to park."

The heavy love making went on only to be interrupted by Musher's alarm clock and coffee pot. They awakened, she went in for a shower and climbed back in bed naked. He showered and returned the same way. The lovemaking resumed. They nibbled on the goodies from the fridge and drank coca-cola. They smoked, made love, and then made love again. At 1700 she said, "Got to go Lover Boy. I am due at the club for work in one hour." She showered and dressed and as she was getting ready to leave said to him, "I get off at 2200. Do you want me to come here?"

"Oh please do. Yes, yes, please do."

She blew him a kiss and said, "Rest, I will be back after work."

CHAPTER 175

It Is Time To Move On

This past month and a half had been wonderful. His golf game had made him some money, he had put on some weight and his strength had increased considerably. On top of all that there was Sunshine who was like the cherry added on the top of an ice cream sundae. Just about every day they drove somewhere to see the sights, eat lunch and play tourist. They had even managed to spend three days in a beach resort in Key West. The time had come to move on. He still had over thirty days before he was due to report to the POE at McQuire AFB but he was getting too accustomed to Sunshine and the non-working good life.

One of the guys Musher played golf with was the Passenger Services Officer for McCoy. Musher had told him that his next assignment was in England and asked what he knew about McQuire AFB, the POE.

"Most likely when you check in they will schedule you for one of the departing troop ships. The ships are staffed by civilians who are members of the Maritime Service. Even as a Master Sergeant you will be billeted in the open bay far below the main deck. You will sleep on a pull down rack stacked sometimes as high as six bunks. You are given a pillow but no pillow case or bed sheets. Passenger comfort is not a concern upon a troop ship. The mess halls will be extremely crowded by those who do not get sea sick and the meals are a much lower quality than the crew eats. You may also be given a detail to perform during the crossing. The crossing will most likely take eight nights and nine days."

"I am air force, don't air force people fly?"

"There are two ways air force people fly. They have a much higher travel priority than yours or they buy a ticket on a commercial aircraft. Believe me a trans-Atlantic flight is expensive. On top of all that you would need a passport."

"How expensive?"

"If there is a seat available in coach around four hundred for a one way ticket. In first class it would be about one thousand dollars."

"How do I make arrangements to go over on a commercial bird?"

"If it were I this is what I would do. I would book a seat on the SAC courier aircraft which makes the rounds stopping here on Thursday, two days from now. I would get off it at Westover AFB, Springfield, Massachusetts which is about one hundred miles west of Logan

International Airport in Boston, actually, East Boston. I would check the boards at Logan for flight schedules and you probably would find that BOAC (British Overseas Airways Corporation) flies one in and out of Boston every day. After I decided when I actually wanted to leave I would go to the ticket counter with my sad story. The sad story is, "My mother and Father were seriously hurt in a car crash last night in London and they may or may not live. I was just released from a North Korean (they would understand the Korean War was still going on) prisoner-of-war camp and have not seen them in over two years. I must see them before they die." Be sure you are not in too neat a uniform with all your decorations and if possible have tears in your eyes. You must have only your passport and your small carry on luggage. You finish your story with, "Can you please sell me a ticket on your next flight to London?" There may have already been a vacant seat on the flight of your choice and it would have been a routine transaction. What you did was take a little edge just in case seating was a difficulty. Does that sound logical to you? By the way, if you are going to try it make sure you have at least a two day growth of beard when you approach the ticket counter. One last thing, if it works I don't care how many cartons of cigarettes and how much money you take with you but the British government has limits. When I go to England I take two cartons of cigarettes, spread my money all over my uniform pickets and declare no more than six hundred dollars, all of which is in my pocket of choice. Do you think you could pull it off?"

"I am sure I could but what about my golf clubs, B-4 bag and other stuff?"

"Did you forget I am the Passenger Services Officer. I will have your things crated and sent to the POE at South Hampton. You told me you had shipped a little TR-6 and South Hampton is where you would go to pick it up." He stepped away and came back with a baggage receipt. He tore off Musher's part and gave it to him. "On the back I have written Marty Halloran. She is the Red Cross agent at South Hampton. Those are her daytime and quarters telephone numbers. She is American and most cooperative with any and I mean any request you may have. If you are leaving on Thursday be here at 0930 hours. You could always wait a week and do it next Thursday. If you come bring all the items you want shipped to South Hampton. They will be in place within five days from Thursday. I'll be here. See you then. Right now I need to go back to work."

Thursday it is. Tonight I tell Sunshine. It won't be easy but as usual I will lie. Tomorrow I will play and then take all my stuff back to the room and pack. My story at the golf course will be that I am forced to cut my leave short because of my parent's health. I will stay out of the NCO Club so I won't have to see Sunshine before I leave.

The light knock on his door came at 2220. As expected it was Sunshine. She hardly had both feet in the room before she starting peeling clothes. He was bare-ass in his bathrobe fully expecting what Sunshine would do. The sex was good. He had fucked her everywhere except in her mouth. He had sucked her pussy into pussy heaven but she constantly refused to suck his cock. He was determined that tonight she would suck his cock. If she would definitely not suck his cock that might be a way to break off this relationship and be gone before she realized he had left Florida. He constantly worked into positions where his cock was in close proximity to her mouth but his encouragements to her simply did not work. No matter what he tried or said she would not take his cock in her mouth. He mounted on her chest and spoke, "I have done every sexual thing that pleases you and you will not do one of the things that pleases me most. If you won't suck my cock I will need to find someone who will!"

"I can't. Musher, I simply can't. I used to suck my ex-husband all the time. He loved it. When he was drunk he would bring his friends home to let them watch me suck his cock. It progressed so that they watched and then took turns while I sucked their cocks. If I didn't he beat me. I have given as many as ten blow jobs without a mouth wash in between. The thought of sucking a cock destroys my inner self. I am sorry but I cannot help it. You can do anything else to me but I will not suck your cock."

Musher leapt off the bed, gathered her clothes and threw them at her as she lay on the bed crying. "Get dressed and get out. I am going in the bath room to jerk off. That will be about as good as you are. Now get out." He listened as the door opened and closed. She was gone. He locked the door and told himself that was easy. I'll ask Pro to spread the word that I actually left because of a romantic difficulty with Sunshine.

CHAPTER 176

England Here I Come

As usual Musher was early at Base Operations. His golfing buddy took the items to ship to England. "The courier aircraft is a C-54 converted for passengers. There are five others going on the same aircraft. There are plenty of seats. I am up to my butt in paperwork so let me say goodbye now. It was a pleasure to meet you and especially to play and watch you play golf. For someone who is, if you excuse the expression, just learning you are miraculous. Stay with it and good luck in England."

Musher boarded along with the other five passengers. The aircraft was almost empty so he was able to use a double reclined seat as a couch. The courier aircraft stopped at three other SAC bases before it arrived at Westover AFB, Massachusetts. Musher spent the night in the BAQ and left early the next morning for Boston. When he got to Logan he checked the boards and sure enough BOAC had a flight leaving at 2100 hours for Heathrow Airport, London. Musher was in a dilemma. He had plenty of time before his leave was up, he wanted to see his mother, he wanted to see Fanucci, he wanted to see his sister, he wanted to thank Caesar for Captain Melke, he wanted to know about Freddie but he harbored the fear of seeing them all, reliving his experiences and then leaving again so quickly. He made a decision. When he knew he was leaving he would call his sister for few minutes and get some updates. He was ready to leave tonight if he could. It was time to visit the BOAC ticket counter.

Before going to the ticket counter Musher went into the bathroom and put a little soap in his eyes and then rinsed them vigorously. There were two ladies working the counter and he told one his story while the other listened intently.

"We have available seats on tonight's flight. May I see your passport and any leave or transfer to England orders you may have?"

He handed her everything he had. The two ladies conferred and started the ticket writing process.

"Sergeant we are going to charge you the coach rate but are going to upgrade your ticket to first class at no additional cost to you. You will probably sleep better in the larger first class accommodations and hopefully look cosmetically better when you see them. Your aircraft leaves from Gate 32 at Ten P.M. Please be at the gate not later than Nine-thirty. Where is your luggage? Only that little bag you are carrying? You may carry that on the aircraft. Here is your ticket and boarding pass. Your boarding pass shows your seat number. At this time there is no one scheduled to sit beside you and if that holds out you will be able to stretch out to sleep. We hope your parents recover and remember you can go to the BOAC Passenger Service at Heathrow for any assistance you may need. Good Luck and May God Bless You."

He went to one of the telephone stations where they place the call for you, you take it in a private booth and you pay the charges when you finish. He stepped into a booth, the phone rang and he said, "Joanna this is your favorite brother."

"Musher where are you, are you all right, are you on your way here, are you out the service, tell me, tell me before I simply drop dead." Musher heard the click of another telephone and knew her husband was listening. He greeted her husband warmly with a thank you for taking care of my sweet sister.

"Joanna, I am in London on a duty assignment. I am well, it may be some time before I can come see you. My release from the military is still a good way off. Your turn, how's Mama."

"She's healthy and smiling. The old man has terminal cancer and if it is possible he is drinking more and more. The doctors give him six months. He is mellow, probably because of the booze, not working, just under Mama's feet all day. Mama cannot understand where her money is coming from but we keep her in the dark. Our other sister and I visit her at least two times a week each. Her eyes are fading but other than that she is good. We, you that is, bought her one of those new television sets with the largest screen available. It is her constant companion. I watch your bank account and only take what I use for Mama. With the interest earning you have over seventy thousand dollars in the account. My family is good. The boys are in school and I have gone back to work on part time basis. Uncle Fanucci is ill and not expected to last another year. Your friend Freddie is back in jail. Somehow or other he was released after his last murder conviction but he is back in jail for another murder conviction. The story is he is a hit man for Caesar. I don't stay in the old neighborhood any longer than necessary."

"Joanna, I want you to do a couple of things for me. First take three thousand dollars from my account and spend it on yourself. Take another two thousand for your husband and the boys. Second I want you to get a message to Fanucci for him to get to Caesar thanking Caesar for Melke. Fanucci and Caesar will understand. I must go now they are telling me I am on this overseas phone line too long. Hug and kiss Mama for me and try to make her understand I love her and would have come to see her if I could have. Please keep where I am to yourself. It would benefit my well being. I love you and yours. Goodbye." He did not wait for an answer he hung up the phone, paid his charges and went to the nearest bar for a drink.

He had a couple of drinks, walked to Gate 32 and waited for his boarding call. This was a really plush aircraft. After take off the stewardess came and showed him to take the arm rest from the center of the two seats and together they were almost as large as a couch. They reclined to close to the prone position. The stewardess brought him cokes, blankets and pillows. Dinner would be served in about two hours. Would he like some snacks for nibbling before dinner? She brought an array of goodies. He slept for almost three hours and was afraid he had missed dinner. From what he could see no one else was eating. "You looked so tired we wanted you to sleep as long as possible." She set his seat trays with table cloth, china and heavy silver utensils. The tablecloth and napkin were Irish linen. From the on board menu he selected filet mignon in a peppercorn sauce. He declined the water and would drink Perrier. He finished the first steak and was offered another. He settled for an extra dessert of chocolate ice cream. The stewardess told him there are shaving facilities in the bathroom if he cared to use them. The dinner was so filling he passed on the coffee. He smoke a couple of Lucky Strikes and fell back to sleep.

"Sir, it is time to wake up. We will land at Heathrow in thirty-four minutes." He had slept for over another four hours. Two cups of coffee and two Lucky Strikes and he was ready to face the world. The landing was water glass quality. Since he had only the small bag and his passport and papers were in order, he was through customs very quickly. Standing outside the terminal he asked himself, "What in Jesus's name do I do now?"

He took the advice of the BOAC counter people in Boston and went to the BOAC Passenger Service desk. He expressed his need to get to South Hampton and was told the three alternatives. He passed the rental of car and driver, he passed the arduous bus ride and settled for the train. A taxi took him to Charing Cross train terminal, the train took him to South Hampton and another taxi to vehicle acquisition terminal. The distance from Heathrow to South Hampton was not very great but the time to get to South Hampton was. The vehicle acquisition terminal was closed for the day. The VAQ was very crowded with the personnel who had docked at South Hampton today from a very rough troopship crossing. Here being a Master Sergeant had some rewards. He was quartered in a private room with another Master Sergeant who had been on the troop ship. Musher had no other clothes so that after his SSS he was obliged to redress in the ones he had traveled in. He made a prolific use of his cologne.

570

His roommate could not wait to go to the dining hall and sit in a stationary chair rather than standing while trying to eat. He spoke of the rocking table trying to eat low quality food. They went to the dining hall and dinner took them almost an hour. His roommate who by this time said he was called Smasher from his football days questioned Musher. "Were you able to eat on the way here?"

"I only really ate twice."

"The damn sea was so rough we were not allowed to go out on deck, did you manage to step out?"

"I didn't even think about trying to step out."

"I am going to RAF Mildenhall to be the first sergeant of the supply squadron. It's about eighty miles north of London. That will be a hell of a train ride from here. Where are you going?"

"To an administrative headquarters in London call South Ruislip. I have a car to pickup tomorrow that I shipped from Japan. If you want you can ride as far as London with me."

"I appreciate that. My family is coming and meanwhile I will see about quarters at Mildenhall and buying some car myself. What time are we leaving?"

"Just as soon as I can get the car, get it serviced and get my personal goods which were shipped from McCoy AFB."

"You sound like you get around, what do you do?"

"I am a B-29 Aerial Gunner."

"In an administrative headquarters?"

"You figure it out."

Smasher took a close look at Musher's blouse, knew the Korean War was still going on, and said, "I think I have."

CHAPTER 177
Take A Week Before Reporting For Duty

The car was waiting for him. He inspected its condition and signed all the papers. The next stop was the base service station where they washed it, waxed it, and filled it up with petrol. (You and I call it gasoline). Before Musher could drive it off the POE he was obligated to visit the on base office of the RAC (Royal Automobile Club). Here you got your windshield sticker which proved you had paid the tax on the vehicle. American military servicemen who brought cars in when assigned to England were exempt from that tax), your front and rear license plates which would remain as part of the vehicle as long as the vehicle was operated on a British road and your collision and comprehensive liability insurance. Musher was now ready to roll. Musher picked up his crate, making sure he retained the claim check with the ARC (American Red Cross) lady's information on it, and put his stuff in the boot (trunk). They went to the VAQ to pickup Smasher's luggage. Fortunately he only had one B-4 bag and they were able to fit it in the boot along with Musher's stuff. It was near lunch time and since the dining hall was open twenty four hours a day they decided to eat well before they hit the road.

Four and one half hours later they were at Charing Cross, one of the main train terminals in London. Musher parked and walked in with Smasher. After seeing Smasher off Musher walked through the terminal until he was approached by a "trader of valuable items."

"Yank do you have anything to trade?"

"Twenty one hundred American dollar bills. If you are interested?"

"I am definitely interested. With the sterling pound at two dollars eighty cents American each one of those notes is worth thirty-five pound fourteen shillings. The lot is seven hundred fourteen pounds. Just about two thousand American."

"That may be so but I want fifty pounds for each one hundred dollar note. Just about twenty-eight hundred American. My demand is not negotiable."

"I agree let us go somewhere private where we can do the deal."

"Let's do it here in the open. I have my part ready in my pocket. It is important that I tell you this. If you try to screw me in any manner, if not today, someday soon I shall return and kill you. If you do this deal well you will be in line for many, many more trades of valuable items. It is your choice."

The Trader clandestinely counted twenty-eight hundred pounds and handed them to Musher in exchange for the twenty one hundred dollar bills. Musher did not count the pound notes. He could see in the Trader's eyes that the Trader believed his promise. He drove to Piccadilly Circus, selected a hotel, gave his car to the valet, checked into a small suite, over tipped the bell hop and unpacked. There was nothing in his personal belongings that looked British and he wanted to try to blend in. After all he spoke close to the same language as the Brits. In his earlier trip to London when the wing was TDY to Wyton he had done some shopping in the mercantile called "Marks and Spencer". He changed from his uniform and went to Marks and Spencer. He studied the way the men around his age were dressed and he purchased a complete wardrobe to match what he saw. He had a bell hop take his packages to his room while he went into the Pub (a bar to us Yanks). It was almost empty but it had what he was looking for, dart boards and some house darts. He practiced hitting his target and doing the chalk math in his head. It felt as if he still had it but it would take practice to get back the old hand eye coordination. Back in his room he decided to order room service, get a good night's sleep and be Mister Tourist as of tomorrow morning. He left a wake-up call for 0700 with a full breakfast.

Musher was already up when the phone rang. "Sir this is your seven o'clock wake-up call. Your breakfast will be at your room in fifteen minutes."

The room was chilly to him and he had on one of the new cashmere sweaters he had bought. He made a note to himself, "Get a robe and slippers." Breakfast was typically British, eggs, bangers (sausage), potatoes, heavy toast and a large pot of hot tea. It was almost 0900 when he entered the hotel lobby. He approached the concierge. "I would like to engage a car and driver for at least the next five days. Can you arrange that?"

"Is it for in London use or is it possible you will leave greater London?"

"Mostly for London use but I want the ability to take a longer drive if I so choose."

"The car with a driver on a twenty-four hour basis costs nine pounds per day plus petrol and any expenses which may be incurred. When would you like the car and do you want it for twenty-four hours a day?"

Twenty-four hours a day for twenty-four dollars! "Now and yes."

"Sir please do not misunderstand me. This type of engagement requires advance payment of the daily rate. I would need forty-five pounds in advance."

Musher counted out fifty pounds and gave them to the concierge. "The additional five pounds are for you to encourage you to look after me while I am here."

"Sir that is not necessary. I will always do my very best to take care of you."

"What is your name?"

The concierge handed him a business card, "Phillip Mason, Concierge, New London Hotel." It listed two telephone numbers and a promissory statement, "I can fill all your needs on very short notice."

"Sir anything you want at any time Phillip will make it appear. Thank you very much. Your car and driver will be here in ten to twenty minutes."

CHAPTER 178
I Am a Tourist

The concierge suggested that Musher convert some pound notes into lesser denominations. He advised Musher keep pocket change consisting of six pence (American equivalent of seven cents); shilling (American equivalent of fourteen cents); half crown (American equivalent of thirty-five cents) and the ten shilling paper note. (Ten shillings' value is half a pound note, the American equivalent of one dollar forty cents)The hotel doorman came to Musher, "Your car is here". He turned and scurried to be there to open the car door when Musher appeared. Based on guidance from the concierge Musher tipped him one shilling (fourteen cents)."Good morning Governor. My name is Cecil Cody and I am called "Cody". I know every inch of this city and will drive you around safely. Where to Governor?""Show me the United States Air Force Administrative Headquarters in South Ruislip." The building was on the other side of London in a much quieter area. There were no signs posted to identify the building. There were no flags flying in front of building and no other trappings which defined the functions housed in this building. "I have seen enough. Just drive around and let me look at the real London and not just what I saw when I was last here."Cody took him to East London's Mile End. It was the final stop on the Tube (subway) and the area had taken a terrible beating during the German blitz of England. WWII had been over for almost eight years and Mile End looked like it happened last night. The buildings which were habitable were scarred by the flash burning of a detonating bomb. He didn't count them but it looked like there were hundreds of people, men and women, armed with a brick pick hammer busily trying to recover bricks for future construction.He made a stop at Marks and Spencer for a pair of pajamas, a heavy bathrobe and some slippers. It had been a long time since he lived in a cool much less alone cold climate. They drove around with Cody pointing out the notable places, buildings and statues in London. "Cody, take me to a good restaurant." He drove to Soho and stopped in front of the "La Cabineri". Inside the restaurant you would never have known this was a country which was still suffering from not enough of almost anything. La Cabineri was richly decorated. The waiters wore tuxedos. Lunch was "Pollo Marsala" (chicken in a light white wine sauce), fresh Italian bread and salad. The meal was well prepared, excellently presented and superbly served. Back in the car

Musher felt he could easily take a nap."Cody are there any golf courses in London?"

It is the called the "New London Golf Course". It is owned by the same people who own your hotel."

They drove to the golf course so that Musher could see what it looked like from the outside. It was formerly an estate of a low ranking member of royalty who was unable to financially no longer afford to keep up the buildings and grounds. The main house had been converted into a Clubhouse facility complete with all the trimmings of a hotel. The course was carved out of the estate grounds taking full advantage of the topography. It had been opened for play for about six years and had matured into a quite decent facility. Musher had Cody drive to the main clubhouse but not stop."Please take me to my hotel. When we get there please wait for me." A bell hop took his packages to his room.He went to the concierge. "Phillip I just came back from a drive to the New London Golf Course. I understand it is owned by the same people who own this hotel."

"That is correct. Membership is limited and very expensive. While you are a guest at the hotel I can arrange for you to play there. Your charges would be billed to your hotel account. If you were to play there your charges would be three pounds green fees ($8.40), one pound caddy fee ($2.80), ten shillings for a locker and use of the shower ($1.40) plus whatever else you may spend in the dining room and pro shop. (A total of $12.60 plus expenditures) With exception of what a player may tip his caddy actual money is not exchanged at the club. There is also a dress code. Players are required to wear "Plus Fours" (knickers to you and me), a jacket, shirt and tie. Are you interested in playing there? If you are when would you like to play and do you have an established handicap?""Yes I am interested. My established handicap is four. (He thought he would give himself some wiggling room). I would like to play somewhere around ten o'clock tomorrow morning." (Give the day a chance to warm up. He planned to be on the driving range at nine.)Phillip was on the phone for a minute or two. "His name is Signore Muscarello. He speaks American English." "They will be expecting you." Musher gave him a two pound tip and thanked him for his help.In the car he said to Cody, "To a clothier where I can buy golfing attire." He told the clerk at the clothier, "I am going to play golf for my first time in England and I do not have the proper attire. I have my own clubs and white golf shoes. Please pick out everything else I will need."

"We will begin with a cap and jacket. Do you have any color you prefer?"

"I have a preference for the darker blues."

The clothier looked at Musher, went to a clothing rack and returned with three jackets each a different shade of dark blue. Musher selected the one he liked best. Back to the rack went the other two jackets and the clothier returned with three different caps. "It is most important that there is a coordination of jacket, cap and tie." Musher didn't think any of them were attractive but the clothier explained that it was the proper type cap for golf. Musher asked the clothier to choose one, which he did without hesitation. Shortly he was back with shirts and ties. After those selections he returned with knee length stockings which matched the tie. The next garment was the "Plus Fours". Musher' body was an "off the rack" body so the only real choice was color. They settled for a pearl gray. The final three additions were a belt, suspenders and sweater vest which matched the plus fours.The clothier looked at Musher and said, "Your white shoes are probably beautiful. Only in mid-summer do we wear anything white. To finish the ensemble you will need different shoes." They went to a different part of the store where Musher tried on various types and colors of shoes. He finally settled on wing tip black lacers. The clothier commented, "Those are the ones I would have chosen for you. Let me help you get all these items to a dressing room. We must make sure everything fits properly."Musher emerged in sartorial splendor. Because of his "off the rack" body everything fit without tailoring. If he didn't speak you could easily believe he was British and from one of the higher class families.His bill was one hundred eighty-six pounds. ($521.00 American) Musher paid him two hundred twenty pounds ($616.00 American). "The extra payment is not a mistake. No change please. The extra payment is for you in appreciation for your help with these clothes. I would also appreciate it if you would make up four additional outfits equally as coordinated." (A 34 pound tip was probably equal to his months pay)He was most thankful and bubbled, "Yes Sir, they will be ready this time tomorrow. Unless you need them tonight and I will get them done tonight." He helped Musher get all the boxes out to the car. Cody put them in the boot."Please take me to the hotel. When we get these boxes to my room you may leave and I will look for you here at 8 A.M. tomorrow." The doorman assisted emptying the boot and a bell hop took his packages to his room. He tipped them one shilling each. He walked to Cody and put two pounds in his hand. "You did a good job."

CHAPTER 179

Golf Is Golf and Golfers Are Golfers

Musher ate breakfast in the hotel dining room and read the London Times while waiting for Cody. He arrived promptly at eight o'clock. The golf clubs and his shoes were put in the boot. He had put extra cigarettes and candy bars in his golf bag. He tipped everybody around him one shilling. As he got into the car Cody reached in with a large mug of hot tea, "It's a long ride. I thought you might like a cup of tea. If I may Governor, you look like a fashion model from one of them men's magazines."

The time it took to get to the golf course seemed shorter than yesterday. Cody was not talking, just driving. When Cody pulled up in front of the club house they were greeted by two attendants. One took Musher's golf bag, the other his small bag and golf shoes. Cody pulled the car into an area designated for him to park and settled in for the day. The attendant who took Musher's shoes and bag handed him a key and said, 417. Your name will be on the locker."

Musher stepped into the pro shop and almost collided with a gentleman holding out his right hand. "I am Marshal Thompson, Head Pro and Greens Superintendent." Pointing to a young man behind a cash register he declared, "This is Emile he takes care of all the paper work and is the club accountant. He has everything ready for you to sign. We have arranged for your caddy and there are range balls waiting for you on the range. Your tee time is ten past ten and your playing partner is the President of the Club. I and another gentleman named Forrest Whitaker will make up the foursome. We will meet in our 19th hole at nine forty-five. Let Emile do his paperwork and feel free to do as you wish until nine forty-five." Musher signed a bunch of paperwork, changed into his golf shoes and headed for the range.

His caddy was an older gentleman named MacInnes. Musher took his five iron and started swinging slowly. His golf muscles were a little tight and he did not want to strain them by hard full swings. He kept changing irons and types of shots he wanted to hit. When he felt loose he hit his four wood, his three wood and driver. He concentrated on the quality of his swing. He took three balls and headed for the putting green. The greens were different than Florida, Hawaii or Japan. The putting green looked easier to read but this was only the putting green.

When he went into the 19th hole the other three members of the foursome were drinking tea. They stood and Marshal did the introductions.

"Gentlemen this is Signore Saverio Muscarello, who prefers to be called Musher. Musher, Sir Christopher Kraft, Admiral, Royal Navy Retired, President of the Club, who prefers to be called Admiral; and, Mister Forrest Whitaker, Chairman of the Board, Barclay Bank, who prefers to be called Whit."

The Admiral was first, "I understand you are an American, why the "Signore"?"

"It was the concierge at the hotel trying to make me out to be something I am not. I am sure he did not intend to do anyone any harm."

Whit, "How valid is your four handicap? Where have you been playing?"

"It is valid, sometimes I play much better but most of the time I am right there. Recently I have been playing in Japan, Hawaii and Florida. It has been over a week since I last played in Florida."

"Are you a man who bets on his golf?"

"I am."

"What stakes will you play for?"

Musher thought of Fanucci's poem once again. *I will play any man, from any land, any game he can name, for any amount he can count.* "Most any amount."

"We play individual Nassau for ten pounds. You have forty pounds at risk for each player and one hundred twenty pounds over all. Is that acceptable?

"Lay on MacDuff and damn be he who first cries hold enough."

It was very difficult to beat all three at Nassau when you must decide each hole who should win or tie. In any case he beat each one one up on each side. His stroke score was seventy-five. None of the three were capable of playing to their posted handicap. Even the Pro was a shaggy golfer.

The caddie fee was in his bill so he watched to see what level tip these three gave their caddies. Each one gave a ten shilling note. Musher discreetly gave his caddy two pounds. MacInnes pretended to be showing Musher something about his clubs when he said, "Laddie, I have seen good swings in my lifetime. None of them were any better than yours. Managing your winning over all three of them was a beautiful thing to see. I hope I can caddy for you again sometime."

"If you are here tomorrow so shall I. I hope for around a ten o'clock tee time."

The others had gone into the bar to settle up. Musher sat with them and ordered a coke. No such luck. He settled for a gin and orange crush. Without malice or angry looks each passed him forty pounds. Pro said, "With a little

579

instruction and practice you could be a much better player than a four handicap."

The conversation turned to the round. They commented about some of Musher's "lucky" shots and a few putts he made under pressure. All three told of the many reasons they did not play better. Musher had not been playing golf very long but this was a familiar tune with familiar lyrics.

No matter where they play or who they are basically golfers are golfers.

Musher asked Pro to try to set him up for tomorrow at ten.

CHAPTER 180
Add A Couple of Days Leave

Musher had a new plan. He would add another two days before reporting for duty. He still has plenty of time before he is required to report for duty at South Ruislip. After Friday he would drive his own car. He would tell the hotel he is staying three more nights beyond the original five. He would report to South Ruislip Monday morning. The missing component was female companionship. He would talk to Cody before talking to Phillip.

At the golf course he found that today was the day the ladies invited all their golfing friends from other clubs to come to The New London. The hostesses made some simple tournaments only to be able to give prizes to the guests. Emile told Musher,"From ten until eleven fifteen the first tee is closed to everyone except the ladies and their guests. I have a twosome of two daughters of one of the members who are going to tee off at nine thirty six. After that the tee closes. Would you care to join the girls?"

"Why not?"

MacInnes was waiting on the range surrounded by women of all shapes and sizes. "Do you play today Lad?"

"Nine thirty-six." Musher went to the putting green which was even more crowded than the driving range.

At nine thirty Musher and MacInnes were waiting at the first tee. Two tall, lovely, full grown women dressed identically down to the golf bags and head covers stepped to him. "We are the Kraft twins. I am Jane and she is Jill. We believe you are going to join us. Is that correct?

Musher was awe stricken and could barely say yes.

"We play from the men's black tees. Please feel free to play from wherever you choose. Would you like to be first off the tee?"

"Ladies first."

Both hit adequate drives. Musher hit his three wood seventy yards past either of their balls. No comment from the ladies. They both hit excellent second shot layups. Musher waited for the group in front of them to get off the green. The ladies looked at him like, "Who is this buffoon? It's over two hundred fifty yards to the green." They heard the crisp snap of a ball being hurtled from the center of the face of a persimmon wood club. They watched it travel in a line directly to the green only to land and go no farther. The ball plugged seven feet short of the green in the frog hair. (the finely manicured grass surrounding the edge of the green)

Both sisters hit third shots which ended up on the green one fifteen from the hole and the other eighteen feet from the hole. According to the rules, a ball which plugs in a fairway may be marked for its location, removed by the player and cleaned. The player may then take a one club distance (most players use their driver) from the spot where the ball plugged and make a free drop of the ball no closer to the hole. Musher took advantage of the rule and made his drop parallel to the plugged spot staying in the frog hair but no closer to the hole. MacInnes counseled a putt rather than a pitch. Musher read the line with the help of MacInnes and stroked the putt. It stopped short dead in the hole. He tapped in for birdie. Neither lady made the birdie but both made par.

All three of them made par on the next six holes. The eighth hole was a two hundred thirty five yard par three which required two hundred yards to carry over the water and the sand traps which protected the green. Both ladies hit driver, carried the hazards but were not on the green. MacInnes said, "This hole needs a high cut shot long enough to hit the left side of the green and spin right. Do you have that shot Laddie?"

"We will know in a minute. Two iron please."

"No Laddie, four wood. Tee it up high and let it fly."

Musher took MacInnes' suggestion and the ball ended up four feet from the hole. A simple tap-in birdie. Both ladies made excellent pitch shots. Jane's went into the hole for a birdie and Jill's tapped in for her three. All three made par on the last hole of the front side.

Jane, "We usually stop for a cool drink and a cigarette. Do you mind?"

"I don't mind if we don't hold up the people behind us."

"You must be kidding. It's our mom and three of her friends who measure their game in rides. You know, "How many times did I get to ride between shots?" We are not a bad threesome, one two under par, one one under par and the other even par. You're quite the player. Been playing long?"

"Not long enough. I make too many mistakes."

The back nine was uneventful. Both ladies were one over par and Musher was one under par.

They we walking off the green when Jill said, "There is a black tie formal dance here tonight. Will you be here?"

"I am afraid not. I am not a member. I am staying at the New London Hotel so they let me play here."

"With that swing you can play anywhere you wish. Please come tonight as my guest. Black tie, around eight thirty. OK?"

Musher used one of the many phones in the foyer to call Phillip. "I need a complete black tie ensemble for tonight. I am on my way back to the hotel now." When he was back at the hotel he said to Cody, "Here is two thousand pounds. Please pick up the things at the clothier. Pay whatever he asks and ad fifty pounds for him." He was joined by Phillip as he passed through the lobby. In the room waiting were all the clothes for the evening and a valet who would help him dress. "Sir this is Francois. He has been a gentleman's gentleman for many, many years. If you will buzz my desk when you are ready to dress he will join you. These items are not on your bill. At your convenience you can settle with me personally." Phillip and Francois left. Musher thought, I am down to eight hundred pounds or less. I must go see The Trader tomorrow.

Cody came to the room about 1815 with boxes and two bell hops to help him carry all the boxes. Musher flipped the bell boys a shilling each. "The cost of your clothes was eighteen hundred seventy pounds. I gave him that plus the fifty pound tip you directed. Here is your change of eighty pounds."

"Keep twenty for yourself and put the rest on the dresser. Do what you wish but when I come down at seven-thirty to go to the New London Golf Club I would like you to put on your best chauffeur act. Can you do that?"

"Yes sir." He left.

Musher bathed and was wrapped in his robe when he buzzed Phillip. Francois appeared and laid his clothes out on the bed. The dressing was a remembrance of Hereford. He asked Francois to unpack his new clothes and put them away. He gave Francois a ten pound tip and filled his pockets with his necessities including a six pack of condoms. At precisely seven-thirty he passed through the lobby to exit the hotel. Phillip smiled and gave him a thumbs up. When he exited the hotel his car was waiting with Cody in his best chauffeur duds holding the car door open for Musher.

The arrival at the New London Golf club was almost ceremonial. The Admiral, his wife and the senior officers of the club had a reception line which greeted every guest. When Musher reached the Admiral during the handshake the Admiral said, "I am so glad you could come. My daughters tell me you put on quite an exhibition on the golf course today. We will have a drink together later." Musher thought that may not be a sign of good things to come. His first stop was at the bar. "What soft drinks do you have?"

"Sir I have coke and seven-up."

"I will have a seven-up with a slice of lime in it. Anytime either I or anyone wants a drink for me they will say gin and lime and you will make seven-up with lime." Musher pushed ten pounds towards the bartender.

"Yes sir, one gin and lime coming up."

He turned from the bar to find Jill coming towards him. "I am glad to see you could make it. May I have this dance? Bartender make him a fresh drink and keep it for him." She practically pulled him onto the dance floor. The music was slow and cradled herself in his arms. The music stopped. Light applause and the music began again. A Tango beat. She looked at with the "can you do this or should we get off the floor?" His thoughts went to his mother Filomena and the hours she worked with him so that he could dance well and to just about every musical beat. Musher did not answer. He whirled her into an open space and danced the tango as if he were George Raft or Caesar Romero whom he had seen do the tango many times in the movies. It wasn't until the music stopped and the applause began that he realized he and Jan were the only people who had been dancing. Jan curtsied to the audience while Musher simply blushed. That was a new kind of attention for him.

They went back to the bar to have a cool drink. Jane came to them and said, "It's my turn." He was back on the dance floor doing a Viennese Waltz followed by a slow dance. Jane cradled the same as had Jill. How identical are these twins?

"We are going swimming with our friends. Are you coming with us?"

"It is far too cold for me to go swimming. Besides I don't even have a swim suit."

"Silly, the pool is inside the club and the water is heated. We had hoped you would swim with us and stay the night. We reserved a room for you here in the club. Dad and Mom wanted you to join us for a round tomorrow after brunch. We took the liberty of having your chauffeur put your golf things in the room and Jan and I have put golf clothes in the closet. Against his will we released your driver with the promise that we would see that you returned to your hotel safely. We have taken care of your swim suit need. It is in the room with a robe and slippers. Come we will go change and knock on your door when we are ready."

It was not long before they were at the pool. There were no others there. They must be on their way.

"Musher are you ready?" The twins kicked off their slippers and disrobed. Musher's eyes nearly popped out of his head. Their swimsuits were their birthday suits. They turned and dove into the water.

"Come on in the water is fine."

"Where are your friends who were coming too?"

"We didn't tell you, we don't have any friends. Come on in and be friendly. Your bathing suit must match ours."

Musher stripped and went into the water. They fooled around in the water racing from end to end and the girls beat him every time. They were very athletic. He couldn't stay in the water any longer. He was bordering exhaustion. When they reached his room he said goodnight and opened his door. Jane and Jill slipped into the room before he could close the door. The key was turned into the lock. They dropped their robes and spread-eagled on his bed. Exhausted or not he remembered Blanchard and what it had been like with two women. He dropped his clothes and lay between them alternating his head movement to kiss each pussy. It was a night to remember.

The phone rang in his room, "Come to breakfast. Our tee time is eleven twenty." When he entered the dining room the Admiral, his wife and two daughters were sitting at a table with a fifth place setting waiting. The Admiral rose and shook hands with Musher. "Glad you could make it. We are looking forward to a good round. Have some breakfast." Musher wondered and surmised that if you are president of a very exclusive club you could play a ninesome if you so desired.

Admiral and Missus Admiral rode a cart. She played from the lady's tees and he from the men's. Musher and the girls played from the black tees. A normal round takes four hours or slightly less or slightly more. This round took six. They were really slow but no one behind them complained. When they finally finished it was time for tea. They agreed to meet back downstairs in one hour. He couldn't put on the tuxedo so he stayed in his golf clothes with patent leather black shoes.

During tea the Admiral began his questioning. "Tell us about yourself."

"I am a Master Sergeant in the United States Air Force." When he told them he could see the change of expression on all four of the Kraft family faces. It read, "My God he is not one of us!" At that point he coughed and said, "I am sure that I am catching a cold which always seems to become pneumonia. I hope you will not be offended if I leave before I contaminate you all." No one voiced an objection. "My driver was released I need transportation to the hotel." The Admiral whispered something to the waiter and then said, "A car and driver will be waiting for you outside."

Finally he was back in his hotel room and standing under a warm shower. He had not eaten much at the golf club. He ordered a steak, baked potato, salad and two bottles of lager beer from room service. (Lager was the only British beer served cold) While eating dinner he knew he needed a new plan.

First thing tomorrow he would visit the Trader of Valuables.

CHAPTER 181

A New Plan

Musher needed a new plan.

Phillip had come to him at breakfast to suggest that he no longer try to play golf at the New London Golf Club. Phillip told him that his job was threatened and would end if another enlisted man was sent to play at the New London Golf Course. He told Phillip he understood and he would see him as soon as he returned from his visit with the Trader of Valuables.

"What are you trading?"

"Twenty American one hundred dollar bills. Are you interested? If you are what is your offer?"

"More than you received for a similar trade. What did you receive?"

"Fifty-five pounds Sterling for each note."

"I will pay sixty."

"Twelve hundred pounds?" (American equivalent of $3,360.00)

"As you Americans say Cash on the Barrelhead.'"Phillip let me tell you what I told the other trader. This is not meant to insult you but to make sure you understand that if you try to beat me in any way in this deal you will not live long enough to enjoy any of the spoils of your work. I will certainly kill you. If you understand tell me when and where we do the deal."

"In your room in ten minutes."

"At your desk now. I have my part ready in my pocket. You have five minutes to get your part ready at your desk. If you cannot do it this way then we cannot do it "

"I will see you in five minutes." In five minutes the deal was done. Twelve hundred one pound notes really fill your pockets. Musher went back to his room. He counted his finances. He still had twenty American one hundred dollar bills, seven hundred thirty-eight one pound notes and now another twelve hundred one pound notes. He figured the safest place for the bulk of his cash would be in the little bag he carried on BOAC. The bag would not be out of his hands until he could find a better solution. He would store eight hundred pound notes in the bag and eleven hundred thirty-eight in his pockets. He would put ten American one hundred dollar bills in the bag and the other ten in his pocket.

He needed a new plan.

Phillip must be paid this morning. He would do that on his way out. He would return the tuxedo ensemble at the same time.

Tomorrow was the last day for Cody and the car. He would have Cody drive many routes from Piccadilly to South Ruislip. He must learn the routes so that he could drive his car around London without always being lost. He would ask Cody to select the best Chinese food restaurant in London and when they got there he would insist Cody join him for lunch. As a last gesture he would give Cody a fifty pound tip.

He would stop at the Royal Automobile Club and purchase a good set of road maps for travel in England, Scotland and Wales. His first trip would be to Scotland, the home of golf. After today he would still have ten more days before he was due to report at South Ruislip.

The day after tomorrow he would check out of the hotel and begin his venture to Scotland.

"Phillip, tell me what I owe you. I don't want an itemized list just your figure."

"Nine hundred pounds settles all accounts." ($322.00 American)

Musher paid him, thanked him for his help. Part 1 of the plan is done.

He went to his car where Cody was there holding the door. "Cody, starting tomorrow I shall be driving my own car. Today I want to learn all the ways I can get to South Ruislip using this hotel as the base point. Cody drove six different routes, driving them five times each. Musher was studying landmarks and road signs. Finally he asked Cody to take him to the best Chinese restaurant in London. As Cody parked Musher said, "Come with me."

Musher ordered an array of dishes making sure that Cody liked the dish before it was ordered. Watching Cody trying to use chopsticks made Musher sympathetic. He remembered POW Camp #6 where he first tried eating rice with chopsticks. He had a knife, fork and spoon brought for Cody. He told Cody of his intended trip to Scotland but he would be back in seven days because he would need to find a place to live since there are no government quarters at South Ruislip. Cody insisted Musher take a couple of his business cards and that Musher call him when he came back to London. "I am sure I can help you find a place at the right price."

Cody asked permission to drive to his home because he wanted his missus to meet the Governor. Pulling into his driveway Musher recognized that he was in Mile End, not more than two miles from the USAF South Ruislip headquarters. Missus Cody, Alice was petite and soft spoken. Cody introduced her to the Governor and she curtsied beautifully. She insisted he have "a cuppa" and a few biscuits. (cookies to you and me) He did not protest too strongly. She liked to talk and he was a good listener. She did not ask questions of him and he appreciated that. Cody was getting nervous about being home while being paid so he finally suggested they leave to avoid the traffic. Musher thanked Alice for the tea and biscuits and hoped he could return the hospitality some day. Cody took the most direct route to the hotel. The route which passed directly in front of the USAF headquarters building. They stood in front of the hotel trying to say goodbye. Musher complemented him on his ability and behavior during their five days together. In the final handshake he pressed fifty pounds into Cody's hand, turned and went into the hotel.

He went to the registration desk, "I'll be leaving in the morning. Please have two bell hops at my room at nine. Also have my car serviced and brought around by nine. I will settle the bill with cash."

He started packing and once more he was amazed at just how much clothing and other items can be put in a B-4 Bag. Finished for tonight he went to the hotel dining room for dinner.

In the middle of his dinner a middle aged man approached and asked if he could join Musher for dinner. "I detest eating alone." Musher said, "Please do. I am called Musher."

"I am James Boone, American Tool and Die of Albany, New York. Did you notice the poker game in the room off the side of the hall? I went into look and there was money all over that table. I watched a while until I realized they were playing what we called $20 and $50 only it was in Sterling, American, Deutch and some currencies I could not even recognize. Do you play poker Musher?"

"Sometimes."

"I love to play but those stakes are a little too rich for me." When they finished dinner they went into the poker room to watch. There were six players in the game and they were playing only five card draw Jacks or better. There was not a community dealer, each took his turn to deal. The ante was ten dollars but the first bet was twenty and raises could be for fifty. There was no limit on how many raises could be made on each card. Musher watched very closely for any indication of card manipulation. It was very obvious that two were partners and there were two pair of partners. One of the partner pairs said, "Either one of you want to sit in. We have room for one more. We are playing two pounds ante sterling, seven and eighteen sterling, what Americans call five dollar ante, twenty and fifty dollars. No limit to the number of raises and we only play five card draw nothing wild, jacks or better." Boone was quick to say no thank you but Musher said, "I would like to join." He sat and put five hundred pounds on the table.

He played his conservative game and gained a little ground over a long period. It was watching the partners and knowing when to call and when to fold. He couldn't determine if the two pairs of partners were really a foursome team or if each pair of partners was working independently. It was getting late and he had not made much money for his time. It was his deal and the time to make money. Of the seven hands he dealt one member of each pair a good hand, he dealt the two independents a good hand and he himself a potentially good hand. Pair 1A opened for twenty, Independent 1 called and raised fifty, Independent 2 called and raised fifty and Pair2A called and raised fifty. Musher called the one hundred seventy pounds. Pair 1A, the original opener was not to be undone he called all the raises and raised another fifty. Independent 1 folded, Independent 2 called the raises and raised another fifty. Pair 2A called and raised another fifty, Musher called the five hundred fifty pounds. The raises stopped, the other two players called. The pot was fourteen hundred ten pounds (Three thousand nine hundred forty-eight dollars American) before the players had drawn any cards, if they wanted or needed any cards.

"Cards gentlemen." Pair 1A stood pat. Independent 2 took one card. Pair 2A took one card. The dealer (Musher) took one card. The opener, Pair 1A bet fifty, Independent 2 called, Pair 2A called and raised fifty, Musher called the one hundred dollar bet to him. Pair 1A called and raised, Independent 2 called, Pair 2A raised, Musher called the one hundred dollar bet to him. The same betting cycle continued for six rounds before Musher realized all four had been partners. At one point Independent 2 ran out of money and the pot was set aside limiting how much he could win. Pair 2A started the new pot with a fifty dollar call and a fifty dollar raise.

It was Musher's time to bet. "Gentlemen I can see you are both men of character and will continue this call and raise sequence until one of you runs out of money. May I suggest since it is my turn to bet that I bet an amount equal to the greater sum of your independent money and if the one who does not have enough to cover my bet then we will have a second pot for the one with the lesser amount of money. If neither can call my bet then we will have three separate pots for this hand each player only able to win the pot in which he has money. If that is agreeable please count your money."

The bets went as discussed. There were two pots. It was now time to see the cards. Pair 1A showed four aces and a king kicker. Pair 2A showed a straight flush from the three to the seven. Musher showed his usual straight flush from the six to the ten. The partnership got its ass kicked. Musher asked the two independents to stay for a minute. He quickly counted his money and was pleasantly surprised He counted thirty-six hundred pounds

Sterling. Subtracting his five hundred pound investment his net profit is thirty-one hundred pounds Sterling. (Eight thousand six hundred eight dollars American)

"How much did you guys lose?"

"Together we lost seven hundred forty pounds." (Two thousand dollars American)

Musher counted out seven hundred forty pounds. "You were victimized. Those four play as two teams but were really only one team. They helped me kick their ass by each one wanting to be the hero who won the big pot. Take this and leave. Remember you don't play poker with strangers." Even with the gesture he still made over six thousand dollars profit for the night.

Boone said, "That was great. Do you believe you must give some to get some? I do." "Goodnight Boone, tomorrow is going to be a tough day." He had his little bag clutched in his arms. During the poker game he kept control of it by keeping it between his ankles.

He had not only completed part two of the plan, he had far exceeded any of the happy results from Part 2. Part 3 begins tomorrow.

CHAPTER 182
I Am On My Own As a Tourist

He drove away from the hotel feeling very secure in his life.

According to the RAC it was six hundred fifty kilometers (one kilometer is equal to one eighth of a mile) to Edinburgh Scotland. They estimated a seven and a half hour drive. Little TR-6 was cruising right along but Musher was starting to feel cold despite the fact that he had the heating system turned up as hot as it would go. He pulled off to the side and decided where he would get off the main road and into a town or village whichever was there. His luck was still good. The town had a Marks and Spencer. A very cordial sales woman listened to his tale of woe about the temperature in the TR-6. She smiled and said, "Your first little sports car?" Musher nodded. She led him to a section of the store called Drivers Lane. There displayed were all types of what they called Drivers Coats. He settled for two fingertip length coats. One Alpaca lined (kind of like the sheep skin lining in his high altitude cold weather flying gear) the other with a standard inner lining. His eye caught a waist length alpaca lined leather jacket. He swore they must have converted RAF clothing. He purchased the jacket along with two hats, one alpaca lined with ear flaps, the other a standard lining with ear flaps. He added three pair of gloves, one for cold weather driving, one for standard driving and one for warmer weather driving. The hardest part of the shopping was not the paying for his goods because things seemed very reasonable to him, but carrying all the packages and fitting them into the TR-6. Throughout the shopping and the checking out the little black bag never left his hands.

He sat in the car and thought, if it was estimated seven and half hours to Scotland and I have already eaten up four of those, I would get to Scotland in the dark. He felt like the logistician who planned the wing TDY move from Roswell to Wyton. Takeoff in the dark, land in the light. He would modify the process and make his take off in the light and land in the light. Where could he RON? RAF Mildenhall is less than two hours away. He would visit Smasher at Mildenhall.

He inquired where to find the orderly room of the Group Supply Squadron. The Air Policeman asked about the USAF windshield sticker from Japan. He passed Musher through with instructions how to find the orderly room. Musher walked into the orderly room only to be faced by Master Sergeant Spencer Cohan, better known as "Smasher."

"What brings you here?"

"I left London heading for Scotland and the TR got cold. By time I could stop and buy the right gear it was around lunch and if I kept going I would be driving mostly in the dark. Since I am on an eight day trip I changed my route to come see you."

Smasher turned to the orderly room Chief Clerk, "I am going to the NCO Club, the BX and then my quarters. Take care of the place."

Musher had a breakfast lunch, omelet, toast and coffee. As they were leaving they passed the stag bar and the loud noises of a crap game. "It's just the start of the daily game. It will go until morning or even later. Yesterday was pay day and some of them feel like millionaires. Musher tugged Smasher into the room. He wanted to see what kind of action there was in a non-flying unit. There were a couple of guys trying to dominate the game with money. Not a bad technique unless you bet the dice wrong and the shooter is a wild horse fucker. The shooter was in short sleeves with a large handful of money. He yelled, "Smasher when are you going to pay me the hundred you owe me?" Musher passed his black bag to Smasher and then boomed, "Five hundred the shooter is wrong! The room was quiet while the other players tried to decide if they wanted into this act. Unanimously they stood quietly and watched. Musher followed up to the Loud Mouth, "Five hundred not enough for you, five hundred more if you have any balls."

Loud mouth said, "Show me the money." Musher put ten one hundred American dollar bills on the table. Your turn to show. Loud mouth emptied pockets and counted and when he reached one thousand dollars he said, "You're on." He rattled the dice in his hands, said some expressions imploring the Goddess of Luck and released the dice to the table wall farthest from him. What the crap shooters would call "Two Stars". A pair of fives for a point of ten. The next roll caromed off the wall and Musher exclaimed, "Star green, half of fourteen, a loser in the main."

Musher looked at Smasher, "Would you pick up the cash, pay him his hundred and give him a hundred for car fare." Loud mouth was coming hard around the table to get to Musher. Musher did his best street routine, the side step, the kick in the balls, the punch to the Adam's apple and a knee to the face to finish the job. It was over in seconds. Musher spoke to the room, "Is there anyone else who thinks he should come beat my ass? If there is let me tell you, he will recover, the next person will not."

Musher and Smasher went to the BX. Smasher had some cigarette ration coupons. Musher loaded the little bag with goodies and cokes for his drive to Scotland. He would top off his tank at the base service station where gasoline was ten cents a gallon instead of the one dollar six cents for an imperial gallon on the local market.

Musher and Smasher were back at the NCO Club for dinner. Friends of Smasher were courteous but not their usual bubbly selves. Tonight was the night the local girls and women were transported into the NCO club to dance with and entertain the NCOs. Smasher told him that most of the females were just really trying to find a G.I. to marry and get a free ticket to "the land of the big BX." Musher knew Smasher was faithful to his wife so he made the excuse of being very tired and asked if they could leave.

CHAPTER 183
Traveling the Countryside

In the kitchen he found a note from Smasher. "Early formation, just plug in the coffee and there is some coffee cake in the breadbox. Stop in to say goodbye and tell me when you will be here again."

He did his morning SSS, dressed and had breakfast. He put three hundred dollars in script on the table and added to Smasher's note. "Not much at goodbyes. I took your phone number and next time I will call before I come. Take LoudMouth's money and spend it on your wife when she gets here. Don't use it to gamble, remember you are a football player not a gambler."

While servicing the TR he thought, I will visit Dukie. It's only forty kilometers.

The morning was warm and comfortable when the TR stopped in front of Dukie's house. With small bag in hand Musher knocked and it was answered by Hereford. He looked as if he had seen a ghost and had trouble getting out his words. "Master Musher, come in, come in, everyone will be so happy to see you." The Duke was coming down the grand staircase when he heard Hereford's welcome. He hurried to the door and hugged Musher.

"Do come in. Hereford please get the bags and put them in Musher's old room. Come my boy and let's have some tea. Hereford tea please." In the library the Duke told of how they had heard that Musher was killed in the Korean War.

Musher's response was classic Mark Twain, "The rumor of my death has been greatly exaggerated." "I did have some tough times and I was not able to get out of the Air Force because of a presidential executive order." The Duke's eyes thirsted for more details. Hereford brought tea and sandwiches and Musher had time to gather his thoughts.

He began at the point where his wing returned to Roswell from the TDY to RAF Wyton. I had very few months before my discharge and in anticipation of my discharge I was replaced on my aircrew. I was forced to do clerical work which I intentionally did poorly while voicing my opinions of the air force and my superiors. Then came the blow, The Korean War. All discharges were frozen. As an act of vengeance for my behavior I was transferred to a combat wing which was getting ready to go overseas and make combat strikes against North Korea. My aircraft was shot down (a little poetic license) I was captured and spent fourteen months as a prisoner of war. Following my release from the POW camp I was promoted to Master Sergeant in accordance with air force regulations governing the loss of aircraft in combat and survival of POW status. Over a year was spent in Japan recuperating and while I was there I learned to play golf. Finally after getting my weight from the one hundred nineteen pounds I weighed at release to a less skeletal look of one hundred sixty pounds the air force decided it was time I went on a convalescent leave. I asked for and received assignment to England. I added thirty days of my accrued leave to the sixty day convalescent leave and started for England. On the way here I spent a couple of days in Hawaii playing golf and then almost a month more playing golf in Florida. I have been in London for almost a week. I was staying at the New London Hotel in Piccadilly, seeing the sights and playing golf at The New London Golf Club. Everything was rosy until they discovered, through my response to "what do you do". I told them of my military life. From that answer everything went topsy turvey. They asked me to leave the club and the concierge at the hotel told me my playing golf at the club would no longer be possible. Last night I stayed with a friend and his family at RAF Mildenhall. Counting today I have seven days before reporting to the USAF Headquarters at South Ruislip, London.

Enough about me fill me in on the Duke of Gloucester and his family."

"The Duchess passed away about six months ago. Cerebral hemorrhage. The girls are young ladies and being sought for marriage by any number of the young royal gentlemen. Dukie and the Willingham girl were married ten days ago, are on their honeymoon in Paris and will return here tomorrow. Hereford and the rest of the staff are still with us, God Bless Them. I still cannot beat Willy at snooker but he talks about you all the time. I hope you still play as well but we will see about that later. How long have you been playing golf and how well do you play?"

"I would say close to eight months. I believe I play extremely well. The course at The New London Club was relatively short and only on two rounds which were intentionally played poorly did I shoot seventy-five. All the other rounds were par or better."

"Do you think we could get Willy again? He is an ardent golfer and about a four handicap. You and I will play tomorrow at my club and see what you can shoot there. That is if you want to play golf tomorrow."

"Can I be Master Sergeant Muscarello or must I pretend to be otherwise? If I must pretend I do not wish to play."

"You must always be who you are. There are a great many clubs in England which follow the same snobbish rules as The New London Golf

Club. We will settle with The New London Golf Club sometime soon. Now, why don't we play a little snooker?"

Musher still knew the drill but his hand eye coordination had diminished slightly. He was still far better than Willy or anyone like him but he doubted seriously if he could break one hundred plus.

Hereford had laid out dinner clothes from Dukie's closet. The conversation at dinner was social and generally devoted to the courtship of the Duke's daughters and their suitors. The Duke dreaded the thoughts of their marriages and moving into new homes with their husbands. According to him his only consolation would be that Dukie and bride would live here with him.

In the game room the Duke challenged Musher to 301. Here again Musher's hand eye coordination has diminished but he still gave a good accounting of himself. The Duke yawned and remarked, "Off to bed. Big day at the golf course tomorrow. I will see you at breakfast."

Hereford was waiting in his room. "On behalf of myself and the rest of the staff we sincerely thank you for your gift to us. It was totally enjoyed by all the staff. Shall I start the shower now?"

His last thoughts before falling asleep, I need more snooker practice, I need more dart practice and I surely hope I play well tomorrow.

CHAPTER 184
A Day Playing Golf

Hereford came in carrying a tray with hot tea. "Sir, the Duke is waiting breakfast for you." Musher did a quick SSS. Hereford had laid the golf attire on the bed. When Musher was dressed Hereford exclaimed, "You are quite the dapper you are." Musher asked Hereford to go tell the Duke he would be right down. Hereford took his golf bag and shoes and remarked, "These will be in the boot." Once alone he emptied all his cash onto the bed. He put five hundred pounds in his trousers and stashed the rest away securely in the room. He was not a trusting soul.

At breakfast the Duke spoke only of the forthcoming golf day. He would introduce Musher as his visiting guest. Today they would ride a cart and play as a twosome. The Duke didn't want Willy to hear about it if Musher played very well. The name of the golf club was The Estates Golf Club. It was on properties owned by the Duke and Willy.

The Head Golf Professional was introduced to Musher as Peter MacTavish, a former player on the United Kingdom Professional Golfers tour. The Duke told him that he had an important meeting this afternoon so he would like to go off as quickly as possible and he and his guest would play as a twosome. In the cart riding towards the first tee the Duke whispered, "We skipped the range and the putting green just in case someone was watching. After the first hole we will play from the tips. (As far back as the tee box extends). We will play the men's tee on the first hole. From the first tee hit a four wood."

The Duke may be royalty but he definitely has a hustler's blood flowing through his veins.

Despite the Duke dictating which club to hit and where to aim the shot Musher managed to shoot one under par. Left to his own choices and decisions he felt he could easily shoot three or four under par. Especially since all the five pars were short enough for a good drive and at worst a five iron to the green. The Duke did not play every hole, instead he watched Musher and some times asked him to hit a second ball which would not count for score.

They were having a Lager and Crisps (potato chips to us Yanks) when Willy came in from his round. He excused himself from his group and came to sit with Duke and Musher. Musher stood as Willy approached they shook hands and Willy sat down. He said, "I am most pleased you are not dead. I didn't know you played golf. Do you play as well as you played snooker?"

"No. I have only been playing for about one year."

"I hope you will be here long enough for us to play a round. Right now if you will excuse me I must rejoin my group and pay my losses."

The Duke sighed, "Those three that he plays with are best described by the French word "Poisson", fish. They continually lose to him and not intentionally. They are seven or eight handicap players and they play scratch Nassau with him. I think it was one of your American circus operators who said, "There's a sucker born every second." Musher, I think Willy might be ripe for the taking. His heart is full of revenge and when you told him that you have only been playing one year his eyes lit up like a neon sign. Excuse me while I invite him and his family to dinner tonight. Dukie and Mary should be home also. He will not be able to resist."

The Duke returned with, "They will be there about seven. You look like you did not get enough golf today. If you would like to play another nine or so I would be glad to drive the cart for you. Most members are gone and even if they were not if we are going to take Willy it will need to be tomorrow."

Musher played the front nine from the black tees and shot thirty-one, five under par. The Duke could hardly contain himself. When they were back home Dukie and Mary had not yet arrived. Musher excused himself, went to his room and took a nap. It seemed he had hardly closed his eyes when two gruff arms were shaking his shoulders. "Wake up Sleeping Beauty, time to talk to Uncle Dukie." They hugged and shook hands. Dukie insisted on being filled in about Musher's life. He told Dukie the same story he had told the Duke. That seemed to satisfy Dukie's curiosity. Hereford came in and announced, "It is time to get ready for dinner." Dukie left saying, "Mary and I will be in the library if you come down early."

Musher was first in the library. He was sipping a scotch and soda when in came Dukie and his bride. Musher rose, bowed to Mary and said, "It is a pleasure to be here with such royal friends." All three chuckled. Dukie filled in Musher with all the details since their last meeting. He teased that Mary had given him an ultimatum, either marry her or find his sex somewhere else. He was now managing most of the family businesses and actually getting better at it with his father's tutelage. He and Mary would practice making a baby every chance they got. Remember only because the Duke wanted a grandchild. With his hand over his mouth he muttered "Sex isn't really that much fun."

The Duke came in and Mary just disappeared as the Duchess before her had done. The Duke could hardly explain Musher's ability with a golf club. He spoke of today's practice round and final nine. They had been joined for a few minutes in the 19th hole and the Duke had invited Willy and family for dinner. When Musher told him he had only been playing golf for less than a year Willy looked at Musher like the fox who just got the job to guard the chickens. After dinner tonight we are going to try to engage Willy in a golf match for a lot of money. Inside he is still burning from his last tromping by Musher and so badly wants revenge. Hereford announced the Willinghams were arriving. The three men greeted them in the foyer. Willy, his Duchess and his daughter Ann accompanied by one of her suitors, Hemingway the son of the Duke of Nottingham. Introductions and niceties were exchanged before the men adjourned to the library.

The dinner conversation was dominated by Hemingway. He had graduated from Cambridge University and was now studying to be a doctor. At least one male member of the lineage has always been a physician. Willy tapped his glass, "We have not publicly announced it yet but very soon Hemingway and Ann will announce their engagement and set a date for the wedding." The men rose with a glass in hand, "To Hemingway and Ann". Dinner ended and the men went to the game room while the ladies went to the study.

On the way to the study Musher whispered to Dukie, "I know this is not a polite question but just how rich is Willy?"

"If the Crown needed a loan they would seek him before any bank. I would venture a guess that in his residence he keeps one million pounds for immediate use."

In the game room the men, all except Musher, were smoking cigars and drinking brandy. Musher was smoking Lucky Strikes and drinking coco-cola. Hemingway looked at him like, "Typical American colony boy."

"Musher, how about a little snooker and let me get my money back?"

"I am afraid not Willy for two reasons, one I don't play as well as I used to, and two, I could not afford to play for such stakes. Remember I was backed, it was not my money at risk."

"Then how about a friendly game?"

"I have not changed that much. I still only play games for money."

"How about a golf match tomorrow, say for one thousand pounds?"

"Yes, I can do that."

"Here's where the Duke broke in. "Willy, I backed him last time and I will again this time. You gave me the fifty thousand pounds and you may try to get it back from me."

"That certainly is a bet. Eighteen holes, match play, strict rules of golf, from the black tees. I will try for a ten o'clock tee time. (Like you would have a problem when you own fifty percent of the course and one of your playing partners owns the other fifty percent) My friend the Duke of Gloucester and his son will make up the foursome. Peter MacTavish will come along as the Rules Officer and Scorer. There will be no coaching on the course except by your caddy who is considered a member of your team. The losing party will pay cash at the end of the round. Does anyone have anything to add? Then it is settled. Ten o'clock tomorrow morning."

When Willy finished Musher felt like he should be getting a second for this duel to the death. Willy gathered his family and left. The Duke, Dukie and Musher waited until they were sure he was gone before showing any joy. Musher assured the Duke, "I will win but not by a very large margin. I will not make the mistake I made with him when we played snooker. He will be able to walk around the club with his head high saying, I almost got him, I almost got him." He recalled Fanucci one more time, "You can shear a sheep many, many times but you can only skin him once."

"Gentlemen, breakfast will be at six thirty. We want plenty of time on the range and putting green before we go to the first tee."

CHAPTER 185

Shear the Sheep

It was eight in the morning when they arrived at the golf course. The Duke went into the pro shop while Dukie and Musher went into the 19th hole for a cup of tea. Already sitting there was Willy, Hemingway and Peter MacTavish. Polite good mornings were exchanged. When the Duke came Willy told him Hemingway had stayed overnight just to watch the match. Musher thought, "Bullshit, he stayed to fuck Ann all night. Certainly no one could blame him. She was pleasant thoughts in Musher's memory." Peter went into the pro-shop and Willy to the driving range.

"Boys we will reverse our warm-up routine. As long as he is on the driving range we will be on the putting green. When he quits we will swap. He is too much of gentleman to try to watch Musher on the range." As the Duke predicted the warm-up routine went smoothly.

On the first tee MacTavish had them draw a number from a hat. Willy drew the 1 and was first to tee off. He hit an excellent drive and picked up his tee smiling. It was now Musher's turn. He thought of Fanucci, "The most important thing you can do when playing a hustler is get ahead. Make him chase you just to try to get even much less ahead. Most hustlers have the fear they are being hustled." The drive was long, with a little draw and at least forty meters past Willy. For this par five Willy hit a layup shot to the ninety-one meter marker. Musher hit a three wood within six meters of the pin. A little of the wind went out of Willy's sails. Willy made a great pitch and tapped in for birdie. Musher made a silk stroke and sunk the eagle. He is one up but he needs more.

The next hole was a long par four. Musher's drive left him within one hundred nineteen meters of the pin. Willy's drive left him at one hundred fifty-five meters from the pin. Willy's second shot was right of the green and in a sand trap. Musher's second shot was left of the pin by six meters. Willy almost holed his sand shot but tapped in for a par. Musher made the birdie. Two up made Musher comfortable for his plan.

They both made par on the next three holes until they came to the island green sixth hole. It was two hundred ten meters to the center of the island. Musher made a display of taking a three iron. His shot landed on the green and rolled to a stop. He watched Willy take the bait. Willy's three iron fell short and in the water. From the drop area he made a four. Musher two putted for a three and was now three up. From here he would coast until they finished the front nine with him just two up. The back nine scenario was played so that Musher ended one up after the eighteenth hole. The Duke and Dukie had quit playing back on the third hole and were just two more spectators. Everyone shook hands and they headed for the club dining room. Well not quite everyone. Hemingway excused himself for the long drive home but it was easy to see that he was frustrated by the "colony boy."

In the dining room Willy gave Musher one thousand pounds. To the Duke he handed a heavily stuffed envelope. During lunch they replayed the round. Willy congratulated Musher on his skill but if it had not been for some long lucky putts Musher made the outcome could have been different. Everyone agreed that Musher had the luck today. MacTavish the pro allowed that he was particularly impressed with the distance Musher got from his clubs. He even suggested that with a good teacher Musher should get out of the air force and play professional golf. With that Willy suddenly had to leave for an afternoon appointment. Musher spoke to him in condolence," I was lucky today. It would have taken very little for you to win. Thank you for the match I enjoyed it very much."

Willy, always the gentleman replied, "You are very good. I feel no shame having been beaten especially by such a small margin. Goodbye." Musher smiled inside, he had left the man his dignity, not his money, but his dignity.

In the game room the Duke counted out fourteen thousand two hundred eighty-six pounds. Add the thousand pounds Willy had paid him and it was not a bad days' work. ($42,800 American) I must get a wedding gift for Dukie. There was a dinner and dance at the Estate Golf Club tonight and Dukie insisted Musher go with the family. The Willingham family will be there.

Musher stashed his new money with his old. Hereford dressed him for the occasion. At the club they were seated with the Willinghams. He danced with all the ladies but mostly with Ann. At the table she offered to give him a tour of the club facilities.

Anyone who has read this story to this point can figure out what happened when they came to the first dark alcove.

Almost an hour had passed when she suggested they return to the table, "After all did you forget I am soon to be married?"

Tomorrow he would return to London and settle in. If he stayed here any longer it would only cause trouble with people he loved.

CHAPTER 186

Sign In For Duty

At breakfast Musher announced he would leave today for London. He still had five days before he was due to sign in but he wanted to be sure he would be early rather than risk the chance of being late. It was only about one hundred twenty-five kilometers and when he is settled they can all feel free to visit.

The Duke had hoped for more golf and bridge. You know Mary is a better bridge player than Dukie. Dukie added that he had hoped they would go horseback riding.

"Maybe in the future if you will let me come back to visit you. I am not much at goodbyes so can we say them here?" After breakfast a lot of hugging, kissing and handshaking. Hereford was waiting for him in the room. Most everything was packed. Musher clandestinely recovered his money stashes from throughout the room. When Hereford finished packing he said, "I shall take these down and have your car serviced and brought to the front."

"Just a moment please Hereford. I want to buy Dukie and Mary a wedding gift. Have you heard them mention anything they would like?"

"Yes there is. Mary has asked for a crystal statue which she wants to display in the library. It is expensive and Dukie has asked her to wait before buying it."

"How expensive is it?"

"With taxes and all it is about four thousand pounds." (About eleven thousand dollars American)

"Do you know where to get it?"

"Yes sir."

Musher counted out five thousand pounds. "Hereford please take this and buy the statue. Put a simple card in it which says "With my love, Musher". Can you do that? The extra thousand pounds is for you and the staff as an early Christmas gift."

Musher slipped out the front door, shook hands and gave a hug to Hereford, started the TR and headed for London. In less than two hours he was getting change to use the pay phones. "Cody, this is Musher. I am going to sign in at South Ruislip. Will you be available later today?"

"When you finish at Ruislip, come to my house for a snack. I will be here waiting."

Musher rented a thirty shillings (four dollars twenty cents American) room to clean up, change into a uniform and get his papers in order. At worst he would have a place to sleep tonight. He approached the reception desk and gave the Sergeant his papers. He was asked to have a seat. Shortly thereafter a muscular Technical Sergeant strutted towards him. "You must be Master Sergeant Muscarello. I am Gideon Thorpe, your new first sergeant. Where is your gear? Is it secure?"

"With the exception of this bag everything is in the car."

"Give me your car keys." Gideon looked to the sergeant at the desk, "Take his car around the back and put it in the secure area. Put the keys in my office when you finish. Muscarello, what do they call you? I am generally called Thorpe. OK Musher let's go have a snack and talk."

They went into a small but well equipped cafeteria. The Fire Marshal sign limited its capacity to forty people. The cafeteria had table service so Gideon ordered tea and rye toast. Musher ordered the same. When they were served Gideon began. "You have me, my squadron commander and even the 7th Air Division commander in a dither. You are an aerial gunner assigned to a place where there are no airplanes. On top of that you are to continue to receive flight pay until further notice. Do you have some other specialty that we are not aware of ? I can see by your blouse that you are a combat veteran and your record says you were a POW in China for fourteen months. Do you know why you were sent here?"

"Our air force figured I had stayed too long in Japan while becoming a person after prison camp. My body has reacted well but our air force is not sure that my mind has. I sometimes lose mental control and become a violent killer. I asked to be sent to England because my memories of England were good from the TDY I had spent here with my bomber group. I am to continue my psychiatric visits until three psychiatrists say I am totally stable. That's as much as I know and can figure."

"There are no government quarters here. We are paid a twelve dollar per day per diem for quarters and one dollar thirty-three cents for meals. This cafeteria is only open from 0600 to 1600, Monday through Friday. Even if you could eat all your meals here one dollar and thirty-three cents would starve you to death. I am positive you know what it is like to be hungry." Gideon saw a bright light in Musher's eyes and quickly retreated to another subject. "You have a car and you will be given a key to the secure area. We have our own filling station there where petrol is ten cents a gallon versus seven and six (one dollar five cents American) for an imperial gallon on the market. Why don't we go to my office to get your keys and a key to the secure area so you can go find a place to stay tonight. The squadron commander is not here and will not be in before ten in the morning. If you can come in about nine I will give you a tour of the facility and set you up with ration cards, etc. We don't keep a very tight schedule."

Musher pulled up in front of Cody's house. Cody and Alice came out to greet him. Alice could have almost been Italian. The minute a visitor came into her house out came the tea and biscuits instead of coffee and cake. They sat in the kitchen and Musher told of his experience at his new duty assignment. Since there were no quarters at South Ruislip he needed Cody's help to find a place to live. He chose not to live in a hotel although with the per diem he certainly could afford it.

"Have you thought about lodging? You Americans call it boarding."

Musher thought about Priscilla and her boarding house. He would love one just like that. "I have stayed in boarding houses before and find it very pleasant."

"Lodging in England during these times is hardly anything you can compare with a first class boarding house in America. Here the lodger gets his private room, shares the bathroom with the family, gets tea and fried bread served in his room for breakfast but does not take any other meals with the family. If he chooses he can get his laundry done. Most of the houses do not have a shower facility and limited hot water. It is considerably less expensive than any other form of living facility."

"Let's talk about this. I could always shower at South Ruislip. When I used the latrine there were sinks and showers. I could take most Monday through Friday meals in their cafeteria. I would require a safe place to park my car. Everything else I could live with providing my room was not the size of a cardboard box. Do you know of such a place?"

"A retired Royal Air Force Sergeant Major and his wife live next door. They live totally on the first floor. There are only two ways into the house, either through the front or the back door. Either way you must pass into the first floor to get to the stairs leading to the top floor. The second floor is a very large bedroom with many windows, a small den with no windows and a half bath. (A sink and a commode) There are shilling meters in the two rooms. (A shilling meter requires you put a shilling in the slot for the gas to come on. You must ignite it and it will burn gas for heat for a given time.) I have told him about you and suggested that you might be a candidate as a lodger. As for secure car parking you can park along side mine on property he and I own jointly. Would you like to go and see the place?"

The door knocker was answered by a robust man with one of the largest handlebar moustaches Musher had seen in England. Once they were inside Cody introduced Master Sergeant Saverio Muscarello, commonly known as

Musher to RAF Sergeant Major, Retired Alfred Tandy, commonly known among his peers as "Dandy Tandy". His wife stepped forward and introduced herself as Eloise Tandy. "Musher wants to see the upstairs. Is it all right if we just go up?" Before they could take the first step Eloise was apologizing, "It needs a really good cleaning. We seldom go up there." Cody and Musher continued up the stairs. Two steps creaked rather loudly.

This bedroom is certainly not a cardboard box. The windowless room would serve well as a storage closet. He would need to buy a bed, dresser, sheets, pillow cases, a night stand, some blankets and maybe even a comforter. He would contract Eloise to put up drapes which he would buy.

"They heard Dandy's voice, "If you buy the paint I could do this whole floor in one day."

Musher turned to Cody, "With some work this will do very well. Let's have a "cuppa" and discuss finances." Dandy put the first proposal on the table. "You have the entire second floor as your quarters. You buy the paint and I will repaint the entire floor including the baseboards and ceiling. If you wish I can get carpet for the two rooms in any color you choose. The rental rate is five bob (a shilling) a day with laundry service and four bob a day without laundry service."

"Does that include hot tea and fried bread served in my room every morning?"

"That will cost an extra two shillings per week."

"Here is my counter proposal. Cody will oversee the project. He and I will acquire the paint, brushes, rollers and what ever else you need to paint the entire apartment including the ceilings. We will have that in your hands today. How long will it take to finish the painting? One day means the morning after tomorrow morning I can move in. Is that correct? Good. Tomorrow Cody and I will purchase all the furnishings I want in the apartment. If I transfer to another location in England or when I go back to the states all the furnishings will be yours. Eloise will go with Cody to pick out drapes or curtains for the room. You will have another shilling heater installed in the bathroom. I will fill a container with four hundred shillings to be used for heating. At the end of each month you will tell me how many shillings are required to begin each month with four hundred in the container. I will be allowed guests both male and female without interference from either of you. Dandy you will be expected to keep my car clean. Eloise you will be expected to keep my laundry and the room clean and orderly. For these services I will not pay five bob a day. I will pay ten bob a day, fifteen pounds a month (Forty-two dollars American. Less than four days per diem. If these terms are agreeable here is one hundred pounds to cover the first two months plus.

Dandy put his arms around Eloise, popped her butt and said, "Agreeable but only if you buy a bed without a lot of squeaks when you move."

Musher said to Cody, "We must get rid of the staircase squeaks. How else can I slip in and out without being noticed?"

Eloise gave him keys to both the front and back doors. Musher and Cody went off to get the painting supplies. When they returned the apartment had been scrubbed and was ready for painting. Musher asked that after the ceilings the windowless room be done first. Cody and Musher left again for the furniture store. Musher was able to pick out everything he wanted and scheduled the delivery for early morning the day after tomorrow. It was getting close to tea time. Musher bought a large quantity of fish and chips and a case of Lager beer. At Cody's house the six of them ate, laughed and told entertaining stories. Musher left for his overnight hotel room.

CHAPTER 187
My South Ruislip Assignment

It was hardly 0800 when Musher had checked out of the hotel, put his car in the secure area and was eating breakfast in the cafeteria. He was joined by Gideon Thorpe. 'You are an early riser?"

"Yes and I try very hard not to miss a meal. Some complex left over from prison camp."

"I talked with the 7th Air division senior medical officer yesterday afternoon about your need to continue counseling. The nearest facility where you can get your treatment is RAF Station Lakenheath which is about two hours north of here. To do this treatment, which we must according to our orders, you would need to leave South Ruislip every Monday, Wednesday and Friday around 0900 for an 1100 hours appointment. Considering your appointment would be at least one hour and then you would eat lunch before heading back here, the drive back here would be slower as it always is when heading south. At best we could expect you in the headquarters some time after 1500 hours. At 1600 hours we close shop for the day. Think about that while I show you the facility."

The headquarters was on two floors. The top floor was the 7th Air Division Commander and his staff. Hardly anyone had any reason to visit the top floor. The main floor had the cafeteria, a latrine equipped with a steam room and showers, a reading room of reasonable proportions and the offices of the support unit. There was a heavy metal door guarded by an air policeman. "This door leads to the basement communications center. It is highly classified and none of us has ever even seen the door open. That's the facility. I trust our squadron commander will be here, it is almost 1030 hours."

They entered the squadron commander's office. In the center of his desk was a large name plate, Captain Jeffrey Todd, West Point Class of 1946. He had neither pilot or navigator wings on his chest. As a matter of fact his blouse was basically clean of all meaningful decorations. Gideon, "Sir this is Master Sergeant Saverio Muscarello our most recent addition to our unit." Musher saluted and Todd returned his salute most casually. Musher thought, "Oh Oh, this titless WAF is going to be a problem."

"Sergeant Muscarello I have read your record. Most impressive. Our orders regarding you are very clear. Sergeant Thorpe has told me of the continued need for counseling and the only place you could get such counseling from the air force. He also tells me that beyond aerial gunnery you do not have any other skills. Is that true? Sergeant Muscarello to be very honest with you I have no idea what to do with you for the two days a week you might be here in the headquarters. Do you have any suggestions?"

"No sir." He still had not asked Musher to sit.

"Certainly Sergeant Muscarello you must have some suggestions."

It was time for the act. Musher erupted into a screaming fit, "You fucking people are all alike. You say you want to help me and then you put the pressure on me because you can't figure out what to do and don't really give a shit what happens to me. Well fuck you Captain I will get rid of all you back-stabbing non-caring officers. I will go upstairs and see if there is one officer there who cares."

Gideon had his arms wrapped around Musher. Musher put up a token resistance. Captain Todd, "Sergeant please sit down. I know we can work this out."

Musher sat and began to cry.

"I honestly don't know what to do. I want to help but I don't know how. Why don't you go with Sergeant Thorpe and I will try to figure out what to do. Rest assured we will help in any way we can."

Gideon took Musher into his office and gave him a glass of water. All the orderly room staff had heard the outburst and they were buzzing with gossip. Musher and his uniform were wet as if he had dove into a water tank. "Musher take the day off. As a matter of fact take enough time to get settled before you come back."

"Can I get some cigarettes?"

"What brand?"

"Lucky Strikes."

Gideon motioned to one of the clerks to come into his office. He handed him a ration book and two script dollars. "Four cartons of Lucky Strikes." Musher was reaching in his pockets to give Gideon the money. "Let's just say it is a welcoming gift from me to you." When the clerk returned Gideon said, "Musher why don't you leave now. I will see you when I see you."

Musher thought to himself that could be the code, *"I will see you when I see you."*

CHAPTER 188

I'll See You When I See You

Musher took his B-4 bag into the building latrine, brought out some civilian clothes and did his SSS. The little bag never left his sight. He filled the TR with ten cent petrol and headed for RAF Lakenheath. After lunch in the NCO Club he went to the Base Education Office. There was a lone Master Sergeant there. "Sergeant I am Master Sergeant Saverio Muscarello stationed at 7th Air Division Headquarters in London. Headquarters does not have an education office and it was suggested that this office was the most complete, well run education office in the United Kingdom. I would like to take the college level GED test. Can you help me?"

"Can you prove who you are and where you are stationed?"

Musher showed him his assignment orders and his passport.

"We can administer the test on most any day convenient for you. It is four hours long. We generally suggest that it be taken in the early morning. Did you have a day in mind?"

"I thought if it were possible I would stay tonight in the VAQ and we could do the test tomorrow morning."

"We can do that providing you are in uniform and here not later than 0730 hours."

"Thank you Sergeant, I will be here in uniform."

Musher drove around until he found the base tailor shop. He showed his uniform to the attendant and asked if it and the shirt could be pressed while he waited for them. Fifteen minutes and forty cents script later he was in his car looking for the VAQ. "Just tonight, I have an appointment at the Base Education Office at 0700 tomorrow. I don't have an alarm clock could I get a wakeup call for 0530 tomorrow?" He paid the fifty cent fee and headed for his room. The room was self-contained. Small refrigerator, coffee pot, radio, alarm clock and full bath with shower. There were towels stacked in the bathroom.

It was early in the day so he thought he would take in a movie. He was so strung out he hardly heard the characters and had totally lost the story line. From sheer disgust he left the base theatre headed for the NCO Club. This club was typical of any combat wing club where the aircrews are here on TDY. Every wall was loaded with slot machines. There was a crap game going in the stag bar along with two poker tables. One section of the stag bar was devoted to dart boards. This club is active. Being who he is Musher could not resist the temptation to kibitz the poker tables. Before long he filled a vacant seat.

The Red Headed player said, "Dealer's choice. Five stud high or low, seven stud high or low, wheel is best low. Jacks or better not progressive and there is a joker in the deck for aces, straights and flushes. Two dollar ante, half pot limit. Two hundred takeout."

The first three hands were five card stud and his cards were so bad he just folded. The next three were draw and he could not call the opener. It was his turn to deal. Under no circumstances would he win this pot. Even if he were dealt a pat royal flush he would fold before the draw. He won one small five stud pot which just got back his ante's. The cards were getting better. The Red Head dealt seven card stud high and low. Musher's two hole cards were the ace of diamonds and the joker. His face up card was a five of diamonds. He simply called the bets and raises. His next card was the five of clubs. Again, he simply called the bets and raises. The next card brought him a four of diamonds. He simply called the bets and raises. His fourth up card was the deuce of diamonds. He simply called the bets and raises. He has a baby straight flush but he remembers how many times he has set someone up with that hand only to beat them with his higher straight flush. If he just chose low and nobody else had a wheel he would win one half of the pot. Most of which was not his money. He simply called the bets and raises. The seventh card came face down. Musher made a pretense of squeezing a look and changed his facial expression to one of "oh shit. I missed." First bettor checked, Musher checked and Red Head bet the limit. First bettor folded and Musher refused the raise. The rule of the game is that the last person to make a bet, not a call, but a bet must be first to declare which part of the pot he intends to win, either the high part, the low part or both parts. If he declares for both parts and is tied or beaten on either part he loses and the pot goes to the rightful winner or winners.

Musher declared, "I play both."

Red Head showed four kings. Musher showed his straight flush for high and his wheel for low. The blood vessels in Red Head's neck looked like they were going to burst. Musher spoke inside his head, "This asshole is going to do something stupid and in the process of defending myself I will blow my GED test and who knows what else. Oh well I cannot control his mind but if he makes any kind of an aggressive move I will probably kill him in self-defense."

Musher was saved by two of the other players who were most likely friends of Red Head. They restrained him physically while he continued to verbalize nasty names and remarks. I doubt if Red Head knew they saved his life. Musher picked up his money stuffed it in his bag and went into the dining room.

Musher was well into his dinner when two men in flying suits approached him. The taller one spoke, "You are Musher aren't you?"

"Yes I am."

"You don't remember us do you?"

"No. Please help me."

"I am Master Sergeant Jack Carson and this is Master Sergeant Richard Brighton. We were your students in the RCS CFSC class at Smoky Hill. We followed you best we could because of the screwing you took on reassignment. Everyone had written you off as dead in the B-29 explosion over North Korea. We are certainly glad to see you here, alive and well. Was it you just had the run in with Big Red at the poker game? Do you mind if we join you? Fill us in we are interested for your welfare. We both owe you for our promotion and this choice assignment."

"What is your assignment here? Are you here TDY?"

"No, we are permanent party. We are gunners on the combat loaded B-50s parked far away from the regular base traffic."

"What are you doing with combat loaded B-50s? Are they the ones with the carburetion engines and not the rocker box fuel injection like on the old B-29?"

"Yes they are but we cannot talk about what we do. At least we do not talk about it in the NCO club. Fill us in from Smoky and what you are doing at Lakenheath. Are you here to join our unit?"

Musher gave them the synopsized version of Roswell, Spokane, Okinawa, Prison Camp, Japan and now on convalescent leave. "I am at Lakenheath because tomorrow morning I am taking the college GED. My assignment is Headquarters 7th Air Division at South Ruislip in London. Where there are no aircraft but I still draw flying pay. In case you are wondering and it is not visible in these clothes it is Master Sergeant Musher." They both silently applauded.

"What time is the test and for how long?"

"0800 for four hours. If I use four hours I must just as well have stayed home."

"We hate to eat and run but we have a 2100 station time. We will meet you here tomorrow for lunch. Good luck with your test."

Musher paid his bill and went to the VAQ. A good shower and off to bed.

CHAPTER 189

Two Steps Towards a College Degree

Musher entered the Base Education Office at 0715. He was smiling when saying good morning. The same master sergeant was there today as was there yesterday. The difference was that yesterday he was looking at a young guy in civilian clothing who could have easily been a titless WAF. Today he was looking at a polished Master Sergeant with a chest of combat decorations. He walked around his desk with his hand extended. "Dewey Wojeski, are you ready?"

They went into an adjoining classroom where Wojeski explained the test taking rules. He guided Musher through filling out the test answer sheet. At precisely 0800 Musher opened the first of four test booklets. Wojeski stayed in the room which was required by AFIT (Armed Forces Training Institute) who graded and evaluated the tests. It was declared that time was up and Musher put down the pencil. He wasn't sure if it was easy and he complicated it or he didn't know didily shit about the subject so he rapidly guessed his way through each part of the test.

When he put on his blouse his shirt was wet with sweat. Wojeski asked, "What do you think? How do you think you did? It will be two weeks before we get any results. Where do you want the results sent?"

"Keep them here. I will be coming here quite often for medical treatment and I will personally pick them up. Thank you for your help."

"Sergeant Muscarello we have an extensive University of Maryland undergraduate program here on the base. The next time you are up here why don't you come in and we will talk about it."

"Thank you." To himself, I have a much more grandiose undergraduate degree in mind.

Carson and Brighton were in the dining room waiting for him to join them for lunch. They asked how the tests went and would he be available for a small party at their squadron operations tonight? It's a 1700 hours early party with no liquor. Some crews have 2200 hours station times."

"What's the occasion?"

"I am afraid you can only find that out if you come to the party." They had been staring at Musher's uniform and his decorations. "If you don't have a flying suit with you a uniform will do. One of us will pick you up at the VAQ at 1700."

"OK but right now I must go to the base hospital for a treatment. I'll see you at 1700."

At the reception desk he asked to see the hospital administrator or hospital commander whoever was available. When questioned why he wished to see either he responded, "A very personal matter."

"I am sorry sergeant they only see visitors on an appointment basis."

Time for the act. "Listen you dumb shit you either get one of them or a lot of people around here will regret your "I don't give a fuck about you" attitude." A full colonel came rushing towards the scene. "What's going on here?"

"Ask this bitch who thinks she runs this fucking air force. I want to see the hospital administrator or commander and I don't have a fucking appointment."

"Easy son, I am the hospital commander, Colonel Howard Fuchs. Why don't you come into my office and let's take care of whatever it was you came here for." Sitting in the Colonel's office smoking a Lucky Strike and sipping water Musher put on as good an act of calming down as he had done in outburst.

When Colonel Fuchs thought Musher was ready he asked him what he could do for him. Musher told him he was assigned to London with the provision that he receive psychiatric help three times a week until three doctors declared him fit to terminate treatment. He was told this was the best place to receive that treatment and since it was less than two hours from South Ruislip he was here trying to arrange a treatment schedule. He tried to glass his eyes and said, "That non-caring bitch told me I could not see you or the hospital administrator without an appointment. She didn't ask if I wanted an appointment she just said I could not see either of you."

"What is your name?" Master Sergeant Saverio Muscarello. The Colonel picked up his phone, dialed and then said, "Phil this is Howard can you come to my office now please." A light knock and entered Lieutenant Colonel Phillip Crisalucci. "Sergeant Muscarello this is the head of psychiatric services. Please tell him what you told me." Musher finished and Colonel Fuchs asked Phil, "Do you see any problem accommodating Sergeant Muscarello?"

"None sir. If the sergeant will come with me to my office we can arrange a schedule to fit his needs." He rose and turned towards the door. Musher stood and said, "Thank you Colonel. I still would get rid of that bitch out front."

In Crisalucci's office he was asked why the USAF thought he needed psychiatric counseling. Musher told him he believed it was because he was a

614

POW in China as part of the Korean War and he has a tendency to lose it when things don't go so well.

"What name shall I use in our conversations?"

"Musher, what shall I call you?"

"When we are in session I am Phil. Since you need to be here three times a week what is a good schedule for you?"

"Headquarters 7th Air Divison is two hours from here. If we could schedule for 1500 hours I would only be away from my job one half a day and I could be back in London before it is pitch black."

"That is easy enough. I will not be your doctor but we have some excellent doctors on our staff. When do you want to start your visits?"

"Monday is fine. Report here before 1415 and I will introduce your doctor. Please don't frighten our receptionist anymore than she already is."

"Thank you Phil. I will see you on Monday."

Musher went to the base clothing store to purchase two more uniform shirts. At the VAQ he checked in for another night. He kept a goodly amount of money in his pockets and stashed the rest in the VAQ. At 1700 he was standing outside waiting for Carson and Brighton. They came in less than a minute, he boarded and they headed for the far operations center.

Musher was the only one there not in a flying suit. He was greeted like a long lost brother. He would never remember all the names of his peers. He made sure he knew the squadron commander's name, Lieutenant Colonel Charley Stride, call sign Strutter. Carson called for quiet. "Before we get to the reason for this get together I want all of you who do not know him to meet the best, I mean the best, B-29 Aerial Gunner in the entire United States Air Force, Master Sergeant Saverio Muscarello known and loved by us as Musher." Applause and cheers.

Strutter called for quiet. "Everyone knows that the United States Air Force aircraft do not invade Russian sovereign borders to do airborne spy work. Today one of those non existent flights encountered a MIG-23 who felt brave and made a pass at our non-existent aircraft. His rounds punctured some surfaces but nothing critical. Our boy, Master Sergeant Brighton fired some non-existent ammunition and destroyed the MIG. There will not be any headlines acknowledging his work but we all know he deserves our cheers and praise. He raised his glass, To our boy, Master Sergeant Richard Brighton." Applause and cheers.

That short praise told Musher what this unit did.

CHAPTER 190
You Will See Me When You See Me

Musher drove up to his new digs and saw the furniture lorry being unloaded. He parked where Cody had told him, unloaded everything but his golf bag and shoes and carried them upstairs. Dandy had done an excellent paint job, Eloise had put up the window drapes and the place was spotless. The furniture delivery men had just placed the last piece into the "flat" and were leaving. Musher went outside with them and gave each a two pound tip. When he reentered and going upstairs he noticed that there were no squeaky steps. The steps had been covered with the same carpet that covered the floors in the flat. Dandy and Eloise were waiting for him to arrange the furniture. When it was in place Eloise made the bed. The clothes dresser had been put in the windowless room. Dandy was unpacking and soon realized there was no way to hang the clothes in that room. He left and returned in thirty minutes with two long poles and some mounting blocks. He apologized to Musher for not having recognized the need. Tomorrow he would take down the clothes and paint the poles to match the rest of the room. Musher thought, it is not as pretty as the Duke's but it is functional.

Everything was in place and Musher realized he needed a good sitting chair. He would have Cody get two, one for his use and one he would keep in the windowless room for when he needed it. While he was at it he would have Cody get a dirty clothes hamper. The windowless room was a blessing. He checked and the windowless room had two electrical outlets. Maybe Cody could find a small refrigerator and put it in the windowless room for his cokes and other goodies. He would add five pounds a month to offset the additional cost for electricity. He lit a Lucky and realized that he did not have an ash tray. The commode in the half bath would be the temporary ash tray. Dandy had said it would be a week before the new shilling meter could be installed in the bathroom. He would have Cody get a medicine cabinet to install in the bathroom. He assessed the flat one more time and was truly pleased. It was time to visit Captain Jeffrey Todd. As he put on his uniform he realized that he did not have a mirror. He would have Cody get a full length stand alone mirror. Properly placed it could give some great views of the room.

On his way out he stopped in the kitchen where Dandy and Eloise were having "a cuppa". He told of his plan to buy a refrigerator and how he would pay five pounds more per month to offset the additional electricity cost. Dandy insisted that five pounds was far too much. Musher ignored him and left the room. His car was noticeably cleaner. Dandy again.

Cody answered his door knocker. Musher handed him a list of things he wanted Cody to buy and gave him one thousand pounds to use. "It's far more than I should need."

"You can always bring me the leftovers. Get four hundred shillings for the meters. I don't know what you smoke but here is a carton of Lucky Strikes. Got to go now."

It was after 1000 when he parked in the secure area. He entered Thorpe's office and asked to see the squadron commander. Thorpe escorted him into the squadron commander's office. Musher saluted, "Sir, permission to speak with the squadron commander."

Todd motioned for both Musher and Thorpe to sit. "Sir I want to apologize for my outburst the other day. No matter how I try occasionally I will lose control and make a complete ass of myself. I know I need psychiatric help. With your permission and my medical records tomorrow I will go to Lakenheath and arrange a treatment schedule. Sir, you must understand that at times these sessions will mentally drain me and I may spend as much as twenty-four hours regaining stability. Reliving the months of a Chinese prison camp takes it toll. I want you to know that under those circumstances I would probably spend the night in the Lakenheath VAQ or somewhere along the route coming back to London."

"Sergeant I am most pleased that you recognize what needs to be done. I must admit I was a little scared the other day. I have your medical records in my desk and I shall give them to you. Of course you have my permission to travel to Lakenheath and be gone from duty here whenever it is necessary. It's not like you were filling a critical position here. These are your medical records. Is there anything else?"

"No Sir. I truly appreciate your understanding. I will keep Sergeant Thorpe appraised of the situation. Again, my apology and thank you." Musher thought, "He's like the psychiatrist in Japan, he doesn't care what I do as long as he doesn't know about it or be involved with me." Now I can go to Step 3 of my undergraduate degree program.

In Thorpe's office Musher spoke as one G.I. to another. "I am glad your Captain is so understanding. With the latitude he has given me even you with all your knowledge of air force regulations could ever say I was not granted permission to make independent choices. You didn't give me any ration cards yesterday. I appreciate your gift of the cigarettes but I am old enough to take care of my self. When and how is payday?"

Thorpe handed Musher a six month ration card, a USAF identity card showing his duty station as South Ruislip and a charge book for purchase of petrol and petrol products at the in-house station. "Payday is the last day of the month. You will be paid in script. There is no pay formation. You can come to me anytime between 1000 and 1500 to get your pay and settle any debt you may have with USAF. I agree with you but I honestly believe Captain Todd is solely interested in your welfare. He does not live by the book himself and we are lucky if he comes to the office once a week. He drinks a little and he has an appetite for women which seems impossible for him to satisfy. He would never give us any trouble."

Great, from here on you will see me when you see me.

Before leaving the headquarters Musher did his SSS. Back at his place Cody had returned with all the purchases and placed them in the master room. Dandy had mounted the medicine cabinet and used one of Eloise's bowls to hold the shillings. Musher was evaluating his position and there were a couple of things he thought might be necessary. He needed a car which would attract less attention and give him more space. It must be right hand drive with a reasonable petrol capacity. He would ask Cody to search for one. He changed from his uniform to civilian attire. Suddenly the car thing became most prominent in his mind. He went next door and knocked. Eloise answered the door and invited him in for "a cuppa."

Cody had over four hundred pounds on the table as Musher's change. Musher gave him a ten pound tip for his efforts. "I have another job for you." Musher explained what kind of car he wanted and asked Cody to search for one. "I will be going away for a couple days it might even three or more days before I return." Musher gave him three thousand pounds to have as good faith money if he found a car which he believed was suited for Musher.

His next stop was a pay phone. Because it was a long distance call he went to the place and pay shop to which Cody had given him directions. The telephone was answered by Hereford. "This is Musher, May I speak to the Duke please?"

"Musher is something wrong? Where are you?"

"I am in London but I would like very much to see you. May I come tomorrow?"

"Of course, plan to stay the weekend."

"Thank you Sir, I will be there before noon."

CHAPTER 191
Step 3 Towards a College Degree

It was 0900 before Musher was on the road to Wyton. Along the highway one of his rear tires blew out. He was fortunate that in less than an hour an RAC (Royal Auto Club) Road Patrol vehicle came his way. Another half hour passed before the support RAC had called arrived on the scene. The spare was mounted, the blown tire was mounted where the spare came from, he paid four pounds for the work and he was on his way. Since England did not have speed limits the temptation was to go full throttle to try to make up time. He rationalized that would be stupid. He would risk a serious accident to meet a non-existent schedule. It was just past one when he pulled up in front of The Gloucester House. Hereford met him and took his bags. The Duke shook hands and hugged him. "I was just sitting for lunch. Dukie and Mary are playing golf and the girls have gone to London. It's just you and me." Dukie knew that routinely they ate lunch promptly at noon.

When they were alone at lunch the Duke questioned Musher about his visit.

"I have told you about my life but I did not tell you that I am required to have psychiatric care three times each week for at least the next two years. My treatment is only available at the USAF hospital at RAF Lakenheath. My treatments are scheduled for Monday, Wednesday and Friday at three o'clock in the afternoon. My squadron commander has not given me any assignment at the headquarters but has given me carte blanche authority to control my own duty hours whenever I find it necessary. I have taken an Air Force Institute for Training (AFIT) general education development examination and will be awarded a college equivalency rating of both the freshman and sophomore years. I could enroll in the USAF extension program operated for the University of Maryland. Since I am going to have so much time on my hands and no real duty I would like to try for an undergraduate degree from Cambridge University. I have no idea how to apply or if they would even consider a student with my educational background."

The Duke, "Willy and I are both on the Board of Regents for Cambridge University. We will speak to the Dean of Students about you and see what can be done, if anything can be done. Do you have proof of your educational background including the AFIT examinations?"

"Not with me but I will post the documents to you on Tuesday."

"When I receive your post Willy and I will visit Cambridge. If there is no more to your visit let's enjoy lunch?"

While they were eating Dukie and Mary came in. At the sight of Musher there were exchanges of hugs and kisses. "We are famished, may we join you?" Mary could not stop thanking Musher for the statue.

Dukie, "Dad can the four of us play golf tomorrow? Musher, you are staying right?"

"We will play at ten o'clock. Breakfast at seven-thirty. Right now I know Musher has had a rough morning and I certainly would like a nap myself. You two need to work on having my grandson. I will not live forever."

Hereford awakened Musher for dinner. The SSS was stimulating. Dinner dress was not formal tonight. Dinner lasted almost two hours. Nothing had changed, the men to the game room and the women disappeared. For a couple of hours they fooled with the darts, snooker and gin rummy. Musher was extremely tired and asked to be excused.

At breakfast Musher begged off from the golf. He was running a slight fever and did not feel well. The Duke had Hereford put Musher to bed and the family physician summoned. Doctor Wallace Robertson's diagnosis, "He has a viral infection of unknown origin. I have injected an antibiotic and most probably he will be well in less than twenty-four hours. Get as much liquid into his body as you can. Check his fever every hour until it is normal. I have given him a sedative and he should sleep for at least the next twelve hours. If he doesn't improve, call me."

The Duke shared Musher's secret with Dukie and Mary. He told why Musher had come and promised if it were at all possible he and Willy would get it done. During the next ten hours it was necessary to change Musher's pajamas and the bed sheets and blankets four times because Musher had sweated so much it were as if water had been poured over him. Most of the night the Duke slept in a chair in Musher's room. For no explanatory reason he believed that Musher's relay of his secret to him placed such a strain on him that his body could not fight some long lingering virus.

Musher awakened about 0500 feeling well and craving a cigarette. He saw the Duke in the chair and decided he would lie in bed until either the Duke woke up, Musher would watch for that, or until someone other than he awakened the Duke. It was not too long when the Duke stirred and coughed. He headed for the bathroom and when he returned Musher was sitting up in bed.

"You look well my boy. You gave us all quite a scare."

"My apologies" Musher did not know why he had become ill but this was a good opportunity to enrich the story. "I have special pills for these attacks but they were in my little bag and I could not seem to put the words together to tell anyone."

"I am sure Doctor Robertson will be very happy to know he used the right anti-biotic without knowing his enemy. You must be famished. We'll go down and have an early breakfast. Come down when you are ready."

Musher needed a shower. The sweating had left him feeling sticky and dirty. When he came out of the shower Hereford was waiting there with some sporting attire. Everyone else was also there for early breakfast. The Duke had made the rounds reporting Musher's health. Musher ate like a starving wolf.

Dukie, "Are you well enough for a round of golf?"

"As I told your Dad these attacks come and go and I have pills to control them. Yesterday I simply did not recognize the signals and didn't take the pills. When it struck I could not speak the words to tell you of the pills. The attack has passed and I am just plain old simple me. Whoever that is."

The round was fun. Musher made no attempt to play extremely well. He generally under-clubbed his shots in order to stay in the same shooting range as the other players. Despite all the goofing around he still shot one over par. In the middle of lunch the Duke looked directly at Musher. "Dukie and I want you to leave the USAF and become a full time professional golfer. We are prepared to absorb all expenses. We will split any prize winnings evenly between you and us. Your end of the prize money will be pure profit. We will establish a residence for you in Ireland and therefore avoid the murderous income taxes here in the United Kingdom and the United States. We will commit to a five year personal services contract with renewal options for both parties."

"Sir I am extremely flattered. Even if I wanted to get out of the USAF because of my medical history it would probably be a while before I would be certified mentally capable and be discharged. True I have played some excellent golf around other amateurs and club professionals but on the tour these are men who are playing for their bread and butter. They will present an entirely new level of golf. You may be wanting to make an unwise investment."

"As far as getting you released from the USAF it would be as Dukie says, "a piece of cake". As far as being a strong enough player to play competitively and win why don't we test the water? In two weeks there is an open tournament at The New London Golf Club. It will attract the better players from the European and British tours. There are sponsor exemptions for deserving amateurs. I will make sure you are listed as a deserving amateur. You would not be able to win any prize money as an amateur but you could win a memorial trophy and at the same time break it off in the asses of those snobbish owners of the club. Are you willing to try?"

"For you Sir anything."

"Good, seven days before the tournament we would expect that you would move into The Gloucester House. If you feel you need a coach we will get you the best. Whatever you want we will provide. It's a done deal then. We will not concern ourselves with any formal agreements until after your first competitive tournament."

CHAPTER 192

These Guys Are Really Good

Musher had his AFIT results. He received full credit for two years college education. Most of those credits would apply to liberal arts undergraduate degrees only. He had requested a copy of his high school transcript from the states. Along with the request, the money order for the fee and postage return (twice as much as he thought it could be) he included a self addressed envelope directed to Thorpe at the headquarters. It still had not been received and the Duke was on hold. When he last saw Thorpe he told him what might be coming and to hold it for him. He covered the need by saying "I am considering enrolling in the University of Maryland on-base extension course undergraduate degree program." He laid the basis for his extended absence which would last anywhere from seven to ten days. "You know I have been receiving psychiatric care for over two weeks now. The doctor is going to send me to a private clinic for further evaluation and consulting about my case. I can't tell you where it is because I don't know and I cannot tell you when. I suspect it will be this next week or so."

Thorpe reinforced his safety net. He in essence repeated Todd's guidance and his we will see you when we see you.

Musher told Dandy and Cody that he was being sent on a detached service assignment to another unit for the next seven to ten days. That simple statement started the speculation machine. "Maybe he is really in the air force office of special investigation (OSI) and he is going on assignment?" "Maybe he belongs to one of the other Sneaky Pete outfits?" "Do you wonder where he gets his money? He spends like he has an endless supply." When Dandy checked Musher's closet and found all his uniforms still there, he put more fuel on the fire with Cody. They sincerely debated whether they should contact British MI-6, the counterpart to the OSI.

Musher moved into The Gloucester House. He kept his treatment appointments at Lakenheath and when not there he practiced his golf. The Duke had engaged a well known American professional who was visiting England to identify any areas where Musher should work and to help him improve those areas. He helped Musher improve his sand game by at least five hundred percent. Gone was the fear of the sand trap.

The Gloucester House was consumed with the approaching tournament. The Duke had gotten a sponsor invitation for Musher. At dinner Musher commented, "Sir, the professional help you got for me improved my same game very significantly. There is one other thing which I believe would help my game. When I played at The New London Club I used the same caddy all the time. His name is MacInnes. Can you arrange that also?"

"My boy the tournament director is a member of the House of Lords in Parliament. So am I. Consider it done."

"Practice rounds are Tuesday, the Pro-Am Wednesday and the first scoring round Thursday. Tomorrow is Monday. Tomorrow we go to London. I have five suites reserved in the New London Hotel. One for our staff and Willy said he might be able to come to watch so I reserved a suite for him. Anything anyone of you spends in the hotel just sign your name to the bill. Do not tip any of the hotel staff." Musher took Dukie aside, "Why no tipping?" His answer, "When we check out Dad makes sure all the staff is tipped according to the service they provided."

When the family Rolls-Royce stopped in front of the hotel with the servants and the luggage car pulling in behind it bell hops and porters appeared from everywhere. Hereford took control of the hotel staff. Musher was the last out of the Rolls and was immediately recognized by the hotel doorman. He tipped his hat, smiled and said, "Sir, I am most happy to see you. Remember anything you need you can count on me." The Duke went to the registration desk while Musher slipped away to speak to the concierge. Phillip came from behind his desk to shake hands with Musher. "I thought I recognized your name as one of the players. Please do well so we may gloat over that fucking asshole Admiral."

The Duke motioned to Musher to join them. "We might just as well have lunch while the suites are prepared for us. Following lunch the four of them repaired to the game room and played bridge for the rest of the afternoon. The Duke was correct Mary was a better bridge player than Dukie. At tea time the Duke suggested they stop playing and take a short nap. "We will meet in the dining room at seven. It was an excellent bridge session."

Following the normal brandy and cigar everyone retired to their rooms. In his room Musher dialed Phillip. "This room is empty and cold. Can you suggest something to warm my cockles."

A light tap on his door and he welcomed a tall, blond statuesque well dressed lady. She entered the room and without comment removed all her clothing. Standing before him as naked as the day she was born she said, "Do you want the lights on or off?"

When the family car stopped in front of The New London Golf Club entrance once again porters appeared from nowhere. MacInnes was standing there waiting for Musher. He took the clubs, took off his hat and said, "I knew you were a winner. This week we shall prove it. I shall be on the range."

The Duke dictated, "I shall register you and pay the fees. Get your shoes on and head for the range." The hair on the back of Musher's neck rose. "This guy is good at giving orders and he is trying to control me. Nobody controls me. Never again will anyone control me."

Musher's practice on the range would be considered no better than poor. His practice putts were even worse. MacInnes, "Lad it's just another round of golf. Why don't we go sit and smoke a cigarette." They were no sooner on a bench and he had lit a cigarette than they were joined by Duke et al. "Sir I don't want to seem disrespectful but you must give me space. You are spectators and I am a player. Your crowding has my alpha waves juggled. If you want me to win let me be the independent player that I am." Musher was saved by MacInnes, "Sir we are due on the tee."

For the practice round he was paired with a professional he had never heard of. That was no surprise. The pairing directors would hardly put an amateur on a sponsor exemption with a well known pro. He was smiling with a hand extended, "I am Tommy Bass."

"I am Saverio Muscarello. Please call me Musher."

"We generally play a little Nassau on the practice round. Are you up for that?"

"What did you have in mind?"

"Twenty-five pound front, back, double overall."

Musher looked at him, "Lay on MacDuff and damned be he who first cries hold enough."

"What did you say?"

"Shakespeare from MacBeth. You're up."

The Duke et al had a four passenger golf cart and followed him throughout the round. They stayed well back as observers. They were the only spectators for this group.

When the round finished Musher had shot sixty-four and had Tommy Bass talking to himself. He would give the hundred pounds to MacInnes.

He was in the 19th hole having a coke with Tommy when The Duke et al joined them. "What do you think of my boy?" There he goes again, does he think he owns me? I will play my best this week and stall him until he gets me into Cambridge. I will never play professional golf for him.

As they were leaving for the hotel Musher looked at the practice round board. There were a bunch of sixty-fours. The highest rounds were in the eighties. This score meant nothing.

CHAPTER 193

The Tournament Begins Today

It was Musher's first Pro-Am. He was paired with three players whose handicaps went from fourteen to thirty-two. They constantly sought advice on how to improve their game. Musher tried but he didn't seem to be much help to any of them.

His entourage, the Duke et al, were at the first tee to watch the play. No four passenger golf cart today you must walk if you want to watch. It was an early tee time (the first day the lesser notables play early) and he knew he would not remember the names of the other three players in his foursome. MacInnes was at times encouraging and always correct in his advice. Musher played smoothly and finished the eighteen three under par. He gave MacInnes some money for lunch and went into the 19th hole to have lunch. Naturally he was joined by the Duke et al. The conversation from them would make a person believe that a three under round was a failure. He excused himself to go to the range. The Duke spoke, "Don't stay too long. You need your rest for tomorrow." Here he goes again. Between the driving range and the putting green Musher practiced for three and one half hours. When they were in the family car the Duke was not happy and did not hesitate to say so. "You knew I had to make an appointment and you intentionally delayed our leaving the golf course. You were not considerate."

Musher digested those words and said to himself, "I should tell him what I think and just leave. Right now he is too important to my game plan." Musher apologized for losing track of time.

The next tournament round was another three under. The cut was plus 2 and ties.

Tee times for the weekend were based on your individual standing for the tournament's first two rounds. Musher was in the tenth twosome off the first tee. He was only five strokes behind the leader. There were eighteen other golfers between him and the leader. Musher lit up today and turned in an eight under sixty-four. When all the players were in Musher was tied for the lead at fourteen under.

The Duke and et al were ecstatic. In the 19th Hole the conversation was just about every shot Musher had hit. The Duke must have sensed he was upsetting Musher so he no longer was authoritive but anything he thought was posed to Musher as a question for his approval. Musher could not wait to get to the hotel where he planned to have his cockles warmed.

At the hotel the Duke suggested they have dinner in the hotel at seven. Musher dissented, "I am going to order dinner in my room and get a good rest. I will see you at breakfast." No one made any comment.

Musher showered and crawled in bed to nap. Sleep did not come easy as he replayed today's round mentally emphasizing his strengths. At 2200 Musher was ready for dinner. After dinner he was ready for dessert so he called Phillip. Dessert was better than the meal. A shower and back to bed to rest.

Hereford was at the door. Musher took a quick SSS and went to breakfast. Everyone was there and in a great mood. No one talked golf. MacInnes was already on the range waiting. Musher was hitting wedge shots when MacInnes said, "Here comes the enemy, Eddie Leach. He is just about the best on the British Tour and you have him worried. Look at his eyes. He must have drunk himself to sleep last night. Can you imagine what the press would say if he lost to a first time sponsor exempted amateur. Just play your game and he is yours."

Musher was first off the tee. They both played very well and were still tied when they reached the eighteenth tee. All the other players had finished and six of the finishers were in the club house two shots behind the co-leaders. Both hit excellent drives. Musher was just slightly ahead of Eddie. Eddie's approach shot was on the green but not very close to the pin. Musher stood at his ball not thinking about what club or what type shot but what should he do. If he were to win this tournament it would be the lead story in every London paper. Certainly some of the 7th Air Division golfers would recognize if not his face surely his name. If he finishes second he can expect the same treatment; however if he were to blow this hole and finish either fifth or six there would still be a story but in no way would it show his picture. The spectators were getting impatient. Musher selected his club, lined up for a flight to the green and then made his swing. The ball started towards the green but suddenly turned left and into the pond beside the green. With the drop penalty he was hitting four. The pitch settled just short of Eddie's ball. Eddie stroked his putt. It lay on the edge of the cup. He tapped in and knew he had won the tournament. Musher's first putt was long, the second was short and the third finally fell into the hole for a seven and a drop to eighth place. There was pleasant but meaningless applause. After signing his card he headed for the locker room.

In came the Duke looking like he had been dipped in red paint. "What happened out there? On the seventy-second hole you fall apart?"

627

"I don't know what happened. Maybe it was the pressure that comes with the thought of winning from the big boys? I don't know."

"By all standards you did very well for a sponsor's exemption amateur. We will find you more tournaments to get over the pressure feeling."

"Sir can I have a hundred pounds? I want to pay my caddy."

The Duke gave him the money and said, "We will wait for you in the car."

Musher apologized to MacInnes while giving him the hundred pounds.

"Son there must have been a very good reason why you intentionally blew the eighteenth hole. You may fool all the others but I know you intentionally blew it. I watched you change your grip to create that viscous hook. I won't ask why for I am sure I would not understand. My heart is heavy to think that one of the best golfers ever to tee it up does not want to play professional golf. Take care of yourself and if you ever change your mind you can find me here. I would go anywhere to caddy for you."

MacInnes had tears in his eyes as he walked away.

CHAPTER 194
We're In

For the rest of the day Musher lamented his failure to do better at the tournament. He carried that "woe is me, nobody loves me" routine to breakfast. He told everyone he would be leaving before lunch to go for his medical treatment. All anyone did was either nod their head or grunt. As he was leaving he again apologized to the Duke and promised to play better.

After his treatment he drove directly to his flat. He was halfway up the stairs when Eloise suggested he drop the bags to have "a cuppa". In the kitchen holding up two newspapers were Cody, Alice and Dandy. None of these snaps flatter you and the articles don't either. Was that your detached service assignment?"

"No that was because I had some free time and certain people wanted to see how well I would play against Britain's best golfers. They were not very impressed after the eighteenth hole." With that he went to bed.

Musher had been able to get two flying suits from his friends at Lakenheath. The Lakenheath tailor was quite accustomed to making flying suits look pretty. He did a good job for Musher and was well rewarded. Musher bought a red baseball hat and had the tailor embroider 98-S22 on its crown. (98-S22 was his crew number from the 98th Bomb Wing). On the crown of his hat he placed the pin showing his rank of Master Sergeant. He wore them when he went to see Thorpe. Thorpe immediately held up a newspaper to show Musher the story. It was the same as the one Dandy had. "Is this your clinical evaluation?"

"No that has been delayed. That was just me trying to placate some friends who had dreams of me being a professional golfer."

"I received an envelope containing your high school transcript. You were quite the student. Nothing but "A's" for four years. What happens now?"

"I continue my treatment and apply for the undergraduate program. Did I miss payday?"

"Don't bullshit me. You knew damn well today is payday. Why else would you be in those flyboy clothes?"Musher settled his petrol debt and headed for the small BX. He bought these items in pairs: Soap flakes, coffee cans, boxes of British tea, cartons of Pall Mall cigarettes, boxes of candy bars, cases of coco-cola, cases of orange crush, boxes of saltine crackers and cases of sardines. He added bottles of gin, vodka, rye whiskey and scotch.

With the help of a BX employee he loaded everything into his car. He practically had to force the boy to take a tip. Dandy helped him get his purchases upstairs to his flat. He instructed Dandy to take the soap flakes, coffee cans and boxes of British tea. Give one to Eloise and the other to Alice. The Pall Mall's are for you and Cody. I wonder how Cody did about the car. He didn't even mention it. Tomorrow he will bring his papers to the Duke and see if he can help me before he realizes I don't want to play golf for a living. Especially not for him.

Cody reported no luck trying to find a car but he would keep looking.

Musher arrived early at The Gloucester House. He told the Duke he was going to the range to practice until his treatment later today. He handed the Duke his educational papers and added, "I thank you for any help you can give me."

"This weekend there is a two day tournament for amateurs at one of the local clubs. Should I register you or not?"

"Please do. I believe you are totally right when you say I need more competitive experience with better players."

"Do you want me to bring MacInnes here to caddy?"

"That would be great. I can bring him up Friday."

"That will not be necessary. One of our cars will bring him and Hereford will make him comfortable. After the Thursday practice round I want you to stay here. Is that a problem?"

"No sir. Today I will tell the doctor I cannot make Friday's treatment session and I will be one hundred percent golf for this tournament." He was sure he detected a slight smile on Duke's face.

Musher left for his treatment. He would be very early but the atmosphere at Lakenheath would be more relaxing than at The Gloucester House. He was having lunch when his two buddies from the hush-hush squadron sat down beside him. They were both dressed in civilian clothes and if they didn't speak could easily pass for Brits.

"You two look very British. What's with the civvies? Where are you going?"

"We have a four day pass and we are going to London. We have been there before and seen the sights. This is solely an I&I visit."

"When you get to London have the cabbie take you to The New London Hotel. Talk to Phillip, the concierge and tell him you are Mister Smith and Mister Jones. Tell him you are the personal guests of Musher and that you are not allowed to spend any money for anything you want or do in the hotel. He will see that you are well taken care of. My thanks to you both for your treatment and caring."

At the end of his treatment Musher advised his treating physician Doctor Donald Parsons of his planned absence from this coming Friday's session. He did not meet with resistance. He returned to his flat, packed some clothes and told Dandy he would be gone until at least late Sunday night. He arrived at The Gloucester House at 0750 Thursday morning. MacInnes was already there and having breakfast with the Duke. Musher joined them. The Duke continued his interrogation regarding MacInnes golf life and asked for a true opinion of Musher as a golfer.

"In my thirty years as a caddy, and I have caddied for some of the major name players in major golf tournaments, I have never seen a better, more consistent swing. He has the potential to be number one in the world."

"What do you think caused the collapse at The New London Club?"

"I surely don't know but I think it was the pressure of being tied with best British golfer and facing a chance to win having never won any tournaments before. I will say this. The upcoming tournament is purely amateur. He will win the tournament by at least six strokes. If you can find a taker bet everything for me you intended to pay me. If you can, take odds that he will win by at least three strokes."

The Duke followed Musher throughout the round. Musher and MacInnes did not keep score. Some of his intentionally shaping shots to an imaginary target made him look like a hacker. Friday he played equally poorly and the bookmakers placed him at eight to one. There were seventy-two players in the field and he was rated as eight to one. The Duke had spread his bets to a series of bookmakers in England. He had bet two hundred fifteen thousand pounds, including ten thousand for Musher and five thousand for MacInnes. At the end of the first round Musher was the leader by five strokes. The second round ended with Musher the winner of the tournament by twelve strokes. The awards ceremony was quick and quiet.

Back at The Gloucester House the Duke gave MacInnes forty thousand pounds (one hundred twelve thousand dollars American) as his winnings. He asked if MacInnes would consider leaving the London area and become the permanent caddy for Musher. "Just say when and I will be here." The Duke escorted him to the family car and he was on his way home. MacInnes had earned more in two days than he would in two years.

Another two weeks went by without any remarkable incidents. Musher had settled his debt to Phillip for the care he had given his two buddies. At his most recent treatment he was presented a note which had the Duke of Gloucester seal on the envelope. "Please come to see me at your earliest possible convenience." No signature was necessary. Musher stayed at the VAQ that night and the next day at 1030 hours he was at The Gloucester

House. Hereford escorted him to the patio where the Duke, Dukie and Willy were waiting for lunch.

The Duke, "What a beautiful day to play golf."

Musher thought, "Is that the reason for the hurry-up and get here note? I doubt it."

"Willy and I knew you would want to hear the good news as soon as possible. We have spoken to the Dean of Admissions at Cambridge University and he is willing to allow you to attend if when you meet with him you answer his questions correctly. At that meeting he will quantify the number of AFIT credits which may be used in your DRS (Degree Requirement Summary) depending on what major you may choose. He will prepare a class schedule again depending upon the major concentration you select. There is the matter of tuition and books. We trust you can afford to attend Cambridge University. If you cannot, talk with me and Willy before you decline attendance. Our one reward for our efforts and future support if necessary is that you continue to work on your golf and play the amateur tournaments we schedule until you finish your schooling. We estimate that as one tournament per month. How does that strike you?"

"I think your offer is most gracious and for me to thank you for your assistance is beyond my vocabulary. When is the meeting set for? I will try very hard to answer the questions correctly. What happens if I fail his evaluation?"

"The meeting is scheduled for this coming Thursday at ten o'clock in the Dean's office. My dear boy you cannot fail. Your interview is what you Americans call "filling the squares. Rest assured you will be admitted."

WE ARE IN !!

CHAPTER 195

Balance Golf, Education and the USAF

The next two days passed agonizingly slow. On Thursday Musher was standing outside the door marked, "D. Underwood, Dean of Admissions." Musher knocked gently and entered. Sitting behind a huge maple desk, dressed in the gown of a Doctor of Philosophy was Miss Doris Underwood, Dean of Admissions.

"M'am, I am Saverio Muscarello."

"You are on my calendar. Do you mind if I call you Musher?"

"No M'am."

"Please call me Dean. M'am makes me feel old. Do you think I am old?"

"No Dean."

For the next hour the Dean outlined Musher's credit received for his AFIT GED. The academic major he selected was Philosophy. His classroom schedule was Tuesday, Wednesday and Thursday each week from eight in the morning until one thirty in the afternoon. His DRS plan would have him graduate with a Bachelor of Philosophy in eight semesters. The upcoming spring and summer I and II. The fall semester, the winter semester, the spring semester and the two summer semesters. A total classroom attendance time of sixteen calendar months. The Dean gave him a list of books to purchase and a printed schedule of his classes. Before she dismissed him she preached a few caveats: If you miss too many classes I will drop you from our student roster. If you are accused of cheating the presumption is that you did. If you cannot disprove the allegation I will drop you from our student roster. Over and above your AFIT credit you must earn fifty four credits here at Cambridge University. If you fail two of your four courses in any semester, I will put you on probation. If you fail two courses in the subsequent marking period I will drop you from our student roster. Cambridge University requires high standards of academics and conduct. If you are still desirous of coming to this institution take these papers to the Bursar and meet your financial obligations. Can you meet those obligations? My two cousins, The Duke of Gloucester and the Duke of Willingham have deposited a very tidy sum in your student account. I will be monitoring your progress. Good day Musher."

At the student book store Musher gathered the books the Dean had put on the list. He added pens, pencils and ruled notebooks. The student cashier reviewed his purchases and said, "Some of these are for courses you will take in subsequent semesters. Are you sure you want to spend this much money now?"

"What's the total?"

"Two thousand eight hundred eighty pounds sterling." ($7,280.00 American) Musher counted it out from his little bag. He paid a clerk five pounds to help him get his purchases into his car. His next stop was the Bursar's Office. Again he paid cash for the upcoming semester. In comparison to the tuition and fees the bookstore was a bargain. He directed his car to The Gloucester House where he would report the day's activities.

Musher was so excited when he was relaying his day he had difficulty following the algorithmic logic of his meeting with Dean Underwood. When he finished explaining his meeting the Duke suggested he might want to go to the club and hit balls or play a few holes to get his focus on the upcoming tournament. "MacInnes is waiting for you at your car. Remember if you need anything at the club just sign for it. By now they all know who you are."

MacInnes looked as happy as dog whose master has just returned home and is petting him. "Are we winning again the week Laddie?"

"We had better or this golden goose will stop laying golden eggs and start laying balls of shit."

CHAPTER 196
Nothing Lasts Forever

It was difficult to believe how long he had been enrolled at Cambridge. There were only the last two summer semesters to complete before Musher had his undergraduate degree from Kings College, Cambridge University. MacInnes was living in the area of the Duke's golf course. Musher was still getting his flight pay and plenty of money as the Duke continued to bet heavily upon him finishing in the top three of any golf tournament in which he played. That included nine professional golf tournaments where he was invited on a sponsor's exemption. He managed to keep the USAF at bay with the assistance of First Sergeant Gideon Thorpe.

Sooner or later this big bubble must burst. Nothing lasts forever. It was sooner than later when Gideon told him of the replacement of Captain Todd, the squadron commander. The new squadron commander wanted to know who the master sergeant is that is on the roster but does not have a job assignment in the headquarters. He insisted Gideon bring him in immediately. Musher told Gideon that he needed ninety days or less to finish at Cambridge.

Gideon, who recently had been promoted to master sergeant, looked at him coldly, "When Todd was here if the shit hit the fan I could push everything towards him. This new commander, Major Victor Mooney, is here every morning at 0800 and stops by to check out every evening at 1630. With him gone I have no protection and as much as I like you I am not going to throw away my career to further yours. You will report here tomorrow morning at 1000 hours."

"Sir, Master Sergeant Muscarello reporting as ordered."

"Sit down please, Sergeant Thorpe, please stay." Musher was evaluating the new Major just as he was evaluating Musher. He had a West Point Academy ring on his hand, Navigator wings on his breast and Korean War decorations on his chest. He was not going to be easy. He continued, "I have read your record closely and I respect your time as a POW. These are the original orders which assigned you here and you still draw flight pay. I took the liberty of speaking with your psychiatrist at Lakenheath and he tells me you have improved so greatly that your treatments have been reduced from three times a week to two times a week. He also says that he believes you may stop the treatments without risking your health. Do you agree with him?"

"Sir, I certainly feel better. I trust Doctor Crisalucci did not discuss any of the contents of any of our sessions."

"No, he was most careful about what he said. He believes a panel of three psychiatrists would release you from further treatment. Are you willing to be evaluated by a panel?"

"Yes Sir."

"Good I will work with Doctor Crisalucci to do the evaluation as soon as possible. I am told it may take as long as a month to get the three together. Meanwhile you can report to Sergeant Thorpe every morning at 0800 until the panel is established."

"Sir, what will my duties in this orderly room be?"

"I am sure Sergeant Thorpe will find things to keep you busy."

It is time for the act. Musher jumped up from his chair and started bellowing at the top of his lungs, "Just because you can't fly anymore and have become a titless WAF you want to make one out of me. No fucking way Major, I am either going back to an aircrew or getting out of this air force. I prefer to be on an aircrew but with assholes like you dictating what I will and won't be it ain't worth being a fucking master sergeant". He started tearing off his wings, his ribbons and his chevrons. In the process he knocked over much of the office's small furnishings. Sergeant Thorpe restrained him and took him into his office. Sat him down and talked to him gently. "He didn't know how vulnerable you are. We all know because we have seen you explode before. You cannot see him but he is in his office throwing up into his waste basket. He has probably just figured out why Captain Todd left your care and custody to me. I expect in a matter of a couple of days he will have another talk with you. Right now, go try to straighten up that uniform and leave the headquarters. Come see me in a couple of days."

Musher went into the latrine and smiled. He thought, "I should have been a movie actor. James Cagney could not have played that role any better." The next time I see Crisalucci I will give him hell for discussing my medical condition with anyone. Maybe if I do it with the right act it will give me an edge if I need to persuade him to do something.

Musher played and finished second in the weekend tournament. Monday at 0930 hours he was in Gideon's office. Gideon, "It won't go away, let's go in. Forget the fancy reporting just take a seat."

The three of them sat silently in Mooney's office and nobody spoke. It was like a game of chicken, whoever speaks first flinches and will get a punch from the other two. Major Victor Mooney flinched. "Sergeant Muscarello I may have been a little hasty the other day insisting that you spend your time in the orderly room. Since you and I agree that you are ready for the three doctor panel I would not want to cause any real change in your circumstances which would make the panel an unfair evaluation. I want you to continue whatever it was you were doing until the evaluation by the panel. I am asking Sergeant Thorpe to continue as your main contact with the squadron. I have asked him to contact Doctor Crisalucci to make arrangements for the panel. I am told it will take at least forty-five days to appoint such a panel, for them to study your history and to assemble at Lakenheath. Do you have any questions?"

"No Sir. Sir let me apologize for my behavior the other day. I see by your decorations that you flew combat in Korea. I don't know why you are now assigned an administrative job but I am sure your purple heart gives me a good clue. Instead of insulting you I should be admiring you for your devotion to the air force. Only someone with extreme loyalty to the air force could accept such an assignment and continue to function as a valuable asset for the air force. Please accept my apology." Musher thought to himself, "You couldn't find this much bullshit in a Texas corral."

"Thank you sergeant. We are combat brothers in arms."

Back in Gideon Thorpe's office Gideon almost laughed, "You are as full of shit as a Christmas turkey. He ate every word of your self degradation. Your mouth should be in a circus. OK you got your stall. You said you needed ninety days to finish your undergraduate degree. We have at least the first forty-five in the bag. Talk to Crisalucci and maybe he will be able to stall it even longer. The time it will take for the panel to write its review and have the report medically evaluated will be at least another month. It seems to me you have made your goal. Remember none of this is set in concrete so stay loose. I want Mooney to feel he is on top of this so come see me at least once every week. *Get out of here and I will see you when I see you.*"

CHAPTER 197

Reassigned To the States

Musher began his session with Crisalucci with a question. "Doc isn't everything we discuss and I tell you in the strictest of confidences and not available to anyone else without my permission?"

"That is true. There are exceptions such as for other medical staff assigned to your case but they are bound by the same confidences."

"Can you tell me why you would discuss my treatments and medical condition with my new squadron commander at South Ruislip?"

"What I told him was harmless. Nothing of any consequence."

"I know you told him I was ready for the panel of psychiatrists? Are you telling me you don't believe that is discussing my medical condition? I want you to know that as a result of your talking with him he is pushing for the panel to be assembled and the evaluation take place. I understand it will take at least forty-five days before the panel can be assembled. I need for the panel to assemble in no less than sixty days. I also need the panel report to take at least thirty days before you present the panel's recommendations to me" Musher told Crisalucci about the timing for him to earn his undergraduate degree in philosophy from Cambridge University. "Can you help me out?"

"Of course. I didn't bring you this far along just to watch you fail. As a patient, you are my pride and joy. I have known about your clandestine attendance at Cambridge and your weekend golf tournaments ever since you suggested we drop the Friday treatment and change from three treatments each week to two. Granted my handicap is twelve but I follow the local golf tournaments and the British Golf Tour results."

True to his word the panel was appointed and convened sixty-six days from the date of his meeting with Crisalucci. During that time Musher went along as if nothing had ever happened with Mooney or Crisalucci. The panel was made up of one US Army psychiatrist from Germany, one USAF psychiatrist from an air base in Italy and a prominent civilian psychiatrist from London. The evaluation lasted almost four hours. Musher maintained absolute control of his emotions. He did not want to fail this evaluation. After the panel Crisalucci told him the panelists would return to their regular practices and it would take about two or three weeks before each would independently submit their findings to him.

638

At one of his last classes he was handed a note from Dean Underwood. Musher went there after class, knocked gently on the door and entered. She motioned him to the couch. She sat beside him and took his hand. "We are so proud of you. You have completed your DRS and will be awarded your Bachelor of Arts degree at graduation."

"Dean Underwood may I receive my diploma separately from the graduation ceremony. I am sure you know I know very few of my classmates, I have never socialized with them and I would not add anything to their joy. Whereas I did this strictly for me I would enjoy the serenity that comes with being alone with someone or something you enjoy."

"Spoken like a true philosopher. My cousins and I thought you would enjoy hearing your accomplishment verbalized especially since you are graduating Magna Cum Laude. Whatever you wish will be done. The physical degree document and the transcripts will be here with me in about two days. Stop by at any time and I will have them ready for you. Maybe sometime we could get together for a drink, or better yet you will let me fix dinner for you. Think about what is under this robe and we'll talk about us when you come for your diploma."

On his next visit to Crisalucci they discussed the three independent reports he had received from the panel members. Each was positive in his remarks about Musher's mental health. They saw no reason to continue mandatory treatments but must always be aware of a possible recurrent need. "That's the sum and substance. I will close your file and forward it to be kept with your records."

"Have you forgotten I have all my official records? You have only that portion which was begun at this hospital. If you give me the reports and your hospital records they will be with my official records."

"It is not normal but since you have the records what can it hurt?"

"I do have a problem that maybe you can help me solve. I have been here for a long time. It has been a good time but it is time for me to leave. I know 7th Air Division will be glad to let me go stateside, I know you have had enough of me to deserve a break but since you know about my golf exploits you will understand my problem. The Duke of Gloucester and the Duke of Willingham have treated me as if I were a son. They have made an endless amount of money betting on me at golf tournaments; however, they were responsible for me getting into Cambridge. They did it because it was their plan that after graduation I would play professional golf and make them a lot more money. I never wanted to play professional golf but I did want that degree. My problem is how do I escape the clutches of the Dukes?"

"That is no real problem. I will write you a letter it will be the only copy so you must destroy it after it has served its purpose. The letter will say that you have failed your patient evaluation and you are to be reassigned to a facility in the United States for further more intense psychiatric treatment. It will direct you to report to your squadron commander as soon as possible. Do all your housekeeping chores. When you want to spring the letter on the Dukes I will date it. I will do a second letter to your squadron commander which simply states you have not been stationed in the United States for a very long time. The panel recommends immediate reassignment."

"Can I wait for that letter? It will be the nexus of my plan." Fifteen minutes later he had in his hand the letter addressed to his squadron commander. Tomorrow he would put the plan in play."

CHAPTER 198

The Reassignment Process

The plan was quite simple.

He visited Gideon and showed him the letter from Doctor Crisalucci. Together they went into see Major Mooney. Mooney read the letter at least twice and each time the lines around his eyes pointed farther upward with joy. "This will get the bastard out of my hair."

"Sergeant Thorpe please take Sergeant Muscarello to division personnel and help him get done whatever needs to be done for a smooth relocation. Take this letter and when you are done file it with his official records."

Sergeant Thorpe went to Master Sergeant John Hogan the NCOIC of Division Personnel and showed him the letter. "We need to move on this as quickly as possible."

"For you Giddy, with this infamous dude I will do his paperwork personally. Sit down gentlemen and let's begin." They went through a number of routine questions and every now and then an important one would be asked. "What is your AFSC?" (Air Force Specialty Code)

"Aerial Gunner"

"Would you consider cross training to another specialty?"

No." He didn't like the sounds of that question.

"Where in the ZI (Zone of Interior) would you like to be assigned?"

"Texas."

"There are two possible air bases where aerial gunners are utilized. Biggs AFB in El Paso and Carswell AFB in Fort Worth. Which would you prefer?"

Musher thought a bit and said, "Carswell." He figured he already knew Biggs and Juarez maybe there is something new in Fort Worth."When will you be ready to leave this headquarters?"

"I need three days to take care of my obligations."

"We will book you out of South Hampton on the first vessel following the next three days."

"Sergeant Hogan can we hold off booking a berth at South Hampton? I was hoping for a ten day delay enroute which I may spend here in England playing some golf. I would sign a waiver or something making me responsible to report to my next duty station on time. Is that possible?"

"We can certainly do that but you must remember such a waiver is prima facie guilt if you fail to report on time. I will have your orders authorize a

641

ten day delay enroute. If you drive to Carswell you will receive a mileage allowance from the normal US POE. Do you want any advance pay? That's about all we can do today. Come back at 1000 tomorrow and we will have your documents ready."

Musher and Gideon thanked him. "I did it for Giddy, not for you."

Gideon, "I will see you in my office not later than 0945 tomorrow. Get gone."

It was only 1040 hours and only two hours to Mildenhall. Time for a visit to Smasher. This time when he walked into Smasher's orderly room he was in full uniform and the staff acted differently. "Sergeant Cohan is at an NCO meeting in the NCO Club."

The NCO meeting in the NCO Club was a full blown crap game. Musher watched Smasher who appeared to be ahead. A tap on the shoulder, a surprised look and "Can you tear yourself a way for a little bit?"

Over lunch Musher told Smasher of his impending reassignment. He stressed that they wanted to schedule him to return to the states on one of those ships out of South Hampton. "Smasher, do you know somebody in Passenger Services who could get me on a flight so I can skip the ship?"

"I can do better than that if you have a valid passport. Do you?"

Musher whipped it out and placed it on the table. He had brought it in case he was going to buy a commercial ticket. He knew for sure he wasn't steaming the Atlantic in a rusty scow.

"My friend has access to pre-paid seats on BOAC. Let's go visit him."

"Meet Musher. The guy I talk about. He needs a favor. Can you get him a ride to the states on BOAC? Musher this is Master Sergeant Dante Vess, NCOIC."

"For you I can. I have one available seat tomorrow night and one available three nights from now leaving Heathrow at 2200 hours. I presume he has orders and a passport."

"Passport yes. I will have orders tomorrow morning."

"That eliminates tomorrow night and if I don't have your orders by 2200 tomorrow it will eliminate the one three nights from now. After that seats on BOAC are as rare as hen's teeth. Let me see your passport. It's OK. If you can bring your orders between noon and 1800 I will be here."

Everyone shook hands along with the thank you's. Musher, "I will definitely see you tomorrow."

He and Smasher parted and he made the TR head for Lakenheath at greatest possible speed. He met with Crisalucci and told him of today's happenings. In ten minutes he had the letter he would show the Dukes. He thanked the doctor for all his help. His next stop is The Gloucester House. He would not be there long.

In the library he showed the letter to the Duke. (Making sure that after the Duke had read it two or three times it was back in his possession) Both the Duke and Musher sat with looks on their face which would remind the world of the two hound dogs sitting on the coon but couldn't find the coon. They were totally lost about what to do next. The Duke's plans were shattered unless Musher played in the states. The Duke never asked where he was being reassigned but Musher knew he could find Musher in a matter of minutes. He told the Duke he was leaving tomorrow night and softly left the library.

It was still early enough to reach Cambridge to pick up his documents and see if he could find out what was under Dean Underwood's robe. In the Dean's office he said first things first. He looked at his diplomas and the other documents and it actually caused an erection. On her way to the couch she locked and dead bolted her door.

"Show me what's under the robe."

"You will need to find out for yourself." He disrobed her and she was perfectly shaped and very solid for a woman her age. She reminded him of Major Blanchard at Yokota. He put a hand gently on the top of her head. She did not need any more encouragement to move downward. He returned the favor and they enjoyed each other for the next hour.

After the cleanup he detailed his reassignment and that he would be leaving tomorrow night. He told of his visit to the Duke and the sorrow of being forced to leave. He must go back to London tonight.

CHAPTER 199

Farewell, It Has Been

The next morning he was knocking on Cody's door. "I need to go to my headquarters and then to RAF Mildenhall and back. Are you available?" "

Musher was in Gideon's office promptly at 0930. Together they went to see Hogan in personnel. After signing a bunch of papers including the transportation waiver he received five copies of his reassignment orders. 7th Air Division finance was just down the hall and with his orders he was permitted to exchange script and sterling for American dollars. The largest denomination of American currency used for the conversion was the twenty dollar bill. He had over two thousand dollars in script and twenty thousand pounds sterling. He put the conversion money in his little bag, a cash conversion of over fifty-eight thousand dollars American. To Gideon his goodbye and thank you was brief but sincere.

Cody parked in front of the passenger terminal at RAF Mildenhall. Musher left his black bag with Cody while he went in to solidify his seat on the BOAC flight one more night from now. Beyond the desk clerk he could see Vess sitting in his office. He tapped on the glass door window and Vess came to meet him. "Let's go to the counter. Give me your passport and your orders." Less than ten minutes passed before Vess came back to him, "Here are your passport, your orders and your authorization to fly from Heathrow. Present those and your baggage at the BOAC desk not later than 2000 before the flight. Again, the flight is tomorrow night, Thursday, 2200 hours takeoff, Flight Number 1415. Any questions?"

"No Sergeant." He expressed his appreciation and went to use one of the base phones. "Smasher, it's Musher, are you free for lunch? Great I am on my way to the NCO Club now."

Cody had not been in an NCO Club before and he was like someone who goes to New York the first time and stares at the buildings and the glamour of the city. In the dining room he was most impressed with the menu. Smasher joined them and they made small talk throughout the lunch. Musher handed Smasher a small package. "This is for your Missus." Smasher could not resist looking in the box. The top prize for one of the amateur tournaments that he had won was this beautiful ladies diamond brooch. Smasher started to voice an objection when Musher placed a hand over his mouth, "How cute do you think I would look wearing that?" Everyone laughed and the tense moment passed.

Cody pulled the car into its parking place. Musher told him to get Alice and come next door for "a cuppa". Musher spoke loudly enough to be heard as he opened his entryway, "Eloise, please put on the tea Cody and Alice are coming for "a cuppa". He dashed upstairs took off his blouse, gathered a few things and headed for the kitchen. Just like the Italians serious business was always done in the kitchen.

"You know I am leaving for the states tomorrow night. Cody I must be at the BOAC terminal not later than seven-thirty to check in. I know you will take care of me in that regard. We are doing this now so that we won't have sad looks just before I leave. I have enjoyed every moment of your hospitality and friendship.

Dandy I know you have a driver's license but not a car. I shall give you my TR. I shall also give you sufficient funds to register, pay the taxes and insure the car for the next two years. There will also be a little extra money for petrol. Cody knows the procedures and will take you through the process.

Eloise anything which I cannot fit into my B-4 bag will remain here as your property. You have made this flat most enjoyable. It is my suggestion that after I am gone you visit Master Sergeant Gideon Thorpe at the headquarters. Tell him of the flat and its availability. Be willing to accept either a single lodger or a married couple. When you tell him of its availability be sure you quote a price of three pounds per day. Each person at the headquarters receives almost five pounds daily to live "on the economy".

Cody, Alice, I am sure Eloise will share with you anything I leave behind. Since I don't have anything directly for you and you both have been so good I will leave to you fifty thousand pounds. ($140,000.00 American)

Let me say I have learned to love you. You are as close to a family as I have had since I was fifteen years old. God Bless You." The women cried, the men tried to stifle any tears as Musher went upstairs to lie on his bed.

The next day was arduously long. Finally Musher was at the BOAC desk to check in. His B-4 bag was checked but his little black bag never left his hands. The flight to Logan Airport in Boston was long but uneventful. During most of the flight he reminisced about his time in the United Kingdom. He thought of his lifestyle, the royalty he met, the golf, the girls, the new friends he had made, his attainment of a Cambridge college degree and he inwardly smiled. *Farewell, it has been simply great.*

Standing outside the terminal he wondered, "What do I do now?"

SECOND  LIEUTENANT

JUST BECAME
A LFER

I do solemnly swear to bear true
faith and allegiance
So Help Me God

There is a massive difference
between stripes on the sleeve
and bars on the shoulder

BOOK 7

647

CHAPTER 200

In Or Out?

He had ten days to get to Carswell. It's over nineteen hundred miles if he chose to drive. Driving straight through at reasonable speeds would take about thirty hours. The big question for him was, "Did he want to stay in Boston for awhile?" It would be nice to see his mother and his sister, Caesar, the guys at The Bucket and maybe even Freddie. As a side benefit he could get at least fifty thousand cash for his little black bag. He was low on cash now. Who knows how much money anyone would need when facing such a long trip.

He went downtown to the hotel he had stayed at when he was here before. He paid for two nights. Do I change into civvies or do I stay in my uniform. I will stay in my uniform. From his room he phoned his sister. "Hello Joanna, guess who will be in Boston tomorrow? I am leaving London tonight."

Between her crying and babbling he hardly understood a word. "Let us pick you up. You stay with me and mine. Are you all right? Are you a civilian now?"

"No you cannot pick me up. I am traveling incognito. Meet me at Mama's tomorrow at eleven in the morning. Do me a favor, go by the bank and get me fifty thousand dollars in twenty dollar bills." He successfully dodged her question about his civilian/military status. "Got to go. See you a Mama's. Don't broadcast my arrival. Goodnight, I love you." It hit him that he had told her he loved her. It was not his way. It was not a bad way.

Musher knelt in front of Caesar and kissed his ring. "You have my loyalty forever." Caesar rose and hugged Musher closely.

"Come we shall have a snack." They were in the kitchen picking on pastries and in walked this most dapper, physically fit looking gentleman. "Musher you remember my consigliore Martin Melke."

Musher was out of his chair and hugging Melke before Melke realized what was happening. "Godfather I owe my very existence to this gentleman. Next to you there is no one to whom I am more grateful."

"Come Musher let him have his breakfast."

Musher spent almost two hours filling the gaps for Melke and The Godfather. *Then came the bomb question. "When will you be out of the air force?* We have a place for you in our organization. Since the death of Fanucci, God Rest His Soul, we have been looking for the one we can bring into the organization with the explicit goal of him learning our business and eventually taking over Fanucci's role. We have decided that it was always Fanucci's intent to bring you in as a bookie until you learned your way around. We have decided you are the man we have been looking for. *So, when is your discharge date?"*

"I don't really know. I have been past my discharge date twice. Once because of Hairy S. Truman and the other was my choice because I wanted to finish my degree at Cambridge. Until I get to Texas and talk with the personnel people there I am afraid I don't have an intelligent answer."

Caesar, "We understand. How are you planning to get to Texas? Have you considered driving? Martin can make one phone call and you will have the car of your choice. It would be totally clean and all the papers would be originals. Think about it and talk to Martin. Right now I must ask you to excuse me I have people waiting."

"Musher if you could have any car you wanted what would you choose?"

"I would probably choose a Baby Blue Coupe de Ville Cadillac with white leather interior and power everything including air conditioning. It would be too expensive for me."

Melke, "Have I ever let you down and not delivered what I said I would deliver. Tomorrow at three in the afternoon meet me at this garage." He handed Musher a paper with an address on it. "I need to be at the same meeting with the Boss. See you tomorrow."

Musher went to The Bucket. It was early in the evening but all the action was in play. The Keeper hugged him warmly and announced his presence. There were warm greetings and for every greeting two questions. The questions ranged from the stories of his death to his status, a civilian or what? They finally let up when he took off his blouse to join the nine ball game. These were not the country hick hustlers he had seen in so many places, these were real pool shooters who asked for no quarter and gave none. After almost three hours he was either slightly down or slightly up. Either way the difference could not be more than fifty dollars. He went to the neighborhood pizzeria for the dinner he had missed. There was a liquor store close to the hotel. He bought some cold cokes and goodies. He was exhausted but every time he lay down and try for sleep he was visited by Caesar and Melke. With those visitors and his time lag from England his sleep was fitful.

CHAPTER 201
It Is Time to Leave Boston Again

His Mama could not stop crying and hugging and kissing her baby. He could be seven foot tall and forty years old but with Italians the last born is always "the baby". It took a lot of talking to convince Mama he was all right. He was in civilian clothes so that helped considerably. Not long after he arrived at Mama's so did Sweet Sister. They hugged, kissed and finally all three settled at the kitchen table for coffee and pastries. Musher answered every question as best he could without getting into too much detail. Mama's only concern was when he would come home for good. As part of his stories he repeatedly interspersed the fact that he would not be here long. He was due back with the military very, very soon. He begged off dinner with Mama and Sweet Sister with the pretense that he had a meeting at Hanscom AFB. "As a matter of fact I may have to fly out tonight right from there."

Musher noticed that Mama now had a telephone. Every day she talked with her daughters and she had learned how to make calls. The telephone ranked above the television.

Sister had brought a paper bag which she gave him. One peek and he knew what it was. "After my taking those papers (money) from the box (the bank) there are still fifteen thousand clippings left in the box. When I leave here I must stop at the grocery store to pick up fresh vegetables. I am sure there will be fresh vegetables and everything is fine. I like to get my vegetables there. You know Mama goes to church regularly and if there was anything she needed to make her life better she would hear it from the pulpit. She would tell me and maybe we could figure how to get it for her."

Poor Mama she heard it all but did not understand any of its meaning. What is it they say, "Ignorance is bliss."

"Time to go. I want to visit Fanucci's grave." Mama added," And your father's." Musher pretended he didn't hear her. It took five minutes to get out the door and only after he promised to call Mama regularly.

He hailed a cab to take him on the half hour ride to the cemetery. There he handed the cabbie two twentys and asked him to wait. Standing before the tombstone he could not control the water dripping from his eyes. He spoke to Fanucci's spirit, "You were a much better father to me than my own. What you have taught me has carried me through very difficult times. I loved you and respected you. I will cherish our times together until the day I

651

join you once more." He silently recited the Our Father, the Hail Mary and the I Believe in God. Before leaving he spoke to God, "This is a good man. His path may have been different than most others but he never disrespected you or those who believe in you. Keep him close to you. I besecch you that when I come to you he will be there to greet me."

Time to eat. Deep thoughts always made him hungry. He took the cabbie to lunch at the No Name on the wharf. It had been a very long time since he had steamers (small clams), fish chowder (the dish for which the restaurant was famous) and steamed lobster. He even had a beer with his lunch but prohibited the cabbie from having one. There was just enough time to get to Melke's garage. When the cabbie dropped him off he gave him another five twentys. He was feeling financially strong again.

Melke met him as entered the garage. They took an elevator which went down and opened to what looked like a car dealership with all various makes. Melke led him to a Baby Blue Cadillac Coupe de Ville. "Look it over and tell me what you think."

The car was gorgeous. It was love at first sight. Musher's mouth salivated as he slid behind the wheel. "It's everything anyone could ever want in car."

"The title, the papers, the VIN (vehicle identification number), the state registration and the license plates are all legitimate. Your insurance papers are also in the glove compartment. The boys did a first class job. They also made a few modifications. The little bench seat behind the driver and passenger has been somewhat changed." He pulled the seat forward and exposed two compartments. "This compartment contains license plates for New York, Pennsylvania, both the Virginias, North Carolina, Kentucky, Georgia, Tennessee, Louisiana and Texas. With each set of plates is the title, registration for the state and an insurance policy. There is also five one hundred dollar bills attached to each license plate package. As soon as they can get your picture they will make you a driver's license for each state.

Melke opened the other compartment. It was the equivalent of an infantry man's combat load. Two loaded automatic pistols with one round already in the chamber ample clips and spare ammunition. A loaded sawed off shotgun with two boxes of shells, three hand grenades and two K-Bar (commando one edge serrated the other edge razor sharp steel) knives. Musher thought, "This is scary."

"What do you think Musher? Have I delivered as promised?"

"Far beyond any of my expectations. It's beautiful and certainly well equipped but as I told you I cannot afford it."

"It is a gift from The Godfather. You made him proud in the El Paso area. He has the highest regard for you. He is having a family dinner tonight and wants you to join them. It's not formal. Do you have a dark suit and the trimmings?"

"Yes but it is in dire need of pressing before it could be worn."

"I will have one of the guys take you to your hotel. Make sure you look good. Be waiting outside at five thirty. See you then."

The ride to dinner took almost an hour. Melke told him he could pick up the car and licenses anytime of day. Musher tried to explain that he felt he should leave tomorrow. "Nineteen hundred miles is a lot of driving and he did not want to drive straight through."

Melke told him that would be all right but do not mention it tonight. I will tell The Godfather."

There were only six for dinner. The Godfather, his missus, his two daughters, Melke and Musher. The Godfather's two daughters, Josephine and Christina would not stop traffic but they were attractive. Josephine, the older, looked at Melke like "why aren't we married?" Christina was about Musher's age. She acted very shyly. The dinner was very pleasant and the conversation very light. Shortly after dinner Musher asked to be excused saying he was still tired from the flight and the excitement since he arrived in Boston. He did all the pleasant good-nights and thank-yous ending with the kissing of the ring.

In his hotel he packed. Tomorrow he would leave Boston.

CHAPTER 202

Carswell Here I Com

Musher took a cab to the garage. He and his luggage were taken down below. He was given his Massachusetts driving license and told all the others were with their respective packages. He was given a set of car keys and told there was an emergency set mounted under the left front fender. On the front seat were maps showing the complete route to Fort Worth, Texas. There was a change dispenser mounted on the dash board on the driver's side and it had been filled with quarters. The car was totally serviced. These people were very professional. He thanked everyone he possibly could and headed the car out of Boston. When he was on the highway headed to New York he suddenly felt very relieved. At the first major rest stop he stashed his cash. He kept almost eight hundred in his pockets and stored the rest right along side the two automatic pistols in the special bench seat compartment.

Each night he stopped and rested until morning. He was averaging four hundred miles a day, ten hours on the clock. He remembered the military daily TPA (travel by private automobile) required three hundred miles a day. On the fifth day he was downtown Fort Worth. He still had two full days before he was required to report. As usual he was hungry and one of the billboards coming into Fort Worth advertised the Hilton Hotel and the famous steak house, The Cattlemen's Club. He checked in had the porter take his bag to his room and the valet to put his car in the covered garage. Both reacted to the tip with a robust, "Yes Sir." Musher headed for the Cattlemen's Club and a large juicy steak with all the trimmings.

The meal relaxed him so much he took a nap with his clothes on. He cleaned up and went to the Cattlemen's for some dinner. Sitting in the lobby smoking his Lucky Strikes he stopped one of the bell boys. "What do people do in Fort Worth when the sun goes down?"

"Women are plentiful, but not inexpensive. If you are extremely wealthy there is a poker game on the third floor where the buy in is one million dollars. If you are a card player without that kind of wealth there is a private club close by where there is gambling action of all kinds. Of course as a last resort you can drink until you get drunk and pass out. Fort Worth is pretty much like any other city."

"Tell me more about the private club and the gambling."

"Never been to it myself. Way over my head. There is a one hundred dollar temporary membership fee. I have on occasion sent other guests there and I have never had a complaint. Did you wish to go? I can make a call and they will be expecting you."

"Please make the call."

He handed Musher a card. "Show this to the cab driver and again when you get to the club. The club has no markings but every hack in this city knows it. If you have any other wishes my name is Kenneth and I am here until three in the morning." Musher handed him two twentys.

Musher went to his car and took ten thousand dollars. How stupid of me to ask for twentys. I must convert these others very soon. Kenneth was right, one look at the card and the cab was on its way. It was only a few blocks from the hotel but Musher gave the cabbie a twenty dollar bill. He showed the card at the club door and was admitted. For his hundred dollar temporary membership fee he received a card which expired at the end of this calendar year.

"Sir, is there anything special you are looking for?"

"Not really. Is it all right if I walk about and get accustomed to the room?"

"There are other rooms if you don't see anything you like in this room."

Musher strolled and watched. The gambling was pedestrian. It was designed for heavy volume without individual killing losses. Catering to the "wanna be" gamblers who could afford at most to lose five hundred dollars in any one visit. At the poker tables the house cut the pot collecting from each ante, Black Jack was limited to a twenty-five dollar bet and the crap table was limited to a fifty dollar bet on everything except the center hard ways, etc., those bets were limited to ten dollars each. The place was a gold mine without the hard work.

Musher spoke to the doorman. "All the games are here but they would have a hard time holding my interest. Might there be poker in the other rooms?"

"We have pot limit five stud with a two thousand dollar buy. We have pot limit seven stud with a two thousand dollar buy. We have pot limit five card draw jacks or better with a two thousand dollar buy. We have no limit draw jacks or better with a five thousand dollar buy."

"May I kibitz before sitting?"

"You may but you must be careful not to disturb the players. If you find you want to join a game please come see me."

Musher went to the pot limit five card draw room. There were four active tables of players. He studied each table. Three of the four tables had an empty seat. He decided which one he wanted to join and went to the doorman. Musher apologized that his funds were in twenty dollar bills. "Is there a way to convert these?" At the cage the cashier inspected the twentys and converted eight thousand to hundreds and fifties.

There was not a house dealer. Each player dealt at his turn. At the table there was only one player who Musher saw palm a card, deal a second and fake a deck cut. He appeared to be the big winner and a hologram bullseye Target suddenly appeared on his shirt. Musher had won a couple carefully avoiding any hand dealt by the Target. Almost two hours had gone by and Musher's buy of two thousand was now at seven thousand plus. He decided now was the time to destroy the Target. He kept four players in the deal with the first one being the opener and Target making a substantial raise. Every one called and Musher asked, "Cards?" Opener checked, number two folded and Target bet the pot. Musher called and raised the pot. Target called and raised what little he had left. Musher called. Target showed a straight flush to the seven. Musher showed a straight flush to the ten. Target left the game. Musher also left the game. He estimated the pot was in the twenty thousand dollar range. The house cut one thousand from the pot. Musher gave the doorman two hundred and asked for a cab to the hotel. While they were waiting for the cab doorman said, "Sir when you come again call me I will have one of our cars pick you up. Here is my card."

Passing through the lobby stopped Kenneth the bell hop. He handed him ten twenties. "This is your share of the night. Kenneth, the weather is so beautiful is there anywhere I can play golf?"

"As a guest of the hotel you have priveleges at Colonial Country Club. You can have guest services call early tomorrow and they would make the arrangements." Musher handed him another twenty.

He asked Kenneth to come to his room in fifteen minutes to take some clothing to have it pressed. He would need it very early in the morning.

CHAPTER 203
Texas Golf Is Different

It was early and he had already spoken to Guest Services and was having breakfast in his room. "This is Guest Services. We have arranged for you to play at eleven o'clock if that is agreeable to you. May I call back and tell them to expect you?"

"Please do."

Would you like one of our cars to drive you?"

"Yes please. I will be down in ten minutes."

It was a twenty minute drive to the entrance to the pro shop at the Colonial Country Club (CCC). He was greeted by a petite blond who offered her hand and said, "My name is Amanda Wilson. I am one of the golf professionals on the staff here at the Colonial Country Club. I didn't see any equipment when your driver let you off."

"Yes I just came from an extended period in the United Kingdom. I gave all my equipment to my caddy when I left four days ago."

"We have some you can use."

"If it's all the same to you I would like to buy some new equipment."

"Why don't we fit you for shoes, a glove and a hat? There are demo clubs on the range. It would be wise for you to try them until you feel which are right for you." Very shortly they were on the range and Musher was hitting balls. By the end of the second bucket his swing was looking very good.

Amanda, "I can see you are a player. Did you decide on which clubs?"

"MacGregor copper faced stiff C-6 irons and MacGregor persimmon stiff shaft D-2 woods. I will pick a bag and you can put in two dozen balls, tees and another glove." In the pro shop he chose the bag he wanted and the head covers for the woods. While Amanda was loading his bag he was getting the feel of the putters in the rack. He settled for a putter identical to the Bullseye he had left in England.

"I placed your bill as part of your hotel bill. Is that all right with you? The way you look any one would think you are a touring pro. I had my clubs put on with yours if you don't mind playing with a girl." They played from the black tees. She hit the ball farther than ninety-percent of the male low handicap amateur golfers. This course was longer than he had ever played before. It wasn't the distance that made it so difficult it was the water hazards, the out of bounds proximity to the best position on any given hole, the height of the trees bordering the fairways and above all the speed of the greens. He struggled and ground out a seventy-four. Amanda had seventy six.

They were in the 19th hole having a coke when Amanda said, "It doesn't get too dark around here to play until at least eight thirty. Want to play another round?"

"Let me take a bathroom break. I will be back in less than five minutes."

"The second round was better for them both. Musher had a better understanding of the course and the greens had lost some of their speed. Amanda shot even par and Musher a four under sixty-eight.

They sat in the bar watching the night settle in Texas. "How long will you be at the hotel?"

"Just tonight and tomorrow night."

"Would you like to play again tomorrow? If we tee it up around eight we could play thirty-six before dinner. Does your schedule allow that?"

"I certainly would. Right now I need to find a ride to the hotel."

"That's not a problem. Give me a few minutes to change and I will be ready. We will just keep your clubs and shoes here until tomorrow."

Amada drove a coupe, not a Cadillac coupe but a coupe. On the way to the hotel Musher asked, "If you don't have any other plans how about having dinner with me. I have tried the Cattlemen's Club and everything was top shelf. Come on up with me while I shower and change into something more conservative."

They left Amanda's car at the hotel and took a cab. After dinner at the hotel Musher asked if she would like to come up for a nightcap. "I must get home. She gets very upset when I am this late. See you in the morning." Musher thought, "That explains a great many things."

CHAPTER 204
It's Tough To Hustle a Hustler

Musher drove his own car to the golf course. He was early enough to have some toast and tea before going to the range to loosen up. Amanda was already in the 19th Hole sitting with two young men about Musher's age. "Musher this is Ryan Tolliver and Bradford Pennington. They are tour rabbits. (A person who is not a member of the tour. A rabbit plays every Monday hoping to qualify for the two or three slots available for the current week's tournament) I have asked them to join us. The tour is coming here in two months and they are taking this opportunity to play practice rounds here this week. Do you mind?"

"Certainly not I am a guest here myself."

Tolliver spoke first, "Brad and I generally have a Nassau when we practice just to keep us concentrating. Would you be interested in a hundred dollar Nassau?"

"With you?"

"With both of us."

"How about this. This morning you and I play a five hundred dollar Nassau. This afternoon Brad and I will play a five hundred dollar Nassau."

"Do you want strokes?"

"No. I do want automatic two down presses and a caddy of my own." He was wishing for MacInnes.

"OK with me. Brad, how about you?"

The morning round against Ryan Tolliver was a walk in the park. He was two up and one press at the end of the first nine. After the back nine he was two up and one more press. By his count he won three thousand dollars. The afternoon round wasn't much different. Three way win on the Nassau and one press on each side, another three thousand dollars.

They were in the bar to settle up. Tolliver and Pennington both ashamedly said they could not pay. They acknowledged the debt but simply did not have the cash.

Musher asked them if they knew what happened in the real world to gamblers who cannot pay their debts. Let me help you understand, first they forfeit all their worldly goods as payment of the debt. If that is not enough to satisfy the debt they are put on a payment plan with a significant interest rate. If they fail to meet a scheduled payment they will receive a visit from a collector called Bruno. If he does not collect he will leave the gambler with a series of broken limbs and integers. You don't have any worldly goods I would want and most probably even your van would not satisfy the total debt. Here's my offer. Starting today your debt interest rate is five per cent weekly. Your repayment schedule is twenty percent of your combined winnings until the debt is paid. If you go one month without a payment of any size your vig (the interest rate) will increase by one quarter of one percent. If you ignore your obligation you will receive a visit from Bruno. You will know him when you see him. He is a mountain of a man with a flat nose and cauliflower ears. Since Amanda was party to your poor attempt to hustle a hustler she will be your contact. She will have an address where you will send the payments. My staff will monitor your progress and keep me advised. Now if you need money to go out and earn your living playing golf I would be more than happy to advance you any given sum and add it to your obligation. All the original loan conditions will exist."

"Could you loan us a thousand dollars each?"

"Of course but there is no us. You are like Siamese twins, joined by the shared debt. What affects one affects the other." He handed Tolliver two thousand dollars. "I give it to you because if the hustle was not your idea you were its spokesman." He asked the waiter to have his car brought up and his clubs put into the trunk. "You three can pay this bill. Thank you for the competition it makes me wonder if I am in the wrong profession." He changed shoes and headed for the hotel.

CHAPTER 205

Life As An Aerial Gunner at Carswell AFB

The Air Policeman directed him to the 11th Bomb Wing Headquarters. He signed in from leave and was asked to wait. It would be a few minutes before the Wing Director of Personnel would be available. "You may smoke if you like." Almost an hour passed before Musher was escorted into the WDP's office. Musher reported very militarily and was asked to sit. "Am I right that you just came from England?" Yes Sir. "Sending a B-29 Aerial Gunner to Carswell is like sending coal to Newcastle. We are in a transition from the B-36 and its crew of thirteen aerial gunners to the B-52 and its crew of one aerial gunner. We had thirty-nine B-36s. You do the math. Over five hundred gunners, well qualified, loyal air force personnel and we have a need for less than fifty. The other wing here at Carswell, the 7th, is doing the same transition. Together we have over nine hundred gunners, well qualified, loyal air force personnel that we neither have a job for nor a place to reassign them as gunners. Throughout the Strategic Air Command the transition to the B-52 has begun. I have read your record closely and we can make three choices available to you. Choice 1, since you have passed your discharge date twice we can process you for discharge immediately and you will be a civilian in ten days. Choice 2, you can contend with the rituals of a no position, no purpose senior NCO and hope for a reassignment or retraining to an AFSC which you would like. Choice 3, until someone far above me decides what to do with as many, many aerial gunners who are looking for guidance, you can join your brethren at the NCO Club every day and pass the day away doing whatever the NCOs do in their club. Pending a personnel action you will be assigned to the 20th Bomb Squadron. Choice 1 is available for the next one hundred eighty days. After that you must either reenlist or accept a discharge.

You deserve a better deal than this. All of the aerial gunners deserve a better deal. I am sure you know if it were I there would be a better deal but I am just a flunky who is maybe one or two steps higher than you are in the flunky chain. You have one hundred eighty days in which to decide which of the choices you will make. If you don't come back to see me about a discharge then I will presume you have taken either Choice 2 or Choice 3. Good luck Sergeant Muscarello."

One of the personnel clerks met him as he left the DP's office. "I am to escort you to your new squadron. Your new first sergeant is expecting you.

661

We can walk but if you have a car we can ride." When the clerk saw Musher's Cadillac he stopped in his tracks and dropped Musher's records folder. Musher recovered the folder and took it with him into the car. At the 20th Orderly Room Musher told the personnel clerk, "I can take it from here. You should go back to the headquarters. Walk very slowly." The young man left without a question about Musher's records.

Musher went into the orderly room and to the desk of the first sergeant. The name placard read "Master Sergeant Michael Dunton". "Sergeant Dunton", Musher waited until Dunton looked him in the eye," I am Saverio Muscarello assigned here today as an aerial gunner." Dunton picked up his phone and dialed a number and when it answered, "Did you send me another aerial gunner today?" "Give me his name and serial number. Thank you. See you at supper." "That was my wife she is the DP's secretary."

"I am sure you know we have aerial gunners coming out the gazoo. Give me your paperwork."

"I don't have it Sergeant I presume they will send it from personnel."

"Our barracks is next door. Just take a bunk and make yourself at home. Master Sergeants don't pull any details in this squadron. Tomorrow morning you will go to the 20th Bomb Squadron 0800 roll call on the flight line. Unless something different happens all masters and techs will be released after roll call but are on standby. They are restricted to the air base. We all know if it were necessary we can find them in the NCO Club."

Musher went into the barracks and looked it over. It was clean but almost full. It would best be described as Spartan. Back in the orderly room he asked Dunton, "Are there any rules against me living off station?"

"No but since you are bachelor and the air force is not asking you to live off station you cannot receive a quarters or ration allowance. Other than that if you meet all your requirements it is no different than any other person who lives off station."

Musher needed one more stop before he began his search for a place to live. At squadron supply he asked for issue of two flying suits. The supply clerk looked puzzled and summoned his Technical Sergeant NCOIC. The NCOIC took one look and said, "Musher right? I was at Smoky when you were. We never knew each other but I witnessed your pool and snooker exhibitions. I am Charlie Louden. What's it been two years, maybe a little more. You must have done something right from staff to master sergeant during that time. Where have you been?"

"Korea and then England. Just arrived here today and I need some clothes until my stuff gets here. Can you help me?"

"I'll be right back." He came back with two new flying suits, a B-2 leather jacket, a pair of brogans, three pair of socks and a black baseball hat with the 20th emblem on the crown. Sorry I don't have rank pins but they are at the BX. Will I see you for beer call at the club after work?"

"I can't say yet. I need to find a place to live. I don't want to live in the squadron barracks. If I can I will be there. Do me a favor Charlie don't talk about me. I don't have the talents I used to have. Prison camp took a lot out of me."

Musher went to the NCO Club to enroll in membership and pay his dues. He read the club bulletin board where people advertise cars for sale, houses for sale, houses to rent and rooms to rent. There were a couple of possible room rentals and they were located near the base. He called both of them and set up visit appointments for later this afternoon. A quick stop at the BX for a hat rank pin and lunch.

One of the room rentals was actually two rooms and a private bathroom. The entry was from a side door and was totally separated from the rest of the house. The main room was a fully furnished bedroom. The second room was not much more than an eight by eight foot large closet with a small refrigerator and a two burner hot plate. It could have a separate telephone line installed but it would be at his expense. There was parking for his car right along side the entry door to the house. The rent was a basic three hundred fifty dollars a month, four hundred fifty a month if he wanted maid service and laundry. If he paid six months in advance it was four hundred twenty-five. Any advance payment would not be refundable if he moved. It was totally clean and available right now.

Musher counted out two thousand five hundred fifty dollars and said, "This is for the first six months. I need to move in now so I will have somewhere to sleep tonight. I am sure you can see I am a Master Sergeant who just arrived from England today. My name is Saverio Muscarello but everyone calls me Musher."

"We are Angelo and Maria Vasquez. Maria will get you the keys to this door and I will help you get your things upstairs. If after you are in and you either need something or have a question don't hesitate to talk to us. Our last tenant was with us for two years before he was discharged. Are you a lifer?"

"Right now that is a very difficult question to answer."

CHAPTER 206
Me, A Dog Robber?

It had been three weeks since Musher arrived at Carswell. Sergeant Dunton had been correct. He went to roll call every morning and was released as soon as it was over. Carswell did not have a golf course but it did have a driving range. Every morning he went to the driving range and practiced for at least two hours but most of the time he practiced for three hours. He would SSS at the NCO Club put on a clean flying suit etc. (he had been given two additional flying suits by his Smoky buddy the NCOIC of squadron supply). Lunch and then join the boys in the card room and play whatever game was available. The stakes were not high but it was good way to pass the day.

He was playing twenty-five cent Booray (one of the great card games to come out of Louisiana) when suddenly everyone in the room stood up. "Carry On." The command to carry on came from the 11th Bomb Wing Deputy Commander Colonel Charles Rowe. The last time Musher saw him was when they boarded the aircraft on the day they were forced to bail out over North Korea. He was a First Lieutenant then and now a full Colonel in just over two years. Musher remembers he was one of Hairy S's boys and now he is a lifer. He must have done many things right in the past two plus years. He came to Musher's table, all stood up as he looked straight at Musher. "I just heard this morning you were assigned to this wing. How long have you been here?"

"Three weeks Sir."

"You knew I was here and you didn't come to see me?"

"Sir, master sergeants don't make calls on full colonels."

"What are you doing here?"

"The same as the other gunners, I am waiting for reassignment."

"Very good. Tomorrow morning you will pick up my vehicle at the motor pool and be at my office by 0800. You are my new driver."

"Colonel, I don't want to dog-rob for anybody." Flag officers, Brigadier General and above are authorized an aide who is a commissioned officer. Full colonels take this privilege by selecting an enlisted man to be their personal driver. This technique was learned from the British forces where all officers have a "batman." The batman not only drives his car if he is authorized one, he also shines his boots, makes sure his clothes are always ready, runs errands for him and lies to protect him when lying is required. In the US Forces it was called "dog-robbing".

"Sergeant I didn't hear anybody ask you what you wanted. Do not be late to my office. Wear a Class "A" uniform." With that he left the NCO Club.

Musher parked in the space reserved for the Deputy Wing Commander and was in his office area at 0745. There was an attractive young woman behind the desk guarding his office. "My name is Pat Barnett, I am Colonel Rowe's secretary. You must be the new driver. I have heard so much about you I feel I know you. Please call me Pat and if you don't mind I will call you Musher. Come, let me show you your cubby-hole." She opened a door which led into a very small office which contained a small desk, two chairs and a telephone. "When you are in the office this is where you will be. Feel free to make it as pleasant and as comfortable as you wish." She closed the door behind her.

For two hours he had been sitting in this room trying to keep from ripping the doors off the hinges and heading for his discharge at personnel. The phone rang and when he answered Pat said, "The Colonel needs to go into Fort Worth. He will be outside in five minutes." She hung up.

Like any other dutiful dog-robber Musher went outside and stood by the right rear passenger door. As the Colonel approached he held open the door and saluted. The Colonel nodded and went into the car. When Musher was behind the wheel the Colonel said, "To Fort Worth." About three miles short of Fort Worth the Colonel said, "At the next major intersection turn left." Away from Fort Worth? Four miles farther the Colonel said, "Turn in at the entry way." The Wellington Arms Hotel. He stopped at the entry to the hotel. Before leaving the car the Colonel told him this meeting would probably last at least three hours. "You may do whatever you wish to pass the time but be here at 1500." Four hours from now. He was on the perimeter of Fort Worth and the only thing he remembered passing was a strip shop mall.

While eating lunch he asked himself who he thought should pay these unnecessary expenses. No matter how he tried he kept coming back to himself. At promptly 1500 he picked up the Colonel. There was no conversation during the ride back to headquarters. "Was it really a meeting or was it a broad?" There were no tell tale signs on the Colonel except that he looked tired and was dozing in and out during the ride.

At 1700 Pat was on his phone. "You may leave now. Return the vehicle to the motor pool. They will clean and service it. I will see you tomorrow at

0800." He returned the car and the motor pool attendant said, "Your ride will be here in a moment."

"Thank you but I live off base and I brought my car here this morning." That will be my routine. Please make sure the Colonel's car is ready by 0700."

CHAPTER 207

A New Phase of Dog-Robbing

As usual Musher was early for work and so was Pat. Musher went into his office and unloaded his little black bag. Lucky Strikes, an ashtray, a Zippo lighter, two decks of cards and a host of cookies to put in the desk draw. Next trip it will be a small coffee pot and maybe a small radio. It looked like he would be here for at least the next two months. After that, who knows?

Pat rang and said, "If you want coffee we have it out here. Help yourself." Maybe he wouldn't need the coffee pot. He went to get coffee and on his way back to his office Pat said, "Make sure your cup is here at the end of the day for the office cleaners." What a bossy broad. Knowing the Colonel's propensity for pussy he wondered if he was banging her.

Just before noon he was summoned to the Colonel. "Musher I am having a small party at my house tonight. The senior officers of both wings and the air division will be there. They will bring their wives. A total of twelve people. I want you to go to my house and setup the bar, check the liquor and liqueur stock and serving items for the party. The kitchen staff will take care of the food and kitchen clean up. Dinner will be 2000 so we can expect guests from 1830 on. If you need liquors or liqueurs see Captain Lawrence, the Class 6 manager and he will give you what you ask for and charge it to me. If you don't have a white shirt, cummerbund, black tie and black pants see Mr. Felix Womack, the BX Manager and he will fix you up and charge it to me. When you finish getting ready you may leave the car at the motor pool. I will see you at my house not later than 1630. Any questions? Then be on your way."

The Class 6 manager obliged his requests without hesitation. He already owned everything the Colonel had mentioned but this was a good chance to get a second outfitting free. Everything was in his car and he was in the NCO Club by 1500. He was at the Colonel's house by 1545 and when the doorbell was answered it was by a heavenly looking woman in her late twenties. She was beautiful. "You must be Musher. Can I give you a hand?"

"Thank you. Please show me where the bar is."

"Is that your beautiful Cadillac? If it is please park it alongside the house."

When he returned she was in the bar putting away the liquor and liqueurs. Musher was filling the ice well and putting the rest in the freezer.

"Please fix me a tall, light vodka and tonic with a lime. " It was just after four in the afternoon. Is she showing off or is she a lush? Time will tell.

"I am going to bathe and dress. Please make yourself at home." Musher did just that. He poured a coke, found a comfortable chair and smoked Lucky Strikes.

The guests arrived just as Rowe predicted and the men drank either martinis or scotch and water. Not much skill required to take care of those orders. Particularly since Musher had opened a quart of gin and put one half ounce of vermouth before resealing it and putting it back in the freezer. He had done the same with a quart of vodka. The ladies were the difficult ones. A Singapore Sling, a Fuzzy Navel and a Pina Colada. After dinner the drinking became heavier. Even the ladies switched to such standards as gin and tonic, vodka and tonic and just plain vodka. By 2300 the kitchen staff was gone and only the partiers and Musher remained. The music became softer and the dancers danced closer. No one seemed to be dancing with his own spouse. Every now and again a couple would drift towards a bed room. The party broke about 0230. Personally Musher didn't think any of them was fit to drive even though it was a short way since they all lived on station. He cleaned the area. Since there was no extra pay for this he took a bottle of vodka and a bottle of scotch and headed for home. Tomorrow was Saturday and he was going to find a golf course.

CHAPTER 208

Six Weeks Have Gone By

Monday morning Musher was sitting in his office practicing card palming when Colonel Rowe walked in without so much as a knock. "You did a good job the other night." He put one hundred dollars on Musher's desk. "In addition to that little reward keep track of your hours and we will get you free time to make up for it. Colonel Traxler, the 7th Bomb Wing Commander is having a little party at his house Friday night and he would like you to tend bar for him. Why don't you see him sometime today or tomorrow and if you agree to do it take off whatever time you need to get it ready."

Musher called Colonel Traxler's office for an appointment. "Come in after lunch. He will see you some time this afternoon." At 1300 Musher was at Traxler's office. He was announced and immediately seen by Traxler. "Musher you did a great job at Lowe's. I want you to do the same for me this Friday. The guest list will be the same, the timing will be the same and of course the kitchen staff will take care of everything except the bar. You will have the same authorities at the Class 6 store and the BX. I will call my wife and tell her you are coming by this afternoon. Is that all right?"

"Yes sir. Please tell her it won't be any sooner than one hour. I want to return Colonel Lowe's car to the motor pool to stop anyone from saying I am using it for either his personal use or my personal use. Sir, may I be excused?" A salute to Colonel Traxler and he went out the door smiling.

Mrs. Traxler was a very attractive woman. He remembered her from Lowe's party on her knees between Lowe's legs. He surveyed the liquor and liqueur stock and left to get supplies. At the BX he bought another two shirts, another cummerbund and tie and had it all charged to Colonel Traxler. The Friday night party at Trexler's was the same as the one at Lowe's. Drinking, dancing and sex. Every Monday thereafter Colonel Lowe would give him a hundred dollars and tell him who was holding the party this upcoming Friday. This went on for the next four Fridays.

The party for the fifth Friday was at the home of Brigadier General Horace Wellman, Commander of the 8th Air Division at Carswell. It was the first time the General had hosted a party although he and his wife had been at all the other parties. Musher was there early to make sure everything was right. The General came home early, came into the bar and asked for a strong scotch and water. He said to Musher, "Pour one for yourself and come keep me company. You have been very closed mouth about your

669

Friday night duties and we appreciate that. You are a young master sergeant with a great combat record and I am told by all who know you that you are very bright. Why are you not an officer? Why have you not gone to OCS? Don't you have the education? Can't you pass the entrance examinations?"

"Sir I have passed the OCS examination twice with the highest stanine scores that can be earned. I have an undergraduate degree in philosophy from Kings College, Cambridge University, England. I have made a combat bail out from a B-29, been a POW and survived those fourteen months. Despite all that I am always an alternate for a class but I am never selected. I am an alternate for the upcoming class in September. If I don't get in this class I will be over the age limit to ever go so I will leave the air force."

"We cannot afford to lose good men such as you. Come to my office Monday morning. I will tell Lowe you will be late for your duty."

The weekend dragged on as Musher waited for Monday morning. At 0800 Monday he was in the reception area of General Wellman's office. When the General walked in he and the secretary rose. He motioned for Musher to follow him and he said to the secretary, "Get me the Chief of the Air Training Command." He was sipping coffee when his phone buzzed, he picked up and said, "Good morning Bill I need a favor. I have a master sergeant who should be at least a major." While he was talking he handed Musher a pad and pencil. He mouthed, Full name and serial number. "We are on the brink of losing him to civilian life because he is always and alternate for OCS but never selected. Worst of all if he is not in the September class he will be age ineligible and the air force will lose him. Can you help us out?"

"Bill I owe you another one. Thank you and when you speak to Mom tell her I love her. Take care." He hung up the phone and commented to Musher, "It helps when your brother is the Chief of the Air Training Command. Your notification of acceptance into OCS will be here in a day or two and you will enroll in the September class. When you get to OCS it will be tough, there is nothing more than the sadistic commissioned officer staff enjoys more than washing out a warrant officer or a very senior NCO. Good Luck. No thank yous. The air force will be the benefactor of my call."

The first thing he did was tell Colonel Lowe about General Wellman's call to his brother who is the Chief of the Air Training Command. "Sir, may I take the day off? I am so uptight and have so much to do I don't think I would be of any value to you."

"Of course you can. Drop my car at the motor pool and take today and tomorrow off. You will make a fine officer."

His next stop was to tell the Wing Director of Personnel. He already knew. "Musher I will contact you when your official orders to OCS come. You will then sign a one year service extension. When you graduate OCS you will be discharged and sworn in as an officer. If you fail OCS you will be returned here to finish the one year extension."

CHAPTER 209
I Need Caesar's Blessing

Everything was breaking his way. He should be happy. He still had the problem of his words to Caesar and their plans for him. The more he pondered a life as one of Caesar's chosen the more he wondered if he could carry a gun and maybe do some of the things Fanucci had told him about. He must face Caesar and tell him he will abide by his decision. He must do this quickly.

When Colonel Lowe came to the office Musher was waiting to see him. "What's up Musher? You don't look well."

"I talked to my sister last night and my mother is very, very ill and asking for me. May I have some leave to make a quick trip to Boston?"

"Sit down while I make a phone call." He dialed and then spoke, "Good morning Horace (the 8th Air Division Commander) I think today may be the right day for us to go to 8th Air Force headquarters. (Westover AFB, Springfield, Massachusetts) We could RON tonight, do our business tomorrow, RON tomorrow night and be back here on Thursday. Trust me, the RON's would be most pleasant. There is another consideration, Musher's mom is very sick and he needs to see her immediately. We could drop him off at Logan and pick him up there Thursday morning. You need to put some time on your aircraft. Do you think we could do this?"

"Yes Sir, Musher and I will be at base ops at 1030 hours. Thank you. OK Musher you heard the jist of the conversation, go pack and be at base ops at 1000. I will take care of the paperwork." He buzzed Pat and she came in as Musher was leaving.

From a phone in the Logan Airport terminal Musher dialed a number he had a long time ago committed to memory. "This is Saverio Muscarello, Musher. I need to talk to Martin Melke. I am at a public pay phone, KEN-6606. I will wait here." He settled into the phone booth to wait. It took a half hour before the phone rang and he answered identifying himself.

"Hello Musher, what's up?"

"I need to see you. I need your counsel."

"Do you remember the garage? Come to the garage now." The line went dead.

He was escorted upstairs to Melke's office suite. "He has someone with him please have a seat." Musher sat trying to rehearse how he would explain his feelings to Melke without being disrespectful or ungrateful. Melke's office door opened and out walked two men who Musher recognized, the Scaparetti brothers. Moments later Melke came out and gave Musher hugs and handshakes. They were hugging as Melke's door closed behind them.

"OK Kid, what is your serious problem that would bring you here from Texas?"

"I have been offered the opportunity to be a United States Air Force officer. To take the opportunity I must sign an enlistment extension of one year. I am aware of my obligation to The Godfather and you. I would not do anything to negate those obligations. Achieving the status of an officer would culminate all the efforts I have given to the air force. It may be my vanity. I never targeted this opportunity but now that it has been offered I truly would like to do it. I seek your counsel because I have great faith in yours and The Godfather's judgment. If you could speak to him on my behalf whatever he decides is best for him and you will be what I will do."

"I will speak to him. Do you have a deadline to make this decision?"

"My General was going to a meeting in Springfield so he gave me a ride to Logan. He will pick me up at Logan Thursday morning at nine. I must sign whether I accept or decline before midnight Thursday."

"Are you staying at your usual hotel?"

"I have not checked in yet but I will be there tonight."

"If I don't contact you then tomorrow morning around ten call me at the usual number. It is great to see you. Everything will work out for the best."

Musher stayed in his hotel room just in case Melke was trying to reach him. He ordered delivery pizza and coke. About nine-thirty there was knock on his door and he opened it to the hotel clerk holding out an envelope. Inside the envelope it said, "Be in front of your hotel at ten in the morning."

At ten a car pulled up and Musher got in. It was Melke. "We are going to the boss' house. He wants to talk with you personally."

In the library Musher knelt and kissed the ring. The Godfather got up and hugged him and whispered, "I am so happy to see you. Please sit. Martin tells me of your opportunity and says you are worried about letting us down. Don't be worried. Climbing from the street to become a military officer is an accomplishment for anyone. We want you to do well and if there is anything we can do please tell Martin. I asked for you to be here so I could personally reassure you of our confidence in you. Are you enjoying your Cadillac? Now, go see your Mama." Musher knelt and kissed the ring again.

CHAPTER 210

Officer Candidate School

Musher stopped at the main gate to Lackland AFB, San Antonio, Texas and was directed to the OCS area. He parked in the student lot whose car license plates were from all over the United States. An extremely sharp looking cadet opened his door, "Good morning. Welcome to OCS. Let me get your bag." According to instructions Musher had only his B-4 bag and it was lightly packed. Everything else he owned was secured in his car. "May I have your car keys? We will put your car in the permanent student parking lot." Together they walked (almost marched) to the OCS Orderly Room. His escort told him he would wait outside with his bag. The sign in process was done by other OCS cadets. Everything moved so smoothly and so well. When he and his escort reached his assigned barracks he was shown to a room. A room set up for two people but at this point he was alone. His escort opened a wall closet cabinet and it had a 1505 shirt (the name of the air force summer uniform). He was asked to change from his duty shirt into the plain shirt. Another technical sergeant joined him in the room with his escort and he was given he same instructions. "Relax gentlemen, we will see you shortly."

Musher took a Lucky from his newly opened package and sat on the bed to light it. About the time he had struck the Zippo three cadets entered the room screaming. One at him, "What are you doing? Did anyone give you permission to smoke? Do you think we lie down anytime we wish? Put those cigarettes and that lighter in the trash can. Get on your feet and come to attention. You call that attention. You look like a ruptured duck. Head up, chin down, stomach in, feet at a forty-five degree angle, arms by your side, palms along the seam of you leg. You are disgusting. What is your name?"

"Master Sergeant Saverio Muscarello."

"Wrong! You are Cadet Muscarello. The first word and the last word out of your mouth will be Sir. Is that clear? What is your name?"

"Cadet Muscarello."

"Don't you have a first name? Try again. What is your name?"

"Cadet Saverio Muscarello."

"Dummy did you forget about the sir already. Try again."

"Sir, Cadet Saverio Muscarello, sir."

"Don't you have a middle initial?"

"Sir, no sir."

"Then your middle name is NMI (No Middle Name). Try it again, what is your name?"

"Sir, Saverio NMI Muscarello sir."

"Have you already given up being a cadet? Try it again."

"Sir, Cadet Saverio NMI Muscarello, sir."

Musher's room mate had been getting the same interrogation. Musher wasn't sure how much longer he could stand at attention. It had been some time since he had stood at attention at all.

"What is your room mate's name?" "What do you mean you don't know? How do you expect to communicate in a gentlemanly fashion? We are going to leave you. Find out about your room mate and we shall return."

"My name is Saverio NMI Muscarello. What's yours?

"George K. Mawakana."

The three Nazi henchmen returned. "Tell me your room mate's name."

"Sir, George K. Mawakana, sir."

"Is his middle name "K"? What is his middle name? " The three left.

"OK George what does the "K" stand for?"

"Lulu ooo cow e kah vay que" (Hawaiian phonetic) Musher tried to say it but stumbled badly.

They returned. "All right Cadet Muscarello what does the "K" in your room mate's name stand for?"

Musher tried, "Sir, and repeatedly unsuccessfully pronounced George's middle name."

"I will give you a pass on this one until this evening's retreat formation. Now, drive into the hall and get on the wall." ("Drive" was the OCS synonym for move, march, go, or any other verb requiring movement)("On the wall" was an attention position requiring heels on the base board, butt, shoulder blades and back of the head touching the wall with the head up and the chin down)

The interrogation continued with different interrogators constantly standing just inches from your nose and screaming the questions. It's OK if they yell but if one of them touches me I am going to rip his heart out. Musher tried one of his POW techniques. You hear but you don't hear. You are aware enough to answer a question if asked but you give whatever answer makes your interrogator happy providing you don't break the faith with yourself. Somewhere during however long the on the wall session lasted a more dominant voice was yelling, "Fall out for lunch. Move it, move it, drive, drive, drive." The OCS Group was divided into six squadrons. Each squadron was forty-six cadets strong counting both the upper class and the new students. Musher was in third squadron. It didn't take long to arrange the second class into proper height distribution. It composed the second half of the squadron formation. The march to the dining hall was long, hot and filled with nothing but criticisms from the upper class members controlling the march.

At the dining hall the cadets were required to stand in line at parade rest and come to attention before taking a step forward and then returned to parade rest. No talking while in line or in the dining hall unless it was a response to a question. When they entered the dining hall Musher and others were diverted from the serving line to another serving line. There he received a tray containing a four ounce steak, four ounces of vegetable accompanied by two glasses of milk. He was seated at a table with a large placard which read "Fat Boys Table". The upper class cadet sitting at the head of table recited, "You are all over weight by at least fifteen pounds. This will be your standard meal until you are physically fit." This was not the air force dining hall to which Musher had become accustomed. There were no plates and silverware it was back to segregated metal trays. There were no silently moving people to serve coffee and handle the bussing of the tables. There were no Luckies after eating. Eating here was hardly a pleasure. He guessed the next two hundred seventy meals would be equally unenjoyable.

The afternoon was spent marching from place to place to pick up the items required for the training. Of course during all the marching there was the constant criticizing and yelling. It seemed none of the upper class knew how to talk, they only knew how to scream. With everything stored in their rooms the class went to the ramp for close order drill. (The ramp was a two hundred yard by one hundred yard rectangle with an asphalt surface) The COD continued until it was time to go to dinner. A quick wash up, then came the aggravating march to the dining hall and the same meal with the same amount of enjoyment.

It was 1830 when the announcement came. "G.I. Party. All cadets of the second class report to the day room." It wasn't a standard G.I. party because these barracks were top drawer. Only the latrine bordered on a standard barracks. With the exception of two in this squadron before coming to OCS all cadets were either tech or master sergeants. G.I. parties were nothing new except this place added a new wrinkle. No scrub brushes, they used tooth brushes instead. The entire latrine was rinsed with isopropyl alcohol.

It was 2145 when they were once again assembled in the dayroom. "In fifteen minutes you will be in bed. You will stay in bed until morning. There will be no "night crawling". (Night crawling is defined as getting out of bed for any reason or getting under the blanket with a flashlight to read) Wake

676

up is at 0500 and you are not to get out of bed before the lights are on in your room. You will have three minutes to shower, shave and shine. One minute to make your bed and square away your area. You will be on the street ready for inspection in fatigues and field jacket at 0505. Listen for "The Minute Caller." He will tell you how much time you have, the uniform for the day and who the OCS officer of the day is. This is a duty done by two of your classmates, one on each floor and everyone will get his chance. The Minute Caller will stand at attention with his left arm at shoulder height with his elbow at a ninety degree angle from his arm and parrell to the floor. His call is, "Gentlemen it is 0500 hours. You have five minutes to reveille formation. The uniform for the day is fatigues with field jackets. The Officer Candidate School Officer of the Day is Captain Henry Camp." At the next minute and every subsequent minute the announcement will be made. The last call will be when you have one minute to fall in for reveille. The Minute Caller must stand at attention throughout his routine and he must keep his arm in its proper position. It's time for bed. 0500 will come early."

Musher thought, "This guy must be crazy. I can hardly shave in five minutes never mind do all the things he said must be done. Christ this is like being at infantry basic training again."

CHAPTER 211

Meet the Plumber

The first morning in the latrine was a memorable moment. The Minute Callers were allowed to get up fifteen minutes early. On the latrine sink shelf they had spread shaving cream the full length of the two sink stations. They had scattered razors along the shelf next to the shaving cream. Clumps of tooth past were also on that shelf. Musher followed the lead of the cadet in front of him. Grab a handful of shaving cream and smear it on your face, take a razor and make four passes. He made two on the cheek area and the other two on the neck area. Some toothpaste on your finger and rub your teeth while getting in the shower. Don't take off your underwear just get into the showers which were already running with tepid water. No soap, no shampoo, just get under the water long enough to be totally wet. Rub the towel across your body but mostly on your underwear while running to your room. On with the fatigues, sox and boots. Make the bed as best you can. Get on your knees and use your hands to wipe and dust the floor and the room. Put on your field jacket and hold your hat in hand while you drive to formation. Musher was among the first few to fall-in. He immediately was bombarded by upper classmen trying to make his life miserable. He was wet, cold, tired and had not had a cigarette since he signed-in to this crazy nut house. He was a master sergeant, he deserved better treatment. While these thoughts were in his head an upper classman was in his face.

"Mister you don't have to put up with this crap. You are a master sergeant, a decorated combat veteran. You could go in and put on your shirt with those master sergeant stripes and end all this right there. A baby blue Cadillac, back on flight pay and a house full of women. Why give it all up just to be a second lieutenant? Come with me, we will fall out and go smoke Lucky Strikes. You can sign the SIE paper (SIE is Self Initiated Elimination) and be what you were, the playboy who had it all. Should we leave?"

The upper classman's barbs and disrespectful talking did nothing more than stiffen Musher's resolve. To himself, "I'll be here to piss on your grave."

Breakfast was not any more pleasant than the two previous meals. The food was good but Musher was starving. He missed his goodies. After breakfast they returned to the barracks for shit details and to make themselves more presentable than they were at reveille. It was 1000 hours when the new cadets were seated in the OCS auditorium. There was that soft Ten Hut when the School Commandant Brigadier General Rollins Walker and his staff took positions on the stage. BG Walker, "My apologies for not greeting you yesterday but I was called to Air Training Command headquarters. What I say today is pretty much what I would have said yesterday. Welcome to OCS. You are the most deserving airmen, WAFs and warrant officers the USAF has to offer. Just to give you a slight idea of how hard this course is yesterday two hundred and nine of you enrolled here at OCS. This morning there are one hundred ninety-eight of you left. You cannot succeed here if you do not have the determination to withstand discomfort and pain. One last thought, there are one hundred ninety-eight of you sitting here right now. The others were SIE's. I am authorized to award one hundred eight second lieutenant commissions. Look around you. Basically one out of every three of you will not graduate as an officer. If you think we are being hard in our training and academics it is simply because we want the very best officers we can produce. Most of you were halfway to retirement eligibility. Your presence here says more for your dedication and loyalty to the USAF than any peace time act I know. I must leave now but I leave you in the hands of our Chief Tactical Officer Captain Alselmo Rodriguez." Again there was that soft Ten Hut when the School Commandant left the stage.

Musher heard the people behind him talking, "My buddy graduated from here six months ago and he told me to watch out for Captain Rodriguez. He is so entwined in monitoring cadet activities he sometimes forgets about taking his medicine every day. Behind his back they call him The Plumber because he washes out so many of the wash outs. He is far more dangerous than the academics."

Captain Rodriguez, The Plumber speaks," Me and the rest of the commissioned staff tactical officers assigned to your squadron will get to know you as we would our children. We will be in your pockets all day every day. Our job is to separate the wheat from the chaff while we teach the wheat to be strong leaders. Not all men are born as leaders. God gives them the basic talent and we prove God was right. Those who do not survive to graduation cannot blame God, he gave them the tools and they dropped the tools along the way. Your next two weeks will consist of close order drill, physical fitness and basic officer skills. All that begins right now. Ten Hut. Fall-out."

CHAPTER 212

The Pressure Stays On

The Plumber did not exaggerate. Each day was fifteen hours long and began with the morning inspections and hassle. At least eight of those hours were devoted to a combination of Close Order Drill and Physical Training. Shin-splinters, a condition caused by the shin bone's attendant tendons being stressed and creating minuscule separations from the shin bone inducing great pain while walking and even greater pain while marching. It is only cured by living through the pain and continue to march until the splinters heal themselves. This condition led to fourteen SIE's.

The dining experience had not become any better despite the fact that Musher had lost thirteen pounds and was eating with his regular squadron. The dining room displeasure was compounded when you were selected by your squad leader to be "The Table Gunner." It was the duty of the Table Gunner to solicit the drink choices of each member of the table and to procure such choices before he could begin his own meal.

Of course we must not forget the "Three Piece Rule." When meat is part of the meal (which it always is) there can be no more than three pieces of meat on your plate at any one time. You must keep the size of each individual bite so small that if you are asked a question while you are chewing a bite you may take three more chews and swallow without gagging and choking to death.

As Table Gunner when it was your squadron's turn to deliver the evening meal proclaiming the wonder of the upper class and if you were selected as the Table Gunner from your squadron to do so, you would go to the center of the dining room, climb onto a table and using your most loud and deepest command voice deliver, "Gentlemen, your attention please. There are (the number of days left before the upper class graduates) until the absolute and total salvation of the United States Air Force." All cadets would rise from their chairs and make outlandishly loud noises effectuating the statement. You may be asked to repeat it three or four times.

Musher could not stand to hear "on the wall" but he did it because he was going to graduate. The second class was on the wall and one of the upper class was asking questions of the wall flowers. He was particularly close to the face of one cadet when he asked him, "What are you famous for?"

"Sir, I am a doctor in a window factory, I take care of the panes. Sir."

The upper classman was joined by another classmate and together they got in the face of a cadet who had been a Chief Warrant Officer. "Look, here is our ex-CWO. Haven't figured out why a CWO would want to be a second lieutenant." The upper class has been on the CWO as often as possible for almost no rhyme or reason. "OK Mister, what are you famous for?"

"I cut toilet seats in half for half-ass upper classmen."

Pow, pow, he had decked both of them and headed for his room. He could not be seen but you could hear the ripping off of his cadet shirt and the closet doors slam. He came back into the hall wearing his CWO shirt and popped the nearest cadet he could reach. It took four to harness him and they led him into the day room. The rest of us were commanded to stay on the wall. We never saw the CWO again.

For sure the class size is now one hundred eighty-three.

Every barracks had a basement which was referred to as The In-house Obstacle Course. After dinner a cadet would be selected to run the obstacle course. One of the course obstacles was a long trough filled with filthy water and other smelly things and at one end there was a football. The cadet was required to crawl in his shorts only to the end of the trough, acquire the football and crawl back to the beginning point. It sounds messy but it was compounded by the fact that the cadet was blindfolded. There were other equally disrespecting obstacles but this was the worst and generally saved for the last. For the rest of the class the after dinner shit details continued until 2145 hours before they released you for the day. You could not lie or sit on your bed during those fifteen minutes and at 2200 you were in bed. It was a grind.

Five more cadets did the SIE number.

Our class was now one hundred seventy-eight strong, or maybe one hundred seventy-eight weak.

CHAPTER 213
Recognition

During the last phases of those two grueling physical and mental weeks of training we had another nine SIE's. The class total was now one hundred sixty-nine. On the Friday night which ended those two weeks Flight 161, 3rd OCS Squadron had a routine unpleasant dinner experience. Only a few of the upper class had come to dinner. When Flight 161 returned to its barracks it was greeted by an order to fall in at the day room. The day room was almost pitch black but the flight managed to get in without killing each other. When the lights were turned on the entire upper class was there cheering for the second class. The cadet squadron commander spoke, "You gentlemen have survived where others have failed. We salute you and welcome you as brother future second lieutenants. Remember, when we all graduate we will all have equal rank and be no more to each other than just second lieutenants." There was a lot of handshaking and hugging and pats on the back.

Life at OCS had just taken a major turn for the better.

The following Monday the schedule became Revielle, Academics until noon, Physical Training for the first part of the afternoon, Close Order Drill for the latter part of the afternoon and Retreat to end the day.

Discipline at meals had not changed, you must still eat square meals (A Square Meal: Anything which you intend to put in your mouth from your plate the utensil must travel forward parrell to the plate, make a ninety degree angle turn upward, make a ninety degree turn left towards the mouth and then a ninety degree down turn to be at the starting position once more. Even water or milk glasses must follow the same procedural route) The Table Gunner concept and the nightly proclamation of the wonders of the upper class continued in full force. One of the most noticeable changes was the after dinner to lights out time. Very seldom were they bothered by the upper class. There was homework to do, maintenance of clothing and for some letter writing. Musher thought the change was wonderful because smoking was allowed in the day room while studying there and the day room had a coke machine.

Every Saturday there was a parade and the OCS cadet body was part of the Lackland Air Force Base parade. The parade complement of permanent party and basic trainees was about ten thousand airmen. OCS had without fail won the appearance and marching pennants every week since who knows when. With white gloves on their hands highlighting the precision of the arm swing and their spectacular uniform appearance it was no contest. After the parade OCS returned to its norm. Saturday afternoon was always a G.I. party. Sunday was a little different. Reveille was at 0700. It was without a critical inspection. At breakfast second class was allowed to have coffee, linger and smoke cigarettes until church call. Musher was ready for church call as he lined up with the Methodists. No Catholic ups and down for him. Sunday afternoon was the same COD and PT. Dinner formation was no different than any other dinner formation.

Friday nights brought a new school requirement. All OCS candidates were required to go to the OCS Club for an evening of entertainment. Married candidates whose wives were living locally while they were in OCS were allowed to have their wives join them at the club. At 2200 they were allowed to leave the club with the caveat that they must be in their room not later than 0030 hours. Among their fellow candidates they were known as members of "The 4H Club, Half Hour of Horizontal Happiness." One attendance night two cadets drank too much liquor and became offensive. Despite the fact that they were escorted to their barracks by upper class members of their squadron they were gone from the group. The class size shrunk to one hundred sixty-seven.

Academics consisted of Air Power, Logistics, Geo-Politics, Understanding Communism, World Geography, Leadership, and a non-graded speed reading course. None of these courses had he taken at Cambridge. He must study hard. One of the dangers of the grading method used at OCS was that it graded examinations "against the curve." (For example: All the students take the exam and all but one student answers all fifty questions correctly. All the students who had all the correct answers receive a one hundred percent score but the student who incorrectly answered just one of the fifty questions fails.) OCS allowed only three single subject examination failures during training and if two were in the same subject it was cause for immediate dismissal. Single subject examinations were administered weekly after the first three weeks of the course.

By the end of the tenth week of training the class size was reduced to one hundred fifteen. Fifty-two had fallen via academics. There were only two more weeks of academics. By the end of the two academic weeks the second class was down to one hundred eight. The upper class graduates ninety-eight in just three weeks.

The commissioned tactical officers are interviewing candidates for the rank positions when the second class becomes the first class. The interview committee is headed by The Plumber. Along with many others Musher is called for interview. When he finished the interview he was not sure how he had done. He knew his military bearing and speech had been impeccable. There was one question The Plumber asked that he was definitive in his answer but he read trouble in the faces of the panel.

Two days before the first class' graduation the second class was assembled in the OCS auditorium. The cadet officers of the first class were on one side of the aisle and the second class was on the other. The Plumber was on stage with the rest of the commissioned officer tactical staff. "Today we announce the new system operators for the upcoming first class. When we call the name and position both the new designee and his counterpart will meet in front of the stage. The graduating candidate will give his rank designator to his successor. Please hold all applause until we finish. The first designee for Flight Lieutenant, 1st Squadron is Alexander Pastore. The Plumber went through all the rank positions for each squadron. The six squadrons were divided into two groups, he name the new group commanders. The candidate's voted choice for the Honor Council. He read off the four names. Then came the appointee for Chaplin's Assistant. Everyone was waiting for the next four appointees to be named.

"Adjutant to the OCS Corps, Cadet Major William Gambell."

"Director of Materiel for the OCS Corps, Cadet Major Hewitt Hammon"

"Director of Operations and Training for the OCS Corps, Cadet Lieutenant Colonel Saverio Muscarello."

"Commander of the OCS Corps, Cadet Colonel Barry Addicott"

"Gentlemen my congratulations. Now we can do the applause."

The first class was thunderously loud. They knew that now it would be almost impossible to keep them from putting on that gold bar unless they did something so terribly stupid they did not deserve the commission.

The second class, now the first class was equally if not louder than the people they were replacing. They knew that all the hard times were basically over and soon there would be a new second class and their time to be "the cock of the walk."

Musher was disappointed. He needed to know what made Addicott a better commander than he would have been. He resigned himself to the fact that he would never know.

CHAPTER 214
A Fourteen Day Respite

The first class had graduated and was gone. Musher moved from the 3rd Squadron barracks to the OCS Wing Staff Headquarters. His room was much larger and he did not share with anyone. He had a telephone. The day room was furnished much nicer than the squadron day room. The headquarters day room had a television set, a radio, goodies machines, soft couches and a pool table. He was not required to make any reveille appearances or march to the dining hall. He was not scheduled into any squadron exercises or functions. With the exception of maintaining his academic standard he was free to roam wherever he pleased on the pretext that he was "checking on the training." Like the first class before him the heels on his shoes had been changed to wood so that when he brought them together to return a salute there was a very loud click. Many afternoons he roamed through the OCS area simply to encounter other cadets who would salute and he would enjoy returning it.

For the staff which commands a military parade there is a marching move called "Change Post." When all the troops are in position and the reviewing officers are on the reviewing stand the parade commander moves onto the parade ground with his staff. Their first alignment is the parade commander facing the reviewing stand and his staff behind him as if he were a quarterback in a football "T" formation. Musher's position was directly behind the commander and the other staff members were positioned one on Musher's left and the other on his right. The parade commander reports to the senior reviewing officer, "Sir the parade is ready."

"You may begin." Now the parade commander must face the troops to give his commands. This is where the "Change Post" is executed. Musher's job was to whisper just loud enough for the commander and the staff to hear his command. The maneuver is simple it is the timing that makes it look good or very bad. The simple maneuver: On "CHANGE" the staff behind the commander does a right face. On "POST" the staff right winger steps off with one step forward and a column left move. The two remaining staffers follow his lead. The staff right winger now takes three steps along his new line. The two remaining staffers are still following his lead. The staff right winger now makes a column left move. The two remaining staffers are still following his lead. The staff right winger now takes three steps on his marching line. The two remaining staffers are now on the same line as he is.

They halt as one, count to three and together make a left face. The parade commander has made an about face and is facing the troops with his staff behind him. After receiving the reports from all the squadrons and groups they execute another Change Post so the parade commander will be facing the senior officer when he reports. "Sir, all personnel are present or accounted for."

"You may pass in review." They execute another Change Post so the parade commander will be facing the troops when he gives the command *"Pass in Review."*

The OCS Wing staff had practiced the Change Post enough times to feel confident that when they take the parade ground they would not embarrass the OCS Corps but would make them proud.

There are fourteen days until the next class reports to OCS. Most of the candidates took leave for the period. Musher didn't have any place he really wanted to go so he did not. He had just about everyday free. It would be a good time to play some golf. Lackland had an excellent course. He used a locker at the golf course to change into golf clothes which like everything else he owned was stored in his car. He approached the starter slipped a five dollar bill in his hand and told him he was looking to play. "Wait on the range, I'll take care of you." The starter came to get him and took him to the first tee. "You will join these three gentlemen." Musher did not know what to do. He recognized all three, it was The Plumber and two other OCS tactical officers.

"Good morning Mister Muscarello. Of course you know these other two gentlemen. Are you a golfer or are you here to pass time?"

I can't let these three think they intimidate me. "Yes I am a golfer and before the three month layoff a good one."

"What was your handicap before the layoff?"

Give yourself a little cushion. You don't know how good these guys might be. Fuck it, tell them what you believe. "At least as low as anyone of you three and most probably lower."

"Good. Then you will join us in a little ten dollar sixes. Long and short for the first six."

Musher played erratically. Seven birdies and two eagles and shot seventy-two. Eleven minus scores but the other nine holes were beauties. He managed to win two sixes and lose one for a ten dollar win. At lunch in the 19th Hole when they were settling the wins and losses The Plumber said to him, "You must be a hell of a golfer when you play regularly. Have you played professionally?"

"No, but I have played many, many amateur tournaments and some professional tournaments when I was stationed in England."

"What is your all time low amateur handicap?"

"Plus two." His three playing partners let out deep sighs. One had shot eighty-five, one ninety-one and The Plumber seventy-eight.

"We have an eight o'clock tee time tomorrow would you like to join us? During the break we try to play every day because our time is just as jammed as the candidates when the course is going full steam."

"I thank you and I will be here if the crick don't rise. Right now I need to go back to the range and practice. My right hand is acting lazily." Musher insisted on paying the lunch check on the theory that winners pay. He was shocked that as he was leaving all three stood up and shook his hand. He hit a couple of buckets and putted until dark. Have dinner at the golf course and then be in bed early. He would sleep well tonight.

For nine of the next eleven days Musher played thirty-six holes each day. Most of the rounds were with The Plumber and the other two tactical officers. On the days he didn't play it was because he was involved in the preparations to receive a new incoming class. His on duty relationship with his three golfing partners would not in any way reveal that they were on a first name basis on the golf course. He helped them with their games and you could see the improvement as the playing days went by.

The respite was over. Put away the golf clubs, the golf clothes and get back into full time Officer Candidate Lieutenant Colonel Saverio Muscarello. One of the side benefits of being friendly with three of the five members of the OCS position selection committee was that he found out why he had not been selected as OCS Wing Commander. He was right, it was the one question that did him in. The Plumber told him he would be a great combat leader but as a senior officer you must know when to enlist the aid of the chaplin and on that day he did not.

CHAPTER 215
Three Days to Graduation

There were only three days until he became a second lieutenant. The academics were over, the physical training was over, the close order drill was over and the only significant thing before graduation was the designation of the OCS cadet appointments and rank. The final standings in the class were published. Musher finished second in academics and first in tactical exercises, overall second. New assignments would be issued the day before graduation. Musher knew there was no flying school for him. He was now twenty-seven years old and the flying school limit was age twenty-six and one half. He had applied for a waiver and it had been denied. The air force was full of wanna-be flyboys who were much younger. His class was simply herding the second class and waiting to graduate.

The graduation ceremony was heart throbbing to him. When he walked across that stage to get his commission and then be sworn in as an officer he just simply cried inside. As he was leaving the auditorium he ran smack dab into Brigadier General Horace Wellman who had gotten him here and Colonel Lowe. Both had been at the graduation ceremony and he had not seen them. BG Wellman, "Musher these were my first gold bars." He pinned them on Musher. "I have a reservation at the O-Club. I am starving." The lunch service for a visiting Brigadier General was better than any five star restaurants could provide. During coffee Wellman said, "I suppose you are wondering why you don't have assignment orders. I would not do this unless you wanted to. I want you to be my aide de camp. You will meet all the right people and it certainly would enhance your career."

"General, Colonel Lowe, I am deeply grateful for what you two have done for me. Sir, I did my time as a dog-robber and I don't want to do it ever again." Wellman and Lowe pushed back their chairs, got up and left without saying a word.

Oh Boy Musher, you did it this time. Your next assignment will be a beauty.

CHAPTER 216

Back To Lowry AFB

Musher had been at OCS Personnel for most of the morning while they tried to figure out where to send him. He did not want any Air Force Specialty Code which kept him on the WAF side of the flight line. It was finally concluded that he would be best suited as a Munitions Officer working in a bomb assembly and storage area. It was for him the best of the options and he agreed to enter the field of Munitions. The technical training school was twelve weeks and it was conducted at Lowry AFB, Colorado. The next day he was on his way to Lowry with a fifteen day delay enroute and three days POV travel time. On his way out the front gate he thought "It's sixteen hours to Denver but only eight to El Paso and just a couple miles from there to Juarez. El Paso here I come."

It was late afternoon when he stopped in front of "Bruno Bottecelli's Car Repairs and Storage" garage just a few hundred feet short of the Juarez checkpoint. "Is anybody in here?" The big man who had been there the last time Musher was there recognized him and gave him a hug. "What can we do for you?"

"I am on my way to Denver but I thought I might stop in Juarez for a couple of days and get my ashes hauled."

"Enjoy yourself. We will take good care of this beautiful Cadillac."

He booked a room at the Florida Hotel for two nights. The cost was seven dollars. The room rate had gone up fifty cents a night. He wondered what else had gone up. In the bar with his first tequila sour he found out the price of drinks had gone from ten cents to fifteen cents and the price of a quickie from one dollar to two dollars. He couldn't wait to spend two dollars. He had three tequila sours and for each one he spent another two dollars. He had a typical Mexican dinner, pollo, rice and frijoles. Shortly after dinner he went to bed in the hopes of a late night visitor. She came in silently and worked him over completely. He pressed a five dollar bill in her hand and patted her butt. After she left he felt if he never had sex again it would be all right with him. It just could not get any better.

The next day he had breakfast at the little diner next door but couldn't figure out what he would do for the rest of the day. He was sexually drained and no female body could interest him. He was smoking a Lucky when he read the ad on the table. *"Tired, need pep, visit Slumber Land. Wet and dry steam. Full and partial body massages. Full liquor bar. Full Japanese style Jacuzzis.* " Let's try that.

Slumber Land was equal to its advertising. He sampled all of it s offerings except sex. He rebuked any attempt to entice him. When he left he was feeling beautifully clean and relaxed. As usual he was hungry. He returned to the American food restaurant where he had eaten once before on the premise that no one would remember him. If anyone did remember him they certainly did not show it. He ate like a wolf and when he returned to the hotel he lay down to rest and fell sound asleep. Somewhere during the dark of night he had a silent visitor. It was almost impossible for him to believe but the sex was better than it was last night. He passed her ten dollars and she left as silently as she came.

At 1000 he left the breakfast diner. His car was there and the big man was holding the driver's door open for him. When Musher was settled in the car the big man reached through the window and put a shoe box size package in his lap. Sitting on top of the wrapped package were five one hundred dollar bills. "We would appreciate it if when you get into Colorado just find a small town and drop this package in the mail. Have a safe trip." With that he left, Musher pocketed the money and headed for the Biggs AFB dispensary. The dispensary staff was totally different than when he was last there but they were every bit as polite and accommodating.

When he left Biggs he drove the Baby Blue towards Denver. Along the route he came to a small town in Colorado named Willow Way. He dropped the shoebox in the outgoing parcel box and left town as quickly as possible without attracting attention. Since his first package drop he had lost some of his own discipline. He memorized the mailing and return addresses. During the drive he contemplated the contents of the package. He knew he was being unwise but being alone on a seven hundred plus mile drive one must do thinking or the trip would seem endless.

It was almost midnight when he checked in at the BOQ. The room wasn't any better than VAQ's he had stayed at during his enlisted years. He was so tired he didn't really care. Just get to bed and look at tomorrow when you wake up.

CHAPTER 217

Take a Vacation

In the morning at the VAQ desk he showed the clerk his orders assigning him to Lowry. The airman told him he would be staying in the student BOQ which was just next door. He paid his last night's one dollar BOQ fee, his eighty-four dollar twelve week BOQ fee, took the keys to his new room and went next door. The room was sparsely furnished but it was large enough, had good closet space and a private latrine with shower. It was on the first floor and coming in the back door it was only five steps from the entryway. It was only for twelve weeks.

In the well equipped dayroom he found many pamphlets describing the tourist places in and around Denver. To him one of the more interesting was the US Army Fitzsimmons Hospital and its eighteen hole golf course. Lowry did not have a golf course. Since he had not signed in and still had fourteen days before he must sign in on the fifteenth day maybe he would try the Fitz Golf Course after breakfast. At the O Club he was one of very few in civilian clothes. It brought a great many looks from the diners. "I need a new place for breakfast."

At the Fitz GC he was greeted most warmly. He explained that he was a student a Lowry but had almost two full weeks before he was due to sign in and he wanted to use his golf swing after a long layoff. The Fitz pro, Mickey Vane told him there were no caddies, no carts but he could rent or buy a pull cart. "This is a hospital golf course which exists strictly to help patients rehabilitate. What is your rank?"

"Second Lieutenant."

"It is four dollars a day green fees and you can play as much as want. The driving range is closed every day from 1000 to 1200 hours. Patients are on the range with instructors. Just about every day except Saturday and Sunday the course does not get much use. Weekends are different. If you want to play on the weekend tell me and I will fit you in some where. I am pro, starter, greens keeper and general flunky. I sneak out during the week when I can and I was just getting ready to go. Would you like to join me?"

The Fitz 19th hole did not have a bar or a restaurant. It had vending machines. Musher got two cokes and they sat to have a cigarette. Pro scored sixty-five and Musher sixty-eight. "For a guy with a long layoff and no warm-up you played pretty darn well. Have you played professionally?"

"No. I took up the game in Japan to rehabilitate from a Chinese prison camp about three years ago."

"At least three years in the air force and you are still a second lieutenant?"

"I have only been a second lieutenant for almost two months now. Before that I was a master sergeant with almost eleven years military service."

Musher played golf just about every day all day. He had most of his evening meals in the O-Club. In the O-Club stag bar there generally was a poker game every night. It was not a big game. It was usually five card stud, ten and twenty, three raise limit, two dollar ante with each player taking a turn dealing a hand. It was the kind of game where a good player could earn a living but never get rich. Musher watched and the big winner was a hustler. Not a good hustler but he was a hustler. He dealt seconds poorly and his palming technique was awful. Musher tinkered with the thought of busting his ass but told himself to mind his own business. If those dumb suckers wanted to give him their money that was not one of his concerns. Musher watched the game every night for three consecutive nights and it was always the same winner. The other players were not the same. There were so many student officers and officers here on TDY the O-Club could have four or five tables going at any time. For some reason there was only one. Each Friday night the table stakes went from ten and twenty to pot limit, five dollar ante, three raise limit, a five hundred dollar buy-in and each player taking a turn with the deal. It was time to get into the game. Everyone declared at least one thousand as their table buy except Cheap Hustler who declared three thousand and Musher who declared five thousand.

So many times during the game Musher wanted to defrock Cheap Hustler but that was not his intent. He let him keep cheating to win and build up his cash. There were no chips in this game it was all good old American Cash (Money orders and American Express traveler checks were acceptable) It came time. Seven players, three got trash, two playable first two cards, Cheap Hustler a good looking hand and Musher a potential winner. Things went as planned. Next card First player bet twenty-five. Numbers 2 and 3 folded. Cheap Hustler raised to one hundred twenty-five. Number 5 folded and number six raised to two hundred. Musher called, first player folded, Cheap Hustler bet one hundred. Number 6 raised to two hundred. Musher and Cheap Hustler called. The third and fourth cards were bet the same way.

On final card Cheap Hustler looked good. He could be holding a strong flush or a straight flush to the eight. He bet more than three quarters of all the money he had on the table. Number 6 folded. Musher asked Cheap Hustler to count his remaining money. He looked quizzically at Musher and Musher said, "I intend to raise you out of that chair." When he told how much money he still had in front of him Musher called his bet and raised the exact amount Cheap Hustler said he had left in front of him. Cheap Hustler was evaluating Musher's cards and told himself he probably has a straight flush but his up card says it could go to the nine. The longer he thought the more he convinced himself that Musher had a straight flush to the nine. Musher was prepared for whichever decision Cheap Hustler made. Cheap Hustler finally turned down his cards and did not call.

Musher laughed, turned over his cards and he had a pair of nines. As he was gathering the pot he said, "My boys my Uncle Fanucci once said it takes four things to be a successful gambler. One, a little luck. Two, a little skill. Three, the time to devote to winning; and Four, no fear of losing your money. Our friend lost one of the four and gave away the pot." Of course no one else knew it but Musher had palmed the card which would have turned his pair of nines into a nine high straight flush.

That single game provided enough cash to take care of all his expenses at Fitz or any where else in the Denver area. Come Friday morning he must sign in at Lowry.

CHAPTER 218

Munitions School

Musher had been processed in on time and was given a map of the school complex showing his classroom and was told to report there at 0730 hours Monday. At 0715 he was sitting in the classroom with his uniform fully decorated. There were six other second lieutenants also sitting there. They seemed to be a friendly group among themselves but also they seemed to ignore him. The classroom door opened and in came a Chief Warrant Officer in his fully decorated uniform. As the CWO perused the class Musher recognized that he knew the instructor and the instructor knew him.

"My name is Chief Warrant Officer William Park. I will be your instructor for the next twelve weeks. My background is aerial gunnery and I have been teaching this course for over three and one half years. We have class Monday through Friday from 0730 to 1130. What your schedule is after class will be decided today when you see the scheduling officer for the Basic Military Officer Training Course. Later I will give you a sheet showing the location of his office. You must report to him between 1300 and 1530 hours. Each Friday we will have an examination covering the course material. The content of the examination will be cumulative from today until the day before the examination. As college graduates with degrees in Engineering the air force expects that you will not make any less than an eighty percent grade on any single exam. If you fail any exam you will be given remedial training. If you fail the same exam on your next testing you will be removed from this training class. At the end of today's class I will give you a course syllabus and your study materials. We will try to keep the course as casual as possible. You may call me Mister Park or Chief. I will call you by your last name without a rank designator. Do any of you have a problem with that? Now let's tell each other a little about our selves. Begin with you. Please stand up."

"Robert Holden, ROTC (a four year college program named Reserve Officer Training Corp. Maybe one step above the Boy Scouts.), University of Texas, commissioned second lieutenant last Monday, reported for active duty last Friday. I graduated from U of T as a Civil Engineer, Magna Cum Laude, Hook 'Em Horns."

The other five were not much different. They were all ROTC graduates in some form of engineering and all were either Summa Cum Laude or

694

Magna Cum Laude. Each one had been an officer for seven days and this was his first day of active duty.

Then came Musher's turn. He stood in all the splendor of his uniform. "Saverio Muscarello, called by most people Musher. For over ten years I was an enlisted man, a master sergeant, an aerial gunner on B-29s, and a POW during the Korean War. I am highly decorated, I was commissioned from Officer Candidate School over a month ago, I am too old for flying school so I ended up here. I am a graduate of Kings College, University of Cambridge, England. I graduated Magna Cum Laude."

It was easy to sense the awe of the other students. Park broke the spell. "There is no smoking in the classroom. We will take a ten minute break in every hour. This is a good time for one. If you want to smoke you may step outside."

Musher was the first outside and in those ten minutes smoked two Lucky Strikes. The rest of the class mingled together and just basically ignored him. Alone again,.... naturally.

Class resumed and Park handed out a syllabus, an examination schedule, books, notebooks, study guides and practice exams. The morning was devoted to how to read a technical order, the USAF part numbering system and general discussion of the course.

At 1130 hours Park dismissed all of the class except Musher. When all the other students were gone Park came to Musher with handshakes and hugs. They had served in the same bomb wing at Smoky Hill AFB. Park had witnessed many of Musher's exploits in the NCO Club and had actually been a student in Musher's RCS CFCS class.

"Was Munitions the best you could do?"

"It's a long story. I pissed off a Brigadier and a full Colonel who were trying to help me and I wasn't smart enough to recognize it."

"Musher you understand that when you finish here you will be sent to a bomb dump to do administrative work. It will be on the right side of the flight line but in overall it will border on being a titless WAF."

"I will figure a way to change my AFSC when I finish here."

"Listen to me. There is a way if you want a high risk, high reward career. The top student of this class will be given a chance to attend the US Naval School for Explosive Ordnance Disposal. (EOD) You know, disarming bombs, recovering duds, disposing of dangerous munitions and lots of other good jobs."

"These kids are accustomed to studying. They don't have pussy on their minds. I doubt if I can compete with them."

"They can't beat you if you will use the Park system faithfully. Our tests are multiple guess and marked on a bubble sheet. When I give a test you will fill in the blanks about name, rank, serial number and class number. You will not darken one bubble on the answer sheet. You will look industrious during the test time period. You will not finish first nor will you finish last. When you turn in your answer sheet you will make sure you hand it to me face down. I will put my plastic marking template on your test and with my blue on one end red on the other pencil I will score your test. It will be no surprise to me that if you faithfully follow the Park system you will end this course without ever having missed a single test question. Fuck the ROTCie Officers. I can't help you with the Basic Military Officer Training Course. There you are on your own. The Captain in charge is another ROTCie. He is not rated (a pilot, navigator or aerial observer) and he has been in the air force less than three years. He wears his National Service Defense Medal (given to anyone on active duty for at least one year) as if it were a red badge of courage. Good luck. See you tomorrow, don't be late. You and me cannot socialize until you finish this school. Do you play golf? If you do maybe I will see you at Fitz on the weekend."

He was greeted by one of his classmates as he entered the dining room. "Come sit with us. Did Park hold you and give you hell?" That question was followed by a series of others mostly about his time in the air force. He dodged most of them. He did it by pretending he was interested in their college careers and time in ROTC. One of them asked the sixty-four dollar question. "Were you the one in the poker game last night who bought a very large pot on a pair of nines?"

"Guilty."

"We have been talking about your Uncle Fanucci's formula to avoid being a loser and being a winner. We have been questioning each other about it to make sure it stays in our long term memory. Do you play any other card games? Do you play bridge?"

Musher nodded yes and they left for the BMOC Training Officer. They were in a room with about twenty other second lieutenants while the Captain briefed the program. The briefing lasted almost an hour before he dismissed them and told them to be here tomorrow after class and lunch. Musher followed him to his office. Just before entering his office he turned to Musher, "Can I help you with something?"

"Sir, could I have a private minute in your office?"

"Come in and have a seat."

Musher remained standing and asked, "Captain can you see this blouse. I graduated from OCS just over a month ago. I am an ex-master sergeant, a

POW from the Korean War and have more time in the chow line of this man's air force than you have in the service. Do I look to you like after eleven years in the air force I need to attend a BMOC?"

"Well it is our policy that all second lieutenants attend the BMOC."

"Fuck your policy. Let me tell you my policy. When I encounter a titless WAF who proudly wears a single NSDM on his uniform and I think of when I bailed out of a burning B-29 over enemy territory I cannot hear his policy. Keep in mind I was once in the infantry and did more Close Order Drill in a day than you did marching in your ROTC unit in your entire college career. I have been serving my country since your mother was giving you an allowance. I promise you, if you order me to attend BMOC I will. I will disrupt that program so badly it will look like a failure. I will do it in such a manner as to make sure you do not have grounds to expel me. I had lunch with my classmates and they adore my background. What do think the other ROTCies will do when I undermine your instructors?"

"I can see you do not need the BMOC. You could join my staff and be a BMOC instructor."

"Fuck that. I have had all the training I need for quite some time."

"Here's my deal. When class dismisses and the others go to lunch you will disappear and not be seen around this air base. If your classmates question you why you are not at BMOC and what you are doing you better come up with some convincing stories. If any part of this agreement leaks out I will blacken my own eye and tell them you attacked me. I will insist on a court martial. Striking a superior officer can get you some serious time in Leavenworth. Now, get the fuck out of here!"

Musher followed his order. At the BOQ he changed clothes and went to Fitz to play a little golf.

CHAPTER 219

Dispatched Service With the U.S. Navy

The remainder of the twelve weeks of Munitions School was literally a walk in the Park. (No pun intended) He paid close attention in class, he looked studious and every now and again if he could figure out an intelligent question he asked it. None of his classmates were surprised when the final results were posted and Musher had not missed a single question on any examination. His classmates received assignments to various locations in the ZI (Zone of Interior, the lower forty-eight states). Musher's order gave him a five day delay enroute plus five days travel time to report to the Commanding Officer, US Naval Explosive Ordnance Disposal School, Indianhead, Maryland. In his Baby Blue it was seventeen hundred miles. He figured he could go to Junction City and see Priscilla that would cut five hundred miles so he could stay two nights and still have eight days to get to his assignment. From a phone both he told Priscilla of his plan.

"Sorry Musher. I remarried my ex-husband and I am afraid if he saw you he would kill you. I think of you often but it has been a long time since you said you would call. Drive safely." She hung up the phone. He smiled, "I can't win them all."

He debated driving to Georgia to see the Bilderbooks and show off his new commission and see Emily. That would be an extra five hundred miles. If he were going to drive an extra five hundred miles he would go to Boston to keep peace with the Godfather. Let's just steer the Baby Blue East and see what happens along the way. It was almost seventeen hundred miles to Andrews AFB in Washington D.C. It was major highway all the way. If he did ten hours actual driving today he would cover at least six hundred fifty miles, and do it again tomorrow that would be thirteen of the seventeen hundred. On the third day he would be in the BOQ at Andrews and could rest. Weather permitting he could play golf for four or five days. Indianhead was only about forty miles south of Andrews. At 1600 on the third day he checked into the BOQ. The room was very well furnished, large, with telephone service and private latrine. He had brought his chest of goodies into the room. In the large arm chair he opened a coke and picked on some goodies. He smoked a couple of Luckies and then lay on the bed to rest a minute. He awakened at 0200 still in his clothing. He just turned over and tried to go to sleep again.

Breakfast at the golf course was the prelude to his next four or five days. He talked to the starter about playing and emphasized his wish to play with a five dollar bill. "Pay your fees and I will call you on the P.A. system if you are on the range. What's your handicap?"

"My handicap is Zero and yes I do like to wager on the game."

"It won't be any trouble getting you off. The money players generally play between 0830 and 0930. We do not have caddies. When I have a game for you I will call you. Give me a name to call."

"Just call me Musher." He had time to hit a bucket and do some practice putting before his name was called.

"These gentlemen will be your playing partners. This is Patrick Hauge, Jeff Miller and John Spurgin. Our new guest is called Musher. Everyone is scratch so it should be a good round. Please give me a ball so I can toss for tee off order on the first tee."

They had about six minutes to wait. Jeff said to Musher, "We usually play ten dollar Nassau because there are generally only we three. With you here we could play sixes. Do you have a problem playing fifty dollar sixes?"

"My only problem is if you don't accept American money." They all chuckled.

Musher worked very hard to make sure he was on the winning team for all three sixes. It was not easy to do that and still keep his score from being too low. It was only a hundred fifty dollar win but that will pay golf expenses for today. They were sitting in the 19th Hole when Jeff said, "You have a great looking swing and touch. Have you played professionally?"

"No, never. This is only my second year of playing. I started learning as a therapy when I was recovering in Japan."

Jeff continued, "These guys can't play tomorrow but I can. Would you like to join me at say 0900?" He and the others started to rise to leave. Musher grabbed the lunch check, "Winner's pleasure. Jeff, I will be here in the morning."

Musher played every day for four days. Every day he won enough money to pay expenses. Most of the guys he played with carried a one, two, three or four handicap and generally could not play to it. Musher gave strokes and controlled the Nassau bets so it was, "If I had made that one putt I would have beaten you Musher", or "If you hadn't made that lucky chip in I would have beaten you Musher." At the end of the fourth day's playing he announced that today was his last round because tomorrow he must go to Indianhead and sign in to the EOD School.

CHAPTER 220

Explosive Ordnance Disposal

It was 1025 hours when Musher stopped at the entrance gate to the United States Naval Propellant Plant, Indianhead, Maryland. The gate sentry was a US Marine looking splendidly like a recruiting poster model. Musher showed his orders and was directed to the office of the USAF Liaison Officer. He parked as close as he could and entered the building where the USAF Liaison office was located. Just inside the entrance was the quarterdeck (Naval term for where the receptionist controls access into the building). He checked Musher's orders and buzzed someone on the phone. In a few minutes a staff sergeant came to the access door, the quarterdeck Petty Officer buzzed the access door and Musher moved inside. "Sir, I am Staff Sergeant Johnston Ihrig, clerk in the Liaison Office. Please come this way." He escorted him to the Liaison Officer who took Musher's salute and then stood, "I am Lieutenant Colonel Willard Peterson. Welcome to EOD School. Please sit. Smoke if you like while he relit his pipe.

Your class begins Monday. Today Ihrig will get you signed-in, a school identification card and setup in the BOQ and generally tell you where everything is on this station. Tomorrow morning, the first Saturday of every month, the Naval Commander of this school holds a personnel inspection. Full Class "A" uniform with authorized decorations. You report here at 0730. Inspection is at 0830. After inspection you are free until your first class day, Monday. The first part of the training course is held in this building. Classroom hours are from 0800 to 1630 with breaks in between. The school uniform is fatigues and brogans. Flying suits are not permitted but organizational head gear (baseball caps) is. I will probably only see you on inspection days or if you need something from me. Good Luck. You have two very important things to remember. We are guests of the US Navy and they write the rules. The other, failure of this course will probably get your commission revoked and you out of the USAF." He stuck out his hand to shake, Musher saluted and left his office.

After answering a ton of questions and signing another ton of papers Ihrig handed him an EOD School I.D. showing his name, rank, serial number and class number. EODS 58D. "Shall we go?"

Ihrig had him drive around the station pointing out the various items he felt Musher need to know. One of the places they past, cuddled inside the base housing area was a nine-hole golf course.

"Is the golf course active?"

"Not so much during the week because everybody is working and the students don't have time to play but on weekends there is always something doing. The officers' wives probably use it more than anyone else. It is only a nine hole with two tee boxes for each hole. It is fairly well maintained and there is no charge to use it. There are no golf carts it is either pull or carry your golf clubs yourself. There is no clubhouse just a small building with a few golf supplies and a head. (Head is the Navy term for latrine, or bathroom) Sir, do you play golf? The school Skipper (Navy for commanding officer) is a golf fanatic. During the week he must go to at least three or four other places to play."

In front of the BOQ Ihrig said, "Registration is just inside the door. Enlisted men are not allowed in the BOQ unless directly ordered to do so. After you register there will be a couple of "white hats" (Enlisted men below the grade of Chief) to help you with your baggage and direct you to the student parking lot. You can see the BOQ is directly across the main street from the Officers Club. It is also less than a ten minute brisk walk from the main school building and our office. The BOQ rooms do not have telephones but there are base telephones and pay phone booths in the large day rooms on each of the three floors. Our office extension is written on a number of the papers that I gave you. If I can be of any help please call me."

Musher would be on the third floor (there were no elevators) and he would share his room with another member of the class. Whoever signs in next is his room mate. There were already six other officers signed in for EODS 58-D. He was provided a room key, a mail box number and a mailbox key. He signed a paper authorizing the BOQ to have the air force pay his monthly "Comrats Allowance" (the amount of money paid to an officer for eating meals at his own expense). The dining hall was on the first floor. He was advised that the air force would be billed whether he ate there or not. Dining hours were posted at the entrance and he was given a copy of the serving times. He was also given a menu for the remainder of the month and told he would get an updated menu in his mail box every two weeks. Laundry service is available for two dollars weekly. Drop well identified laundry into the laundry chute on his floor every Monday and it will be returned on Thursday. The "Maid and Towel Service" was one dollar per day. There was a community Head and Showers on each floor. He was expected to settle his BOQ account on the last day of each month.

Two white hats helped him get his gear to his room. He overrode their objections when he gave each a ten dollar tip. He took his car to the student parking lot and removed all the cash stashed in various locations. As he

701

climbed the three flights of stairs to his room he thought, "I would not want to do this many times each day."

At dinner he sat with three other air force officers. Two captains and a first lieutenant. They were not members of his class and if nothing went wrong they would finish the twenty-two week school in less than five weeks. They were in the nuclear weapons half of the school training and told just how difficult it is. After dinner they would go back to the school to study and would study all weekend for Monday's examination. "I better enjoy this weekend it doesn't sound like there will be many more for the next five months." He climbed those three flights, showered and went to bed.

CHAPTER 221

Let the Good Times Begin

He was early for inspection formation. He was greeted by Ihrig holding a "MUSCARELLO" name tag. "I noticed yesterday you did not have one. The Skipper is anal about detail so I figured I would get you one. You owe me two dollars." With that he pinned it on Musher's blouse. Musher handed him a twenty and said, "Give me the change when I ask for it."

The inspection was not very stringent. Musher had groomed for an OCS inspection. The actual inspection time was less than thirty minutes. The troops were excused by 0915. What to do until Monday? He decided he would try the on station golf course. When he pulled into the small, unsurfaced parking lot there was still some space for cars. He signed the golf course log which recorded play and was told to either see if there were others he could join or he could go out alone when the first tee was open. Not very much discipline regarding the play but the course was here for enjoyment. There was no driving range or practice putting green.

As he was standing outside a threesome was just making the turn for their second nine. The apparent leader asked, "Are you alone. If you are you are welcome to join us for the back nine." Musher viewed this as a chance to meet new permanent party personnel.

"I would very much like to. My name is Saverio Muscarello but everybody calls me Musher."

"I am Roland Brownstone, that is Stanley Cashew and he is Angelo Montano. We are going to hit the head and grab a coke. We will go very shortly."

Musher studied the first hole. It was a par three of one hundred fifty-three yards from an extremely elevated tee box. When the group teed off each hit a seven iron. All were in the frog hair surrounding the green. Musher hit a wedge to the center of the green. No one said anything but all three looked at him with, "Are you kidding me man?" The green required a lot of work. Musher managed to make par while all three made bogey. This green is not a test of anyone's putting skill. All the holes were short including the two par fives. On one Musher hit drive and eight iron and on the other drive and seven iron. He had difficulty putting but still shot thirty-two for the nine. There were some tables set in the shade of the trees around the first tee area. The three were settling their Bingo-Bango-Bongo debts from the round. (A game played by amateurs for longest drives, first on

703

greens, least amount of putts on the hole. Usually played for anywhere from ten cents to twenty-five cents a point)

While they were sitting smoking and drinking cokes Musher was bombarded by the same questions. "Had he played professionally?" etc. He gave his stock answers. "We will play tomorrow morning at 0800 if you care to join us."

"It will be my pleasure."

"You mentioned that you were staying in the BOQ. We presume you are one of the new EOD students for the class that begins Monday. We are not affiliated with the school. We work on the other side of the Plant. Listen tonight there is a dinner dance at the club. If you wish come to dinner with us and our wives. Cocktails are at 1900, dinner at 2000. The occasion is formal. If you don't have formal attire your dress uniform will be OK." They shook hands with Musher and Brownstone said, "Don't forget tomorrow morning."

Musher asked the petty officer at the BOQ registration desk, "My Mess Dress (the air force term for its most formal uniform) badly needs steaming and pressing. I want to go the O-Club function tonight but the way it looks I wouldn't be seen in it in my own room. Is there a place where I can get it steamed and pressed and my dress shirt pressed?"

"Sir there is no such place on the station; however, we have a couple of stewards (Navy enlisted men) here who are as good as any commercial cleaner in the country. Tell me your room number, I will give you ten minutes then one of the stewards will come to get your garments. Be sure to give him your uniform plus cummerbund and shoes. He will return them all in less than two hours. "

"That's great. How do I pay him?"

"Sir this is not a service provided by the US Navy. This is something the stewards do to make a little extra money."

"Can you suggest an amount?"

"Sir, anything less than ten dollars would be insulting to them. If you wish to ingratiate them and have them eager to do your bidding this is your chance to show how much you appreciate their efforts."

"Musher thanked him and left a ten dollar bill on the counter as he started up the stairs.

At the O Club Musher went to the bar for a seven-up and lime. He gave the bartender ten dollars and told him the routine for the order "gin and tonic". "Run me a tab and I will catch you before I leave." He approached the maitre d' etre and asked for Bobby Brownstone.

"Do you mean Commander Brownstone?" His group was already seated in the dining room having a drink at the table. He approached them and noted the table was set for eight. The men rose, Stanley Cashew was Lieutenant Commander Stanley Cashew, Executive Officer for Commander Brownstone. Angelo Montano was Major Angelo Montano US Army, Commanding Officer of a Liaison Group.

Commander Brownstone, "Ladies this is USAF Second Lieutenant Saverio Muscarello, but we all call him Musher." He pointed, "My wife Bunny, Missus Cashew, Bonnie and Missus Montano, Maria. Please sit and let me order you a drink."

"No thank you sir. I already have one and I must confess I am not much of a drinker at all."   "We have been telling the ladies about your beautiful golf swing and if I could play as you do I would be out of this man's US Navy just as quickly as I could be. It is amazing that you have only been playing for such a short time. What is your secret?"

"Sir, I don't have a secret. Like every other sport, if you have hand eye coordination and work at it you will be better than average in a very short time. I worked at it diligently and still work at it every chance I get."

"Have you met the school Skipper yet? When we tell him about his newest student he will bubble. Be careful he will have you out playing golf when you should be studying. We three are all EOD qualified and know from first hand just how tough the course is. For tonight, eat, drink and be merry."

The dinner conversation was gay and Musher danced with all the ladies. About 2130 a striking brunette joined the table. Now he knew what the eighth place setting was for and why they wanted him to join them for dinner. "Musher, this is my sister-in-law Nirvana Brownstone." When all the girls were at the powder room Brownstone told Musher that Nirvana was a widow. Her husband had been a sub-mariner and was in the accident at the North Pole. It was almost two years ago and she just recently has been going places with them. When the girls returned Musher began dancing with Nirvana. The two of them danced and talked as if there was no one else in the room. When the evening ended Musher told Nirvana he wanted to see her again.

"Tomorrow afternoon if you want to see me again."

"I could play chauffeur and you could show me all the places outside this station. I am playing golf with the boys and I should be able to shower and be wherever you are staying by one-thirty. I heard you say you were staying with Commander Brownstone. Shall I come get you about two?"

"I will be waiting for you."

705

There were hand shakes and light kisses good-night. "See you on the tee in the morning."

Musher walked back to his BOQ and climbed the three flights of stairs. As he lay in bed the only thing on his mind was Nirvana. He felt about her very differently than he had ever felt about any woman.

CHAPTER 222

Life Style Changes Tomorrow

"There is no intelligent bet we can make with you. We have our Bingo-Bango-Bongo but you would eat us up alive. The only gambling golfer around is the school skipper."

"You guys make your bets and I will just practice. I am thankful for the company. Speaking of company your sister-in-law is really something special. We are going on the local tour after lunch."

"We know, we know. That's all she has talked about is Musher this and Musher that. You really impressed her."

He played and practiced but his mind was not on the game. After the round they could tell he was itchy.

At 1330 sharp he parked the Baby Blue at Brownstone's house. She heard the car and came out in a white halter, bare midriff and white shorts. Musher was struck. He had difficulty getting out of the car to hold the door for her. When he was back in the car she leaned over and kissed him lightly on the cheek. "What say Musher, shall we begin with the Lincoln Memorial?" It seemed they had just parked the car and started sightseeing when it was already six o'clock. She suggested, "Let's go to Waldorf."

"I will go with you any place you want to go."

Route 301 took them to Waldorf. Remember the saying, *"You can get your kicks on Route 66, but you get your fun on Route 301."*

They went for Maryland style crabs to a crab house in Pope's Creek. Musher had never had a spicy Maryland Crab but after that meal he vowed to do it over and over again. The only drawback to such a meal is that you must work to open the crab and extract the meat inside. One of its advantages was that it was slow eating and gave lots of time for conversation. The crabs and drinks were so cheap he felt like he was stealing. Slot machines were legal on 301 and in the restaurant they were going full bore from the time they walked into the crab house until they left. It reminded him of Tachikawa where the slot machines were so profitable the NCO Club had to almost give things away to stay within their allowable profit limit.

At her door she thanked him for a wonderful day. He took her in his arms and kissed her. This kiss was different from any other kiss he had known. He knew the sensation of a lust kiss, a sex kiss and this was neither. It was a warm blending of two personalities into one body. "Tomorrow I start school and if it is everything I have heard there is no telling when I will get the chance to see you again. I will call. Better I should go now before we do something we will regret later."

It took some time before he could fall asleep.

CHAPTER 223
This Is a Tough Twenty-two Week Course

Musher's class assembled in the briefing room. The class size was thirteen, three air force captains, two air force lieutenants, one army lieutenant, five air force enlisted men, one army enlisted man and one navy enlisted man. A whispered Ten Hut brought them to their feet.

"As you were. My name is Commander Ted Coody. I am the commanding officer of this school. I sometimes favor a day off but rarely. I say that to you because for the next twenty-two calendar weeks you will be thankful for the few days off and what little time you find for yourself. It is no secret that this is a tough. tough course. I and the rest of the staff are here to help you through the tough times. We want you to pass. If you were not the best your service has to offer, you would not be here. If you did not have the nerve to be willing to face an explosive device designed to kill you, you would not be here. If you had not already shown your commitment to the United States military forces, you would not be here. I want to leave you with two thoughts. Number 1 forget about any type of social life while you are a student; and Number 2, when you think you have studied long enough, study for another hour." With that closing he left the room.

The next person to come into the room introduced himself as Lieutenant Maximillian (Max) Gomez. (A US Navy Lieutenant is the same rank as a Captain in the three other services) I am the Curriculum and Standards Officer for the school. You will receive a syllabus for the course but let me give you a brief picture.

Twenty-two weeks from today you will finish the course. Phase I, the first nine weeks will be devoted to conventional weapons, the common term for which is "iron". Those nine weeks will take place in this compound. The next two weeks will be spent learning "Rigging and Digging" (explosive devices recovery methods), booby-traps and sabotage. That section of the course is taught at a location here on the propellant plant property known as "Stump Neck". The final test for Phase I will be held with live explosives on one of the demolition ranges at Eglin Air Force Base in Florida. That test including travel will last for one week. You will be given five school days off between Phase I and Phase II.

Phase II will make you capable of working with Nuclear Weapons. You will learn the outside and inside of every nuclear weapon in the United States arsenal and each weapon's rendering safe procedure in the event of an inadvertent arming of the weapon. To protect our country, while you are in Phase I you will be investigated to receive a higher security clearance than Top Secret. It is called "CNWDI", Critical Nuclear Weapons Design Information. Without that clearance you will not be allowed into Phase II. During your five school days off you will receive new security badges. Phase II is taught in the secure sally-port (a physical enclosure completely enclosed with heavy duty wire consisting of two gates. One person at a time is in the sally port while credentials are verified) building across from here. It is referred to as "Division 6".

Throughout each phase you will be given weekly examinations. The minimum passing score on any examination is seventy. In the event you fail an examination you will be given tutoring and study time to retake the examination. If you fail the retake you will appear before an evaluation board to determine if you should be held back or dismissed from the school. Obviously since attendance at this school is voluntary you can withdraw from this school and return to your unit at any time you choose. When you complete the school both officers and enlisted men will receive an effectiveness report for their personnel file.

Scheduled classes are from Monday to Friday beginning at 0800 hours and ending at 1645 hours with a forty-five minute break for lunch. Generally speaking individual classes are for fifty minutes and whenever possible you will be given a ten minute break between classes. If you wish you may "brown bag" your lunch. There are areas in the building lunch room located on this floor where your properly identified lunch may be stored including refrigerator space. There are also vending machines but no change makers. The building lunch room is a designated smoking area. Smoking is allowed only in the designated areas.

While you are in the student mode in the classroom environment you will be addressed by your last name without your rank. Each instructor will tell you how he wishes to be addressed. Each class must have a Class Leader. Your most senior officer is USAF Captain Walter Moon and ergo your class leader. Congratulations Captain. Today we are as lenient as we will get throughout the course. It's 1030 hours let's adjourn to the lunch room and when I finish this paperwork I will come get you and show the way to your first class."

In the twelve minutes it took Max to return Musher smoked three Lucky Strikes. The class was mingling and commenting about the start of today. Captain Moon was so layback he hardly whispered when he spoke. When asked to speak louder he joked, "I never really say anything important enough to hear."

The first class set the tone for the course. The instructor, Master Sergeant David Addicott, US Army was in fatigues which were pressed to perfection. "As long as you are in this class I want you to sit in the same seat you are in now unless I direct you otherwise. Today we will start with the identification of US bombs delivered by aircraft. On each desk is notebook filled with lined paper. There is also a book entitled "US Bombs Delivered by Aircraft"(USBDbyA). We shall go through that book chapter by chapter and you may make whatever supplemental notes you may need. Do not be bashful, if there is something I have not made clear or you don't understand, stop me and we will discuss it. The only thing that matters is that you learn. Who knows, one day you may be my partner in the field and I want to know you know what you are doing." We started with chapter 1 and went until he said, "Lunch break. Be in your seat NLT 1245 hours."

Musher was so hungry he practically ran to the BOQ. The staff was ready for the students. Lunch was served quickly and was very good. He ate like a wolf and it was only 1220 hours. He went to talk with the same petty officer who had helped him with his mess dress and said, "Running here from the school for lunch is a pain in the ass is there anything we can do?"

"Sir the boys make a few dollars packing box lunches which are delicious. They charge three dollars for each lunch because they buy the ingredients rather than steal from the Navy. They label each box and it is ready at breakfast each school day."

"How do I sign up?"

"You pay me two weeks in advance and I take care of all the details."

"Two weeks is five times three times two or thirty dollars." Musher reached into his pockets and counted out six hundred fifty dollars. "Here is my enrollment fee for the next twenty weeks and a fifty dollar gratuity for you for being so knowledgeable and supportive. I do not need a receipt. Are we together on this?"

"Sir, consider it done. I thank you on behalf of the stewards and above all a big thank you from me."

Musher was in his seat at 1240 hours. He had a good lunch and some Luckies and would have preferred to lie down for a nap. When Addicott came into the room he took the roll with one glance and immediately started where he had left off at lunch. He was a good instructor. He kept the explanations from being dry by introducing the various explosives used in each bomb and where in WWI or WWII the bomb may have been used and its aircraft delivery system. At 1600 he stopped talking and announced, "We are going to have a little quiz to see what you have learned and remember about what we have covered today. It is not multiple guess. Use your notebook paper to write your answers. There are only ten questions and you have twenty minutes. Begin when you receive the questionnaire."

At 1620, "Please put your pencils down. Here's the plan. I will tell you the correct answer. When we leave you will take your unclassified USBDbyA book to your billet and will get the page and figure number which explains the answer. First thing tomorrow we will discuss the answers. Class dismissed."

Walking back to the BOQ with Captain Moon, the class leader, he asked, "Do you agree that this is only the beginning difficulty level and it will get a lot tougher?"

"I would hope so. So far it is easy to understand."

He had time before dinner to call Nirvana. When she answered he tensed. He couldn't understand the feeling but he loved it. "Hi, I have a little time before dinner and wanted to talk with you. I cannot get you off my mind. I have never felt like this."

"I am afraid I am in the same boat. I was useless at work today my mind continually drifted to yesterday and you. Can I see you tonight?"

"I am afraid not. I have two tons of homework and studying to do. I don't want to fail and I am sure you don't want me to fail."

"By no means. I was warned that you would not have much of a life as a student." From that point on they coo-ed and made small talk until Musher said the dinner bell was ringing. "If I can I will call you tomorrow. Please take care of yourself and know that every moment of weakness is devoted to thinking of you. Kiss, kiss, goodbye."

After dinner Musher worked on his assignment. It was not difficult but it was time consuming. The worst part was that of the ten questions he had missed four. That would be a failing grade. He cannot afford that. When he finally got to shower and get in bed his head ran those four missed questions by time and time again. His sleep was fitful. He had never failed any exam before.

CHAPTER 224

Nine Weeks Is an Eternity

The entire nine weeks of Phase I required all the time Musher had just to absorb it all and give the correct answers to questions. Not only did they learn the US munitions but munitions from countries all over the world. When they studied fuzes they were required to know which fuze generally went with which bomb, how the fuze worked and how it could be rendered safe. Close to the end of the nine weeks they were given an examination which consisted of one hundred pieces of material. They were required to answer the most probable source of each piece and its probable use. Musher was thrilled to pass that one and even more thrilled to have made eighty-two.

Starting this coming Monday they would begin two weeks training at Stump Neck. The days became longer because of the bus rides to and from the Stump Neck area. The cold weather was settling in and Stump Neck bordered the Potomac River. Every day the instruction staff would booby trap just about everything which the students would be exposed to. When you missed a booby trap or failed to render it safe properly a flash bulb would go off and everyone would yell "Hoorah". He learned that with the exception of electrically controlled explosive initiation there were only four ways a detonation could be set off. They are Pull something, Push something, Pull and Push something and Push and Pull something.

The hardest, coldest part of the two weeks was Rigging and Digging. In the woods that surrounded Stump Neck a bomb with an active fuze was buried three feet in the ground. The entry path was visible but there was no knowledge given about the type of bomb. It was a class project and the class was provided two shovels, two axes, one pulley and one hundred feet of rope. The task was to defuse and extract the bomb with the tools provided. They began the project first thing in the morning and the class day would only end when they finish the project. A member of the class, Lieutenant Stephen Richards, U S Army was a civil engineer by profession. He took command of the project and everyone else subordinated their thoughts on how to do the job. He briefed the class on his plan. Extensive digging and earth moving was required and every member took turns. By lunch the bomb and the fuze were visible. They agreed on the type and name of the bomb and the rendering safe procedure (RSP). They had been told the bomb was live and so was the fuze. Captain Walter Moon spoke *the EOD Creed,*

713

"He who makes the most money takes the biggest risks." He instructed the rest of the team to withdraw to safe cover and he went into the hole. The RSP said to use his hand to unscrew the fuze being careful not to press on the fuze nose. It took a couple of tries before Moon could firmly but gently grasp the fuze. He turned it out and climbed out of the hole holding the fuze above his head like the Olympic Torch. He was greeted by cheers. With the fuze arming pin replaced by a nail found in the area it was securely placed where it presented no danger.

Richards declared the hard part was done and this was a good time for lunch and cigarettes. They pooled their foodstuffs and water, ate lunch and smoked cigarettes. Back at the site they rigged a tripod of chopped trees, hung the pulley and passed the rope through it. The bomb was knotted with the rope and pulled from the hole. The RSP for the bomb was PUCA (Pick Up and Carry Away).

As if they were being constantly watched when they had the area secure two instructors appeared and congratulated them on a job well done. They were commended for the efforts as a team and Captain Moon's execution of the EOD Creed. When they were back in the warm classroom shack Musher asked the Navy Chief in Charge, "Chief do we have any coffee?"

"In the corner."

"Chief, where is the cream and sugar?"

Musher was looking towards the Chief whose head appeared to be on a swivel when he turned and stared at Musher and bellowed, "Sonny, anybody who needs cream and sugar doesn't need coffee!" A truly memorable moment.

What a great way to end Stump Neck.

Tomorrow they would be bussed to Pawtuxket Naval Air Station where they would board a Naval transport flight to Eglin AFB, Florida. The TDY (or in Navy terms DS (dispatched service) was for a week. Maybe they would get to relax. How wrong can one guy be. From the moment they were billeted the training and testing began. The first afternoon following a short orientation they learned the proper method for disposing of small caliber ammunition. They actually burned a significant quantity. Dinner was structured. The entire class ate in the enlisted dining hall. In the day room of their quarters they had a class on anti-disturbance butterfly bombs and the various methods which could be used to clear a contaminated site.

The next day began at 0500. They were billeted in a squad bay and each was responsible for his area. After breakfast they rode a bus for over an hour out to one of the explosive disposal ranges located in far reaches of Eglin AFB. The observation bunker, designed to protect its inhabitants from any detonations on the range, contained a classroom. They were briefed on the twenty pound fragmentation bomb with the seven degree mushroom fuze installed. These were anti-personnel bombs which armed the minute they left the bomb rack and the safety wire was pulled. If they did not detonate on contact and lay on the terrain any seven degree movement of the fuze in any direction would most probably cause detonation. The RSP for this fuze was the use of Dental Plaster of Paris. Build a trough around the fuze and another test trough in close proximity. Fill the fuze trough with Dental Plaster of Paris at sufficient depth for it to enter the fuze access where the arming wire had been withdrawn. Let the DP of Paris harden and it will prevent the firing pin from reaching the first phase of explosive. Fill the test trough with the same DP of P and use that to know when the DP of P is sufficiently hard to unscrew the fuze from the bomb without a detonation.

The instructor demonstrated the procedure. The class adjourned to the bunker observation window. "Most students think they are doing this exercise with inert fuzes and bombs. Captain Moon there are eight different setups on the range. Take this Carbine and fire at any one of them. Do not try to hit the bomb, just its surrounding area. Tell me the number of your target."

Moon went to the firing position, said "Six" and fired. The bomb detonated.

"Now gentlemen if any of you wish to withdraw from this examination, please do so now." There were some wavering looks but no one withdrew. "We have your thirteen names in this hat. Each of you will draw one and he will be you partner for this exercise. I will partner with the thirteenth name."

Musher drew Gunners Mate Petty Officer First Class James Fricke. Each team was given DP of P, one quart of water and a Kabar (combat) knife. Musher said, "In accordance with the creed I will honcho the first exercise. You will be my observer and keep me from doing something stupid." Only one team at a time was allowed on the range. Musher was eager so he volunteered to be first. He had no trouble making the troughs or mixing the DP of P. He gritted his teeth as the DP of P poured into the fuze. Within five minutes the test trough was so hard it could not be penetrated with the Kabar. "OK Fricke, go back to the bunker. There is no need here for the two of us." Fricke did not hesitate to leave.

Musher felt a sensation which he thought was the same as Moon's when it was time to unscrew the fuze. It took him three times to wrap his hand around the fuze and unscrew it. When he withdrew the fuze it did not go boom so he knew he was successful. According to instructions he brought the fuze, the bomb and the remaining supplies back to the observation bunker. Musher looked at the clock in the bunker, they had been at their site for thirty-two minutes. The next team went onto the range. The cycle was repeated until all teams had done one RSP. With the exception of one person each of the class members completed the exercise. The air force captain who had worked in base supply could not bring himself to unscrew the fuze. At the end of the day when they returned to their billet the captain was gone. The class had gone from a Baker's Dozen to an even dozen. The stress of the day had Musher exhausted. After dinner he did his SSS and went to bed.

In the EOD building day room Captain Bernie Rabbit spoke. "Today we will strip and dispose of rockets." Only God knows how many rockets they stripped and burned. They were also shown how the rocket motor could be used as disposal explosive. At the end of the day it seemed the class had barely dented the pile of 2.75 Pod Fired rockets. It was the rocket of choice for training fighter pilots.

The third and fourth day were devoted to the use of TNT, C-4 Plastic explosive and prima cord. On the morning of the fifth day there was a critique of the week's activities. Everyone had been waiting for a written exam. Captain Bernie Rabbit told them that when they passed the M-20 defusing they had passed the course. Later that afternoon they boarded for the flight back to Pawtuxket NAS. When the bus from Pawtuxket pulled up in front of the EOD building the class was told, "You have Saturday and Sunday off. Report to Division 6 at 0730 hours Monday morning. Do not forget your security badge."

Musher could not wait to call and see Nirvana. He did a quick SSS and was at Brownie's door in less than forty-five minutes. When she answered the door he grabbed her and kissed her and then kissed her again.

"Please Musher, what will the neighbors think?"

He thought about Rod but could not say it, but he could think it, "Fuck 'em and feed 'em frijoles." They drove out the main gate and headed for dinner in Washington. In a small, quiet restaurant he whispered, "Nirvana I love you. Will you marry me?"

"I love you. Yes I am joyous about marrying you."

"I have nine more difficult weeks of school. If you will wait we will be married as soon as I finish. Tomorrow we will come back to Washington and I will buy you an engagement ring."

"She looked at him and coyly said, "Why make that awful trip. Why don't we just stay in Washington tonight?"

CHAPTER 225

Big Time EOD

Musher and friends were at the Division 6 sally port at 0730. As they were passed through they were directed to a classroom. When the class was convened there were now only ten. One of the air force enlisted men did not receive his CNWDI clearance. The blackboard read "Introduction to Nuclear Physics for Nuclear Weapons Design." Along side it said, "Captain Marco DiPaulo."

"These next two weeks will be devoted to your learning of the elements of a nuclear weapon, how and why it works and making you sufficiently knowledgeable to discuss nuclear weapons. You will the learn the element chart symbols for elements in a nuclear weapon, you will learn about fusion and fission, explosive implosion, nuclear generators, barometric devices and the "Y" curve. These two weeks will be equal to one semester of nuclear physics in most any college in the United States. Since all this material here in Division 6 is classified top secret or higher you must come here to study and study you must if you expect to pass. Does anyone in this group have a degree in nuclear physics? We will have a quiz every morning concerning all the material we covered up to the end of the class the day before. These quizzes will not be graded or marked for or against you. The serious exams will come each of the next two Fridays at 1500 hours. I am sure you all know the consequences for failure. Each night after dinner Musher and all but one of the rest of his class came back to Division 6 to study. It was obvious that one air force sergeant had resigned himself to the fact that he could not pass the Intro course. He would prefer it be said the nuclear physics was too much for him rather than he voluntarily dropped from the school. The remaining classmates also studied the first full weekend. The study and the ungraded daily quizzes were the primary reason the nine in the class passed.

There was a two day break before the cooker pot began again on Monday. Musher was determined to spend his two days with Nirvana. They set the wedding date and she started making arrangements for a reception at the O-Club. The Brownstone family was happy they liked Musher.

The next seven weeks of nuclear weapons training were mind boggling. Every moment not in class was spent studying. He managed to squeeze in some phone calls but he had not seen Nirvana since the two day break. Today the scores for yesterday's final examination in Division 6 were posted. Everyone passed, some better than others, but everyone passed. Tomorrow he would get his certificate of successful completion, his EOD breast pocket badge and his new assignment orders. The class was sitting in the day room drinking cokes and smoking cigarettes. It reminded him of his OCS days when they had Community Study and Review. (CSR: otherwise known as Cokes, Smokes and Relax). He was approached by a yeoman who told him Commander Brownstone needed to see him and was waiting across the street in the other EOD building. The watch on the quarterdeck told him which room the Commander was in and Musher burst through the door laughing and hugging Mrs. Brownstone. What was she doing here? The Commander asked Musher to sit.

"There isn't any easy way to say this. Nirvana was driving to Washington to buy some things for the wedding and your honeymoon when an oncoming car crossed into her lane and there was a head-on collision."

"How badly was she hurt? Is she in the hospital? Why are we sitting here, let's go!"

"Musher, I am afraid she was killed. She was dead at the scene."

Musher rocked in his chair incapable of accepting Brown's statement as truth. He broke down and amidst his tears, "It can't be we are getting married tomorrow evening. Everything is set. There must be a mistake. Was the identification positive? Did the other car driver son-of-a-bitch die too. If he hasn't he soon will."

"The four people in the other car were also killed on the scene. Why don't we go to my house and settle down as much as we can?" The three of them went to Brownie's house but everything reminded him of Nirvana and he just couldn't take it. It was raining outside but that meant nothing to him as he walked towards the BOQ. He locked the door to his room and used a chair to brace it from opening. He lay on the bed and cried himself to sleep. The next day there was a memorial service in the base chapel but Musher was too deeply destroyed to attend. For three days he stayed in his room without eating, a bath or even a cup of coffee. He did not care if he lived or died. *Unsurprisingly he was alone again.*

CHAPTER 226
I Need To Get It Back Together

On the morning of the fourth day he looked in the latrine mirror and said out loud, "You have been fucked before and you always manage to get up and fight." He did his SSS and he almost looked human. He called Sergeant Ilhrig at the USAF Liaison office and asked him if he could bring to his room all the papers he needed to sign and check out from EOD School. The next call was to the yeoman at the registration desk. When he identified himself there was a sincere tone of happiness in the yeoman's voice. "Could your stewards do two things for me? Bring me a very healthy breakfast and wash and service my car so I can get on the road?" Very quickly he was eating a large American breakfast. He had not finished eating when Sergeant Ihrig was at his door. He expressed his sincere condolences. All his papers were in one folder. His new assignment was England AFB, Alexandria, Louisiana. Heaven knows how many papers he signed. The important facts were he had a certificate of completion from EOD School, a new badge for his breast, a five day delay enroute and four days POV travel time When he finished with Ihrig he gave Ihrig a one hundred dollar bill and his thanks for all his support through school. The stewards helped him get his gear into the Baby Blue. At the yeoman's desk he was told his account had a credit balance and he was entitled to a refund. He told the yeoman to keep it and in addition he placed five one hundred dollar bills. "This is for you and the stewards. Again, I thank you all."

In his car he sat extremely depressed. He had no one he could turn to for love and understanding. He decided he would take the shuttle from Washington National to Logan, rent a car and surprise sweet sister. He would spend tonight and two more days with her and on the fourth day take the shuttle back to Washington National. That would give him five and one half days to cover the twelve hundred miles to Alexandria, Louisiana and still another day in the event of a mishap or emergency.

Sweet Sister answered the door and she looked at him in awe. "You are so handsome and an officer in the air force. Come in, come in." She hugged and kissed him and for the first time noticed he had his B-4 bag in his hand. "The boys will double up and you can take the elder's room. How long can you stay with us? My husband and the boys are at a school hockey game and won't be back for at least three hours." She guided him to the elder boy's room. "You get settled while I fix some coffee and something for you to eat. If that's your rental car you can just leave it where it is."

At the kitchen table he told her about Nirvana, his marriage plans and Nirvana's death. He cried like a baby and she consoled him as best as she could. For almost two hours he continuously sobbed and at the end he felt better for it. He needed to be hugged and loved and Sweet Sister provided both.

For the next two days Musher spent playing with Sweet Sister's boys, chatting with Sweet Sister's husband and just generally doing nothing. Sweet Sister had Mama to dinner and that was a most pleasant night. Mama cried a lot and laughed a lot. On the third day Musher told Sweet Sister he had to leave to get to Lousiana on time. He took the shuttle back to Washington, picked up the Baby Blue and started the drive to Louisiana. He didn't drive very long each day because he had a number of days before he had to sign in to his new assignment. It was beautiful country. He stopped every day in a nice hotel, ate a good dinner, tried to get sleep but most of all he tried very hard not to think of the past.

On the eighth day he was sitting at the main gate at England AFB. Above the main gate was a huge sign which said *"Welcome to England AFB, Pilots are the only people who count, Everyone else is expendable."* That certainly was a welcome to a new assignment. He reported to the Base Personnel Officer who then sent him to the 401st Fighter Wing Commander, the author of the sign at the main gate. The Wing Commander was Colonel Jason Dillard, call sign "Bald Eagle."

Musher reported to Dillard in his best OCS style. He had on a plain uniform. "Lieutenant have you ever ridden in a fighter aircraft?"

"No Sir."

"I am sure you saw the sign at the gate. Be at the 334th Fighter Squadron Ops at 0730 tomorrow morning and you and I will take a ride. Do you have an altitude certification card? Good. I will see you in the morning. Take the rest of the day to get settled and be on time in the morning."

Musher checked into the BOQ and was given a two room suite. He was so tired he barely unpacked, did an SSS and fell into bed. He was wide awake at 0530. He showered again, put on a clean flying suit complete with his 98th Bomb Wing baseball cap, brogans and aviator glasses in his pocket. The only things he put in his flying suit was some money, his Luckies and his Zippo He had breakfast in the Airman's Dining Hall for seventy-five cents and caught the base bus to the 334th. They were expecting him. The rigged him out with a girdle (a stomach, waist and legs pressure suit), a brain bucket (a helmet fitted to his head by air pressure and equipped with an internal headset receiver and transmitter) and a back pack parachute. At the aircraft the crew chief helped Musher into the cockpit and made sure he was properly connected and strapped in. Musher was in the rear seat of an F-100D, the two seater model of the F-100 used for training and orientation rides. At just about 0825 "Bald Eagle" strutted to the aircraft and started the engine. He made no preflight checks. Later Musher found out he was known for "Kick the tires, light the fires and the first one off is the leader and flying safety is paramount."

He spoke to Musher on the intercom, "Are you secure?" "Tower this is Bald Eagle taxiing for takeoff." Tower responded with takeoff data as Bald Eagle rolled to the active runway. As he turned onto the active runway, "Tower Bald Eagle taking off." There was no request in his statement. He was taking off. When he started rolling and kicked in the afterburner Musher's stomach felt like it was pressing through his back. At lift off the flaps came up and the control stick was pulled straight back into Bald Eagles crotch. At forty thousand feet he leveled off and spoke, "How are you doing? Are you all right?" No matter how badly Musher may have felt he said, "Yes sir, doing fine."

The word fine had just barely gotten out of his mouth when Bald Eagle stood the F-100 on its left wing and started a steep dive. "We will go to the Claiborne Bombing Range and make a low level strafing run". He called the range to tell them he was coming in and if there was any other traffic clear it. He was coming from the northwest at five hundred feet He leveled the F-100 at two thousand feet and then continued his decent to five hundred feet. They came across the range at five hundred fifty knots. When the guns fired the aircraft shook and at the end of his run he pulled the stick into his lap and climbed to fifteen thousand feet before getting straight and level. "What do you think of that run?"

"Fascinating. Better than any roller coaster I have ever been on."

Bald Eagle climbed to forty thousand feet and contacted Claiborne Range. "I am coming from the northwest for a LABS maneuver." (Low Altitude Bomb Strike maneuver. At the bomb release point the aircraft is tilted up on a fifty degree angle and when the bomb is released it is pitched to the target and preset to detonate at a given altitude.) "Clear any traffic. I am on my way in now." With that he dropped the left wing and went straight down leveling off at two thousand feet. From there he descended to one hundred feet and came across the range at one hundred feet and five hundred fifty knots. At the bomb release point he spoke "bombs away" and sucked the stick back into his lap. They went into a direct climb to fifteen thousand feet at which time he rolled the aircraft to the left and onto normal position as they raced away into the direction from which they came. After one minute he pulled the stick back in his lap and took the aircraft to forty-thousand feet. Musher felt for shit but was determined he would not get sick.

"What do you think?"

Time to ingratiate with this Wing Commander. "I can better understand the sign at the gate and now I believe in it. I am jealous that I was too old for flying school. This is the life of a tiger."

"Let's go home." As they approached the air base, "Tower, Bald Eagle, low fuel emergency, clear the traffic." Tower gave him landing instructions and he did the seven second approach technique where you break the pattern every seven seconds to touchdown. Just short of the runway he dropped the flaps and at touchdown released the drag chute. As he turned off the runway he dropped the drag chute to some waiting ground crew members and he taxied into the position from which they started. The aircraft was chocked and he and the Bald Eagle were deplaning when two civilians headed for the aircraft. They were from the Federal Aviation Administration center in New Orleans. "Colonel, you have too many low fuel emergencies. We are here to dip your tanks." Bald Eagle turned to the two air policmen who had escorted the civilians to the flight line and said, "If they touch this aircraft, shoot them." He turned to Musher, "Come with me." Musher followed like an obedient dog.

Inside the squadron ops day room they had coffee and Bald Eagle smoked a cigar. That was his cue so Musher lit a Lucky. "Tell me what they call you and tell me about your time in the service."

"Sir, my full name is Saverio Muscarello. I am called Musher. I have been in the military service for almost twelve years. I was in the Army and transferred to the air force as an aerial gunner. I was also an inflight air refueling reel operator in the first B-29 tankers. During the Korean War I was a ring gunner on a B-29 before we were shot down. I spent over a year in a Chinese prison camp. With the exception of today the other two real rides were one, a B-29 full power on stall at twenty-two thousand feet with the aircraft being recovered at nine thousand feet; and, two was a free fall bailing out of a burning B-29 at eighteen thousand feet. Neither of those compares to the ride you gave me today. Sir, I thank you."

"You are very welcome. You will be a great addition to these fighter wings. Get changed into a class "A" uniform and report to the Base Commander. I will give him a call and tell him to expect you."

Back at the BOQ Musher did a well needed SSS. The ride had sweated him so much and kicked the shit out of him so badly that he wanted to lie down and sleep. He put on a fully decorated Class "A" uniform and reported

722

to the Base Commander Colonel Robert MacFee. As usual he reported in his best OCS manner. "Lieutenant Muscarello you have a very impressive service record. Colonel Dillard called to tell me what a welcome addition you would be to the fighter wings. My problem is there is no slot for you in the fighter wings and I already have an EOD officer in the bomb dump. What I need is a Base Supply Officer. I want you to work there until the present EOD officer is discharged in six months. I will call Lieutenant Colonel William Bell to let him know you are coming. That will be all." Musher did as his training said, "Salute smartly and get on the boat."

At base supply he was ushered into Colonel Bell's office. He reported smartly and Bell returned his salute. He never offered Musher to sit down. "What am I going to do with another second lieutenant in base supply? I already have four and I can hardly keep them busy. What do I do with you?" He sat pensively and finally said, "I've got it. I have a request to supply one junior officer to the Rand McNally Corporation to learn about something called computers. Since you were not here yesterday I will not miss you tomorrow. In the morning report to Base Personnel to get your orders and instructions. When you return you will be the project officer to convert our base supply from a manual operation to an automated operation." Again, Musher saluted smartly and got on the boat.

CHAPTER 227

Rand McNally For Computer Training

The training will be held in Phoenix, Arizona. Phoenix is thirteen hundred seventy miles, twenty-one driving hours west of Alexandria. His orders gave him five days delay enroute and five days POV travel time. The main highway route went through El Paso, Texas on the way to Phoenix. What an enticing thought. He signed-out after lunch so today did not count as one of his nine day total. It was nine hundred fifty miles, fourteen driving hours to El Paso. If he drove nine hours today he would cover just about seven hundred miles and be able to rest from 2200 to 0600. He would be in El Paso tomorrow before noon. Two nights in Juarez should set him straight for awhile.

Everything went as planned and he pulled into Bruno's garage just before the Juarez bridge crossing. He was met by the big man who assured him all would be taken care of. Musher left all but three hundred dollars of his money stashed in the Baby Blue. By nightfall he was checked into the Florida hotel, had been in Florida Club and had taken two trips to the back room. Later that night he had his mystery visitor and then he slept until noon the next day. Day 2 was a repeat of Day 1. At noon on Day 3 in Juarez he was leaving for Arizona. He was not surprised to find the big man by the door of Baby Blue with a package in his hand. He held out the package, "When you cross into Arizona drop this in a small town." On top of the package there were five one hundred dollar bills. Musher left Juarez and headed for Biggs AFB for a treatment. He used the VOQ to shower and change clothes. From the VOQ set a course to Phoenix four hundred twenty-five miles away. He dropped off the main highway to post the package. He was sure nobody paid any attention to him as he dropped the package in the outside mail box and then immediately and quietly left town. At 1800 hours he checked into the Phoenix Star Hotel as prescribed by his orders. He was given a roster of seven other officers who would be attending the course. In addition to the roster he was given a clip on name tag and asked to wear it until his classmates knew him and he knew them. The name tag did not prescribe a rank it simply said his name and USAF. He was billeted in a small suite on the top floor overlooking the City of Phoenix. His orders prescribed taking breakfast and dinner meals in the hotel dining room. His luncheon meal would be provided at the RM (Rand McNally) training facility. In the dining room he joined three other gentlemen wearing similar name tags. There were introductions and questions about where each was stationed. All the others were base supply officers. Musher made it clear he was an EOD Officer and had to explain EOD.

After dinner the four of them played bridge until almost midnight. These were excellent bridge players. Musher needed to learn how to control four hands of thirteen cards each. That will take a lot of practice.

CHAPTER 228
A New Air Force Specialty?

After breakfast a RM van drove the students to the training facility. The students had been asked to wear a Class "A" uniform for the first day but would wear civilian clothes every day after that. Musher was the only second lieutenant. All the other students were one captain and six first lieutenants. Their Class "A" uniforms showed only the NSDM (National Service Defense Medal given to any one with at least one year of service) Musher's uniform was laden with Aerial Gunner Wings, his EOD badge and with three rows of ribbons. He was not the most senior in rank but his military service exceeded the sum total of military service for his other class mates. The RM briefing officer was highly respectful to Musher's uniform.

The orientation went like this. The classroom course is twenty weeks. Class will be held Monday to Friday beginning at 0800 hours and ending at 1145 hours. Lunch will be served here at the facility and following lunch the students will be transported to their billet. Students who have their own car may drive their car to the facility and following lunch would be released on their own. The highlight portions of the course will be the learning of three computer languages, BASIC, FORTRAN and COBOL. Students will learn the code for each language and will actually compose a computer program in each language. In addition they will learn to punch machine cards to sort materials in the program data base and how to process the cards for an answer. There will be some homework but it will be limited to memorization projects. There will be no graded examinations during the course. At the end of the course each officer will be awarded a completion certificate with a course summary printed on the reverse side.

For the fun side of attendance for those who play golf RM has a relationship (fifty-one per cent ownership) with the Sun Valley Golf Club. You may get a temporary golf club membership card following this class. You will have no expenses to play golf there but if you choose to buy items in the pro shop you will receive a twenty-five percent discount. Your membership card will show you the Pro Shop and Starter telephone numbers. They will assist you however they can.

A new gentleman came into the room. My name is Wes Hardin. I will be your primary teacher and class monitor. If you have any academic problems I am the man for you to speak to. Remember we want you to succeed. You have three books. One for each of the three computer languages you will learn. They are yours. You may write in them as you choose we only ask that you use a pencil so that if your notes need correcting it can be easily done. We will spend the rest of today discussing the computer language named BASIC, Beginners All Purpose Symbolic Instruction Code.

At 1145 hours Hardin said, "That's it for today. You may take all or any of your books with you or you may leave them here. Let's have lunch."

The conversation at lunch centered on the morning's class and introduction. Musher broke the trend when he said, "Just as soon as I can I am going to play a little golf. Do any of you play?"

Two of the three were players. The question had been heard at the adjacent table. One of the diners said, "I do. May I join you?"

By the time everyone changed clothes, had placed their gear in Baby Blue and drove the thirty minutes to the Sun Valley Golf Club it was almost 1400 hours. There was plenty of time to play eighteen if they did not spend time on the range and practice putting green.

It was a great golf course and the weather could not have been more beautiful. It sure seemed this was going to be a very pleasant TDY.

CHAPTER 229

I Am Ready To Reorganize Base Supply

Learning the three computer languages was actually fun. They were all based in numbers and Musher loved the use of numbers. He and his classmates first wrote simple programs and eventually wrote more complicated programs for the effective operation of a base supply complex. The use of computers was a totally new concept and they were standing on the ground floor with the authors of the computer language. The actual installation of such a computer in the individual base supply was not scheduled for six months after they completed the course. During that time as the lead officer for the conversion of their particular air base supply they would control the challenge and implementation of the programs.

Between the fact that the course was so enjoyable and the golf filled in the time he was not in class or studying Musher hardly noticed that in two days the TDY would end. He had made some close friends of the seven other students in the class. He wondered if he never worked as an EOD officer would it really bother him. He knew that this project would give him all the traits of a titless WAF but somehow the thought did not bother him that much. RM held a small party to celebrate the successful completion of the course and presented each student with documentation to prove his attendance and successful completion.

On the third day Baby Blue was headed for Alexandria. Musher had no intention of stopping in El Paso he was eager to get to England AFB and begin the reorganization of base supply. He stopped for one night and on the second driving day completed the fourteen hundred miles to Alexandria. Since he had only been TDY his BOQ rooms had been held for him. He couldn't wait to unpack do a SSS and get some sleep.

The next morning he was sitting with the Base Supply Officer Lieutenant Colonel William Bell telling of his TDY and outlining a broad base plan to automate base supply. Colonel Bell was surprised and pleased with the plan and gave Musher a private office to further develop the implementation milestones for his plan. It was expected that the computer would be installed in six months which gave Musher five months to be ready for the computer. No sooner was he established in his new office than he began working on the milestone plan.

For the next four days he was consumed with his reorganization plan. On mid-morning of the fourth day he was told to report to the Base Personnel

Officer. The purpose of his visit was two fold. One, he had completed his time in grade as a second lieutenant and effective this date he was promoted to the grade of first lieutenant. The Base Personnel Officer pinned the new silver bars on Musher. The second purpose was spoken by the Base Personnel Officer, "We have an immediate levy for a qualified EOD officer to report to Tachikawa AB in Japan. Our other EOD officer is scheduled for discharge and that leaves you as the only person available to fill the emergency levy. You will leave for Tachikawa in two days. Return here tomorrow at 1000 and we will process the paper work. I have already told Lieutenant Colonel Bell and he wants you to turn over all the materials for your base supply reorganization program. I suggest you do that when you leave here. Other than that there is no need for you to return to base supply. Get your personal affairs in order and I will see you in the morning."

Musher turned in his reorganization plans and books to base supply and no one even said goodbye or wished him luck. At his BOQ he packed the items he was shipping to Japan and a box containing a note and items from Baby Blue to ship to Sweet Sister. He loaded them into Baby Blue went to ship to Sweet Sister because he could not deliver the stuff for Japan to transportation until he received some orders tomorrow.

By 1130 the next day Musher was finished processing out. The Bald Eagle had heard of Musher's plight so he had set up for tomorrow for himself and a wing man to fly Musher to Travis AFB, California the POE for the Far East. With the exception of what to do with Baby Blue Musher would be ready to go as soon as he dropped his things at transportation for shipment to Tachikawa AB. When his goods were at transportation he headed for Alexandria to sell Baby Blue. The best offer was insulting but he was up against it. Since he had not paid for the car whatever he got for it was more than he paid. He did manage to get the car dealer to give him a ride back to the air base. There was nothing for him to do so the rest of the day just dragged by.

He was at the 334th Fighter Squadron Ops early the next morning and was outfitted for the flight in the back seat of the F-100D. His B-4 bag was in the luggage compartment and he was secured in the back seat when the Bald Eagle and his wingman climbed into their aircraft. Bald Eagle asked of Musher's welfare and spoke his regrets for losing such a welcome addition to the fighter wings support team. Bald Eagle did his usual take off routine and he and his wing man rolled down the runway together and climbed to forty thousand feet. Bald Eagle spoke, "In about two hours we will do an inflight refueling. Not like the old hose method you are familiar with but with a KC-135 boom system. It will be fascinating for your first time and we will have our tanks filled in less than two minutes. With the refueling we can go directly to Travis with enough fuel left over to cover two alternate landing sites if there is a problem.

Inflight refueling had come a long way since Musher's days in the B-29 gravity hose. Bald Eagle landed at Travis and stayed only long enough to get Musher on the ground, say a sad goodbye to Musher, have his fuel tanks topped off, file a new flight plan and head back to England AFB. Musher checked into Overseas Passenger Service and within two hours was on a transport aircraft headed for Tachikawa, Japan. The aircraft stopped at Hickam long enough to drop some passengers and get some new ones. The next stop was a one by two island named Wake. The aircraft was on the ground just long enough to take on fuel and then take-off for Japan. They landed at Tachikawa just after dark. He was taken to the BOQ and told to report to the Base Personnel Office in the morning.

The total enroute time was twenty-nine hours. Musher was exhausted. He remembered the O-Club was close. He had dinner there and headed for a SSS and the sack.

A SIX BAGGER

TACHIKAWA
WAKE ISLAND
VIETNAM
8TH AF G.
MARRIAGE
GUAM

BOOK 8

CHAPTER 230
At Least I Am Assigned As an EOD Officer

At 0800 he reported to the Base Personnel Officer Lieutenant Colonel Jonathan Ayers. His paperwork was processed. He could not resist asking what caused the immediate urgent levy for an EOD officer. He was told there was no immediate urgency. Someone stateside had misconstrued the air force personnel levy. You must have been at an air base where there was more than one EOD officer against a Table of Equipment and Organization which authorized only one EOD officer. He was escorted to the Base Supply Officer Lieutenant Colonel Michael Stallingsworth. At Tachikawa the EOD Officer was also the Officer in Charge of the Base Munitions Area and supplies under the supervision of the Base Supply Officer.

Colonel Stallingsworth who insisted he be called Michael when there were no other officers, enlisted men or civilians in their presence, and he insisted on calling his newest first lieutenant Musher. "Musher, do you speak Japanese?"

"No sir."

"I want all my officers to be able to speak and understand conversational Japanese and to read and write Romanji Japanese. There is a six week saturation Japanese conversational course taught in Tokyo which is only twenty-six miles from here and thirty minutes on the direct train from Fussa City. Cab fare to Fussa City from the BOQ is five hundred forty yen including tip. (540 yen equals $1.50 with yen at 360 to the dollar. Black market yen is 720 to the dollar which would reduce your daily fare to and from the train to $1.50 round trip. The train fare is 180 yen (black market yen at 25 cents each way) Your transportation costs will be two dollars American, five days a week for six weeks or a total of sixty dollars. Can you handle those costs? If not I will be glad to assist you. The air force will pay for your school supplies and school attendance fees. Are you all right financially?"

"Yes sir."

"Come by after lunch and I will give you all the paperwork you need to attend school and to be away from Base Supply while you are a student. Check with me every two weeks and tell me how you are doing. A new class begins the day after tomorrow, Friday, meanwhile I will see you this afternoon."

It was spring in Japan and it was beautiful golf weather. He might have to buy another complete set of golf gear rather than waste the beautiful weather. It had been some time since he was last here but he thought he would give it a try. He called the Tachikawa base motor pool and asked for transportation to Yokota. Within fifteen minutes a car and driver picked him up at Base Supply. At the Yokota golf course he was remembered by the Japanese staff in the Pro Shop. "Nite-Tie I need new equipment." He selected the same equipment he had originally bought when he was last here. Now that he was permanent party at Tachikawa he paid for a locker, club storage and range fees. He did not have script or yen so he used American one hundred dollar bills. He had time before he was due at base supply so he talked with the locker room attendant Nite-Tie 2. "Does Nite-Tie 6 still work here and is she available?"

"Yes and yes." He escorted Musher into the proper private room.

Nite-Tie 6 immediately recognized him and the good times began. He gave her an American five dollar bill tip. He paid Nite-Tie 2 with an American twenty dollar bill. His clothes were freshly laundered and pressed and his shoes glistened. He had a sandwich while he waited for his transport to take him to Tachikawa Base Supply.

With his "freedom papers" he went to his BOQ for a nap. He had tomorrow off. He would go play golf and see if Nite-Tie 2 could help convert some American hundred dollar bills to yen at a good rate.

When he awoke from his nap he went to the O-Club to join and have dinner. As usual there was a good band playing soft dance music during dinner and a number of Round-Eye (Caucasian or Negro) women eating dinner alone. After Nite-Tie 6 he did not have any inspiration for sex. Instead after dinner he went into the Stag Bar and joined a pot limit five card draw game. He played ultimately conservative, never won a hand which he dealt and never won a really big pot. By time it was bedtime he had won enough small pots to pay for all his golf purchases. In the next few days he would win enough to buy a car. He wished he had Melke to help him buy the car but he would be forced to do it on his own. Oh well, it will not be his money he will use to buy the car and get it on the road. In the Stag Bar there was a bulletin board offering items for sale. Among them was a 1951 two door Chevrolet Coupe allegedly in fine condition with new tires and recently had an engine overall. "Owner forced to sell. Must make immediate return to the states. Make an offer. Contact Captain Summerall, can be seen at Base Supply, Phone Ext 811. Best offer in next thirty hours."

Musher was up early and at Base Supply when Summerall drove up in the Chevy. Musher confronted him and asked about the ad in the O-Club.

Summerall raved about the car and Musher asked what was the least he would take for it in American cash.

"Make me an offer."

"Five hundred."

"Small cars like this are hard to find in this country. I will take fifteen hundred." About that time Lieutenant Colonel Stallingsworth, the Base Supply Officer walked up and said, "Musher he paid three hundred for the car and he leaves tomorrow." Summerall looked shocked. Musher said, "My offer of five hundred stands." They went inside and did the paperwork. Musher gave him five one hundred dollar bills and made sure the bill of sale and the title were clear and properly signed for transfer to him. As he was leaving he stopped by Stallingsworth office to thank him for his help. Stallingworth drew him a map where he must go to register the car in his name and buy the on-base and off-base insurance. He also told him the name of a Japanese worker here in base supply who would exchange yen for American dollars at the seven hundred twenty rate rather than the legal three hundred sixty rate.

Musher still had his international driver's license and now he had his own personal transportation. Tomorrow he would play golf and spend time with Nite-Tie 6. On Friday he would drive himself to the train at Fussa City and to his BOQ at the end of the day. Weekends would be his to do with as he pleased. The next six weeks would be one big vacation and a great learning experience.

He was right. The school went by quickly but he was now able to converse in Japanese and to read and write Romanji. (Romanji was the use of English characters to form phonetic words which when spoken gave the full sound of Japanese.)

At the end of the course he reported to Lieutenant Colonel Stallingsworth with "Konichi-wah (Good Day) Michael-san."

CHAPTER 231
My First Assignment As An Officer In Charge

Monday morning he reported to Michael. "Come Musher I will take you to your new job. You will be the Officer-In-Charge of the base bomb dump. I will have my secretary call and tell them we are coming and I am bringing their new boss." Musher expected a drive away from the air base to protect the air base in case of a detonation at the bomb dump. The bomb dump wasn't more than a five minute drive from base supply. The bomb dump consisted of two buildings enclosed with a chain link fence and one entry and exit gate. In the main administration building the bomb dump staff was aligned and at attention. Michael introduced the staff. "Technical Sergeant Richard Downey is your NCOIC. Yoko-san is your secretary. These sixteen airmen are your field staff. I will leave you now and Sergeant Downey will fill you in. Good Luck Lieutenant. I know you will do well."

"Lieutenant may I dismiss the airmen back to their duties and Yoko back to hers? Can you and I speak in your office?"

They adjourned to Musher's office. His NCOIC began. "Sir let me tell you about your predecessor and how he ran this bomb dump. This bomb dump contains only three items. It stores caliber .45 ammunition for automatic pistols, caliber .30 ammunition for carbines and smoke signal grenades. It is our mission to be ready to issue these items in the event of a declared emergency. Once each year we inspect each squadron which has such items on hand. There are eighteen locations on Tachikawa which we are required to inspect and submit a report on each location. We have six certified inspectors who do three inspections each month throughout the year. You might say we are overstaffed for our mission. Everyone knows it including your boss the Base Supply Officer.

Your predecessor was a golfer who loved the game. Each day of good weather he would go to Yokota to play golf. At the turn of the ninth hole he would call me on the telephone for a status report. If I needed him to sign documents or whatever he would play the second nine and call me again for confirmation of his need and the approximate time he would be here. He ran this bomb dump that way for eighteen months. There was no doubt that the Base Supply Officer was aware of his operational technique because he never made a surprise visit here and always gave us at least six hours notice that he was coming. During the non-golfing weather and season the lieutenant had a telephone in his quarters and he would sleep in. I think that more than half the time he had a woman in his quarters. He spent the rest of the day at one of the six base movies or in the officer's club playing cards. He was a strong poker player. He played just about every day or night. Now I can do the same for you and assure you that you will never get in trouble as long as I am here. If something should go wrong, which I sincerely doubt, I am ready to take all the heat."

Musher was astounded at Sergeant Downey's revelation. He fully accepted the operational program. "I will need a telephone in my BOQ. Here is my BOQ room number."

"I will take care of that. There will be one installed before today is over. Take this paper, I have written the telephone number for the dump and for me. I suggest you go to the billeting office and get yourself a maid. If you want any additional furniture tell me."

"There is one immediate thing I would like. A much larger bed."

"That too will be taken care of. Call me around 1400 to check in."

Musher left heading for the billeting office. "I need a personal maid. She must speak English and help me with my Japanese. I will pay the going rate for a full time maid exclusively working for me." He interviewed three and selected one named Susie-san. She rode with him in his car to his BOQ parking spot. She immediately started cleaning his two rooms and bathroom. She made a list of cooking utensils she needed and all the other things to equip his bedroom and his cooking and eating area. The next day Musher gave his list to Sergeant Downey and when he returned from Yokota the place was fully furnished and clean. Even the telephone was installed. All his items had been unpacked and neatly stored. He called Sergeant Downey to give him his telephone extension number but the NCOIC was full briefed on the status of the phone and his room. He dismissed Susie-san until tomorrow. She hesitated and asked, "You no want me to help with your shower?" "No thank you I will see you tomorrow when I come back from Yokota."

At the O-Club bar before dinner he met a good looking woman and asked her to dinner. She was a first lieutenant nurse at the base hospital. The dinner and dancing was simply great. They ended up in his BOQ for a drink and they spent the rest of the night together doing the deed. During the night Musher called a cab for her to take her to her quarters. He promised he would call very soon.

He knew he was lying.

CHAPTER 232
How Good Can Life Be ?

The entire golf season went by without any incident at the bomb dump. The base storage inspections reports were made and Musher signed them for turn-in. Michael, the base supply officer, made some routine visits but not without first having given plenty of advance warning. One time he brought the base commander to see how well kept the facility was. Musher was there for each of those visits and Michael bragged upon his leadership abilities.

One afternoon which he was spending in his rooms with a gorgeous kindergarten teacher his phone rang. He was wanted at the Base Commander's office ASAP (as soon as possible) He dressed quickly and was in the Base Commander's waiting room in less than twenty minutes. When he was ushered in he gave his best OCS salute and reported. "Sit down Musher and let me tell you a story. You know that we have a small detachment on Wake Island staffed by EOD personnel from here in Japan. Each Thursday a MATS (Military Air Transport System) aircraft stops at Wake on its way to either Kadena AB in Okinawa or Yokota AB in Japan. You know our international treaties do not permit us to keep nuclear weapons in the far east. The crates on board are generally aircraft engines or aircraft engine parts. Our EOD people check the cargo for any hazardous condition which may exist. The aircraft is only on the ground for a couple of hours and then it is on its way to one of the two bases I just mentioned. It is imperative that those crates are inspected without sacrificing the integrity of the aircraft engines and assuring they are ready for further travel. When the inspections are complete and the fuel tanks topped off the aircraft will depart for its next stop. Two days later the aircraft will be returning to the states and once again it will stop at Wake to insure the crates full of aircraft engines going for repair are fit to travel. All things being normal the EOD workweek is roughly six hours.

There is another duty which consumes a great deal of the EOD crew's time. During WW II Wake was held by the Japanese. The island was a target for the US Navy's ships big guns firing eight inch shells. Each shell contained two hundred eighty-two pounds of high explosives. For whatever reasons many of the rounds fell short of the Wake Island beaches and did not detonate. Instead they eventually washed ashore and our EOD team did the disposal. The disposal was very simple. The FAA (Federal Aviation Association) had a PT Boat which had been converted into a rescue boat.

738

Each Saturday the PT was taken outside the reef and run to keep her in shape. When there was a shell to dispose our EOD people would lash the shell to the deck of the PT and ride with it outside the reef where the water depth approached six thousand feet. The shell was lowered over the side and the disposal was complete.

An eight inch shell had washed up on the beach. There was no reason why the disposal should not have been done in the routine manner.

The disposal was not done in a routine manner.

The on site EOD officer was a second lieutenant recently graduated from EOD school. While at school he saw a demonstration using sand bags to channel the detonation waves upward and in a given direction. He told the EOD team enlisted men that it was his intent to dispose of the eight inch shell using the sandbag channeling method. Each of the enlisted team members told him the risk was too severe and there was nothing to gain even if he was right. Despite their arguments he ordered the sand bagging. As a protective method the enlisted team went to the island communication center and sent a message to FEAF (Far East Air Force) headquarters detailing the lieutenant's plan and voicing their objection. By time the message could be received and processed the disposal shot had been made. As a result the Troposcatter Antenna (a large antenna constructed with a large number of individual transmission and receiving antennae combined into one large antenna) was severely chopped by casing fragments hurled through the air and in the direction of the Troposcatter Antenna. Loss of the antenna gave loss to the US Coast Guard Loran Facility. (Long Range Navigation Signals used to guide ships and aircraft moving on or through the South Pacific air space) In addition it broke a number of windows in the grade school for the children of FAA (Federal Aviation Association) employees and caused severe panic among the children. It also rocked the control tower and knocked out the GCA (Guided Control Approach)

The island governor, a GS-19 appointed by the President of the United States was so furious he wanted the EOD function off the island and unequivocally stated that no longer would USAF aircraft be allowed to land on Wake for fuel. He was not privy to the actual purpose of the landings and he could not be told.

After the story was told the Base Commander instructed Musher to get his things together and be ready to leave for Wake within two hours. His job is to mend the fences with the island governor at any cost. Secondarily put that young second lieutenant on the aircraft he gets off so they can get him off the island before he is shot or hung. There is no time for processing orders. The paperwork will catch up with him.

He parked his car by his BOQ, packed very lightly with just about everything he owned that would be good in extremely hot weather. Six hours later his aircraft touched down at Wake Island. As he was deplaning he hustled the young lieutenant aboard the aircraft and gave the pilot the signal to leave immediately. He was greeted by the EOD team and each one kept saying how they were against the shot and so notified FEAF. Musher consoled them and assured them they were in the clear.

The island governor approached Musher screaming obscenities and threatening his very life. No matter what Musher said or did to console the governor he refused to be quiet. "Be in my office in one hour. It will take me that long to write all the orders for you and those enlisted men to get off my island."

The EOD team had a pickup which they used to take Musher to his quarters and waited to drive him to the office of the Island Governor. The governor had calmed down somewhat and conceded that Musher was not at fault for the incident but he wanted that second lieutenant severely punished. Musher assured him that the lieutenant would most likely receive a general court martial and be removed from the USAF. That seemed to quiet the governor even more.

Before long they were drinking iced tea and talking about their homes in the states. The conversation came around to how little there was to do on this island and much of the time was spent playing table tennis Filipino Style or playing bridge. "Musher do you play table tennis?"

"No sir but I am sure I will learn while I am here."

"Do you play bridge? That stupid lieutenant was the twelveth person to make for a Michigan rotation. If you play how well do you play?"

"Yes I do play. I have been a life master since I was fourteen years old."

"Superb. Come to my house for dinner tonight at 6:30. The bridge game is at my house tonight." Peace had come to Wake Island. Musher went to the communications center and filed a report with the Base Commander at Tachikawa and the Chief of FEAF.

Fortunately for Musher the dress was casual. Dinner was excellent and half the players played bridge decently. Musher paired with the island governor and together they just walked through the competition. After the game the island governor asked Musher to help him apply to the American Contract Bridge League for registered status for Wake Island. That status would allow them to have duplicate bridge games and earn points for recognition in the ACBL.

When it came time for him to go to his quarters one of the married ladies whose husband was at home baby sitting the children offered to drop him at his quarters. He obligingly accepted. It was a direct route from the governor's house to his billet. Instead she took a perimeter road which traveled around the one by two mile island. In a secluded spot she stopped her pickup and shut down the truck. She removed her skirt and her underpants. She turned on the overhead lights in the pickup and said, "Do you like the looks of my pussy? Let me see yours."

Musher took off his shorts and under pants and his dick was standing straight up. She reached for it and guided him into her pussy. He was barely inside when he ejaculated. She looked at him in disgust until she realized he had not gone soft and was moving in and out of her. She worked him until she could no longer hold off and she let it all go. The feeling of her coming caused him to come. They stayed entwined for as long as they could. Shortly thereafter they did it again. She had towels in her truck and two canteens of water. She washed them both clean. Her washing of him caused him to harden. She put her head in his lap and sucked his penis until he came. She used the second canteen to rinse her mouth. She put his head against her pussy and he licked his best. When she came she sighed deeply and rinsed herself with the second canteen. She told him that when she got home her husband would want to eat her pussy and it must be clean for him. He was not smart enough to know she needed more than he could give her but it made him think he had her satisfied.

She dropped him at his billet and said, "If you want I will be here tomorrow night after it gets dark."

"I will be waiting outside."

CHAPTER 233

Wake Island
Five Months Is a Long Time

There wasn't a heck of a lot to do on Wake. With the exception of the two flights each week, one going into the Far East and the same one leaving the Far East for the states the only other thing to do was train. One and one half days each week were devoted to what to do and how to do it if there was an incident on the island. The rest of the time was pretty much just generally doing nothing. Occasionally a "non-sked" (non scheduled tourist flight) would stop for minor maintenance or fuel.

Musher became friendly with the LORAN Station Skipper, Coast Guard Lieutenant Junior Grade Fred Pace (the same rank as Musher). He taught Musher how to sail a twelve foot skiff inside the lagoon and close to shore around the island. They were too smart to venture outside the reef in the little twelve footer. They swam a lot but were very careful not to be in the swimming lane of the big wing flapping sting ray. There were Filipino stewards who worked for and served the FAA. From them he learned to play table tennis Filipino Style. The aircraft which passed through Wake were more than happy to bring things from either Okinawa or Japan depending upon their destination. Musher and Fred kept their two officer officer's club well stocked with booze and beer. The membership fee for any transient officers was either two cases of beer or two fifths of any type booze. In return, providing you mixed your drinks with water, drinks were on the house.

On one occasion a non-sked had engine trouble and landed on Wake for repairs. One of the rules for non-skeds was cash on the barrel-head for any parts, fuel or other accommodations. The cargo on the non-sked was forty-two female school teachers touring the Far East. The engine parts for repair would take at least eight days to come from the states. The Coast Guard male complement was eleven white hats and one chief. They were in heaven. A few of the passengers were sex oriented and the Coast Guard enlisted and Musher's four enlisted men were in heaven. Musher and Fred entertained the tour leaders in their officers club. Musher found it difficult (but most enjoyable) to handle the new pussy and keep up with his regular island companion.

The parts arrived on Wake, the engine repairs were made and the aircraft was test hopped. Tomorrow the group would leave and continue on their tour. The next morning the aircrew was doing their preflight when they noticed a lengthy vertical cut in the vertical stabilizer. It was obvious that someone had climbed the vertical stabilizer, penetrated the surface and slid down holding the knife tightly. When the repair part came, approximately eight days from today, it would mean another test hop. There was no way to determine who the perpetrator was but it would not have been hard to guess.

The beach parties continued. The non-sked was finally repaired and left for the rest of its tour. The island settled down into its routine boredom. Four more months went by and Musher was relieved and returned to Japan.

CHAPTER 234
Life Resumes At Tachikawa

Everything at Tachikawa was as if he had never left. The weather had turned warm, Sergeant Downey had run the bomb dump no differently than he would have if Musher had been there and his BOQ was clean and fresh. He reported to the Base Commander and told him of the events during his time on Wake (not all of the events). He made a similar report to his boss the Base Supply Officer. Michael, the base supply officer, told Musher he looked drained and beat. It must have been caused from the constant hot sun on the island. Mike suggested he take a week off and just rest. Maybe play some golf but mostly just rest. After the week off he reverted to his agreement with Sergeant Downey and went back to the easy life of a bomb dump officer with a great NCOIC to take care of running the railroad.

He had been playing golf and just generally doing nothing but chasing women and seeing movies. One day as he finished the round and was checking in with Sergeant Downey he was told to report to the OSI (Office of Special Investigations) at 1500 hours today. Back at his BOQ he did his SSS and dressed in a neatly pressed properly adorned with badges and ribbons Class A uniform he reported to the OSI. He was nervous. He knew he had done many things which could entice the OSI to look at his character and security clearance. No matter how deeply he thought he could not come up with one single incident which would warrant OSI special agents to want to talk with him. Maybe it had something to do with the packages he dropped in mail boxes.

At his appointment time he was shown into a private room where two gentlemen in civilian clothes were seated opposite him at the table. There was no introduction of names the conversation went like this:

"We are representatives of an organization being newly formed to do clandestine work. We have studied your files and decided that you are well fit for our organization. This is your opportunity to join our organization. Do you choose to volunteer?"

"Tell me about your organization and what my role would be as a part of it."

"The specific data is highly classified and you can only be told its contents if you volunteer to join."

"Are you telling me I join first and then I find out what it is I have joined?"

"That's it. We can only tell you it is not an organization for girls and the it coincides with the lyric, "I want to be an airborne ranger, I want to live a life of danger." That will give you some idea of what to expect. You have one minute to decide whether to join or go back to your assignment."

It didn't take Musher two minutes to decide. That certain something in the heart which says, "I am indestructible" caused him to say, "I volunteer." He signed a bunch of papers which he hardly read.

The spokesman for the two in civilian clothes said, "You have two days in which to settle your personal affairs. Be here at 1400 hours two days from today. You will receive orders giving you a PCS (Permanent Change of Station) to Atsugi, Japan. Everyone who needs to know about your transfer will be told when you are gone. You will receive further instructions at Atsugi. You are not to discuss this matter with anyone or tell anyone about your relocation. If you must store items until you return to Tachikawa take them to transportation and fill out the storage tag with the identifying code JJP0001. This will keep your items in a secure area until you call for them. You can store your car with the same JJP001 code. Pack light without civilian clothes. Limit yourself to your B-4 bag. We will see you here in two days at 1400 hours. If you don't show we will know you changed your mind and we shall act accordingly."

Musher had no idea where they were going or for how long. He decided he should make the best of the two nights before he reports for the unknown. He selected two females who would make great, easy company for one night each. He took each one to dinner and back to his BOQ. Who knows how long those two adventures must last.

At the reporting site he joined six other guys. They exchanged their uniforms for plain coveralls and jump boots. They boarded an enclosed truck and then loaded into a C-11 aircraft. When they and all their luggage was in the aircraft it rolled for take off. Everyone knew Atsugi was just barely an hour away in flight time and they were already in the air for over two hours. After three more hours the aircraft intercom buzzed on. "Kadena Tower this is C-11 JJP0001 requesting straight in approach." The conversation which ensued between C-11 and Kadena Tower brought the aircraft in with the help of GCA.

The passengers downloaded with their luggage, boarded a six-by and were dropped off at a barracks. "Stow your gear and get back in the truck. We will go have lunch." The seven guys plus four instructors were the only persons in the dining hall. "No talking during lunch. There will be plenty of talking when we are back in your barracks."

When they were back at the barracks all the doors were closed and there was one of the instructors guarding each entrance to protect it from unwanted visitors. "We apologize for the ruse regarding Atsugi but this project is so highly classified that we are taking every precaution to protect it contents. Your storage tags are coded JJP0001. The translation is "Jungle Jim Program, 0001, the first team of the program. There are seven of you. Your team leader is US Army Infantry Captain Nicolas Arias, called The Greek. His deputy is USAF EOD First Lieutenant Saverio Muscarello, better known as Musher. The communications officer is USAF First Lieutenant Anthony Bono, called Tony. The other half of the EOD team is US Army Sergeant First Class John Bachus, called Jack. The other half of the communications team is Communications Specialist US Navy Petty Officer First Class Claude Wilson, called Willy. The two riflemen, sniper and combat medics combined are USMC Corporal Hans Fernanys, called Kraut, and USMC Corporal Domenic Carse, called Pope. We prefer that you refer to each other by nickname. Do not express rank or military service connection.

After dinner we will have ground school on how to properly bail out of an aircraft and properly land either in water or land. Right now "Let's squeet."

Parachute ground school training was interesting and informative. Musher wished he had had this training before he bailed out of the B-29. Maybe he would not have been so scared. Everyone was glad to get into bed. 0430 will come very early.

CHAPTER 235

Now I Am a Paratrooper

Once again the dining hall was empty except for the instructors, Greek, Musher and the rest of the team. After breakfast the team was at the parachute shop being fitted for a back pack parachute and a chest reserve chute. There was a final lesson on the proper tightening of the chute straps. Improper fitting of the chute straps and when the chute popped open you would probably sing soprano for the rest of your life.

The aircraft was at nine thousand feet over the water when the command came to "stand-up and hook up." "Check the man in front of you." The jump master checked the last man in the stick (The stick is the name for the jumpers from the first out the door until the last out the door) The ready light came on and the stick began the Teaberry Shuffle. Named after a chewing gum of its time each jumper shuffled his feet in small steps heading for the door. The jumper's last move was a right turn at the door and with his arms folded across his reserve chute he followed the man in front of him out the door. Since the chute release was attached to the static line in the aircraft the chute opened when the static line reached its maximum length. For anyone who was making his first jump the shock of the chute opening was almost inexplicable. It did not take long for the chute to settle and begin its downward float. The really tricky part came when your feet touched the water and you released the chute from your body and swam away from the chute so you would not get tangled in it. Not all of the team did a clean release but there were instructor divers in the water waiting to help anyone who had difficulty. When all the team was out of the water, into a transport boat and finally standing on land you could hear the sighs of relief and exhilaration. One hour later they did it again. Then they did it again for the third time. Each time it was easier and the team did not require any help from the standby instructors. The last two jumps of the day were over a good size land clearing. These two were really easy. The five jumps qualified the team members as jumpers and they were awarded a parachute badge to wear on their uniform along with any other badges, such as the EOD badge and the Aerial Gunners Badge.

After lunch the team was excused for the rest of the day. To the man they went to the barracks did a SSS and slept until dinner. After dinner they were in the barracks day room attending a lecture on the types of knives available and the correct methods of killing with a knife.

The next morning was spent using various types of firearms. The afternoon and the next two days were devoted to physical conditioning. On the evening of the fifth day they met the project officer for the project Jungle Jim. He was an Army Major with a long history of clandestine combat. He explained the mission of Jungle Jim. The team would be the first of three to enter into South Vietnam as couriers for the US Embassy. Their role would be to penetrate North Vietnam and destroy selected targets. Penetration would be to either walk in and out or to jump in and be extracted by some method other than walking. Under no circumstances was any member of the team be taken. He emphasized that under no circumstances was any member of the team to be taken alive.The next afternoon the team entered Saigon, South Vietnam and reported in to the US Embassy. The in-country briefing showed the areas controlled by the South Vietnamese forces and the area controlled by the Viet Cong. The map gave the impression that the South Vietnamese forces were controlling more territory and had a good chance to win their war. The team was taken to an arsenal within the embassy and were given the opportunity to select their weapons of choice. Everybody on the team selected a foreign made weapon called Schmizer. Caliber .9MM hand held automatic weapon similar to the US Grease Gun. The clips held sixty rounds. When the clips were rosebudded (three clips taped together for easy removal and insertion of a full clip) the weapon had one hundred eighty rounds and the ammunition chest pack held six more clips. The combat load was five hundred forty rounds. Three team members carried sixty pounds of C-4 plastic explosive. Two team members carried five thousand feet each of prima cord. (Prima cord is an explosive cord which looks like clothesline but detonates at one mile every second. Its primary use was to attach a detonator to it and attach the prima cord to the plastic explosive.) The two EOD personnel carried cushion packed manual blasting caps and safety fuse.) On his web belt each team member also carried two grenades, a foreign made small arms pistol, two KABAR knives, two canteens of water and a can of bug repellant spray. The repellant cans were painted black for camouflage purposes. The team did not wear helmets. They wore soft hats generally referred to as "Aussie Hats". In every hat was a pack of foreign cigarettes, water proof matches and a stringer of amphetamine tablets. In each boot there was two small packs of coffee each large enough to make one canteen of coffee. Also in each boot were four atabrine tablets for purifying rice patty water to make it potable. It was not difficult to understand why each team member had to be in great physical shape with a great amount of stamina.

When the team left the embassy they were billeted in an out of the way small hotel in a Saigon area called Cholon. Cholon was basically a Chinese community and they tried to stay uninvolved with the war. Musher's love for the Chinese kept him armed all the time and as the saying goes, "sleeping with one eye open."

Almost a week went by before they received their first mission. Just north of Phu Bai began the DMZ (Demilitarized Zone). On the other side of the DMZ not too far into North Vietnam was a fuel storage area consisting of five fuel tanks. This fuel depot served to provide fuel for all vehicles sneaking through the DMZ and traveling with troops and supplies into South Vietnam along the guerilla route known as the Ho Chi Minh Trail. The team jumped just north of the fuel dump with full combat load. Their arrival was unnoticed. They buried the chutes and headed south to the fuel dump. There were three guards at the dump. Greek and the two marines disposed of them handily. Musher, his EOD person and the assistant communications sergeant helped rig the tanks. When the C-4 was in place and the prima cord knotted to kick the C-4 the team withdrew to the maximum length of the prima cord. Musher attached two safety fuses and blasting caps to make sure the detonation would go. Musher whispered to the team "Fire in the Hole" and lit off the safety fuses.

Within a minute Musher discovered his mistake. When all five tanks blew simultaneously Musher realized he had not put any delay between the tanks. The team was over a mile away when the tanks blew but the heat wave was so strong it took the eyebrows off the team. It knocked off their hats but since they were all shaved bald it just heated them up. No one cursed at Musher. The cursing and teasing would come later. The team made tracks heading south under the cover of night. During the day they stayed hidden and waited for nightfall to travel again. They crossed the DMZ using the Ho Chi Minh trail. As soon as they were clear of the DMZ they broke off and headed for Phu Bai and the safety of South Vietnam. They did not stay in Phu Bai. There was a helicopter waiting to take them to Saigon. At their billet they drank three fifths of scotch and critiqued the operation. There were no written reports to be done. Everyone only got up to eat, shower and go back to bed. The team rested for two days before they received another mission.

This mission was to destroy the ordnance from a crashed B-26 and destroy the aircraft so that there was no material left which could be useful to a guerilla force. The crash had occurred at Nam Cam on the southern tip of the South Vietnam peninsula. There was very little guerilla combat in that portion of the peninsula. The common name for the area was "Father Hoa (pronounced "Waaah") Country." Father Hoa was a Catholic priest who had seen the communist takeover coming in North Vietnam so he gathered all his parishioners and their families and led them to the sanctity of the deepest part of South Vietnam. It was common knowledge that anything which happened in Father Hoa Country he immediately had the full story. Greek knew of the Father's reputation for knowing so our first stop was to see Father Hoa. Greek explained the team goal and sought Father Hoa's help.

"Yes, I know exactly where it is and I have had my people guarding it until you came to do whatever it is you will do."

"Will you take us to it?"

"Of course but for a price. My price is two hundred M1A1 Caliber .30 rifles and ten thousand rounds of ammunition."

"Done, but only after we finish our mission. When we see the aircraft and recover the ordnance I will radio Saigon and the rifles and ammo will be here the same day."

Both parties delivered on their word. The team made a lot of loud booms. The rifles and ammunition arrived the same afternoon Greek had notified Saigon. Back in the Saigon billet the team drank three fifths of scotch, showered and went to bed.

For a year the team did similar missions and was pleased that not one team member received a scratch and every mission had been successful.

It was now late 1960 and every person in the world knew that US forces were teaching and guiding ARVN (Army of the Republic of South Vietnam) forces. There was a major influx of US Army ground forces and a buildup of USAF air power. Just as the Army was disguised as teacher and logistics people for ARVN the USAF forces were similarly disguised as teachers and guidance personnel for VNAF (Vietnamese Air Force). The Jungle Jim program was terminated. Musher was asked to stay another year and transfer to the newest 2nd Air Division in South Vietnam as the EOD Officer for all of Southeast Asia. He was promoted to Captain.

Because there were no truly experienced EOD officers in Southeast Asia the EOD concept was different than in the USA. At every major airbase in South Vietnam and Thailand there was a team of enlisted EOD personnel. When an incident occurred in either South Vietnam or Thailand Musher would go to the nearest major air base pick up the resident team and the necessary equipment and explosives. He and the team would go to the site and take care of whatever needed taking care of. When the incident was complete Musher would write a letter to the Commander of the EOD enlisted team congratulating them on their support and fine work. Many a promotion came because of that letter.

The 2nd Air Division aircraft inventory was B-26's and T-28's which had been mothballed in Arizona and were reworked for combat in Southeast Asia. Unfortunately the electrical systems were not that reliable. At times you could press the flaps up on the B-26 and the nose guns would fire. The landing gear switch sometimes turned on the landing lights without raising the gear. As a result of these electrical screw ups there were a lot of crashes and pilots being killed. One day Musher was called into the office of 2nd Air Division Commander, Brigadier General Leyland Trotter. Trotter said to Musher, "You know how many crashes we have had recently. They are being reported as Pilot Error. You and I know better. Since you are the Reclamation Officer on most crashes doesn't it seem to you more honorable for our pilots to be remembered as shot down by enemy fire?"

"Yes Sir."

"That will be all Musher."

Musher confiscated a Russian AK-47 and lots of ammo from the captured weapons storage locker. Everybody turned their heads when he was doing it. On his next reclamation project Musher brought back a good size piece of the control panel which had been shattered by AK-47 rounds. He filed his combat loss report with the evidence of the control panel. During the next six months he filed seven such reports with different parts of the aircraft saturated with AK-47 punctures to support his theory. His last recovery was near a place called Ba Xse (Baa Say) in the Mekong Delta. When his chopper brought him to Tan Son Nhut Air Base in Saigon the chopper was met by two USAF Air Policemen.

"Sir, are you Captain Muscarello?"

"Yes I am."

"Sir, may we have your weapons?"

"No, you may not." As he said that he heard the sound of the forward slide putting a round in the chamber of a caliber .45 automatic. He looked at the weapon pointed directly at his chest and changed his song. "Of course you may" and he handed over his weapons. The air policemen guided him into their jeep and took him to 2nd Air Division Headquarters. As he passed through the outside office going into General Trotter's office, the General's aide sidled up to him and whispered, "Musher, keep the faith." When he entered the office he immediately noticed General Trotter was not sitting behind his desk. The four star General Commander of the Military Army Command Vietnam was perched in his place. Musher went to salute but was interrupted by the MACV Commander saying, "Take this scum bag in the next room, read him his rights and bring his dumb ass back here when you finish."

Musher was accompanied into the next room by Colonel Herbert Korenstein the Judge Advocate General for 2nd Air Division. Musher, they have you cold for the seven false combat loss reports you have filed. Sign these specification sheets and just keep your mouth shut for anything but yes sir or no sir. If a question needs answering I will answer it for you." With that they returned into the main room. Musher noticed two men in civilian clothes sitting along the wall. The US Army Judge Advocate General read the specifications and to each one Musher pleaded guilty. The MACV commander spoke, "Take this excuse for an officer out of my sight. We will have his General Court Martial as soon as I can arrange it. Until then he is arrest to quarters."

When Musher got back to his hooch both his room mates had been moved out. Outside his door an air policeman was assigned for a twenty-four hour watch and escort. He was allowed to go to the Officer's Latrine and to the Dining Hall. Other than that he was restricted to his hooch. It went on for almost three weeks before he was summoned to General Trotter's office. In the waiting room outside the General's office he was greeted with applause and pats on the back. In the General's office he started to salute and report when the General interrupted. "Musher you look for shit. Have a drink. I suppose you would like an explanation. How many of the spec sheets did you sign? I doubt if you know. Here they are. Use the waste basket and burn them all."

"Can I have one for a souvenir?"

"Burn them all. Here's the deal. Our flying safety officer writes and tells his wife what you are doing and how great it is. She tells her dad, but her dad is a US Senator. One of the two civilians who was sitting in the room. They come here to investigate. Once they know the story everything ends. It's all over. You will be taken care of by me and the MACV Commander. We both figure we owe you one and anything within reason we will grant. Don't waste the chip on a transfer or some other weak piece of shit. Save it for a big one. Meanwhile we think you have been over here too long. I am going to rotate you back to the states to a nice quiet job. You will have a number of decorations coming to you but we will not give them to you here. They will do you a lot more good to receive them in the states."

In three days Musher was rotated to the US and assigned to the 99th Bomb Wing (SAC), Westover AFB, Chicopee, Massachusetts.

CHAPTER 236

The 8th Air Force Inspector General

Musher checked into the 99th Bomb Wing (SAC) and was further assigned to the 24th Munitions Maintenance Squadron (MMS). There was another B-52 bomb wing also assigned to Westover AFB. To top it all off there was a full EOD Detachment assigned to a portion of the air base called Stoney Brook. Stoney Brook was where the nuclear weapons were stored and the EOD team trained. The squadron commander of the 24th MMS, Lieutenant Colonel Ephraim Marshall resented having an EOD officer. He gave Musher the job of writing the squadron policy manual for use of the two man concept policy. The basic core of the two man policy was that no single individual was to ever be near to a nuclear weapon; and, if there was any task to perform on a nuclear weapon there must be two men who equally understand the task to be done and who are equally capable of doing the job. The squadron commander wanted a policy manual to teach the policy complete with unclassified pictures and stories. He had designated Musher to author the project and placed Musher in a cubby hole office without any windows. It was more like a broom closet with a desk and chair.

Musher had been working on his first draft for almost three weeks when the squadron commander came in and said, "You and I are wanted at the Wing Commander's office now. What did you fuck up this time? Maybe they are going to court martial you for something. No, my luck's not that good."

When he entered the 99th Bomb Wing Commander's office, Colonel Neil Burroughs greeted Musher with hand shakes and pats on the back. From the Wing Commander, "Captain, we did not know we had such a hero in our wing." The decorations from overseas had arrived and the SAC boys had not seen such decorations since the Korean War. The room went quiet as the Wing Adjutant read the list of awards and decorations. Included in the list of decorations were a Bronze Star with V for combat award and one oak leaf cluster for the second Bronze Star for a second combat award. Two Purple hearts for combat wounds, the USAF Individual Commendation Award, the Presidential Citation for Outstanding Behavior in a Combat Environment, a United States Army Combat Infantry Badge with Combat Wreath awarded by the US Army Commander of the Military Army Advisory Group for Southeast Asia, the Vietnam Campaign Medal with three silver stars, The

American Expeditionary Medal for Southeast Asia and the Republic of Vietnam Presidential Citation for Valor.

At the end of the list there was major applause and the commander of the 24th MMS stood there with his face red. He had entered the USAF straight from West Point and he was neither a pilot nor a navigator. His blouse showed a National Service Defense Medal and some other meaningless ribbons awarded to West Point graduates so they at least look like they know something about the US Combat Forces.

The 99th Bomb Wing Commander spoke, "This calls for a parade. Two Saturdays from now and we shall award the medals and commendations on the parade ground."

Musher asked to speak. "Sir I truly appreciate your desire to recognize my awards. As you know I was enlisted for over ten years and if there was anything I detested it was a Saturday morning parade to give some officer some medals which we wondered if he even earned and the parade fucked up an entire weekend. Can't we just do a quiet presentation ceremony here in your office?"

The Wing Commander was not pleased. "If that is what you want Captain then that is what we will do. All the other senior officers from the air base will be present if you do not object. We will do it in my conference room Friday at 1000 hours. This group is dismissed except for you Captain Muscarello." When all the others were gone Colonel Burroughs questioned Musher about Vietnam and his job and time assigned there. Almost two hours went by before the "interrogation" ended. Burroughs asked Musher what he thought of the 24th MMS.

"Sir, you should not ask a question to which you may not want to hear the answer."

"Tell me!"

"I don't know about the squadron. Colonel Marshall has me in a closet writing a manual for the Two Man Policy in the 24th. No matter what I write he tears it apart and constantly insults my intelligence and devotion to duty. The man is a fucking asshole. More than once I wanted to beat his ass but the thought of the stockade and a general court martial has kept me in check. There is almost no doubt in my mind if I stay there I will end up beating his ass and maybe killing the cocksucker. Sir I don't know if you know it but I spent fourteen months in a Chinese prison camp during the Korean War. While I was doing that this fucking asshole was getting an allowance from his mother. When I came out of prison camp I made myself a new life philosophy. If I wanted a cigarette I would have one. If I was hungry I would get something to eat. If someone tried to intimidate me I would simply kill him. I am afraid I am on that edge again."

"Captain I will not let that happen. Between you and me I always thought Marshall was a wimp and used his rank to delude himself into believing he was not. For a West Pointer he is a sorry excuse. He is jealous of a Mustang like you but he is as far in the rank structure as he will ever go. Hang in there and on Friday I will have some good news for you. Take the rest of the day off." He stood and shook hands with Musher. Musher saluted and left.

On Friday the conference room was packed. The eighth air force commander and his staff, both wing commanders and their staff, the base commander and his staff, three newspaper reporters with cameras in hand, the commander and officers of the 24th MMS and Musher. The room went silent and the 99th Bomb Wing Executive Officer read each citation and Colonel Burroughs pinned the medal or ribbon on Musher's blouse. By the end of the ceremony medals, ribbons and his Army Combat Badge were hanging from his breast pockets. The end brought a standing ovation.

The Eighth AF Commander Lieutenant General Anthony Rossetti came to shake Musher's hand and said, "Welcome to Eighth AF Headquarters." He was followed by Brigadier General Elmer Riller, "Welcome to the 8th AF Inspector General Team. Your transfer orders are being cut now." By the time everyone had come to congratulate Musher and shake his hand he was exhausted with the praise. Even the 24th Commander came to shake hands. When he did Musher holding his hand very tightly leaned in closely and whispered, "Fuck you asshole. When I come to inspect the 24th I will put your ass out to dry." He loosened his grip and said, "I think you are queer."

CHAPTER 237
Life On the Inspector General Team

Musher met with the Inspector General, Brigadier General Elmer Riller for about as long as he had met him at the awards ceremony. The real Honcho of the team was Colonel George Williams. From him Musher got a broad picture of the team and its activities. The team generally went out on inspection on Sunday afternoon for a period of six days. Only Colonel Williams and the team Chief Clerk Master Sergeant Phil Dunnelly knew the destination of the team. All members were required to pack for both hot and cold weather. Each team member would bring two B-4 bags each appropriately packed. Normally the team would return on late Friday afternoon and would report for duty Monday morning. The 8th AF Commander and the significant staff members of 8th AF Headquarters would be briefed on the inspection findings later Monday afternoon. If everything went smoothly as it usually did, the team would be off on Tuesday and Wednesday. Thursday would be devoted to getting all materials ready for the next inspection. Friday and Saturday would be days off and the team would report ready to depart on Sunday at 1300 hours. When the team was at an inspection site the work day was generally five days at sixteen hours each day. That eighty hour work week did not count Friday which was generally four hours in the base theatre while Colonel Williams briefed the inspected unit on the results of the inspection. The team would fly out Friday and the airborne time could range from two hours to twelve hours. Total road time was usually ninety-four hours. The schedule as outlined for time at 8th AF Headquarters sounded easy but the ninety-four hours in six days was not easy.

If the weather was right when the team was at home the days off were spent playing golf. Any team member below the rank of Lieutenant Colonel who did not play golf was the office guardian during the routine duty day. On the days when the weather did not allow golf the team met at the 8th AF Physical Conditioning Unit and worked out or played badminton. The married team members did not always come to participate in the team sports.

During the home period at least two times one of the senior officers would host a dinner party followed by a general party. Musher always made it a point to go the dinners and bring a case of fine quality wine.

Almost a year went by. When there was no team activity Musher spent his nights in the O-Club playing cards when there was game or drinking his favorite liqueurs. It was late July and Musher was sitting on his favorite bar stool when in walked Lieutenant Colonel Harden who Musher knew, his wife and a third lady of striking beauty and poise. Musher asked the bartender, "Chester, who is she?"

"Don't know. I have never seen her in here before. She is just a young girl."

"Young girl my butt. She is twenty-five if she is a day. I'll bet you tonight's tab she is at least twenty-five."

You're on. Prove it."

Musher walked to where the trio was sitting, greeted Colonel Harden and his wife then turned his attention to the blond beauty. "May I borrow your driver's license for a minute? I have made a bet with bartender that you are no older than twenty-three. I need your license to prove I am right."

"Yes you may borrow my license but I am afraid you are wrong."

Musher took the license, walked to Chet and came back to the table shaking his head. "You certainly don't look any older than twenty-three." He insisted on buying the table a drink for interrupting their pre-dinner drink. Harden asked Musher to join them and he had accomplished the first step of his goal. He accomplished the second step when they invited him to join them for dinner. After dinner they sat in the bar having an after dinner drink when Mrs. Harden said she had to get home the sitter would be worried. Musher offered to take their guest home and the guest agreed to the ride.

Musher's best technique with women was to encourage them to talk about themselves and listen attentively. He finally managed to get her name, Melinda Kelly and her phone number. She told him she had an early shoot in the morning and could they please leave. He did not press the issue of an early shoot. She lived with her father in a nearby city and he walked her to her front door of her house like a perfect gentleman.

CHAPTER 238
Wining and Dining

Musher called Mrs. Harden to find out more about Melinda Kelly. "She is a fashion model and the television and radio spokeswoman for Narragansett beer. She has consented to model some outfits at the Officers Wives' Fashion Show next week. At a shoot, the name given to a camera session, she is known as a "one take". For that ability she is highly paid. She probably makes more in one day than an Air Force Captain on Hazard Pay will make in a month. She has never been married and we don't even know of one serious romantic affair." Musher thanked her for the information.

He tried to call her at her home but all he got was her father. He told him who he was and he was trying very hard to know Melinda better. Her father, John Kelly, was willing to give her a message. She should be home by three to three thirty. Musher said he would call again. That evening he finally reached her but she was tired and was going to bed early. "How about tomorrow?" (It was Wednesday and he was off all day)

"I have another shoot tomorrow which will end about five in the afternoon. If you want to pick me up there I would be most happy to see you." She gave him the location of the shoot.

No matter what he did to pass the time the day was long, long and longer. When it came time to pick her up at the shoot he was forty-five minutes early and impatiently waited. As she got in his car the day brightened and his life seemed so much better. He suggested the O-Club for dinner. At his corner of the bar he asked her what she would like to drink. "Whatever you have is all right with me."

Musher drank what is called a "Bird Bath." A "Bird Bath" is a very fancy crystal glass which holds a triple gin martini. Chet served them, Musher said Cheers and took a sip. Melinda drank the glass empty and said, "May I have another?" Musher and Chet looked at each other and Chet served her another. That one went the way of the first one. Again she said, "May I have another?" Musher did not know how to react. Either this girl is a lush or she has no idea what a martini can do to you, much less the equivalent of nine martinis. She said, "Please excuse me while I go to the ladies room." As she stood she grabbed the bar and said, "Please take me home." She walked out of the club like a perfect lady and they left the air base on the way to her home. On the way she said, "I think I am going to be sick." Musher gritted his teeth, thought about his new Thunderbird with less than two hundred miles on it and said, "Not in this son-of-a-bitch you're not" and she didn't. He walked her to the front door where she was met by her father who said goodnight for both of them. Within the hour he was back at the club where he and Chet laughed about this non-drinker and the Bird Baths.

Oh well he will call her tomorrow to see if she is still alive.

Her Dad answered the phone and Musher asked for Melinda. "She's alive. If you listen closely you will the wail of death and her wishing to die. What did you feed her?"

"She had nine martinis. I think she had never had one before because she chug-a-lugged them. I give her credit she behaved like a perfect lady and didn't get sick in my new Thunderbird."

"Well she's paying for it now. Call back around dinner time and if she is still alive she may want to talk with you."

CHAPTER 239
Goodbye Bachelorhood

Musher and Melinda had been dating exclusively for just about five months. One night while sitting together on a warm couch Musher said, "I guess you know I love you. Do you love me?"

"Yes."

"I want to marry you, do you want to marry me?"

"Yes."

"OK. Today is Tuesday what do you have scheduled for Thursday?"

"I have nothing until after Christmas and then I have some personal appearances during the New Year festivities."

"Good, I have been doing some research and if I wear my uniform we can go to Vermont where they will issue us a license and we can be married the same day. I will make a call to our flight surgeon and have the blood tests in the morning. You can tell your dad if you wish but other than that let's keep it to ourselves."

Thursday morning they drove to Brattleboro,Vermont and paid the twenty-five dollars for a license. Without too much trouble they found a Justice of the Peace who did marriages in his home. His wife served as the witness and he charged twenty-five dollars. By noon on December 23rd they were Captain and Mrs. Saverio Muscarello.

"I know you are Irish but among Italians there is a very large celebration on Christmas Eve. It's called the dinner of seven fishes. Each year one of my sisters hosts the occasion and everyone in the family brings something special. Let me call my mother and find out which sister is hosting this year."

"Hello Mama, it's Saverio."

"Whatsa matter? Are you OK?"

"I am all right. I just want to know who is having Christmas Eve this year."

"Your sister Joanna. Are you coming home?"

Musher had not been home in years. "Only if I can bring my wife."

He could hear Mama crying and saying out loud, "Thank you My God, he is saved."

CHAPTER 240
Why Me?
I Am the Junior Munitions Officer

Everything was going well on the IG Team. Melinda had been welcomed with open arms and Musher was no longer the odd ball male at team functions. His inspection skills had greatly improved and his nuclear weapons skills had risen even more proportionally. He was as happy as a lark. When things are going that well, look out the sky is about to fall. He, his IG, and Colonel George Williams, the IG Honcho were summoned to the office of the 8th AF Commander.

"I have here in my hand a Top Secret document dealing with combat effectiveness of the largest Munitions Maintenance Squadron in the world. Recently the Strategic Air Command IG Team did an ORI (Operational Readiness Inspection) of that MMS and the only reason they did not fail the squadron was because it is heavily involved in the B-52 bombing of Southeast Asia. The bomb loading crews are having too many dropped bombs on the ramp, and hung bombs in the bomb bays when the 52's return from a combat mission. Because so many of our wings go TDY to Guam SAC wants us to send a munitions officer to find out why that squadron is doing so poorly and what it will take to square it away. Musher I have selected you to do that job. I will give you a letter of introduction to the present squadron commander and he will give you his fullest cooperation. When you figure out what is wrong brief the squadron commander and give him your recommendations to solve the problem. You will report directly to me upon your return. Be ready to leave tonight. We have a KC-135 tanker going to Guam at 2200 hours tonight. Be on board. Your orders and my letter will be waiting for you on the aircraft. Good luck. Remember how important that squadron is to the successful completion of the war in Southeast Asia."

Musher told Melinda he was going on a short TDY. He expected to be back in a week. She helped him pack a B-4 bag of warm weather uniforms and one set of civilian clothes. It was a ten thousand air miles flight to Guam. He arrived at 1800 hours local time. He went to the base motor pool showed his orders and requested transportation to the 3rd MMS Control Room. He was driven to the control room which bordered the bomb dump and other MMS functions. He was allowed to enter the control room without challenge. The operation was being controlled by Technical Sergeant Claude Adkins and Airman First Class Robert Stackhouse. Musher asked, "Where are the officers on this shift?"

"Sir there are none. We have contact telephone numbers if we need one of them."

"Which of the EOD officers is on the flight line for the recovery of the strike force and the launch of the next strike force?"

"Sir the flight line is covered by one of our three highly competent EOD Master Sergeants."

"Let me see if I have this straight. This squadron loads six B-52s with one hundred eight 500 pound bombs four times each day. This squadron recovers six B-52s from a strike mission four times a day. The Maintenance Supervisor, a Regular Air Force Major, and the Squadron Commander, a recalled reserve Colonel go off duty at 1700 hours. There are nine officers assigned to this squadron yet there are no officers on this 1700 to 0600 hours shift or anywhere on the flight line. From 1700 hours until 0600 the next morning you are in complete charge of the control room. Of the nine officers three are EOD officers assigned to the squadron yet none are on this shift and an EOD master sergeant is responsible for EOD flight line activities and any EOD problems which might arise on the base. Is all that a true summary? I want you to write down that summary and both you and A/1C Stackhouse sign it as true to the best of your knowledge and belief. I will date it and witness your signatures." When the statement was signed and witnessed Musher made ten copies. He gave each of the airmen a copy and put the rest in his pocket. "When your shift ends in the morning I want you to stay here. I noticed the squadron operates it own coffee shop. Have breakfast there and I will pay for it. I do not want you to tell anyone I have been here. If you do it will be very difficult for you when I find out you have. I will be here before your shift ends."

Musher checked in at the BOQ, did a SSS and caught a couple of hours sleep. At 0530 he was in the squadron coffee shop having bacon, eggs and toast. There were three airman and one staff sergeant assigned to run the coffee shop. Two of the airmen were AGE (Aerospace Ground Equipment) mechanics. This was one of the squadron areas which bordered on failure but was given a marginal rating for reasons which Musher knew. The oncoming Shift Master Sergeant took the roll call and of the sixty-nine enlisted personnel assigned to this shift twelve were absent for sick call, four others on injured status which kept them from full duty work and four operating the squadron coffee shop. Slightly less than thirty percent of the enlisted personnel work force was not doing munitions maintenance squadron work. The load was placed on the remaining seventy percent of the shift enlisted personnel work force.

At about 0800 the squadron commander, the maintenance supervisor and the other officers drifted in and immediately went to the coffee shop. Musher approached the squadron commander and asked to see him alone in his office. The squadron commander insisted that the maintenance supervisor be present. In the privacy of his office Musher gave the squadron commander the letter from the 8th AF Commander and a copy of the statement which he elicited last night in the control room. Both the 3rd MMS senior officers turned livid with rage. "Who do you think you are coming here and rating my operation. We just had a SAC IG inspection and we passed."

"Sir I am here because of that inspection. If you read the 8th AF Commander's letter I have been charged to find out what the problems are that make this squadron weak, report them to you, offer any recommendations I may feel worthy and then leave and go back to the states. You will have my report by 1500 hours and I shall be on my way back to 8th AF Headquarters at 1900 hours tonight. My job is not to tell you how to run your squadron, my job was to study and report to the 8th AF Commander what I believe to be wrong with the squadron. I can tell you this now. My report will be a two liner. "This squadron lacks leadership from all its commissioned staff. The weakest links are the two senior officers assigned to the squadron." That is also the report I shall give the 8th AF Commander. Musher went into the orderly room and typed his report. He dated and signed it. Then he made six copies. He put the original in an envelope for the squadron commander and hand delivered it to him. "Sir, it took less time to write it than I thought." He saluted and left.

He checked out of the BOQ, turned in the pickup he had been using and went to Base Operation to board the KC-135. They made one stop at Hickam AFB and landed at Westover AFB before noon. Musher went directly to his boss the IG. Colonel Williams the IG Honcho sat in. Musher showed them his report. When asked to defend his conclusion Musher handed him the certified statement from the two airmen working in the control room. He also handed him a written analysis of the availability and use of the enlisted personnel flight line work force.

The IG made one phone call. When he hung up the telephone he said, "We see General Rossetti at 0900 tomorrow. Musher be prepared for some hard questions. Go see your pretty wife. Be here tomorrow at 0730 hours for coffee."

CHAPTER 241
Don't Talk When You Should Listen

Musher was at the IG's office at 0715. Additional copies of the statements, the analysis of the use of the work force and the two line report were made so that no matter how many people the 8th AF Commander may invite to the debriefing there would be copies for each attendee. The three of them drank coffee while the IG and his Honcho fired off the wall questions at Musher. Most of the questions had nothing to do with the meeting but were designed to attempt to rattle Musher's confidence. At 0845 the three of them were in General Rossetti's waiting room. When they went in the IG reported for all three. The IG and his Honcho sat but Musher was left standing.

The 8th AF commander began, "I have read your two line report and looked at the supporting documents, is there anything else you wish to add?"

"No sir."

"If you were I what action would you take?"

"I would replace the 3rd MMS two senior officers."

"Replacing both seniors at one time would cause reverberations that would be detrimental to the mission. If you could only replace one which one would it be?"

"Sir, the squadron commander. The attitude and behavior of the squadron is a direct reflection of its top leadership."

"To replace him would give rise to the familiar cry that he was the scapegoat but not the real problem. I am afraid Musher the thing to do is to replace the Maintenance Supervisor. Do you think a strong Maintenance Supervisor could square away the squadron?"

"No sir I do not. Not as long as the poor leadership of the squadron commander could undermine the efforts of the Maintenance Supervisor."

The 8th AF Commander continued, "So do you think that a strong Maintenance Supervisor who could operate without the interference of the squadron commander could resolve the issues and bring the squadron up to par?"

"Yes sir."

"Musher how soon could you leave for a Permanent Change of Station to Guam?"

"Sir I don't want to sound like a wimp but I have spent five of the last six years on remote duty with the two most recent in a hot combat zone. I recently married and I would like some time in the states with her before I go back into a combat zone type environment. If I am not mistaken the unaccompanied tour in Guam is eighteen months. Even if I were to fly her there at my expense there is no suitable housing for her. Sir, please reconsider your choice."

"Musher I am afraid this is one of those times when no matter how sympathetic I am to the persons involved in my decision I must put all sympathies in the background and think of the mission. I believe you are the best man for this job and therefore my reconsideration still appoints you to the job. There are some things I can do to help make the job easier. First we will change the tour to an accompanied tour for twenty-four months. I can use my influence to get you on base housing at Anderson. I can use my influence to have your wife join you on Guam within thirty days from the day you leave for Guam. With that settled here's the deal. The current Maintenance Supervisor will rotate to the states before you can get to Guam. I will give you a one of a kind letter for the squadron commander which in essence tells him he will remain the squadron commander in name only but will take his directions from you. The letter will tell him that if that arrangement is not suitable to him I shall have him rotated to the states and assigned to the pentagon where he will be just one more colonel errand boy and he can do no damage to the air force. Each week I will want for my eyes only a short report of your progress. Now how soon can you leave?"

"Sir, whenever you say."

"We have a flight of eight B-52s leaving for Guam two nights from tonight. Colonel Riller will make sure you are on one of them, that all the paperwork is done for you and he will have my letter. Good luck Musher. I shall wait to hear from you." With that the IG, his Honcho and Musher went back to the IG's office.

Colonel Riller, "Musher look at this like the break of your military career. Do the job well and there is no telling where it might take you. Take the rest of today off and tomorrow as well. Check in with me at 0900 on the day of your departure. Be sure to tell Melinda that we will support her and do everything to make sure her relocation goes smoothly."

On the third night Musher was listed as a passenger on the flight leader's B-52. For some reason take-off was delayed six hours. Landing on Guam would be around midnight the next day. With the dateline change they would land on local time the day before they left the states.

CHAPTER 242

It Won't Be Like the Bomb Dump
at Tachikawa

Musher went to the Base Motor Pool and on the strength of his orders signed out a pickup truck. It was pouring rain, he had his two B-4 bags in the front seat and per his instructions from the 8th AF Commander he headed for the 3rd MMS squadron commander's residence. It was 0200 hours. Standing in the rain he rang the doorbell and waited for Colonel Bergstrom to answer the door. He was greeted by "What the hell do you want?" Musher handed him the letter from the 8th AF Commander. He took the letter, went inside to read it and left Musher standing in the pouring rain. Shortly he came back, handed the letter back to Musher and asked, "What do you want to do?"

"I want you to implement your recall plan for all officers and master sergeants to report to the squadron briefing room ASAP. It is now 0305. I will time the response and attendance at the recall." Musher headed to the squadron control room. The same tech sergeant and airman were running the control room. "Are you aware of the emergency recall for officers and master sergeants?"

"Yes sir. We are calling everyone now."

"Send them into the squadron briefing room."

He went to the squadron coffee shop. "Make plenty of coffee. We are having an emergency recall of all officers and master sergeants. Set up coffee and accouterments in the briefing room. There is no charge. We will write it off as a combat necessity."

It was 0435 when the last of the recallees came into the briefing room. Four of the personnel did not show. The control room tech sergeant said he was unable to reach the four absentees. The squadron commander introduced Captain Muscarello as the new Squadron Maintenance Supervisor. "There is a pad over there, I want everyone to sign and print his name on their way out. I will see you all at 0600 roll call."

In one and a half hours the shift roll call took place as usual. With the exception of the master sergeant who took the shift roll call and gave out assignments for the day every other master sergeant and officer was back in the squadron briefing room. Musher began, "We are going to make some personnel changes and we are going to make them now. We will begin with flight line operations.

We have two EOD officers who are here TDY and we have one permanent party EOD officer plus me. You three EOD officers will go to that bowl and pick a slip. The slips are marked A, B and C. From this moment on you will be known by the letter you pick out of the bowl. I don't care what your name or rank is. You will be known as EOD A, or EOD B or EOD C. This way you will constantly be reminded what your job is here. We have six EOD qualified master sergeants. You will pick from the bowl next to the officers bowl and from that moment on you will be known as EOD Sergeant D, etc. Nine fully qualified senior EOD personnel is enough for any organization. According to the squadron records in addition to you nine there are eleven additional enlisted men who are also fully qualified EOD technicians. According to my quick calculations there is no reason why there is not at least one EOD officer, one EOD master sergeant and two EOD qualified airmen on duty with a primary station on the flight line twenty-four hours a day. You three EOD officers work out a duty schedule for EOD people and have it on my desk by noon today.

The last of the flight line operations is bomb loading. We have a total of thirteen munitions officers. Most of you have little skill and have received very little training from the more experienced officers and sergeants. That stops now. You six, go to the large bowl and draw a slip. Henceforth you are FMO-A (Flightline Munitions Officer) You other five are FMO–B through FMO-F. You first six master sergeants go draw a letter. You will be known as FMS-A (Flightline Munitions Sergeant) through FMS-F.

We now have plenty of flight line supervision assigned. I will discuss my flightline expectations later. Now for the bomb storage area, bomb assembly area and transport of the bombs to the flight line for loading. Every other function we do is useless if we cannot assemble bombs and get them to the flightline when we need them. I consider the preparation of bombs for loading onto strike aircraft as one of the primary responsibilities of this squadron. The other primary responsibility is to load them onto aircraft and properly fuze them. You two are BDO-A (Bomb Dump Officer) and BDO-B. You four master sergeants are BDS-A (Bomb Dump Sergeant) through BDS-D.

You lieutenant and the master sergeant sitting next to you are assigned to the AGE Shop (Aerospace Ground Equipment). In the last IG inspection the shop almost failed. It bordered on failure because of the physical condition of the equipment. You are known as AGEO-A and AGES-A. You have plenty of AGE technicians who know how to keep the equipment in good shape but suffer from lack of supervision. I will be watching you two and the shop very closely.

The heart of operations is the control room. It coordinates the actions of the squadron yet it is left with a tech sergeant as its chief of operations. He may be very good at what he does but he is only one person. I am assigning three officers who will be known as CRO-A (Control Room Officer), CRO-B and CRO-C. In addition I am assigning two master sergeants CRS-A and CRS-B. I am also assigning six airmen.

Everyone in this room has an assignment. I will discuss what I expect from each group as soon as possible. Until such time as your unit is functioning to my degree of expectation none of you will be known by rank or name. This is a major step towards major improvement of this squadron. All right gentlemen you are dismissed let me see you work it out in your section. I will be monitoring every action every day.

Now it is time for the administration and administrators. Musher took the squadron adjutant and the first sergeant and they went to visit the troops living quarters. They were abominable. The buildings were Quonset Huts igloo style metal. They cooked in the Guam sun and they were not air conditioned. There were not enough fans to keep the air circulating in the building. They smelled of stale sweat and unbathed inhabitants. They were double decked bunks and each person barely had room to sit between the bunks. At this point in time the troops were working twelve hour shifts seven days a week. He would change that as soon as possible. He asked the first sergeant, "How many of these hell holes billet our airmen?"

"Sir there are one hundred twenty-six bunks in each Quonset Hut. Our people occupy six such huts."

"Do all enlisted grades live in these Quonset Huts?"

"No sir. Only airmen below the grade of staff sergeant."

"Where do those others live?"

"They live in the permanent party barracks which were here before the big influx of troops."

"How many of our troops live in those permanent party barracks?"

"About two hundred."

"First sergeant, do you live in the permanent party barracks?"

"Yes sir." The first sergeant could tell Musher was planning something and he knew it would involve his and the other two hundred troops becoming less comfortable in favor of some airmen becoming more comfortable.

He thought about when he was the Munitions Officer at Tachikawa and how his staff lived.

768

Most of the airmen who worked here in the bomb dump assembly areas were not even in the munitions field. They deserved better living conditions. It was time for his first report to the 8th AF Commander.

CHAPTER 243

The Squadron Is Getting Better and Better Each Day

Melinda had been here for almost two months. She was his saving grace after almost sixteen hours every day seven days a week running around the squadron. The months had gone by and the statistical reports were favorable.

The AGE shop had improved the condition of the MJ-1 Bomb Loaders so much that they were able to limit the flight line stock to fourteen. The users babied the AGE to the extent that the MJ-1's came into the shop after a loading shift on the flight line and when they were run through the post-op check there was very little need for any maintenance. The AGE officer and master sergeant were back to using their name and rank instead of the AGE code.

The B-52 had two external pylon bomb racks which carried eight 500 pound bombs on each pylon. When Musher's ramp supervision program went into place it took a loading team seventeen minutes to load and fuze one pylon. The time now had been reduced to eight and one half minutes to load and fuze one pylon. More impressive was the fact that in the past two months there had not been a single bomb dropped onto the ramp during the pylon loading process. The bomb bay loading and fuzing time for ninety-two 500 pound bombs had been reduced by thirty percent without a bomb or fuze incident. The flight line officers and master sergeants were close to getting their rank and names back. The loading and fuzing time needed to drop another eleven percent without any incidents.

The bomb assembly time had been reduced by fifteen percent but that was about as much as he could hope for until the pneumatic impact wrenches could last longer and the sockets did not wear out so quickly. The troops in the field maintenance shop were desperately trying to improve the impact wrench situation. Still Musher did not waiver from the goals he set because the goals were realistic.

Probably the most visual improvements were in the control room. The staff had developed flight line portrayals depicting which aircraft were to be loaded, where the aircraft was parked awaiting loading and when the loading time would commence. They had developed a special control room staff position to monitor and control the positioning of the bombs and fuzes for loading the scheduled aircraft. There was always an officer in the control room to handle special situations. With the guidance of the master sergeant who was also always in the control room the flight line activity went very smoothly.

Musher could not say too many nice things about the EOD teams. He clearly understood the difficult role they played in defusing and downloading hung bombs to get the bomb bays ready to be loaded for the next strike. So far the EOD flight line activity had been truly dangerous and hard, sweaty work to defuse the hung bombs and to down load the hung bombs for inspection at a revetment safely removed from the active flight line.

During the eight months that Musher was getting the squadron in shape the ladies of the Officers Wives Club were falling deeply in love with Melinda. She was active in the officers wive's club programs. The club was getting ready to have its annual fashion show and Melinda had been asked to be the lead person. She knew how much time and effort were required to have such a show and she did not want to get that involved. She really had no choice. The club members starting with the Air Division Commanding General's wife and the board of directors hounded her until she acquiesced. It was not an easy time for Melinda and she came to Musher for advice and consolation.

"When we first married I asked you what my role was as an air force officer's wife. At the time you told me I did not have an air force active duty role. You were the officer and I was simply the officer's lady. Your squadron commander's wife is driving me crazy about the fashion show. She suggests models who would be better suited to show pear shaped clothes and whose looks do not compare with the looks of the wives of some of the younger officers. Every day she offers me some suggestions which might have looked good in Podunk, Arkansas but hardly in a cosmopolitan city. I just don't know what to do."

"Ignore her and do what you believe is right."

The fashion show was a smashing success. Musher had a temporary ramp built in the officer's club so that the models could walk a runway and be seen by all the attendees. Melinda had written the description of the garments in the most fashionable terms she remembered from her days walking the ramp. There were fifteen hundred members of the wive's club in attendance and just about each individually congratulated Melinda. That night Melinda and Musher had dinner at the O-Club with the 3rd Air Division Commander and his wife. Musher could have stayed home for all the notice he received during that night.

The next day Musher came home to find Melinda crying and she looked like she had been crying all afternoon. "This afternoon I had a visit from Mrs. Bergstrom, your squadron commander's wife. She dressed me down most severely for not using any of the models she suggested or any other suggestion she had made. The show was so successful it made me very angry and I remembered what you had told me on how to handle any officer's wife who tried to pull rank on me. I let her finish then simply walked her to the front door and said what you had told me, "Blow it out your ass lady." With that I slammed the door in her face."

Musher consoled her that she had done the right thing. They went to bed early after dinner and he showed his love for her. She drifted off to sleep and he lay there thinking what a day tomorrow will be.

As usual Musher was at the squadron very early. He was greeted by the first sergeant. "The Old Man (the squadron commander) is already here and wants you in his office the minute you get here."

Musher walked in saluted and said, "Good morning sir. You wanted to see me?"

He did not invite Musher to sit. "Did you know my wife visited your wife in your quarters yesterday afternoon?"

"Yes sir."

"Did you know my wife criticized your wife for not using any of her suggestions in the recent fashion show which your wife produced and directed.?"

"Yes sir."

"Do you know what your wife's response was to my wife's criticisms?"

"Yes sir."

"Your wife had the audacity to tell my wife to blow it out her ass. What do you think of that?"

"I think my wife said exactly what any other wife should say if some rankless wife tries to intimidate another wife of an air force officer."

"Did you know I could have you court martialled for causing a breach of military etiquette?"

"I think that would be cute. Can you see yourself on the witness stand as the complaining officer telling the court that I am being court martialled because of something my wife said to your wife in a totally non military environment. Colonel I would like to see that."

"Maybe a court martial would not work but you are up for promotion to major and I must write an officer effectiveness report (OER) telling the promotion board what I think of you as fit for promotion. That OER will be lower than the Mach Number on a helicopter." (Mach Number is how they measure the speed of an aircraft. Mach 1 is the speed of sound. A helicopter Mach Number is generally around .15 The maximum OER Number is 4.0)

Musher knew this prick would not hesitate to attempt to try to destroy his career. Musher wanted to be a Major.

Later in the day Musher went to MARS (Military Amateur Radio System) to place a person to person telephone call to Brigadier General Leyland Trotter at the Pentagon. Musher forgot about the time change and when Trotter answered the phone it was 0200 his time. "Musher this better be good."

"Sir I am on assignment on Guam. I was personally placed here by the 8th AF Commander. I am running a squadron where the lieutenant colonel commander is my puppet. He has taken a hate to me and my wife and wants to destroy my chance to be promoted to major this upcoming cycle and my becoming a regular officer. Sir, I would like both of things to happen."

"Goodnight Musher. You will hear from me. Remember I am a man of my word."

Four days went by and each day his squadron commander whispered soft digs about his future in the air force. On the evening of the fourth day Musher was summoned to the MARS station to take a telephone call. "My name is Colonel Chancellor. I am General Trotter's aide. This message is from General Trotter and your Army General friend. Your name is number sixteen on the promotion list to major and your name is number nine on the list of officers to be appointed into the regular air force. If you leak one word of this it will all go away. Your friends want you to know their debt is paid and they wish you the best of luck. Goodnight Captain." The line went dead.

Musher was astounded. All he had to do was keep his mouth shut and stay out of jail for the next forty two days and he will be a regular air force major. He had to tell Melinda so she would be relieved of any guilt she felt.

CHAPTER 244

No More "Mother May I"

On the evening of the 41st day Musher took out his highly pressed best gabardine uniform. He decked the uniform with every badge, medal and ribbon he was authorized to wear. In the morning when he dressed he looked like the poster boy on a recruiting billboard. Everyone knew the date officer promotions would be announced. Everyone also knew that the night before that date an "Eyes Only" TWX (an electronic message) was sent to the senior officer on the installation. The following morning (the 42nd day) those persons to be promoted would be summoned to the senior military officer's office.

Musher was in the control room when the squadron commander came in. "Musher what are you doing in those glad rags. There is no way you will be called today. Your OER guaranteed that."

About the time the squadron commander finished his venominous remarks the controller said, "Captain you are wanted at the ADiv's (Air Division Commander) office ASAP." Musher looked at Bergstrom, his squadron commander, shot him a bird and laughingly left the control center.

At the ADiv's office there were six other persons. The chief of the weather squadron who was promoted to Lieutenant Colonel and the Squadron Commander of the Armament & Electronics Squadron who was also promoted to Lieutenant Colonel. The other four gentlemen and Musher were all being promoted to Major. The ADiv had the new rank insignia for each person and he pinned them. Musher was the only one in full dress uniform. The ADiv whispered to him, "I like a confident officer." Musher thought, "General if you only knew."

When the seven of them were in the ADiv's waiting area the new weather Lieutenant Colonel spoke. "Promotion party at the O-Club beginning at 1730 hours. Open bar until the last person orders a drink. We split the tab seven ways and have each of our parts put on our club bill. Any suggestions or disagreements?" Everyone nodded in consent. "See you at the club. Right now I am going home to share this with my wife." The other six thought the same and did the same.

At 1615 the control room reached Musher at his quarters. "Sir you had better come to the control room now. We have a circumstance which requires your presence." Musher was dressing and wondered what could be so important as to warrant his presence. In eighteen minutes he found out.

His squadron commander had suffered a heart attack and was taken to the base hospital. Musher calmly said, "Just carry on as if he were on leave in the states. There is no reason to panic or change our routine operation. I will go to the base hospital, check on his condition and send the info back to the control room which will keep everybody apprised of his status." Inside Musher said to himself, "With any luck the cocksucker will die."

The attending physician said the heart attack was most probably brought on by the severe stress of managing the worlds largest MMS and keeping it on the right tract. Musher knew inside it was not that because Bergstrom had done nothing to run the squadron. It was most probably because he realized that he was only a puppet and everyone on the air base knew he was relegated to the position of flunky for Musher. To top it off Musher's promotion told him who had the influence and where he had it. Musher's report to the control room reported that Bergstrom would be in the hospital for a few days and then would be shipped back to the states.

The promotion party went as scheduled and every officer on the airbase who could get away from a duty was there helping to celebrate. The talk of the night was Bergstrom's heart attack and the apparent rise of Musher to the position of squadron commander. He would no longer have to make sure he didn't upset the apple cart. He would be the known boss and he would no longer have to say, "Mother May I."

The next morning Major Muscarello was summoned to the 2nd Air Division Commander's office. "Musher I know you will understand but I wanted you here so I could discuss it with you personally. I know all about your assignment here and the super job you have done. I want you to take over as the squadron commander but only on a temporary basis. The slot calls for a Lieutenant Colonel or a Full Colonel and you are neither. Everyone knows you can do the job and probably do it better than any new squadron commander. Unfortunately the USAF cannot afford a Major in a higher rank TO&E (Table of Organization and Equipment) slot. I know you understand. It will probably take a month or two before the new squadron commander will report. Meanwhile you name your own Maintenance Supervisor and train him to function as well as you have done. When the new squadron commander gets here you will be here for a few months until you have him trained on how to keep your squadron as effective and efficient as it has been. During those few months you can take Melinda on a couple of R&R's after which we will reassign you to the states. We will also forward decorations to your new assignment as recognition of your efforts here. You have my personal appreciation."

Musher stood, did what OCS had trained him to do, saluted smartly and got on the boat. Not very happy, but very disciplined.

CHAPTER 245
The Last Days on Guam

The squadron was functioning smoothly and Musher had lost some of his aggressiveness. His appointed Maintenance Supervisor made up for most of Musher's spirit. He was thrilled with his new job and tried to mimic what he learned from Musher. Musher's home life was good. Melinda was president of the OWC (Officers Wives Club) and because of that she and Musher were invited to every major function held on the island. Nobody at the functions really cared whether he was there or not because his wife kept the people there transfixed with her beauty and poise.

The new squadron commander will be here next week. He was a West Point Lieutenant Colonel named Benjamin Stover. He had no combat experience but he had been a squadron commander of a SAC MMS. His experience was with nuclear forces but none with iron. Musher thought it will be OJT (On the Job Training) for Stover. Musher spent two weeks almost living in Stover's pocket teaching him the routine of the squadron.

Musher managed to go to the Naval Station and play golf a couple of times each week.

He and Melinda took a six day R&R to Taiwan. On the way to Taiwan Melinda got to sit in the co-pilot seat on the KC-97 and actually fly the aircraft for fifteen or so minutes. Since the OWC did over a million dollars worth of commodities purchases with Taiwanese companies for their gift shop and Melinda signed the payment checks she was treated like royalty. When she and Musher walked the streets of Taiwan her blond hair and striking beauty brought men to stop them and ask if they could have their picture taken with her. The memorable moment came when she and Musher were having lunch in the most lavish restaurant high on the fortieth floor of the prominent hotel. The violins were playing softly when the building began to shake and rock. The violins stopped, all the silverware became silent and people just stared at each other. The shake seemed eternal but was just a few seconds. Musher put money on the table and he and Melinda walked the stairs down to the ground floor. There they met a couple who had come on the same airplane and they had not noticed any shake on the ground. Others to whom they spoke had not noticed any shake.

Musher and Melinda felt better when their aircraft was in the air on its way back to Guam.

Musher devoted another two weeks working with Stover before he and Melinda went on another R&R to Japan. Musher gave Melinda a choice. We can go to Tokyo and stay at the American hotel and live like tourists; or, he would take her to most of the places he went before he met her. She wanted to go to where he used to go.

They took the train and then a ferry to the island of Enoshima. No English was spoken there and they would live like the natives. Their western clothes were traded for Kimonas and Geta (Gay-Tah), the name for Japanese shoes. Most of their meals, especially Sukiyaki were cooked in their room by the Japanese hotel keepers. During the day they walked around the island and enjoyed the serenity. Musher's Japanese came back enough for them to do whatever they chose. They bathed in their room in privacy because Melinda was hesitant to go to the public baths. Musher finally convinced her to go to the public bath along with all the other Japanese women. The islanders were so friendly and her striking beauty and body kept them all in awe.

It was time to leave for Tachikawa and the aircraft back to Guam. Melinda did some shopping in the kiosks at Tachikawa. When they got back to Guam Musher took another day off to rest from his restful vacation.

Musher was summoned by BG Trotter the 2nd Air Division Commander. "Musher you have done a fine job with the transition of the squadron to the new administrators. I personally wanted to tell you about your new assignment. You will be assigned to the US Naval School for Explosive Ordnance Disposal at Indianhead, Maryland. The naval skipper will decide what they can best use you for but with your background and experience whatever they ask of you you will surpass their expectations. When you get there you will be awarded The Legion of Merit and another cluster to your AF Commendation Medal. Will you and Melinda be ready to go in two weeks? My wife is planning parties for Melinda and I know the squadron is planning activities for you. You will be contacted by my personnel staff to help with all your arrangements. Again, my personal thanks and the thanks of General Rossetti (The 8th AF Commander)"

The next two weeks were like another vacation. Melinda was busy with the OWC and Musher was busy with the squadron functions. Finally, they were on board an air force transport aircraft and landed in California. They processed through customs and headed for the nearest Cadillac dealer.

THE LAST OF THE
MEMORABLE MOMENTS

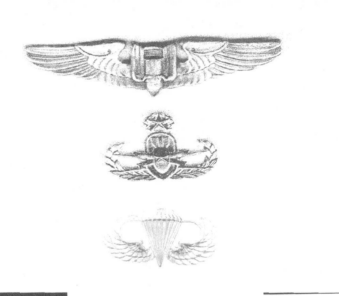

BOOK 9

CHAPTER 246
Some Things Never Change

Musher and Melinda had talked about a new Cadillac and a leisure drive to Indianhead, Maryland. They were at the Cadillac dealership and had fallen in love with the new four door sedan. They separated themselves from the salesman and discussed the merits and drawbacks to a three thousand mile drive which would take at least two full days behind the wheel. If they managed to drive four hundred miles per day the trip would take over seven days. If they took a flight the trip to Washington National Airport would take about six hours. They figure they can always buy a Cadillac anywhere. They booked the red-eye special leaving at 2300 hours tonight. In the morning they checked into a hotel in Washington, ordered room service breakfast, showered and went to bed. They both slept through to dinner which they ordered from room service. For a late snack they ordered real chocolate ice cream and whole milk. In the morning they had breakfast in the room. There were two Cadillac agencies located fairly close to the hotel. At the first dealership they found the car they wanted and it had all the bells and whistles. To close the deal at their price and quickly they paid cash. It took almost one hour to do the paperwork. They were back at the hotel before noon and checked out again paying cash to settle their bill.

Musher remembered his way around so they went to Waldorf and then to Pope's Creek for a lunch of Maryland Spicy Crabs. They drove to the Propellant Plant Main Gate at Indianhead. Musher showed his orders and was permitted entrance. They drove around wondering where they would live. There were no hotels or motels outside the gate. The nearest motel was in Waldorf. They drove to Waldorf and rented a motel cabin for the night. In the morning Melinda stayed at the motel while Musher went to sign in with the USAF Liaison office.

There was still a yeoman at the quarterdeck who checked Musher's orders and who then called the Liaison Office for an escort. The escort was Master Sergeant Pepe Martinez. Musher was introduced to the Liaison Officer Lieutenant Colonel William Faulkner.

"Pepe will take care of all your paperwork. Let's you and I go see the Skipper while he is still here. The school skipper was Commander Hawthorne Brooks, referred to as Hawk. Faulkner made the introductions. Hawk told Musher he would be assigned as the Assistant OIC of Division 6.

Then he asked the two most serious questions, "Do you play golf and if you do what is your handicap?"

"Sir I have not been playing very much. I was scratch but I would figure I am now about a two or a three."

"Colonel Faulkner we will give Major Muscarello the old Forrestahl House." The house was originally built during the WWII years to give then Secretary of the Navy Forrestahl a place to escape from the hustle and bustle of war time Washington. It was smaller than most of the houses on the station but it was right on the Potomac River and had all the comforts of home.

The next day the Muscarello family moved onto the station. The house was sparsely furnished with all top grade furniture. It had a fire place and a large bath and shower area. The kitchen was well supplied and the house had a basement with a complete sleeping area and full bath. There was plenty of room for the Muscarello family and the house sat next to the ninth tee of the golf course. Their first night on station they were invited to the EOD School Skipper's house for dinner. The skipper's house was a short walk across the eighth fairway from the Muscarello home. The evening was spent with the men talking golf and the women talking about the station activities and the OWC.

The school and Division 6 were just a short walk from his house. The best part of the next morning Musher spent finishing his check in paperwork and getting his security badge. The school skipper escorted Musher to Division 6 and introduced him to the Division 6 OIC, USN Lieutenant Commander Willis McGraf. Nothing had changed since Musher's last time he was here as a student. After the Division 6 walk through the skipper told McGraf, "I am taking Musher with me there are some other things I want to show him. If he is not here tomorrow that means he is with me." Everyone in Division 6 knew they were off to test Musher's golf skills.

Fortunately the hold baggage the Muscarello's had shipped as soon as they knew their assignment location had arrived and was in the house. Musher unpacked his golf equipment, put on his golf shoes and walked to the first tee. Hawk was already there and impatiently waiting to tee off. At the end of the round Musher had shot one under par and Hawk had shot two over. Hawk said, "Tomorrow morning we will drive to Andrews AFB and play. I am sure there must be something that you need to check with the air force at Andrews. We go in my car in uniform and change our clothes at Andrews. Tell Melinda that tomorrow night we dine at the O-Club. The reservation is made for you two to sit at my table. The dress is not formal but it is jacket and tie for men and cocktail dresses for the ladies.

That evening Musher and Melinda went to Pope's Creek for Maryland crabs.

CHAPTER 247
Two Comfortable Years

The following two years could not have been more comfortable no matter what. By the end of the first year the Muscarello's had a baby girl named Christine Filomena Muscarello. She was named in honor of her two maternal grandmothers. Melinda's dad came down from Massachusetts regularly and he played golf with Musher and the skipper. With every new Division 6 class Musher taught the first week, "Nuclear Physics for the Design of Nuclear Weapons." He attended all the Skipper's inspections. At his first one he was presented the decorations he had earned on Guam and at each subsequent inspection he stood tall with the rest of the commissioned staff. Life was almost too good to be true.

When something is too good to be true it generally isn't.

One day he was asked to see the air force liaison officer Faulkner. "Musher I have orders here for you to be reassigned to Vietnam. I know you did three full years in combat there so I presume this is a mistake. Why don't you call air force personnel at Randolph and get this matter corrected." He used the privacy of Faulkner's office.

"This is Major Arturo Costa how can I help you?"

Musher identified himself by name, rank and serial number. "I want to talk to you about a transfer order I have received telling me I am going back to Vietnam for another one year tour. There must be some mistake. I have done three tours there, a long tour in Guam and have only been back in the states for a little over two years. I know lots of guys with the same rank and AFSC who have never been to Nam. Get one of them."

"I am sorry Major but you are the most eligible for this duty."

"How can I be the most eligible if these other guys have never been?"

"Your last three assignments out of the ZI were on a volunteer basis so they don't count as foreign tours and therefore you are the most eligible non-volunteer. Sorry but that is in accordance with AF Regulations." He quoted the regulation cite.

Musher hung up. That same day he drove to Andrews to the base personnel office and read regulations. He talked the new orders over with Melinda and confessed to her that he did not think he could stand another year of wet and dirty clothes, amphetamines for energy, heavy drinking to come down off the amphetamine high and dodging bullets in a war he was sure we could not win. Another major consideration in his decision was the new baby.

The next morning he was on the phone with Major Arturo Costa at USAF Personnel. "I read the regulation you cited and you are perfectly correct. I also read some other regulations and you tell me if I read them correctly. Am I not a Regular USAF Officer?"

"Yes you are."

"Do I not have more than twenty creditable years for retirement?"

"Yes you do."

"Do the regulations not say a regular officer with twenty or more years of creditable service for retirement purposes has seven days in which to accept an assignment or apply for and will be granted an honorable retirement from active duty?"

"Yes they do."

"Do those same regs allow the officer to select a retirement date up to but no longer in the future than one year?"

"Yes they do."

"Do those same regs also say that during the selection period of pre-retirement the officer cannot be transferred from his duty station?"

"Yes they do."

"At this time I opt to select retirement one year from this date. Do you have that properly recorded?"

"Yes I do. We will begin the paperwork and be in touch with you."

Musher did not tell anyone of his plans but when the AF Personnel contacted the liaison office it did not take long for the word to spread. The next day Musher was contacted and advised his reassignment orders would be there shortly. When he queried about the no transfer from duty station provision he was told he was not going to be transferred from the duty station he was only being reassigned to another AF unit on the duty station. His orders would explain it all.

His official reassignment orders sent him to the other side of the propellant plant as the commander of an EOD unit which wrote rendering safe procedures for newly developed weapons. The unit consisted of him, a secretary and four senior sergeants. He would be there until retirement but a new commander would be there within a couple of weeks. Everyone at the EOD School agreed the non-volunteer regulation was stupid but it was a regulation. The school skipper agreed but he told Musher he would need to vacate his house since it would be required for his replacement who would be here in a week.

He talked it over with Melinda and they decided Washington would be a good place for post-retirement living. He would easily be able to get a job and if necessary she could go back to work until they were stable as civilians. At a civilian golf course one day with the school skipper Musher and skipper played with two real estate agents. At the 19th Hole Musher told of his impending retirement and his need for a house. One of the agents said he had the perfect place. A Colonel stationed at the Pentagon was undergoing a nasty divorce and was willing to give up the house to someone who would take the equity and payments rather than have his credit standing ruined. The house was in Silver Spring. Musher made meeting arrangements for tomorrow so that he and Melinda could look at the house.

The house was fabulous. Seven bedrooms on a tri-level frame, three fire places, a two car garage, two large patio areas, a large back yard and even cedar closets, a play room and servant quarters on the base level. The agent agreed to pack the closing costs into the new mortgage. The mortgage would be an assumable G.I. loan at a very low rate. They would move in with no out of pocket expense. They could easily afford the mortgage payments and the operational costs of the house. The only draw back was that it was fifty-seven miles one way to the plant at Indianhead. Musher was not worried, he did not intend to make that trip every day. The deal was closed in four days. The Muscarello family was settled in the house in six days.

As predicted the new detachment commander arrived in three weeks. He looked over the workload and said to Musher, "We have a lot to do." Musher looked at him and said, "What's this we Kemo Sabay do you have a mouse in your pocket?" After that day nobody missed Musher and he just skated along until retirement.

CHAPTER 248

The Last Memorable Moment In a Twenty-three Plus Year Career

The year went by quickly and in a very few days Musher would be a civilian. There were a few get togethers and farewell parties given for Melinda by the OWC and a couple for Musher from the EOD school and the people at his detachment side of the propellant plant. Certainly nothing spectacular and far from Musher's dream of retiring as a general officer with his farewell address given by the President of the United States. It will always just be a dream.

On his actual retirement date in true US Navy style he was piped over the side and passed between the saluting side boys of the officer corps from all branches of the service. He wept and knew how much he would miss it all as he passed between them with the boatsun's pipe cracking the silence of the moment.

His last truly memorable moment.